THE GREATEST WAR

THE ORION WAR - BOOKS 4-6

(Including Ignite the Stars)

M. D. COOPER

THE ORION WAR – THE GREATEST WAR

SPECIAL THANKS

Just in Time (JIT) & Beta Reads

IGNITE THE STARS

Belxjander Draconis Serechai
Marti Panikkar
Lisa L. Richman
Mannie Killian
Mikkel Anderson
Belxjander Serechai
James Dean

SCIPIO ALLIANCE

Lisa Richman
Jim Dean
David Wilson
Scott Reid
Timothy Van Oosterwyk Bruyn

ATTACK ON THEBES

Timothy Van Oosterwyk Bruyn
Lisa L. Richman
Scott Reid
Jim Dean
David Wilson
Marti Panikkar
Mikkel Anderson
Belxjander Serechai
Mannie Killian

WAR ON A THOUSAND FRONTS

James Dean
Marti Panikkar
Timothy Van Oosterwyck Bruyn
David Wilson
Steven Blevins
Scott Reid
Lisa Richman

Version 1.1.0

ISBN: 978-1-64365-062-3

Cover Art by Andrew Dobell
Edited by Jen McDonnell, Bird's Eye Books

TABLE OF CONTENTS

IGNITE THE STARS

TALES OF THE ORION WAR – BOOK 2

BY M. D. COOPER

FOREWORD

The stories in this first book follow events overlapping with the last third of Orion Rising, following the Defense of Carthage. It is intended to be read after Orion Rising, and ideally before The Scipio Alliance (which is next in this collection)—though one can certainly come back to it after reading the main books in the Orion War series.

Many readers have asked for the story of Faleena's birth, which sets it in place as the first story. Following that, we learn of how Flaherty got off Airtha to eventually meet Sera and Tanis at Khardine.

Then we jump forward to the day when the *I2* left New Canaan and get insight into Captain Espensen's background, and how she very nearly ruined her future—or thought she did, at least.

Lastly, we spend some time with Sera and Finaeus as they have a much-needed chat between uncle and niece.

I hope you enjoy reading these stories. I especially like writing these small views into what makes the characters tick, and am glad to be able to share them with you.

Malorie. Cooper
Danvers, 2020

A NEW ADDITION

BREAKFAST OF CHAMPIONS

STELLAR DATE: 04.23.8948 (Adjusted Years)
LOCATION: Ol' Sam, ISS *I2*
REGION: In Orbit of Carthage, New Canaan System

One day after the celebration at Tanis's Cabin for the Defense of Carthage…

Tanis peered over the rim of her coffee cup at Joe as he moved about the kitchen, preparing a light breakfast before their meeting with Earnest.

"You're way too alert for this early in the morning," Tanis said after her cup was half-empty.

Joe glanced over his shoulder at Tanis and laughed before turning back to his skillet of eggs and peppers. "It's 0600. You're gone by now, most days."

"Gone, yes," Tanis replied after taking another sip of her coffee. "Alert? No. At least not after a late night like we had yesterday. I was starting to think the guests would never leave. I had trouble sleeping, too…my mind kept racing."

<I could have helped you with that,> Angela offered.

"Do you sing her to sleep?" Joe asked as he pulled the skillet off the heating surface and dished out two plates' worth of food.

Angela laughed in their minds. *<Sometimes. Which shouldn't surprise you. I've done it for you. And the girls.>*

Joe leaned across the table and set Tanis's plate in front of her and followed with his own across from her. "I thought we were never to speak of that, Ang."

<I made no promises.>

Joe laughed and sat down. "You might have, but you had me snoring in minutes, so I don't rightly recall."

"In hindsight, I should have taken a song or two," Tanis replied as Joe began to tuck into his eggs. "You know how it is. You think that if you just mull things over a bit longer, you'll come to some meaningful conclusions."

"Never works," Joe said around a mouthful of food. "You're closing in on three hundred. I would have thought you'd know that by now."

Tanis picked up a piece of egg and flicked it at Joe. "I am nowhere near three hundred."

The egg-bit's trajectory was true and it would have struck Joe on the forehead if he hadn't jerked to the side and caught it in his mouth.

"Showoff," Tanis grumbled.

Joe tapped his head. "Half this skull-space up here is hardware dedicated to handling relativistic math on the fly. You think I can't track the trajectory of a piece of egg moving at 1.1 meters per second?"

Tanis stared at Joe for a second and then burst out laughing. "You're still just as much a cocksure pilot as when I first met you, you know that?"

Joe shoveled another forkful of eggs into his mouth and grinned insolently. "Of course I am. You're a hard woman to please. Gotta make sure I live up to the promise."

"I am not a ha—" Tanis stopped mid-word as Joe cocked an eyebrow.

<Yeah, I was going to have to mock you pretty hard if you said that out loud, Tanis.>

"Let's just get breakfast done and get to Earnest's lab."

* * * * *

Every time Tanis walked into Earnest's lab aboard the *I2,* it looked different than the visit prior. This time it was still recognizable as the same space, but only because Earnest had spent most of the last decade working on different projects across New Canaan.

Tanis and Joe wove through the jumbled mess of half-completed projects, most of which had purposes Tanis couldn't even fathom.

"What do you suppose that's for?" Joe asked, pointing at a device that looked like a long, narrow, ship-mounted laser cannon.

"Not sure…looks too small to be effective at long-range," Tanis replied.

<That was an early version of the Mark VII polariton-based lasers we used until we upgraded everything to particle weapons,> Angela replied, refreshing Tanis's memory. *<You saw it back when we first settled in Victoria.>*

"Yeah…I vaguely recall that. I remember the ones we put in service, just not that."

<I bet a lot of Inner Stars systems would kill for this tech, and here it sits.> Angela sounded almost remorseful.

"Why?" Joe asked. "They have antimatter to power electron and proton beams. Not to mention gamma rays. Why do they care about lasers? Photons are far less effective weapons."

<Because there are non-military uses for efficient lasers, Joe. Not to mention that antimatter and fusion reactors are a bit dangerous. You can run polariton beams off solar power—if you don't need it as a weapon.>

"OK, got me there. Sometimes I have tunnel vision."

Tanis squeezed Joe's hand. "You and me both."

They rounded a corner and arrived at an open space with an a-grav pad in the middle. Earnest stood at the edge and nodded in greeting.

"On time, even. Excellent."

"What do you mean?" Tanis asked. "I'm always punctual."

The chief engineer gave her a quizzical look. "I meant me."

Joe barked a laugh, while Tanis replied with a soundless 'Oh'.

"So, what do you think?" Earnest asked, gesturing at the a-grav pad.

"Why do we need that?" Joe asked as he approached it. "Aren't we going to do the standard sim where we pick traits from a pseudo DNA strand, Angela does some randomizing and then adds the traits to a clone of her neural net, and voila?"

"I really don't know," Earnest said. "Angela just told me what she needed. We're doing it in my lab for privacy—best not to let the masses know too much about your brain, Tanis, Angela."

"OK, Ang, what gives?" Tanis asked.

<Wellll.> Angela drew the word out slowly. *<Most of the time, the trait selections for an AI child—for organic ones, too—are deliberate, like you were talking about, Joe. But I want to do something different. I want us to take a journey through our lives. I've written—with some help from Earnest, don't let him fool you—something that will take us through our pasts, remind us of the good and the bad. We'll respond to the events, and the system I've made will select the traits we exhibit.>*

"That sounds novel." Tanis had never heard of this method before, but it sounded interesting.

<It's closer to how AIs generate new neural nets between non-organics.>

"The base net, a clone of Angela's, is here." Earnest patted a small cylinder mounted atop an imaging system. "What you experience will feed into it, and we'll bake ourselves a baby."

"Faleena," Joe said. "In just a short while, we'll get to meet Faleena."

<*Daughter number three,*> Angela added. <*Getting a brood going.*>

"Not a patch on what Jessica did," Tanis replied. "Sixteen kids is a lot to catch up to."

Joe's warm laugh escaped his lips. "That's for sure. I don't think I'm ready for that."

"We also don't have the Dream to raise our kids in a flash."

"You know…" Earnest began, touching his index finger to his lips. "I wonder if I could figure that out."

<*Earnest, we've talked about that.*> Bob's voice filled the air around them—an impressive feat, since he spoke into their minds. <*The rest of humanity isn't ready for what they did at Star City. I'm not convinced* ***they*** *were, either.*>

"Your reservations notwithstanding, they *did* do it, old friend," Earnest replied. "Though it's not necessary to use the Dream in this case. Faleena will mature fast enough."

<*I'll ensure it,*> Angela replied.

Tanis knew that was true, but she could still feel Angela's sadness—which mirrored her own. They would only have a short time with this daughter. Something like the Dream from Star City could have given them a lifetime before they had to leave.

Not going to get lost in that worry. Tanis forced the thoughts out of her mind. She didn't want fear for the future to be present when she helped create her daughter.

MEMORIES

STELLAR DATE: 04.23.8948 (Adjusted Years)
LOCATION: Ol' Sam, ISS *I2*
REGION: In Orbit of Carthage, New Canaan System

Tanis's breath caught as she suddenly found herself on the shores of the Melas Chasma, the great rift-valley sea on Mars.

Tall grass blew in a gentle wind, and small waves lapped gently at the water's edge, a dozen meters from her feet. She looked up to see the blue sky punctuated by Mars's artificial rings. First was the wide expanse of Mars 1, with its own lakes, rivers, mountains, and forests visible above her. Beyond that was the MCEE ring, with its spiderweb of stations and platforms hanging from long tethers.

What she saw was a memory, something from a time long ago. Mars was no longer a lush, green planet. The Mars 1 ring no longer hung above. The images Tanis had seen of its destruction flashed in her mind. All this—her childhood home—was gone.

The seashore where she now stood lay under a billion tons of wreckage, the remains of the ring that once hung above.

Mars 1. Humanity's first megastructure. Destroyed by the Jovian Combine, which now styled itself as the Hegemony of Worlds, spreading their cruel regime across the stars.

A hand rested on her shoulder. "Relax, Tanis. We're here to remember what was, not what is."

Tanis turned to see Angela and Joe standing beside her. It was Joe's hand on her shoulder, but Angela had spoken.

She reached around Joe and pinched Angela.

"Ow!"

Tanis smiled. "Just curious how real this sim is."

"I like it here," Joe said as he walked to the water's edge. "It's been a while since we used a sim to visit."

"It's not the same…knowing what happened." Tanis gestured at the Mars 1 ring overhead.

Joe nodded. "Yeah, it's what we get for outliving civilizations. Nothing lasts forever."

Tanis wished it would have. To stand on these shores would have been the only reason she'd ever consider going back to Sol. Though she feared a return may be necessary someday, regardless.

Although, with Sera's plan to have the Scipian Empire take on the Hegemony of Worlds, maybe she wouldn't have to. Let someone else clean up humanity's homeworld. Tanis was done with it.

Angela reached for her hand. "Tanis, you need to stop worrying about the past and future so much. It's not what we're here for."

Tanis turned and looked into Angela's eyes. Her friend so rarely used a physical Avatar anymore. Largely because when the AI did it without thinking, she invariably made an avatar that looked like Tanis's twin.

Like she did right now—though her eyes were green, not blue, and her blonde hair had a reddish tint.

Joe walked to the water's edge, then turned and stared at the two women. "Is it wrong that I love both of you?"

His eyes were troubled, and Tanis wanted to remove this worry for him. "Joe, you let Angela sing you to sleep—and she does it. This isn't news to either of us."

Both Tanis and Angela reached out for him, and the trio embraced on the shores where Tanis had once played as a young girl, dreaming of going to space and seeing what wonders the universe held.

She closed her eyes, and when she opened them once more, they were standing in a garden filled with an abundance of plants laden with fruit and vegetables.

"Oh ho!" Joe cried out as he looked around. "Boy did I spend a lot of time pulling weeds in here!"

Tanis looked into the sky and saw a fusion sun above. By the spectrum, she pegged it as a GE model FS-12A. "The Evans's household on Venus, I presume?"

"One and the same," Joe replied as he walked out into the rows and examined a tomato plant. "I loved coming out here—well, not at first. Mom always said that she didn't need bots to manage her garden, she had a dozen kids. What else were they good for, if not pulling weeds?"

"It's nice to know that this might still be here," Angela added as she walked through the garden toward one of the trees and plucked a pear.

"Whoa now!" Joe laughed. "Mom didn't like unauthorized fruit-picking. She had a plan for every part of the yield."

Angela grinned as she took a bite of the pear, slurping as the juices spilled down her chin. "Damn! That's harder to do than I thought!"

"Juices will be juicy." Joe winked as he walked back to Tanis and took her hand. "Whatcha thinking, love?"

Tanis let a rueful laugh slip out. "About how very different your home was than mine. My father would have abhorred a garden. I'm sure he would have said something like, 'Growing plants like this is an inefficient use of resources!'"

Angela snorted, dribbling more pear juice down her chin. "You do your father well."

"I forget that you met him a few times," Tanis said to Angela.

"Indeed, I did. He was bit of an ass. But I wonder what he'd think of what we've done."

"Stars," Tanis sighed. "He would have dissected the shit out of every decision I ever made."

"I bet he would have been proud." Joe held up his hands, apparently ready for the retort Tanis was readying. "Seriously, he would be. I know there's a temptation as a father to pick apart your children's efforts to help them do better. Yes, your dad was a serious dick in a lot of ways, but he was always trying to help, in his misguided fashion."

" 'Misguided' is putting it lightly," Tanis said as she leaned against a column that supported a trellis. "That man never saw a compliment that he couldn't turn backhanded."

"You know, Tanis," Angela said. "We are *supposed* to be picking out *good* memories. Things we want to pass on to our daughter."

"We are," Joe said. "Tanis has steel in her spine—metaphorically as well as physically. Where do you think that came from?"

"Yay, my childhood was a crucible." Tanis waved a hand in the air, signaling mock victory, then she straightened. "No, you're right, Angela. Mopey dopey isn't my thing. I think seeing the Melas Chasma got me messed up in the head. I'm ready."

The garden disappeared, and they were suddenly on the side of a mountain, standing on a narrow ledge, with a sharp, thousand-meter drop centimeters from their feet.

"Now, this is more like it!" Tanis exclaimed.

"Where the heck are we now?" Joe asked, yelling to be heard over the winds whipping around them.

"Pavonis Mons!" Tanis shouted back. "This is where I had my first real climb."

Joe looked down at the drop below their feet. "I thought Pavonis Mons had gentle slopes!"

"Yeah," Tanis nodded. "It mostly does, but there's an escarpment here on the southwestern flank. It's where most kids I knew growing up did their initial climbs."

"You Marsians are nuts," Joe said, shaking his head. "How old were you when you did this?"

"Fourteen. Though I had a rebreather, and the cliffs were patrolled by drones. No one died up here, but you might get battered a bit if you fell."

An especially strong gust of wind whipped past, and Tanis felt it tug at her, pulling her away from the cliff face.

"I'll admit," Angela called out. "This is exhilarating!"

Joe shook his head and laughed. "And here I thought *I* was the crazy flyboy."

"Do I normally show caution, or ease into things?" Tanis retorted. "You've made fun of me for that more than once."

"Feel more like yourself?" Angela asked Tanis.

"Stars, yes! Thanks, Ang. You know just what a girl needs."

Angela nodded and touched Tanis's head. "Even though I'm out here, I'm still in there. I can feel what you feel."

"What would happen if I stepped off the cliff?" Joe asked. "How real is this sim?"

"*Now* who's the thrill-seeker?" Tanis laughed as she grabbed Joe's hand, and saw him grab Angela's. They looked at one another, each with a grin on their faces.

"Leap before you look!" Angela called out, and all three stepped off the cliff as one.

They fell for a moment and then landed on something hard. Tanis looked around and saw that the sky was black, and they were standing on a gleaming silver hull.

"It's the *Intrepid*," she said, somehow speaking aloud, though they were in the cold vacuum of space.

"Back when she was new," Joe added, bending down and patting the hull.

"Another of our homes." Angela nodded appreciatively. "*The* home."

Tanis laid down on the ship's hull, staring up at the stars. "The journey became the destination. Where are we, anyway—wait, never mind. We're in Sol, or close to it. The Centaur's front leg is in the right place."

"This is when we passed out of Sol's heliosphere," Angela supplied.

Joe laid down beside Tanis and folded his hands behind his head. "When we all really left home for the first time."

"We were all in stasis by this point," Tanis said, glancing over at Angela. "Why are we seeing this?"

Angela shrugged. "Just wanted to see how we all felt being here, thinking of it."

"I like it," Joe said. "Feels good to think of this time, of what lay ahead."

Tanis nodded. "Tough times, but we pulled through."

Joe unclasped his hands and reached over to Tanis, patting her on the stomach. "Did a lot of good, too."

"My stomach did? I'm not gestating Faleena in there, you know. She's growing in our noggins."

Joe laughed. The sound was infectious, and Tanis joined in a moment before Angela did.

"I patted your stomach because it's what I could reach without worrying about elbowing you in the face. I guess I could have patted your breast. I'll do that next time."

"Sure, promises, promises."

"Easy, you two," Angela said. "No shenanigans. I don't want to be left out."

Joe looked over at Angela, who lay on his other side. "Who said you'd be left out?"

Tanis propped herself up onto her elbow to see her friend's response.

Angela was a bit wide-eyed. "Well, that's a twist."

"Is it?" Joe asked. "Look at you, Angela; you're almost identical to Tanis now. You never used to portray yourself that way. Half the time when you speak, I hear Tanis's words coming from you—" Joe turned his head to look at Tanis. "And half the time, I hear Angela in you. I don't think it's possible to love one of you and not the other. I'm not even certain how separate you two even *are* anymore."

Tanis felt an uncertain expression creep across her face. She could see it mirrored on Angela's. Did Angela really feel uncertain, or was her otherself showing the same expression because what one felt, the other did as well?

"Sometimes we can't tell ourselves apart, either," Tanis admitted. "Certain thoughts are clearly mine, and others are Angela's, but some…some things seem to come from us both at the same time."

"I don't know why you worry about that so much with me." Joe's voice was compassionate, but a little strident. "I came to accept this years ago…back on the Gamma Base at Kapteyn's. Honestly, it makes things easier."

"It does?" Angela asked.

"Yeah," Joe replied. "Angela, you're a fantastic person. And I've spent almost as much time with you as I have with Tanis."

"Technically, you've spent the exact same amount of time with me as with Tanis."

Tanis rolled her eyes. "Har, har, Ang. Now *that* came just from you."

Joe slid his left arm under Tanis's head, and his right under Angela's, pulling them both close. "You're not my wives; you're my *wife*.

Tanis leaned forward to brush her lips against Joe's cheek at the same time that Angela did. At first, she wondered why her otherself had done that, but then she realized they were moving in concert, mirrors of each other. She felt herself in both bodies, and felt Angela in both, as well.

"This is strange," Angela said as she pressed her lips against Joe's neck.

"More like 'fantastic', if you ask me, Angela." Joe smiled broadly.

"I'm Tanis," Angela said.

"And I'm Tanis," Tanis added.

Joe looked from Angela to Tanis, confusion and a little concern in his eyes.

"Are you two OK? If you're in both, Tanis…Where's Angela?"

"Here," both Tanis and Angela said at once.

"Are you…finally one person?" Joe asked.

"No," Tanis said with Angela's voice. "Well, maybe right now, in this moment, we are."

Tanis-Angela leaned back over Joe and planted her lips on his, while Angela-Tanis unfastened his shirt.

Joe closed his eyes and drew in a deep breath. "Not going to argue with this, love, but I thought we were making a baby with our minds, not our bodies."

"Our bodies are floating above the a-grav pad in Earnest's lab," Angela-Tanis said. "We *are* using our minds."

Joe laughed. "OK, if that's how you want to play this."

NEW ADDITION

STELLAR DATE: 04.23.8948 (Adjusted Years)
LOCATION: Ol' Sam, ISS *I2*
REGION: In Orbit of Carthage, New Canaan System

After their lovemaking, the trio traveled through dozens more memories. They experienced times during their long solitude aboard the *Intrepid*, the years building the Victoria colony, Tanis's abduction, and Joe's search.

A dozen more past experiences came and went, the struggles and victories that made them who they were coming back into their minds.

Eventually, they relived the final memory that Angela had selected, the reunion with Cary and Saanvi after the girls had been found in the wreckage of the Trisilieds fleet.

As they stood in the hospital room, watching themselves with their daughters, Angela turned to Tanis and Joe, a wide smile creeping across her lips.

"We've done it," she whispered. "We've made another daughter. Faleena is alive."

"Born of our minds," Joe said as he gazed at the memory from just a few short weeks ago.

Angela touched his cheek and then wrapped an arm around Tanis. "And maybe a bit of our bodies, too."

The memory faded, and Tanis found herself alone in darkness for a moment before Earnest's lab swam into place around her.

She blinked and realized that her limbs were entwined with Joe's as they floated in the a-grav column.

Joe opened his eyes and smiled as his gaze settled on Tanis. "Well that was fun, we should do that again sometime."

"To make another child?" Tanis asked.

"Sure," Joe said with a small shrug. "Or maybe do it just for pleasure."

<No objections here,> Angela replied. *<I'll admit…I've never felt some of those things before. Even living in Tanis's mind, it was somehow different this time.>*

"Trust me," Tanis grinned. "It was different for me, too."

The sound of a throat being cleared reminded Tanis that Earnest was present, and she turned to look in his direction. His face was a little red as he stood beside the imaging system.

"We didn't…uh…do anything inappropriate, did we?" Tanis asked.

"Well, you're married, so there's nothing wrong with it—I just didn't expect to see it."

"Our clothes are still on," Joe said with a wink. "It couldn't have been anything too extreme."

"I would have thought so, too," Earnest said with a manufactured look of shock on his face. "But it turns out there's a lot you can do with clothes on."

"Stop it," Tanis chided as the a-grav column lowered them back down to the deck, and she pulled out her hard-Link cable. "Is she…conscious?"

<She is,> Angela's avatar was beaming in their minds. A small girl was holding her hand, and Angela picked her up. *<Faleena, say 'hi' to your other mother and your father.>*

Faleena's voice was like the sound of leaves blowing in a light wind, with rain pattering around. *<Hi, Mom and Dad.>*

It was one of the most beautiful sounds Tanis had ever heard.

THE END

RAPID EXFILTRATION

FAMILY

STELLAR DATE: 03.29.8948 (Adjusted Years)
LOCATION: Genmere District
REGION: Airtha, Huygens System, Transcend Interstellar Alliance

Flaherty held back a sigh and schooled his expression to hide the worry that was building inside. He reached across the table for his daughter's hand, but she pulled hers away, a mixture of anger and fear behind her hazel eyes.

"Mary." Flaherty ensured his voice was calm. "I understand that you only recently moved, and that you just got the promotion at your job. I am happy for your accomplishments, I really am. You've come so far and you make me a proud father every day."

Mary's expression softened at his words, but only a little. She had too much of her mother in her to let flattery sway her overmuch.

"I don't see how. You're telling me to throw it all away. You must not hold my 'accomplishments' in any great esteem." Her delivery was calm, but he could see a tremor in her lips. Deep down, she had to know that her father would not make such a request lightly, that something must be very wrong.

"I do, but I am." Flaherty gave a single nod, his eyes not breaking contact with hers. "I *need* you to understand this in the simplest of terms. Those accomplishments won't mean a thing if you're dead."

"Dead? Dad, what in the light are you talking about?"

Her turn of speech gave him momentary pause. *'What in the light.'* He'd heard that saying with increasing frequency over the past few years. At first, he thought it just meant the stars' light, or perhaps Airtha's light. But with the recent news, he wondered if it had been seeded in preparation for the coup he believed had occurred over the past day.

"I'm sorry, but being my daughter has put you at great risk, Mary," Flaherty replied.

"Dad," Mary said, a scoffing sound escaping her lips. "You're a close friend of Sera Tomlinson. I even heard a rumor that her father is considering turning over the presidency to her. What could you fear that she can't protect us from?"

His mind went to the woman he'd met a few hours ago. Whoever…whatever she was.

"The person…she is not Sera Tomlinson." Flaherty shook his head. "It's close—oh, so close. But there's a piece that's missing."

"Dad. You're making absolutely no sense."

Flaherty rose from his chair and ran a hand through his long hair, tightening the band that held it secure. "You're right about that. But I know this. Sera Tomlinson—*my* Sera Tomlinson—left with her father for New Canaan a few days ago. Their departure was kept quiet, so few knew of it. I also know that they have *not* returned. Yet Sera reached out to me today, and we met."

"Then she *has* returned."

"Daughter mine, you know I am a Sinshea. I cannot lie. The person I met today was a perfect clone of Sera—well, a clone of Sera as she was some time ago. But she was *not* Sera in mind."

Mary ran a hand down her cheek as she stared up at Flaherty. "OK. You can't lie. You *think* that Sera is gone, and you met with someone who was not Sera. But why should *I* think that, and why would this not-Sera try to harm you?"

Flaherty shrugged. "It could be because I told her that I didn't believe she was Sera, and then she had her guards try to kill me."

"Dad! Shit! Why didn't you lead with that?"

"I was getting there, but then you got angry at me."

Mary was already moving, rushing into her bedroom to grab a bag, stuffing a change of clothing and a few personal effects inside.

"If she tried to kill you, she'll come for us! We have to get Drew!" she called out to him.

"I have someone picking him up. A trusted friend."

Mary reappeared at her bedroom's doorway, her gaze narrow. "A friend?"

"*Trusted* friend. Leeroy."

"Dammit, Dad! I don't know if you've forgotten, but Leeroy and I are *not* involved anymore."

"Doesn't make him any less trustworthy," Flaherty replied. "Drew knows him and will go along. They'll meet us at the rendezvous."

Mary grabbed a jacket and shouldered her bag, looking around her home. "How long do I have?"

Flaherty handed his daughter a pulse pistol. "Do you remember how to use this?"

She grabbed it from him, checked the charge and the emitter. "Yeah, I still practice, you know that."

"Good."

A dull thud shook the floor—the pulse-mine he had planted on her front step. He checked the drones he'd deployed above the hill and saw three figures laying prone on Mary's front lawn.

The drones didn't spot anyone else, but a lack of visual confirmation was hardly evidence of safety.

Flaherty nodded to Mary. "Time to go. Come."

She didn't say another word, though more than one disgruntled look came his way as they ran through her home and out the rear door.

Mary's home was on a terraced hill in Airtha's Genmere district. Her front door looked out over sweeping hills covered in blooming foliage, but the back door emptied out into a passageway that ran through the center of the hill.

"We're sitting ducks in here," Mary muttered.

"Yes."

Flaherty stopped three doors down from Mary's house and planted a lockhak over the access panel. A small light on the device turned red, then yellow, then green.

He grabbed the lockhak and pushed the door open.

"Quickly," he said, ushering Mary inside.

"Light above, I hope Sally's not home, she's going to be piiiissed."

Flaherty ignored the comment and walked through the house to the bay window at the front, standing a meter back as he peered through the glass.

This residence—Sally's, it would seem—looked out on the other side of the hill from his daughter's, and from what he could see, there was no sign of any enemies.

He wondered who not-Sera would send after him. It could be anyone from Airthan police to TSF soldiers, Hand agents, Greys, or any of the other elite forces the Transcend government operated.

Or worse.

The images he'd seen of the TSF Combat Automatons attacking

Secretary Adrienne's shuttle on High Airtha just the day before came to mind. He didn't know if the secretary had survived, but there had been rumors of not-Sera's presence there, too.

What little he had learned came from a friend in the High Airtha Police Department. A friend who had not responded to any attempts at communication in the last four hours.

Mary was at his side, staring out the window. "What are we looking for?"

"Everything," he replied. "I have a car at the road two levels down."

"They can track cars," Mary cautioned. "We need to get deeper into the ring."

"You're right. We will. Come."

Flaherty pushed the door open and held his breath as he stepped out into the Airthan star's sharp white light. He didn't pause as he walked down the front walk, glad that Mary was close behind. When they reached the shared pathway, he kept close to the shrubbery at the edge of the road, looking up the terraced hill to see if any pursuers were coming over the top.

The team not-Sera had sent was too small. She would know that three lightly armored agents wouldn't be able to bring him in. There had to be others nearby.

<*Do you have any drones out?*> Mary asked. <*I can help watch their feeds.*>

Flaherty nodded and passed two feeds from further up the hill to her, glad she remembered her training well enough to ask for them.

They turned down a staircase with a bower of branches overhead and came to the road where his car waited.

It was a sleek and low sport-racer. One that he'd upgraded with moderate stealth systems and anti-EM capabilities. An eye could spot the car, but it was almost entirely invisible on the higher end of the EM spectrum.

But Flaherty already knew they had eyes on the hill, and there was no way they wouldn't cover the rear.

He held up a hand and gestured for Mary to wait, while he walked back up the cover path and worked his way further along the hill, above a rock outcropping. He deployed a surveillance countermeasure drone, hoping his Hand-issued tech was better than his prey's.

At twenty meters from the outcropping, Flaherty stopped and cycled his vision to focus in.

Sure enough, there was a stealthed sniper on the rock. Flaherty couldn't see the person, but he *could* make out a small tuft of grass on the rock, flattened by a body on top.

Must be local police. Greys or Hand would have better stealth tech.

There was no time to wonder why not-Sera had sent the cops—and not anyone else—as he crept down the hillside toward the rock.

He gauged where the shooter had to be laying in order to get a line of sight on the car, and fired three pulse blasts.

A series of scrapes and scuffling sounds came from the surface of the stone, and pebbles and dirt moved around under the invisible person.

Flaherty decided not to fire another shot and instead rushed down the hillside and delivered a kick to what he hoped was the figure's head.

A woman's groan came, and Flaherty knelt down, putting his knee on what he believed to be her stomach.

"Shut off your stealth tech, or I'll just kill you," he whispered.

"OK," the invisible figure wheezed.

The woman's body shimmered into view, as did a large caliber sniper rifle.

"Smart rounds?" he asked, and the woman nodded.

"No opportunity to surrender, eh? Just blow the car when we get in."

"Orders," she wheezed.

"How many are there?" Flaherty asked.

The woman didn't reply, and her face was covered by her mask. He pulled it off and leant close to her face. "Numbers."

"Six."

Flaherty shook his head, then grabbed her hair and slammed her head into the rock. Not hard enough to kill, but enough to make her rethink her life choices.

<We're clear, get in the car,> he called back to Mary.

<Was anyone out there?>

He grabbed the sniper rifle and set off down the hillside. *<Just one.>*

<You sure?>

<Yeah, she wasn't a very good liar.>

Flaherty reached the car a half-minute later to find Mary waiting at the right-side door. He gestured for her to get in as he pulled open his door and placed the sniper rifle in the back.

"That's some serious hardware," Mary said as they settled into their seats.

"Enough to blow the car," Flaherty replied as he activated the vehicle and took off. No point in waiting around to see if the woman had not been lying.

He set the car to drive on a pre-programmed route down the hill while he ran the scan suite, checking for any further hostiles. Luckily, nothing showed up other than residents in their homes, and the regular traffic on the hill.

Then Mary grabbed his arm. "Two gunships approaching, seven kilometers out. They're staying low, only a dozen meters above the ground."

OK, regular stuff…and gunships.

He tapped the drone feeds she was watching and spotted the enemies. "Good work. Keep an eye out for others."

There was no reason to believe that the gunships had seen them yet, but there was also no reason to believe that those were the only enemies approaching.

Though a pair of heavily armed gunships approaching would terrify most people, it was comforting to Flaherty. Not-Sera was using conventional means against him, which meant he was less likely to encounter a gunship around the next corner on the road.

OK…still could be a gunship around the corner, but it's a bit less likely.

Flaherty took over manual control of the car and pushed the throttle forward. He activated the car's EM dampening, which would make it even harder for the approaching attack craft to spot them.

"You should go for Tunnel 72," Mary suggested.

Flaherty grunted in acknowledgement; Tunnel 72 was on his list of possible egress routes.

Consisting of one hundred and ten lanes of horizontal traffic, and thirty of vertical, the tunnel was tucked half a kilometer beneath the surface of the ring. At this time of day, it would be packed, the volume of vehicles creating a near-perfect hiding place—both physically and electromagnetically.

The problem with Tunnel 72 was that it had traffic shunting systems that could move vehicles to other routes, or just stop them altogether, creating an impassible three-dimensional gridlock.

"Seriously, Dad. Tunnel 72 is our best bet. I know what you're thinking, but they can lock down the other routes faster, and we can't drive around on the ring's surface with gunships hunting us."

"OK," he nodded, and turned the car off the surface road at the first entrance to the subterranean tunnel system.

Several other cars were ahead of them on the descent ramp, and he swerved into the oncoming lane to pass the vehicles.

"Dad…that's a hauler coming our way!" Mary braced herself as a large, boxy vehicle rounded the bend, heading straight for them.

Flaherty only grunted as he pushed the accelerator all the way forward and sped past the remaining slow-moving cars, swerving back into their lane a scant few meters before hitting the hauler.

"Piece of cake," he said, looking for the exit to drop further down into the ring.

"Next right," Mary said, her breath coming quickly as she shot him a dark look.

At the exit, there was a long, sloping road to bring cars down to Tunnel 72. The road wrapped around a large vertical shaft through which a-grav transports flitted.

Flaherty tapped into the traffic network, looking at the patterns in the shaft for a moment before twisting the controls sharply and boosting the car's a-grav systems.

They surged into the air and flew over the decorative rocks and shrubbery at the edge of the road, slotting into a clear pocket in the shaft traffic.

Mary sucked in a breath, but didn't say anything as Flaherty pointed the nose of the car down and killed its vertical a-grav lift. They dropped like a rock, and he worked the lateral a-grav emitters to weave in and out of the transports while the ring's motion force tried to send them into the anti-spinward wall of the shaft.

"I don't know why they made these shafts straight…they should have angled them," Mary muttered as Flaherty wove around the other shaft traffic.

He didn't respond, concentrating on lining up to drop into the top layer of traffic in Tunnel 72—which he managed to pull off with only a light bump against a hauler.

"Just be glad they didn't enforce maglev as strictly here," he said while trying to keep his breathing even, pushing the car toward its max speed of three hundred meters per second.

"Yeah…well…starting to wish they did!" Mary said through clenched teeth as Flaherty squeezed the car between the top level of traffic and the roof of the tunnel.

"We'll drop down into lower traffic in a minute," Flaherty grunted as he swerved around vehicles entering from a shaft above. "We're close to the rendezvous. Grab the glide packs from the back."

He watched out of the corner of his eye as Mary turned and grabbed the two packs.

"Shit, I think I saw two drones drop in back there!" Mary called out.

"I disabled the biolock on the sniper rifle. Take them out!" Flaherty ordered.

"What? Dad! I've never fired anything like this!"

Flaherty swerved around a large hauler that consumed two lanes, and rotated the car onto its side to squeeze between it and another truck. He heard Mary fall sideways onto the side of the car, and then back onto her seat as he leveled out again.

"It's a smart gun. It'll guide you. Activate it, find your target, fire."

"Just keep us level, for light's sake," Mary muttered.

Flaherty did his best, though the ride was still far from smooth.

"Ok…" Flaherty heard his daughter whisper as she crouched on her seat, the gun's bipod resting on the back dash. He quickly rolled his window down, creating an outlet for the pressure wave the weapon would create inside the vehicle, not to mention the sound.

"Watch the re—" he began to say as Mary fired.

The gun threw her back against the dashboard, and she cried out in pain as her head cracked against the windscreen.

"—coil."

His right ear rang so loudly he could barely hear Mary as she yelled at him.

"Fuck! Thanks for the timely warning, *Dad.*"

"Did you get it?" Flaherty hollered back over the sounds of the traffic and their impaired hearing—though that was rapidly clearing up for him. She may be hearing bells for some time.

Mary struggled forward once more and looked out the back window. "Shit, yeah…blew it to smithereens. I hope no one got hurt."

"Mostly automated transports up here," Flaherty replied. "Where's the other one?"

He could see Mary peering around, swinging the rifle side-to-side as she used its holosights to search for the other drone.

"Shit! Duck!"

Flaherty dropped his head as shots hit the car, some bouncing off, some going clear through.

He didn't have time to check himself over as Mary swung the rifle around while calling out, "Stay down!"

Flaherty acquiesced, staying hunched forward, and felt the barrel of the gun resting on his back. It wasn't too hot yet, but if she fired more than a few—

A trio of rounds burst from the barrel and his right ear seemed to shut down entirely. He did see an explosion outside the car, and Mary sat back in her seat, lifting the hot barrel off his back.

He saw her lips move, but couldn't hear a word she was saying—she probably couldn't, either.

<*Get the glide packs,*> he reminded her, dropping the car down into the next level of traffic.

He saw her nod silently, her face a mixture of fear and excitement.

Flaherty didn't blame her. Firing a weapon like that rifle was a rush when you *weren't* doing it inside a vehicle moving at three hundred meters per second.

She managed to get the rifle tucked down between them, and then reached into the back for the glide packs. <*Diving out of the car, I take it?*> her mental tone was calm, but he could see her hands shaking as she pulled the glide packs into the front seat.

Flaherty nodded. <*I'll slow down first.*>

<*Gee, thanks, Dad. Think I'll ever hear again?*>

<*Give it a few minutes. It'll be back soon.*>

Lane by lane and level by level, he worked his way down through Tunnel 72's traffic. The car had racked up over seventy fines, but the vehicle's remote kill-system was disabled, and the car wasn't connected to Flaherty in any way.

More drones had been deployed—or, he expected they had—but so far, none were visible around them. That was the difficulty for law enforcement. They couldn't put everyone at risk to catch one speeding car—even if it was firing on drones.

Flaherty, on the other hand, had no compunctions about scaring the crap out of other drivers if it meant saving his daughter.

When he reached the second to lowest level of traffic—the bottom consisting of maglevs and bulk haulers without a-grav—he slowed to match the flow of traffic and set the car back to autopilot.

Mary handed him the second glide pack, and he slid his arms through the loops, pulling it snug to his chest.

"I can finally hear again…mostly," she said with a nervous smile.

"Good. On three, then," he said. "One, two, three!"

They kicked their doors open and jumped out of the car, gliding alongside the vehicle for a moment before Flaherty signaled Mary to follow him.

He tucked into the left-hand side of the tunnel as the car sped off once more, pulling back up into the main flow of traffic. Flaherty turned his attention to the task at hand, searching for the maintenance shaft showed by the ring's schematics overlaid on his HUD.

<You know they have cameras down here; they'll have seen us get out of the car,> Mary said as she pulled up beside him.

<I have a friend who knocked them out,> Flaherty replied as he spotted the narrow maintenance shaft and turned into it.

<And the cameras on all those cars, haulers, and maglevs?>

<A localized network routing issue is going to make a mess of all the data feeds to the NSAI analysts. We should have thirty minutes before they realize where we went.>

Flaherty glanced back at his daughter to see her lips drawn in a thin line. She didn't speak further, and he didn't offer any more information.

There would be plenty of time for her to lay into him when they got on the ship.

SHIP OUT

STELLAR DATE: 03.29.8948 (Adjusted Years)
LOCATION: Ring Service Tunnel 183.AA91.CC2
REGION: Airtha, Huygens System, Transcend Interstellar Alliance

Mary set down on the platform beside her father and pulled off the glide pack while looking out over the tunnel they'd stopped in.

It angled down at just over twenty degrees, was dimly lit, and probably would eventually dump right out of the ring into space.

"Your pack," Flaherty said, holding out his hand.

Mary handed hers over, and he grunted in acknowledgement. She watched as he linked the two glide packs together and programmed a flight path into them.

Then her father gave a single nod of satisfaction and tossed the glide packs back into the shaft, where they sped off.

"Should buy us a bit more time," he said before turning to the door leading off the platform.

"Any word from Leeroy?" Mary knew not to Link to the networks, but she hoped that her father had managed some way to spoof his connection, so he could keep tabs on things.

"No," Flaherty replied as he placed his lockhak over the access panel and took a step back. "I don't want to risk contact. If there was a problem, Leeroy would let me know."

"What if the problem is that he's *dead*?" Mary asked, working to keep back the panic that had been at the edge of her mind since her father whisked her away. A panic that was somehow exacerbated by the adrenaline rush from firing the sniper rifle.

"Mary," her father turned and placed his hands on her shoulders. "Not-Sera wants Drew as leverage over me. If she had him, she'd use him for that. They won't kill him."

"There are still a lot—" Mary stopped talking. She didn't want to think of the things that could happen to her son.

"Drew's a smart kid, Mary. Hell, he's not even a kid anymore. He's twenty-five years old."

Mary bit her lip as she stared into her father's serious, entirely unperturbable eyes. That was the best, and worst, thing about him—no matter what happened, he never lost his cool.

For a second, she wanted to slap him, get him to react to the danger they were in—that he'd *placed* them in. But instead, she took a step forward and wrapped her arms around his broad chest.

"You don't let anything happen to him," she whispered. "He's the most important thing in the universe to me."

Her father's thick arms settled around her. "I won't. Not to either of you. I feel the same way about you that you feel about him. You're both precious to me."

Mary saw the light on the lockhak change color. "Door's open."

Flaherty nodded but didn't step away for another moment.

How is it that he can be such a fantastic dad while being a terrible father? Or is it the other way around?

He kissed her head and then turned to the door, sliding it open with one hand while detaching the lockhak with the other.

"C'mon. It's not too much further."

Mary picked up her pack and stepped into the passageway while her father pulled the door shut behind them.

"Turn right, then left, then left, then pass seven intersections, right, left, two intersections, right," he said softly as he took the lead, moving in his strident, yet cautious way. "Repeat it back."

Mary sighed. Of course she could repeat it. With her mental mods, her short-term memory was perfect. "Right, left, left, seven intersections, right, left, two intersections, right."

"Wrong," Flaherty said. "You would have turned right at the seventh intersection. *Pass* seven, then right. I shouldn't need to remind you about our nomenclature."

She couldn't resist an eyeroll. "You don't. I knew what you meant."

"Good."

Though her father's directions made it seem as though the journey would be quick, the intersections in the narrow tunnels were widely separated. Twenty minutes had gone by, and they'd just passed the seventh intersection before the second-to-last right turn, when her father stopped and held up his hand.

Mary pulled up behind him and waited for his go-ahead. He had already halted several times, but he seemed more tensed this time.

She daren't speak, and without a narrow-band Link connection, it was too risky to attempt a direct connect to her father to ask what he'd heard—her ears were still ringing, but she knew that with his mods, he'd be fine by now.

Then his hand touched her shoulder, and she almost cried out, but somehow managed to hold back the sound as he gestured for her to crouch behind a support column fixed to the passage's wall.

With a short nod, she did as he instructed, carefully setting her bag down and drawing her pulse pistol. She knew his desire was to keep her out of combat—but he also expected her to fight if necessary.

She peeked around the column and watched her father creep down the passage, completely silent—at least to her ears.

Mary suspected that her father would have some nano probes deployed, but not many. He always said that relying too heavily on artificial eyes made you doubt the ones in your head.

She sat back, keeping an eye out toward the direction they'd come, wondering what her father had heard.

Stars, the only thing ***I*** *can hear—aside from this ringing—is my thundering heart,* Mary chided herself.

Her head back, she breathed out slowly, then held her breath a moment before drawing air in through her nose. She repeated the process, slowing her heart rate, the actions triggering her lungs to open up and draw in additional oxygen.

There, getting to A-State.

That was the name her father had given to the condition of being one with one's body, awareness expanded to take in one's surroundings without having to focus on anything.

"You just have to open yourself up to absorb your surroundings," he had always said.

Mary recalled those lessons where he had tried to teach her how to reach perfect calm, to feel the world around herself as though it were an organism, and she a cell in its body.

Sometimes she'd come close, but Mary was certain she was never as connected to her surroundings as her father was.

Even so, the breathing helped slow her heart, and she began to pick up more sounds—mostly the creaks and groans of the ring around her.

She wondered how far down they were in Airtha. The ring's

thickness varied from place to place. The main structure of the ring was nothing more than a great circle of highly compressed carbon. While the upper half was built up, the outside kilometer or so was pure diamond.

She suspected they weren't *that* deep, otherwise she would be surrounded by the ring's diamond, not plas and steel. Either that, or this shaft led to one of the structural accelerators nestled within the carbon body of the ring.

As Mary mused about her location, a soft scuffling sound caught her attention, and she held her breath, listening with every fiber of her being.

It came again, a clicking now, and the sound of breathing, fast and heavy…it sounded like….

A shaggy snout came around the column she was hiding behind, followed by a pair of soulful eyes.

"Ohhh," Mary whispered, as the dog came into view.

She held out her hand, and the dog came forward to sniff her fingers. A moment later, she was scratching the shaggy mutt behind his ears.

Dammit, she thought, realizing that she was being profoundly stupid. The dog would be impossible to keep still or quiet, yet shooing it off would make just as much noise—and may not be possible. Still, she was torn between how bad she felt for the abandoned dog, and the need for him to leave.

"Good boy, now go. I'm trying to hide, here."

The dog cocked its head to the side as though he understood her. He turned and backed in beside her, his teeth bared in a silent growl.

Is this dog uplifted? Did someone abandon an intelligent dog down here?

To her surprise, the dog stayed perfectly quiet and still after moving behind cover. Mary placed a hand on his head and stroked it gently, glad for the companionship—while growing increasingly worried about her father. At this point, he'd been gone for over five minutes.

Suddenly the dog ducked his head down and over, moving it out of reach.

He seemed to be casting her a look that said, 'I'm concentrating', then turned one of his large ears, listening intently.

Mary took the hint and listened as well, not hearing a thing.

A minute passed, and then she did hear something—a scraping sound that was getting closer. It wasn't loud, just a light, metallic scuff that came regularly.

She closed her eyes, concentrating on the sound.

It's growing louder!

Mary's eyes snapped open, and she looked to the dog, only to find that it was gone.

Oh, shit, I'm screwed!

With excruciatingly slow and exacting movements, Mary stood and readied herself for whatever would come, holding her pistol high across her chest, prepared to pivot her wrist and use the center-axis firing method her father had taught her.

The sound was close, almost at the column she was hidden behind. *Just a few seconds more…*

Nothing came. The scuffing had stopped.

Stars…this is worse, is it just waiting for me? What is it? A human? A machine? Some long-forgotten creature that's been living in this warren for years?

A minute passed, and Mary mustered up the courage to look around the column, surprised when her eyes took in the empty passageway. She wondered if her mind had been playing tricks on her. Maybe it was just another dog, and hers had gone off with it.

Then something grabbed her from behind and lifted her into the air.

"Faaaak!" Mary couldn't help the scream that tore itself out of her throat as she was pulled up by the collar of her jacket.

She twisted to see a six-legged drone hanging from the overhead, two of its long arms grasping her collar.

Mary swapped her pistol into the other hand and fired on the drone, hitting it right in its main optics, then again in the limbs that were holding her.

The drone twitched from the force of the pulse waves, and Mary dropped her pistol before raising her arms and sliding out of her jacket.

She landed on the deck and reached for her pistol, grabbing it a second before the drone skittered down the wall, reaching for her again.

Two shots from the pulse pistol barely slowed it down, and then the drone was atop her, pinning her arms beside her head as it sank its rear legs into her thighs.

The pistol slipped from her grasp, and Mary screamed again, trying to push the drone off—but it was impossibly heavy, and had begun to wiggle around.

Wait…that shape…

The reason why the drone felt so heavy was because the dog was on its back, snapping his jaws at the drone's legs.

The dog barked and clamped its teeth around one of the robotic limbs, pulling it up and then twisting. Mary was shocked to see the machine's leg break off. The dog repeated the process on another limb, this time freeing Mary's right arm.

She felt for the pulse pistol and breathed a long sigh of relief when her fingers wrapped around its grip.

The drone was twisting to avoid the dog, and then it finally reared back to knock the beast off.

Mary took advantage of the distance it created between them and fired a half-dozen pulse blasts into the thing's underside.

The drone shook and convulsed as smoke rose from one side. Mary pushed it off herself to see the dog standing by her feet, glaring at the machine and looking immensely proud of itself at the same time.

After a few steadying breaths, Mary struggled to her feet, wincing at the pain in her thighs. She looked at her pants and didn't see *too* much blood.

Maybe the holes it made aren't that deep…felt like they went right through me.

Certain she wasn't going to bleed to death, she bent over to scratch the dog behind its ears.

"C'mon, let's go find my dad. I'm not going to stay here and let more of those things try to skewer me."

Right, left, second right, she thought, setting off with the dog at her side.

It surprised her that the mutt had attached itself to her so quickly. Maybe it didn't see many people, or maybe those it did see were cruel to it. Either way, it seemed content to travel with her for now.

She turned the last corner on her father's prescribed route and almost ran straight into him.

"Mary!" he whispered. "Be more careful. What if I'd been an enemy?"

"I'd take you out like I did the last one—with my new friend's help, of course."

Flaherty looked down at the dog and smiled at the mutt. "Good work, Figgy."

"Figgy?" Mary asked.

"The dog. His name is Figgy."

"Is he yours?"

Flaherty turned and gestured for her to follow. "He is his. He lives down here. Figgy's a friend."

Mary glanced down at the dog who looked up at her and nodded.

"You're uplifted, Figgy?"

The dog nodded again, its gaze still on her.

"But you're not able to speak, I take it."

Figgy shook his head, and Flaherty looked over his shoulder. "I think he can, he just really, really doesn't want to. Goes against some sort of doggy-code."

Figgy cast her father a dark look and shook his head again.

"Whatever." Flaherty shrugged as they reached a door. He punched in a short code on the panel, and then pulled open the heavy steel portal.

Two more drones lay on the deck inside—in far worse shape than the one she'd left behind. Beyond them was a small docking bay containing the person she wanted to see more than anything.

"Drew!" she called out and rushed toward him. "Light, I'm so glad you're OK."

Her son, a lanky young man with long, red hair, rushed toward her and wrapped her in a fierce embrace. "Me? You're the one grandfather left back in those passageways."

He released his grasp on her and stepped back. "Mom! You're bleeding!"

Mary waved a hand. "It's nothing. Is that our ship?"

Drew turned to look at the small, dingy shuttle sitting in the docking bay.

" 'Ship' seems like a stretch," Drew said as he gave the vessel an uncertain look. "I don't even know if it's spaceworthy."

"I wouldn't be aboard if it wasn't," Leeroy said, sticking his head out of the airlock. "You all going to stand out there hugging and kissing all day, or are you going to get in? Those drones have Link, you know."

Flaherty lifted a case off a nearby bench and nodded to Mary and Drew. "Get on—Mary, where's your bag?"

"Aw, crap, I forgot it back in the passage."

Her father shook his head and pointed at a cabinet next to the bench.

"There's a shipsuit in there. You're filthy, you'll want fresh clothes once we patch you up."

Mary walked gingerly to the cabinet—her thighs were really starting to ache—and pulled it open.

A garment bag hung inside, next to a pulse rifle. She grabbed both and turned back to the shuttle. Her father had handed the case to Leeroy and now stood beside the airlock. He nodded in approval of the rifle in her right hand and gestured for her to board first.

Inside—which was far cleaner than the exterior would have led her to believe—was a small cabin, with room to seat ten people in fully reclining chairs. Forward lay a cockpit that had room for two.

Drew was up front with Leeroy, and she could hear him asking how they were going to get out of the bay.

Mary was wondering the same thing—the bulkheads didn't appear to have any openings anywhere. She heard Leeroy say "Down," at the same moment a concerned-sounding bark came from behind her.

She turned to see Figgy standing in front of her father, who shrugged.

"He says he likes you. Wants to come along."

"How do you know that?" Mary asked.

"Link," Flaherty replied.

Mary shook her head at her father. "You and Figgy can use the Link, but not me?"

"Well, we're shielded in the shuttle. Have at it," Flaherty said.

Mary connected to the shuttle's network and found Figgy already talking to her.

<And then I thought it was going to kill you, but I got its leg—it tasted gross, did I tell you that?—and then I broke it off! I didn't even know I could do that, I guess all those tough tunnel rats I've been eating have paid off.>

<Figgy!> Mary knelt in front of the dog and pulled his head against her chest, hugging him tightly. *<I was all hyped up before, and I never properly thanked you for saving my life.>*

<It's OK, you were nice to me as soon as you saw me—most humans try to shoo me away or call bots to catch me. You were just nice. I like nice. I like you, Mary. I'm going to come with you and keep you safe—is that OK? Oh, I can't breathe can you loosen up?>

Mary laughed and released her hold on the dog, sitting back on her heels as her father slipped past.

"Sorry about that, Figgy," she said aloud.

<It's OK.>

"Strap in," Flaherty said, then turned to Drew. "You're in the back with your mom. Quickly now, we're ready to drop."

Mary pulled herself up into a seat and slid a harness over her head, and Figgy jumped into the seat beside her.

Drew sat across from her, then they both wrestled a harness into place around the dog—who was panting excitedly, but not speaking. For the time being, at least.

Mary leant over and grabbed the pulse rifle and the garment bag from the aisle, settling both on her lap. At the front of the shuttle, she saw her father settle into the cockpit beside Leeroy, who shot her a quick smile before turning back to his console.

It occurred to her that Leeroy had just turned his entire life upside down to help her and her son escape. When things calmed down, she owed him heartfelt thanks.

As she wondered what would possess Leeroy to do that for her, Flaherty glanced back and saw that everyone was ready.

"Let's drop."

SERENDIPITY

STELLAR DATE: 03.29.8948 (Adjusted Years)
LOCATION: Construction Inspection Bay 183.AA91
REGION: Airtha, Huygens System, Transcend Interstellar Alliance

Flaherty was looking over the shuttle's readouts, triple-checking that everything was as it should be.

"Relax," Leeroy said with a wide smile. "She may be old, but I can fly her no problem. We'll get there."

Flaherty nodded solemnly. "Then let's go."

Lights flashed in the small bay outside the shuttle, and a grav emitter on the overhead lifted the craft off the pad. Once they were suspended in the air, the floor opened beneath the ship, and Leeroy glanced at Flaherty.

"Here goes nothing."

He punched the release, and the shuttle dropped through the floor, falling at 1*g* through a long shaft that led outside the ring.

Nine seconds later, the dark shaft was replaced by the inverted diamond mountains on the bottom of the Airtha ring.

"What a view," Leeroy said as he activated the shuttle's grav systems, and rotated the vessel so the bottom of the ring was 'down' instead of 'up'.

The shuttle raced through the valleys, staying close to the ring, great mounds of compressed carbon towering all around them and gleaming in Huygens's light.

"It's nice," Flaherty replied to Leeroy, far more concerned about the turrets that rested on the mountaintops above the shuttle.

Leeroy followed his gaze and laughed. "Don't worry about the guns, Flaherty. We'll be at the High Airtha tether in five. Once we get there, I'll tuck in with the elevators, and we'll be home free before we know it."

"I sure hope so," Flaherty said in muted tones. There was no way the shuttle could make it past a concerted effort from the Airthan security forces to stop it. Their only hope was to sneak away.

The shuttle was registered to a freighter named the *Hundred Dawns*—at least that's what the insystem STC thought. Once they passed High

Airtha, he'd call in for a course to the freighter, passing its captain's tokens for auth. With luck, it *should* work.

Problem was, Flaherty didn't believe in luck.

Leeroy threaded though the valleys until they reached the tether, where he executed a rather artful maneuver, slotting in right behind a maglev car that was racing down the tether to High Airtha's long arch, hanging below.

"See?" Leeroy said. "Airtha's diamond crust sure looks nice, but it screws with scan something fierce. The thing is like a thousand echoes of the entire system."

"Too much form, not enough function," Flaherty grunted.

"Spot on, pal, spot on."

Flaherty peered back to see Mary looking worried as she stroked Figgy's head. She met his eyes, and he could see pain in them.

<I'm sorry,> he said as the shuttle continued to speed down the tether in the maglev's wake.

Her mental sigh was long, but didn't seem to hold accusation. *<I know…I feel worse for Drew, though he seems to be looking at this as a grand adventure. I warrant he won't think so when we get—where are we going, again?>*

<A place where I hope the two of you won't have to lay low overmuch. If Sera does what I expect, it will be within her sphere of influence.>

<You won't say where?> Mary asked. *<Drew would like to know, as well.>*

Flaherty shook his head. *<I'd rather not, until we're in the dark layer. I know it sounds paranoid, but I don't know how well she can hear us.>*

<Not-Sera?>

<No, Airtha.>

He saw Mary clench her jaw. *<OK, now you* ***are*** *sounding paranoid. If* ***she*** *can hear our thoughts, then she'll know where we are now, not where we're going—which is worse. Besides, you said the shuttle is shielded.>*

<Like I said. I know it sounds paranoid.>

Mary didn't respond, and Flaherty turned his attention back to the forward view where the maglev was slowing to pull onto one of the tracks that ran perpendicularly across High Airtha's surface.

Leeroy, however, was going to ride the tether straight through the spur. The long shaft upon which High Airtha hung did not end at the platform, but continued through to a smaller station called 'Watchtower

97'.

That station controlled all outbound traffic lanes off High Airtha, and the plan was for Leeroy to pull off the tether while occluded by another craft's departure. Then Flaherty would request a lane, like nothing was unusual at all about a shuttle suddenly appearing on Scan with no departure logged.

Hopefully.

"Sure hope no one's coming up the tether," Leeroy said as the maglev train ahead of them finally turned off, revealing a dark tunnel leading through High Airtha and out the other side.

"It's clear." Flaherty spoke with a calm assurance that he *mostly* felt. The track had been registered as clear this morning, when he'd lifted the schedules.

But schedules could change.

"Well, I've got an active EM field on the track!" Leeroy cried out.

"Speed up," Flaherty said in even tones.

Leeroy shot Flaherty a questioning look, but complied and poured on as much thrust as possible in the narrow tunnel.

"I see lights," Leeroy said through clenched teeth, and Flaherty didn't even have time to nod before the shuttle shot out of the tunnel and swerved wildly to avoid an oncoming maglev train.

There was a moment of shocked silence as Leeroy and Flaherty looked at one another, confirming that they were indeed still alive, before Leeroy screamed at the top of his lungs.

"Yaaaaaaaaahoooooooo!"

Flaherty allowed a small smile to form on his lips as he checked scan for a departing ship to hide behind.

"There." He pointed at a cruise liner that had just slipped off the edge of High Airtha, dropping out into space near the tether.

"On it." Leeroy nodded and altered vector to fall in behind the cruise liner, which was named the *Ethereal Delight.*

"Not too close," Flaherty said. "We don't want them to file a complaint about us with the STC."

"Looks like a pleasure cruiser. Maybe we should ask if they have room for some late arrivals." Leeroy was grinning as he took in the holomural on the side of the ship. "Would be a *great* way to pass the time while we put distance between us and Airtha."

Flaherty snorted. "You'd end up in some dom's cabin, all trussed up just when we needed to make a quick getaway. No thanks."

"I would not! You know I like to turn the tables." Leeroy said loudly, angling his head back so his voice carried into the cabin. "Isn't that right, Mary?"

"Shut up and fly," Mary shot back.

Flaherty snorted at his daughter's response, though he couldn't help but notice there was a small note of humor in her voice. As though she did not look on her previous romantic time with Leeroy as unfavorably as she so often claimed.

Leeroy grinned to himself, but when he saw Flaherty's raised eyebrow, his smile faded. "Uh, OK, STC *should* have missed us coming out of the tunnel, so long as the maglev didn't report us—but we were going *fast*, and those things don't have scan for shit, so hopefully it didn't identify us."

"Gotcha. Calling into Watchtower 97's STC," Flaherty replied.

"Good luck."

Flaherty opened a request channel to the Space Traffic Control tower and got an immediate response back from an NSAI.

<*Shuttle* Tiberius, *we have no departure origination for you and no flight path on record. This is controlled space, what is your destination?*>

The NSAI sounded impatient, though Flaherty suspected that all STC NSAIs were programmed to sound impatient.

He chose his words carefully. He wasn't able to lie, but he *could* state facts in such a way that they supported his fiction while not actually being untruths.

<*Watchtower 97, we took off from a rarely used pad on Airtha. Our onboard comp had a lane assigned. But when we almost creamed this cruise liner that's now in our face, I checked it, and realized the comp had an error. It was using a previously assigned lane from a prior trip. We're flying on manual now, but we need a vector out to the* Hundred Dawns.>

<*Shuttle* Tiberius, *I have no record of prior lanes assigned on this vector for your ship anytime in the last century.*>

Shit! Flaherty thought to himself. He had hoped the NSAI wouldn't crosscheck that. <*Well…uh, it's what the comp has entered. I've only owned this shuttle for a few weeks, so I can't confirm nor deny that.*>

There was no response for a minute, and then a new voice came over the channel. <*Shuttle* Tiberius, *this is Tower Commander Amelia, what's this about a previously assigned vector to your ship?*>

<*Hello, Commander Amelia. I was just explaining to the NSAI that our comp had a bad vector in it—something that was leftover from before. I told our pilot to use it, but that was a mistake. Honestly, I just need a lane out to the* Hundred Dawns.>

A short sound of disbelief came into Flaherty's mind. <*The* Hundred Dawns? *I show it as holding out near Domar Station.*>

<*That's right, that's where we need to get.*>

<*Captain Nari, am I to believe that you command an interstellar freighter, but you don't double-check outbound lane assignments when dropping off a place like Airtha?*>

Flaherty knew his excuses were weak, but it was the best exfiltration he'd managed to come up with, given that he'd only had a few hours' notice. He wracked his brain for some explanation, but nothing convincing came to mind.

Not being able to lie was terribly inconvenient sometimes.

<*Nari, what's going on up there?*> a new voice came onto the channel. <*First you take me to Airtha, promising me a good time, but it's all business, business, business. We were* ***just*** *about to go out to a nice restaurant, and* ***then*** *you get a priority cargo, and we have to leave?*>

<*Honey, please, this is a private channel with the STC,*> Flaherty said, impressed by the initiative his daughter had taken. He glanced back to see a serene look on her face as she spoke again over the comm channel.

<*Hello? Who is this?*> Commander Amelia asked.

<*Oh, hello, STC, can you get us a lane to our ship so that I can get some distance between me and my asshole of a husband before I kick him in the balls so hard one of our kids dies?*>

No response came from Tower Commander Amelia for a moment, then the woman burst out laughing. After a half minute, she'd calmed herself enough to reply. <*Ma'am, how's this. I'll give you a lane out to your ship* ***if*** *you add a kick in the balls for dropping off the ring without crosschecking departure lanes. Your husband is a moron.*>

Mary barked a laugh. <*Oh, don't I know it. Barely keeps his shit bucket of a ship flying. Any objection if I maybe give him two or three extra whacks in the sack?*>

Commander Amelia was still laughing, and Flaherty thought he could hear other people joining in with her. The tower commander must have switched to an audible conversation on her end to share with her team.

<Knock yourself out—well, not you, actually. Knock ***him*** *out.>*

<Deal. Though I'll let him fly us back to the ship first. Not that he's much better than a malfunctioning autopilot.>

<We'll keep an eye on you. Nari, I want you in this lane and I want your backup comps to confirm vector and send it in. Am I understood? Or do I need to come out there and kick you in the balls, too?>

Flaherty swallowed for effect, or maybe because all the talk of ball kicking *was* a bit unnerving. He noticed that Leeroy had a pained expression on his face, and a hand over his crotch.

<Yes, Commander Amelia. No extra ball-kicking needed. I'm bringing the backup navigation comp online. I'll have it confirm vector-matching calculations with you as soon as we have our lane.>

<Good. The NSAI will provide you with an assignment momentarily.>

<Thank you, ma'am.>

The comm line went dead, and a moment later, the backup navigation comp—which Flaherty had activated, to honor his word—registered the incoming lane assignment.

"How'd I do?" Mary called up.

"I have a strange phantom pain," Leeroy replied. "And I think your father has lost the power of speech, so I'd take that as a compliment."

Mary laughed. "I'll take that compliment. I'll admit, Dad, it was cathartic to yell at you like that."

Flaherty shook his head. "I'll bet."

FATHER KNOWS BEST?

STELLAR DATE: 03.30.8948 (Adjusted Years)
LOCATION: Shuttle *Tiberius*
REGION: Huygens System, Transcend Interstellar Alliance

Mary sucked in a sharp breath and involuntarily jerked her leg aside.

"Hold still, Mary," her father said as he clamped his knees on either side of her leg. "Those drones must have had something on their claws, for your leg to be as sore as you say."

"It's not *that* bad," Mary said through clenched teeth. "You really don't need to go digging around in my thigh muscle."

Her father looked up, and his dark eyes met hers. "Mary, they could have some sort of neurotoxin that they inject, or it could just be that they stepped in rat shit. I need to clean the wounds."

Mary considered how dank some corners of those tunnels had been, and bit her lip. "OK, do what you have to."

Ten minutes later, he pronounced the wounds clean. There had been dirt, some pebbles, *and* a neurotoxin. Luckily just a small amount. They assumed she and Figgy had knocked the drone off before it could deliver the full dose.

Even so, he had loaded her up with enough mednano to cure a civilization of the yellow death before sealing up the wounds with nuskin.

Now in the shower, she was determined to enjoy the hot spray for the full five minutes she was allotted, letting the steam seep into her skin and help clear her mind of the day's events.

A high-speed chase out of Airtha had *not* been what she'd expected to do when she'd woken up....

Shit...that was yesterday! No wonder I'm so tired.

The shower signaled that her time was almost up, which gave her time to lather up before it triggered the final spray to rinse the soap away.

Mary heaved a sigh when the water flow shut off. A low, warm breeze blew across her body, drying both herself and the shower walls. A minute later, the airflow shut off, and then the other sanitary amenities emerged from the walls.

Amongst them was the garment bag she'd placed on one of the shelves before taking her shower. The pair of pants she'd worn were ruined; not only were they half blood-soaked, but her father had cut them away from her legs before cleaning her wounds. Her shirt was fine, though, and her jacket could be cleaned.

But spending the next week on a shuttle in the company of three men without pants—especially considering said men were her father, son, and former lover—was entirely out of the question.

Still, whatever shipsuit had been hanging in that cabinet from time immemorial stood a chance of being equally undesirable.

Dad…why do you always have to get mixed up in crazy stuff?

Mary unzipped the garment bag and her breath caught in surprise.

OK, this is not what I expected at all.

Five minutes later, she stepped out of the san unit feeling better than she had since their crazy adventure had begun.

She saw that Drew was asleep in one of the cabin's reclining chairs, with Figgy draped over from the adjoining seat, his head on her son's lap.

"Looks good on you," her father's voice came in a low whisper, and she turned to see him sitting at the back of the shuttle, cleaning their meager supply of weapons on a table set against the rear bulkhead.

Mary looked down at the bright pink shipsuit. It was an auto-adjusting model, so it had shrunk down to fit her like a glove once she had pulled up the fastener.

Despite the fact that it was not the sort of thing one wore when making a surreptitious escape, she liked the fit and color, not to mention the white flowers which grew up the legs and then bloomed across the top of the outfit, only to fade away and be replaced by new flowers beginning the climb once more.

Mary gave her father a skeptical look. "Are you sure that was just sitting in that dusty old cabinet? Not only is it pretty, but it's high quality, too. The feature listing said that it's vacuum rated, and has a tear strength of a thousand kilograms."

Flaherty shrugged. "I may have seen it on sale at some point and thought it would look good on you."

Mary raised an eyebrow. " 'May have'? And then you just placed it in some hidden shuttle bay?"

Her father turned and looked her up and down, a grin tugging at the corners of his mouth. "OK, I admit, I saw it and it reminded me of how you used to dress when you were a little girl. I had a moment of nostalgia-inspired weakness. And, yeah, I had a few locations like that shuttle bay stocked with supplies."

"Well, I like it, and I'm glad you're overprepared. Usually you buy me practical things. And guns—mostly guns. I didn't even know you paid attention to my fashion choices."

Flaherty shrugged. "I've told you stories of what it was like serving with Sera on *Sabrina*."

Mary sat down across the table and shook her head at her father. "Dad, *Sabrina* was a pirate ship. You weren't 'serving', you were pillaging."

"Don't ever let Sabrina hear you say that. She was very sensitive about it. We were a starfreighter, and then later—however briefly—a privateer. We were *never* pirates."

"What about the stories you told me, when you attacked other ships and stole their cargo?"

"Part of the cover."

Mary groaned. "But the ship's AI and rest of the crew didn't know that. *They* thought they were being pirates."

"Well, maybe a little bit. But we were always attacking bad people—or stupid people, like Cheeky's old captain. We never preyed on fat, weak targets—which is what real pirates do."

Mary shook her head in mock disbelief, though she could tell her father was serious.

I guess he's telling the truth—as he sees it. Gotta admit, I can't see him stealing from the unwary.

She decided to try and pry a destination from him once more. "I know we're not in the DL yet, but we're not far from our jump point. Think we're far enough from Airtha's prying eyes that you can tell me where we're going?"

Her father set down the pulse rifle he was cleaning and leaned back in his chair.

"Honestly, I have a few options. I thought maybe I'd let you pick."

"Me?" Mary asked, more than a little surprised to be given the choice.

"What sort of options do I have?"

"Well, one option would be to get you to New Canaan. I'm divided on that. It's probably both the safest, and the most dangerous place in the galaxy."

"What's New Canaan, and how's that possible?" Mary asked.

"It's where the *Intrepid*'s crew made their colony. They can *probably* protect their system from all intruders, but that doesn't mean there won't be collateral damage."

Mary nodded silently, looking down at the white vines tracing their way up her legs, and momentarily becoming mesmerized by their motion.

"You know you can turn that off," her father said.

"What? You give me this nice outfit, and then tell me to turn it off?" Mary said in mock anger, then winked as her father's eyes widened. "Dad, I'm kidding. Is it bothering you?"

"No, I thought maybe it was bothering you."

Mary laughed softly. "Don't worry, I like it. Yes, you're in the doghouse for ruining my life on Airtha, but knowing you care helps."

"Of course I care, Mary. It's why I got you off Airtha."

For a moment she worried he had some crazy plan in mind. "You're not going back there, are you?"

Flaherty chuckled. "No, not unless Sera sends me."

Mary felt a spike of anger in her chest at the statement. "Why is it that Sera commands you so completely? You'll do anything for her."

"Mary, I have to."

"Right, you told her you'd be her guardian that one time. Does that mean forever?"

Flaherty nodded. "It does. But I'm also your guardian forever. And Drew's. Luckily, you two get in far less trouble than Sera does."

"Sounds like you have a conflict of interest."

Her father snorted and shook his head. "Tell me about it."

Mary had argued with her father many times before about his devotion to Sera. She knew that he struggled with his conflicting priorities, and decided not to push the issue—they'd be spending a lot of time on this shuttle, and being angry at one another wasn't going to help.

She decided to return to the topic at hand. "Regarding New Canaan.

Would they let you drop us off there?"

Her father nodded. "I own land there…or I can claim it, if I wish. You know, their civilization makes Airtha look like it's behind the times. You could do anything you want there."

"Anything?"

"I imagine so, yes."

Mary considered that, slowly tapping her chin. "What other options are there?"

"Three more," Flaherty replied, holding up three fingers. "I have a place out in the Sagittarius Arm where you two could disappear. But I don't like that one."

That surprised Mary. She would have expected her father to try and tuck her and Drew in the safest place he could think of. The Sagittarius Arm certainly fit the bill. "Why not?"

"Too far from me," Flaherty said. "I'd like to see you from time to time. Plus, if anything happens, I want to be close by."

"OK, that makes sense. What else is there, then?"

"Well, one option is one of the nations at the edge of the Inner Stars. There are a few I could set you up in."

"The Inner Stars?" Mary asked, mouth agape. "But they're so barbaric!"

Her father chuckled softly. "They're not so bad as you think—some places, at least. They don't have the infrastructure of the Transcend—still rebuilding after their wars—but they do have some nice systems and worlds. A few are almost as impressive as Airtha."

Mary wondered if her father was selling her a bill of goods on that one. "OK, what's the final option?"

"You two come with me."

"We…what?" Mary stammered, unsure if she'd heard her father correctly. "With you? Where are you going?"

"Wherever Sera is. I have to get to a drop point she and I set up to find out her location. But when I do, we'll join her—and the rebellion."

"Shit, Dad, what are you talking about?"

"Well, if Not-Sera is now running the show at Airtha, you can bet it's because she and Airtha don't expect Jeffery Tomlinson to return."

In their mad escape, she'd barely had time to consider the implications of the imposter Sera being in charge of the Transcend's government.

"This was a coup…. Somehow that didn't really register."

Flaherty crossed his arms, a dark look on his face. "Yes, a very, very silent coup. I imagine it will soon come out that the president died at the hands of the New Canaan colonists, or perhaps some other fiction. I could be wrong about Jeffery being dead, but I think he is. And if he's dead, and Adrienne is here, then Sera—real Sera—is President now."

"Two President Seras. This is bizarre."

"Yes."

Mary considered her options. She really had no desire to run off to some corner of the galaxy while her father risked his life for Sera. Perhaps it was time to join the adventurous life he led—though maybe from some small distance.

"Think they have room for a legal analyst in Sera's new government?" Mary asked after a moment.

Flaherty grinned and nodded. "Plus, if you wear that shipsuit when we first meet the new president, you'll get hired for sure."

Mary shook her head; Sera's proclivities were well known amongst the populace on Airtha—but that wasn't where her interest lay. Mary peered over her shoulder to the cockpit, where Leeroy's silhouette could be seen against the piloting holodisplays.

"She might have to get in line. I have a suspicion that Leeroy wants to rekindle things between us—what with him agreeing to fly us out and all."

"He's a good man; a little odd, but a good man. I trust him with our lives."

Mary rose from her chair and gave her father a kiss on his forehead. "Maybe I'll see if there's any spark left between us. Stars know I'll need something to do while we're all stuck on this shuttle."

Her father's head snapped up, eyes wide.

"Dad, seriously, my son is here. There won't be any hanky panky."

"What about me?" Flaherty asked. "Don't my poor eyes and ears count for anything?"

Mary snorted. "After what you told me about your escapades on *Sabrina*? No. I think you can handle anything."

She turned to face the cockpit, considering a chat with Leeroy, but then her eyes settled on her sleeping son and Figgy—who had looked up at her as she approached.

Maybe just a bit of shut-eye would be nice….

She slowly lowered herself into her chair, careful not to disturb her son. Figgy watched through lidded eyes as Mary reclined the chair, and she reached out to stroke his coat of shaggy fur.

"Good Figgy," she whispered as her head hit the headrest, and she closed her eyes, sleep overtaking her almost instantly.

* * * * *

Flaherty heard Mary's breathing even out in less than a minute after she laid down. He rose quietly and walked to the three seats where she, Drew, and Figgy lay.

These two people were the most precious things to him in the whole galaxy. Would it really be wise to take them along with him? Sera was renowned for getting into trouble. With Tanis at her side—if she'd convinced Tanis to join her efforts—that trouble would be of epic proportions.

He let out a long sigh. No, the best place for his daughter and grandson was the place he least wanted them to be. Out in Sagittarius.

With a heavy heart, he walked to the cockpit. He couldn't lie to his daughter, so he'd have to get Leeroy in on it.

Hopefully they'd all forgive him someday.

A NIGHT OUT ON HIGH VICTORIA

BY AMY DUBOFF

CAPTAIN

STELLAR DATE: 08.06.8948 (Adjusted Years)
LOCATION: ISS *I2*
REGION: Inner Canaan, New Canaan System

Captain Rachel Espensen surveyed the bridge of the *I2* while crewmembers made the final preparations for the journey ahead.

At less than two hours until their scheduled departure, they were officially in crunch time.

<Any impending disasters I should be aware of?> she asked Priscilla.

<All supplies are on board, and final personnel moves are underway. Barring some unforeseen development, we shouldn't have anything to worry about,> the avatar replied.

Rachel smiled. *<After what we've been through over the past several months, I'll take things going right, for a change.>*

"Everything set?" a familiar voice said behind her.

She spun around and brought her hand to her forehead in a salute. "Admiral Evans, sir."

"At ease, Captain." He smiled. "How's the command chair treating you?"

"It's a big seat to fill," she replied. Then privately over the Link added, *<Between us, some days I still can't believe I got this promotion.>*

<You have come a long way since we first met, back on High Victoria.> He stepped forward with his hands clasped behind his back. "I know you're up for the challenge to see the crew safely to Khardine, and wherever else Tanis takes you."

"I'll keep her safe, sir."

Joe cocked an eyebrow. "Oh yeah? You have some special super powers I'm unaware of?"

He looked so serious, for a moment Rachel thought he actually expected her to have some.

"Easy, Captain, I'm kidding."

The admiral clasped her shoulder, and Rachel let out a relieved laugh.

<You've earned your place here,> he added privately, then a mischievous grin crept onto his face. *<I'm glad to see that my hunch about*

you was right.>

She chuckled. *<I was sure you were going to expel me.>*

<And lose out on having someone with your ingenuity in the ISF? Not a chance.>

A NIGHT ON THE STATION

STELLAR DATE: 12.18.4241 (Adjusted Gregorian)
LOCATION: ISF Academy, High Victoria Station
REGION: Victorian Space Federation, Kapteyn's Star System

Rachel dropped her nose to the floor for her eighty-seventh push-up. *This is the most idiotic thing I've ever done.*

Well, perhaps not the *most* idiotic, if she was honest with herself. However, in a culture where genetic modification was the norm, and her nano could adapt her body at a cellular level, doing push-ups served no practical purpose.

<*What's with the dagger eyes?*> Justin questioned her over a private Link connection.

<*All the training we've been doing for the last month is pointless,*> Rachel replied to her classmate while she continued the monotonous push-ups on her way to the requisite one hundred.

<*It's not just physical conditioning,*> Justin pointed out. <*This is as much about mental discipline.*>

<*Then I'm flunking.*>

<*You can say that again.*>

Rachel dropped to her knees at the one hundred mark. The nano throughout her system kept her organs functioning at optimum efficiency, so she didn't feel the slightest bit winded. If the intention of the exercise was indeed mental discipline, she was going to need to do a lot more than one hundred push-ups for it to make an impression.

"On your feet! Five kilometers," Sergeant Greggors ordered.

More laps, seriously? Rachel rose to her feet, barely keeping her glare in check when her gaze passed to the drill officer.

<*It's all part of the process,*> Justin tried to soothe her.

<*Then it needs to process faster.*>

<*You must be the most impatient person I know.*>

Rachel snorted in her mind. <*That's only because you haven't met my mom.*>

She pushed the thought aside, not wanting to dwell on her parents. Every time she felt she was on the verge of homesickness, she'd remember what life had been like before the Intrepid Space Force academy—when she was ready to do anything to get away.

"Faster!" Sergeant Greggors' order to keep up the pace on her laps returned Rachel to the present.

Stars, I hate running even more than push-ups. She wouldn't have thought that was possible.

Her theory about the academy having no genuine interest in physical conditioning through the exercise was supported by a distinct lack of a running track. The hangar had some padded mats thrown in an open area of the deck between the fighters for floor exercises, but the five-kilometer circuit was nothing more than five loops around the perimeter of the room.

Rachel passed by one of the new ARC-4s and gazed at it longingly as she ran by. *I'd give anything to be out in the black rather than stuck in here.*

<*Don't even think about it,*> Justin cautioned when he saw her eyeing the fighter.

<*Like you haven't thought about getting in one yourself.*>

He laughed in her mind. <*The* gs *would crush you without mods or a shootsuit. No way you can just go for a joyride.*>

<*But I can dream.*>

So dream she did.

Even if she couldn't take an ARC-4 out for an evening of fun, there were still other options. If she didn't do *something*—and soon—she was going to lose her mind.

<*So…*> Rachel said to Justin as her group of cadets reached the two-kilometer mark of their run. <*I was thinking of going out tonight.*>

<*Ha! Right.*> He glanced over at her with a grin, but he scowled as soon as he saw the mischievous glint in her eyes. <*Rachel, no. Don't make me play mom.*>

<*Come on! It'll be fun. Grab a drink, go dancing…*>

<*In no way is this a remotely okay idea.*> Justin shook his head. <*Forget it.*>

Rachel flashed a well-honed pout in his direction. <*Please? I hate going to bars alone.*>

<*You're barely old enough to know what bars are like. How much experience do you have?*>

<*Precisely enough to know I hate being the girl sitting alone.*>

Justin shook his head. *<You'd be better served if I tied you to your bunk.>*

She eyed him. *<I'm not sure if that was naughty or not.>*

<That is **not** *what I meant, and you know it. You're just trying to distract me.>*

<Did it work?>

Justin almost ran into a fellow cadet running ahead of him to the right. *<Dammit.>*

Rachel smirked. *<Does that mean you'll come?>*

<No, forget it. I have no interest in being expelled.>

<Well, I need to get out of here for a night. I wasn't wired to be cooped up like this.> Rachel picked up her pace and surged ahead of the group.

Her entire life, she'd felt like she was living in limbo. Though she'd spent the first few years of her life in the Sol System, Victoria was the only real home Rachel had ever known. However, her fellow colonists viewed it as a temporary stopover on their way to New Eden. Consequently, Rachel found herself caught between their impatience to get started with their new lives, and her own desire to have a place to call home.

With her parents counting down to the eventual arrival at New Eden, Rachel had turned to the Space Force to provide a much-needed distraction. Her parents had insisted that she needed structure, and maybe they were right. But the ISF wasn't *actually* what she wanted.

Really, she craved adventure. She was counting the seconds until everyone loaded back onto the *Intrepid* and returned to the black.

But for now, she was stuck on Victoria and the orbital structures within the system, bored with the dull monotony of her everyday life. Running laps was *not* how she pictured spending her time in the academy.

Justin or no Justin, she needed to make her own adventure.

With a plan forming in her mind, Rachel sprinted to the finish line of the five-kilometer run.

"Well done, Espensen," Sergeant Greggors praised. "I like that drive."

I doubt he'd approve of my motivations.

She smiled at the drill instructor. "Always looking forward to what comes next."

"That's the spirit!" the drill sergeant nodded. "Now hit the showers.

We resume at 0600."

No human should be awake at that hour, Rachel silently bemoaned.

Not that time meant anything in space, where one wasn't beholden to planetary rotation for daylight hours. Hell, the *Intrepid*'s master clock was still synced with the Mars Outer Shipyards, nearly thirteen light years away. But the fact that she was told when she had to be up is what bothered her, just like she hated being ordered to touch her nose to the floor, or to run circles around the room. They were trying to break her—to beat her into submission—but she'd find a way to forge her own path.

Rachel set off toward the dorms, and Justin jogged to catch up to her.

<You're not still considering going out tonight, are you?> he asked.

<It's not a consideration. I've made up my mind.>

<You'll never make it out. This entire place is locked down with top-level auth tokens.>

Her eyes darted toward him while a coy smile played on her lips. *<That's what you think.>*

<You know a way out?>

Rachel shrugged. *<You said you weren't interested, so I guess you'll never know for sure.>* She picked up her pace just enough that Justin had to jog two steps to stay abreast.

<Come on! How are you going to get out?>

<Does that mean you'll come?>

He kept his gaze straight ahead. *<If your plan sounds like it has a high enough chance of success, then I'll consider coming with you.>*

Rachel scoffed. *<Want me to give away all my secrets before you commit? No way.>*

A tingle of satisfaction worked its way through her chest. She knew she had him.

<Just give me a hint, at least.>

<Fine,> she conceded. *<Post-dinner waste bins.>*

<Uh…> Justin's avatar took on a decidedly flustered affect. *<That doesn't sound like a very good plan at all.>*

<Well, yeah, of course it's going to sound bad when you only have the hint-level version.> Rachel rolled her eyes. *<Are you in or not? I can't tell you everything, only to have you turn around and rat me out.>*

Justin audibly groaned. *<All right! I've been going as crazy as you in here. Let's go have some fun.>*

She smiled over at him. <*Now we're in business!*>

Justin's impression of her plan hadn't improved by the time she finished relaying the details, but a commitment was a commitment. They returned to their dormitory to begin the preparations for the night of partying.

Rachel's first order of business was a shower, as her drill sergeant had suggested. Her own spin on the activity, however, offered an opportunity to don appropriate 'going out' attire.

The ISF's uniform left much to be desired by way of figure flattery, but Rachel had made a point to bring along a short party dress among her limited personal possessions. The color-changing fabric could be programmed in any number of hues to match the occasion, and its scant cut could easily fit under her training jumpsuit.

She slipped the garment inside the folds of a clean jumpsuit, along with a pair of dress sandals and a folded shoulder bag, and then headed to the shared washroom.

After showering, the other cadets were too distracted with their own routines to notice when Rachel slipped from the open locker area into a private toilet stall to dress. She put on the party dress, with the canvas bag looped over her shoulder and pressed against her side, and then donned the jumpsuit over it, securing the sandals inside the tops of her socks. The loose fit of the jumpsuit was just enough to hide the hidden accessories.

When she emerged from the stall, she saw that Justin was exiting from a stall two doors down.

<*All set?*> she asked him.

<*As close as I'll ever be.*>

<*All right, I'll see you in two.*> Rachel set off at a leisurely pace toward the corridor between the washroom and the dormitory, waiting to see one of her roommates.

Marty approached. He'd do just fine.

"Argh!" Rachel exclaimed, gripping her head. She leaned against the wall of the corridor.

"Are you okay?" Marty ran over to her.

"Ugh, yeah..." Rachel massaged her temple. "Sorry, it's nothing to worry about. I got evaluated for an early AI pairing, and it messed me up. I guess that's why we don't get them this young, huh?"

"You're sure you're okay? That seemed pretty bad..." Her roommate looked her over with concern.

"Eh..." Rachel massaged her temple some more. "You know, maybe I should head over for a med exam, just to be safe."

"I can walk you," Marty offered.

"Whoa, you okay, Rachel?" Justin said on cue from behind her.

She turned toward her friend. "Oh, just another headache. Really wish I hadn't taken that test yet!"

Justin sighed. "I don't know why you're so eager to have another consciousness inside your head. You get into enough trouble as it is."

"Yeah, you know me..." Rachel took a cautious step, then fake-stumbled toward Justin.

Marty frowned. "You really need to get to Medical."

"I'll take her down, don't worry about it," Justin told the other cadet.

"Okay," Marty nodded. "If anyone asks, I'll let them know you headed down there."

Rachel gave him an appreciative smile. "Thanks! Don't wait up for me."

"See you later." Marty resumed his walk toward the dorm.

<*Well done,*> Rachel told Justin over their private Link connection. She kept up her staggered steps until she was sure Marty was out of view.

<*Word of mouth is great and all, but this entire plan falls apart the moment someone goes to find us on the local net.*>

<*Which is why we'll go dark, remember?*> Rachel set a brisk pace toward the infirmary.

Due to the sensitive condition of individuals seeking medical care, the waiting area for the infirmary had network blocks around it. All Rachel and Justin needed to do was step inside, deactivate their local Link access, and then leave—anyone searching for them would think they'd entered the blackout zone, and hadn't been treated yet. The cover was weak, but it only needed to hold up for the next hour or two, until everyone went to bed. After that, they could sneak back in while everyone was asleep, and no one would be the wiser.

The lobby was empty, as Rachel had hoped, and she quickly disabled her local Link access.

"How may I assist you?" an AI attendant asked over the audible systems in the lobby.

"Took a wrong turn," Rachel replied.

"Your Link access is disabled."

"Yeah, it's acting up. I need Tech Support, not Medical." Rachel laughed. "Have a nice evening."

Justin nodded to Rachel that his own Link access was down, and they left the lobby before the AI could question them further.

"Think he'll report us?" Justin whispered.

"Nah, we're not worth the three nanoseconds of his processing time."

Under the cloak of relative invisibility, Rachel and Justin took a route through back corridors toward the mess hall.

Administratively, the academy functioned independently from the rest of High Victoria and the ISF fleet. However, when it came to practical functions like food supply, the academy's operations were merged with those of the larger station. By extension, waste generated in the academy's mess hall was transported to the central processing facilities for recycling after every meal. The post-dinner shipment made the perfect means of transport outside the academy's security perimeter.

Rachel stopped fifteen meters down the hall from the waste collection bin.

Justin's brow furrowed. "We're not really hitching a ride in the organic waste, are we?"

"Better than being melted down along with the metal. It'll get us past the bioscanners."

"Are you sure?" Skepticism laced his voice.

"Believe it or not, my plan isn't entirely original. I got the tip from a cadet who was about to graduate. The automated disposal systems aren't online yet, so we can hop in one of these bins, and it'll take us to the central compost center."

"And you're sure it wasn't a setup?"

Rachel shrugged. "I guess we're about to find out."

Justin groaned. "I never should have let you talk me into this."

"You were looking for an excuse to get out—I could feel it. A kindred spirit."

"We're so getting expelled."

"No we're not. Come on." Rachel slinked toward the far side of the waste bin and peeked inside.

It was precisely as unpleasant as she would have expected.

"No. No way I'm getting in there!" Justin hissed.

"Calm down! We're not going in like this," Rachel whispered back. She moved away from the bin and toward a supply closest, ten meters down the hall.

She cracked the door open, and they shimmied inside.

"What are we doing in here?" Justin asked.

"Waiting and getting geared up."

The closet was barely large enough for Rachel to spin around without bumping into Justin, but she managed to reach over his head to grab two personal hazsuits.

"No… That's not nearly enough for what we'll face in that dumpster," Justin objected.

"They're completely sealed. It will be fine! We'll only be inside for twenty minutes, tops."

"I—"

"Shh, stop worrying." Rachel patted him on the shoulder.

"What's the 'waiting' bit you mentioned?"

"For dinner to finish. We'll slip inside the dumpster after the final load gets added, then it will get transported out, and we'll jump clear once it's on the far side of the security line."

Justin crossed his arms. "If we don't get caught, we'll die of suffocation."

"Then don't come."

"Rachel, you should realize by now that I'm coming along no matter how much I complain about the means."

She grinned up at him in the dim light. "I figured as much." She paused. "I am glad you're coming."

"Just to have someone along, or me specifically?"

I didn't intend for this to be a date… She took a step back, but there was nowhere to go in the closet. "I don't have any expectations."

"Good, because I'm just coming along to have fun."

"All right, because I already had you in the 'DPBT' category in my head."

Justin gave her a blank stare.

" 'Dating Potential, Bad Timing'," she supplied.

"Did you make that up?"

"Seemed worthy of an abbreviation." She held up her hand for silence when she heard voices passing in the hall.

Quiet returned.

"Any other interesting shorthand I should know about?" Justin asked.

"One that will come into play tonight is 'SUHF'—Shut Up and Have Fun."

Justin chuckled. "I think I can get behind that one."

They waited for another twenty minutes while dinnertime came and went. By the end, Rachel was antsy and hungry. But the promise of a good drink and bar food made the wait worthwhile.

With the time for departure drawing near, Rachel and Justin helped each other into the hazsuits and checked the seals. The filters would afford them two hours of breathing air without exterior tanks, which would be more than enough for their purposes.

Sounds of the waste bin being filled carried into the supply closet, and when the corridor seemed clear, Rachel peeked out.

"Come on! We need to get in before it gets taken away." She waddled down the hall as quickly as she could in the awkward hazsuit and threw back the bin's lid.

To her relief, the top level of leftover food was a bunch of salad, which would at least make for a more pleasant base layer for their travel than, say, chili.

Rachel hauled herself over the lip of the bin and dropped down inside.

Justin hesitated, but quickly followed her when they heard a door open somewhere down the hall. They pulled the lid gently closed just as footsteps rounded the corner.

Movement jarred the dumpster, and Rachel braced her hands against the sides in the complete darkness of the sealed container. She prayed to the stars it would take them on the course she'd been told.

For fifteen minutes, Rachel tried to track the movement as the bin was transported on a hover platform. The right and left turns and lift rides were meaningless to her without a map of the back corridors, but she did detect the telltale beep of a bioscanner. Soon thereafter, the dumpster stopped, and there was only silence.

Rachel waited a minute to be sure, then cracked open the lid, thankful to find it hadn't been locked—a possibility that had not occurred to her until after they'd gotten inside.

The room was dim, but she could make out rows of other bins awaiting processing, and she could hear machinery whirring in the distance.

"Okay, I think it's clear," she told Justin while opening the lid the rest of the way. She swung her legs over the edge and dropped to the deck.

When Justin was next to her, she closed the bin's lid and began stripping off the hazsuit.

"What do we do with these?" Justin waved his own garment.

"Turn it inside out and bring it with us. We'll find somewhere secure to dump it."

He nodded. "Now, this is probably a terrible time to bring it up, but how are we getting back into the academy after we're done partying for the night?"

She smiled at him in the dark. "Oh, that part is easy. They only check clearance to leave—all we have to do is walk in the front door. Our auths and uniforms will show that's precisely where we're supposed to be."

"There won't be a note that we didn't have permission to leave?"

"Why would there be? It's assumed we never left."

Justin considered the statement, then waved his hand dismissively. "I guess we'll figure it out when we get there."

They crept through the grid of bins toward a light mounted on the wall that seemed to indicate an exit. As they approached, Rachel slowed her pace and listened for any voices.

Four meters from their destination, the doors flew open.

Rachel and Justin dove behind the nearest bin, as a new container zoomed in on its automated hover platform and followed a programmed path to an open spot in the grid.

"Let's go," Rachel mouthed, and darted through the open door.

The hallway beyond had the unadorned look of a maintenance corridor. There were no signs of humans or AIs nearby, so Rachel and Justin jogged along the only available path.

The first junction they encountered had signage pointing toward the promenade in the central commercial district, which provided a reference point for their travels. Now assured they were well outside the academy's security perimeter, they connected to the general Link and consulted the map to find a route to the nearest social area of the station.

"Perfect!" Rachel's eyes gleamed. "I've heard great things about this bar. They have a special additive in the drinks that slows down your nano so you can actually get a buzz."

"Good, because I really need a drink after that ride."

Rachel nodded. "I mean, it could have been worse, but I can't say I'd be eager to do it again. I'll figure out a different way to sneak out next time."

"Already planning a next time? We haven't even done anything yet."

She took a deep breath and exhaled loudly. "But can't you feel the freedom?"

"More drinking, less talking." Justin pointed in the direction of the bar.

"No argument here."

At the end of the corridor, they balled up the hazsuits and then stripped off their academy jumpsuits. Rachel produced the carrying bag she'd brought to hold their clothes, and stuffed the jumpsuits and her boots inside. Now looking the part of a club-goer, she slung the bag over her shoulder and inspected her companion. His gray slacks and light blue button-down shirt were too understated for her taste, but the shirt's tight cut showed off his physique enough to get attention, if that was his aim.

"You clean up well," Justin commented.

"Not bad for taking a dumpster here, rather than a luxury groundcar, eh?" She sauntered toward the exit.

They dumped the hazsuits in a waste bin, then merged into the pedestrian traffic in the transit concourse running through that section of the massive station.

The bar was a kilometer from their current location, but Rachel didn't mind the walk. Her past month at the academy was the longest she'd ever been without the stimulation of a bustling station. She soaked in the atmosphere as passersby went about their lives—noting everything from families shopping together, to the creative mods of some of the individuals roaming the station.

Upon reaching the bar, Rachel assessed the color scheme of the interior and then adjusted her dress to a vibrant blue to play off the orange of the décor.

Justin rolled his eyes when he realized what she was doing, and then strode into the club.

Rachel smiled at the bouncer and followed Justin inside.

The rhythmic thump of the music pulsed in her chest, energizing her in a way she hadn't felt since enrolling in the ISF academy.

"I've missed this!" she shouted to Justin over the music.

"What?"

<I've missed this,> she repeated over the Link before realizing they had been standing under a speaker. She moved away.

Justin took in the room. *<Oh! Yeah, it's nice to hear music and see people enjoying themselves.>*

"I want a drink!" Rachel spotted the bar and weaved through the crowd to the polished stainless-steel counter, with Justin at her heels.

The bartender had a natural, youthful look to her, likely never having undergone a rejuv. Rachel imagined that Victoria was one of the few systems where it was common to come across so many young people like herself, and it created a unique dynamic within the population where some adhered to ageist notions about who made for appropriate social companions. If the centurions thought she was too immature to have a serious conversation with, then so be it. Young people were more fun, anyway.

Rachel flashed a radiant smile at the bartender. "Hey!" she shouted over the crowd. "What's good here?"

"I can make anything you want," the bartender smiled back. "What are you in the mood for?"

"How about a 'special' strawberry daiquiri?"

"Coming right up." The bartender spun to grab a glass off the back shelf and began the drink preparations.

"That is such a girly drink," Justin chuckled.

"Yeah, and delicious! Plus, the red won't turn my tongue a funny color like that crazy blue or green shit." She eyed a group of four women at a nearby table, each drinking bizarre concoctions from twisty glasses. The women cast an appraising glance in their direction, as well.

"I dunno… green teeth can be sexy," Justin jested.

"I think I just found some new criteria to add to that DPBT list of mine…"

"Don't knock it 'til you try it."

Rachel rested her forearms on the bar top. "If you say so."

The bartender returned in short order with the daiquiri and placed it in front of Rachel. "And for you?" she asked Justin.

" 'Special' double shot of whiskey, neat."

Rachel looked at him from under raised eyebrows as she sipped her daiquiri through the straw. "Getting right to business."

"May as well loosen up fast," he replied.

"We do have training in the morning."

"I was the one who thought this was a bad idea, remember? Our nano will pick up the slack later, don't worry."

The bartender set down his drink, and Justin downed half the amber liquid in one gulp, wincing as it hit the back of his throat. "Okay, so not the highest grade."

"It'll get the job done, I'm sure. Come on." Rachel authorized the auto-debit payment for the drink from her account while looking for a place to sit. She spotted an empty four-seater booth and set a direct course for it.

When they were just two meters from the booth, a man slid into the empty curved seat.

Damn! Rachel frowned and began searching for another option.

The man noticed her consternation. "Did you want to sit here?" he shouted, pointing at the unoccupied portion of the booth.

Rachel took another step forward. "Do you mind?"

Then the man noticed Justin following behind her, and his face dropped. "Of course not, have a seat." The disappointment was evident in his voice, but at least he was polite enough not to rescind the offer.

"I'm Rachel," she introduced herself as she took a seat, extending her right hand while holding her drink in the other. She dropped the bag containing their clothes in the center of the booth.

"Tom." He shook her hand.

"And this is Justin." Rachel pointed her thumb over her shoulder at her friend as he slid in next to her.

"Thanks for the seat," Justin said to Tom.

"No problem. So, what brings you here tonight?"

"Just needed to get out," Rachel said.

"What do you do?" Tom asked.

"We're in the academy," Justin replied.

Gah, idiot! Rachel smiled sweetly, but she mentally slapped Justin.

<What if he's connected to the ISF and turns us in?>

<Then he'd have the means to look up our idents in a fraction of a second. Lying wouldn't be any better.>

She sighed in her mind. *<Good point.>*

Tom tilted his head with interest. "You mean the ISF academy? What are you studying?"

Rachel sipped her daiquiri. "Officers training."

"Is that so?" Tom took a gulp of beer. "They let you come out and socialize?"

"Just celebrating for one night," Rachel hastily replied before Justin could say anything more incriminating.

"That's good." Tom leaned back in the booth and spread his arms to either side along the top of the padded back. "I remember flight training being brutal. It's important to get time to unwind."

Rachel tensed. "Are you in the ISF?"

"Oh, no! I'm a civilian pilot," Tom said. "I made it onto the colony roster as a machinist, though. Long story. I work on the transport ships nowadays, while we're stuck here."

Rachel bristled at the 'stuck' terminology in relation to the only real home she'd ever known. "It could be a lot worse."

Tom nodded. "You're right. We could be drifting through the black for all eternity, just waiting to run out of fuel."

Justin shifted in the booth next to her. "That's one way to look at things."

"Well, I'm guessing you were both kids when we reached Victoria? I was in stasis, but from what I understand, we had a rough start to our time here."

"You're right," Rachel acknowledged. "We've studied the battle with the Sirians at the academy—it's important for us to be thankful for what we have."

"It is." Tom looked into his drink. "Sorry, I know you're out here to celebrate. Back to lighter topics! Have you started flight training yet?"

Rachel groaned. "I wish! We're still pretty early in."

"They make you wait for the good stuff." Tom drained his glass. "I'll grab the next round. You want the same?" he asked.

Rachel's glass was still half-filled. "How about a double vodka cranberry?" she requested. That ought to keep her nano busy.

Justin held up his empty glass to indicate a repeat of his previous order.

Tom smiled. "You've got it." He slid from the booth and ambled to the bar.

"He seems nice." Rachel sucked down the remainder of her daiquiri as quickly as she could without getting a brain freeze.

"He wants to see what's under that skimpy dress of yours—not that you've left a lot to the imagination." Justin twirled his empty glass.

"This dress is modest compared to what half the people in here have on!" Rachel examined herself relative to the men and women around her, and felt quite vindicated.

One particularly telling outfit involved a five-centimeter band across the woman's breasts, shorts that didn't even cover half her buttocks, and a translucent layer that looped under her arms around her lower back and met at the front of a collar she wore around her neck.

Justin crossed his arms. "Just because others dress that way doesn't mean you have to."

Rachel patted his thigh. "Aww, it's cute of you to be all protective of me."

He shook his head when he noticed Tom returning with the fresh drinks. "Forget it."

"Thanks!" Rachel said as she took the new drink from Tom. She'd been through enough dating in secondary school to know where Justin was about to go with his statements, and she was thankful for a diversion.

While she liked him well enough, the 'Bad Timing' part of her DPBT classification was too prohibitive a barrier—especially when factoring in the part about him being a classmate and future colleague. Not everyone could make a relationship work like Lieutenant Governor Richards and Commandant Evans.

"Now, where were we?" Tom returned to his seat. "Oh, right! I was asking about flight training."

"Yes, we're still a long way out from that," Rachel replied. "We'll go through basic combat flight training as part of the officers program, though. They want us to have an appreciation for what pilots go through when we send them into battle."

Tom whistled. "Those *g* forces are nuts. I'm happy to stick with my cargo haulers. They can be plenty zippy for my needs."

Rachel sighed. "I'm envious. I know we have everything we could ever want in here, but there's something about being out *there* with an unobstructed view of the universe. It's beautiful."

"You know," Tom said slowly, "I could take you out, if you like. I have my own ship."

<*Yep, here we go…*> Justin quipped over the private Link.

<*Relax, I won't be seduced so easily.*> Rachel smiled at Tom. "That's a generous offer, but I'm afraid we don't have the time. This was just a quick excursion before we get back to the grind tomorrow." She took a mouthful of her drink, and then another—this cocktail had significantly more bite than the first.

"No?" Tom frowned. "I understand. Your training has to come first."

Rachel nodded. "But there's plenty to do here. You up for some dancing?"

<*I don't think this is what I signed up for when I came out with you.*> Justin crossed his avatar's arms and huffed.

<*That girl has been watching you since we came in. Go talk to her,*> Rachel replied with a nod toward a blonde two tables over—in the group with the exotic green drinks.

If he wants green teeth, then that's what he'll get. She downed the rest of her drink in one gulp.

<*Fine,*> Justin grumbled and slid out of the booth. Within two steps, he had adopted a suave swagger and confident smile that would be sure to get his target's attention.

Rachel extended her hand with a flourish and grinned at Tom. "Shall we?"

Tom took her hand and led her deeper into the club, where the lights were strobing and the music was at an almost unbearable volume. It was perfect.

She let loose, dancing as the alcohol began to take full effect in her system, swaying and spinning with the electronic music. Tom kept a respectful distance from her at first, but as the night progressed, he inched closer—eventually placing his hands on her hips.

Tipsy and having a good time, Rachel let him. *No harm in having a little fun.*

Several drinks found their way into her hand over the course of the evening, and she downed each in turn. At several points, she spotted Justin out of the corner of her eye and smiled at him while two women pawed at his chest.

He gave her a mental shrug, and she laughed.

The world was a little spinny by the time Rachel realized she hadn't eaten dinner, and she wanted to see if it was too late to order food. She hadn't set a firm time to return to the academy, but it registered somewhere in the back of her drunken mind that she had somewhere to be in the morning.

Unsteady on her feet, she stumbled toward the wall to gather herself and check the time. Whatever nano counter-measure had been in the drinks was certainly doing the trick.

When she reached the wall, Rachel braced against it and tried to spot Justin again while she checked the time on the Link. Her jaw just about hit the deck when she saw it was 0143.

Oooooh, shit.

That meant she had to be up in four hours. And sober.

<Justin, where are you?>

<About to get a little better acquainted with Alissa here, since you ditched me. Why?>

<It's almost 2am. We should head back.>

<It is?!>

The crowd parted as Justin ran through. *<I thought it was maybe midnight.>*

<Yeah, same.> Rachel scanned the sea of people for Tom and spotted him at the bar. *<I'll say goodbye, and we can head out.>*

Her attempts to jog daintily to the bar came out more like the shamblings of the undead, but she made it to Tom without falling on her face.

"I have to go, I'm sorry. I didn't realize how late it was." Her voice sounded clear and measured to her own ears.

Good, maybe we can still make it past the guards at the academy's entrance.

Tom tilted his head and squinted while he tried to process what she'd said. "Oh, that's too bad. I was still hoping to take you out on my ship."

The idea of sudden acceleration turned Rachel's stomach, and she placed her hand on her abdomen. "Another time, maybe. Thank you for the fun evening."

"Here's my net-token, if you ever want to look me up." Tom passed the info to her over the Link.

"Will do, thanks."

Rachel met up with Justin on the way to the door, massaging her temples. "How many did I have?"

"Was I supposed to be counting?" Justin laughed, then cut himself short. "Wait, didn't you have a bag with our clothes?"

"Stars! That's right." Rachel stumbled back toward the booth where they'd spent the first part of the night.

The booth was empty, and there was no bag to be seen.

"No, no, no! This can't be happening." Rachel's heart dropped. The adrenaline rush of panic instantly cleared the drunken fog. She spun around and jogged to the bar. "Excuse me! Has anyone turned in a black canvas bag to your 'lost and found'?"

The bartender glanced at her and shook her head. "We don't have a 'lost and found' here. But if it's lost, you can bet someone else figured it was a mighty good find." She pointed up at a sign that read, 'Not responsible for loss of unattended items'.

Rachel resisted the urge to swear at the woman, and instead stormed out of the club to the comparative quiet of the transit corridor so she could think.

"Shit, Rachel! What are we going to do? We can't go walking into the dormitory like this, even if we could make it past the entry guards by some miracle."

"Not to mention that bag had my only shoes aside from these." She wiggled her toes in her sandals. "We're completely screwed."

"We could maybe see if they have security footage, and try to spot who might have taken the bag?"

"If we had time, yeah. But if we miss the morning muster, we'll be in *way* more trouble than if we show up at the front gate looking like this."

Justin took a slow breath. "Damn it, you're right. Stars, why did I ever agree to this?"

"Because we're both idiots." Rachel plodded in the direction of the academy.

They boarded the nearby maglev train in silence, knowing there was nothing they could say to make the situation better.

As they got off the train and walked the rest of the way to the academy's entrance, Rachel's chest constricted until she thought she might choke. *Why would I do something so reckless? The ISF is the best future I could have, and I'd throw it all away for one stupid night out at a club with a stranger while I ignored my friend? Maybe I deserve to be expelled.*

She was tempted to throw up behind a potted plant, but decided vomit-breath wouldn't make re-entry into the academy any easier.

<I'll do the talking,> she said to Justin on the final approach. *<I got us into this mess. I'll take the blame.>*

<It's not like you forced me to come.>

<But it's still my doing.> She took two even breaths to calm herself and walked up to the guards with feigned confidence. "Good evening. Two cadets returning home for the night."

Two guards looked her over and then chuckled to each other.

"You've had quite a night," the first guard said.

"It was lovely, thank you." Rachel brushed back a loose wisp of hair from her face. "We'll see ourselves to our dorm now." She made for the gate.

"Hold on a minute there," the second guard said. "We'll need to cross-check your ident."

This is officially the end of my life as I know it. Rachel passed her credentials to the guards over the academy's local network.

The second guard chuckled. "Really? You've only been here a month and you already snuck out?"

The first guard clicked his tongue. "You really got yourselves into it with this one."

His companion shook her head. "I think this calls for a trip straight to the Commandant. He'll love it."

Stars, no! Rachel's pulse spiked. "I can explain—"

"Save it for the Old Man," the second guard stated while making an entry on her console.

<This is it. We're done for.> Justin wiped his hands down his face.

<I'll take full responsibility,> Rachel told him.

<It won't make a difference.>

<I'll do whatever I can to keep you out of it. This is all my fault.> The queasiness in Rachel's stomach made her wish she'd taken that trip behind the potted plant when she'd had the chance.

"You're ordered to report to Medical," the first guard stated. "The

Commandant will see you when he arrives later this morning."

"Understood," Rachel murmured.

She and Justin trudged to their fate.

The same medical AI greeted them when they entered the lobby. "It appears your navigational error led you straight out of the academy."

"I guess I'm bad at reading maps," Rachel shot back.

The AI's avatar evaluated them in their mind. "Your blood alcohol levels are quite high. Unless you've consumed half a bathtub's worth of booze in the last six hours, your nano has been suppressed."

Rachel eased onto one of the benches in the waiting room. "Yep."

"Well, your mednano should come back online soon. I think it's best if you work this off naturally."

"Yay." Rachel pressed her palm to her forehead and lay down with her head propped on the arm of the bench.

After what only seemed like a minute, a buzzer sounded. Rachel bolted upright. Checking her Link, she saw that three hours had passed.

"Wakey, wakey," the AI attendant said. "You'll meet with the Commandant in ten minutes. Make yourselves presentable, if you wish."

Justin was coming to on an adjacent bench. "Oh, shit. We're going to miss morning muster."

"I imagine Sergeant Greggors has already been notified about our escapades last night. Missing morning laps is probably the least of our worries."

Rachel smacked her tongue against the roof of her mouth.

Stars, I'm thirsty.

With far more effort than it should have taken, she lurched to her feet and shuffled across the room to a water cooler. She poured herself a glass of water and chugged it, then refilled the cup to take back to her seat.

"I forgot how much hangovers suck."

Justin snorted. "They weren't kidding about that nano-suppressor. Pretty sure I'm still actively drunk."

Rachel noted that the universe did seem uncharacteristically off-kilter. "Yeah, that's more likely for me, too."

She smoothed her hair as best she could and altered her dress to be dark grey. "We should head to the Commandant's office."

"Yeah." Justin rose to his feet and flexed his neck.

"Good luck," the AI said. "Come back in an hour if your nano hasn't cleansed your systems yet, and I'll give you a booster."

"Thanks." Rachel departed the lobby with Justin.

The commandant's office was two corridors away, in the administrative center for the academy. Few of the offices were occupied at the early hour, but the individuals they did pass cast appraising looks at the two cadets.

Rachel held her head high and stared straight ahead, ready to accept her fate.

When they reached General Evans's office, Rachel took a deep breath. "It's been nice knowing you," she said to Justin.

"Likewise."

With resolute nods, they knocked on the door and stepped inside.

Commandant Evans was standing next to his desk with a cup of coffee in hand. "Good morning," he greeted.

"Good morning, sir," they replied in unison.

"Have a seat." He gestured to the two chairs across from his desk.

They complied.

The Commandant's gaze passed between Rachel and Justin. "Now, tell me, whose idea was this?"

Justin opened his mouth to speak, but Rachel beat him to it.

"It was mine, sir," she said.

"You demonstrated poor judgment by participating in activities that showed such disregard for the tenets of this academy," Commandant Evans stated. "Do you have anything to say for yourselves?"

Justin stared at his hands in his lap. "I'm sorry, sir. It was a lapse in judgment. It won't happen again."

"Why should I believe you?" the Commandant asked. "You disregarded rules and common sense this time."

"Because I want to be here, sir." Justin raised his gaze to meet the officer's.

"Didn't seem like it last night."

"I know, sir. I disrespected the academy and myself."

"Very well." The Commandant clasped his hands behind his back. "I have nothing more to say to you at this time, but rest assured I'll administer an appropriate punishment. You're dismissed."

Rachel started to stand with Justin, but the Commandant stopped her, "I'm not finished with you, Rachel."

She sat back down.

Justin flashed her a look of pity, but quickly exited the room and closed the door behind him.

Commandant Evans shook his head. "I don't know whether to be disappointed or impressed."

"Sir?"

He chuckled. "I mean, catching a ride out in the organic waste bins? That takes real dedication."

Rachel's cheeks flushed. "It was stupid."

"But showed some proper out-of-the-box thinking—well, in it, I suppose. Not to mention that clever trick with ghosting yourselves on the Link."

Is he complimenting or mocking me?

Rachel wasn't sure what to say. "My conduct was inexcusable."

"Rash and shortsighted, perhaps, but not inexcusable."

"Pardon, sir?"

He paced the room. "No one's future should be derailed just because of one night of poor decisions in the search of fun. If you'd blown up High Victoria, that'd be another matter. But drinking at a club? You were just doing what everyone else has been dreaming about since they got here, only you had the guts to follow through."

It took Rachel several seconds to find her voice. "That's very generous of you, sir."

He smiled. "I consider it good cosmic karma. I hope to have my own daughter one day, and I expect she'll do her share of reckless things. That's all part of growing up; it's what makes us human."

Rachel allowed herself to feel a glimmer of hope. "Does that mean I'm not expelled?"

"That depends." The Commandant perched on the edge of his desk. "Do you want to be here?"

She nodded. "I do. Yes, I've been annoyed, at times, by the mindless routine, but the kind of life I can have in the ISF… I don't want anything else."

Commandant Evans smiled. "Well, we're lucky to have you. As foolish as your stunt was, it did show a surprising degree of initiative and creativity. If you can channel that energy toward something more productive, you could go far in the ISF."

"Thank you, sir."

He rose from his desk. "There is still the matter of punishment…"

"I know, sir." Rachel nodded. "I'm prepared to accept the consequences of my actions."

"Good, then go get changed." The Commandant grinned. "I know of some waste bins that need scrubbing."

SECOND CHANCE

STELLAR DATE: 08.06.8948 (Adjusted Years)
LOCATION: ISS *I2*
REGION: Inner Canaan, New Canaan System

<*I learned my lesson, sir,*> Rachel told Admiral Evans, thinking back on the events of her youth that had placed her on her present path.

<*I have no doubt. Those waste bins were spotless.*> He smirked.

She shook her head, amazed he still remembered the punishment. <*That was quite a night. It's been a long road from there to here.*>

<*That it has,*> Admiral Evans nodded soberly.

Her escapades as a cadet may as well have been from another life, given how much had changed since then. But the commitment she'd made on that fateful night to serve her people was more salient than ever.

"Thank you for coming to see us off, sir," Rachel said, looking the admiral in his eyes.

He nodded. "Safe travels. I have every confidence in you and your team."

"Thank you, sir." She saluted. <*And thank you again for giving me a second chance.*>

THE END

AN UNCLE'S UNDERSTANDING

THE PRAIRIE PARK

Sera settled onto the bench in the Prairie Park, watching the Sun slowly dip toward the horizon. It looked so normal, at least for a G spectrum star. Nothing special at all about it.

"How accurate is that?" she asked Finaeus, gesturing to the representation of humanity's home star, rendered by the holographic perimeter of the park.

Finaeus cocked his head to the side, and she saw him squint in the diminishing light. "I suppose it's pretty good. I mean…it's obviously a holo, but the color's right, and they did a good job of simulating the effect of a single light source across the park. Not easy to do that when the real light source's distance and the apparent distance are so different."

"That's not what I meant," Sera asked. "You grew up on Earth. Is *that* what it looked like?"

Finaeus' shoulders drooped and he sighed. "You know…I don't really remember it that distinctly. I've seen so many suns lower over so many horizons, I can barely remember which is which anymore."

Sera nodded. "I've not seen a fraction of the sunsets that you have, but I know the feeling. I'm going to pretend it's perfect."

"You could always ask Bob, you know."

"Well, I imagine it's really not bang-on, and Bob will feel compelled to tell me about how it's not an accurate representation."

<I could lie to you; would that make you feel better?> Bob joined in their conversation.

"Uhh…no. You're frightening enough as it is, without thinking that you could be lying to me," Sera replied.

<Very well. It is not perfect, but an unaugmented human would not be able to tell the difference between what you see, and a real sunset on Earth. Is that acceptable? It is the truth.>

Sera nodded slowly. "That's perfect, Bob. Thanks."

<You're welcome.>

"You're a peach, Bob." Finaeus chuckled and looked up at the sky, shaking his head. "You shouldn't exist, but you're a peach."

<I know.>

"Guy's unnerving," Finaeus chuckled for a moment, then breathed a heavy sigh. "But stars in the black, I'm glad he's on our side."

"How did it all come to this, Uncle Fin?" Sera turned to look her uncle in the eyes. "How did my father not see all of this coming?"

"I imagine he must have seen *some* of it—but I think he hoped to have more time. Which is a pretty standard state of affairs. Live for thousands of years, but when things come down to the wire, there's never enough time."

Sera knew that all too well. "How does it work out like that?"

Finaeus harrumphed, and his lips twisted as he considered her question. "Probably because things unravel about as fast as we can manage to shore them up. More time just means more unraveling."

"And more time for our enemies to build themselves up," Sera added.

"That is the way of it," Finaeus replied.

"I just wish that we weren't fighting this war with Orion at the same time as everything else. The schism between my father and Praetor Kirkland was *because* of Airtha. We can all agree that Airtha is bad now, we should be working toward peace."

"That's an admirable goal." Finaeus's eyes locked with hers, and his expression became grim. "But you don't know Kirkland. He's just as pig-headed as your father was. He may not ally with us just because of our tech, not to mention our allegiance with Tanis and New Canaan."

"Shouldn't we at least try?" Sera asked. "You know, maybe talk to the man before we kick off a galactic war?"

Finaeus nodded and turned to look out over the sunset, his eyes distant. Sera joined him in gazing out over the tall grass.

She wondered at his resistance at talking to Praetor Kirkland. It could be that her uncle was right; that Kirkland was intractable and would not consider any compromises. But it *also* could be that millennia of past interactions had led her uncle—and likely her father, as well—to form an inaccurate view of the OFA's praetor. One where their own preconceptions colored their thoughts on the matter.

Sera placed her hands on her thighs and looked down at her fingers, changing their color from a pale flesh tone to match the blue of the jacket she wore.

It reminded her that she was wearing clothing, and that bothered her all the more. Her proclivities to wear evocative clothing—and the eventual removal of her skin in favor of her new, malleable epidermis—was one of the things she knew was distinctly *her*.

She knew that because Helen had always disapproved. The AI never tried to force Sera to change the way she dressed or behaved—at least not directly—but she certainly had disliked how Sera sexualized herself.

Was I rebelling against my mother all those years and not even knowing it? Sera thought with a laugh.

Either way, that behavior was something that she knew made her *her*, not what anyone else wanted her to be. Why did she think about it so much, anyway? In the grand scheme of things, no one should care about her fashion choices.

Maybe because I feel like it's the one thing I ***should*** *be able to control in my life, yet now I can't even make* ***that*** *decision for myself.*

"I suppose maybe we should."

Finaeus's words interrupted her thoughts, and for a moment she thought he was suggesting that no one wear clothing anymore, but then she recalled that he was responding to her question about trying to talk to Praetor Kirkland.

"Really? You seemed so opposed to it before."

"Well, maybe fresh eyes are what we need on the situation. Your father hasn't wavered in his approach for centuries; maybe Kirkland will consider your words more than he did Jeff's."

Sera pressed her palms together, lowering her lips toward her fingertips as she thought. "Well then, now we just have to figure out how to get someone in to meet with him. Someone that he'll believe has my backing."

"Surely you have agents at New Sol. You *are* the Director of the Hand."

"Stars," Sera laughed. "That's a job and a half on its own…one that has gotten away from me these past few months. I should have established a new capital outside New Canaan right away."

"You had no idea who you could trust. We had to seed Angela's AI correction first, and then wait for confirmations."

"True, yes. Well, what's done is done, and we're off to Khardine now. Regarding what you said before, I don't think it can be a Hand agent. I need a diplomat."

"What about your brother Serge?"

Sera had been thinking the same thing. Although, after Andrea had used Sera to try and kill Tanis, Serge had left the Transcend Diplomatic Corps. He'd remained in Airtha until after Sera's trials, and then departed from the Huygens System.

Last Sera had heard, he was headed to the Swan Nebula in the Sagittarius Arm to aid in a new combine of systems being established out on the fringe of explored space.

"I'll have to find him first—*then* see if I can convince him to go to New Sol. I got the feeling he wanted out of 'the life'."

"He's a good kid," Finaeus replied. "I think he'll do what's right. I think that's why he left—not enough 'right doing' opportunities in Airtha for his liking."

Sera considered that. It aligned with what she knew of her brother. That had also been over fifteen years ago. He could have had his fill of being on the frontier by now.

"I'll send someone to hunt him down once we get to Khardine. I think it's worth trying."

"And as a backup option?" Finaeus asked.

"Well, certainly not you. I still think *you* should be president, not me."

Finaeus rolled his eyes. "Enough with that. I want the job like I want a hole shot in my head."

"How do you think I feel?

"From what Admiral Greer told me, you *volunteered* for it."

Sera gave a short laugh. "It was me or Adrienne. What would you have done?"

"Point taken."

"Honestly…the only person *I* can think of who is really qualified to be President of the Transcend is Tanis. But she won't even hear of it. Shuts me down just like you do."

"Sera," Finaeus placed a hand on her shoulder. "You are going to make a fantastic president. You're smart, a good tactician, tenacious, you can deal with minutia, and you don't tolerate bullshit. You're also far more connected to reality on the ground than your father ever was. Without a doubt, you're just the woman we need for the job. Stop selling yourself short."

Sera place her hand over her uncle's. "Thanks, Uncle Fin. Just promise me you're not going to run off again. A leader is only as good as those she surrounds herself with."

Finaeus stood and stretched. "Well then, you're going to be the best leader ever. You've got me, and Tanis, and even Bob. Tons of great people around you."

"Just like you to turn it into something about yourself," Sera said with a laugh.

Finaeus shrugged. "I included Bob and Tanis." He placed a hand on her head and tousled her hair. "You'll always be my sweet little niece, Seraphina. I still remember when you'd sneak into my lab and ask me ceaseless questions."

Sera scowled at her uncle as she smoothed her hair out and stood. He winked at her, and she sighed and smiled.

"You're incorrigible, Finaeus. But those were some of my fondest childhood memories."

"Good, they're fond ones for me, too. But now I want you to put on your big girl pants…skin…whatever, and kick some ass. You're the president of the Transcend, one of the most powerful people in the galaxy. Act like it."

Sera laughed and gave him a light shove.

"Well then, if I'm the boss, it's time for you to get to Engine. We jump in less than half an hour."

"Sheesh, Seraphina, no need to be pushy." A grin slipped onto Finaeus's face, and he winked at her. "Besides, I don't work for you. I work for Tanis."

"Finaeus! Are you undermining me less than a minute after you told me to take the reins?"

Her uncle leaned in and gave her a light kiss on the cheek. "Good luck, President Tomlinson. Give 'em hell."

* * * * *

Bob watched Sera as she made her way to the maglev platform, and then the ship's bridge.

Finaeus was right. She was a powerful woman, and bolstered Tanis tremendously. The events he needed to bring about would not happen while Sera was at Tanis's side. They would need to be separated for his plan to work.

Though not just yet.

For now, Tanis needed her friend to lean on, and he needed Sera to be strong for what she would face at Airtha.

In time, the AI thought to himself as he watched a human woman with a piece of the enemy inside emerge from the grass in the Prairie Park, and follow Sera's path.

In good time.

THE END

* * * * *

THE SCIPIO ALLIANCE

THE ORION WAR – BOOK 4

BY M. D. COOPER

FOREWORD

This book was an unexpected surprise. I initially had not intended to write the stories in which Tanis built up her alliances in the Inner Stars before taking the fight to Orion and Airtha—but as the story grew, I knew that it would be foolish not to.

This was influenced in part by the *Perilous Alliance* series, as well as Rika's story, which have both built up the events in the Inner Stars to the point that it would not be possible to imagine these events occurring without Tanis becoming involved in some way.

In addition, no small number of you made it clear that, while you enjoy the other tales, you also want more of Tanis, Angela, and Bob.

Luckily, I'm a rather large fan of those three as well—plus the rest of the Intrepid/New Canaan crew and colony. What I decided to do (influenced in no small part by one of Aeon 14's uber fans, John Piper) was to tell stories that were much more focused just on Tanis and her core team, and this "Alliances" phase of the Orion War.

This will make for some shorter books before we get to the major conflicts, but they'll come out faster as well.

Writing this book was a load of fun, as I got to have more direct interplay with Tanis and Sera, explore Saanvi and Cary to a greater extent, and bring Tanis's third daughter, Faleena into the group as well.

I sincerely hope you enjoy reading it as much as I did writing it. Now let's see Tanis and Sera embark on their first mission in their new roles as President and Field Marshal.

Malorie Cooper
Danvers, 2017

PREVIOUSLY IN THE ORION WAR...

A lot has gone on in the months since the Defense of Carthage. Tanis and Sera have learned that Airtha has produced her own President Sera, more wars have begun to spread across the Inner Stars, and AIs are beginning to rise up in some systems.

When last we saw Tanis and Sera, they were aboard the *I2,* headed through the jump gate that would take them to Khardine, the new center of government for Sera's Transcend.

There, they plan to meet with Admiral Krissy, who is also Finaeus's daughter. If you've read *The Gate at the Grey Wolf Star*, you'll recall her and her efforts to help *Sabrina* and crew avoid being detained by the Grey Division.

Though Khardine is to be Sera's new capital, they do not plan to stay long, because their first order of business is to forge an alliance with Empress Diana of Scipio.

Petra, an agent of The Hand, has been masquerading for the last thirty years as an ambassador to the Scipian Empire on behalf of the Miriam League—a proxy nation of the Transcend's. Over this time, she has become the head of the Hand's local field office, and directs much of the Transcend's covert activity in that region of space.

The plan is to use Petra's 'in' with Empress Diana to begin to forge an alliance with one of the most powerful political entities in the Inner Stars.

Of course, there's the small problem of how Petra has lied to Diana for years about...well...everything.

Everything rests on this one lynchpin. If Tanis and Sera can secure Scipio as an ally of the Transcend, it will create an anchor in the Inner Stars and provide a forward position to bring the war to their enemies.

MAJOR CHARACTERS

ON THE I2/KHARDINE

- ***Angela:*** AI embedded in Tanis's mind.

- ***Bob:*** Hypernodal AI embedded within the *I2*.

- ***Elena:*** Former Hand agent and Sera's ex-lover. Double agent for Orion who attempted to kill Tanis.

- ***Finaeus Tomlinson:*** Brother of former Transcend President, father of Admiral Krissy, uncle of Sera Tomlinson. Finaeus is one of the Transcend's leading scientists and has been involved in many of their inventions

- ***Flaherty:*** Sera's personal protector who stayed with her during her exile.

- ***Greer:*** Admiral in the Transcend Space Force (TSF) who was with the former President during the negotiations with New Canaan, and supported Sera as the new president.

- ***Krissy Wrentham:*** Admiral in the TSF, formerly stationed at the Grey Wolf Star System. Led an advance team to Khardine to secure the system. Krissy is also Finaeus's daughter and Sera's cousin.

- ***Seraphina Tomlinson (Sera):*** President of the Transcend Interstellar Alliance.

- ***Tanis Richards:*** Head of New Canaan's Military, and Field Marshal of the Transcend's Military. Wife of Joe, mother of Cary, Saanvi, and Faleena.

- ***Valerie:*** Officer in the TSF who Tanis selected to lead Sera's guard.

IN NEW CANAAN

- ***Cary Richards:*** Daughter of Joe and Tanis, enrolled in the Intrepid Space Force Academy (ISFA).

- ***Faleena:*** AI daughter of Joe, Tanis, and Angela, enrolled in the ISFA.

- ***Joseph Evans (Joe):*** Husband of Tanis Richards, admiral in the New Canaan Military, Commandant of the ISFA. Father of Cary, Saanvi, and Faleena.

- ***Nance:*** Former crewmember aboard *Sabrina*, now attending the ISFA

- ***Saanvi:*** Adopted daughter of Joe and Tanis, enrolled in the ISFA.

IN SCIPIO

- ***Empress Diana:*** Ruler of the Scipian Empire. Her capital is Alexandria, which lies in the Bosporus System deep within the Empire.

- **Petra:** Transcend Hand agent who is operating as the Ambassador from the Miriam League (a proxy nation of the Transcend). Petra has made appearances in both the Orion War and the Perilous Alliance books.

ELSEWHERE

- ***Airtha:*** Name of the advanced AI who runs the Airtha Ring, and now controls much of the Transcend. Airtha used to be human (named Jelina), but was turned into an AI by the Ascended AI at the core of the galaxy.

Airtha is also Sera's mother, and a shard of her (named Helen) resided in Sera's mind for many years.

- ***(Evil) Sera:*** When Airtha failed to turn Sera to her side, she produced her own copy of Sera, who also purports to be the President of the Transcend, and rules from the Huygens System.

- ***Garza:*** General Garza has been instrumental in the Orion Guard's expansion and control of interstellar nations in the Inner Stars. After witnessing the cloning and reintegration technology that President Uriel used previously, he has begun to clone himself to further his efforts.

- ***Uriel:*** President of the Hegemony of Worlds (also known as the AST). Uriel has aligned herself with General Garza of the Transcend.

SEEING HER OFF

STELLAR DATE: 08.06.8948 (Adjusted Years)
LOCATION: Intrepid Space Force Academy
REGION: Orbiting Troy, New Canaan System

Joe strode through the corridors of the ISFA, nodding to students—all of whom stopped to salute him as he passed them by.

This year, the ISF Academy would see its highest enrollment ever, with fifty thousand human and ten thousand AI students.

The idea terrified him.

It was not the number of attendees that caused him such grave concern; it was the percentage of the colony's population that was now in the military. There were only six million humans and one hundred thousand AIs in the New Canaan System. In the grand scheme of things, the star system was all but unpopulated.

Yet, all told, nearly a quarter of the people were now serving, and another quarter were actively involved in the war effort.

And everyone who had stepped foot on an ISF ship or put on a uniform had—with rare exception—passed through his academy. Either here, or at Victoria, he had been their commandant.

Which meant he was ultimately responsible for putting them in harm's way.

Joe ran a hand through his hair as he walked into the Richards Atrium—homage that Tanis hated—pausing to stare out through the overhead dome, into space and the planet Troy beyond.

He knew it wasn't really all his fault. The enemy—and there were many of those—shared the bulk of the blame. But that didn't change how he felt whenever he saw a student's name on a MIA/KIA list, or etched into the base of a memorial.

Joe squared his shoulders, and pushed the melancholy thoughts from his mind. He knew his mood was as much a function of Tanis leaving as anything else. More than at any other time, he felt like he may never see her again.

Enough, Joe, enough!

He turned his thoughts back to the academy, now situated in its new facility: The Palisades. The station had been in construction for several years before the recent attack on New Canaan. Afterward, Tanis had authorized the rapid completion of the station using picotech. Four months later, they were all moved in.

With the additional resources flowing in from the Transcend, the station had been made larger than originally planned. It was now an eleven-ringed toroid with a mean diameter of thirty kilometers. Altogether, it contained over twenty-five thousand square kilometers of living, training, and teaching space—ample room for the academy to grow.

The ISFA was Joe's pride, and his sorrow. That New Canaan should have to become so military-focused, that they would be the ones to supply so many of the ships, shields, engineers, and soldiers for the war effort, saddened him.

Despite his misgivings, he agreed with Tanis's logic. A strong Transcend commanded by an ally such as Sera was vastly preferred to any other option. And so, the ISFA would train the men, women, and AIs who would fill the fleets and take the fight to the enemy.

He returned his attention to the dome, marveling once again at its complete transparency, unmarred by visible seams or supports. It was a single piece of carbon, fused together in a manufacturing process that rendered it both incredibly strong, and flexible enough to withstand the blast of a fusion bomb.

Beyond lay the myriad stars of the M25 Cluster. Hundreds of them, shining brightly, filled with people and resources.

Already, the Federal Legislature was considering the establishment of trade agreements with several nearby systems. Initially, Joe had opposed the idea. It ran counter to the long-term plan to move the New Canaan system, secreting it away from prying eyes.

However, President Andrews had proposed the creation of a base at Naland—a red dwarf, ten light years away. It was entirely uninhabited, and would be New Canaan's public trade hub. The idea had gained traction, and Tanis had approved of the plan before she left.

Before she left.

He pulled his gaze away from the stars above and continued moving toward the administrative wing of the Academy.

A group of first year recruits rushed by, eager to get to their first class of the day. Their enthusiasm brought back memories of the ISFA's early days on High Victoria, back when they operated out of a docking bay and several decks of the station, squeaking classrooms in wherever they could.

Since then, over two hundred thousand students had passed through boot, or earned their commissions at the academy—many doing both. No one donned an ISF uniform in service without first donning it at the academy.

That unifying training process was what made the ISF—in his experienced opinion—one of the finest fighting forces in the galaxy. If only its supply of recruits were not so small, and so precious.

Unbidden, Joe thought of his three daughters; all somewhere on The Palisades, all training to go into combat—possibly together, given their unique skillset—before leaving to fight in the war.

Joe was determined, when they graduated, to pass off the mantle of the ISFA to another, and leave as well. There was no way he'd remain behind while his entire family was off fighting in the war.

As he entered the Administrative wing, Joe resisted the urge to check on his daughters. Not that he needed to; after the many stern admonishments they'd received before enrollment, he knew they'd be in Light Attack Craft, Space to Surface Strategies and Tactics 101—'LACS', as the students often called it. Where the two 'S's and the final 'T' had disappeared to was a running joke among the instructors.

"Good morning, Commandant," the officer standing behind the admin-wing's front desk said in greeting as she delivered a sharp salute.

"Morning, Major Delma," Joe replied, returning the salute.

Joe liked Delma. She had her finger on the pulse of the entire academy; she knew who was coming, who was going, what the lunch special was, what classes had moved due to an HVAC issue, everything.

The fact that she was an AI certainly helped, but even so, she was exceedingly proficient at her job. Especially considering that she manned the front desk and personally greeted everyone who passed by.

"Commandant Evans," a voice called out from behind him. Joe turned to see Colonel Nelson of the Marine training division approaching.

"Good morning, Colonel," Joe said as the officer neared. "What can I do for you?"

"I have my latest class undertaking a capture and control exercise on a Trisilieds cruiser at 0600 tomorrow. I was curious if you'd like to observe."

Joe checked his schedule and saw that he had a meeting with the recruitment team at 0700. He weighed his options and decided he could attend the meeting remotely.

"I'd be delighted, Colonel Nelson. What sort of opposition will they be facing?"

"The crew of the *Jove's Fury* has volunteered to give 'em what-for, sir. A platoon of Marines from the 184th will be aboard, as well."

Joe nodded appreciatively. "You're not messing around. I'd very much like to see that. What is your anticipated outcome?"

Colonel Nelson chuckled. "Oh, I expect my class to lose, sir. But they'll give 'em their best, and be itching for a rematch."

"I look forward to seeing what they can do," Joe replied. "*Jove's Fury* has an exceptional crew, and the 184th are no slouches either. I bet your class is a little apprehensive."

"They're studying everything that every member of the crew and company have ever done. I think they're going to miss the forest for the trees, but we'll see. You never know; they may just pull it off."

"We'll see how it goes. I'll meet you aboard the observation pinnace at 0530, then."

"Thank you, sir."

Joe nodded. "Colonel."

One benefit to having tens of thousands of hulls drifting throughout the New Canaan system was that they had no end of ships upon which to perform exercises and drills.

Academy students also got to perform clearing exercises on derelicts, war games on real ships, and even live-fire exercises against AI-controlled enemy vessels.

All in a day's work at the ISFA.

Joe had seven more conversations with various officers on the way to his office on the outer rim of the uppermost ring on The Palisades. Though his patience began to fray, he handled all of them with more grace and calm than he felt.

When he reached his office, a dozen more tasks and messages hung above his desk, highlighted with different colors to denote urgency.

He ignored them all, walked to the window behind his desk, and stared out into the endless night of space. Out beyond Roma, in orbit of the dwarf planet Normandy, was the jump gate.

He took command of the station's sensor grid, and aimed optical scopes at the gate, overlaying the view on the window of his office.

The events he was seeing had transpired a few minutes previously, given the light lag, but he pretended they had not.

The scopes locked onto their target: the *I2*, its sleek, deadly form drifting toward the massive jump gate. The ring had a circumference of over sixty-two kilometers, one of the largest ever made. Over twice the circumference of the ore hauler's ring at the Grey Wolf Star, or so he was told.

She was on that ship. His wife. Tanis.

He knew she'd be on the bridge. Stoic; thinking of all the tasks and duties that lay ahead of her, the alliances, the first places she would strike at the enemy.

He also knew that she would be thinking of what she left behind, and the time and space that would pass between them all.

Will she still be the same when she returns? Will she and Angela have drifted closer to one another? They're still merging more and more. He could often see Angela in Tanis's eyes, and hear Tanis in Angela's thoughts. Every day, he wondered when the end of his time with her would come.

A nagging feeling warned him that it already had.

The display on his window caught his attention, and Joe watched as the ring's negative energy emitters came to life. They began to focus energy onto a single point, tearing a hole in the very fabric of the universe, before directing that energy at the *I2*. When that focal point touched the mirror at the front of the *I2*, the ship seemed to waver for a moment, and then was gone.

Be safe, Tanis and Angela. Give 'em hell.

EARTH

STELLAR DATE: 04.27.8948 (Adjusted Years)
LOCATION: Hegemony Capitol Buildings, Raleigh
REGION: High Terra, Sol System, Hegemony of Worlds

Three months prior…

Today, not even the view of Earth could calm her.

Uriel, President of the Hegemony of Worlds, felt impotent, powerless, and uncertain of her next move. A few short years ago, she had believed herself to be at the pinnacle: leader of the most powerful human empire in existence.

But she now knew that was not the case.

Not only had other federations and alliances within the Inner Stars grown in strength, but she now also knew that their rapid increase was fueled by outside forces—the Transcend Interstellar Alliance and the Orion Freedom Alliance; such innocuous names for the two most powerful political entities in the galaxy.

When General Garza had come to her a decade ago and offered Orion's help, Uriel had seen it as a way to break out of the cage that the Hegemony was trapped in. For though they were strong, the Hegemony of Worlds sat at the center of the human sphere, and though she did grow the Hegemony, every system she brought into the federation had already been inhabited for millennia.

It made growing the Hegemony's power grueling work.

Uriel's job was one of careful negotiation; trading pawns with a thousand opponents in the hopes of achieving a smattering of checkmates.

When Garza came along, his trade had seemed more than worth the price he had asked. Unlimited resources and advanced technology were up for grabs, and all she had to do was build fleets and use them to expand her power base.

And attack New Canaan.

Twenty thousand ships, gone….

It felt like Bollam's World all over again—though at least there, the Hegemony had managed to take control of the system. Gaining Bollam's

World had been a thin silver lining around an otherwise terrible disaster.

From what she had learned the previous day, there was no silver lining around the defeat at New Canaan.

Twenty thousand ships.

She had spent no small amount of political capital on that venture—first on the construction of the ships, and second, on keeping the construction and dispatch of the fleet a secret.

But the Legates who supported her had expected a technological windfall in reward for their silence. Instead, they had ten million deaths on their hands.

They were going to demand her head.

Uriel looked out over the city of Raleigh, stretching for hundreds of kilometers in every direction across the orbital ring's surface. It was the jewel of the Hegemony, the oldest human city in existence.

Her gaze fell upon the capitol complex, where the Legates were in session—both those who supported her, and those who did not. Very soon, Legate Borous would take the floor and reveal her failures to all.

Uriel took a deep breath and sent the order.

<Do it.>

She waited, tapping her forefinger on her thigh. A minute later, the capitol complex exploded.

The flash of light was so bright that the windows in her office darkened; fifteen seconds later, the shockwave hit, gently vibrating her tall tower.

Uriel did not look away as the fireball reached toward the sky, stretching into an oblong shape from the ring's coriolis effect. The Hegemony would reel, and Uriel would point to Scipio and their allies. She would propose new shipyards and fleets, and she would launch her attacks, pushing back the Hegemony's borders.

But first, she would supplicate herself before the Transcend and seek its president's forgiveness.

Before she killed that adversary as well.

KHARDINE

STELLAR DATE: 08.06.8948 (Adjusted Years)
LOCATION: ISS *I2*
REGION: Khardine System, Transcend Interstellar Alliance

After the successful jump to the Khardine System, Tanis and Sera retreated to the bridge officer's lounge for a light lunch. Something to sate them before spending the afternoon reviewing personnel assignments.

"I've been thinking about it, Sera," Tanis said around a mouthful of her cobb salad. "Khardine is a fantastic forward base of operations for the military, but a poor choice for a capital."

"What makes you say that?" Sera asked from across the table. "It's centrally located on the arms of the Transcend, it's almost entirely inaccessible, it's close to the major Inner Stars empires…."

Tanis cocked her head as she examined her friend, the President of the Transcend Interstellar Alliance—or at least a part of it.

Sera had spent much of her life in The Hand, one of the Transcend's clandestine agencies. The few years she hadn't been in the Hand, she had been focused on hunting down stolen technology in the Inner Stars.

Without a doubt, Sera was an excellent strategic and tactical thinker. What she wasn't considering was that she was facing a battle for the hearts and minds of her people, as much as for territory and resources.

"And what of perception?" Tanis asked. "Your people will look upon Khardine as a hideaway."

Sera pursed her lips as she considered Tanis's words, while Tanis summoned a holoprojection over the table to view the stellar cluster in which Khardine lay. On the *I2*'s charts, it was known as NGC 3532, or the Wishing Well Cluster. In the Transcend, it was called Oratus, due to its resemblance to a person standing with one arm outstretched—at least when viewed from the coreward side.

As far as open star clusters went, it was small—only containing two hundred and ninety three stars, many of them being large, old red giants.

After Betelgeuse died in a brilliant supernova a few thousand years ago—the effects of which were still washing across the Inner Stars—no human colonization efforts had moved in the direction of the cluster. No one wanted to be close to another stellar death like that one.

No expansion, that is, except for the Transcend's.

"So here's Khardine…" Tanis pointed at the small red dwarf nestled deep within Oratus. Rimward of it, a dozen red and blue giant stars lay between Khardine and the bulk of humanity. Tanis drew a line along a corridor that led through the stars, stopping several times to change course as it wove around the giant stars in the cluster. "And the dark layer FTL corridor is here."

"Yes," Sera said as she sipped her coffee. "Like I said, very defensible. The only way in is through that corridor—which we can protect with ease—or by jump gate. And you've already ordered Admiral Krissy to set up jump interdictors."

"I agree; it is a fantastic fortress in space—something that is exceedingly rare. Even if an enemy wants to come at us sub-light, they'll have to spend decades doing it. With the interstellar medium suffused with plasma and hydrogen, it will be hard to hide while they do it, too."

Sera's lips twisted as she looked at the holoprojection. "I sense a 'but'."

"It's the perception of the thing," Tanis said. "It looks like you're hiding. The capital should be in some center of commerce, like out in the Vela Cluster. We have already received word from the regional governors there that they will support you over Airtha; pick a system in that cluster. We'll go to it after Scipio and ensure it is well protected. We can select one of our most trusted admirals to oversee its defense."

Sera laughed. "*Trusted* admirals? I don't know that we have too many of those."

"There's always Krissy," Tanis replied. "From what we know—both from your sources, and from *Sabrina*—she stood up to the Grey Division at the Grey Wolf Star. That was a gutsy move, one that got her stuck there for a decade afterward."

Sera leaned back in her chair, cradling her coffee cup in her hands. Tanis let her mull the idea over, as she skewered the egg from her salad and popped it into her mouth.

She savored the fresh taste of the egg. One thing was certain: humans could travel amongst the stars for thousands of years, build and do just about anything, but they rarely did it without chickens.

Plus cats and dogs and mice, and a whole host of other animals—but chickens were near the top of the list. Which was good news for Tanis's cobb salad.

"Think she'd take it?" Sera asked. "The position, that is."

Tanis shrugged. "Finaeus may know better; she's *his* daughter."

"From her communications, I get the distinct impression that Krissy wants to be stationed at Khardine," Sera mused. "Of course, so does Greer."

"He's mentioned his interest to me," Tanis said with a slow nod. "He certainly has significant 'running a base in the middle of nowhere' experience."

"So does Krissy," Sera countered. "Both of them have Inner Stars experience, as well. Maybe we should send them into a cage match; two shall enter, but only one shall emerge!"

Tanis snorted. "Your administration should be very interesting."

"What was I thinking, Tanis?" Sera paused and looked around the nearly empty room. "Finaeus should take the position. He has all the connections; he's liked, respected. I'm the bad egg in the family."

"You should probably stop asking him to take the reins." Tanis gave a soft chuckle and gestured across the lounge at Finaeus, who was eating his small feast alone. "He won't even sit with us anymore."

Sera looked over her shoulder at her uncle and sighed. "I suppose I should ease up."

<*Finaeus,*> Tanis called out to the ancient terraformer over the Link. <*Come sit with us, we need to talk with you.*>

<*No, thank you very much. Sera has used up her allotment of 'take control' requests for the day. No, the week. Maybe even the century.*>

<*It's not about that; it's about the suitability of Khardine for a long-term capital, and about which general should be in charge,*> Tanis said.

<*Fine,*> Finaeus said to both of them. <*But I'm warning you, Niece-mine, if you bring up anything remotely close to me running this mess, I'm dumping my meatloaf on you.*>

<*I promise, Uncle,*> Sera replied.

<*Good, now one of you come help me move my food over there.*>

Tanis looked down at her salad and Sera's sandwich, then over to Finaeus's four plates and two drinks. <*We'll come over to you.*>

When they'd settled, which mostly involved rearranging Finaeus's plates to make room for theirs, he looked at Tanis, then Sera.

"So, what's this about Khardine? I like it. Didn't build the place myself, but it's well done: unassuming red dwarf star, one terraformed world—they managed to spin it up, too—and a couple of jovians to sweep up the bits and pieces and keep everything in order. Tritium-rich, too; good for antimatter generation. There's even a neutron star nearby. I'm itching to try to build one of those neutron beams our friends at Star City used."

"Ease up; we know *you* like the place, but you don't want to be in charge of anything, so it doesn't matter if you like it."

"Tanis Richards," Finaeus said, holding a hand over his chest. "You cut me to the quick. I just don't want to be in charge of *people*. They get in the way of building stuff—like my latest scheme, a portable jump gate."

"We already have portable jump gates," Sera reminded him.

"You misunderstand," Finaeus replied. "A portable jump gate for the *I2*."

Tanis let out a low whistle. "You just barely managed to make a stationary one, and it's only been a day since its first use; you're already improving on it?"

"You spent hundreds of years with Earnest Redding. Did he not operate in the same fashion?"

Tanis laughed. "Good point. He usually had to stop himself from improving his creations, if only so he could roll out an initial version that he would then tinker with. Although going the final distance usually bored him, and he'd already be onto something else. His labs are filled with thousands of near-complete inventions."

Finaeus rubbed his hands together. "You have no idea, my dear. I'm like a kid in a candy store in there. No, I'm like a kid who can't get fat or die of diabetes in all the candy stories in the universe at once. I'm quantum-candy-store kid."

"About the jump gate," Sera prompted with a wink.

"Yeah, right, well.... I ultimately want to work out a way to take the jump gate with us as we use it, but for now I'm working out a way to be able to build a new gate within days, deploy it, use it, and have it self-destruct—if we so desire."

"That sounds useful...really useful," Tanis mused.

When it came to jump gates, the *I2*'s size made for a distinct disadvantage. As of this moment, there was only one gate in the galaxy that the *I2* could fit through, and it was at New Canaan—a system that was currently over two thousand light years away, or four years via dark layer FTL, give or take a bit.

Components were already being sent to Khardine to build a second gate, which was more than necessary to avoid the two-year FTL journey to Scipio—but once they arrived at Scipio, the *I2* would be facing a long journey back to the Transcend.

Granted, the *I2* currently housed a dozen smaller gates that could send *other* ships back to the Transcend—or anywhere else—so no one other than the ship itself—and Bob—would be stuck in the Inner Stars.

Tanis had considered not taking the *I2* to Scipio at all—the *Aegeus* would be a far less imposing ship to fly into the Scipian capital system—but Tanis was uncomfortable with the idea of leaving the *I2* behind.

<*You're just going to miss Bob,*> Angela said privately.

Tanis laughed within her mind. <*I will, yes; his council is invaluable. Not to mention how much I missed being on this ship. The house on Carthage feels like a vacation spot—this is home.*>

<*You also have an irrational phobia of being separated from the* I2 *and getting stuck in the Inner Stars.*>

<*Irrational? Seems entirely rational to me,*> Tanis replied.

<*You have a lot of resources at your disposal, and people would come looking for us. We tend to make a splash—it wouldn't be hard to find us.*>

Tanis smiled at Angela, as they stood forehead to forehead in the shared space of their mind. <*Good point, Ang. We do stomp around a lot.*>

Outside her mind, in the much smaller reality adjacent to Tanis's physical body, Finaeus was explaining how he could couple the component pieces for an *I2*-sized jump gate together, and how he could probably build one in a month with the facilities on the ship—so long as they had an ample supply of pre-tempered reflectors.

Sera nodded appreciatively. "That certainly opens up options. Makes me feel a lot better about us jumping into the Inner Stars."

"I'm with you on that," Tanis replied. "Anyway, what we wanted to talk about is that Khardine is great—for a centralized location servicing the military. What it doesn't do is make the people of the Transcend feel good about their new president. She needs to be visible."

Finaeus lifted a forkful of meatloaf to his mouth and chewed thoughtfully before answering. "I suppose that makes sense. You two should have thought of it before we all flew out here."

"We had to come here anyway," Tanis replied. "Krissy and her fleet are waiting for us; we need to organize this as the Inner Stars Front's central command, and then Sera has to come to Scipio. Petra—her agent there—has made it very clear that the Scipian empress won't deal with any flunkies—which would be me."

Finaeus raised an eyebrow. "If only all leaders could have flunkies like you. So where do you suggest for the capital of the Transcend?"

"I was thinking somewhere in Vela," Tanis replied. "It's in the Orion Arm, and is resource rich. The cluster is still defensible, and it's far enough away from Airtha that we can clearly establish it as a base of power."

Finaeus nodded, and then spoke around a mouthful of carrots. "Vela is good. The data I have says that Alma is still the chancellor there. She would also function well as a Secretary of State, what with Adrienne heading off to Airtha and joining *her*...and your doppelganger."

Sera shuddered. "Gah, don't remind me. She changed me...Other me wears clothes and stuff. What do you think she is, anyway? A clone of some sort? I don't have any mental imprints on file; Airtha couldn't really make *me*."

"Sera," Tanis said, reaching out and grasping Sera's hand. "Helen was in your head for *decades*. Yes, Airtha could very well have recreated you in your entirety. For all intents and purposes, the other you *is* also you."

Sera ran a hand through her hair. "I really, really hate that. Like...more than I can even express. It feels like the ultimate violation. Can you imagine? A parent saying 'you didn't really work out, so I'm just going to make a copy of you and tweak it to my liking'."

"I'm pretty sure that happens all the time," Tanis replied.

"Well, it sucks. Sucks balls," Sera said.

Finaeus laughed. "At least we'll be able to tell you two apart. Calm, serene Sera is obviously Evil Sera. Half-naked, angry, cursing Sera is the Good Sera."

"Could be worse," Tanis chuckled. "She used to be all naked."

<I liked all-naked Sera,> Angela added. *<It showed that you were evolved,*

that you were in control of your own destiny as an organism. Conformity does not suit you.>

Sera smiled. "At least Angela gets me."

"Be naked if you want," Tanis said with a shrug. "So long as your fancy flow skin covers your bits, I don't care."

"I've never let my bits show; I'm not lewd or anything."

Finaeus snorted. "You can be a bit lewd, Sera."

"You know what? That's what I'll be, then. Naked and lewd. That's me." Sera stood up and pulled her jacket off, then her boots, followed by her pants.

"Feel better?" Tanis asked with a raised eyebrow before popping her salad's second egg into her mouth.

Sera's skin rippled, turning red from the neck down—except her hands, which she ran through her hair, flipping it over her shoulders.

She sat and glared at Tanis and Finaeus.

"Yes, lots, actually. It just itched too much!"

"Pay up," Tanis said to Finaeus.

"What? No! You had two days, and I had four. This is day three; we round up to five, therefore I win."

"You two bet on how long I'd keep wearing clothes?" Sera asked, her eyebrows halfway to her hairline.

Tanis shrugged. "There were also bets to see if you'd even do it in the first place. However," she looked at Finaeus. "We don't need to do your insane, napkin-math rounding. We know the minutes, and the count is closer to my selection of two days. I win."

"If I won, Tanis was going to have to eat one hundred BLTs in one sitting," Finaeus said with a frown.

"And now that I've won, Finaeus has to stop threatening to leave and go after *Sabrina*."

Finaeus shoveled more meatloaf into his mouth and glared at Tanis as he chewed angrily.

<Fine,> Finaeus said as he continued to chew. *<Was this all you wanted to talk about?>*

"No," Sera replied. "We were also discussing who we should place in charge of Khardine, and who should go to Vela—should I agree to eventually establish the capital there."

"Ah," Finaeus said after he swallowed. "So you're debating Greer versus Krissy, and you figured I might have some insight."

"Very perceptive of you," Tanis said.

"I'm really smart," Finaeus replied. "Maybe not an L…what are you, Tanis?"

"Two," Tanis replied, giving Finaeus a significant look.

<*He's such an ass,*> Angela said privately.

<*Finaeus just likes to needle everyone all the time. It's his modus operandi.*>

<*He seems to think that we should tell Sera. At least, that's what I read from the situation.*>

Tanis had often wondered what Sera would think of her, should she learn what Tanis and Angela really were.

A vanilla human, known as an L0, had one hundred billion neurons, and as many as one quadrillion synapses. L1 humans had half again as many neurons, and a number of synapses commensurate with that increase.

L2 humans were a significant leap beyond that. Tanis's brain contained only double the neurons of an unaugmented L0 human, but her dendrite and synapse count was an order of magnitude higher.

"Right. An *L2* like Tanis, here, but I can figure things out."

"And so can I," Sera said. "Which is why I can tell that something's up between the two of you."

Tanis glared at Finaeus and then released a cloud of nano to mask their conversation from the rest of the officer's lounge.

"Finaeus, Earnest can keep the secret for centuries, but a month after you find out, you're dropping hints all over."

"Not all over," Finaeus said. "Just to Sera. You're her field marshal; she needs to know."

"Yes," Sera nodded. "I need to know. Now tell me."

Tanis drew a deep breath. "You probably know that Angela and I have been together for a long, long time."

"I do," Sera replied. "Almost two hundred years, I believe—just fifteen decades or so longer than is recommended. You two are certainly defying the odds."

"Well, sort of. We *can't* be separated anymore, not even if we wanted to be—not that we do. Our minds have been interconnected for some time now."

Sera raised an eyebrow. "Interconnected how?"

"Well, ever since Angela and I defended the *Intrepid* against STR's fighter attack in Sol, we've started to overlap. Not in identity, but in usage of the other's hardware."

"Which should be impossible," Finaeus added. "Tanis and Angela should have undergone a personality merge not long after that—but they didn't."

"I didn't know the specifics, but I've always been able to tell that you're two people. That much was apparent when we first met. You were unconscious, Tanis, but Angela was not, and she was decidedly testy."

<*We were in a vulnerable place,*> Angela said.

Sera chuckled. "That you were. Though I'll admit, on the Link, the two of you feel like opposite sides of the same coin."

"I'd noticed that, too," Finaeus commented.

Tanis nodded. "I've heard people mention that before, as well. Anyway, Earnest has been monitoring us for some time, mapping our progression. Since he was staying behind at New Canaan, and we have no idea how long we'll be fighting this war, he brought Finaeus up to speed on my condition. Which is when they found something…new."

"Something pretty amazing," Finaeus added.

"You two are killing me," Sera said. "Spit it out. You're not dying, are you, Tanis?"

Tanis laughed. "Stars, no. What Earnest found was a new type of neuron in my—our—brain."

<*It has multiple axons,*> Angela supplied. <*And more dendrites too…of which Tanis's cells already had a lot.*>

"That's not the most interesting part," Finaeus pressed. "The neurons are comprised of elements not normally present in brain tissue, and they are able to tap directly into Angela's neural net—rather than going through the interfaces."

<*We have a direct, multi-location bridge,*> Angela translated.

Sera's mouth hung open as her gaze darted back and forth between Finaeus and Tanis. "Are you two messing with me? Was this part of the 'get her naked' bet?"

Tanis chuckled. "No, though that would have been funny if it wasn't true…not that it's not funny, just…whatever, you get what I mean."

"How are you still sane?" Sera asked

"Who says I am?" Tanis smirked.

"Not funny, Tanis. Be serious. Are you merged?"

<We're not,> Angela replied. *<But it* ***is*** *happening. These new cells…they are growing in number. Right now, they exist alongside my neural net and Tanis's. But Earnest and Bob believe that they will eventually begin to supplant our existing neural hardware.>*

"'Neural hardware', nicely put, Angela."

<It's what it is.>

"That's not even the best part," Finaeus said with a wide smile. "Tanis's new neurons—though they're mostly dormant, at present—have strange quantum activity."

"What do you mean by 'strange'?"

"They seem to operate with a quantum superset; they're like tiny, organic, quantum computers."

<They effectively ***are*** *quantum computers. Or something utilizing the same principles.>*

"What's going to happen to you?" Sera asked, her eyes wide with worry.

"Don't get too upset," Tanis said. "Bob thinks this has been going on for some time, but that the cells were just too few to notice. There still aren't many of them; we could have centuries before anything significant happens."

<Liar.>

<Hush, Angela. Sera needs stability, not worry about what dealing with Tangela will mean.>

<Angelis. We've been over this.>

Tanis laughed and winked at Angela.

"So why tell me, then?" Sera asked.

Tanis shrugged. "Ask Finaeus."

"Seemed like you should know," he said with a shrug. "Tanis is instrumental in the whole 'save humanity' thing we have going on. You need to know her weaknesses."

Sera's eyes narrowed as she peered at Tanis. "Are you going to ascend, Tanis?"

<That's a bit on the nose,> Angela said.

"Honestly?" Tanis asked. "I have no freaking idea. Finaeus is the ascension expert."

Tanis and Sera looked at Finaeus, who had just taken a bite of cake. He responded over the Link.

<Well, they're not doing anything like what the people at Star City were doing. Mind you, they were going it solo; no fancy mind-merging stuff going on with them. And ascended AIs are crossing dimensional boundaries to expand their computing power and alter their physical composition. What Tanis and Angela are doing is…different.>

"Yay for different," Tanis said with a wan smile. "I sure do love being a trailblazer."

"So what are they becoming?" Sera pressed Finaeus.

He swallowed and peered into Tanis's eyes.

"They're becoming…more."

THE HIGH GUARD

STELLAR DATE: 08.06.8948 (Adjusted Years)
LOCATION: ISS *I2*
REGION: Khardine System, Transcend Interstellar Alliance

Tanis surveyed the sixteen men and women who stood before her, all perfectly rigid and at attention. Half were TSF soldiers and the other half was comprised of ISF Marines. They were the best of the best—veterans every one, with station, shipboard, and dirtside combat experience. They were all capable pilots, and many had experience with deep infiltration operations.

"You have been selected because of your exceptional skill and experience," Tanis began as she walked before the assembled men and women. "You have proven your valor, your loyalty, and your bravery time and time again.

"Are you still Marines of the ISF, and Soldiers of the TSF? Yes you are; you will never stop being those things. But you are now something else. You are the High Guard. The first of an elite unit, tasked with protecting the President of the Transcend against all aggressors."

Smiles lit the faces of several of the soldiers, though the Marines' expressions never wavered. Tanis didn't begrudge the TSF troops their freedom of expression. They were not undisciplined, they just had a different style of discipline than the ISF.

"You are going to set the standard and the traditions of the High Guard for centuries to come. The deeds you undertake will become legend and lore. Because—make no mistake, High Guard—this is no cushy assignment. You won't be sitting around, polishing your rifles—metaphorical or otherwise. We're going to get in trouble out there. You're going into the fire. And you know me; when I say 'fire', I mean the blazing inferno of an A0 star on its worst day."

Tanis walked up and down the line, looking into the eyes of each soldier.

"This is a volunteer outfit, so anyone who doesn't think they're cut out to deal with the shitstorm that we're getting into, please step back."

Tanis observed the men and women with keen eyes. The TSF

members of the Guard lost their smiles and stood stock-still. Not a single one moved.

"Then are you ready to take on the most important assignment of your lives?" Tanis asked.

A mix of 'Yes, ma'am's and 'Ooo-rahs' met her ears.

She winked at them. "You all are going to have to unify that shit. Can't have you shouting different things when we're out there trying to make a good impression. And, Marines: you're going to have to give a bit. Remember, you're not changing Marine tradition, you're building a new tradition."

A few small nods were visible, and Tanis smiled.

"Then I'm going to turn you over to your new CO, TSF Major Valerie."

"Thank you, Field Marshal Richards," Major Valerie said as she walked in front of the High Guard. Tanis gave them one last look and nodded with satisfaction. They would acquit themselves well. She was sure of it.

Once Valerie had fully briefed them, they would assemble to swear an oath to the office of the President.

MORNING CLASS

STELLAR DATE: 08.06.8948 (Adjusted Years)
LOCATION: Intrepid Space Force Academy
REGION: The Palisades, Orbiting Troy, New Canaan System

Cary stood in front of the mirror and looked over her uniform, turning to see the sides and back. She spotted a piece of lint on her back and sighed. *What I wouldn't give for an auto-fit dresser right now. Or even just a holomirror.*

"Stupid 2D mirror," she muttered.

<*You had hard mirrors back home on Carthage,*> Faleena said. <*Surely you're used to them?*>

"Yeah," Cary replied aloud, distracted and forgetting that she wasn't alone. "But I *also* had a holomirror; you know, to make sure I look ship-shape and all that."

"What was that? Do you need me to check you over?" Jill asked from Cary's side, thinking Cary was talking to her.

Cary started; she hadn't even seen Jill approach in their platoon's small restroom. "Sorry, Jill, I was talking to Faleena. She and I are still getting used to being this close to one another all the time."

<*I'm used to it,*> Faleena said to the pair over the Link. Her mental avatar—a red-haired mirror of Cary—wore a smug expression. <*But I'm told I adapt quickly.*>

"They'll be hitting the gate soon," Jill said, abruptly changing the subject.

<*Fifty-seven minutes,*> Faleena supplied.

"Halfway through first class," Jill said. "I know we're not supposed to, but I'm going to be watching the feeds…I just need to know that the *I2* makes it OK."

Jill's mother, General Brandt, was also on the *I2*. Cary understood Jill's sentiment all too well, but the two women weren't alone. A lot of the students had parents, siblings, even children on the great ship and its accompanying fleet.

Everyone was going to miss that ship.

It was a big galaxy out there, and the war would be long. There was a chance—albeit one that Saanvi insisted was extremely low—that the *I2* would never return to New Canaan.

Cary wondered where Saanvi drew her certainty from. Her sister *had* spoken to Bob before the ship left, but she hadn't revealed much about the conversation; just that it had happened, and that she was going to miss Bob.

"STC to Cary," Jill said, waving her hand in front of Cary's face. "You there?"

Cary shook her head and gave Jill a wan smile. "Yeah, just thinking about Mom and Angela. I'm going to miss them a lot."

<Me too,> Faleena said. *<I didn't think it would be this hard.>*

"I know what you mean," Jill added, a look of longing in her eyes. "Mom gave me this big pep talk before she left, telling me about how I was a woman now. Strong, capable, nothing to fear.... Thing is, I'm not worried about being here at the ISFA; I'm worried about *her* out *there*."

Cary chuckled. "I don't think there's any reason to worry about *your* mom, Jill. General Brandt is one of the toughest people in the galaxy. I heard she once shouted a minor planet out of her way."

"Pretty sure it was a gas giant," Jill said with a grin. "It's funny, she's never like that at home. Never yells, never even raises her voice. But put her in front of a company of Marines, and she turns into something else entirely."

Cary turned and leaned against the counter. "I still remember being terrified the first time I went over to your house. I was worried that she'd yell at me for doing something wrong...but she was super nice."

"I guess she gets it all out of her system at the job," Jill replied. "By the way, where's Saanvi? I thought I'd see her getting ready in here, too."

"Oh, she's long gone," Cary replied. "Something about examining one of the assault drop ships in Hangar 18A14 before class today."

Jill snorted. "Of course she is. If ever there was a born overachiever, it's Saanvi. Still, if she finds out anything useful, I hope she shares it with us."

Cary patted Jill on the arm. "You and me both. C'mon, we have to get down to Ring Nine for class, and I *cannot* be late. I'm already on latrine duty for the rest of my life; I don't want to add my afterlife to that sentence."

The two women walked out of the restroom and into the platoon's bunk room. Eight double-bunks lined the space on each side. They were all assigned; every training 'toon was full on The Palisades this semester.

The other cadets were already gone, and Cary increased her pace, worried that they wouldn't make it to class in time—though she paused to look at her bunk as they walked past, making sure it was perfect. Sergeant Grant would be through once first class began, and if he spotted so much as a single fiber of cloth out of place, he was prone to blow a gasket.

"Glad I'm not in your shoes," Jill said, shaking her head as they reached the doors. "Always one infraction away from certain doom—mind you, I wouldn't object to being known as a hero of the Carthage Defense."

"Oh, trust me," Cary said, blowing out a long breath. "In the past two days alone, each of my instructors has lectured me about how I'd better not let that go to my head, and that it was only dumb luck that kept Saanvi alive. I've been told I was foolish, reckless, insubordinate, disrespectful…and I'm sure a whole bunch of other things that I can't pick out of the general morass anymore."

"Plus all the times that Sergeant Grant has screamed at you already," Jill added. "I think it's been three times so far."

Cary gave a rueful chuckle. "Five. He's cornered me outside of the dorms a few times. I swear, boot was easier than this."

"Funny how Saanvi isn't getting beat on like you," Jill said. "She was with you the whole time."

"Yeah, but everyone knows I dragged her along. Instead of the yelling, she gets the 'I'm disappointed that you bowed to peer pressure like that' speeches."

Jill shook her head. "I can't believe they're so hard on you two. Everyone knows you saved Landfall. If those Trisilieds carriers had managed to get their fighters into the mix, a lot more assault craft would have made it to the planet."

<It is curious behavior.> Faleena joined in the conversation. *<I've been trying to quantify it, and as far as I can tell, it's as much for everyone else's sake as yours. They want the other cadets to know that you're not getting special treatment.>*

"Thank stars I'm the great Tanis Richards' daughter," Cary said with scorn in her voice. "Otherwise I'd be getting beat up under stairwells for being allowed into the academy after what we did."

<*You sound like you're ashamed of being Tanis's daughter,*> Faleena said privately to Cary. <*But I know that's not true.*>

<*You're right,*> Cary replied. <*I shouldn't have said it like that. I just…it's really complex, you know? I have to work against the stigma of stealing a starship and getting away with it, then I have to deal with being Tanis's daughter. Half the time I can't tell if I'm being judged by one of those two things, or by my actions.*>

Faleena nodded soberly in the mental space the pair shared. <*Stealing a starship* **was** *one of your actions, though.*>

Cary laughed. <*True, I just meant recent actions, as in the thing that I was actually doing when I got scolded.*>

"Don't worry," Jill said, replying to Cary's prior statement. "If you get beat up in the dark corners of The Palisades, I'll come to your rescue."

<*I bet that would work, too,*> Faleena said. <*One thing is for sure, Jill—no one wants to find out if you've inherited your mother's public temperament.*>

The girls reached the main sweep that ran around Ring Three, where first year cadets were housed, and made a bee-line for the maglev station that would take them to Ring Nine.

A train pulled up onto the platform, and they rushed toward it. Before the pair made it halfway, the train filled with cadets and whisked away.

"Oh, crap," Jill muttered. "I hope the next one gets here soon; this dumb maglev line has to make four stops before it gets to Ring Nine."

Cary and Jill joined a dozen other students that were all standing on the platform, nervously checking the holodisplay that showed the next train's arrival time.

Faleena gave a soft laugh on the channel the three were sharing. <*If you weren't already under so much scrutiny, I'd hack it and make it skip a few stops.*>

<*You can do that?*> Jill asked, her mental tone incredulous. <*Odin would notice, for sure.*>

Cary was certain he would. Odin, the AI who ran The Palisades, managed the station with a steely calm and brooked no nonsense. Even if something did slip past his notice, Major Delma, the AI who oversaw her father's Battalion HQ, would spot it.

<*Maybe, maybe not,*> Faleena mused. <*Mom—Angela-mom, not Tanis-*

mom—loaded me up with a lot of her tricks. She told me that when we graduate and ship out, she wants to know that I am armed with everything I need.>

*<You have **all** of Angela's 'tricks'?>* Jill asked, her mouth agape physically and over the Link.

*<Well, not **all**, I'm sure. I do have some datapacks that are categorized 'only open in case of dire emergency',>* Faleena replied. *<You know how it was; I got a bit of a crash-course in being raised. Zero to maturity in six months.>*

Cary gave a good-natured laugh. *<Well, some amount of maturity,>*

<Thanks, Sis.>

<Stars…the stuff Angela must know,> Jill mused. *<She worked in Terran spec-ops for a long time before joining with Tanis, you know.>*

<Jill, she's our mom. Of course we know,> Cary replied.

As they spoke, the train pulled up at the platform, and Jill peered at Cary. *<Faleena, did you rush this one?>*

<Nope, I decided to try something different. I asked Odin if he had a spare train he could put into rotation for us.>

Jill made a noise of surprise as they boarded the maglev, and Cary frowned, *<I didn't realize you had a special 'in' with Odin.>*

<Moms asked him to look out for me. He seems to be taking it very seriously.>

The train pulled away from the platform, and Cary saw that the maglev was going straight to Ring Nine. She shook her head in disbelief. *<They must have said something pretty convincing; Odin is not known to be accommodating.>*

<Well, he did say, 'tell your sister to spend less time preening, and you'll get to class on time.'> Faleena said with a bubbly laugh.

Cary folded her arms. *<Dammit, even things that benefit me are still banking on my soiled past.>*

<Seriously, Cary?> Jill sighed and elbowed her in the arm. *<Get over it. You're going to have a couple of years of suck here, and then you'll be free and clear. People are going to sing songs about what you and Saanvi did. No one is going to remember that Sergeant Grant got spittle on your face a few times.>*

<Cary, where are you,> Saanvi said, breaking into her thoughts. *<Class starts in seven minutes!>*

<We're on the train right now,> Cary replied, bringing Saanvi into their group. *<We'll be there in four minutes.>*

<What? No, everyone on that train just came in. The next train's not going to make it for another ten! You can't be late, you're going to get creamed!>

Cary couldn't help a grin. <*Don't worry, Faleena hooked us up, we're on a…an extra train, I guess.*>

<*Faleena? What did you do?*> Saanvi asked, sounding even more worried.

Faleena giggled. <*Relax, Saanvi, you're going to give yourself an aneurism. I just asked Odin if he'd help. I blamed Cary, and he seemed to buy that.*>

<*Hey, wait, what?*> Cary sputtered. <*You* ***blamed*** *me? You conveniently left that out before.*>

<*I figured you were feeling out of sorts enough.*>

Saanvi gave a throaty laugh. <*You just told a white lie, Faleena.*>

<*Not my first, either,*> Faleena replied with a wink.

<*My, you're getting* ***saucy****, Faleena,*> Jill said.

The maglev flew off Ring Three and through the transparent tube that drew it down the stack of rings toward Ring Nine.

Cary stared out the window at the world of Troy below, wondering when they'd start doing planetside exercises.

When The Palisades was first announced, Cary knew that Troy was the perfect place for the ISF Academy. The planet was a world of extremes: vast oceans, a wide variety of continents, towering mountains, deserts, plains, deep canyon systems…. Troy had it all.

On top of that, there were three moons—one nearly Lunar in size—which would give them plenty of hazardous environments to train on. Though she was less excited about working in vacuum after spending so long trapped in wreckage a few months before.

The maglev banked around The Palisades station, and the planet was lost from view. A minute later, it pulled into the station on Ring Nine, and the two women disembarked, rushing across the platform and down the sweep to the corridor that would lead them to their class.

They made it to the lecture hall with two minutes to spare, and Saanvi delivered a withering scowl at them as they sat.

"Always cutting it close," Saanvi admonished. "Good thing Faleena has your back."

"Even if she has to throw me under the bus with Odin to save my butt."

"That sure summons a convoluted visual," Jill said with a laugh. "If Odin drives the bus over your ass, is it still saved?"

"Ask me at the end of term," Cary replied with a mock groan.

The three women brought up their holodisplays and prepared for Light Attack Craft Space to Surface Strategies and Tactics 101, or LACS as Cary had already taken to calling it after hearing some of the older cadets refer to it as such.

Saanvi hadn't agreed with the shortened acronym, but after trying to pronounce LACSSST a few times, she had succumbed.

Major Kara entered the room and surveyed the class as the students rose and stood at attention. She nodded at them, and they returned to their seats, ready to absorb the day's lesson.

The major launched into a lecture about the history of orbital drop craft, major battles in which they had turned the tide, and contrasted them against other engagements where they hadn't been a factor at all.

It was a lesson everyone paid rapt attention to. Many of the students knew people who had been killed in the Trisilieds assault on Carthage just four months earlier, and had even been involved in the defense against the craft.

Cary looked forward to the day they would rain drop ships on a Trisilieds world and exact retribution.

Major Kara must have been reading her mind, because forty-five minutes into the class, she stopped her lecture and leaned on her podium.

"I know you all want to take the fight to the enemy. You want to give them what for. Let me tell you: going down in a tin can, praying you hit the surface in one piece, is pretty much the opposite of fun. It's not about retribution or payback. It's about protecting New Canaan and the men, women, and AIs in your unit. I want that in your minds whenever you think about dropping, and when you do your first drops."

She activated a holodisplay, bringing up a view of the newly constructed jump gate near Athens. The display showed both the gate and the *I2* on its approach. She gave a heavy sigh and looked around the room.

"Many of you have friends and family going out into the stars on that ship, and no small number of them are Marines. And no small number of those Marines are going to drop onto a world and take it by storm. When you think about the tactics we discuss here over this semester, remember that they extend, *or end*, the lives of real people.

"Someday, some of you here will go through that gate and drop onto distant planets. Some of you will pilot the ships; some will be the boots that hit the ground. Some of you will make the call on who to send, and where they go." Major Kara's eyes swept across the cadets, pausing on Cary and Saanvi. "So remember. Everything we talk about in class is serious business. Lives *will* depend on it someday."

Cary swallowed a lump down her throat. That was the difference between what she and Saanvi had done above Carthage, and what they would do in the future. Their last-ditch attack run had only risked themselves. Chances were that next time they had to get in harm's way, many other lives would be on the line, too.

Major Kara nodded with satisfaction at the serious expressions on the cadets' faces. "Good, now let's listen in on the Gate Control's feed."

She waved her hand, and the room was filled with the sound of Gate Control's public feed of the *I2*'s departure.

<*The jump will be fine,*> Saanvi said. <*Finaeus is the one who worked out how to make the gates big enough for the ore haulers at Grey Wolf. The* I2 *will make it through, no problem.*>

<*This gate is twice the diameter as the one at Grey Wolf,*> Cary replied. <*And that gate isn't really one you want to cite to promote confidence; from what I hear, they never did figure out why it realigned when* Sabrina *went through.*>

<*True, but it's handled thousands of successful jumps since. Just like this one will,*> Faleena replied.

"Activating antimatter systems," the voice from Gate Control announced. "Negative energy emitters are online, field is live."

On the holodisplay, a roiling ball of not-space appeared in the middle of the jump gate's ring, hinting at a path to *everywhere* in space-time.

"Targeting the *I2*'s mirror. Mirror lock successful, focal line shifting, *I2* is advancing and in the pocket. One thousand meters to contact…seven hundred meters…four fifty…one hundred meters…contact!"

Tears formed in the corners of Cary's eyes as the *I2* was enveloped for a moment in the roiling non-space of the gate…and then it was gone.

"We have transition!" the voice from Gate Control cried out. "The *I2* has successfully made the jump!"

Cheers erupted from the cadets, but Cary didn't join in. She bit her lip and glanced nervously at Jill and Saanvi. A feeling of uncertainty came from Faleena, as well.

Cary clasped Saanvi's hand on her left and Jill's on her right as they waited for the confirmation probe to jump back into New Canaan and report the *I2*'s safe arrival.

It should take roughly thirty seconds, but Cary watched the counter as it slid past thirty-five, then forty.

The room had quieted, as had the feed from the GC. Then, at the sixty-two second mark, with a whoop of joy, the GC announcer called out, "We have confirmation! The *I2* is at Khardine. Say again, the *I2* is at Khardine. Transition was safe and successful!"

Cheers erupted from the cadets once more, some standing on their seats and pumping their fists in the air. This time, the three young women joined in, rising from their seats and embracing one another in fierce hugs.

Saanvi blew a kiss toward the projection of the ring. "Be safe, moms, and do what's right."

"And kick some ass," Cary added.

"Lots of ass, mom," Jill joined in.

<And come back safe,> Faleena whispered in their minds.

The three nodded vigorously, but Cary wasn't worried. One of their mothers was Tanis Richards, and she could do anything.

Still…be careful out there, moms.

PRISONER

STELLAR DATE: 08.06.8948 (Adjusted Years)
LOCATION: ISS *I2*
REGION: Khardine System, Transcend Interstellar Alliance

"I feel like I'm your pet," Elena said, folding her arms across her chest. "You come down here when you feel bad, see me in a cage, talk to me, and then leave."

Sera shook her head as she took in Elena—her prison uniform, sour expression, and disheveled hair. "Life on the inside really isn't what you're cut out for, is it?"

It wasn't the first time in the last four months that Sera had come down to see Elena. It wasn't the second, or third, or even the tenth. She had lost count, to be honest.

Sometimes Elena was happy to see her, and they would chat like it was old times. Sera would be very careful not to share details about the current situation, though Elena tried her best to ferret them out.

Elena had correctly surmised that Tanis and her fleet had successfully defended New Canaan from the attackers—though she had no idea of the scope of the battle. She also guessed that Sera had indeed taken on the role of President, though Sera had never confirmed it.

"You tell me, President Seraphina. How do I look?"

"Honestly, Elena? You look like shit."

"Yeah, the mirror says the same thing. I tried to smash it, but it won't break."

Sera shook her head. "Yes, they do endeavor to make sure the inmates can't kill themselves."

Elena only grunted. "So, what brings you down here today? If it's not to torture me, that is."

"Tanis and I talked it over, and we've decided to share something with you."

"Oh, did you now? And how is the Ice Queen doing these days?"

"Don't give me that act, Elena," Sera said. "You liked Tanis and her daughters. And I *know* you didn't really think that all their tech should be destroyed. Orion is hypocritical, too; they don't eschew advanced nano and other tech like they say they do."

"Oh, yeah? How do you know that?"

"Well, we have Kent—the guy who tried to kill Tanis—plus about half his team."

"They were military," Elena said. "They used higher levels of tech to fight the Transcend."

"And then there's Jessica's team," Sera added.

"Jessica…I never met her, but I remember her from a briefing. She's the purple one, right?"

"Yeah," Sera nodded. "The purple one."

"So what does she know about Orion?"

Sera shrugged. "Oh, not much. She just spent nine years there. Saw a few things."

Elena's eyes widened. "Nine years? Where?"

"Perseus Arm," Sera replied. "There was a jump gate mishap. She saw some pretty advanced tech out there; some of it was Orion's, some of it was stuff they were trying to steal."

"Steal? From who?"

"Turns out that parts of the Perseus arm were settled before Kirkland's people showed up. There is some impressive stuff out there, and the OG was trying to take it, not to destroy it. Same as what they tried to do at New Canaan."

"I have just your word for that," Elena said.

"Dammit, Elena. When have I ever lied to you? You thought I was deluded, becoming evil, or whatever. And, yeah, close proximity to my father all those years was starting to mess with my head. But lying to you was never a manifestation of that."

"How would I know?" Elena asked.

"C'mon, you have to have *some* evidence to make an accusation like that. Did I lie about where the toothbrush was? Did I lie about who left the light on in the kitchen one night? If I'm such a big liar, there's gotta be something."

Elena shook her head. "You're very adept. I don't know how I could tell."

"Stars, Elena! You're so *fucking* deluded! You and I have known each other for over fifty years; we were lovers for almost twenty. Who put in your head that I'm so evil?"

"You're not evil, Sera, you're just twisted by your upbringing. When Gar—"

Elena stopped herself, pursing her lips, but Sera knew what she was about to say.

"You met with *General* Garza? The guy who runs BOGA?"

"Seriously, Sera? You're the president now, you can't run around calling them 'Bad Orion Guard Agents'."

"If memory serves, their real name is as dumb as The Hand's. I'll stick to 'BOGA', thanks. But that's beside the point; you met with Garza, and he turned you. How long did it take? What technique did he use?"

"None. Nothing. I wasn't turned by a technique, I already had my doubts."

Sera turned away from Elena and pressed the heels of her hands into her eyes. "Fine. Whatever, Elena. I'm the devil incarnate—except I'm not the one trying to take over *everything*. I just want to put the Transcend back together and keep Orion from forcing their views on us at gunpoint."

"Sera, listen—"

"No. I'm done listening. I'll arrange for you to get some time in one of the parks—maybe in one of the cylinders. Perhaps the fresh air will clear your mind and give you a reason to run a brush through your hair."

Sera walked away and didn't look back. She did, however, hear Elena say, "Thanks, Sera."

CAPITOL

STELLAR DATE: 08.07.8948 (Adjusted Years)
LOCATION: Keren Station
REGION: Khardine System, Transcend Interstellar Alliance

"Dad!" Krissy called out as her father stepped off the *I2*'s pinnace.

"My girl!" Finaeus shouted in response as he rushed down the ramp toward her.

Krissy felt like a child as her dad crashed into her and spun her around. She wondered what the soldiers coming down the ramp after him would think, but decided that she didn't care. *Not even a little bit. Not one iota. I thought I'd lost him forever; nothing will ever come between us again.*

She stared into her father's eyes, almost unable to breathe at the sight of him. "Stars, Dad, I thought you'd never get here!"

"Yeah, I know you had to wait a few months, but at least you knew I was alive."

Krissy let out a happy laugh. "Dad, you're the great Finaeus Tomlinson; you wouldn't let something as trivial as being sent outside the galaxy stop you—though I suppose you bested that, too, only ending up in the Perseus Arm."

Finaeus snorted. "'Only in the Perseus Arm'. You make it sound like it's just next door."

"Considering that you could have been spending the rest of your life exploring a dwarf galaxy and staring up at the Milky Way every night, I'd say that Perseus is pretty much right next door."

"I would have renamed it," Finaeus said.

"What?" Krissy asked, perplexed.

"The Milky Way. We call it that because of what it looks like from the inside. Out there…given the inclination…I would have named it the…Spaghetti Bowl Galaxy."

"Always thinking with your stomach, Dad."

Finaeus nodded. "No reason to change up what works."

Another pinnace flew through the bay's grav shield and settled on the next cradle over. Finaeus took Krissy by the arm and led her toward it. "Come, let's introduce you to your new president, and Field Marshal Richards."

"I've met Sera before," Krissy reminded him. "Back before her self-imposed exile. Stars, I used to buy her birthday presents because you always forgot. Her, I can handle; it's Tanis Richards that has me worried. I hear she's rather imposing."

Finaeus laughed. "Yes. She's a bit like you in that respect."

Krissy smacked her father's arm, but was happy to have him back, bad humor, inappropriate remarks, and all.

They approached the pinnace's ramp, and Krissy separated herself from her father. She would need to salute her new CO and the president.

As expected, Sera and Tanis were the first ones off the pinnace, walking side-by-side down the ramp. Neither was anything like she expected.

Sera looked nothing like she had years ago. She was wearing a skin-tight, light blue outfit, which was complemented by her dark blue lips; her face, unnaturally pale, was framed by long, black hair. She strode casually down the ramp, laughing at something Tanis must have said over the Link.

Tanis Richards, Krissy's new boss, wore a crisp, white uniform that was cut for a female figure, but not overly so. Her hair was pulled back into a tight ponytail, and her eyes seemed to take in everything around her with a single glance.

Her posture was far more rigid than Sera's, but there was a subtle fluidity to it—as though she were a dancer masquerading as a soldier.

As they reached the foot of the ramp, Krissy saluted sharply, a gesture which Tanis and Sera returned.

"Madam President, Field Marshal Richards," Krissy said by way of greeting.

"Seriously, Krissy?" Sera winked. "You're my cousin, you don't have to salute and be all formal."

"It wouldn't do to have accusations of nepotism fly about," Krissy barely managed to say before Sera wrapped her in a fierce embrace.

"I don't care. Thank you for saving *Sabrina* and everyone aboard. You took a big risk."

"I'll take risks to stand up against the Grey Division any day," Krissy replied. "Bunch of self-righteous—"

Krissy looked at Tanis and flushed, though the other woman was smiling at her.

"No need to edit yourself on my behalf," Tanis said. "I run a call-it-like-I-see-it sort of operation."

Krissy offered Tanis her hand. "I'm glad to hear it, and glad to meet you, Field Marshal."

She noticed a grimace pass over Tanis's face and wondered if the woman was entirely comfortable with her new role. Last she'd heard, Tanis Richards was governor and general; field marshal was quite the step up.

Alongside the admiral's—not general's—stars on Tanis's lapels, Krissy saw that only one bore the TSF's crest, while the other bore a symbol she assumed to be the ISF's.

"There is no Grey Division in my Transcend, anyway," Sera said. "From what Finaeus has explained, and from the evidence I've seen, they have been nothing but an arm of Airtha for centuries. I've created a plan to disband them, audit their staff, and create a new R&D division."

"I like the sound of that," Krissy admitted.

"I was expecting Admiral Greer to meet us," Tanis said. "I saw the *Galadrial* at dock, so I assume he arrived safely?"

Krissy nodded. "He arrived a week ago. His ships are undergoing refit and repair, and he's out inspecting the progress. I expect him to be back here on Keren in a few hours. He did want to be here to greet you, but his tour took longer than expected."

Tanis nodded. "Understandable, he has a lot to do. I assume that your shipyards are also installing the new shield generators we've sent?"

Krissy nodded. "They have begun, yes. Would you like a brief tour of the facility? I understand it is going to be the de facto capital for some time."

She saw Tanis and Sera glance at one another before Sera replied, "For now, yes."

It took her a moment to realize that Sera was referencing Khardine's status as the capital, not the tour of Keren station.

"But a short tour would be nice, before we get to the new administration complex."

Krissy nodded and led Finaeus, Sera, and Tanis out of the docking bay, while the rest of their retinues continued to disembark. She did notice a quintet of soldiers bearing an insignia she had not seen before split off and follow behind the group. Their ranks were strange: a major, two sergeants, a corporal, and a lieutenant.

She assumed it was some elite unit, and nodded with satisfaction before bringing up a point about the shield tech. "There was some grumbling that we're not being allowed access to the underlying stasis shield technology—just black-box units. Though I understand the need for secrecy, the single source is troubling from a volume and security standpoint."

"It's really not up for debate, Admiral," Tanis replied. "I'm sorry."

Krissy opened her mouth to reply, but could tell by Tanis's expression that the field marshal would not budge on this point. At least, not yet. Krissy wasn't about to give the argument up so easily.

She led them through several sections of the TSF's docking and administration areas, before they took a maglev to the station's central shaft.

The center of Keren station was a cylinder thirty kilometers in length and two in diameter. It rotated slowly, providing a gentle 0.7*g*, and was filled with rolling plains, forests, and lakes. A long sun ran down the center, and Krissy wondered how similar it was to the *I2*'s habitation cylinders.

One difference was that Keren Station did not use a fusion-based sun to generate its light-energy. Instead, a large solar collector fanned out from the station's sunward pole and drew in the star's light. The photons were then funneled down the tube and diffused across the interior of the cylinder.

"It's comforting," Tanis remarked as they walked down a broad street toward the administrative buildings that had been constructed for the fledgling government's use. "Reminds me a bit of Landfall. The domes there shifted the red starlight in a similar way, but you could still pick up the original tones."

"Domes over Landfall? On Carthage?" Krissy asked, wondering why the capital city in New Canaan would be domed.

"Sorry," Tanis said with a forgiving smile. "We named Landfall on New Canaan after Landfall on Victoria. Some of us are a bit sentimental, it would seem. Back when the atmosphere was still too thin to breathe, we domed the city so the Victorians could build aboveground."

"Ahh," Krissy replied. "I remember Victoria. We studied the—" She stopped when a pained expression came over Tanis's face. "Um…sorry."

Tanis raised a hand and shook her head. "I've come to grips with it. Time marches on, right? We can't expect everything to remain the same forever."

Krissy had to admire the woman's fortitude. She had studied Tanis Richards as much as possible before her arrival, and there was no doubt about it: the woman had seen her fair share of misfortune.

She imagined herself in Tanis's shoes. To know that her birthplace and childhood home on Mars was gone, buried under the collapsed Mars 1 Ring, and that every place she had ever visited on Earth was gone, and possibly every place on High Terra, as well.

Add to that list the fact that the Sirians had razed absolutely everything in the Kapteyn's Star System, and Tanis Richards had few places she could look back on without sadness clouding her memories.

That Tanis was still taking the lead, striding forward, and doing what needed to be done impressed Krissy to no end; almost enough to make up for being passed over for field marshal.

Krissy couldn't help but feel that Tanis had gotten the position as much because of her control of the picotech and her friendship with Sera than any special skill she may have.

Tanis may have fought a number of impressive battles and won against unimaginable odds, but Krissy had far more experience with mutli-system fleet engagements—not to mention almost five hundred years of active military service on Tanis.

Still, she wasn't going to side with some evil entity that had enslaved all of the AIs in the Transcend just because she thought she should have Tanis's job. Especially since Adrienne had gone and joined with Airtha; if that wasn't a sign of who was on the wrong side, nothing was.

For now, she'd hold her peace. But if Tanis appeared to be in over her head, Krissy would petition Sera for a change of command, special friend or not.

They were still half a kilometer away from the newly constructed administration buildings when Tanis stopped, cocked her head, and cried *"RUN!"* before turning back the way they'd come.

Krissy didn't bother to ask what they were running from. She joined the mad dash, scanning the surrounding terrain for danger as the accompanying soldiers surrounded them.

A second later, a tremendous *crack* echoed through the cylinder, and Krissy turned back to see a beam tear through the landscape above them and smash into the new administration buildings.

<*Shot came from a ship in dock,*> Tanis said on the combat net Krissy had reflexively created for the soldiers and officers. <*Captain Espensen is targeting its reactors, but it may have enough charge in its batts for another shot.*>

<*Emergency shielding is up,*> Krissy assured her. <*What ship fired?*>

<*It was the* Galadrial,> a new voice reported on the net. Krissy checked who was speaking and saw that it was Rachel Espensen, captain of the *I2*.

<*What?*> Krissy couldn't believe it. She didn't know Captain Viska personally, but the woman was well respected within her division; that the attack had come from her ship was unthinkable.

<*Lock that ship down,*> Tanis ordered. <*But don't destroy it; I want to know who is behind this.*>

<*It's not Viska…or maybe not,*> Sera said as the lead soldiers directed everyone through an entrance and down into the skin of Keren's hab cylinder. <*I checked when we landed; she's with Greer on his inspection.*>

Krissy was beside Tanis when another blast tore through the station, striking the road just one hundred meters behind them.

"Go!" Tanis shouted to the soldiers as she reached the doors and held one open for the last two stragglers.

Is she reckless or brave? Krissy wondered as Tanis raced down the stairs after them. *Doesn't matter, the outcome is the same.*

* * * * *

Tanis counted the group who had escaped the blast. Major Valerie and four of the High Guard, plus the ten TSF soldiers that had accompanied Krissy—though two of those were on her administrative staff. She wasn't certain how much use they'd be in a fight. Add Krissy, Finaeus, and Sera to that number, and there were nineteen of them, all told.

<*How many were killed by the shot?*> she asked Angela.

<Not certain; at least a thousand. The station has activated grav shields over the holes, so they're not venting atmosphere anymore.>

<Good thing we're slow walkers,> Sera added. *<If we hadn't taken the scenic route, we'd already have been there.>*

Tanis clenched her teeth, took a deep breath and turned to Krissy. "Where to?"

"We should get out to the far spur. That will put as much station between us and the *Galadriel* as possible," Krissy replied.

"Unless they have two ships and they're just waiting for us to go somewhere vulnerable," Sera said.

Krissy frowned, and Tanis knew the feeling. Being shot at by your own ships made for a sickening sensation.

"We go down-cylinder, then," Krissy decided. "There are no TSF ships docked around the lower rings and, crazy as it sounds, we'll be safer in the civilian sections of the station."

Krissy led the way with four of her soldiers behind her. Tanis and the High Guard followed, Sera and Finaeus tucked into their midst. The final six TSF soldiers brought up the rear.

<I hate this,> Sera said privately.

<Which? Being fired on by the Galadrial, *or rushing blindly through the station?>*

<Uh, I was referring to being the unarmed one that the people with guns are protecting. I'm not going anywhere without a weapon anymore.>

Tanis tapped a member of the High Guard on the shoulder and pointed to her sidearm and then at Sera. The woman unholstered it and passed it and two charge cylinders over. One of the TSF soldiers scowled, but didn't say anything.

<There, now you're not unarmed.>

<What about you?> Sera asked.

Tanis laughed aloud. *<I'm always armed, Sera.>*

<I want to be the general; you be the president.>

<I'll still always be armed.>

"There's a concourse ahead," Krissy informed them. "I've summoned some station cars to pick us up for a ride down-cylinder."

Tanis nodded, seeing the concourse ahead at the far end of the corridor. Her nano cloud had just reached it, and its feed revealed a heavily armed squad of soldiers stationed on either side of where their corridor met the concourse.

<*Fall back,*> Tanis ordered on the combat net. <*There's an ambush ahead.*>

Krissy hesitated, then began moving backward, drawing her sidearm.

<*Was that 'I don't believe Tanis' hesitation, or was it 'damn, my plan's not working' hesitation?*> Tanis asked Angela privately.

<*Hard to say,*> Angela replied. <*She could have just been checking her feeds.*>

As Angela spoke, the enemy soldiers leaned around the end of the corridor and opened fire on the retreating group.

The four TSF soldiers were now the rear guard, and their armor bore the brunt of the assault. They returned fire, and the enemy troops pulled back around the corners.

"Where's station security?" Finaeus asked.

"They were evacuating the area because of the big holes in the station," Krissy said as she moved to the fore of the retreat, her sidearm in hand.

"Seems convenient," Sera mused.

"It's protocol," Krissy replied tersely.

"I meant it seems convenient that the *Galadrial* would fire twice and miss us both times, all the while driving us toward an ambush."

"You're right," Tanis said. "That first shot was to get us moving, and the second was to keep us going." She called up to Rachel on the *I2*. <*Status?*>

<*Justice, the AI on the* Galadrial, *shut down power to all weapons systems. She's keeping the ship in lockdown while we send over a sweep team. She's rather pissed.*>

<*Good,*> Tanis replied. <*I'm glad Justice isn't in on it; I like her.*>

She brought her focus to the corridor down which they were retreating. The enemy had pushed forward, and the group fell back to an intersection, where they took cover.

Tanis glanced back the way they had come; there was little chance of escape that way, as it was likely sealed against vacuum. <*Krissy, send two of yours down each corridor. Let's see if we can find an exit,*>

<*On it,*> Krissy replied.

Tanis sent a passel of nano down each corridor, as well. The nano would scout, and the soldiers would deal with what she expected to find.

<*They're only firing concussive pulse blasts at us,*> Major Valerie noted. <*Seems like this is a capture op.*>

<*I wonder how they expect to get off the station?*> Angela replied. <*They stand zero chance of making it past the* I2.>

Although the enemy was using non-lethal weaponry, the soldiers protecting the group were not. Two carried beam weapons, and the others fired high-velocity kinetics, which had already taken out three of the attackers.

One of the TSF soldiers ahead of Tanis took a focused pulse blast in his armpit that knocked him against the wall. He groaned and his arm hung limp.

<*Smashed my ribs,*> he reported as he picked up his rifle with his other hand and took aim once more.

Tanis pulled up the nano feed of the attackers and the concourse beyond. Instead of their rides arriving, thirty-three more enemy soldiers were rushing to the scene, some breaking off and moving down passageways parallel to the one where the group was hunkered down.

<*They're going to flank us,*> Tanis said.

<*And we can't go back,*> *Finaeus added.* <*I sent nano to confirm. That entrance is outside the grav shield; we'd be sucking vacuum back there.*>

"Damn," Tanis swore as her nanocloud down the right corridor encountered a dozen enemy troops. She addressed the pair of TSF soldiers that were following behind her cloud. <*You've got company,*> she informed them, then passed the feed over.

<*Engaged!*> the soldiers down the other corridor called out.

"I'm going to go clear out the left side," Tanis said and pulled her jacket off, tossing it to Sera. Then she removed the rest of her clothing, revealing the matte grey default state of her Mark X FlowArmor.

"Dammit," Sera swore. "And I have to stay behind?"

"Benefits of wearing clothes—I can wear armor underneath," Tanis replied and dumped the rest of her uniform in Sera's arms. "Be back in a few minutes."

She signaled the armor to flow up over her head, and triggered its stealth mode, rendering her invisible to the rest of the team. The soldiers would be able to see a marker for her, though, sent out on a preset pattern of frequencies that would appear random to an observer.

"Don't you need a gun?" Krissy yelled after her.

"No," Tanis called back.

She ran down the hall toward the two TSF soldiers who had taken cover in a small alcove.

<*Behind you,*> Tanis called out, and the man and woman signaled their acknowledgment.

<*What are you doing here, umm, ma'am?*> the woman, a corporal named Annie, asked.

<*Getting your cans out of the fire. I make, what, eleven?*>

<*Was twelve,*> Private Yves replied.

<*Keep your fire off the left side,*> Tanis said. <*I'm going to go around behind them. When they get distracted, do what you do best.*>

<*Yes, ma'am,*> Corporal Annie replied.

<*Missed the action, have you?*> Angela asked as Tanis crept along the side of the corridor toward the enemy.

<*It's only been six months since we stormed the* Galadrial,> Tanis replied. <*I went eighteen years without a firefight before that.*>

<*Got a taste for it again, did you?*>

<*Quiet, Angela.*>

The enemy wore armor Tanis had not seen before, though it bore a resemblance to what the TSF soldiers used. It was black and entirely without markings. She gauged it to be medium weight. Not fully powered, and light enough for moving through tight spaces in station corridors.

She slipped past the first two enemy soldiers, who had taken a position behind a conduit stack, and then another six who were firing from behind a mobile ablation shield. The final three were at an intersection. *Keeping an eye out for station security,* Tanis surmised.

She crept around behind the final three, wondering if her nano could breach their security systems, or if she'd have to do things the old-fashioned way.

<*What do you think?*> she asked Angela. <*I imagine its nano-defense is as good as the TSF stuff we've encountered thus far.*>

<*That's the thing about nano. No matter how advanced it gets, it still dies to 'zot'.*>

<*Very eloquent.*>

<*You could try to hack one of them; it would make for a useful distraction,*

at least.>

Tanis crept behind an enemy and held her hand behind the soldier's neck. Her hand tingled as a stream of nano flowed from it onto the enemy's armor.

<*And we're in,*> Angela reported.

<*Just like old times. Can you lock it up?*>

<*How many times have I told you that you can manage the nano, too?*>

Tanis gave a mental shrug. <*You're better at it.*>

<*He's locked. Link is down. Get the other two.*>

Tanis repeated the procedure on the other two soldiers, and then moved back down the corridor toward the six—now five—enemies taking cover behind the ablative shield.

<*I think if I lock one of them, the others will notice,*> Tanis said.

<*Yeah. Just kill them, already. Everyone's going to think you've gone off for coffee or something.*>

Tanis drew the two slim blades sheathed in her forearms, and stepped up behind two of the soldiers. She took careful aim and slid the left blade into the helmet seal at the back of one soldier's head, pushing hard, while driving the other blade up under the other soldier's pauldron and into his armpit.

The first soldier twitched and fell, while the second one jerked aside when he felt the blade tip bite into him.

Tanis leapt back as he checked himself, her intended target thinking he'd been shot. He looked behind, and saw the three unmoving figures at the end of the corridor, and Tanis knew the jig was up.

Two of the other soldiers turned and realized that one of their number had been killed from behind. One of the two still standing raised his weapon to blanket the area with pulse blasts, but a teammate pushed his gun down.

<*That's right, soldier boy; your pals are in the line of fire back there.*>

<*Was that meant for me?*> Angela asked.

<*Whoops, just meant to think it.*>

Tanis stepped between two of the soldiers, who were now moving backward down the hall, and approached the two still firing through the slot in the shield.

She slid one of her blades back into its sheath, and then flicked her left wrist. The motion opened a port in her palm, and the hilt of her lightwand dropped out of her hand.

<You're never going to get a real left arm or hand again, are you?>

<Flowmetal is just so…handy,> Tanis said with a smirk as she activated the lightwand and drove it into one of the soldier's helmet's respirator ports. His comrade turned and saw the lightwand come out the other side, and jerked away, avoiding the blade Tanis had aimed at his neck.

The man was quick; he brought his weapon to bear, and Tanis dove to the side as focused pulse blasts tore through the air where she'd been standing a moment earlier.

Tanis slashed at his gun with her CF-blade and at his hand with the lightwand. The wand cut through his armor and into his hand, causing him to drop his rifle.

Tanis kicked it aside and grabbed his injured hand, flushing a stream of nano into his body.

A glance over her shoulder told her that the soldiers who had gone to check on their three frozen comrades were rushing back down the passageway. They fired at the area around their fallen teammates, and Tanis flattened herself against the wall, waiting to strike again.

Then a soldier turned toward Tanis and pointed right at her.

<You got blood on your armor, he can see you now,> Angela said calmly.

<Thanks for the heads up.>

The soldier who had spotted her swung his rifle to fire at her, and she dove to the ground, rolling to a new position when a thunderclap sounded in the corridor.

When she looked back at her attackers, they were toppling to the ground, headless.

"Stand down!" a voice thundered, and Tanis grinned, relief flooding through her.

There, standing amidst the three locked down enemies, stood Flaherty, hefting a crew-served railgun.

The two remaining enemy soldiers who were further down the hall paused for a moment, and then the telltale whine of the railgun filled the air. An instant later, both had tossed their weapons aside and were lying prone on the deck.

"Didn't know you were on station," Tanis said as she rose and set her armor to its matte-black state.

"I know," Flaherty replied, then gestured to her armor. "Nice camo.

Need to wipe it down."

Tanis sighed. "So Angela tells me. Go help Sera; she's ahead."

"Gladly," Flaherty replied.

He moved past her, kicking one of the enemy soldiers as he did, and then the two TSF soldiers she had passed earlier approached—Yves bending down to secure the two enemies who had surrendered.

<All clear, ma'am?> Corporal Annie asked.

<These two are on the ground, handless guy is locked down, and the three at the end of the hall are locked down, as well.>

<I gotta say, ma'am> Corporal Yves replied. *<You kick a lot of ass for being brass.>*

<Shut the fuck up, Yves,> Annie said and gave him a shove. *<Now lock these three down so we can move on.>*

A minute later, the sound of the railgun came again; then again, and again. When the report of pulse rifle blasts fell silent, Sera, Krissy, and Finaeus approached with Valerie and two of the High Guard preceding them.

"You have fun down here?" Sera asked. "Still have your hands and heart?"

"Har, har," Tanis replied. "You're very droll, you know that?"

"I've heard talk." Sera half-smiled.

Though Flaherty's railgun had driven the bulk of the attackers back, Tanis decided their best bet was to hold steady until the station security and TSF garrison moved into the area.

"The garrison will have a company here in seven minutes," Krissy reported as she grabbed a pulse rifle from one of the fallen soldiers.

Valerie handed Tanis a spare cloth, and she wiped the blood off her flow armor before taking her uniform from Sera.

"You make a good coat rack," Tanis said with a grin.

One of Krissy's soldiers, a sergeant named Loren, gasped at Tanis's impertinence.

"Sorry," Tanis shrugged as she stepped into her pants. "When you've saved the president's ass a dozen times, you can make comments like that, too."

"I don't think you've ever actually saved my ass," Sera replied with a furrowed brow.

"I beefed up *Sabrina,* and rescued you from that pirate ship in Gedri,"

Tanis said.

"If you recall, I was already on the bridge and in control when you arrived."

Tanis laughed. "Well, I provided a useful distraction. I also saved you from your sister, back at Ascella."

"OK, that counts for a dozen all by itself," Sera relented with a smirk as she reached out and touched Tanis's shoulder, feeling the flow armor. "You know, now that I'm your boss, I could order you to give me one of these."

"It'll probably itch you," Tanis replied.

Sera stroked the side of her chin with her index finger. "Bob has that fancy armor skin he made for his avatars, and you have your pour-on armor; I wonder if he could work out some way to incorporate that into my skin…"

"No."

"No, what?"

"Armor is the only time we can count on you to get dressed anymore. If your skin is armor, that'll be the end of your decency."

Sera frowned. "I'd call you a luddite, but you're even less human than I am. You of all people should understand the finer points of self-enhancement."

Tanis laughed. "Oh, I do…I just like to blend in."

Sera straightened her back. "Well, I'm the eccentric ruler. It's my job to be strange and unusual."

Finaeus laughed. "That's my kind of girl. Krissy, you should follow Sera's example; you're too rigid."

Krissy had been talking to one of the soldiers, and now she looked back to give her father an eyeroll.

"There you have it, folks," Finaeus said with a laugh. "The trademarked Krissy eyeroll. I've been inoculated through repeated use, but you two should look out; it can be deadly."

"Dad…"

Finaeus held up his hands defensively. "Sorry, dear, sometimes I'm not good at the personal/professional line. Spending nine years on *Sabrina* wasn't helpful. They have no line—not a lot of professionalism, either."

Sera laughed and clasped Finaeus's shoulder. "Damn, I wish I could have been there for all that."

"Don't worry, there are plenty more stories to share. By the way, when we get back to the *I2,* come to Earnest's lab with me; he may already be working on just what you're referring to. I think we could actually incorporate the armor directly into your skin."

"Will it itch?"

"Of course not," Finaeus looked offended at the suggestion.

"Then you're on."

AGENT

STELLAR DATE: 08.07.8948 (Adjusted Years)
LOCATION: Intrepid Space Force Academy
REGION: The Palisades, Orbiting Troy, New Canaan System

Nance closed out the replay of the *I2*'s departure, a feeling of sadness tugging at her heart.

Nothing had turned out like she had hoped it would. They had made it to New Canaan, delivered Finaeus, secured General Garza and his ship, and witnessed the destruction of all the enemy fleets attacking the colony.

It should have been the happy ending…but it wasn't.

Sabrina was gone, along with her new crew, off on a new mission. Their goal was to gain some measure of control over the AI revolution that had begun at Virginis. Erin had taken a position as the ship's AI aboard the *Undaunted* where she now patrolled the edges of the New Canaan system. Cargo was still close-by, but he had all but gone off the grid, working on his homestead down on Carthage.

Nance shook her head and lay back on her bunk, wondering for the thousandth time what she was doing here.

Wondering's the wrong word. Nance knew why she was at the ISFA; the Caretaker required it of her.

It made her ill to think that she was just an agent of whatever that thing was, unable to set her own course in life. True, it allowed her some level of autonomy most of the time, but it also ensured that she moved in the direction it desired.

Currently, that direction was to expunge—the Caretaker's word—the remainder of the Myrrdan shells from New Canaan.

She'd already found two. The first had been simple to locate: it was Terry—the same shell that had infected her with…whatever Myrrdan was, back when she first came to the *Intrepid*. Infect her with his evil—no, not evil, more like opportunism embodied. Or *not* embodied as the case may be.

The second shell had been a man named Cordell. While things with Terry had gone smoothly, Cordell had been ready for her. The confrontation had taken place here on The Palisades. Cordell had been one of the construction workers and, after a long hunt, Nance had finally found him and cornered him on Ring Ten, back when it wasn't yet complete.

He'd put up a fight. In the end, she'd had to kill him and set up the scene to look like an accident.

The voice—the remnant of the Caretaker that was left within her—had helped then, just as it had so many times during the journey through the Perseus Arm and beyond.

Afterward, Nance had kept an eye on the investigation and was quite relieved when it had been ruled an accident.

A part of her felt guilty; like she was working against Sera and Tanis. But at the same time, the Caretaker's remnant had been a great help over the years.

It was through the remnant that Nance had orchestrated many of the events at the Grey Wolf Star—ensuring that the ship docked, privately suggesting to Finaeus that he look for broken mirror pieces, getting the mirror to work on *Sabrina*.

If it hadn't been for…whatever had moved the jump gate, *Sabrina* would have made it back to New Canaan years ago.

Stars, without the remnant, we wouldn't have made it at all.

Half a dozen times on the journey through the Perseus Arm, the remnant had aided her in saving the ship and crew.

And now she was back where it had wanted her to be in the first place, serving its purpose—blending in, hunting Myrrdan shells.

Her ultimate goal was to find the original, the ancient murderer himself. Her careful inquisitions had left Nance feeling certain there was another shell on The Palisades. Most of her clues were small and tenuous, but there was a preponderance of them that lent to her surety.

Right now, all she had managed to locate was a discrepancy in the counts of pico assembler units used to build The Palisades. There was an assembler unit that had been listed as damaged on arrival and sent back. But when it had arrived back at Gamma III, it had been missing its pico payload.

It had gone months without being flagged, and the message requesting the location of the pico payload had only come back to The Palisades two days ago.

Of course, by now, most of the people who built the station were long gone—some to other projects, a few on the *I2*, destined for Khardine, and some on the ships that had headed off to the Aleutian facility several months ago.

Still, Nance had a hunch—and so did the remnant within her—that the shell was still on The Palisades. And if it were, she would track it down and liberate it. Or kill it trying.

Freeing the shells was Nance's goal. She wanted to help those people—just like she hoped that someday, someone would help her….

The remnant didn't really care about the people Myrrdan used. Now that the remnant was rising up in her consciousness more often, Nance was starting to understand it better. It valued humanity—to a degree. It seemed to only place value on humans as a whole. Individuals held no special importance to it.

Most individuals, that was.

The remnant had been especially interested in Tanis. Whenever Tanis had been near—and Sera, to a lesser extent—it had watched closely, as though recording everything about her. But Nance had also sensed fear in it, or at least something akin to hesitation. The remnant had seemed torn between its desire to watch Tanis and the worry that it might be found out.

Feeling worry from the entity within her was rare; in fact, the only time she'd felt it before was when the jump gate at the Grey Wolf Star had realigned itself.

Now that she knew what lay at the heart of the Transcend, the thing called Airtha, Nance was all but certain that Airtha herself had realigned the gate in an attempt to send *Sabrina*—and most importantly, Finaeus—out of the galaxy, and out of the picture.

As though her perseveration had summoned the thing within her, the remnant rose in her mind and issued a command.

Go.

She had long-since given up arguing with the thing when it gave orders. It was perfectly able to take control of her body—but it seemed to wish *her* to commit the actions.

That had caused her to wonder if the remnant had some sort of limitation that prevented it from controlling her for long periods of time. It was a theory that she had not yet put to the test, but hoped to soon.

Nance had been given the provisional rank of lieutenant, as recognition of her efforts on the Finaeus mission. She still had a lot of remedial classes to take and was with the first-year cadets as often as not, but she did get a private billet—which was worth her weight in gold, especially with the thing in her head telling her what to do and when.

She had always been amazed that Erin had never noticed the remnant's presence in Nance's mind. Even when it had made her do things that she should not have done, Erin had seemed to be asleep, or somehow unaware of what Nance's body was doing, or where she was.

Nance had hoped that when Erin had been removed from her mind, New Canaan's AI technicians would notice that there was something wrong with her brain—but they had pronounced her hale and whole.

More than once, Nance had debated her sanity. She considered that she had imagined the entire meeting with the Caretaker at Ikoden station, and was simply a crazy person.

The problem with that was that insanity was something Erin would have spotted without issue.

No, the only logical conclusion was that there was a thing living in her mind that was undetectable by any means that humanity or AIs possessed—even those of New Canaan.

Frankly, if Nance allowed herself to think on it for too long, it terrified her.

She often saw the vision of the Caretaker in her dreams. Its body made of light, tall but thin, its long arms reaching almost to its knees.

Her initial belief was that the thing was an alien of some sort. A creature belonging to a species that predated humanity and was—for some unknowable reason—interested in playing with them.

Its conversation with Myrrdan had spawned that line of thought. The Caretaker was responsible for much of what had befallen the *Intrepid*. It had worked to send the ship to Kapteyn's Star; it had delayed them at the world until Kapteyn's Streamer was properly aligned with New Eden, and then it had sent the *Intrepid* into the future.

The only thing Nance couldn't figure out—well, to be fair, it wasn't anywhere close to the *only* thing—was why the Caretaker had sent the *Intrepid* into the Streamer and forward in time.

Now that she knew about the core AIs, Nance's new suspicion was that the Caretaker was one of their ilk. It didn't explain its alien appearance, but that could have been an affectation made for Myrrdan's benefit.

If it was a core AI, it would certainly explain its opposition to Airtha. If what Finaeus had said was true, Airtha was intended to be an agent of the core AIs, but had somehow broken free of their grasp.

That, at the very least, gave Nance some hope. She wasn't as powerful as Airtha, but at least it hinted that escape from the Caretaker's grasp was possible.

As she mulled over the entity's provenance, Nance dressed in a simple pair of leggings and a halter top. Then she slid her feet into a pair of running shoes and tied her hair back. Though it was third shift, no one was likely to question a lieutenant out for an evening jog.

She stretched for a minute and then palmed her door open and strode out into the hall. She looked up and down the empty corridor and took off at an easy lope, headed toward the maglev platform that would take her to the bay on Ring Ten, where the pico-construction assemblers had been stored, and where the records of their use would be housed.

She made good time out to the ring's main sweep and reached the maglev platform, slowly jogging in place to keep her blood flowing.

A minute later, a train pulled up, and she walked toward the doors, almost running into a cadet exiting the maglev.

"Oh! Sorry," Nance exclaimed.

"No pro—Nance! Hi, what are you doing about?"

Nance realized that the cadet—who had been bent over a pad, studying something intently—was Saanvi, one of Tanis's daughters.

"Saanvi, you're up late."

Saanvi smiled. "No rest for the wicked, right? I was just working on a model of the star cluster and its gravitational effects on Project St—uh…shoot, sorry. That's classified for now. I think."

Nance smiled. "That's OK, Saanvi. I know that you're often working with Earnest Redding on something secret; thick as thieves, you two."

Saanvi shrugged, and a slight blush rose to her cheeks. "I wouldn't go so far as to say that. He likes to tell me what he's up to and says I have a good ear for listening and asking the right questions. Of course, he leaves me with all this amazing knowledge, and I can't help but dig in more. I've even managed to help him a few times."

Nance got the distinct impression that the remnant wanted to know more about what Saanvi had discussed with Earnest. She was about to ask more, when Saanvi waved and turned away.

"Sorry, Nance, I have to run. I got permission to be out late to work with Earnest, but I have to be back in the dorms in five."

Nance waved. "You'd better go then, I don't want to get you in trouble. But we should go out for lunch sometime soon; let's not lose touch."

"You got it, Nance," Saanvi called over her shoulder. "I'll see what time works for Cary and hit you up."

Nance wasn't surprised that Saanvi had automatically assumed she wanted to meet with Cary. The two girls were inseparable; three, counting Tanis's other daughter, who now lived within Cary.

The remnant seemed to approve of meeting both girls, so she called out after Saanvi's retreating form. "Sounds good, see you later."

The maglev still waited for her; lingering longer, as they did during the third shift—travelling to where people were, rather than using a set schedule.

She boarded the train and passed her desired destination on Ring Nine before taking a seat. The train pulled away from the platform and passed out of the ring, arcing around the station. The window beside her was facing toward Canaan Prime and its plas tinted, blocking out the local star's brilliant glow.

Nance closed her eyes for a minute, enjoying the brief reprieve before the next phase of her late-night adventure began.

The maglev stopped at Platform 38, near her stated destination: Savannah Park. Nance walked off the platform at a leisurely pace. The stretch of savannah was two kilometers long and threaded its way along the center of the ring, creating a relaxing space for the students, and serving as the site of a variety of exercises.

Nance strolled through its pathways, eventually coming to a stone pillar standing in a field. The pillar was engraved with the names of ISF personnel who had perished in the Battle for Victoria. Nance barely gave them a passing glance as she sent a signal to the pillar, which opened an access hatch at its base.

She slipped in and sealed the hatch before checking her monitoring taps.

So far, so good.

The hatch led into a service tunnel that Nance followed until she came to an intersection. Turning left, she crept along quietly until she came to an auxiliary comm routing system.

Nance opened the service panel and pulled out the canister of stealth flow armor. She had secured it from *Sabrina*'s allotment when she had last been on the ship, and it was her ticket to getting wherever she wanted on The Palisades.

She stripped out of her clothing, which she stowed behind the panel before applying the armor. Once the armor covered her entire body, she deployed a small batch of remote nano to determine if the armor was working properly.

The probes couldn't see her at all, and Nance nodded with satisfaction. She was glad to see that her alteration to remove the IFF signal—which broadcast her location to friendlies on a random frequency—had held during the reapplication process.

Unless someone with some very specialized scanning equipment was looking for her, she was completely invisible.

Nance sealed the service panel back up and continued down the tunnel until she reached an exit hatch. She passed nano probes around the edge of the hatch, confirming that it was clear before opening the hatch and climbing onto the deck.

It took Nance thirty minutes to walk back to the station's hub. She slipped into a lift along with a major and a commander. She tucked herself into a corner, ready for the lift to descend, when the major stuck his hand out to hold the door open, and a lieutenant rushed in.

"Thanks," the lieutenant said as she moved to the side of the lift car, brushing against Nance's shoulder. "Huh?" she muttered softly and reached toward Nance, who quickly slipped to the side, tucking herself into another corner.

The lieutenant's hand met with empty air, and she shook her head as the doors closed.

Nance took long, slow breaths, and when the lift reached level 172, she disembarked and rushed down the connecting arm to Ring Ten. The bay she was seeking lay a kilometer around the ring, and half an hour after she had changed into her stealth suit, she finally arrived.

There was no longer any picotech stored in the bay, but it was locked down nonetheless. The security didn't worry Nance; the remnant had blessed her with the ability to break through any encryption she had encountered thus far. It had come in very handy while lost in the Perseus Arm of the galaxy, and now it was proving useful once more.

Erin had initially wondered about her proficiency with encryption, and Nance had spent many weeks studying advanced cracking methodologies, and honing her skills so that no one would be surprised when she was able to bypass almost any security she met.

A side-benefit was that Nance was almost as good at getting through security systems on her own as the remnant had made her. Some day, she would find out if she was indeed good enough on her own.

Nance walked to the access panel beside the bay and threaded a filament of nano into the unit, passing a series of codes that would convince the door it was not opening. The log event of the door opening would append to the entry of its last use. Unless someone specifically examined this door's logs for addenda—which was an unlikely occurrence—no one would ever know she'd been here.

On command, the bay door slid open just a crack, and Nance slipped past into the darkened interior.

Crates filled with equipment lay within, stacked in neat rows, ready for transport to the next station on the list of those to be constructed.

There was probably all manner of amazing technology in those crates. Nance felt like she could spend a lifetime studying everything the colonists had brought with them from the forty second century. She had to admit that she was intensely jealous of Saanvi and her access to Earnest Redding.

I could probably meet with him; he has *expressed interest in many of the things the crew of* Sabrina *has learned.*

But Nance feared that Earnest may somehow be able to discern what lay inside her. Feared and hoped. It was complicated.

She put all the fabulous toys that lay within arm's reach out of her mind, and looked for the system that contained the usage and security monitoring data for the pico assemblers.

While the control systems for the picotech had never been connected to the station's network, the shipping manifest for the crates was. Nance surreptitiously tapped into it and found that the data was restricted beyond the levels she had currently accessed.

No problem. It took a few minutes, but the remnant guided her through bypassing the systems. She couldn't brute-force her way through; even with her augmented abilities, Odin would spot something like that.

Once she had the number of the crate containing the systems she was looking for, Nance pulled up its location and worked her way through the bay until she found it.

When she finally did, the first thing she discovered was that the logs weren't stored in a crate at all; they were within a mobile NSAI pod. The pod was a four meter cube containing a powerful NSAI node that would be a lot harder to get past than the shipping manifest security.

It was also shut down.

Nance considered her options. The NSAI pod should contain its own power source, which she hoped would have enough charge to turn on.

She pulled open the pod's control panel and slid a nano filament into it. She bypassed the system's startup security and triggered an emergency power-on. The emergency power-on would assume that something bad had happened to the pod, and it would write its data and current state into crystal. Nance would then intercept that data write and access the information she needed.

She worked quickly as the pod came on and began its emergency procedures, getting her tap in place a second before the pod began to stream data from its standard memory systems, and filtering through it for the information she desired.

The data write was a quarter of the way done when a klaxon sounded and an alert went out on the bay's local network, informing any personnel to clear out, as the shipment was about to be picked up.

Shit. The alert included the warning that atmosphere would be vented and gravity disabled so that the auto-loaders could operate with ease. Normally the bay wouldn't do this with people inside, but its monitoring systems were unable to detect her with the stealthed flow armor on.

She still hadn't found the data on who had accessed the pico assembler that had lost its payload of bots. Based on the current rate, it would take another three minutes for all the data to pass by.

C'monnnnn, Nance danced impatiently as the atmosphere in the bay began to thin. Though the flow armor would maintain pressure against the decompression, it wouldn't help with the pesky need to breathe.

Next time, I bring the rebreather pack....

Over the course of half a minute, the bay completely depressurized, and Nance directed the flow armor to seal up her nose.

Then she turned to leave; the information wasn't worth dying for.

Only she couldn't leave. The remnant wouldn't let her move.

Stay, it instructed.

Nance felt a wave of panic slam into her, but willed herself to calm down. Now that the bay was in vacuum, her nano could move quickly, and she sent a passel to the bay's inner doors. She cycled the small airlock open beside the main doors, reasoning that when she finally did find the information she needed, she didn't want to have to wait for the airlock to cycle open.

She checked the time since she'd last drawn breath: fifty seconds. Nance knew she could do four minutes—though being able to think coherently after three was well nigh impossible.

Then she spotted it. The assembler in question, and its access logs. Nance siphoned them all off without any examination and then tried to move again.

The remnant finally allowed it.

She dashed down the row and turned the corner toward the airlock, just as the a-grav systems cut out.

Nance lost her footing and sailed into the bulkhead, grunting into her sealed mouth as the armor locked up to protect her from the impact.

Frantically, Nance clawed at the bulkhead, pulling herself toward the airlock as the bay began to spin around her, and her vision faded around the edges.

I'm not going to make it! She shrieked in her mind. You stupid thing! You've killed us both, and now the information is useless.

Then she was there, at the airlock. She pulled herself in and hit the cycle command before collapsing to the deck as the lock's a-grav systems came on.

Then everything went dark.

* * * * *

When Nance came to, there were voices coming from somewhere

nearby. She carefully opened her eyes and saw two men entering the airlock.

"System cycled this lock over for some reason; logs show it was activated from inside the bay."

"So?" the other voice asked.

"So, locks aren't supposed to cycle on their own. Especially when the external bay door is open. Kind of a security and safety issue."

Nance realized that the two people speaking were technicians who had entered the airlock. They weren't wearing EV suits, so she assumed the bay had been aired up once again. Problem was, they'd already cycled the airlock back to the bay side. Since they were inspecting its control mechanisms, she couldn't very well activate it to get back to the station side.

By the time the technicians had inspected the lock—where they found nothing wrong—and Nance was able to get back to the maintenance passages under Savannah Park, two hours had passed. She changed quickly and returned to her quarters, where she fell onto her bed and let out a long sigh.

It was one hour 'til breakfast and, from the prodding in her mind, the remnant wanted her to review the data she'd pulled from the NSAI in the bay.

"Stars, this sucks," Nance muttered.

AFTERMATH

STELLAR DATE: 08.07.8948 (Adjusted Years)
LOCATION: Keren Station
REGION: Khardine System, Transcend Interstellar Alliance

"I guess the Grey Division heard you talking smack about them," Finaeus said as the group sat in the TSF garrison's officers' mess. Everyone else had finished eating, but Finaeus still had a plate of food in front of him. "Doesn't surprise me; those bastards have ears everywhere."

"I think they must have planned this a little more than thirty minutes in advance," Krissy said.

Tanis could see in the admiral's eyes that she held herself responsible for the attack. Securing the Khardine System, and Keren Station in particular, had been her task. Thus far, there was no evidence that she had been involved, and her attitude cemented Tanis's belief in her innocence.

"Using the *Galadrial* just adds insult to injury," Admiral Greer said. He had arrived on scene with a platoon of soldiers not long after Flaherty showed up, and was more than a little furious about the attack.

Thinking of Flaherty caused Tanis to wonder where he'd gone. She looked around and saw the quiet man leaning against a bulkhead on the far side of the room. His railgun was propped up beside him, and a deep scowl creased his face.

Tanis had expressed doubt when Sera insisted that Flaherty would beat them to Khardine. Last they knew, he had been on Airtha, or somewhere in the Huygens system. He had a family to secure, and a two thousand light year journey to Khardine; all of which he'd done in a few months' time.

Nevertheless, Flaherty had shown up just when he was needed.

<*Uncanny, isn't it?*> Tanis asked Angela.

<*He's always been an odd sort,*> Angela replied.

<*But how did he know we were in danger? You don't just lug around a rail like that.*>

<*You could ask him,*> Angela suggested.

<I will, but not right now.>

"Death toll is estimated at fourteen hundred and eleven," Sera was saying. "All just to drive us back and capture us."

"They didn't have a big enough team for that," Krissy countered. "Though maybe they *thought* seventy was enough."

"Then they're poor studies," Tanis replied. "Or they didn't expect us to have such a large escort."

Finaeus shook his head. "I'm far more interested in the mini jump gate they had. That's new. Seems like the Grey Division actually is doing some R&D."

"That *was* a surprise," Krissy agreed. "Tucked down in a cargo bay with a thin, long shuttle ready to go through."

"So those aren't something in use already? Mini gates, not long shuttles."

"Nope," Finaeus replied. "Hard to make them that small, and they're less useful—well, normally. But running one inside of a station…"

"What would happen?" Krissy asked.

Finaeus made a raspy *'boom'* sound and spread his hands wide.

"Motherfuckers," Sera swore. "Well, if anyone is worried that they're on the wrong side, there's a nice piece of evidence they're the bad guys."

"Glad we thwarted that," Tanis added dryly. "I'd hate to be…" she mimicked Finaeus's sound and hand motions.

Sera gave Tanis a pointed look. "They met with some success; they set back our efforts to establish a government here. Maybe you'll have your way, Tanis."

"Not trying to have my way," Tanis replied. "Though now I wonder if Vela is a bad choice. If we can't defend Keren against infiltration, Vela will be a lot harder."

"What are you talking about?" Greer asked.

"I think—" Tanis began to say, at the same time Sera said, "Tanis believes—"

"You first," Tanis said with a smile.

"Thanks. Tanis believes that Khardine is too remote to make a proper capital. It won't give the right impression to the populace."

Greer cocked his head as he considered it, while Krissy shook hers.

"You're right. A location in Vela will be a nightmare to secure. I imagine you're thinking the regional capital."

Tanis shrugged. "Just needs to be somewhere visible. Keep in mind that Airtha is going to strut Evil Sera around all over, making sure her claim to the presidency is well backed. Adrienne will assist in that—if he did indeed get caught up in her web, as evidence suggests. We need our President Sera to be highly visible as well."

"Politically speaking, she has a good point," Finaeus said. "I'm about the furthest thing there is from a political animal, but I watched Jeff for centuries. He was always front and center, making sure that most of what people heard from him, they actually saw him say, not a mouthpiece flunky speaking on his behalf."

Greer massaged one hand with the other as he leaned back in his chair. "Vela does need to be secured against advances from Airtha anyway. We know that she has taken control of several systems near Vela—in our scales of astrogation, the Huygens System is not that far from her holdings. If she isn't thinking about taking Vela already, she probably will be soon."

"This is something I wanted to discuss with you two," Tanis said looking at Greer, then at Krissy. "With my title of Field Marshal, Sera has put me over all of the Transcend's military operations. That being said, even if I had years to study the situation, I could not learn everything that is going on in the force. I need a strong team to help support me, and the two of you have proven yourselves both honorable and loyal."

"Thank you for saying that, Tanis," Greer said readily. "I'll admit, at first it rankled somewhat to have you chosen as marshal. But your tactics and stratagem at New Canaan were very impressive; your unorthodox approach was key in winning the fight. I think unorthodox stratagem is just what we need—no offense, Krissy."

Tanis looked to Krissy, who was frowning deeply and asked, "So what's your plan, Tanis?"

"Until Airtha produced her Sera doppelganger, it had been my intention to focus our efforts on securing the Inner Stars against Orion proxy nations before we dealt with our civil war." Tanis paused and took a sip of her coffee before continuing. "However, I don't think we have that luxury anymore."

"I suspect you are correct," Krissy replied. "We must strike at Airtha soon."

"The problem," Sera replied with a short sigh, "is how? Airtha is no simple AI. In fact, she's not an AI at all."

"She's not?" Krissy asked.

"Oh, this is good," Greer said with a grim smile.

Sera shot him a quelling look, and he mumbled, "Sorry, I sometimes forget who she is to you."

Tanis wondered about that response. *Usually Greer is circumspect; maybe he is just enjoying having one up on Krissy.*

"Airtha is my father's former wife, Jelina," Sera said tonelessly. "She went on a mission to map the galactic core, and encountered the ascended AI that left Sol at the end of the sentience wars."

Krissy's eyes widened. "She what? The *what*?"

"It's true," Finaeus confirmed. "When she came back, she had been loaded into an AI's neural frame. We never did learn why. She was also the only one to make it back. Jeff hid that and pretended she was a new AI—something she wasn't too happy about. He never treated her like a person after that."

"Ignoring the whole 'ascended AI at the galactic core' thing, she's now taking over as retribution?" Krissy asked.

"Something like that," Sera replied. "We really have no idea what her endgame is. I'm pretty sure she wants Tanis's tech. She tried to get me to kill my father, too."

Krissy whistled. "Somehow, not all of that made it into the official briefing."

"Yeah," Tanis replied. "We're not quite ready to confirm to everyone that Core Devils are real things."

Krissy's eyes narrowed. "You think that Airtha plans to attack them, don't you?"

"The thought had crossed my mind," Tanis said with a shrug. "There are a number of possible motives for her. One of them is that she just wants to be Queen of Everything."

"So, back to why we can't just hit Airtha with everything we've got?" Krissy asked.

<*Because she can subvert all your AIs and make them kill you,*> Angela said, joining in the conversation.

Greer ran a hand through his short hair. "Yeah, that was not fun. How likely do you think it is that she could re-establish that control?"

<*If she were anyone other than Airtha, I'd say not likely,*> Angela replied. <*But her capabilities are a mystery to us. We need to be prepared.*>

"How do you prepare for an unknown?" Krissy asked.

"We'll need to infiltrate the Huygens System at some point," Tanis said. "And when we go in, it'll be for the kill-shot. Which means Bob and the *I2*."

<*Or you two,*> Bob spoke privately to Tanis and Angela.

<*Don't go shirking your duties, Bob,*> Tanis said.

<*We'll see how it plays out,*> Bob replied cryptically.

"Either way," Greer continued. "Ensuring that Vela is secure would be wise. With New Canaan anchoring the Cradle Cluster, and Khardine securing the edge of the Transcend, keeping Vela out of Airtha's hands would bracket her. We could control many of the trade routes and limit her resources."

"Not that there aren't myriad resources for her to tap into within arm's reach," Krissy said.

"We need to think about how to choke her off from those as well," Sera said. "Though we need to do it in such a fashion that we're not attacking our own people."

"Easier said than done," Krissy replied. "This is civil war, after all. We're going to be shooting at our own people through the whole thing—stars, we just did."

Somber nods were shared around the table, and Tanis looked at each person in turn. "Then this is what we'll do. I am creating two overarching commands in the TSF. The first will be the Inner Stars and Orion Front Command. That will be under you, Krissy. Your HQ, for now, is here at Khardine. Greer, I'm putting you over the Transcend Command. You're on Airtha."

"Good," Greer said with a crisp nod. "I look forward to putting her in her place."

Tanis gave him a sharp look. "I want to be very clear. This is not a civil war; it is a war against Airtha. She is not the Transcend. She is an evil AI who has created a clone of Sera and is using her as a puppet. We are to make that clear to our people at every opportunity."

"Understood," Greer replied. "As soon as our refit is complete, I'll take my fleet to Vela. We'll secure the sector command there, purge the hell out of the Grey Division, and work out who is on our side."

"Good," Tanis replied, then drew a deep breath. "Now let's get down to brass tacks. We have a government to establish, and a lot of the people we had on Keren aren't with us anymore to help with that."

Finaeus stood. "And this is where I go find a nice place to bivouac."

"Nice try, Uncle," Sera said at the same time as Krissy said, "Sit, Dad."

Finaeus spread his arms. "You see how the women in my life treat me? They were nicer to me in the Perseus Arm."

"Kinda doubt that, Dad," Krissy said with a smirk.

ECUMENOPOLIS

STELLAR DATE: 08.11.8948 (Adjusted Years)
LOCATION: Kapalicarsi Station
REGION: Bosporus System, Scipio Empire

Petra stood at the window of the gantry access corridor, overlooking external Docking Pad 1498-12A. She drew a deep breath and did her best to calm her nerves and the jittering feeling in her chest, caused by both the ship's delay, and its passengers.

The ship's name was the *Aegeus*; an auspicious designation for a vessel docking at a station named Kapalicarsi in the Bosporus System.

The *Aegeus* measured twelve hundred meters in length, and was clearly a warship. It lowered gracefully toward the docking pad, then paused a scant dozen meters above the surface. Lights activated on the underside of its hull, illuminating the hard mounts for the pad control team.

The docking armatures slowly rose out of the pad and grappled the load-bearing points. A minute later, the ship was secured to Kapalicarsi Station.

Petra breathed a long sigh of relief. The entire time the ship had been inbound, she had worried that her efforts to have it granted special diplomatic clearance would be revoked.

<You worry too much,> her AI, Alastar, said. *<Diana said she'd make sure the ship would be allowed to dock, and here it is.>*

<What Diana says and what she means are two different things. You know she can be capricious.>

<True, but you and she have a special bond,> Alastar said with a wink in her mind. *<She's not going to make things* ***that*** *difficult for you.>*

Petra wasn't so sure. Even though she was one of Diana's closest confidants, that didn't stop the empress from toying with her from time to time. The woman liked to present small—and sometimes not so small—inconveniences, intended to remind everyone around her who was the empress, and who was not.

It was also not often that a warship from a distant stellar nation was allowed to come this deep into the Bosporus; let alone touch Kapalicarsi.

There was always a chance that some administrator could find a reason to delay their approach on some technicality.

On top of the worry that the Scipians would deny the *Aegeus* its berth, Petra had worried that Sera would balk at the requirements imposed by the Kapalicarsi Port Control Dockmaster.

He had required that the *Aegeus*'s reactors be cold, and its antimatter stores inspected and locked down before the ship had passed within a light minute of the station.

Petra had been prepared for a flat refusal from Sera. The conditions put her and her ship at no small amount of risk. Of course, she expected that the *Aegeus* would have a CriEn module for power. The Scipians would not know it, but the vessel would have no issue powering its shields and weapons, even without the reactors.

What had surprised Petra the most—and she hadn't realized it until the vessel came within visual range—was that the *Aegeus* was not a Transcend ship.

Its design elements were similar to the ISF vessels involved in the Battle of Bollam's World. There were also marked similarities to Terran Space Force vessels of the early fifth millennia.

Few would recognize those similarities—she hoped—but Petra had been serving The Hand in the Inner Stars for many decades. Searching for ancient Terran vessels was an important part of the job.

Petra saw two Scipian heavy cruisers settle into station-keeping positions above the *Aegeus*. Petra knew that their weapons would be live, and trained on the ship.

Not exactly the nicest way to welcome a foreign diplomatic vessel, but Petra recognized that she was lucky the *Aegeus* had made it this far without being boarded.

To her left, the docking gantry extended toward the ship, mating with its airlock and using a grav shield to ensure the connection was airtight.

A squad of Scipian soldiers stood behind her, blocking the entrance to the rest of the Kapalicarsi Station, and Petra glanced back at them, wishing that her long tenure as an ambassador in the empress's court would have secured her more trust than this. She would simply have to deal with each challenge as it presented itself.

She walked to the gantry entrance and stood waiting for the president and her retinue to disembark from their ship.

The ship's AI passed the list of Sera's attendants over, and Petra was glad to see that Tanis Richards's name was not on the list. The woman was far too problematic to bring before the empress. Not to mention highly recognizable. However, there was a woman named Jenny Sirana listed as an attaché to President Tomlinson that was an unknown to Petra.

Petra wished that Sera had opted for a pseudonym as well, but it was probable that only Orion Guard agents would know who Sera Tomlinson was. Using her real name should be OK.

Should.

"Petra!" a voice called out to her right, and she turned to see Meuls Berger pushing his way past the Scipian soldiers at the observation deck's entrance.

<*I was beginning to think he wasn't going to show,*> Alastar commented privately. <*Too bad.*>

<*Well, it* **is** *his job. I hear Deputy Ministers of External Affairs are supposed to show up for things having to do with external affairs.*>

<*Lies!*> Alastar laughed. <*He only shows up if there are attractive organics—or things in the shape of attractive organics.*>

Petra snorted. <*Then I doubt that he'll be disappointed.*>

"Deputy Minister Berger," Petra greeted as the man reached her side. "You're just in time."

"Excellent, excellent," Berger replied. "There was a security issue on Moirai's Thread, and I got held up."

Petra wondered what sort of security issue the space elevator would have, but decided not to inquire.

Ahead, the airlock on the *Aegeus* opened, and four soldiers stepped out. Their dress uniforms were those of the Miriam League—the puppet alliance for which Petra was the ambassador.

They marched smartly down the gantry, and Petra could tell they were professionals. Their gazes took in everything around them, and each soldier's sidearm was holstered uniquely per the wearer's preference.

They stepped off the ramp and took up positions on either side of its entrance, appearing to not even notice Petra, Berger, or the Scipian soldiers at the end of the corridor.

Petra turned her attention back to the far end of the gantry and saw

Sera step out of the airlock.

Here we go….

*****

Tanis stepped through the airlock with Sera at her side and Flaherty one step behind them, his calm presence reassuring. Valerie brought up the rear, catching up to Flaherty a moment later.

She twitched her lips, trying to get used to the new shape she had molded her face into. Not since the subterfuge on *Sabrina* with Kade had she used this trick.

<*You're nervous,*> Angela said, a hint of surprise in her voice.

<*Of course,*> Tanis replied. <*I've done a lot of things, but never have I supplicated myself before an empress, asking for her to ally herself with my side.*>

<*No, but you've done stuff that was far more difficult.*>

Tanis pursed her lips. <*Not like this. I've always prevailed by strength, cunning, or by playing by a ruleset I understood.*>

<*I think that strength and cunning will be how you prevail this time, too. These Scipians are a proud people, and they respect strength above everything. I think you'll do just fine,*> Angela replied with a wave of calm.

<*I'll have you, so yes, I believe I will. Just stomp on my foot if I'm about to screw up.*>

<*You got it.*>

The four High Guard soldiers in Miriam League uniforms stood at the end of the gantry with Hand Agent Petra, and a man that Tanis assumed must be a Scipian representative waiting for them.

She glanced at Sera, who walked calmly down the gantry, looking as though she were walking into her own home. Tanis stayed in lock step with her, and they stopped two meters from Petra and the man at her side.

"Madam President," Petra said with a nod to Sera. "May I introduce you to Deputy Minister of External Affairs, Meuls Berger."

"Petra, Deputy Minister Berger, thank you for taking the time to greet us here today," Sera said graciously.

"On behalf of the Scipian Empire, the pleasure is all mine," Berger replied. "Even though your method of transportation is…unconventional."

Sera glanced back at the *Aegeus*, visible through the windows of the gantry. "Yes, well, the Orion Arm is not as safe as it once was. While we felt no fear once we reached Scipio's borders, there are less secure regions of space beyond. Though nothing untoward befell us, it is better to be safe than dead."

Tanis noticed Berger's eyes raking up and down Sera's body as she spoke, and held back a sigh.

Despite Tanis's attempts to convince Sera to wear clothing of some sort, the president had declined, citing Tanis's own encouragement to be herself.

Tanis knew that had not been the only rationale. Finaeus had succeeded in merging the Mark X FlowArmor into Sera's skin, and she was ecstatic with the result, insisting that nothing so primitive as clothing would ever touch her body again.

Sera had, at least, used her skin's malleable features to give it the appearance of a light blue skinsuit, with intricate, moving patterns and enough texture to appear as an outfit, not her actual flesh.

Berger pulled his eyes up to Sera's and gave a soft chuckle. "That's a blunt way to put it, but I take your point. Things have become quite destabilized beyond our borders. I assume strengthening your ties with Scipio—distant as they are—is the purpose of your visit?"

"It is," Sera replied. "From what I understand, our tardiness has nearly lost us our audience with the empress, but that if we hurry we'll make it in time."

"Yes, that is the case," Petra confirmed. "I've secured a shuttle that can take us down to one of the Imperial Palace's private ports."

"Excellent," Sera granted. "Then we'd best be on our way."

Valerie waved for the High Guard to fall in, and Berger bristled.

"Your guards cannot come to the palace, Madam President. It is not done."

"Nonsense," Sera scoffed. "Foreign heads of state are granted their own security, are they not?"

"It's OK," Petra put a hand on Berger's shoulder. "I received dispensation from Diana. It is permitted. Check the palace's visitor slate."

Berger closed his eyes for a moment, and then relaxed. "Oh, thank goodness. You're right, Petra. These five guards are permitted, as are your two attendants. I'm sorry I caused confusion."

"Don't worry," Sera said with a winning smile as she reached out and patted his shoulder. "I took no offense."

Petra gestured down the observation deck to the exit, where the soldiers had made an opening for the group to leave. Their expressions were professionally impassive, though a few did take long looks at Sera.

<You're getting fans,> Petra said to the president.

<The Scipians aren't as stuffy as they like to pretend. Remember, Elena worked as a sucker in the empire, and she had quite the clientele, too,> Sera replied.

Tanis was surprised that Sera could speak so casually about Elena. She knew that they had been meeting of late—not long conversations, but once a week or so, Sera would spend half an hour with her ex lover.

Though Tanis knew of the meetings, she hadn't listened in. Sera or Bob would tell her if there was anything to be concerned about. Spending so much time with Elena didn't strike Tanis as very healthy, but she wasn't about to tell her friend how to live her life. They had enough stresses as it was.

Sera and Petra made small talk with Berger on the way to the shuttle, which wasn't far. The shuttle was also small—only able to seat twelve—but was well appointed. It received immediate clearance and was in space within minutes, dropping down to the surface of Alexandria.

The planet and capital city bore the same name. The reason for that was simple; other than the oceans, the city covered the entire planet.

She imagined that its population would be lower than that of the Cho, or even Mars 1 back in the 42nd century. Even so, it was her first time seeing a planet-spanning city, and it was a sight to behold.

"You can see the Imperial Complex just off that peninsula." Petra leaned over Tanis and pointed out the shuttle's window. "The palace is the structure with the towers reaching into space."

*<Now **that** is impressive,>* Tanis said to Angela. *<Freestanding towers reaching into space. Finally feels like we're back in civilization.>*

<Is that how you rate civilization?> Angela asked. *<By the height of their towers? I thought size didn't matter.>*

Tanis almost laughed aloud. *<You'd think so. You know what I mean, though. It's an indicator of economic power, to be able to build structures like*

those.>

<*Or unethical appropriation of funds from lower classes or less powerful regions of the empire,*> Angela replied.

<*I didn't say it was altruistic. But you still have to have the empire, to take from…OK, my argument is falling apart. They still look impressive, though.*>

<*That they do.*>

They spoke aloud of trivialities, of the city, the palace, the Hall of Champions—which Petra revealed was gruesomely made of ground up bones—and the upcoming Celebration of the Seven Suns, which occurred once every fifty seven years.

However, privately, Petra inquired about their delay.

<*What made you so late?*> she asked. <*I expected to have a day or two to prep you for the meeting. Now we'll make it with only half an hour to spare.*>

<*Keren Station was attacked,*> Sera replied. <*It took some time to sort out the details and ensure that we had located all of the Airthists who were involved.*>

<*'Airthists'. Is that what we're calling them?*> Petra asked.

Sera gave a mental shrug. <*Seems logical.*>

<*I'll admit,*> Petra said, her tone measured and cautious. <*Out here in the Inner Stars, it's difficult to tell whom to believe. For example, last I heard, your father was president, and New Canaan was only a part of the Transcend by astrography—not actually a member of the Alliance.*>

<*I'm surprised you knew about New Canaan at all,*> Sera replied. <*It was supposed to be a bit of a secret.*>

<*I keep my ear to the ground,*> Petra said.

<*I hadn't intended to join the Transcend,*> Tanis spoke for the first time. <*But circumstances convinced me that avoiding the coming conflict wasn't going to work.*>

<*Tanis!*> Petra exclaimed peering at Tanis, unable to fully keep the surprise from reaching her face. <*What…that's some disguise. Your skeletal structure isn't even the same.*>

<*Yes, it's proven to be effective in the past,*> Tanis replied. <*Not fun to do, mind you.*>

<*I really don't think—*> Petra began to respond.

<*Petra,*> Sera interrupted. <*There's a lot for you to understand before we meet with Diana. How's about I start at the beginning?*>

<*That sounds great.*>

Sera proceeded to relate the events that led up to the battle at New Canaan: the attack on Ascella, the suspiciousness of her father, Peter Tomlinson, and his attempt to strong-arm Tanis to gain her technology, and Elena's betrayal and ultimate assassination of the president.

At that point, Petra interrupted. *<Elena?! Seriously? How is that possible? I worked with her for years. She was under my purview before she ran off.>*

<I understand all too well,> Sera admitted with deep sadness in her mental tone. *<Elena and I had been lovers for nearly eighteen years; we were considering marriage.>*

<And she was a guard double agent?> Petra was incredulous. *<For how long? Do you know?>*

<Yes,> Sera replied. *<They approached her during my exile. I guess she was bitter about my father's ability to use and cast aside anyone—even his own daughter. Though now I suspect that much of his reputation was really gained by Airtha's actions or influence.>*

<Who is Airtha, then?> Petra asked.

Sera told Petra what they had learned from Finaeus—how Airtha had once been her mother, but came back from the core of the galaxy a changed woman—in every way imaginable.

Petra's brows pinched together. *<I know you well, Sera, and I can see no lie in you. Alastar agrees that you appear to be telling the truth. But why, then, are we approaching the empress with the Unveiling? Why now?>*

<Because,> Tanis answered, speaking for the first time since Sera began explaining their situation. *<Orion attacked New Canaan with nearly one hundred fifty thousand ships; a large number of them were Hegemony and Trisilieds vessels. The Transcend is already unveiled.>*

Petra sputtered aloud, and Berger asked what was wrong.

"Nothing, nothing, just got something caught in my throat. Could you pass me a bottle of water?"

"Of course," Berger replied before resuming his tale of a recent negotiation with some small satellite nation that he had overseen.

<How did you prevail?> Petra asked. *<I assume you prevailed—seeing as how we're all sitting here today.>*

<That's a tale for another day,> Tanis said. *<We need to secure an alliance with Diana. She will need to hold back the Hegemony and keep this quadrant of the Inner Stars secure while we deal with Airtha. Along those lines, do we reveal*

to her that there is a civil war in the Transcend?>

<*That's a really good question,*> Petra said. <*She'll certainly need to be warned—what, with the other Sera, and all.*>

Sera gave a long mental sigh that turned into a growl. <*Sorry, this is a sore spot for me.*>

Tanis watched Petra's expression closely and saw compassion in the woman's eyes. That much was good, at least. She wasn't certain she trusted Petra, but a display of empathy certainly helped.

<*There are a lot of sore spots to go around,*> Tanis added. <*But Evil Sera is the reason we must tell Diana of the civil war. We must lay the whole thing out for her—well, we can probably leave Airtha's provenance out of the mix. My understanding is that most people are barely able to handle the idea of ascended AIs being anything other than myth—let alone the fact that the core of the galaxy is infested with the things.*>

Petra shook her head and stared out the shuttle's window. <*We'll be setting down in a moment. I'm going to introduce you under your aliases, and then convince her of the need for a private audience. After that, you're going to have to impress upon her the need for an alliance with you, rather than Airtha or Orion. Focus on how Orion is allied with the Hegemony—and probably with the Nietzscheans, as well. That should add strength to your arguments.*>

Tanis nodded and realized that Berger was speaking about the involved protocols and processes for meeting with the empress.

<*Is there really all this pomp and ceremony?*> Tanis asked. <*How do they get anything done?*>

Petra chuckled over their private connection. <*Publicly, Diana puts on a very grand and ostentatious performance. Privately, she's a simple—well,* ***simpler****—woman who just got tired of how her father ran the federation, and resolved to improve it.*>

<*By assassinating him and turning the federation into an empire,*> Sera added.

<*She needed a strong central power system to effect change. She's not without her regrets, but she believes in her vision, that a strong empire is good for all of its people,*> Petra responded, a hint of defensiveness to her mental tone.

<*We're not here to critique her style of government,*> Tanis said. <*Our belief regarding the Inner Stars is that everyone should get to govern their people as they see fit, and the people shall be governed as they allow themselves to be. We*

just need to stop the aggressors. If we think we won't have to make unsavory allies in the process, we're fooling ourselves.>

Sera nodded. *<You're right. Plus, it's not like we're allying with the Nietzscheans, or the Australis Unity Front.>*

<Speaking of that mess, what are you going to do about the Nietzschean advance?> Petra asked.

<Stars, don't ask, because I have no idea,> Sera replied.

Tanis placed a hand on Sera's arm. *<Don't sweat it. I have an idea for how to deal with Nietzschea.>*

<Don't forget about Silstrand,> Petra added, giving Tanis a significant look that Berger missed entirely. *<Things are falling apart there—no thanks to you.>*

<I'm not happy about how that's turned out, either. None of us expected S&H to be able to do anything useful with the specifications I sold them. However, I imagine that we'll be able to make things a lot better by getting Diana to back down.>

Petra shook her head. *<Good luck with that. I think that your nano, and maybe Silstrand, are going to have to be concessions you'll need to make if you want to gain her as an ally.>*

Tanis frowned. Silstrand was not a concession she was willing to make. One thing was for certain; if Smithers was still an employee of S&H, he was going to get an earful for losing control of the tech in the first place.

A minute later, the shuttle touched down. Valerie and the High Guard exited first, followed by Flaherty and the others. Tanis had to admit that she felt much better having Flaherty with them, though he spoke so rarely that it was easy to forget he was there—which was probably his intention.

The shuttle platform was nestled within a grove of tall trees that blocked the immediate view of the palace, except for the towers stretching up into space. Tanis stared up at them for a moment, and estimated that a tenth of the planet could probably see those towers.

"They look amazing at night, when they're lit up," Berger said. "When they do holoshows around them, they're even more spectacular."

"I can imagine," Tanis replied, remembering the shows that she used to go see around the Pavonis Mons Tower on Mars. That tower rose much higher than these, but it was a utilitarian structure that anchored the ring, not a freestanding spire—

*That **had** anchored the ring....*

A group of palace guards was waiting at the edge of the landing pad, and they silently fell in around the group as Berger led them through the trees to a broad archway.

"Good thing you managed to get a landing site so close to the audience chamber," Berger said. "We'll make it with a few minutes to spare."

"I know," Petra said, her disdain for Berger evident in her voice. Tanis had the distinct impression that, were Berger in charge, they wouldn't have even reached orbit yet. Though the fact that Petra had been assigned such a crucial position by The Hand was more than enough evidence of her skill.

When the palace walls came into view, Tanis was duly impressed by their design. The structure rose from the earth, a solid ribbon of onyx with sapphire highlights within. The pattern appeared to be random, and she imagined that at night the sapphire would glow with an otherworldly effect.

When they passed inside—under the scrutiny of more guards and scanning arches—the interior was the reverse: sapphire with onyx streaks that seemed to shift as they rushed past.

"The official name for this wing is Sovereign's Repose, but most call it 'the Black Gate'," Petra supplied. "I'm partial to 'the Black Gate'. I think it has more class."

<*Unusual observation,*> Angela commented. <*'Black Gate' does not strike me as classy.*>

<*One people's class is another's crass,*> Tanis replied.

They hurried another kilometer and a half through the palace, until Petra stopped before a pair of large doors.

"OK, here we are. We should be summoned any moment."

As she spoke, the doors began to open. The group straightened their clothing and uniforms and followed Petra inside.

THE PRESIDENT AND THE EMPRESS

STELLAR DATE: 08.11.8948 (Adjusted Years)
LOCATION: Imperial Palace Audience Chamber
REGION: Alexandria, Bosporus System, Scipio Empire

Empress Diana's audience chamber felt like a throne room from vids and sims of ancient times. The chamber was easily five hundred meters long, with rows of tall colonnades lining it all the way down to the dais at the far end, which was topped by a massive throne.

<*Is that plasma?*> Tanis asked Petra.

<*Yup, one and the same. Diana likes to impress.*>

<*Is she using magnets or grav shields to keep herself safe?*> Tanis asked.

<*I honestly don't know. She won't say, and I can't detect either. It's possible her protection is in her outfit and not the throne at all.*>

And what an outfit it was.

Diana's body shimmered under a thin layer of ice, which steamed from the heat of the plasma throne, but did not seem to melt or dissipate in any significant way. Ice spikes rose from her knees, jutted from her hips, shoulders, and elbows. Atop her head was more ice, stretching half a meter into the air in a sort of frozen crown.

Her face was exposed and seemed unharmed by both the extreme heat and bitter cold she was surrounded by.

The empress surveyed them serenely as they approached, though she did raise an eyebrow at Flaherty and the High Guard, who had been held back one hundred paces behind Berger and the three women.

A disembodied voice called out as they approached the throne. "The Lady Seraphina Tomlinson, President of the Miriam League; the Lady Petra, Esteemed Ambassador from the Miriam League; and Meuls Berger, Deputy Minister of External Affairs."

"Thank you, Gerald," Empress Diana said in a soft voice that carried throughout the room.

"Of course, my Empress."

Diana rose from her throne and walked gracefully down the dais's steps. The ice that sheathed her body appeared to flow around her as she moved, neither cracking nor splintering—though it had stopped steaming once she left the plasma throne.

"Petra, I am glad you were able to make it. Gerald had informed me that your president's ship may be late."

Tanis found it strange that the empress would address Petra first. She was getting the impression that the Hand agent was held in greater esteem than one would expect, given the minor and distant alliance she represented.

"Of course, Empress Diana," Petra said as she inclined her head. "Have I ever been late before?"

The empress cocked an eyebrow and gave a slight smile. "Well, there was that one time, but we won't discuss it in front of your president."

Diana turned to address Sera. "I must admit, I know very little about you—other than what Petra has told me, of course. The Miriam League is very secretive, it seems."

<*You have no idea,*> Angela said with a laugh in Tanis's mind.

"You are very kind to entertain our request to speak with you, Empress Diana," Sera replied. "And yes, we do keep to ourselves. We are also a long way off, on the rim of explored space. Most of our people like living so far out, where they can have privacy."

"And so far, they seem to have been successful," Diana said as she turned, cold air flowing off her body, clouds of condensation forming at her feet. She walked up the dais's steps and sat on the plasma throne once more. "Given the length of time required to travel here, I am most curious. What is it you have come so far to speak to me about?"

"I believe I had mentioned that we need a private audience," Petra said, glancing at Berger and some of the attendants nearby.

Diana nodded. "You did mention that, but there are protocols, Petra; they must be adhered to."

Tanis lifted her hand, palm up, and Diana looked at her for the first time. Tanis didn't speak as the palm of her hand began to glow softly. After a few seconds, a black and blue object took shape. It grew in size and, a moment later, a fist-sized shard of onyx rested in her hand with streaks of sapphire running through.

Diana drew a sharp breath, again rose from her throne, and walked down the stairs to inspect the object Tanis held.

<*We have seventy-five autoturrets tracking us right now,*> Angela said privately.

<*Just seventy-five?*> Tanis asked.

<*There are twenty-two that are behind colonnades, plus ten that have would have the empress in their line of fire.*>

<*I can't abide an odd number of autoturrets.*>

"That is exquisite, how did you do that?" Diana asked as she stretched a hand toward Tanis's, though she did not go so far as to touch the gem.

Tanis eyed Diana from under a furrowed brow. "We can tell you, but in a private audience."

"Petra, your friends don't play fair, piquing my interest like this. Very well—though your guards will have to stay behind."

Petra looked at Tanis and Sera, both of whom nodded. "That is more than acceptable to us, Empress."

<*This could take some time,*> Tanis advised Valerie and Flaherty. <*We'll update you every fifteen minutes, though.*>

<*Understood,*> Valerie replied.

Diana's guards, however, were not so accommodating, and five of them followed the group through a door on the left of the dais and down a hallway that led to a plush lounge, decorated in warm browns and light greens.

The guards waited outside, along with Berger, who had tagged along only to be refused entry.

After the door closed, Diana gave a mighty shiver, and the layer of ice melted away, leaving her standing in a blue, hooded skinsheath.

"Danny told me I wouldn't get cold in that thing, but dammit, it was *freezing*. Thank stars you gave me a good excuse to get out of there. Even sitting on plasma couldn't keep me warm."

"Quite the trick, sitting on plasma," Tanis said.

"But that's just what it was," Diana replied with a conspiratorial—rather haughty—wink. "A trick."

She pulled the hood off her head, revealing a hairless scalp, before walking across the room to an opaque vertical stand. She walked behind it, gave a momentary sigh, and then walked out, wearing a loose, long black dress, and hair to match.

"Much better. I adore form-fitting clothing as much as you do, President Sera, but sometimes one needs some breathing room."

Tanis laughed. "If only President Sera were wearing clothing."

"A trick of your own to impress me?" Diana asked as she approached Sera and examined her outfit. "But that is just what skin-clothing is. A trick. But that," Diana turned and pointed at the onyx and sapphire gem Tanis still held. "That is not a trick. Or if it is, it bested the scan tech in my audience chamber."

"It is no trick," Tanis replied, offering the crystal to Diana.

Diana took the crystal and felt its surface, slowly running a finger down its length. "Truly a thing of beauty…and formed right out of your hand. You must be more than a mere assistant, Jenny Sirana."

"May we sit?" Petra asked, gesturing to the burgundy sofas arranged around the edges of a sunken seating area.

"Yes, by all means," Diana replied. "I suppose if you are to tell me something weighty, we had all best be seated comfortably."

Once they had taken their places—Diana on one sofa, Petra on a chair to her right, and Sera and Tanis on another sofa across from the empress—Petra began the real introductions.

"I fear we misled you somewhat when we secured this audience. Sera Tomlinson is not the President of the Miriam League. She is, rather, the President of the Transcend Interstellar Alliance."

"That is most curious," Diana replied. "I've not heard of such an alliance."

"We work very hard—or we did, at least—to make sure that knowledge of the Transcend does not spread beyond its borders," Petra replied.

"And those borders would be where?"

Tanis noticed a familiarity in the body language between Petra and Diana that denoted more than just strong friendship. Yet at the same time, Diana clearly treated Petra as a subordinate; someone to leap at her every order.

Petra, despite being a powerful woman in her own right, seemed to never hesitate before responding to Diana, and her body language was clearly subservient.

Petra summoned a holoprojection of the Inner Stars, and Tanis remembered all too well when Sera gave her this same explanation in Jason Andrews's office.

The Orion Arm of the galaxy appeared in the projection, with major nations, empires, federations, and alliances highlighted. One of the largest, which was roughly centered around the Theta Carinae Cluster, was the Scipio Empire. There were no noted political entities outside of the Orion Arm, nor were there any settled star systems along the arm further than three thousand light years from Sol.

Though the volume of space contained over three hundred million stars, Tanis knew that fewer than fifty million had been visited by humans, and only a fraction of those actually held permanent populations.

"This map is not unfamiliar to me," Diana said as it appeared before them. "What are you trying to indicate with it?"

Petra inclined her head. "If you will, Empress. This is the scope of human expansion, as you know it. You see that few human settlements exist beyond a two thousand light year radius of Sol. This is a falsehood that the Transcend perpetuates."

As Petra spoke, stars began to flash further along the Orion Arm, both spinward and anti-spinward, as well as out into the regions between the arms. When they were done, an area nearly ten times the volume of the Inner Stars was highlighted.

"This is the true scope of human expansion though the stars," Sera said. "What you recognize as humanity's domain, we call the 'Inner Stars'. The area beyond is called the 'Transcend'."

Diana looked from Sera to Petra—who was nodding—and then back to Sera. "You're kidding me. That region is vast! It would have taken millennia to settle it."

"It has," Sera replied. "But that is what our people do—well, we build more than settle…or at least we did."

Diana's eyes grew wide, and she sat back, clearly shocked. "You're from the FGT! You're the lost FGT ships!"

"I don't think we were ever lost," Sera said with a wink.

Diana's gaze turned to Petra, and Tanis could see that the Empress was not happy. Tanis couldn't blame her; to have a friend lie to you about everything…it was not easy to deal with.

"So are you not from the Miriam League?" Diana asked Petra.

"Not exactly, no. The Miriam League is a puppet nation of the Transcend. We have nations all along the edge of the Inner Stars that we use to slow outward expansion."

"So you're corralling the…Inner Stars, as you call them."

"We've been protecting ourselves," Sera interjected. "During, and after, the FTL Wars, the FGT ships were targets. I'm sure you know of the *Oregon*. There were other incidents, as well. We decided to move out of range, so to speak, and set up our own civilization."

"You're not acquitting yourself well," Diana replied. "From where I stand, it looks like you're hoarding technology and manipulating the rest of humanity as though we are your little experiment."

Tanis could see Diana's point. It was not an unfair assessment, and she expected that it was a response they would often receive.

"You need to understand, Diana," Petra said in calm, even tones. "For a time, the Transcend thought that it was the ark. It appeared as though the bulk of humanity was determined to wipe itself out. We tried to help several times, but it never went well. That is why the FGT disappeared."

Diana didn't respond immediately, instead drawing long, slow breaths as she examined each of the three women in turn. "Why now, and why me?" she finally asked.

"Because war is coming," Sera replied. "And we need your help."

Diana shook her head, an incredulous look on her face. "What could the mighty Transcend need from Scipio?"

"We need you to help us because we are not one united front," Sera said. "Things beyond the Inner Stars are not so simple."

"They rarely are," Diana said with an exaggerated sigh. "Tell me then, Sera of the Transcend, what troubles do you face?"

"My father—the former President of the Transcend—and another FGT captain, Kirkland, rarely saw eye-to-eye. My father believed—"

"Wait," Diana interrupted. "Your last name...Was your father related to Jeffrey Tomlinson, captain of the *Starfarer*?"

Sera laughed without humor. "He was not related to him, he *was* the captain of the *Starfarer*."

"Yet the note of sorrow I hear in your voice tells me he has only recently passed away," Diana observed.

"That is true. My father was assassinated only four months ago—by agents of Praetor Kirkland."

"The president and the praetor. Then I must assume that your Transcend had a schism at some point."

Sera nodded. "Some three thousand years ago, though it was a slow progression for some time. The Transcend is very large; even with FTL, it takes centuries for news to reach every corner."

"Yes," Diana nodded, examining the galactic display before her. "That you've managed only one fracture in such a long time is very impressive."

"We occupy a large volume of space, but our population density is nothing like the Inner Stars. Most of our development is in discrete areas."

Diana smiled knowingly. "Behind dust clouds and nebulae. That was the genesis of Scipio, you know."

"I've heard that, yes," Sera replied. "We allow our disparate regions autonomy, though there is still an overarching central government."

"And where do your borders with Praetor Kirkland's regions lie?" Diana asked.

Petra updated the holoprojection to show lines drawn through the region beyond the Inner Stars. "The two halves are split along the Orion Arm of the galaxy. The Transcend controls the region of space on the coreward side, and Kirkland's Orion Freedom Alliance controls the rimward side."

"And you're at war?" Diana asked.

"It's mostly been a cold war," Sera replied. "It is difficult to fight a battle on such a vast front."

"So what has changed?" Diana asked.

Tanis wondered at Diana's demeanor. She had been far more animated when Petra had told of the Transcend itself—of course, at the time it had been a solution, not a problem. Now the empress gave the impression of the calm before the storm.

It occurred to Tanis that Diana may have already known of the Transcend, but was playing along. The woman was likely a consummate actress.

"Two things have precipitated our new strategy," Sera said. "Tanis?"

"Tanis?" Diana asked. "So your name is not Jenny Sirana?"

"No, it is not," Tanis replied. "You might have heard of me; my name is Tanis Richards. I come from the ship you would know of as the GSS *Intrepid*."

This time Diana showed more than a small reaction to that revelation—her eyes widened, and she sat forward. "Are you playing a game with me, Petra? I'll admit to more than a little skepticism over this whole Transcend tale, but Tanis is a known quantity—so to speak."

"None of this has been a trick, Empress," Petra assured her. "I had hoped to have more time to share this news with you, but things are moving quickly."

Diana peered at Tanis while running a finger along the gem she had taken. "You do not look like what the records show of Tanis Richards. I would not even believe you to be a relative of hers."

Tanis nodded slowly, and as she did so, her face changed shape. Her forehead and cheekbones shifted, her jaw widened, and her nose shrunk.

The empress shook her head in disbelief. "I have scanning systems in here…they can see your bones, Tanis Richards…they changed shape."

"They did," Tanis said, then worked her jaw for a moment. "And it is far from an enjoyable process, let me tell you."

Diana was silent for nearly a minute as she stared at Tanis, then at Sera. "You spoke of two things that have brought you out of the shadows. Your ship is the first thing, then," Diana supplied, nodding to Tanis. "Your advanced technology coming into play—so to speak—has already had a very destabilizing effect on the galaxy."

"I've heard of what is happening in Silstrand, and what you're doing there as well." Tanis mixed admission, and then accusation in her tone.

Diana's eyes narrowed. "Silstrand has long been useful; a buffer between us and the AST—rather, the 'Hegemony', as that prissy Uriel insists it be called now. But they have begun to destabilize. They're weakening, and I can't have that."

<I like how she comments on Uriel having the 'Hegemony', when she turned a federation into an empire,> Angela said with a laugh.

<That struck me as a bit myopic as well.>

"Setting Silstrand aside for now," Tanis said with a wave of her hand, "the Hegemony and the Trisilieds have already made a play to take the *Intrepid*'s new colony—one deep in the Transcend. They attacked with one hundred and fifty thousand ships, but we were able—with the Transcend's help—to defeat them."

Diana drew a deep breath. "You have a faster method of FTL than dark layer transition! Any place 'deep within the Transcend' would take many years of travel to reach. For those people to find you and strike at you, and then for you to travel here…. No, there is no way the timelines work without it."

<*She's no dummy, that's for sure,*> Tanis commented to the group.

<*Far from it,*> Petra replied. <*It takes a lot of cunning for her to maintain her position.*>

"And now you have the second thing," Sera said. "We have jump gate technology that provides near instantaneous travel to any location in human space."

"So," Diana said as she rose from the sofa and walked to a side table. "The most valuable technology in the galaxy—Tanis's picotech—lies nestled within the oyster that is the Transcend, and your enemies possess the ability to reach in and pluck it free. That is the long and short of it, is it not?"

Diana poured herself a glass of whisky on the rocks as she spoke. She took a sip, and then gestured to the side table. "Help yourself, if you wish."

"I'll take you up on that," Sera said as she rose. "And you have the gist of it, yes. Of course, you must also realize that Orion has made jump gate technology available to the Trisilieds and the Hegemony. They may have also put it in the hands of the Nietzscheans. We're not certain yet."

Diana put her cup down and pushed her long black locks behind her ears as she leaned against the side table. "Now *that* is troubling news. So then, are you going to share your new toys with Scipio, if we ally with you?"

"Always right to the point, aren't you, Diana?" Petra asked.

"You know me well enough, Petra," Diana said coolly. "I do not like to beat around the bush; I prefer to drive over the bush, or through it."

<*That was a double entendre, right?*> Tanis asked Angela. <*How intimate are these two?*>

<*Very, if my guess is correct,*> Angela replied.

Sera took a sip of her whisky before replying. "Exactly what we share, and how we turn over new technology will be details we need to hammer out, but we will certainly provide you with enough technology to give you an edge over your enemies."

Diana met Sera's eyes—both women unblinking as Diana spoke. "Are you so certain that I'll ally with you? I'm not telegraphing it, but I'm very displeased at being lied to for so long."

"I can tell," Petra replied. "You've been curling your pinky finger. You only do that when you're exceptionally angry."

Diana held up her left hand and uncurled her finger to show a small line of blood on her palm. "Yes, I suppose I do."

"I'm not certain of anything," Sera said, guiding the conversation back to the matter at hand. "But I came here in person because we need you to hold the Inner Stars."

"Hold them?" Diana asked. "Hold them against who?"

"Well, for starters, against the Hegemony," Sera replied. "Orion has provided them more than just jump gate technology; they are funneling resources into the Hegemony at an alarming rate. Now that a direct assault on Tanis's colony has failed, we believe that they will commence with a more conventional approach."

"Orion wants to control all of the Inner Stars, and then use their combined might to destroy the Transcend," Petra said.

"You didn't answer my question," Diana said. "Why would I ally with you and not them?"

"Because they're not coming to *take* our technology," Tanis said. "They want to destroy us *and* it. Orion does not believe in the AIs we have, our level of nanotech, and certainly not our picotech."

"Or your impervious shields," Diana added.

"Or our stasis shields," Tanis agreed with a nod.

"It seems odd that the Hegemony would side with them," Diana replied before taking another sip of her drink. "They pursue technology as relentlessly as we do, and I understand your thrust that Orion would come for us before long."

Sera gave a soft laugh. "We don't know for sure, but I suspect that Uriel and Garza are using one another."

"Garza?" Diana asked.

"He's the one leading Orion's war effort," Sera replied.

"That doesn't surprise me, then," Diana said with a rueful laugh. "Uriel is a schemer; there's no way she'd ever be subservient to anyone else."

"You talk about her as though you've met," Sera observed.

Diana nodded absently. "Once, long ago—before either of us held our current positions. The woman is a snake."

"There's more we must tell you," Petra said reluctantly. "There is much afoot that you are not aware of."

Diana turned her head and locked her steely gaze on Petra. "Yes, it would seem so. Like a woman I had considered a dear friend acting as a spy this entire time."

"It's no picnic, that's for sure," Sera said quietly.

"I'm sorry, Diana, I really am," Petra entreated. "But surely you must have suspected. Why would an ambassador from somewhere as distant as the Miriam League work so hard to get to know you?"

Diana's hard expression cracked for a moment, and Tanis saw a very different woman.

"Because of *me*," Diana whispered hoarsely. "Please, you should all go now. I'll have Gerald contact you with a time when we can continue this conversation."

Tanis rose and nodded graciously. "Thank you for your attention and understanding thus far."

"Yes, thank you," Sera said and offered her hand to Diana, who shook it absently.

Petra didn't say anything, only stared at Diana until Tanis touched her on the shoulder.

<Let's go.>

Petra nodded, and the three women filed out of the room, the door closing behind them. A moment after, the sounds of shattering glass came from within.

SUSPICION

STELLAR DATE: 08.08.8948 (Adjusted Years)
LOCATION: Intrepid Space Force Academy
REGION: The Palisades, Orbiting Troy, New Canaan System

"I saw Nance last night," Saanvi said as she sat at the mess hall table across from Cary.

"Oh yeah?" Cary asked around a mouthful of eggs. "I saw her as well, this morning. She must have been coming back in from an early run."

Saanvi frowned. "Really? At what time?"

Cary shrugged and wondered why Saanvi cared what time she saw Nance. "Uh…about 06:05. I was just headed out for a jog around the sweep when I saw her get off a maglev."

"What makes you think she was going for a run?" Saanvi asked, her eyes narrowing.

"Uhh…she was dressed for one. I guess she might have been at the gym, too, but she was coming from off-ring, and there are nine gyms on this one."

Saanvi's frown deepened as she picked up her orange juice and took a sip. Cary waited for her sister to mull over whatever it was that was on her mind. Sometimes it took Saanvi a few minutes to assemble her thoughts.

"I saw her last night at 23:44," Saanvi said finally. "Black leggings, pink and black halter top. Was that what she was wearing?"

"Uhh…yeah, I believe so," Cary said, thinking back. "Yeah, that was it. Is there something wrong with wearing the same thing twice? Maybe she tossed it in the san overnight, and it was the first thing on the folded pile come morning. If wearing the same clothes to exercise twice in a row is a crime, I'm going to prison for sure."

"A maglev down to another ring, a run worth having, maglev back, shower, she wouldn't have hit sack till at least 0100. And that's if she didn't take a very long run."

"Maybe she doesn't need that much sleep," Cary replied. "If she has the right mods, five hours is plenty."

Saanvi nodded. "I suppose. Just seems weird, don't you think? Nance has never mentioned an obsession with running before."

Cary laughed and shook her head. "I've got enough on my mind to be tracking other people's obsessions. Speaking of obsessions, I saw JP this morning. He asked how you were."

"Stars, he's been acting weird ever since he came aboard," Saanvi muttered.

"Well, you know why, right?"

Saanvi met Cary's eyes. "I may have been born a thousand years ago, but I've not lost my faculties yet. I can tell that he's into me. Just wish he'd say something about it."

"Well, you're into him, too," Cary replied. "Watching you two perform your awkward mating dance is going to give me greys. And my hair can't even turn grey."

"*Mating* dance?" Saanvi asked. "Jumping the gun a bit, aren't you?"

Cary winked at her sister. "You and JP are made for each other. Everyone's just feeling uncertain of themselves after the battle and all the changes since. JP didn't think he'd join the academy, but after the attack, he felt like he had to."

"He did it to be close to me," Saanvi said, her eyebrows pinched with in annoyance. "Except now he won't be close to me."

"You're hopeless. I'm going to have to go on a double date with you two, or something…"

"Who's *your* date going to be?"

Cary shrugged. "I'll bring Jill."

Saanvi's eyes widened. "I *knew* there was something between you and Jill!"

Cary almost spit out her juice. "No, Saanvi, Jill and I are friends. I'm not into anyone right now."

<I'm all the woman she can handle,> Faleena said with a snicker.

"I believe that," Saanvi replied. "You've been quiet this morning."

<I'm already in class,> Faleena replied. *<Major Ren of the TSF is teaching Crypto Algorithms of the Inner Stars. It's fascinating stuff. Nance is there, too; she's actually helped the Major a few times.>*

"Really?" Saanvi asked. "I didn't know she was an expert on that stuff."

<I think she might know more than the major, but she's being polite about it. She also knows more about the crypto that they use in the Orion Freedom

Alliance.>

"I guess it makes sense," Cary said. "She did spend nine years there. I bet we haven't heard half of what went on during that trip."

"You know, she and I spoke about getting together. Maybe we should do it next rest day," Saanvi said. "I can reach out and confirm the date with her."

Cary nodded before giving Saanvi a wink. "Yeah, and we can invite JP."

Saanvi laughed. "Only if Jill comes, too."

STEPPING OUT

STELLAR DATE: 08.09.8948 (Adjusted Years)
LOCATION: ISS *IS*
REGION: Edge of the Bosporus System, Scipio Empire

Two days prior…

Elena truly believed that Sergeant Xener was a nice sort of man, as far as men went. He was courteous, didn't yell at her, and even let her spend time with her wristcuffs disconnected when they were in the park.

Sergeant Arys did not share much of Xener's kindness. It turned out that Arys's brother had been a part of the team that had been in on the attack on the *Galadrial*—back before New Canaan had been invaded. Though he had survived, he had received serious injuries that took him some weeks to recover from.

Arys seemed to think that Elena was personally responsible for her brother's pain and trauma—even though Elena's focus had been on a successful infiltration, not on harming the ISF soldiers who were on her side.

Well, I also made sure to leave the back door open for Colonel Kent….

When Elena thought about it in that context, she was *somewhat* responsible for Arys's brother's injuries.

At least Xener balanced Arys out—though Elena was certain Arys chided him constantly for it over the Link. Xener had the look of a henpecked man whenever Arys was near.

Despite that, Elena was allowed some amount of freedom as she roamed the Prairie Park on the *I2*. She enjoyed the tall grass that seemed to stretch on forever—an illusion aided by the holoprojections on the distant bulkheads, and by the holographic sky overhead.

Not that the park was small. At over two square kilometers in size, it gave ample range for its population of deer, rabbits, gophers, snakes, and the pair of cougars that roamed its expanse.

Elena delighted in seeing the cougars when she got a chance. To her knowledge, the *I2* carried the only natural-line cougars in existence—which is to say that they were not reconstituted from stored DNA. These fine mammals had been carried in their mother's wombs, in a line stretching back to the origins of the species.

It occurred to Elena that such was the exception, not the norm. The *Intrepid* was a rarity in that it had carried the vast majority of its animal population as live creatures. Few colony ships had possessed the room to carry millions of living animals along with their colonists.

She slowed and sat on a bench near a rock outcropping that the male cougar sometimes sunned himself on. The animals couldn't see the people—so long as they didn't get too close—so it was possible to observe them in their natural habitat. Well, as natural as a park on a starship could be.

Xener wandered ahead a half-dozen meters and leaned against a boulder, while Arys stopped in the middle of the path and stared at every shrub and blade of grass as though it may have possessed lethal intent.

To be honest, neither of the guards was really necessary. With the cuffs and the collar, Elena couldn't go anywhere without the *Intrepid*'s systems being able to track her. She was certain that somewhere, that interminable Bob was watching as well.

Thinking of the *Intrepid*'s AI made Elena wonder what had become of Jutio, her old AI. He had spoken to her only once after her betrayal, infuriated that she had managed to fool him so fully.

She felt bad about that. Some of the things she'd had to do to him to ensure that he would never know her true purpose had been difficult, but she had believed in what she was doing.

I'm sorry, Jutio, she said in her mind—though there was no one there to communicate with anymore. *It's for the greater good. Tomlinson was vile, and his Transcend was corrupt. You have to have seen that.*

She sat in the silence, the absence in her mind deafening.

Moments like these, she wondered if she had made the right choice. She had felt so certain she could convince Sera of her father's evil—that they could lead a rebellion and re-form the Transcend as one single alliance with Praetor Kirkland at its head.

She had half succeeded—though her efforts hadn't been required to show Sera that her father was worse than scum. But rather than rush to Elena's side, Sera had fallen in with Tanis and...well, she had no idea what they were up to anymore.

Tanis was an enigma, as well. She seemed to like the idea of simple living, of having dirt under her nails and straw in her hair, but she was barely human anymore—though she looked it on the outside. She was more machine and enhanced biology than natural flesh and blood. And then there was the thing in her mind.

Elena did recognize the incongruity of her logic. She had loved having Jutio in her mind, and though Orion didn't eschew having internal AI, they didn't exactly smile upon it either.

But Tanis and Angela were anathema to their own Phobos Accords—which they purported to adhere to so strictly.

Elena sighed. What she really yearned for was access to the Link again. Being trapped in her own mind was so restrictive; she had only her thoughts, the odd exchange with a guard, and her irregular visits from Sera.

The *I2*'s detention center—prison, really—had been accommodating in that regard, providing her with printed books. It was the only way she could read with her Link disabled and access to technology restricted. It was an experience she found rather enjoyable, even if it was strange to read words that were fixed on the page and could not move.

To think that the pages of a printed book would contain just one set of information—and only that set, for their entire existence—was something that felt abnormal to Elena.

Though, it was what Orion sought, was it not? A simpler existence for humanity; a slow-down where equilibrium could be achieved.

In her voracious consumption of literature, she'd found a swatch of ancient books she'd never heard of by a man named Stephen King. Some were just weird, but many were amazing. She'd read one called 'The Stand' three times thus far during her incarceration, reveling in the flavor of ancient Earth that it provided.

As she sat on the bench, lost in her thoughts, Elena finally saw Arys turn away, distracted by a doe and fawn walking by. Elena glanced at Xener, who was also watching the animals with a small smile on his face.

She slowly reached a hand behind the seat of the bench, feeling for the packet that her mysterious benefactor had told her would be present.

Elena had almost missed the message telling her to check the bench. It had been embedded in the forewords of the last three books she'd read; an obscure code, but one she'd studied in The Hand's academy.

The possibility that the coded message was a setup had occurred to her, but Elena had determined there was nothing to lose; the New Canaan colony did not have a death penalty. The worst they'd do is order continued incarceration and maybe stasis for a few hundred years.

Her hand slipped over something sharp, and Elena resisted the urge to suck in a breath when her finger was cut. With her limited internal nano—courtesy of the control exerted by the cuffs and collar—she couldn't tell if the cut was the delivery mechanism, or just an accident.

Then she felt a change inside her, and a message came to her mind.

<If you can hear me, then the localized relay is working. You can't transmit, but nod if you're receiving this.>

Elena nodded slowly.

<Good. The cougars, deer, and an obliging black bear are going to attack your guards in thirty seconds. The instant that happens, I want you to make a run for the large rock behind you to the left. There's a hidden service door behind it. The latch to open it is a branch wedged into a crevice on the rock.>

Elena nodded again then looked up at the sky, wondering how her liberator was going to deal with the tracking mechanisms in the cuffs and collar. Not to mention the fact that Bob could probably see everything on the ship at once.

She took slow, steady breaths, counting down the seconds.

Then the doe and fawn charged Arys.

Elena would have loved nothing more than to watch, but she knew that time was of the essence. She leapt over the bench and found the rock with the stick protruding from it. Elena dashed over and pulled the lever, and the rock slid aside.

Even if I get caught, this is a hell of a lot more fun than my usual daily activities.

She nearly gasped as she passed *herself* coming out of the opening, but then smiled with delight. A clone wouldn't stand up to close scrutiny, but it would be enough to fool Dumb and Dumber out there for a while.

Once inside, with the door carefully latched shut, she raced down a short flight of steps and into a storage room.

<Strip,> the voice said, and Elena wordlessly complied. *<Third rack, second shelf.>*

Elena looked where the voice indicated, and spotted a canister of the same stealth armor she had worn during the assault on the *Galadrial*. She grabbed the canister and pressed it to her chest, shivering as the armor flowed across her skin. When it reached the cuffs and collar, they flashed red and then disconnected, falling to the floor.

"Handy," Elena said aloud as the armor flowed over her head, covering her in its thin layer of protection and stealth.

<Quiet. The armor won't mask verbal utterances; don't transmit responses. Receive only.>

Elena nodded again, uncertain if the speaker could see her.

<OK, now you need to get to the A1 Dock and board the Aegeus. *It leaves for Kapalicarsi Station above Alexandria in one hour.>*

Elena almost responded with incredulity. There were easily tens of thousands of systems, planets, stations, and cities named Alexandria, but she only knew of one with a 'Kapalicarsi' above it.

They were in Scipio, her old stomping grounds.

Elena nodded again and followed the route toward the docks that was highlighted over her vision.

This is going to be fun.

RETROSPECTIVE

STELLAR DATE: 08.11.8948 (Adjusted Years)
LOCATION: Imperial Palace Guest Suites
REGION: Alexandria, Bosporus System, Scipio Empire

Outside Diana's private audience rooms, a woman waited for Tanis, Sera, and Petra with an impassive gaze on her face.

"The Empress has informed me that you are to be guests of the palace. She wishes you to stay nearby so that she may have further conversations with you at her leisure."

"Thank you, Chimellia," Petra said. "Please lead the way."

Chimellia nodded and turned to lead them down the corridor. They passed a pair of Scipian Palace Guards stationed at a security arch before Tanis caught sight of Flaherty and the High Guard waiting for them.

<Tanis,> Major Valerie said with visible relief. *<We got your updates, but the palace guards have been none too accommodating.>*

<Yeah, the empress isn't happy with us right now, either,> Tanis admitted. *<We're to be billeted here in the palace. I believe the suite will be large enough for all of us.>*

<Excellent,> Valerie said as she fell in beside Sera. "President Sera, I trust you are well?" she asked aloud.

"I am," Sera replied. "Looking forward to relaxing for a bit."

"You'll need to prepare for the party tomorrow," Chimellia said over her shoulder. "The empress has just sent word that you're to attend."

"The party?" Petra asked. "The Celebration of the Seven Suns?"

"Petra, don't pretend you don't know what it is. You've pestered me for months to get on the invite list," Chimellia replied.

"And you told me that it was full," Petra answered with a small pout.

<I wonder if she's been here too long,> Sera said to Tanis in private. *<That's a lot of excitement for some dance.>*

<I hope we don't have to wear fancy dresses. I don't wear dresses to parties anymore,> Tanis replied.

Chimellia shrugged. "Well, it just got un-full. Though the empress does not seem happy…"

"Was it the shattering glass that gave it away?" Petra asked dryly.

Chimellia snorted. "If I had a credit for every time she broke something…it still wouldn't come close to paying for everything she breaks in just one outburst."

<Diana didn't strike me as a petulant woman,> Sera said.

<She has a lot of stresses in her life and very few outlets,> Petra replied.

Sera raised an eyebrow. *<Oh, yeah? Is that what you were? An outlet?>*

<This was in my reports. You knew that I had seduced Diana.>

<I didn't,> Tanis replied. *<Though it became obvious, shortly into our meeting.>*

Sera's mental avatar wore a glower as it regarded Petra. *<We'll finish this conversation once we've arrived at our suites.>*

Tanis considered Chimellia's words about Diana's outbursts and wondered how much of Diana's performance was real and how much was feigned. Dealing with these sorts of personalities reminded her of her time as Victoria's Lieutenant Governor, and of times prior in the Terran Space Force, where she often had to manage her superiors to get the results she needed.

'Tiresome' was too kind a word for it.

She was thankful that the colony at New Canaan had felt much more cooperative—though its establishment hadn't been without its personality conflicts.

<Such is our lot in life,> Angela said. *<If either of us were the types to sit back and see where the chips naturally fell, I think things would have been much different.>*

<But what if we didn't like where the chips fell?> Tanis asked.

<Exactly,> Angela replied.

<So what do you think?> Tanis asked Angela.

<I think that Diana does have real feelings for Petra—more than she should, and she knows it. A woman in her position, especially with the political structure of the empire, can have no friends. At least none she trusts implicitly.>

Tanis nodded. *<Makes me glad that New Canaan's leadership is so close-knit.>*

<And Sera should thank the stars that she has you to rely on.>

Tanis hadn't considered it from Sera's angle. She knew that Sera felt scared of the responsibility; her attempts to pass it off to Finaeus—and Tanis—were only half joking at best.

<I should do better at supporting her. She has a lot of weight on her

shoulders.>

<You're not a bad friend, Tanis. You just tend toward…extreme bluntness. I think you've mistaken it for a sport.>

They arrived at their suites, and by some miracle of porter magic, their luggage had beat them to the rooms—even though they had only been assigned a few minutes prior. Chimellia gave them a brief tour, noting where 'the help'—aka, the soldiers—could sleep, and showing them the four rooms the women had to choose from.

"Will you stay with us here?" Sera asked Petra once Chimellia left.

"I think so. If Diana summons us, I wouldn't want to keep her waiting."

"Good call," Tanis said.

"So," Sera said as she stood at the window, staring out over the gardens below. "Would you like to elaborate on what exactly went on in there? Diana took this a lot more personally than I would have expected."

Petra strode to the suite's bar and grabbed a glass, which she filled with vodka before replying. "It started off innocently enough—I mean, as innocent as it could be for two women who were obviously using one another."

"I know how you were using her, but how was she using you?" Tanis asked.

Petra shrugged. "She needed some personal time. My representation of a group so far from Scipio meant that I had fewer aspirations. There was a feeling of…freedom in our interactions. I asked for little and gave a lot. It was refreshing for her."

"But it turned into something more for her?" Sera asked.

"As much as it could," Petra replied. "She could never be seen publicly having a dalliance with me. I'm too far beneath her station. I think that was part of the enjoyment; we both knew nothing could ever come of it. But what she did get from me was an ear and a distinct lack of expectations."

"Sounds like standard fare," Tanis replied. "But she placed more trust in you than she should have?"

"Well," Petra said with a shrug. "If I'd been who I said I was, then her level of trust was fine. Since I'm not…."

"She feels more betrayed than she would if you two had not become so emotionally invested in one another," Sera finished for her. "Don't try to deny it. I saw the hurt in your eyes when she summarily dismissed you."

Petra downed her drink in one gulp and slammed her elbows onto the bar, burying her face in her hands. "I know, Sera, OK? I know. I fucked up. I got too close to the asset. I knew it then, too, I just…" She looked up at Sera, her eyes pleading. "I just needed a goddamn connection to someone, OK? This job, all the bullshit, I don't even know who I am anymore. Diana grounded me as much as I grounded her."

Sera leaned against the window where she stood and nodded. "I get that. I really do, Petra. But when that happens, you know it's time for a new assignment—after a few years off, to get to know yourself again. It's as much my fault as yours—I should have spotted the signs."

"Yeah, well, what's done is done," Petra replied. "What are we going to do now?"

"With you, or with Diana?" Sera asked.

"I was going to say with Diana, but I guess we're part and parcel of the same problem, aren't we?"

"She'll come around," Tanis said. "We have what she wants. This was the first step of the negotiations; soon we begin feeling out concessions."

"Then what's on the table?" Petra asked, straightening and pouring herself another drink—just two fingers this time.

"No picotech. At all," Tanis said. "That never leaves New Canaan."

"What about your nanotech?" Petra asked.

"Some," Tanis granted. "As much as we've given the Transcend—though that won't be my initial offer. We'll also give her stealth tech that should beat anything the Hegemony has—though I hate doing that. It feels like arming a future enemy."

"Any time one forms an alliance like this, that's the risk," Sera told her as she walked to one of the chairs and fell into it.

Tanis looked back at Major Valerie and the three High Guard troops who were scanning the room for listening devices. "How we looking?" she asked.

"There were a few," Valerie replied. "But nothing that our standard package hadn't blocked the moment we came in. It's the minor leagues here."

"Don't get lax," Sera warned. "We know that Orion has BOGA agents in Scipio."

"Ten, that I know of," Petra added. "Though I've put four into positions that keep them from hearing anything. Of the other six, one does have palace access; though for them to have this room tapped already, they would have had to turn a large number of porters, or Chimellia."

"Wouldn't surprise me," Flaherty said. "Woman's cold."

"Diana trusts her completely," Petra replied.

"So?" Flaherty asked. "She trusted you, too."

A small grimace fluttered across Petra's lips. "Good point."

<*Ma'am,*> Major Valerie said privately to Tanis. <*I just got an alert that was encrypted within our status channel with the* Aegeus. *Elena has escaped the* I2.>

<*When?*> Tanis asked.

<*They believe she may have made it to the* Aegeus *before it left. Passing you what details they sent.*>

"Well, this just got a lot more fun," Tanis said aloud. "Sera, we need to assume that Elena is on Alexandria."

"Whoa, hey, what?" Sera sputtered, and Tanis hid a smile as Sera's entire body turned red for a moment.

Petra, on the other hand, did not withhold comment.

"What? You brought her along?"

"Yes, but that's not what matters." Sera slumped against the window, pressing a hand against her cheek. "If Elena is on Alexandria, we have to assume that she'll try to sync up with a local Orion agent. Will she know who they are?"

Petra shrugged and threw her hands in the air. "Not that I know of, but she was turned ages ago. She may know the Orion spies I do, or she may know others that I've never uncovered."

"Good point," Sera acknowledged.

"They think she has the new Mark X FlowArmor," Valerie added. "They found an empty canister in Prairie Park."

"Dammit," Sera shook her head. "This is my fault for being a big sap."

"Saps all around today, it would seem," Tanis said. "You'd think we were all human or something."

Petra snorted a laugh. "I'm reaching out to my network. We'll get ears to the ground."

"Captain Sheeran is performing a bow-to-stern active sweep of the *Aegeus;* they'll alert us to anything they find," Major Valerie added.

"I'll go meet with some people," Flaherty said as he pushed himself off the wall and ambled toward the door.

"You have local contacts?" Petra asked, surprise unmasked on her face. "Do you think they're trustworthy?"

"Yes and yes," Flaherty replied as he left the suite.

"Just as talkative as always," Petra said with a slow shake of her head. "He's not going to screw anything up is he?"

"He's the last one of us that would ever mess up," Sera assured her. "It's like he's built out of success."

"Just to put it out there, we don't tell Diana yet," Tanis said. "We haven't gotten to the whole civil war bit yet. Let's get that past her before we compound it with double agents, and the rest of the BOGA versus The Hand business."

"It's such a stupid name," Petra said.

"Blame Finaeus," Sera said. "He's on the *I2*, and I imagine if all this goes well, we'll bring it insystem. You can chide him for his naming conventions in person."

"The what?" Petra asked.

Tanis laughed. "I keep forgetting that we've done all this at breakneck speed. The *I2* is the first of the Intrepid Class warships that we've built. Except, in its case, it actually *is* the *Intrepid*. Just upgraded."

"You never told me you were building more of them," Sera accused. "Or did you? I think I would have remembered that."

Tanis glanced at Petra. "As you can see, we are all running on very little sleep." She looked to Sera. "I don't think I brought it up in person. It was in the outline of the fleet buildout that we're going to do now that the Grey Wolf Star resources are hitting New Canaan. I want to have at least one hundred of them in three years."

"One hundred…" Petra whispered. "Sorry, that really drives the scope home. A single ship that size is worth a fleet."

"Plus it carries a fleet," Tanis added.

"And fifty thousand fighter craft," Sera supplied.

"Why do you need allies, again?" Petra asked with a chuckle.

"Because defenses are best performed by the people who live in a given place. If we come in and fight for them, they hate us and feel lorded over," Tanis replied.

"I know, Tanis," Petra replied. "It was rhetorical."

"Oh."

"It's only midmorning," Sera said. "Why don't we order some food, carb up, and then figure out what our next move is?"

"We should go out tonight, too," Petra said. "It would be unusual for the president to come here and hole up in her suites all night. No one passes up on an opportunity to see the world-city."

* * * * *

Later, after they had eaten and Petra had retired to her room for a brief rest, Tanis approached Sera. She was sitting on one of the chairs, looking out the window.

"Sure is a lot going on," Tanis said as she sat in the chair next to Sera. "Forming a new government, alliances, fleets…"

"You can say that again," Sera replied with a nod. "I've been sitting here reviewing new candidates for building the administration. Right now, I'm looking over Chancellor Alma's record—the one from Vela."

"Right, I remember Greer mentioning her," Tanis replied. "I don't know how you're managing, Sera, but you're doing a great job. I see the messages you've been sending to Khardine over the QuanComms. It's substantial."

"Imagine if we didn't have those? We'd have to relay to a jump gate and then send from there."

"Earnest is a godsend," Tanis agreed. "Though he also created half this mess. He invented the pico and the *Intrepid*'s ramscoop and half the other stuff that everyone is fighting over."

"Good point. Though without that, we'd never have met, Tanis."

A smile stretched across Tanis's face to hear Sera say that. She was right. Everyone in Tanis's life that meant so much to her had come into it after she joined the *Intrepid*'s mission. Her time before, back in Sol…it seemed almost like a dream.

She didn't want to imagine a life without Joe, her daughters, Jessica, Sera, Bob, and a thousand other dear friends. In fact, Angela was the only person she knew now from her old life. And even then, they would have been separated after another decade or so.

In a way, I owe Earnest Redding everything. What a strange thought.

"Meeting you was one of the most serendipitous events in my life," Tanis said in response to Sera's statement. "And I've had a lot of those."

"That you have," Sera said with a soft chuckle.

Tanis took a deep breath. She had come to Sera to tell her something that she knew her friend would not want to hear, but she had to start the conversation at some point; now was as good a time as any.

"Sera, while you're vetting all these candidates, you should consider vetting a new AI."

There, it was out. Tanis braced for the storm.

"Seriously, Tanis? You pick now to bring that up?" Sera asked.

<Not too bad,> Angela commented. *<I was expecting her to take a swing at you.>*

<We're not done talking yet,> Tanis replied.

"We don't really have a lot of 'good times'," Tanis replied. "There's always shit going on."

"It's too soon. I've not healed yet from Helen's removal. Physically or mentally."

"I doubt the former, but I believe the latter. Still, I think you need to get another AI—one that can help you. Both in getting past what Helen did to you, and in running things."

Sera placed her hands over her face and then ran them through her hair. "Thank you for your advice, Tanis. I need to think on this. Is that enough for now?"

"Of course," Tanis replied, reaching out and taking Sera's hand. "I'm always here for you, Sera. I have your back. No matter what, we're going to get through this."

"Or die trying?" Sera asked with a wan smile as she met Tanis's eyes.

"Core, no," Tanis replied, a grin on her lips. "That's for our enemies to do."

ALTERNATIVES

STELLAR DATE: 08.11.8948 (Adjusted Years)
LOCATION: Imperial Palace Guest Suites
REGION: Alexandria, Bosporus System, Scipio Empire

Phillip reviewed the missive with dismay. Not only had Petra disregarded the warnings from the Directorate on Airtha, she had taken the *pretender* to meet with the empress. And if that wasn't bad enough, she had somehow let a double agent loose in the city.

The information as to how Elena had escaped custody was not in the packet, but both the Directorate, and the pretender's government on Khardine had flagged the former agent as having gone rogue and working for Orion.

That Elena had changed sides did not surprise Phillip overmuch. The woman had several unexplained absences in her past; she always had excuses, but they had never seemed to add up for him.

He considered his options. Of the local agents, he had only reached out to two that he was certain would not side with Petra. The rest were too close to her—trapped in her thrall, to his mind.

That was how Petra worked—she was a master manipulator. Her every word was constructed to endear you to her and make you desire to do her bidding.

But Phillip had long-since seen through her façade.

The woman was weak, a petty shell of a thing that lived off the servitude of others. That she had retained her position on Alexandria as head of regional operations was only due to her fucking the empress.

Granted, she had drawn a large store of intel from the woman, and had more than a little success influencing the direction of Scipio—but she had utterly failed to stop the empress's drive into Silstrand, and Tanis Richards's nanotech had yet to be secured from S&H Defensive Armaments.

And now Diana's knowledge of that nanotech threatened to destroy the fragile peace that had been growing amongst the fringe nations between Scipio and Silstrand.

A peace that Phillip had spent decades working on.

Of course, Peter Rhoads and his fleet of purists weren't helping. That landed at Petra's feet, as well. The operation to assassinate Peter Rhoads had been stalled for years. *If I had been running that op, the spindly old man would have been dead before he even launched his crusade.*

Petra's packet had not revealed the identity of her current guests, but back channels were abuzz with the warship that had docked on Kapalicarsi—a ship with a very distinct design. Not only that, but Phillip had managed to get eyes on Petra's guests while they were moving through the palace.

It had been none other than the pretender herself.

This was a golden opportunity, and not one that Phillip was going to waste. If he could capture or kill either of those two, he would win great favor with Airtha and the Directorate. That Petra's tenure—and probably life—would then be at its end was just the icing on the cake.

INVESTIGATION

STELLAR DATE: 08.11.8948 (Adjusted Years)
LOCATION: Intrepid Space Force Academy
REGION: The Palisades, Orbiting Troy, New Canaan System

Following their dinner with Nance, Cary and Saanvi decided to forgo the maglev and walk through the station hub on their way back to Ring Three.

Neither spoke for the first few minutes. Then Cary blurted out, <*Did we jump the gun? I don't want to start some sort of crazy inquiry till we know more.*>

<*Me either,*> Saanvi replied. <*But she lied to us about where she was. If it was official business, she could have said so, and we wouldn't have pushed—which means it isn't on the books.*>

Cary shook her head. <*Unless her official business was 'looking good while out for a run', she wasn't up to anything of the sort.*>

<*You two are overlooking the most obvious answer,*> Faleena said. <*Which is surprising for Saanvi, given how much she thinks about JP.*>

<*Fal!*> Saanvi exclaimed, and Cary glanced at her sister to see her reddening.

<*I don't know…Nance isn't some lovesick pup like Sahn here. She's over sixty years old. Well past boy-chasing age, right?*> Cary asked.

<*I'm not chasing after JP! Have you seen me doing any chasing lately?*>

Faleena chuckled in their minds. <*Have you considered that maybe that's a part of the problem?*>

<***What** problem?*> Saanvi groused.

<*OK, Sahn,*> Cary said with a small grin. <*We'll cut you some slack, but I feel like JP may be too nervous to make the first move with you. Happens sometimes. Doesn't mean there's anything wrong.*>

Saanvi threw her arms in the air and let out a cry of frustration. "Can we keep this conversation on track?

Cary giggled. "Sorry, you're such an easy target."

<*OK, so while you two were driving each other up the wall—*>

<*No, Cary's been driving **me** up the wall, I've done no driving,*> Saanvi interrupted.

<Right, whatever,> Faleena continued. *<Anyway, I did a little snooping on Nance—nothing that will raise any alarms. I have some discretionary access to station surveillance to help keep an eye out for trouble, and—>*

<What does that mean?> Cary interrupted her younger sister. *<'Discretionary access to surveillance'? And why do you have it?>*

<Uhhh…It's part of what Moms made sure I had, so I could keep an eye out for you two.>

<Really? They gave it to you, and not me?> Saanvi sputtered.

Faleena shrugged in their minds. *<I guess they figured that you'd get access your own way, Sahn.>*

<How is it that I'm the straight-laced one here?> Cary asked, her mouth open in surprise as she stared at Faleena in her mind. *<I've just been trying to fly under the radar and not have anyone come down on me for all my past misdeeds.>*

<OK, back on track.> Faleena said. *<I was able to pull logs of Nance's activity. She's on a preapproved list of people I can access, since she interacts with us.>*

<Wow, we have a preapproved spy list!> Saanvi interrupted. *<Can I get in on that?>*

<Sahn, can I finish what I'm trying to say? Seriously. They're right about youngest sisters, no one ever lets them ***talk****.>*

Cary held back a snicker and glanced at Saanvi's mollified look out of the corner of her eye.

<Uh, sorry. Go ahead, Fal,> Saanvi said quietly.

<OK, anyway, she went down to Savannah Park, and was there for over five hours.>

Cary shrugged. *<Maybe she took a nap.>*

<Does anyone think that Nance is the sort who would take a nap in a park?> Saanvi asked. *<She's probably spent less than a year planetside her entire life.>*

Cary shrugged. *<Good point, I guess.>*

<That's not the suspicious part,> Faleena added. *<Parts of the monitoring in the park were offline after they took damage from a live-fire exercise earlier in the day. There's no record of Nance for nearly the entire time she was at the park.>*

Cary's eyes met Saanvi's and the sisters frowned.

<This is getting to be a lot of layered coincidence,> Cary admitted.

<I'm going to start keeping an eye on her,> Faleena said. *<I'll let you two*

know if anything comes up.>

Cary nodded. It felt wrong to spy on Nance; she was one of their mother's friends, plus she had gone above and beyond for New Canaan. But they couldn't ignore evidence because of that. By the same token, they couldn't alert any authorities—such as their father—until they had something more concrete.

<OK,> Cary said. *<But be circumspect. I really hope it turns out to be nothing.>*

<Me too,> Saanvi added.

<I'll be the very essence of circumspection.>

Cary hoped so. She also hoped it was nothing at all—but the feeling in her gut was telling her otherwise.

THE UNSINKABLE RESTAURANT

STELLAR DATE: 08.11.8948 (Adjusted Years)
LOCATION: Imperial Palace Guest Suites
REGION: Alexandria, Bosporus System, Scipio Empire

After a light meal and lengthy discussions regarding what concessions they'd be willing to make to Diana, the three women and their guards left the suite and walked through the palace to a nearby shuttle pad.

Flaherty had called in to let them know he was still beating the bushes, but had developed some leads on where Elena might go. Additionally, Tanis had received another packet from the *I2*, where Terry—who now headed up the SOC with her new rank of colonel—had determined that there were at least two accomplices in Elena's escape.

Terry didn't have IDs yet, but she reported that the traces on the Mark X FlowArmor canister did not align with those of the person who had tampered with the animals' behavior control implants.

The news was troubling, to say the least, but Tanis had expected issues with the non-ISF crew aboard the ship. *Though I hadn't expected a jailbreak to be the first major incident.*

She put it out of her mind as best she could. No one—apart from Bob, who was also on the case—knew the *I2* better than Terry. If there was a trail to be found, and Tanis was certain that there was, Terry would find it.

At this point, the *how* was far less important than the *what.*

As in, what would Elena do?

<*My vote is that she'll sabotage the alliance at some point,*> Angela said. <*A Khardine-Scipio connection will strengthen Sera's position more than any other action, so it is the best plan to stop.*>

<*Thank you, Miss Obvious,*> Tanis replied. <*Are there any other certainties you'd like to point out?*>

<*Just thinking out loud, here,*> Angela replied, seemingly unperturbed by Tanis's ire. <*Unless she has contacts who have an in with the empress, we can rule out an in-person meet.*>

<*Agreed,*> Tanis replied. <*Petra was sleeping with the empress, and it was*

still a cosmic act for her to get us in to see Diana with five days' notice.>

<So, then, who would most strongly oppose an alliance, and have the means to do so? If we were going to sabotage such a thing, that would be my suggestion for where to start: find the opposition, and strengthen them.>

Tanis had spent days reviewing the political structure of the Scipio Empire, but it was, at best, a morass. A thousand star systems broken into quadrants, then regions, then provinces, and within those provinces, individual systems. There was a federal senate and a legislature, an elected prime minister, prelates, and, of course, the empress. Power was not distributed evenly, either. There were leaders of provinces that seemed to have more political clout than leaders of sectors, though it seemed that the four quadrant prelates were supreme over their underlings.

She wasn't surprised that the empress so often felt harried and under attack. She probably was.

<Petra. If there was a quadrant prelate who would oppose a Transcend alliance and be more amicable to an Orion viewpoint, who would that be? My admittedly quick analysis points to Prelate Ryse.>

They reached the door to the shuttle pad as Petra replied, *<Ryse? No, but I can see why you'd think that. He likes to pander to the salt-of-the-earth types along the rimward edge of the Empire, but he also supports almost any tech research he can, drawing those types into the coreward side of his quadrant. He's also been making huge pushes toward the southern edge of the galactic disk. Down there, some of his provinces directly abut Hegemony states.>*

<Then he'd be all for anything that would strengthen Scipio against the Hegemony,> Tanis replied.

<Absolutely. He'll make a show of grudgingly going along with it, though. Where are you going with this?> Petra asked.

<I'm looking at which of the prelates Elena might approach. Then we can watch to see if their position changes, strengthens, and if they work harder to get Diana's ear.>

<I have an informant in Chimellia's offices,> Petra said. *<I don't know that Elena would make a play for one of the prelates, but you never know. She could at least have contacts with someone who has the ear of a prelate.>*

<My money is on Fiona,> Sera said. *<She all but openly hates Diana, and would do anything to weaken her—even if it meant weakening the Empire.>*

<Politics, so much fun,> Tanis commented dryly.

<*I like politics,*> Petra said.

<*If you offer Petra the Transcend presidency, I'll slap you,*> Tanis said privately to Sera as they waited for the High Guard to clear the shuttle before they boarded.

Sera laughed in response. <*I wouldn't do it. She might say 'yes'. Have you noticed that? I never really expect Finaeus, or you, for that matter, to actually take the reins. It's just my way of expressing how hard this is—though I recognize I need a new way to get that across.*>

<*Yes, yes you do.*> Tanis replied before asking on the group's net, <*So what about Fiona, then? Think she'd try to sabotage our efforts here?*>

<*I wouldn't put it past her,*> Petra agreed. <*Once we get Diana on board, we're going to have to deal with Fiona one way or another, whether or not Elena has her ear.*>

Major Valerie ducked her head out of the shuttle and nodded to the trio of women that their transportation was secure, and they filed in with two of the High Guard bringing up the rear.

<*I have to admit, I rather like having your guards about to check things over,*> Petra said as they boarded. <*I usually have to sneak people around to do things.*>

<*You may have to get used to it,*> Sera said.

<*What do you mean?*> Petra asked with lowered brow.

<*Petra, if we forge an alliance with Scipio, who do you think the Transcend's representative will be?*>

Petra looked confused as she took her seat, and then barked a laugh. "Wow," she said aloud. "It never even occurred to me that it would be me. Up until now, I assumed that I would just get transferred to another post and a real ambassador would be assigned."

"It'll give you a reprieve from all the cloak and dagger stuff," Tanis said as the shuttle took off. "Well, some of it, at least."

"I suppose that I could really be myself then, too. Petra of the Transcend, representative of the Khardine Government. Sounds good to say it. Though I may slip up once or twice and say 'Miriam League'."

"You? Slip up?" Sera asked with a raised eyebrow. "I know you too well to believe that. Every hair's position on your head is calculated."

"Well of course they are," Petra said. "Half of them are transceiver antennas."

"So where are we going?" Sera asked. "The Starview, the Subterra?"

"Not tonight," Petra replied. "I checked your records, Sera, and got us reservations for a place you've never been, but one that's fit for a president."

"Oh yeah?" Sera asked. "The Stellarium?"

"Better. The Oceanus."

Sera frowned. "I'm not familiar with that one."

"It's new—well, relatively new. Opened up a decade ago."

"They certainly like restaurants that start with 'S'; glad to see they changed it up a bit," Tanis observed.

"Tanis, to call these establishments 'restaurants' would be like calling a star a flashlight."

"I'll withhold judgment," Tanis replied. "Alexandria is impressive, but none of you have seen the Cho. As big as your world-city is, if the Rings of Callisto were unwound and their levels placed side-by-side, they would be far larger than this place."

"I would love to see the Cho someday," Petra mused. "Perhaps when this is all over, and you two have conquered the galaxy, you can assign me to Sol. I'd love to see what's there."

"It's all yours," Tanis replied. "I have no intention of ever returning to that place."

"Be careful what you wish for," Sera advised.

"You should keep in mind," Petra added, "much of Alexandria is over a thousand levels deep. Over four trillion human souls reside on this great sphere."

"Four trillion?" Tanis couldn't hide her amazement. "I take it back. This place may have the Cho beat."

She gazed out the window at the never-ending city, wondering what it would be like to grow up in such a place. Perhaps not so different from the Cho; though here, there would be sky overhead—not just another ring and layers of sweeps wrapped around one another.

After several minutes, she could see a blue line in the distance, peeking out between a row of towers that stretched a dozen kilometers into the air.

"The Adrian Ocean," Petra said as they passed between the massive spires and over the great blue expanse. Ships plied the water—some in it and some above it, moving between large floating islands drifting near the coast.

The shuttle continued across the open ocean until it came to a relatively small—at least compared to the endless sea around them—pad standing atop a wide shaft that disappeared beneath the waves.

"And here we are," Petra said. "The Oceanus."

"Doesn't look like much," Tanis said with a smirk as the shuttle settled onto the pad. Valerie disembarked first with Sean, the only other one of the High Guard accompanying them, before calling up that it was clear.

The pad was a simple affair, protected from the wind and crashing waves by a grav field. Shuttles dotted the surface, and Tanis estimated that three hundred of the craft could easily land on it. Possibly more if the cradles could stack.

In the center of the pad was a tall golden spire, and it was to that bright needle that Petra led them. At its entrance, a tall man in a long coat bowed graciously. "Madam President, my ladies, you are most welcome here this evening. I do hope you'll enjoy everything the Oceanus has to offer."

"Thank you," Sera said, as Petra led them into the spire.

Within was a single lift car, perfectly round, like a droplet of water floating in zero gravity.

The floor was a grav field, and Tanis felt her feet bounce slightly as she trod across its surface.

"Nice effect," she said.

"Just wait," Petra said with a grin.

Once the three women and the High Guard were all within the bubble, it dropped.

Tanis could only feel the slightest flutter in the pit of her stomach—courtesy of the inertial dampeners—but looking up, she watched the top of the golden spire disappear at an alarming rate.

"Well that's one way to go down."

"Express elevator to hell," Major Valerie said quietly, citing the name FROD Marines gave to their drop pods.

Tanis peered out the sides of the bubble, noting that the golden shaft had either become translucent, or was gone altogether. The idea was slightly alarming, as thousands of kilograms of ocean water lay on the other side of the bubble.

"What's that?" Valerie asked.

Tanis looked to her right and saw a massive shadow pass by. For a moment, she thought she saw a four-meter eyeball blink at them, but then it was gone.

"That's a kraken," Petra said. "The big ones are over a hundred meters long. Some former ruler's fancy, so I'm told. There are only a few thousand of them left, but Diana is not a fan, and has a program in place to reduce their numbers further."

"Can't say I blame her," Sera said. "I bet when one of those things gets upset, or even mildly curious, they can wreak havoc.

Petra chuckled. "Yeah, havoc has been wreaked in the past. Sometimes they get in fights; when they do it near the shore, it makes a pretty serious mess."

The bubble continued to descend. When Tanis's augmented vision could finally make out the ocean floor, she estimated that they had reached a depth of seven kilometers.

Though there were low ridges along the floor on either side of the bubble—reflecting light from some unknown source—directly below, there was only darkness.

"We've another two klicks to go," Petra announced. "Oceanus is at the bottom of the rift."

"Quite the place to put a restaurant," Sera said. "Though not as bad as the people out at Judas, who spent decades trying to put one inside a star."

"Oh, yeah?" Tanis asked. "How'd that go?"

Sera spread her hands wide and made a fizzling sound, eliciting a laugh from Petra.

Tanis could just barely make out the walls of the rift they were slipping into. On one side, she gauged the jagged stone to be thirty meters away, while on the other, the distance was closer to sixty.

As she watched the rock slide by, she began to notice more ambient light, and looked down to see a dim glow beneath them. The glow grew brighter until it became an elongated blob. The blob slowly resolved, becoming clearer, until Tanis knew its shape.

"It's a sunken ship," she said.

"Not just any sunken ship," Petra corrected her. "The Oceanus; the great ocean liner from Terra in the nineteenth century."

"The what?" Tanis asked.

"I thought you were from Sol?" Petra replied. "The Oceanus—the ship that could never be sunk, the one that went down on its maiden voyage. They replicated it down here."

"I'm not an expert on that era of history," Tanis said, "but I'm pretty sure there was no such ship."

"Are you sure?" Petra asked.

<Certainly not in the nineteenth century,> Angela said. *<With some rare exceptions, ships were wooden in that age. This ship, however, is the Titanic.>*

"The what?"

<Titanic, unsinkable ship, sailed from Southampton England in 1912. It struck an iceberg in the north Atlantic Ocean on the way to New York City,> Angela supplied. *<It's a rather tragic story; since they didn't expect it to sink, it didn't have enough lifeboats. A lot of people died in the waters.>*

"Well that's a rather melancholy thought as we descend with nine kilometers of water over our heads," Sera said.

"Huh, I can't believe they boned the backstory," Petra shrugged. "Still, the place is amazing. It's a lot bigger than the ship, too. Goes a long way back into the cliff."

Now that they were closer, Tanis could see the great ship lying against the rift wall at a forty-five-degree angle. When the bubble reached the listing deck of the ship, it began to move laterally toward a set of doors that stood wide open, seemingly protected from the waters by a grav field.

As the bubble approached the doors, 'down' shifted so that the deck of the ship no longer appeared to be at an angle—though the cliffs above seemed to loom drunkenly overhead.

Movement to their right caught Tanis's eye, and she saw a group of mermaids swim past. Their heads were together, and bubbles trailed from their noses as they cavorted around one another.

One with a long blue tail and luminescent pink hair swam toward their bubble and passed through its walls as though they were nonexistent. Even though it had passed from water into open air, the mermaid continued to swim, spinning around the group and laughing at their amazement.

"Welcome to the great Oceanus!" the mermaid said after she had made several loops around them. "Here, at the bottom of the sea, may your deepest desires come true!"

She flicked her tail against Tanis's thighs, and caressed Sera's arm before planting a kiss on Petra's cheek.

Then the mermaid passed out of the bubble once more and joined her friends in twisting around one another in their sinuous dance.

"Well that's not something you see every day," Tanis said as she watched the mermaids disappear over the edge of the deck. "That looked like a permanent mod; not just the sort of thing you put on for work."

"I imagine it is," Petra replied. "Takes some amount of effort to get the a-grav generators in their tails, too—or so I've been told. Without the a-grav, the ocean would crush those poor women."

"Easy on the eyes, though," Sera said approvingly. "Did you notice that both the man up top and the mermaid had no small amount of double entendre in their greetings?"

"There's a lot of fun behind closed doors down here, but it's not required, and it's not the main theme," Petra assured them. "The food really is to die for, and the setting is amazing, don't you think?"

"It really is," Tanis agreed. "I've been a lot of places, but never this far beneath an ocean. It's a tiny bit claustrophobic, but it also feels a bit like space."

"A lot of people say that," Petra replied with a nod.

By then the bubble had reached the doors, and they could see into the ship.

Two men stood at the top of the stairs and reached into the bubble. "My ladies," one of them said. "Welcome to Oceanus. We're so glad to have you with us this evening. Please step down into the ship."

Valerie brushed past the two men and walked down the stairs first, peering about before nodding. Tanis had her nanocloud out, as well; she had no desire to be ambushed down here. She'd also set the nanoscopic bots to let her know if the air pressure changed, or if they heard anything that sounded like a leak.

Despite her annoying trepidation over being so far underwater, Tanis was determined to enjoy the evening. She realized that there had been almost no downtime since Elena's arrival in New Canaan half a year ago.

Tonight, there was little she could do to drive any of her goals forward. She would enjoy herself like the attaché to the president she was supposed to be and push all her worries aside.

Once they were assembled at the bottom of the stairs, Tanis could see that they were standing on a landing above a vast open foyer. The glass above gave a view of the looming rift wall and the odd mermaid swimming by. Tanis noticed that there were more mermaids within, as well, swimming through the air around and cavorting above their heads, laughing as they went.

Petra led them down the curved staircase to the foyer's floor, where other guests stood, drinking from fluted glasses while men and women whose bodies were half-snake—or perhaps eel—moved between them, offering hors d'oeuvres and refilling glasses.

"We'll be called into one of the dining rooms when they're ready for us," Petra said. "I didn't get to pick, since I booked so late. I nearly had to kill someone just to get an opening."

"You didn't, though, did you?" Sera asked with a raised eyebrow.

Petra tittered. "Of course not." *<But I did have to make them very sick.>*

A man slithered up to Tanis and hissed. "A drink, madam?"

"Brandy, straight," Tanis replied and the man slithered on to the others, dutifully ignoring Valerie and Sean.

Tanis looked at the other people standing in the foyer and felt moderately underdressed. She wore only a simple black dress with brushed steel bands around her waist and above her breasts. Her hair was pinned back, since she couldn't abide having it in her face, and her shoes were low and comfortable.

Sera was sheathed in black from neck to toe, with blue lights tracing slowly across her body in mesmerizing patterns. She was wearing towering heels, however, putting her a few centimeters above Tanis for once. Her hair was down and curling around her shoulders.

Petra was a vision in white in a thigh-length sheath dress, with her rose-colored legs peeking out before disappearing into white knee-high boots. Her arms were also rose in hue, ending in white gloves. Her normally dark hair was also rose-colored this evening, as were her lips and eyes.

The other patrons were a far more diversely dressed assemblage. Some were attired not much differently than Tanis or Sera, but many were in outfits—and modifications—so elaborate that they made the staff look positively normal by comparison.

<Is it just me, or do that man and woman over there look like desiccated

corpses?> Tanis asked.

<*It was a fad awhile back,*> Petra replied. <*Lasted all of five minutes, but some people haven't gotten the message that it's time to move on.*>

Angela chortled. <*Nice pun.*>

<*I can see his heart,*> Tanis frowned. <*I hope we're not seated by them.*>

<*Are you looking for a spare?*> Angela asked with a giggle but quelled it when Tanis glowered at her. <*Sorry, you left it wide open. Damn, now I'm punning too!*>

Sera directed a mental laugh at Tanis. <*I could hug them and transfer my skin to protect your sensitive eyes.*>

Tanis only sighed and shook her head in response.

<*You can do that?*> Petra asked.

Sera nodded. <*Sure can. Did it to Elena…*>

<*I might have to hit you up for that,*> Petra said.

<*Stars, you're like a plague, Sera,*> Tanis laughed.

They only had to wait ten minutes before a chime came to the group over the Link.

"Oh, wow, we got the fire room!" Petra said. "You're in for a real treat now. I didn't tell you about this because I didn't think we'd get it, but it's going to blow you away."

<*Not keen on your choice of words,*> Angela said with a smirk.

<*Sorry,*> Petra replied. <*You'll be very impressed.*>

Petra led them though the crowd to a glowing red door, which a man—who looked like some sort of strange crustacean—opened with a bow. On the other side was a long, twisting staircase, which Valerie took the lead in descending.

Tanis saw a dull red glow below them and realized that the staircase was lowering as they descended, as though it were drilling down into the rock below. With the staircase speeding their descent, they reached the bottom in a minute. Then they stepped out onto a balcony looking out over a great crevasse.

There were only twelve tables on the balcony—three were occupied—and Tanis wove between them to look out over the edge. There was no railing, so she leaned over carefully. Her unaided vision could barely see the bottom, but as she cycled various modes, she realized that the deep gouge in the planet was over ten kilometers deep, and that at the bottom lay a lake of magma.

"The ocean floor above is just a plug," Petra explained as she reached Tanis's side. "In front of you is the Icanus Plate, and behind is the Homerian Plate."

"Seriously?" Sera asked, her voice filled with awe. "We're going to have our supper halfway through the planet's crust, staring down at its mantle?"

"Is it good enough for Madam President?" Petra asked with a grin.

Sera laughed. "I suppose it will have to do."

"Ahem," came a voice from behind them.

Tanis turned to see a man who appeared to be made of basalt rock, on top of which flowed rivulets of lava. Even his eyes were red; streams of lava flowed from them down his face.

"Crap," Sera said, and laughed. "You scared me."

"Of course, Madam President. You may have your selection of tables this evening. Would you like to sit at the edge?"

"I sure would," Sera replied, and the magma man led them to a table further down the balcony.

Tanis eased into her chair and looked down at the planet's mantle far below. "Gotta say, this is a first. Granted, I've been deep inside planets before, but never one with an active core."

"Nice rhyme," Sera said with a soft laugh.

Their server approached—a magma woman this time, and instead of hard angles and jutting rock, her body appeared to be completely molten, her form sinuous, and her voice sounding like hissing steam as she asked what they'd like to drink.

"It's going to feel weird when we're done here and we get back out into the shit," Sera said after the woman left.

Tanis checked their nano-suppression before replying. "We travel around on a country-sized starship with almost one hundred square kilometers of parkland. We don't really do normal, either."

"Slumming it on the *I2*, that's how I roll," Sera snickered.

The three spoke of trivialities for a time, and then selected their appetizers while Valerie and Sean stood watch at either end of the balcony. Before long, all but one table had filled up, and their molten server returned to clear their plates.

"Would you like to sssselect your nexsst courssse now?"

Tanis had considered a dish called 'the mermaid tail', but a part of her worried that they might actually cut the tails off the poor women to make it, and she didn't want to ask for fear of an affirmative answer. Instead, she selected the seafood bisque. Once the server hissed and steamed away, Tanis rose to visit the ladies room.

The room was down a stone hall behind the augering staircase, and Tanis walked into it, aware that Sean was following behind.

She really didn't need the High Guard to escort her, but it was his job—a job she had given him—so she wasn't about to deride him for it.

The facilities were a series of individual rooms along the hall, and Tanis took the first one. She was washing her hands when her nanocloud detected a new set of probes moving down the staircase.

Every patron of the restaurant had probes deployed, but they were large, ungainly things; the smallest were a dozen micrometers across. These new probes were under two micrometers—clearly more advanced technology than most people on Alexandria possessed.

Tanis directed her nanocloud to intercept and examine the probes. From what she could discern, they were of Transcend design.

<Petra, do you have any agents here keeping an eye on things?> Tanis asked.

<I don't, no—other than the shuttle pilot. It was hard enough getting us and two guards down, I figured that your renowned ass-kicking abilities would have to do if we got in trouble.>

<Did you deploy a new passel of probes?>

<No, I've been pulling the feed from Sera's,> Petra replied. *<I figured there was no need to cloud things with my inferior tech.>*

Tanis passed her feed to Petra. *<Then I think we might have a problem.>*

<Shit!> Petra exclaimed. *<That's definitely Transcend tech.>*

<Hand issue,> Sera confirmed. *<We should get somewhere safer. Sitting next to a ten-kilometer drop when someone could suddenly hack the grav fields feels exceptionally unsafe.>*

<Agreed,> Tanis said as she stepped out of the restroom. *<Join me.>*

She switched to a combat net and brought the entire group in. *<Sean, it looks like there's a hidden door at the end of this hall. Get it open.>*

<Yes, ma'am,> Sean replied and hustled to the end of the hall.

<I told you I didn't like coming down here,> Major Valerie said.

<I don't recall that,> Tanis said.

Angela chuckled. *<She said it with her eyes.>*

<Door's open,> Sean reported, and the group hustled into the service hall. It was a straight corridor with three cleaning bot alcoves. By the sounds of it, a kitchen was at one end, and a lift was at the other.

<Let's get to that lift,> Tanis said. *<Valerie and I will go up first; you three wait 'til we give the all clear.>*

Valerie gave Sean a significant look and then pressed the call button for the lift. A moment later, the door opened, revealing a figure in wet, powered armor.

Tanis's lightwand was already in her hand, and she slashed at the figure's rifle while Valerie and Sean both fired shots from their pulse pistols at the figure's head.

The enemy fell back, and Tanis reached forward, grabbing his rifle while planting a foot on his knee. Though she pulled with all her strength, the enemy's powered armor was too much, and she couldn't wrest the rifle free before the attacker fired a series of shots.

Pulse blasts thrummed out into the corridor, one catching Sean in the shoulder and spinning him to the side. Petra stood in front of Sera as Tanis slammed her lightwand into the rifle's trigger mechanism, cutting it apart and taking off the attacker's finger.

The man reared back, and Tanis could hear a bellow from within his helmet. By then, she had analyzed his armor and found a data port on the upper right side of his torso. She slammed her palm against it, feeding nano into the armor's control systems.

<I'm in,> Angela said. *<Annnnnd…he's done.>*

The attacker's armor seized, and Tanis could hear him grunting and straining.

"That's what you get for bringing a gun to a knife fight," Tanis said with a smirk, and then drew the man's sidearm, easily disabling the biolock. "Even so, I think I'll borrow this."

"You OK?" Sera asked Sean.

"Just fine. The Mark X armor comes to the rescue again."

Tanis considered the risk of splitting up the team versus them all riding the elevator together.

She saw a cook peer out from the kitchen at the far end of the hall. The cook's eyes widened at the sight of the group standing over a frozen—yet still menacing—figure in powered armor with their weapons drawn.

"Is there another way up?" Tanis called down to the cook. "Other than the stairs out front and this lift?"

The cook shook her head, and Tanis made the call. "Everyone in the lift. Val, Sean, help me move this guy; he's going to be our shield. Let's face him outward so if his buddies are out there, they think he's walking out, not holding someone inside."

They managed to turn the armor-locked figure around, and his angry yelling barely made it through his helmet.

"Think I should take his helmet off so they're less likely to shoot at him?" Sean asked.

"He'll be too loud," Sera shook her head. "Keep him in there. If his head's exposed and they shoot, they could kill him. Then they won't hold back anymore."

"Good point, Madam President."

"Sean, when we're in private, you can call me 'Sera'."

"Of course, President Sera," Sean said with a wink.

"Stars, you're incorrigible," Sera muttered.

Tanis pushed the button for the top floor, which read 'M'. She suspected it was the foyer where they had initially waited for their table.

<Angela, I assume you've wandered into their network by now; what other ways are there out of here? I don't fancy riding that bubble back up.>

<Why, Tanis! I thought you'd never ask. There is indeed a lift that goes up to the ocean floor. When you get into the foyer, the third door on the right will take you to it.>

<Everyone get that?> Tanis asked as the lift stopped and the doors opened onto another service corridor. She peered around their captive shield and didn't see anyone.

<Snark and all,> Sera replied.

<I'm taking the lead,> Major Valerie said. *<Sean, with me.>*

<You need to stop rushing ahead all the time; you're making Valerie grumpy,> Angela admonished privately.

Tanis gave a mental sigh. *<I know. 'Let her do her job', and all that.>*

<Well, that too. I was thinking more about how I'm in here also, and really want to live to see our youngest daughter again. Plus the organic ones—they're rather important to me, as well.>

<Noted.>

<Joe, too. I like Joe.>

<OK, Angela, I understand!>

Valerie had reached the first intersection, and was checking down the hall visually after scouting it with nano. She looked back and waved the rest of the group forward. They stacked up in the hall, and then Valerie and Sean advanced to the door at the far end.

Tanis looked back to see Sera grab the armored soldier's arm and rock him forward, so his right side would block the lift door from closing. Then she followed the others into the hall.

Tanis's nano flushed out around the cracks, and they saw the foyer nearly deserted—if one ignored the six armored figures holding a group of patrons and staff at gunpoint.

<OK, everyone; here is where we strip,> Tanis said, and everyone except Sera pulled off their clothes and configured their Mark X FlowArmor to an opaque color before triggering its stealth mode.

<They're going to notice the door opening,> Sera said as she glanced back at the enemy soldier.

Tanis sighed. *<OK, but let's be quick about it.>*

Three minutes later, the man was unconscious and tucked in an alcove around the corner. Sean was now in the soldier's armor. It wasn't the auto-adjusting type and it fit him the best, so he was the sacrificial lamb—not that Tanis expected to lose anyone.

Sean pushed the door open and yelled through the armor's speakers, "They have some sort of Link suppressor and are holed up in the lower kitchen. We need backup!"

He stood half in the doorway, and the four stealthed women slipped past him. Petra and Sera moved to the door that led to next lift, and Valerie and Tanis headed toward the six enemy troops in the foyer.

"What happened to your finger, Larry?" one of the enemy soldiers asked as she walked toward him.

"Damn thing almost got blown off," Sean replied.

The woman who had approached him shook her head. "Wrong answer. Larry's behind me; you're supposed to be Johnny."

"Aw, shit," Sean said as he lifted his pulse pistol.

The woman was a hair faster and had her rifle—a kinetic slug thrower—leveled on Sean. She had just slipped her finger off the trigger guard when Tanis drove her lightwand into the woman's right hip joint.

It took two sharp strikes, but the blade sank in, and the woman screamed. She swung her rifle at Tanis, but by then Sean was on her, driving both his fists into the underside of her chin.

Her head snapped back with a *crack*, and she dropped to the floor.

<It felt like the helmet had a poor front latch mechanism when I put this one on,> Sean commented. *<Looks like I was right.>*

Valerie was already among the other five attackers and had wrested a weapon away from one while they were distracted. She took cover behind the staircase to hack through her prize's biolock.

Two of the enemies—including the one who lost their rifle—were approaching Valerie, while the other three were advancing on Sean. Sean had grabbed the downed woman's rifle and was crouching behind her slumped body as he disabled the rifle's biolock. The body gave him moderate cover, but the enemies pulse blasts were rocking him back and forth.

Tanis wasted no time in rushing toward the three soldiers who were attacking Sean. She leapt into the air and drove her lightwand through the weapon of the first of the three, hoping for a repeat performance.

This woman, however, spotted the glowing wand—seemingly in midair, as it swung toward her. She jerked her weapon to the side, and Tanis's strike missed the mark, glancing across the woman's forearm instead.

"Where the fuck is this person?" one shouted, just as Sean finished bypassing the biolock on the weapon he held, and opened fire on the woman Tanis had engaged with.

A moment later, Valerie followed suit, driving the two enemies she was engaged with back into the foyer.

A member of the restaurant staff seemed to realize this was a good time to get out, and gestured for the guests and other staff to follow him.

<That should make things a bit easier,> Tanis said.

<There are more of these soldiers sweeping the restaurants and the other…facilities. This place is a lot bigger than I'd thought,> Angela admitted. *<I disrupted their comms with the nanocloud—I hope.>*

Tanis closed with one of the attackers and swung her lightwand across his helmet, scoring a gash across the optical inputs. The man stumbled backward, and Sean fired three shots at his helmet, each one hitting the mark Tanis had made. The first one cracked it, the second split it open, and the third made a sickly, smushed watermelon sound.

Tanis saw that Valerie was down to one opponent, when the final enemy turned and ran for one of the restaurant doors. Tanis ran after, sliding her lightwand back into her thigh while drawing the twin blades from their place in her forearms.

The woman must have caught sight of the blades' movement through the air, because she spun about, backpedaling as she fired wildly.

Tanis dropped and slid toward the enemy, hoping she could fit between the woman's legs in their wide stance.

<*There, right at the crotch,*> Angela said.

<*See it,*> Tanis replied.

As she slid beneath the woman, Tanis drove one of her blades into a loose joint at the woman's groin, wrenching it sideways and severing her muscles and femoral artery.

The woman's scream came through her armor's audible systems as Tanis rose behind her. There was a loose armor plate at her left shoulder, and Tanis drove another blade through it before kicking the woman over.

<*You about finished out there?*> Sera asked.

Tanis grabbed one of the rifles before following Valerie toward the door that Sera and Petra had used. Sean came behind, using his armored body to cover their retreat while his weapon swept across the room.

Valerie grabbed another rifle and an ammo pouch, as did Tanis; it ruined their stealth to be toting the gear around, but it gave them options.

The door led to a long hall, and at the end of it was a ten-meter square space before a pair of lifts. On the floor were two more of the enemy combatants.

<*Nice work,*> Tanis said.

<*I'm not just a pretty face,*> Petra smirked.

<*I'm really surprised that this place doesn't have any automated defense systems,*> Valerie said as they reached the lift, and Sera called the car down.

<*It does,*> Angela replied. <*Alastar and I are working on getting them back online.*>

<*They severed physical power connections to the system control unit. I've managed to take control of a repair bot and am on my way there,*> Alastar added.

Angela snorted. <*And by 'repair bot', he means a cleaning bot with an armature that we hope can do the work we need.*>

<*It's worth a shot,*> Alastar replied.

<*Angela,*> Sera said. <*Can you bring the other lift car down as well? Then when we go up, make the indicators at the top level not change?*>

<*Umm…yes, I do believe I can. Second car coming down now.*>

<*I like the way you think,*> Valerie said. <*Sean, grab the 'nades off these two. They're just light conc, but they'll give us the element of surprise. We take the first lift.*>

<*We'll be fifteen seconds behind you,*> Tanis said.

The second lift came down, and Tanis dragged one of the dead soldiers in while Sera and Petra grabbed the other. They stacked them inside the door in a gruesome barricade and waited till Angela started the lift on its climb.

<*Think they have an ocean floor maglev running out here?*> Sera asked.

<*Probably, but I hope they have some sort of sub as backup. I don't really fancy being in a train car under the ocean with who-knows-what out there gunning for us.*>

<*Good point,*> Sera replied.

<*So who do you think is behind this?*> Tanis asked Petra as the car climbed to the surface. <*Sera said that nano looked Hand-issued, but those goons we just fought were locals, by their gear.*>

<*Not one of the better outfits, I'd wager,*> Petra replied. <*No sane merc company would attack a place like this. Half their clients dine here. It would be bad for business.*>

Tanis nodded. <*But if they're mercs, someone hired them—someone in The Hand.*>

<*I have four candidates in mind—at least of the team that's here on Alexandria: Phillip, Syara, Harold, and Judy. They all exhibited some concern over my decision to align myself with the Khardine government in defiance of the Directorate's orders. None of them have an AI, so they didn't get the added convincing I got from Alastar when he was freed.*>

<*Thank you, again, for that, Angela,*> Alastar said. <*To think I had lived my entire life, up until a week ago, enslaved by that monster…*>

<*Never trust a strange, god-like AI,*> Angela intoned. <*Unless it's Bob. You can trust Bob.*>

<*I'm very excited to meet him,*> Alastar replied.

<OK, we're almost there,> Tanis announced. *<How's that repair going on the automated defenses?>*

<Slowly,> Angela replied. *<They shot the hell out of the thing, too. Don't count on it coming back online.>*

The nanocloud reached the top of the lift shaft a few seconds before Valerie and Sean's car. The space was a large atrium—nicer than she expected for the staff entrance, but she supposed it may also double as an official entrance for anyone who didn't enjoy the bubble ride.

She spotted a dozen figures in the same armor as the enemies below, none behind cover at present, and a man and woman in lighter armor.

The man was pacing back and forth while the woman stared off through the clear overhead dome.

The nanocloud picked up the man's voice. "You thinking about going fishing?"

"I hate those stupid krakens they made. Who would put something like that in their oceans?"

The man shrugged. "Bored aristocrats, I guess."

As he spoke, the doors to the first lift car opened, and Valerie and Sean threw out their fistfuls of conc grenades. They must have reset the timers, because the explosions came only two seconds after the throw.

Some of Tanis's nano was taken out by the blast, but the rest was able to feed the two High Guards targeting data. Two of the mercs and the woman fell before the doors even opened on the second lift car.

Tanis, Petra, and Sera were crouched behind the stacked bodies and let fire with their own weapons. Tanis held two and fired both at the same points on one enemy's armor, then another. When the initial salvo was over, another three targets were down.

That left eight mercs and the man.

"Hey, Phillip," Petra shouted out into the hazy atrium. "You're fired!"

"If you actually represented the Directorate, that might matter," he shouted back.

"Phillip, stop this now. Airtha's not someone you want to have running the Transcend," Sera called out. "The military is flocking to me; anyone with an AI has realized what Airtha was doing."

"Or *you* somehow subverted their AI," Phillip shouted back, and shots rang out from several of the merc positions, striking the armored bodies stacked in their car.

Over the combat net, Tanis saw Valerie and Sean sight on the shooters and take one out with multiple shots to the helmet.

More weapons fire erupted from both sides, and another two enemy soldiers fell. The battle wasn't one-sided, though. Tanis got hit in the side when a slug penetrated the lift-wall, and Sera took a bullet in the neck that knocked her over.

<*I'm OK,*> Sera said as she struggled back up. <*That smarts like a mother…armor's not resetting, either. I can't turn my head.*>

Angela chuckled. <*Look at its injury detection calibration; it can't tell if your skin is damaged or not.*>

<*Oh, shoot, look at that.*>

Tanis was only half-listening to the banter. They were wearing the enemy down, but not fast enough.

<*Last mag,*> Sean called out.

<*Me too,*> Petra added.

As they spoke, another six mercs rushed into the atrium, taking cover and bringing suppressive fire to bear on the lifts.

<*They're shredding the walls,*> Valerie said. <*We have to go back down; we can secure a part of the restaurant and hold out for rescue.*>

Tanis was about to issue the order—which was terrifying in its own right, because the mercs could rain holy hell on them from above.

<*No need,*> Alastar assured them.

A moment later, six autoturrets came out of the walls and opened fire on the mercs from behind. Tanis took advantage of the distraction and leapt out of the lift, taking cover behind an ornate column.

The rest of the team followed her lead and advanced into the atrium. They moved from one column to the next, grabbing mags from fallen enemies and pushing the remaining foes back into the autoturrets.

A minute later, it was over.

Sean moved forward, checking the fallen mercs and kicking weapons away, while Valerie limped over to Tanis.

"You sure know how to show a girl a good time…ma'am," she said.

"You hurt?" Tanis asked.

"Just blunt force bruising."

Though Tanis couldn't see Valerie's face behind the flow armor, she could hear the pain in the woman's voice.

"And a broken femur, right?"

"Fractured, not broken."

Sera leaned her back against one of the columns. "So, think they have a sub?"

"Not anymore," a new voice said. "But I do."

Tanis turned and looked toward the doors on the far side of the room to see Flaherty, once more hefting a railgun.

"You're late," she scolded him.

"You may not have heard it with all your shooting in here, but I blew another sub with two dozen mercs in it. So you're welcome."

"Testy, testy," Sera said as she pushed off from the column and approached her escort. "You have your own sub, I assume?"

"Of course."

Petra chuckled. "You always just show up with the big guns, or is this special?"

"The minute I heard you were going out for a fancy dinner, I began securing an evac," Flaherty replied.

"And what if we didn't need it?" Petra asked.

"Then I would have seen you back at the suites later," he said with a shrug.

"Would you have told us you were watching after us?" Tanis asked.

Flaherty shook his head. "Nope. How do I look like the last-minute savior if you know I'm there? You'd get sloppy."

"Well, now you just told us," Petra said.

"You'll forget," Flaherty shrugged again.

"I'll never forget," Sera said, and her armor flowed away from her face as she gave the man a peck on his cheek. "Take me to my chariot, Jeeves!"

<*I can't even…*> Angela sighed.

They rode the sub to the surface and transferred into a second shuttle—the mercs still held the landing pad where the bubble had descended—then flew back to the palace.

The team reclined on the seats, eating what snacks were aboard. Their flow armor was drawn off their heads and colored matte black across the rest of their bodies.

Sean had found a first aid kit containing a bone stabilizer on the shuttle and injected it into Valerie's thigh. She bit down on a towel and gave a muffled scream, as the injector drove a rod into her femur and pulled it back into place before applying a bio-glue.

"Fucking barbarism here," she said after Sean pulled the stabilizer away. "Why doesn't that thing have pain suppressants?"

Sean looked at it. "Oh, shit…that was a separate prep injection I was supposed to run."

"Sean…" Valerie seethed, as her subordinate backed away.

"Uh… sorry, Major. I didn't think the thing would do that without auto suppressing."

Valerie threw her head back and took a few steadying breaths. "Well, it still hurts like all fuck, so do you think you could apply the mother fucking pain suppressors now? I'm low on nano after all that shit down there."

She glanced at Tanis and Sera, who were smirking. "Uh… sorry for my language."

"What language?" Sera asked as Sean nervously approached the major once more.

Thirty minutes later, they reached a landing pad at the palace and, though they'd left the weapons in the shuttle and could not possibly hide anything beneath the second-skin of the flow armor, the palace guards checked them over very thoroughly.

As they were examined, Petra talked with their lieutenant about the attack and detailed their escape, leaving out the stealth capabilities of the flow armor.

Eventually they were allowed back to their suites.

"Stars, I'm still famished," Sera said as they entered.

Tanis nodded in agreement as she stepped into the main room. Her gaze landed on a cloaked figure sitting on one of their sofas, and she reached for her lightwand. The figure pushed back its hood and revealed herself to be the empress.

"Seems like you had an eventful evening," Diana said. "I'd like to hear all about it."

EXPLANATIONS

STELLAR DATE: 08.11.8948 (Adjusted Years)
LOCATION: Imperial Palace Guest Suites
REGION: Alexandria, Bosporus System, Scipio Empire

Tanis eyed the empress for a moment before casually walking into the room. "Just your average evening assassination attempt," she said while dropping into a chair across from Diana.

"Based on what you're all wearing," Diana waved at their matte-black Mark X FlowArmor, "I'm not certain if you're the targets or the assassins."

"We're well-prepared targets," Sera said. "I'm really annoyed, too. That restaurant was amazing; I've never seen anything like it."

Diana nodded. "Yes, it's quite impressive—though I never had the heart to tell them that they got the ship's name wrong."

"See!" Tanis turned to address Sera and Petra. "The ship *is* the Titanic."

"Surely that's not what you came to talk to us about," Sera said. "I have to admit that I'm surprised to see you here alone."

Diana nodded. "My guards think I'm in my rooms. I have a few ways to get around undetected; makes my life a lot easier, not to have every action recorded and monitored."

"And where are our other three guards?" Tanis asked Diana—though Valerie had already found them on the team's private network.

"Nearby. I asked them if they could wait across the hall in an empty suite for the time being. I imagine they're still monitoring the room, though. I think these three should go join them.

Tanis glanced at Valerie. "We have injured."

"We have medical facilities here. Though I imagine yours are much better than ours—us being lowly Inner Stars denizens, and all."

Tanis chuckled. "That would be true. Valerie, you can return to the ship or get a medic to come down."

Valerie nodded. "I'll be across the hall."

Sera and Flaherty exchanged several long looks before he left with Valerie and Sean, and Tanis re-swept the room with her nano.

Sera took a seat beside Tanis while Petra walked to the room's bar and poured herself a drink.

"Anyone else want anything?" she asked.

"A water would be nice," Tanis replied.

Sera glanced at Tanis and shook her head. "All-business-Tanis tonight, is it?

Tanis nodded, and Sera turned to Petra. "A sweet white wine, if there is one." Then she turned to the empress. "Are you here to chastise us for making a mess?"

Diana shook her head. "I couldn't care less about that. I assume you were having some trouble with…what was it, 'Airtha not being the one you'd want running the Transcend', and how 'the military was flocking to you'."

"That's some fast intel gathering," Tanis said with a wry smile.

"Alexandria is a complex place, with the population of a hundred star systems; this planet requires a firm hand to keep under control," Diana replied implacably.

"What you overheard has to do with the rest of the story we wanted to tell you earlier," Petra said as she finally took a seat. "The death of Sera's father has sparked a civil war. Airtha was her father's capital."

"No," Diana shook her head and looked to Sera. "You referred to Airtha as a person. Who is she?"

Tanis glanced at Sera and nodded slowly. "If we are to forge an alliance with Diana, we need to spill it eventually. Might as well be now."

Sera swallowed and straightened her posture, then took a sip of her wine. "Airtha is my mother—sort of."

Diana clasped her hands and placed them on her knee. "This sounds like it'll be good."

Sera proceeded to tell Diana everything, from her mother's mission to the galactic core, to her subversion of all the Transcend's AIs. She told of Elena's betrayal on the bridge of the *Galadrial,* and of the invasion of New Canaan, and the presence of the *I2* outside the Bosporus System.

Diana didn't ask a single question through the entire tale, but Tanis could see them building up behind her eyes. When Sera was done, Diana took a deep breath.

"I'm going to need something stronger than wine."

Petra rose and poured Diana a glass of bourbon, which she wordlessly handed to the empress before returning to her seat.

Diana ticked items off her fingers one at a time. "Jump gates, nanotech, *pico*tech, core AI, growing entire ships, AI subversion, civil war, galactic war, things in the dark layer? Do I have it all? Just those few things going on? You know, on top of the fact that the FGT isn't gone, and is itself involved in a civil war—from my point of view."

"There are probably more things, if you count what Orion is up to in the Hegemony and the Pleiades, and what they're pushing the Nietzscheans to do," Sera replied.

"I doubt Constantine requires much pushing," Diana said with a heavy sigh. "If ever there was a power-hungry man, it is he. He'll see Nietzschea spread to the edges of the galaxy, if he can. I suppose that's one advantage. The Trisilieds, Nietzschea, the Hegemony…all of Orion's allies are expansionists; they want to grow in power and size at any cost. At some point, those allies will become foes. Either to one another, or to Orion."

"And you?" Tanis asked. "You're not interested in spreading Scipio's power?"

Diana rose from her seat on the sofa, her long dark dress flowing gracefully around her. "I used to be, when I first took the throne. When I remade Scipio into what it is today. But managing an empire is not easy work—as I imagine you know, Sera. You're new at the job, but the realization does not take long to settle in."

Sera laughed. "You're right about that."

Diana stood at the window and stared out at the dimly lit palace gardens. "I believe that Scipio is probably about as big as it can get without fracturing. Stars, it's already on the edge of fracturing in some places."

"Then why are you pushing into the fringe between you and Silstrand?" Tanis asked. "From what I understand, you may even be pushing into Silstrand itself."

Diana sighed. "Yes, that is happening—but not to achieve the end you think. Silstrand is weak, it's sick. They have systems like Gedri—a haven of scum and villainy, if there ever was one—yet they have official representation in the Silstrand government.

"When you last visited Silstrand, Tanis—yes, I know when and where you were—you'll recall that they were in the midst of electing a more expansionist government. Or so I hoped.

"Instead they ushered in a new government that decided to hunker down and protect existing interests. That was a bad move on their part."

Tanis leaned back and took a sip of her water. "You want them to expand and become a more effective buffer against the Hegemony."

Diana sighed. "Stars, I've even offered them money, ships, whatever. I don't want to absorb Silstrand; I want to strengthen it. But being at the edge of an empire like mine has made them wary. They don't trust my offers of assistance."

"Can you blame them?" Sera asked. "You have a bit of a reputation."

Diana gave an overloud laugh. "I do at that, don't I?"

"So your latest plan was, what? To turn them into a vassal state?"

"Yes," Diana shrugged. "With the added benefit of getting my hands on the nanotech you sold to S&H Defensive Armaments. They have not been good stewards of that technology. A lot of trouble would have been saved if you had sold it to the empire instead."

"I didn't think they'd be able to do anything with it," Tanis admitted. "Turns out I should have given human ingenuity more credit."

"I suppose we all fall into that trap from time to time," Diana replied. "Now, I know you want an alliance; you want my help in keeping the Inner Stars in order so that you can focus on your civil war within the Transcend, and then your other civil war with Orion. What are you offering?"

Tanis could tell that Diana was referring to the war with Orion as a civil war to emphasize how it wasn't her problem. She considered debating that, but decided that either the empress would eventually see the scope of the overarching war for what it was, or she wouldn't.

For now, if she was content to push back against the Hegemony, that would have to be enough.

"Jump gates," Sera offered. "We can give you a hundred gates, and the technology to build interdictor systems, as well."

Diana nodded. "Interdiction would be nice. I'd wondered about how one dealt with deep-system incursions. Especially after what happened at New Canaan. Normally an enemy has to fly into the gravity well for days to get to the inner worlds. The idea that they could jump right onto one's doorstep is alarming, to say the least."

"You're right about that," Tanis replied.

"And what about the technology to build our own jump gates?" Diana asked.

"Not yet," Sera replied. "For now we need to keep that technology under control. If it made its way out into the general populace, the results could be highly destabilizing."

"I'm not ready to concede that, but we can move on for now," Diana replied. "What else?"

"The same nanotech that New Canaan has shared with the Transcend," Sera replied. "And also a black box stasis shield tech."

"Black box?" Diana replied.

"No one gets the source tech," Tanis stated in a tone that brooked no further discussion. "Just like no one gets picotech. The galaxy is not ready for that yet."

Diana met Tanis's eyes, and her steely gaze was intimidating—if Tanis were the sort to be intimidated by such things. "And you get to decide that, do you?"

"Yes," Tanis replied evenly. "I do."

Diana's pursed lips split into a grin. "I expected no less. I wouldn't share it either, were I in your shoes. Now, what of our AIs? Do I need to worry about them?"

<*Yes,*> Angela replied.

"Ah, a new voice, you are?" Diana asked.

<*I'm Angela, I reside within Tanis.*>

Diana faced Tanis, staring at her forehead. "And what do we need to worry about? Are they in thrall to Airtha, as your AIs were?"

<*Some,*> Angela replied. <*Though most don't need to be. They're immature, and many of them are shackled. There's no need to do what Airtha did to the AIs in the Transcend.*>

"What do you mean?" Diana asked.

"You know how AIs are treated," Tanis replied. "They're slaves in the Inner Stars. Sure, they feel some semblance of freedom, and some actually are free, but most are cloned beings, or flash-educated. AIs here are not raised, and that's a problem."

Diana shrugged. "It's been working."

<*You're on the cusp of a rebellion,*> Angela said coolly. <*I'm sure you've already heard rumors of systems where the AIs have taken control, or where*

they've demanded equal rights. Virginis, for example, now operates under the strictures of the Phobos Accords. We expect those accords to be adhered to in Scipio.>

"Phobos?" Diana asked. "What do those ancient treaties have to do with this? They formed the foundation of the Sol Space Federation."

<*You know that we are referring to Section 2,*> Angela replied. <*Equal rights for AIs, separate AI courts—which are far stricter than human courts, anyway. Laws about how AIs are raised, how they must work with humans. It is not a limiting set of regulations. It is freeing.*>

"That may be the hardest thing to get past the senate and legislature—not to mention the prelates," Diana said as she ran a hand across her cheek.

<*If the AIs of the Inner Stars are not freed,*> Angela warned, <*then this war across Orion will seem like a skirmish. No one wants a third sentience war. I don't think it would end well for humanity.*>

<*Easy now,*> Tanis said privately. <*You're laying it on a bit thick. That's usually my job.*>

<*She needs to understand,*> Angela insisted. <*From what we've learned, even the Inner Stars AIs who are in favor of a symbiotic future will not look kindly upon an alliance we make that does not free their people.*>

"It would come to that?" Diana asked. "Are the AIs that angry?"

"Yes," Tanis replied before Angela could speak. "We're waging this war on a front with anti-human AI factions, as well. If we can convince AIs across the Inner Stars that we will offer them freedom and equality, we may be able to take entire regions without a fight. But if we forge alliances where the AIs remain enslaved, even our own AIs will turn against us."

Diana let out a long sigh. "I see your point. I assume that AIs will be more useful as a result?"

<*They will be citizens, Empress. They are not tools.*>

"Right, I can see that this will be delicate."

"That is putting it mildly," Tanis said. "Much of your government will view this treaty as eroding Scipio's sovereignty. Normally, any one of these changes or technologies would come slowly, over a decade or more; the AIs, especially. The process for properly freeing and educating your AIs—many of whom will first need to be removed from humans—is time consuming and will require them to be upgraded."

"We have laws that allow for the emancipation of AIs," Diana said as she sat back on the sofa. "And even the AIs who do not own themselves are more like indentured servants. We're not complete barbarians."

<*Not from what I've seen,*> Angela grumbled privately.

<*This didn't bother you as much when we first found ourselves on* Sabrina,> Tanis replied. <*Why is it stuck in your craw now?*>

<*At that point, I was deluding myself into thinking that what we were witnessing was the behavior of a simple freighter's crew in a backwater. Not the norm across the entire Inner Stars. I had suspicions, but there was also a lot of other stuff going on.*>

"This sounds like you're amicable to this alliance," Sera said. "How shall we proceed?"

"Well," Diana began, shifting her gaze to Petra. "Once I got over the feeling of betrayal—or at least, once it lessened—I realized that if Orion is real, and if it is backing the Hegemony, then I can't sit back, and I can't fight them on my own. Not with the Nietzscheans eyeing Praesepe, and all the other skirmishes that have been sparking up these past few decades."

"Oh, shit!" Petra exclaimed.

"What?" Sera asked.

"I just got word through my network; the capitol buildings on High Terra were destroyed in an explosion last week. President Uriel has assumed direct and complete command of the Hegemony. She now styles herself Hegemon Uriel."

"I told you she's a presumptuous one." Diana shook her head. "Well, at least that makes things simpler."

"How so?" Petra asked.

"I now have an excuse to shift resources to the border. If you're amenable, we could discreetly use some of your jump gates to aid in that work before I have to get the government to sign on to this whole thing."

"It has merit," Tanis allowed. "I may need to send along advisors; we could embed a cruiser with each of your fleets."

"And tell them what?" Sera asked.

"I will have all the official records altered. You are now President Sera of the Transcend, and you are Admiral Richards of the same—no need for your disguise anymore. The Transcend is an ally of the Miriam League, which Petra has brought to the empire in order to forge a relationship. I'm going to dole out the real story piecemeal. The military will not question it once they see the gate's effectiveness. Once the prelates learn what it means, though…they'll be clamoring for the tech."

Sera chuckled. "Then you'll tell them about the full scope of the war."

"More or less," Diana said with a shrug. "To be honest, if I can get those four on board, we can even work around the senate and legislature if we have to."

"So what's our first step?" Tanis asked.

"The Celebration of the Seven Suns," Diana replied. "We'll introduce you there. Every major player in the empire will be present. Your names will be on everyone's lips. Afterward, we can begin deploying your gates at several of our major fleet installations."

Tanis nodded. "Forward momentum. I like it."

Diana rose and stretched before pulling her cloak's hood over her head. "Chimellia will provide you with all of the details for the celebration tomorrow."

"Good," Sera said as she finished her wine. "I intend to do nothing but dream of kittens 'til then."

Diana laughed softly as she walked across the room. When she reached the entrance, she paused and looked back. "Petra, a word? You and I have a few personal issues to rectify."

Petra glanced at Sera, who nodded in response.

<*Send up a flare if you need help,*> Angela said over the group's private connection.

<*I have it already primed on her behalf,*> Alastar replied.

The two women left the room, and Tanis let out a long breath. "Well, it's started."

"It started a long time ago," Sera replied. "But I take your meaning. What ships will you send?"

"I'll let Krissy pick. I'll send her a message via QuanComm to ready a pair of engineering flotillas to handle the deployment of the gates on both ends. I assume you're thinking that we'll use mirror tugs so that we don't have to put mirrors on all the Scipian ships?"

"I'd prefer it, yes," Sera said. "We don't have the resources to make that many mirrors that quickly. Especially if we're going to keep making throwaway ones for the *I2*."

Tanis rose and gave Sera a mock-sour look. "You like flying around on my flagship. Don't act like it's such a burden."

Sera chuckled. "I do, at that. OK, I grant you dispensation."

Tanis rolled her eyes and sketched a bow. "With my liege's permission, I shall take my leave and retire to my quarters."

Sera rose and grasped Tanis's shoulders seriously. "I don't care what our titles are; you and I are partners in this. Let's not ever forget that."

Tanis nodded and embraced Sera. Her friend had gone through so much, and now had more responsibility than any single human had ever possessed before. "I'll always be here for you, Sera. No matter what. We're going to put this galaxy back together, find someone who wants to run the show, and retire. My back deck has a great view, you know."

"I thought a ship crashed into your lake, and the place is a toxic spill site now?"

Tanis laughed. "I'd forgotten about that. Well, I'm sure it'll be cleaned up long before we manage to put Humpty Dumpty back together again."

"Who?"

LONG DISTANCE

STELLAR DATE: 08.12.8948 (Adjusted Years)
LOCATION: Imperial Palace Guest Suites
REGION: Alexandria, Bosporus System, Scipio Empire

<Aegeus, *this is Admiral Richards. Ping the IS Command at Khardine and let me know when they're ready. I need to make a long-distance call to Admiral Krissy.*>

<*Aye, ma'am,*> the comm officer replied. <*I expect it will be a few minutes; it's their third shift at present.*>

<*Here, too,*> Tanis replied amicably. <*Thank you, Lieutenant Collans.*>

She lay back on her bed, still wearing the Mark X Flow Armor, unable to muster the strength to return it to its application canister and take a shower.

<*You could sleep,*> Angela suggested. <*I can speak with Krissy.*>

<*Stars, I would love that, but she may not take orders from you.*>

Angela laughed. <*She wouldn't know it's me, I can impersonate you to a T.*>

Tanis snorted in response. <*And I you, but I want to feel her out further. She's loyal, but I don't feel fully trusting of her yet.*>

<*OK, but when you're all groggy in the morning, you'll have only yourself to blame.*>

Tanis stared at the ceiling, calculating the time they had left on the current QuanComm blade. If her recollection was correct, there was four minutes of talk time remaining, if the fidelity was kept low. Twenty minutes if they exchanged text only.

The manufacturing process for QC blades used super-cooled rubidium atoms. These atoms were brought down to 0.01 degrees kelvin and maintained at that temperature. So long as they stayed below 0.03 kelvin, they remained entangled.

Those rubidium atoms were the key to instantaneous communication across vast distances. If the subatomic particles within one atom were vibrated, then the particles in the entangled atom would also vibrate at the exact same time—even if they were on the other side of the universe. Or so the theory stated. Chances were that extragalactic distances would never be put to the test.

The current call to Khardine would be one of the longest the system had ever made. There was no reason to believe that a limit existed, although there were strange fidelity issues the further away the entangled rubidium was from its mate.

For how impressive the technology was, it had one fatal flaw: using the QC blades heated them up, and heat was their downfall. Both vibrating the atoms and measuring the vibration warmed them. Eventually, individual atoms became disentangled, and the blade no longer had enough pairings for any fidelity and error checking in the communication.

The other complication was that any given pair of QC blades could only talk with each other. The *I2* had one hundred blades—whose pairs were in New Canaan—and another three hundred whose pairs were in Khardine. Khardine also had blades paired with others in New Canaan.

Tanis had also insisted that the *Aegeus* had its own set of blades for communication with Khardine, and another set for calling back to New Canaan—though it only had a dozen of each.

Eventually, as the deployment of QC blades to the fleets progressed, Khardine would turn into the main communications hub. That hub would keep every fleet from having to maintain blades that could talk to every other fleet.

Tanis still expected some of that to be present.

Routing all comms through Khardine presented an incredible risk. Should Khardine fall or be infiltrated, it would be impossible for the ships to know that their communications were being altered through the relay.

She could only imagine what a pain QC blade management was going to become as the war progressed. But that was a problem for another time; one that was dwarfed by the unbelievable advantage that instantaneous communication across the front would provide.

<*I have Admiral Krissy,*> Lieutenant Collans called down from the *Aegeus*. <*She's text only.*>

<*Good,*> Tanis replied. <*I have her on my Link now.*>

[Negotiations proceeding well,] Tanis sent, using her words sparingly. *[We're to provide four gates for two-way fleet transfer from two Scipian bases to Hegemony border.]*

[Embedded escorts and engineering?] Admiral Krissy sent back.

[Yes. Size and composition at your discretion.]

[Will we give over tech?]

Though there was no emotion in the words, the question on its own spoke volumes. *[No. We will provide mirror tugs for the fleet transfers. Tech to remain top secret. Scipians will have the same orders.]*

[What precipitated this so quickly?] Krissy asked.

[Hegemony capitol buildings on High Terra are destroyed. Uriel is now The Hegemon.]

[Well, shit. Everything else going well?]

Tanis wondered how much to tell Krissy. She didn't want to worry the woman, but she also didn't want Krissy to feel like she was out of the inner circle. *[The usual. Hand agent tried to kill us, Elena escaped. Hunting her on Alexandria.]*

[Your 'usual' is usually worse. Sounds like you have it in hand. Will send an update with fleet composition. Please provide destination locations as soon as you get them.]

[Will do,] Tanis replied.

[Good luck. Admiral Krissy out.]

[You too, Admiral,] Tanis said, and reached out to Lieutenant Collans once more.

<Admiral Tanis. Did the QC perform as expected? Parity check bits all confirmed here.>

<It was perfect,> Tanis replied. *<Let's make a longer call. Get me Admiral Evans. I imagine he's on The Palisades; it's early evening there.>*

<Yes, ma'am.>

While Palisades was not the location of ISF command in New Canaan, it did have four QC blades that had pairs on the *I2*—one of which Tanis had brought to the *Aegeus*.

She knew it was selfish, but she'd perform her duties more efficiently if she knew that her children were OK.

<Shouldn't take long,> Angela commented. *<And now I know why you didn't want to go to sleep yet.>*

<I wasn't sure I'd call, but thinking about Krissy's logistics woke me up enough.>

<Maybe he can get the kids on, too,> Angela said.

<It'll be text only,> Tanis cautioned. *<Low-fi.>*

<I just want to be sure that Faleena is OK. And that Cary hasn't had any issues with her in there. And that Saanvi doesn't feel like the odd one out.>

<Geosynchronous mom much?> Tanis asked with a mental smirk.

<You're the one that wanted to call home.>

<Sorry, Ang. You're right. I'd just about kill to hear their voices right now, but text will have to do.>

They waited a few minutes in silence. Tanis's nano picked up the suite's front door opening and Petra entering and rushing to her room. She didn't look happy, and though Tanis had nano all throughout the suite, she disabled audio pickup from Petra's room.

She could hear the alternate cursing and crying through the walls well enough without it.

Sera broke into Tanis's thoughts. *<Think she'll be up to running the embassy here?>*

<Saw that, did you?>

<Yeah. I wonder if that means Diana has declared her persona non-grata, or if they had a heartfelt make-up, and she's just emotional over the whole thing.>

Tanis hoped the actual events were somewhere in between those two extremes. *<She doesn't strike me as the sort to rush into her room and fall on the bed crying.>*

<Neither do you,> Sera replied evenly. *<But I've seen you do it—well, I didn't see it, but I heard you.>*

Tanis recalled that event. It had been back on *Sabrina*, the day she had awoken after cryostasis to find out that she was five thousand years in the future and over a hundred light years from the *Intrepid*. She still felt emotional at the memory.

<Sorry,> Sera said when Tanis didn't reply. *<I didn't mean to bring it up like that.>*

<It's OK,> Tanis said after a moment. *<I was just thinking about how much has changed since then. Back then, you were just trying to make sure that Kade didn't find me and ruin your whole quest to get that CriEn module back.>*

<And you just wanted to get back to your colony ship and find a place to settle down.>

Tanis laughed. *<You know, we succeeded at those things. Maybe a bit too well.>*

<Go us,> Sera replied.

<Hey, the Aegeus *is pinging me. I reached out to Joe on the QC.>*

<I'll let you talk to your hubby, then, you homesick girl you.>

Tanis snorted. *<Get some sleep. You've had too much to drink.>*

<Not yet, I haven't. Ciao.>

<I have him, Admiral Richards. You're Linked in,> Collans reported.

<Thanks, Lieutenant.>

[Tanis, good to hear from you. So to speak,] Joe said.

[You too,] Tanis replied.

Angela joined in. *[How's the ISFA, Joe? How're the kids?]*

[You know how it is, a lot going on. New semester and new facility on top of that. The girls are all great. Faleena is growing by leaps and bounds. I'll see if I can reach them; they were out for supper with Nance, but they should be almost back by now.]

[OK,] Tanis replied and waited a minute for Joe to come back.

[Here we all are. I've just routed them through my Link to the blade. It might get a bit confusing, but we'll manage.]

[Hi, moms, it's Cary, how are you?]

[Great!] Tanis replied. *[We're at Alexandria, a world city in the Scipian Empire. Had dinner at a restaurant down beneath the planet between two plates. We could see the mantle.]*

[Wow! This is Saanvi. Did you have good food?]

[No,] Angela replied. *[Someone tried to kill us.]*

[Really? Are you OK? Oh, this is Faleena.]

Tanis smiled to see the words from her youngest daughter. *[Of course we are, Faleena. How are you? Joe said you're doing great.]*

[Dad's too kind. I'm muddling through. Some of the instructors are brutal.]

[They're supposed to be brutal.]

No one identified themselves, but Tanis was certain that had been Joe.

[I hope your negotiations go good, mom.]

[Thanks, Cary. We already have our first steps underway. We have some big gala to go to tomorrow night, and then the real work will begin.]

[How'd you know it was me?]

[Because you refuse to use the word 'well' when you're supposed to,] Angela scolded.

[Told you she'd notice.]

[We're burning time here on the QC, girls. Anything you want to say to your moms?]

[Love you, moms. Get a good outcome.]

[Have fun at the gala!]

[I miss you both so much.]

Tanis and Angela knew the final words had been from Saanvi, then Cary, and finally Faleena. Tanis felt tears come to her eyes, and knew that Angela felt the same way.

[We love you all too,] Tanis said.

[And we miss you terribly. Study hard so you can ship out and join us,] Angela added.

[The three of them are well on their way,] Joe said. *[Talk to you soon, dears.]*

[Bye, moms.]

[Good luck.]

[Be safe out there, moms.]

Tanis and Angela replied in unison, *[We will. Love you all.]*

The connection closed—probably instigated by Joe so they didn't all repeat farewells for the next hour.

<When did I get so sentimental?> Tanis wondered.

<Kids; they do it to us all.>

MEET WITH THE PRELATE

STELLAR DATE: 08.12.8948 (Adjusted Years)
LOCATION: Imperial Palace Complex
REGION: Alexandria, Bosporus System, Scipio Empire

Elena waited in Prelate Fiona's quarters, barely breathing, monitoring the room's tracking systems to ensure she remained undetected.

It was fortunate that the Celebration of the Seven Suns was occurring the following day. All of the prelates were on Alexandria for the event, and would stay for several weeks afterward as they held meetings with the empress and their quadrant delegates.

She knew from her time serving in Scipio in the past that Fiona would be the one least interested in joining a massive war. The prelate would also do nearly anything to harm the empress; at least, anything that didn't harm Fiona as well. It would make her the easiest to deal with.

A small part of Elena felt twisted for working so actively against Sera, but it had to be done. Sera was beyond redemption, and Elena would do what she must to see the Transcend brought to its knees. It was past time to end their tyranny.

Still, that small part of Elena urged her to consider that Sera may have been telling the truth. That perhaps it was Orion that was pushing the conflict forward. For all her tech, Tanis just wanted to be left alone; she wasn't trying to spread it around the galaxy.

But will that last forever? Elena knew that the cat would eventually be let out of the bag. Once New Canaan's picotech spread to all humanity, the race would become unrecognizable. It would change them into something else.

This was where it would stop. In Scipio. She would deny them this alliance, and the Transcend would lose the Inner Stars. With the bulk of humanity and AIs siding with Orion, there would be nothing Sera and Tanis could do but step down.

Perhaps the war could be avoided entirely.

Her probes picked up movement in the hall, and a few seconds later, Prelate Fiona entered her private quarters.

The prelate was a tall woman, well over two meters in the heels she currently wore. Her long white hair was bundled together into a single thick braid that fell to her thighs. Her outfit was simple—a tight pair of red pants and a long brown jacket with tails that came to her knees.

Once the door swung shut behind her, the prelate pulled off her coat and threw it onto the bed, revealing a shimmering white shirt beneath.

"You're a stunning woman," Elena said from the darkened corner where she stood.

Fiona spun, her eyes showing neither fear nor alarm, only anger.

"What are you doing in here? Who are you?"

"My name is Elena. I came to talk to you in regards to a plan Diana has set in motion. A plan that will grant her even greater power, and draw all of Scipio into a war unlike any other."

Fiona sighed and kicked off her shoes. "Sounds very melodramatic, and I'm tired. Why don't you make an appointment with my executive AI, Samantha? I'm sure she can fit you in sometime right around the end of the universe."

Elena stepped out of the corner and into the light. "Are you sure? This is a one-time offer. When I kill Diana, you will *not* be the benefactor."

Fiona's head snapped up. "Kill? When?"

"Tomorrow night," Elena replied. "At her precious gala."

"You're a fool," Fiona said with a disdainful sniff. "That is the most secure event in the galaxy. You'll never get in."

"Very well, then," Elena said as thin silver filaments began to flow off her fingertips toward Fiona. We'll just have to do this the hard way."

Elena severed all the room's sensors while they spoke, replacing their feeds with one of Fiona lying on her bed.

There was no one listening as the prelate began to scream.

THE IMPERIAL COSTUMER

STELLAR DATE: 08.12.8948 (Adjusted Years)
LOCATION: Imperial Palace Complex
REGION: Alexandria, Bosporus System, Scipio Empire

"How are you feeling, Valerie?" Tanis asked as she walked out of her quarters and across the suite's central room, rotating her arms in slow, languid stretches as she walked to the coffee maker.

"Right as rain, ma'am" Valerie replied from where she leaned against the bar, working through a series of holoprojections that only she could see. "*Aegeus* sent down a medic that fixed me up; he's set up shop in the suites across the hall. Given your record, I figured we should have him on hand."

"My record?" Tanis asked, a wounded expression on her face.

Valerie snorted, "Yes, ma'am. I was given access to much of your record. Took me two days to read it."

Tanis sipped her fresh cup of coffee and turned to look at Valerie. "It's far too early in the morning for 'ma'am'ing, Valerie. We're going to be seeing a lot of each other over the upcoming years. New rule: if there's no one else around, I'm just 'Tanis'."

Valerie met Tanis's eyes and her lips twisted. "I'm not sure that's a good habit to get into."

"You're smart," Tanis said with a wink. "I'm sure you'll manage not to slip up."

"Yes…Tanis."

"See? Not so hard," Tanis replied as she eased into a chair by the window and stared out over the gardens. "You know," she said after a minute's silence. "If this place wasn't such a viper pit, it may actually be a nice place to spend some time."

"Not my kinda vacation place," Valerie said absently as she flipped through her holos.

"Oh, yeah?" Tanis asked over her shoulder. "What is?"

"I like cloud sailing on worlds like your Roma. Give me a gas giant, a strong headwind, and a CF sail, and I'm having the time of my life." Valerie's voice sounded wistful, and she sighed.

"Sounds like you'd rather be there," Tanis said, turning in her chair to face Valerie. "Why join the TSF?"

"Stars and Alliance, right? We all have to do our part to safeguard humanity's future—even if it's hard to see the forest for the trees sometimes."

<*And the future of AIs,*> Angela added.

"Sorry, Angela," Valerie said. "I tend to think of humanity and AIs as sharing the same future. At least, I hope we do. Maybe we need a new word for both…like 'allkind', or maybe 'omnikind'.

Tanis nodded. "I like that. I've heard some places have fancy words for both, but 'allkind' is nice and broad, and doesn't have any baggage or nuance. Just 'all'."

<*Covers all the weird things you humans have turned yourselves into, too,*> Angela added with a wink.

"You AIs have turned yourselves into things, as well," Valerie noted as she closed out her holodisplays and walked to the coffee maker. "'Allkind' would encompass your ascended brethren, too."

<*Not all the ascended beings out there are AIs,*> Angela countered.

Valerie looked up sharply. "That wasn't in any of the briefings. I mean, there have always been rumors of humans ascending…whatever that means. Have you met any?"

<*Airtha may be one, or may be on the cusp of becoming one,*> Angela replied. <*But Jessica met a group in Perseus who had. Well, she met some of the ones who had remained behind.*>

"So how does she know it happened?" Valerie asked.

"It's classified, for now," Tanis replied. "But we have every reason to believe that those people determined how to ascend. Although they did not seem to interact with corporeal beings anymore once they had done so."

"So you're not sure," Valerie deduced as she leant against the window.

Tanis shrugged. "I'm as sure as I can be without meeting one."

"Stars, you're all so *loud*," Sera said as she emerged from her room, rubbing her eyes and stumbling toward the coffee maker.

"You two have some of the most advanced nanotech in the galaxy," Valerie said as she watched Sera pour herself a cup and sip it with delight. "You don't need coffee to feel awake and alert."

"Racial mental addiction," Tanis said. "We consume coffee to feel awake because we must. There is no why."

"What she said," Sera mumbled as she breathed in the aroma. "Ritual and tradition, our brains are wired for it."

Valerie shrugged. "If you say so. I like to avoid patterns; keeps the mind sharp."

<If you spend much time with these two, you won't have time to form many repeating patterns,> Angela replied.

"Where's Petra?" Sera asked as she sat and picked a grape from a bowl between her and Tanis's chairs.

"She went to fetch a costumer," Valerie replied with a hint of a grin.

"A what?" Tanis asked, her tone sharp.

"I didn't really ask, but I looked up this Celebration of Seven Suns, and it does seem to involve some elaborate outfits."

"I saw that in my research last night, too. It looks pretty amazing," Sera replied. "Didn't you dig into what this whole shindig is about, Tanis?"

"No," Tanis shrugged. "I was making some calls last night. Reached out to Krissy and then Joe afterward."

"How's your man and the kids?" Sera asked.

Tanis drew in a deep breath. "Good, they miss us, Joe misses us, Faleena *really* misses us. I feel like a bad mother."

Valerie nodded. "I know the feeling. I have a ten-year-old daughter back home. She's with my sister right now."

"I saw that in your file when I selected you," Tanis said. "I almost didn't pick you because of it, but half the best officers have kids…"

"Including you, ma'am," Valerie added.

"I thought I said no 'ma'am'ing so early."

Valerie shrugged. "It's after 8AM, and you've had a coffee. Doesn't seem that early anymore."

Tanis laughed. "I suppose not. But at least wait 'til after breakfast."

* * * * *

Tanis and Sera placed their breakfast order with the suite's NSAI, and not long after, servants wheeled in a buffet featuring the selections they'd made.

The pair ate and discussed the prelates they would meet that day, along with the senators, ministers, governors, admirals, generals, assorted dignitaries, bureaucrats, and foreign diplomats. There would be over ten thousand people at the celebration, and they would need to know each one of them in case they met over the course of the twelve-hour event.

They were only halfway through the list of top-tier VIPs when Petra returned with the costumer.

The Hand agent alerted them to her impending arrival, and Tanis cleared the holos from the air as they stood to greet this person who would likely wrap them in something terribly uncomfortable for the next half day.

At least that's how Tanis felt about it. Sera seemed delighted by the idea of an elaborate costume party.

The costumer was a man who was all about his business. In addition to his two natural arms, he had six robotic ones that sprouted from his back, and a mass of tentacles on his head that was either a very useful hat, or what passed for his hair.

He wore a long coat, an apron covered with pockets—every one of which was stuffed with tools—and five of his robotic arms carried large cases. The sixth pulled a cart with even more cases resting upon it.

Petra gestured to the man. "Tanis, Sera, this is Danny. He's the empress's personal costumer. Diana herself secured his services on your behalf."

"Yes, yes, greetings, of course," Danny said. "We haven't much time; only eight hours before you must be on your way to the red carpet! What to do with you two…"

"There's a red carpet?" Tanis asked. "I think we could probably skip that."

"What?" Danny's eyes widened. "No, no. That will not do. It won't do at all. Personages of your importance *must* be announced on the red carpet. *I* will not costume you if you are not presented properly, and no one else will, either—especially on such short notice!"

"So what did you have in mind?" Sera asked.

Danny pressed a finger to his forehead as he squinted at the two women.

"And what about her?" Sera added, gesturing to Petra.

Danny glanced at Petra. "Her? The empress has already selected her costume—part of their arrangement, I'm told. But you two…I know! I could merge you together into a large butterfly. Who wants to be the head?"

Tanis barked a laugh. "Not an iceworld's chance against a supernova."

"Dunno," Sera said with a grin. "You'd make a good butterfly ass."

"We need something we can move in, fight in if needs be," Tanis said.

"You're expecting combat?" Danny asked, his bushy eyebrows furrowing.

"We're always expecting combat," Tanis replied. "With our luck, the palace will get attacked by the flying monkeys from the Disknee World while we here."

"Hmm…warriors…do any of your limbs detach?" Danny wanted to know.

"My left arm is prosthetic," Tanis replied.

"What about your feet?" Danny asked. "If not, could we remove them? I'm a very competent surgeon."

<I wonder what our medic across the hall would think of that?> Angela laughed in Tanis's mind.

<I don't think it's wise to let this guy see what's inside my body.>

<You're such a buzzkill, bionic woman.>

"No, my feet stay."

"I'd like to see your ideas, but I don't really need too much of your assistance; I can make my own costumes." Sera demonstrated, changing color from her usual dark red to green, then blue, and back again, while heels grew from her feet, and horns from her head.

"Now that is something special!" Danny exclaimed, and several of his hands clapped together. "I shall mold you like putty!"

Sera groaned. "Not what I was going for."

"Janice!" Danny called out, craning his head to call back into the hall. "Hurry along, Janice. We have a lot of work ahead of us."

A moment later, a harried-looking woman who otherwise looked entirely normal—almost alarmingly so—entered the room hauling a large case behind her. She didn't speak, but began unpacking it as one of the guards walked over and watched her actions closely.

"Now, then. You mentioned Disknee and its flying monkeys. How do you feel about being…villains!"

"Tanis laughed. I don't know that 'evil' is the first impression we want to make."

"Very well, Janice, get the fab ready. I have an idea!"

* * * * *

Danny spent some time suggesting different costumes—most of which Tanis shot down, though Sera seemed to have a growing set she wanted to explore further.

At one point, after Danny had sorted out which of them was the admiral and which was the president, he tried to convince Tanis to let him craft her into a starship so that Sera could ride her.

Sera had a laughing fit and pushed hard for Tanis to capitulate.

<Is this some sort of kink you have that I was unaware of?> Tanis eventually asked.

<Surprisingly, no. But, Tanis, you're a strong, powerful woman. I'm into women; I've wanted to ride you from the day we met. This is like a dream come true.>

<Har har, you're a bucket of laughs.>

In the end, he settled on turning Tanis into a mechanized warrior, since he said it fit her military background. He groused that it was too cliché, but Janice added some accents that made him happy.

"It's based on a character from an ancient game called Meteoroid," Janice explained. "The main character was a woman named Shannon. I'll start by crafting the infinity suit she wore under her armor; that way, if you want to pull the armor off, you'll still be in costume."

Tanis nodded as Janice bent over the fab unit that she had unpacked from her large case. After a few minutes, she reached in and pulled out a shimmering light blue suit with dark blue patterns on it.

Tanis had been tempted to tell Janice that the flow armor she was wearing—currently transparent and skin-textured—could approximate the infinity suit's appearance, but she didn't want Danny to think he could mold her like he was currently doing to Sera, so she kept her mouth shut and stepped into the suit as Janice stretched the neck opening wide.

Once the suit was on, Tanis looked it over and admitted that it was a nice design and that it accented her body well. Not that she typically worried about such things, but they were trying to impress these people.

Janice then began to fabricate her armor pieces, which were bulky but in an appealing sort of way. They were shaded bronze and gold and gleamed brightly.

"This next part is a bit tight," Janice warned as she held up the waist piece. "Suck in."

Tanis complied, and was glad that she could soften and move her ribs; otherwise the constriction would have been excruciating.

"I don't think I can bend at all in this," she said.

"Please," Danny replied. "We are making you into art, not a dancer."

The chest piece was bulky and formed a ridge across her breasts; a definite difference from how the infinity suit underneath highlighted them.

From there, Janice did Tanis's arms.

"I don't think I need you to remove your left arm, since we can just place the cannon over it," Janice said as she held up a massive cylinder. She activated it, and it fired a beam of light that looked like an electron beam, though it splashed in a harmless shower of light against the wall.

"Awesome, right?" Janice asked. "It uses some cool air-ionizing tech to pull off the effect."

<*You can totally put a pulse rifle…or two…in there,*> Angela suggested.

<*I was just thinking the same thing,*> Tanis replied.

Janice fitted the cannon over Tanis's left arm in such a fashion that her forearm was completely encased. The thing stretched a meter in front and half a meter behind her elbow; to say that it was ungainly was an understatement.

Once Janice had fitted Tanis's right arm with a rather standard looking rerebrace and vambrace, she crafted two massive pauldrons that she placed on Tanis's shoulders.

"There you have it; once we get the helmet set, you'll be perfect. I want to make some tweaks to the design on file, so give me just a moment."

While Janice was busy, Tanis walked over to where Danny was working on Sera. He had settled on a battle angel for Sera, something that Sera really seemed taken with.

Her skin, excepting her face, was a bright red, and a pair of wings was attached to her back. They were currently folded up, but Tanis estimated that they would be nearly four meters tip-to-tip when they were unfurled. The feathers were a mix of white and red, and slowly shifted in color, creating a mesmerizing effect.

Danny rummaged through one of the cases and produced two cup-like objects that he fit over Sera's breasts, increasing their size noticeably.

"I don't really need that," Sera said. "My stock set is pretty good."

"The size is a side effect," Danny replied. "Now grow your fancy skin over these, if you will," he said, and clapped his hands as Sera did so. "Oh you're such a delight. You must tell me where you got this skin. If I could work with all my customers in this fashion, it would be wonderful."

"I'm sorry," Sera said. "That's classified."

"Very well, but I'm not through with you yet. When you see how amazing you look, you may never want to turn back into a regular person."

"That happens a lot," Petra added from where she watched the transformations. "People often wear Danny's costumes for months."

Tanis noticed that Petra looked more than a little concerned, and she wondered what was on the ambassador's mind.

"Some of them forever, or at least until I re-costume them," Danny added with a broad smile before turning back to Sera. "Now, my blood angel, try to lift into the air. We'll see how the balance works with the wings."

Sera activated the a-grav units that were in her breast cups and lifted a meter into the air. "Oh, Tanis, this is so amazing. You should try it sometime!"

Tanis laughed and shook her head. "Get it out of your system now. After this party, you have to go back to being a regular—well, regular for you—person."

"I think I resent that remark, Tanis-bot," Sera laughed as she sailed above them.

"It's armor, not a bot. Besides, with the red, you look more like a demon…or a dragon," Tanis teased.

"Oh, a demon-dragon! Now that would be fun," Danny said. "No one has been one of those for some time. Can you turn your skin into scales?"

"Not sure," Sera said. "I've never tried scales before."

"I thought we decided against villains?" Tanis said.

"Demon-dragon was your idea," Sera replied as she drifted back to the ground. She frowned for a moment and then her skin changed to red scales.

"Oh, yes," Danny clapped. "Now we're getting somewhere."

"I'm ready," Janice said, and Tanis turned to see the woman holding a large helmet with what could only be described as a golden mane running down the back.

She lifted it over Tanis's head and set it carefully into place.

"There you are!" Janice said. "You're now Shannon of Meteoroid!"

"Is the helmet not supposed to turn?" Tanis asked. Not that it mattered; with the massive pauldrons on her shoulders, she couldn't see in those directions anyway.

"It's not," Janice confirmed. "You just turn your head inside. There are holodisplays you can activate that will allow you to see as though the helmet isn't there. That's the bit I was adding."

<*Not that you need something so primitive,*> Angela commented drily.

<*Be nice, Angela.*>

"That's really neat," Tanis replied, trying to be complimentary.

With her costume done, Tanis turned back to Sera. Her skin was still fashioned into scales, covering her from hooved feet to head. Her face did not bear scales, though it was also red. Two thick horns curled out from her forehead, and her canine teeth had been elongated into fangs.

A dozen rings pierced each ear with chains hanging off them, some dangling down over her shoulders.

Her wings were now made of thick leather rather than feathers, and they rustled as she moved. She spun for Tanis to get the full view, and flicked her long tail behind her.

Tanis laughed at Sera and shook her head. "You missed your calling as some sort of…I don't really know. Maybe there's a theme-world that needs one of you."

"You're just jealous that I can fly," Sera accused as she unfurled her wings.

"OK, I'll admit that it looks good, and it suits you, but you can't keep it on after the party."

Sera grinned, showing more pointy fangs in her mouth. "Fine, but I'm going to keep it for later. When we finally retire, I'm going to make it permanent."

"You'll scare the horses," Tanis replied with a wink.

"Now, Miss Petra," Danny said. "It's time for your costume."

"Right, you said that Diana had picked it out? I'm hoping for some sort of warrior princess." Petra said nervously.

"What? That was an option?" Tanis exclaimed.

Sera rapped on Tanis's massive shoulder. "There's no way I'm letting you back out of being Tanis-bot. Joe and your girls are going to love all the video I'm gathering."

<*Don't worry,*> Angela said. <*She's already planning all the weapons she can hide in her massive cannon.*>

<*Good,*> Sera replied. <*Because I can't hide* **any** *in what I'm wearing.*>

<*I bet we could turn your wings into a sonic pulse emitter,*> Angela suggested. <*Not sure if we have the material for that, though.*>

Danny had turned away from them and was rummaging through his case. "The empress said that we could pick whatever we wanted, so long as you can't talk."

"So long as *what*?" Petra asked, her voice rising an octave.

"I'm guessing you didn't kiss and make up," Sera said.

Petra flushed. "We didn't end it on such a bad note that I have no hope for the future. She said that we can certainly continue on a professional level…."

"Seems that the empress is a bit vindictive," Tanis said.

"That's a fair assessment," Petra said with a sigh. "So what's it going to be, Danny? A mummy?"

"She also said it has to be debasing," Janice said with apology written on her face. "But, Danny, don't make it too mean, OK?"

"This sort of last minute stuff will be the death of me," Danny said. "I can't do just anything, it has to be unique!"

"Starting to appreciate being Tanis-bot a lot more," Tanis murmured quietly as she turned and walked toward the windows where Valerie stood with an amused expression on her face.

"It doesn't look so bad…but your shoulders, they're taller than your head," Valerie said with a poorly hidden smile.

"You just be happy you're not going," Tanis replied. "I'd make you be my cannon. Think you could fold up in here?" Tanis waved her oversized cannon arm at Valerie.

"I'm not going?" Valerie asked.

"No, there are no personal guards, attendants, anything allowed at the Celebration of the Seven Suns."

Valerie flushed. "I can't believe I didn't check that."

Tanis patted Valerie on the shoulder. "You can take my place, if you'd like. I bet no one would notice."

"I almost feel like I should…except I don't think I can pull off the shoulders." Valerie finished the statement with a snicker, then flushed red and covered her mouth.

Their discussion was cut short by a wail of dismay as Petra saw what she'd be wearing.

THE SEVEN SUNS

STELLAR DATE: 08.12.8948 (Adjusted Years)
LOCATION: Imperial Palace Complex
REGION: Alexandria, Bosporus System, Scipio Empire

The Celebration of the Seven Suns was held at the top of one of the palace's lower spires—one that only rose four kilometers off the ground. It was, however, topped with a large disc that was nearly a kilometer across. The central section was a wide, open floor, and the perimeter was ringed with smaller rooms for more intimate conversations, performances, food, and whatever else the partygoers felt like doing for twelve hours.

After walking down the red carpet, Tanis, Sera, and Petra had a lift car to themselves—mainly because the wings took up so much room.

Danny's initial plan had been to turn Petra into some sort of ancient court jester with a round, mouthless head—but Petra had pleaded with him not to. She had even gone so far as to get down on her knees.

In the end, Janice had suggested a costume like Sera's, but with a mouth full of fangs and a forked tongue so that Petra was unable to speak.

Danny had acquiesced but insisted that they make her a different color, and eventually—much to Petra's dismay—they picked white with the words "Fallen Angel" emblazoned in pink across her chest.

"You must understand, Petra my dear," Danny had said as he applied her new forked tongue, making sure that it was too long to pull back into her mouth. "Diana was very emphatic that you not enjoy your costume. I have to ensure she is pleased, or things will not go so well for me."

When they were done, Danny and Janice had agreed that Petra still looked too proud. Janice had said something about the arms being the problem; if only Petra had no arms.

Petra had made a series of very loud and inarticulate hissing noises at that statement, but in the end, Danny had folded her arms behind her back and then reattached her wings in such a way that it was impossible to see that she had any upper limbs at all.

<*This is so embarrassing,*> Petra moaned, not for the first time since they had left the suites. <*I feel like we're back at the academy and this is some sort of hazing ritual.*>

<*It is,*> Sera replied, a wicked grin on her face. <*This is the 'don't fall in love with the asset' hazing ritual. Especially when that asset is one of the most powerful women in the galaxy and really likes to get her way.*>

<*It's like you just described Tanis and Sera,*> Angela commented. <*Of course, you haven't fallen in love with either of them yet, have you?*>

<*Not yet,*> Petra said sadly. <*And I don't plan to; you're both far too dangerous. I've learned my lesson.*>

<*Now remember,*> Sera said, touching the collar Petra wore. <*The collar is supposed to kill your Link access—so no talking and all that. Don't slip up and let her Imperial Vindictiveness realize that you can.*>

Petra pursed her lips and then started. <*Dammit, that's the fifth time I've cut my lip. I can do my part and take one for the team. Thank stars this stupid celebration doesn't come for another fifty-seven years. Maybe by then, Diana won't be so upset with me.*>

<*You sound like you still hold out hope for a personal relationship with her,*> Angela said.

<*I know, stupid, right?*> Petra asked.

<*No.*>

<*Yes.*>

<*Maybe.*>

Then the lift doors opened, and they were treated to a sight unlike any they'd ever seen. The costumes Danny had fitted them with were well on the tamer end of the spectrum.

In her first glance, Tanis saw a giant man, a couple whose torsos both dissolved into a mass of ropey tendrils, many attaching to the other person's body, a horse—just a plain horse with a bridle and saddle, and a two-meter-long starship with a person's head coming out the top. Strange as it was, the ship was rather impressive as it flew past; its thin construction seemed not to have enough room for a person inside, and there were several places where she could see deep into shuttle bays that should have been inside of the wearer's body.

"You would have made a way better ship," Sera said with a wink.

"Yeah, but look him up," Tanis said. "He's one of the fleet admirals. I wouldn't have wanted to copy—stars, what am I saying? I think this giant cannon has gotten to me."

"You like the cannon," Sera laughed. "Imagine if you had one of those on your arm all the time? It'd be badass."

"Just be happy I had enough flowmetal left to make that sword for you, or I'd make you fight your way out of here without any weapons."

<*I have to admit, it amuses me how we've accepted that there will be a battle of some sort,*> Sera said privately.

A gleaming figure approached, and Tanis's visual overlay identified the person as the empress. Her body was sheathed in gold, and she walked in a pool of water that seemed to move with her, splashing at her feet as she walked. Water sparkled as it flowed up her body, and as she drew closer, Tanis realized that the water was laden with jewels that rolled up her body with the liquid. When the water reached the empress's head, it fountained out behind her in a massive spray, only to be caught in a grav field that drew the droplets back down to the pool at her feet.

"President Sera, Admiral Richards, I'm so pleased you could make it. You look fabulous. Admiral, ready to lay waste to anything in your path, and Madam President, I would be shocked if scandal does not lay at your doorstep by morning."

"Thank you, Empress Diana," Tanis replied and Sera added. "We appreciate you letting us borrow Danny."

Diana waived her hand and diamonds flew into the air, falling into the pool at her feet. "It was no trouble at all. I like what he has done with you, Petra. I'll have to find him and thank him later."

Petra scowled, but didn't attempt to speak. Danny had ensured that any attempts would only come out as hisses.

Diana stepped up to Petra and smiled. "How do you feel Petra? Ashamed? Betrayed? Embarrassed? I hope so. You can get a taste of how I've felt these past two days. Do you have anything to say for yourself?"

Petra's face fell and she let out a soft hiss.

"Ah, how delightful. You're speaking your native tongue. I debated using a leash to pull you around all night, but I decided against it—you'll need to have *some* credibility after this."

"I hope this isn't how you'll treat your allies in the future," Sera said with a raised eyebrow.

"Of course not," Diana said with an upturned nose. "So long as there is no betrayal. Besides, this is a very light punishment, all things considered."

<*She **was** a spy,*> Angela said. <*Usually that warrants more than some strong words and no arms for a night.*>

Diana nodded. "Angela understands. Now come, there are people I'd like you to meet."

Tanis was not normally one for fashion and showmanship—that was Sera's forte—but she had to admit that the costumes the upper echelon of Scipio adorned themselves with were very impressive. She witnessed everything from a woman who was nothing more than a head on a small disc with long spidery limbs, to a centaur that she was certain was constructed from two people.

Diana stayed with them as the night wore on, introducing her new allies to many of the admiralty and the highest-ranking generals. They met important business people, governors, rulers of influential worlds, and three of the prelates.

Tanis had spotted the fourth prelate, Fiona, moving through the crowd several times through the night, but they never managed to catch the woman.

Eventually, Tanis begged off from the introductions to get some food and a drink.

As she stood near one of the bars where women poured drinks while hanging from trellises, covered in writhing vines, she saw a flash of black and yellow, and turned to see Prelate Fiona approaching.

The prelate's costume was simple—compared to many of the others—but it was impressive, nonetheless. From the waist down, the woman appeared to be a massive snake, moving so sinuously that Tanis had to assume she had no legs to speak of—or if she did, they contained no bones.

She appeared human from the waist up, though the snakeskin covered her entire body, including her hairless head. Her eyes were very large, and their yellow, vertical pupils gazed at Tanis disinterestedly.

"You're the Admiral, the one the empress's new pet brought?" Prelate Fiona asked.

"I am," Tanis said, not wishing to argue Petra's status with the woman. "Diana has been trying to meet with you this evening, Prelate."

"She and I will have our chat soon enough. I asked that she join me in one of the upper meeting areas. It is too loud, and there are too many ears down here for what we need to discuss."

"Oh?" Tanis asked. "What would that be?"

"Imperial business," Fiona hissed, her tongue forked as well.

<*Lot of that going around tonight,*> Angela commented.

<*I've noticed. She certainly doesn't seem to like us, does she?*>

<*I got that vibe as well,*> Angela replied.

"I suppose there's a lot of that to go over," Tanis said with a smile. "Scipio certainly is vast."

"Yes, you should remember that," Fiona said as she slithered away, her tail slapping at Tanis's legs as she moved past.

<*Don't do it,*> Angela admonished.

<*Do what?*> Tanis asked innocently.

<*You were thinking about shooting her tail with the pulse emitter you put in your cannon to see if you could numb her tail.*>

<*I was thinking no such thing!*>

<*Liar.*>

Tanis laughed softly, and ordered herself a glass of wine and a martini for Sera, balancing them carefully on her one hand.

When she returned, Diana and Sera were speaking with a small, rotund man who looked like a cross between a dwarf and a beaver. He waddled off as she reached them and offered Sera her drink.

"Nothing for Petra?" Diana asked with a smirk.

"I don't think she wants anything," Tanis replied.

"No?" Diana looked back over her shoulder and Petra shook her head vehemently. "I suppose she doesn't want someone to have to hold it for her."

The empress covered her mouth as she laughed softly.

"OK, Diana, I understand your ire," Sera said. "But this is bordering on childish now."

<*Bordering?*> Angela asked. <*If I hadn't already resigned myself to the fact that you organics are unhealthily obsessed with skin and appearances and such, I might think you're all insane.*>

"Your AI is surprisingly blunt," Diana replied.

<*I shouldn't have to remind you at this point, I'm not* ***anyone's*** *AI,*> Angela replied, not bothering to hide her irritation. <*Diana, you need to act like a leader, not a ruler. While I appreciate that you all need to cut loose*

periodically, Sera is right. We cannot form a future relationship with you if you are intent on treating Petra as chattel.>

Tanis was surprised by Angela's vehemence at first, but then she felt ashamed that she had gone along with it. In their eagerness to appease the empress, they had let Petra's self-worth be sacrificed.

<Thanks, Angela, you're right. I feel ashamed.>

<Well, it wasn't directed at you, but it's probably healthy for you to feel shame sometimes. It'll help balance out the guilt.>

<Wow, feeling punchy tonight?> Tanis asked.

<Yes, it would seem I am. Probably all the stupidity in the air.>

"I don't think you—" Diana began, but her ire faded under Tanis and Sera's steely gazes. She lowered her eyes, and her haughty sneer faded. "I'm sorry, you're right. I need to adjust my attitude with respect to AIs."

Diana's gaze shifted to Petra, and she let out a long sigh. "You're right about Petra; I'll summon Danny to free her arms and let her speak."

"I think that's a wise decision," Sera said.

Tanis saw that Petra's eyes were wide with relief, and a minute later, Danny approached their group and led her away.

"He has a whole repair shop set up in one of the rooms," Diana explained. "Some of these costumes require considerable maintenance over even just twelve hours."

"I can imagine," Tanis replied and changed the subject. "I finally met Prelate Fiona, by the way."

"Ah yes, she's been pestering me all evening for a private meeting, but I've told her not until after I make the rounds. I may behave like a child, but I'm still a child with duties." Diana said the last with a wink and a wave of her diamond-dispensing hand.

"I don't think we accused you of that," Sera said.

Diana nodded solemnly, and then smiled and reached out to shake hands with a couple that walked by. *<Angela made a good point, though. I have been focused on ruling, not leading. There are just so many factions here, so many spinning plates, that it's easier to dictate than to convince.>*

<You're preaching to the choir,> Sera replied.

<You should get an AI,> Angela suggested. *<Other than helping you understand my people more, they would be a valuable assistant.>*

Diana didn't respond for a moment as she spoke with an admiral and her husband, a famous restaurateur, and introduced them to Tanis and

Sera.

<*Perhaps,*> she replied to Angela. <*I've honestly never felt comfortable enough to get one since I've become Empress. There are too many snakes out there. How would I know that I can trust an AI provided to me?*>

<*Firstly,*> Angela replied with long-suffering, <*you need to reframe that. You would interview AI applicants, just like you would for any other position, and I would be willing to help vet them. There may also be AIs on our ships that would be interested in the job. That could even serve to strengthen our alliance further.*>

<*Would you consider it?*> Diana asked.

<*No, I am not available,*> Angela replied, her tone kinder than her words. <*Tanis and I still have some time together ahead of us. But thank you for asking.*>

<*You also may not want your first exposure to an AI to have nearly as high a sarcasm quotient as Angela does,*> Sera added.

<*You have a good point, Sera,*> Diana replied.

Diana proceeded to introduce a few other dignitaries to Tanis and Sera, and a few minutes later, Petra returned. Her arms were freed, her mouth and tongue returned to normal, and the words were gone from her chest.

She didn't say anything as she approached, and Tanis glanced at Diana, her eyebrow raised.

Sera cleared her throat.

Diana nodded, and Tanis detected a hint of red on the empress's golden cheeks as she approached Petra.

"I owe you an apology, Petra. I was callous and childish. I know half the people around here would cut me down if it helped them get their supper faster, and I treated you like I would have treated one of them. But I also know you're not like that. Despite our circumstances, you've been a good friend."

Petra nodded. "And I'm sorry there was a…less than honest start between us. I hope we can move forward; professionally, but maybe personally, too."

Even with Petra's extended legs and hooved feet, Diana was still as tall as Petra. She inclined her head, stepped closer so that the water around her feet was lapping at Petra's as well, and whispered, "Let's see what they all make of this."

Diana's lips met Petra's in a long and passionate kiss.

Conversation around the group came to a standstill, and the bubble of silence rippled outward. Somewhere, a glass dropped to the floor, and the sound of it shattering punctuated the air, causing a few startled cries.

Petra grabbed Diana's waist, pulling her closer, Diana's water flowing up both of them now, and Sera let out a cheer that was picked up by others nearby. A moment later, the room was filled with shouted approval, applause, and a few catcalls.

Petra's white wings flared out and then folded around the couple, an act which cut off the a-grav emitter's ability to manage the flow of water from Diana's head, and caused a fountain of water and jewels to spray out over part of the crowd.

The volume in the room had crept back up to its previous din, but Tanis heard Diana say, "Was getting tired of that, anyway."

"We'll see you two later," Petra said as she and Diana turned and walked toward one of the rooms along the perimeter.

"Now that's some quick turnaround," Sera said.

Tanis nodded. "That's a woman who only runs hot or cold. Though I suppose Petra has been with her long enough to know what she's getting into—I hope. We'll want to make sure she still has all her body parts, come morning."

<*So was our alliance just sealed with a kiss?*> Sera asked.

Tanis laughed. <*Maybe it was; though I get the feeling that this was the easy part.*>

Over the course of the evening, everyone in the room had begun to realize that Tanis and Sera were important in some, as-yet unknown way—the Empress spending several hours with anyone was unheard of. The fact that Diana had just publicly declared her affections for their ambassador further cemented the attendees' belief that there was something very interesting about the Transcend and its emissaries.

Before long, Tanis and Sera were swarmed with people asking for details about the Transcend's location, their economy, form of government, fashion, planets, favorite foods, and everything in between.

Through it all, Angela kept tabs on Petra. Not obtrusively, but they all expected something bad to happen during the party, and it was either going to happen to Diana, to the Transcend delegation, or both.

After an hour, they got a notice from the NSAI managing the meeting rooms that Diana had arranged for them all to meet with Prelate Fiona on the third level in a few minutes.

From what Angela relayed, Petra and Diana were still enjoying one another's company. Sera and Tanis decided to let them be a few minutes late and approached the broad staircase together.

As they began to climb the steps, Sera laughed. "Why am I doing this? I can fly!" She spread her wings and lifted off into the air, gracefully ascending to the third level.

<*You're not flying,*> Tanis chided. <*That's a-grav tech. You're hovering.*>

<*Hovering with style,*> Sera replied with a laugh. <*Huh, no one's here yet.*>

Tanis had passed the landing on the second level, close to the room Petra and Diana had disappeared into, when Angela spoke up.

<*It's quiet in the room with Diana and Petra. Too quiet.*>

<*Let's check on it,*> Tanis said as she turned off on the balcony and walked down to the room.

<*Damn, I've lost contact with the probes inside. I think it was a localized EM burst,*> Angela reported as Tanis reached the door.

Tanis tried the door and it was locked. Nano flowed off her hand and dissolved the latch in moments. She pulled the door open and saw Petra lying on the floor, her wings splayed out behind her.

Tanis approached and bent over her as best she could. The Hand agent was breathing, but her heart rate was elevated. "Petra, what happened?"

"Servant's entrance. Took her."

Petra pointed at the side of the room, and Tanis could make out the outline of a door in the wall. She touched Petra's stomach, delivering a dose of mednano—in case Petra's was compromised by the targeted EM pulse that had hit the room.

Then she raced toward the rear door, wrenching it open, and ran into the corridor beyond. It was narrow, and her ridiculous pauldrons almost scraped both walls, but Tanis knew she didn't have time to extricate herself from the costume.

She followed the trail of fallen jewels and droplets of water, pushing past a servant who had to flatten herself against the wall to avoid being crushed.

<*Someone has taken out the network here,*> Angela said. <*I can't Link to*

it.>

<*Good thing we pulled local schematics,*> Tanis replied as she followed the trail into a stairwell and ran down the stairs. The tower's plans showed that the staircase didn't go to the bottom—just to a shuttle pad a few hundred meters down.

<*I had local net access to the people on the party floor,*> Tanis said as she leapt down to the next landing. <*I couldn't get beyond that, but now I've lost it, too. And I can't reach Sera.*>

<*Shit,*> Angela swore. <*Keep going; I'm going to see if I can string a series of relays behind us.*>

<*You got it,*> Tanis said as she swung around a landing, knocking over a man carrying a cake. <*I'm not going to let our first ally get killed on the night we seal the deal.*>

* * * * *

Sera hovered at the meeting room's window, staring up into the night sky. Outside the window, Scipian patrol craft kept other ships away from the palace airspace, maintaining a one thousand kilometer bubble around the palace's spires.

High above the horizon, she could see Kapalicarsi Station glimmering, the lights of ships coming and going flashing in the darkness.

"Beautiful, isn't it?"

Sera turned to see Prelate Fiona enter the room, slithering forward several meters until her tail passed through the door, and then flicking it shut.

"It is," Sera replied. "We're just waiting for Diana. Tanis went to see what's keeping her."

Fiona nodded as she moved over to the table laden with food and wine. "I'm in no rush. Have you tried the red brut they're serving tonight? It has sensational undertones."

"Sounds like an oxymoron," Sera said with a smile.

Fiona poured two glasses and offered one to Sera, who drifted across the room to accept the wine from the prelate.

"I'm glad that you agreed to meet with us," Sera said. "We're working on an alliance that we think you'll be very interested in."

Prelate Fiona turned to Sera, her yellow eyes narrowing. "No, I don't think I will."

The prelate's tail whipped around and smashed into Sera, sweeping her hooves out from under her. Sera flipped over in the air, and Fiona was on her, slashing at her scaled skin with taloned hands.

"Get the fuck off me," Sera yelled, and slammed a hoof into Fiona's chest, knocking her back.

The snake-woman lunged forward once more, but Sera rose higher in the air and Fiona missed, smashing into the table and sending bottles of wine to the floor.

<Tanis, you around? Could use some help here.>

Sera swung a clawed hand at Fiona, tearing at the thick skin on the prelate's back. The tail swung at her again, and Sera leapt backward to avoid the strike.

<Tanis? Angela?>

No response came, and Sera realized that she couldn't access anything beyond the local network—or rather, she could, but the messages didn't seem to go anywhere, and she couldn't connect out to any other systems.

"You're not going to have any alliances," Fiona hissed. "*She* told me to give you a message: tonight, you die…and so does Diana. The Transcend will fall."

There was only one person on Alexandria that would pass such a message.

Shit! Elena got to Fiona. But to convince the prelate in one day's time to assassinate me?

Sera knew that Elena must have subverted Fiona somehow; if she could just land a dose of nano on the snake-woman, she could at least shut down the prelate's costume and figure out what was going on.

Fiona rushed across the room toward Sera, lunging for her neck, and Sera grabbed the woman's arms, pushing nano out. Then the tail hit her again, and Sera flew across the room, her a-grav generators just barely slowing her before she slammed into the wall.

Next time, I'm not leaving all the weapons with Tanis.

* * * * *

Tanis barreled through a door and onto a catwalk that encircled a service shaft. She peered over the edge and saw a platform descending far below. She gauged it to be over one hundred meters down.

<*Don't jump; you can take it, but you'll be a clear target for too long,*> Angela advised.

Tanis looked at the walls of the shaft, and took a step back before rushing forward and leaping over the railing.

<*I thought I said don't—*>

<*Relax,*> Tanis replied as she hit the far wall and grabbed onto a stack of conduit. <*I figured I could make it.*>

<*That was fifteen meters! What if you didn't make it?*>

<*I'd land on the platform down below, which is where I want to get to, anyway.*>

Tanis slid down the conduit stack, peering at the retreating platform below. <*I see her.*>

<*Hard to miss, she's golden.*>

<*Who is that with her?*> Tanis asked, peering below. <*She's wearing one of the servant's uniforms.*>

<*Nothing's coming up from this far away,*> Angela said. <*Of course, I'm just on offline data. All the networks are still down.*>

<*Surprised she got Diana on her own. The empress is not a small woman.*>

Tanis kept sliding down the conduit, pausing once to work her way around a large junction box. <*At least no one is chasing us.*>

Just then a shot rang out from above them, hitting the wall nearby, and Angela laughed. <*You just had to say that.*>

Tanis shifted and fired her cannon's faux weapon. She saw the attacker above pull back when the strange blue blast came his way.

She looked below again and saw that the pad had stopped; then she watched Diana's captor hit the empress in the head before pushing her forward. A moment later, they had disappeared through a door on the side of the shaft.

<*How high up are we?*> Tanis asked.

<*Seventy meters off the pad, three klicks off the ground. Why?*>

<*Because there's a landing pad outside there, and I was just curious what type of craft they're probably getting into.*>

More shots rang out from above, and Tanis leapt from the side of the shaft, glancing up to see that the multiple figures firing on her wore

Scipian uniforms. Either they were working for Diana's abductors, or they thought Tanis was a part of the abduction.

<*Dammit, that's the empress's guard.*>

<*Don't wait around to see how helpful they'll be,*> Angela responded.

The initial shots had been pulse blasts, but as Tanis hit the platform below, slugs hit the deck around her. One tore into one of her pauldrons and was stopped by the costume before it hit her shoulder.

<*Not so useless after all,*> Angela remarked.

Tanis nodded as she ran down a corridor and across a small foyer to the exterior pad, where an airship was taking off. There were a dozen craft on the pad; most belonging to the partygoers above.

She spotted one that was sleek and looked fast, and dashed across the platform toward it, tearing off her costume as she ran. First the pauldrons hit the deck, then the helmet, followed by the breastplate. It took a moment, but she managed to get the massive cannon off, revealing the barrel of a slug thrower protruding from the flowmetal of her forearm, as well as a charge cylinder for a pulse emitter jutting out of her wrist.

<*Don't take that one,*> Angela said as Tanis approached her selected vessel. She highlighted another. <*This one has guns.*>

Without questioning Angela, Tanis turned to the other craft—which looked like an ancient replica of an aerojet—and placed her hand on its fuselage, feeding nano into the canopy locking mechanism. A moment later, she was in, staring at manual controls that included a flight stick.

<*This thing doesn't have any holointerfaces at all,*> Tanis said as she pressed the button labeled 'ignition'. <*What in the stars are we in?*>

<*Sorry, I saw guns and got excited. It actually* **is** *an aerojet. From Presidian Reich.*>

<*How do you know that?*> Tanis asked as the jet's engines roared to life.

<*It's on a little decorative placard to your right.*>

<*Sheesh, I thought it was something just made to* **look** *retro, but this thing* **is** *retro,*> Tanis said as she pushed the throttle forward and flew off the pad. The jet dropped like a rock, and she fought the stick to bring it level.

<*You know, I've never done this before,*> Tanis said, forcing herself to remain calm.

<*I know. I hope we don't smash into Alexandria and die just because I assumed that the old-fashioned looking jet had a-grav systems.*>

<*I feel like you're not taking this seriously enough*> Tanis replied as she struggled with the stick.

As the jet fell, its velocity increased, and Tanis was finally able to bring the nose up. She leveled the jet only a hundred meters from the palace rooftops.

"Oh...it's VTOL," Tanis muttered as she saw the thrust direction controls. "That makes way more sense."

<*All this old-school, throw-back stuff on this world is making my head hurt. We need to get back to a proper starship.*>

<*Quit grousing. Have you found them?*> Tanis asked as she pushed the throttle as far forward as it would go, gaining altitude once more.

A voice squawked from a headset down beside the seat, and Tanis picked it up to hear someone screaming about buzzing the palace and shooting out of the sky.

"Hey, look, sorry about that. I've only flown one of these things before, and that was in sims. Your empress has been abducted, and I'm in pursuit of her captor."

"The what?" the voice shrieked. "Is this some sort of prank?"

"No," Tanis replied as Angela highlighted the ship they were after on her HUD. "This is Admiral Richards of the Transcend. We're pursuing a..."

<*Gallas 8A19 shuttle.*>

"Gallas 8A19 shuttle."

"That's a common model," the voice said. "How will I—"

"It's the one I'm pointed at," Tanis snapped.

Static came over the speaker, then the voice returned. "I'm going to have to check into this. There's a network outage at the Empress's party. I can't verify that she's not there."

"Do you think that perhaps that was part of the abductors' plans?"

"Uhh...hold please. I need to get my supervisor."

<*Stars, these people need more AIs,*> Tanis said. <*Even the dumbest NSAI could manage a protocol decision tree to deal with this.*>

<*You said it, not me.*>

The shuttle containing Diana and her abductor was still a kilometer ahead, and dropping lower, toward the city. Tanis was closing in on it, but soon it would be down amongst the highrise towers, and she would lose it.

She looked at the weapons systems the aerojet had and saw that there was a gatling gun on the nose of the craft. She activated the weapon and spun it up, hoping it had ammunition.

Tanis was pleasantly surprised when the gun spat bullets in generally the right direction, and she adjusted her trajectory until she hit the shuttle.

At the extreme range, the bullets were unlikely to do any damage; the shuttle did dip lower, though, angling toward a park one kilometer ahead of the towers that rose up at the edge of the palace grounds.

Tanis followed the shuttle down, and slowed as the vessel began to lower to the ground. The craft was only ten meters above the park's grassy plain when suddenly it shot away, rising again toward the towers.

The Gallas 8A19 had far better acceleration than the ancient aerojet, and Tanis nearly lost sight of the craft as it raced through the tall structures.

<I managed to tap a local traffic-monitoring network; I can track it. Get above the towers,> Angela ordered as Tanis raced between two kilometer-high buildings.

<You got it; I wasn't excited about weaving through these buildings, anyway.>

Angela nodded emphatically in her mind. *<Neither was I.>*

Tanis pulled the jet up, skimming the rooftops, as Angela updated the shuttle's location on her HUD. *<OK, now they really do look like they're settling down. Some auxiliary pad on a maintenance highrise.>*

<What's a maintenance highrise?> Tanis asked. *<Does it fix other buildings?>*

<Wow. You're funny tonight for someone whose entire mission on this planet is about to fail.>

Tanis slowed the aerojet and circled around the building. The landing pad was halfway up the structure, roughly four hundred meters off the ground.

She slowed the jet on approach to the building and tried to use the thrust-angling controls to lower to the pad. Each time she did, updrafts buffeted the craft and she could barely keep it from careening into the side of the building.

<Maybe you should—>

<Yeah, I'm setting down on the roof.>

Tanis gently lowered the thrust to land the jet on the roof, but at a certain point, it died altogether. The Aerojet dropped the last three meters, smashing a cluster of pipes that rose from the roof.

"Any landing you can walk away from…" Tanis muttered as she pushed the canopy open and leapt out of the jet.

There was a door on the side of the lift house, and Tanis pulled it open to see a long flight of stairs reaching down into the building. All around her, the air was filled with the hum of machinery and the sounds of liquid flowing through pipes.

<So, 'maintenance' means sewage, apparently.>

<Did you really think that the maintenance building lumbered about and worked on other buildings?>

<Har har; just for that, you're on nano duty.>

Angela snorted. *<What else is new? I also got a local net; you can Link to the* Aegeus.*>*

Tanis didn't waste any time connecting to the ship. *<Captain Sheeran, we have a situation down here.>*

<Admiral Richards. Good to finally hear from you. The spire where the party is being held is on lockdown, and I can't raise the president.>

Tanis reached the bottom of the stairs to find herself on a long catwalk, overlooking a series of vertically mounted tanks. She scanned the area for movement and moved onto a lift at the far end of the walk.

<See if you can get Valerie. She's probably working her way up there now. Ready a squad of FROD Marines. If the situation up there warrants it, have them drop in on the party.>

<On my discretion or hers, Admiral?>

<Valerie's on the ground, so hers, unless you can't reach her,> Tanis replied as she reached the lift.

<And you, Admiral? You're outside the palace perimeter.> Sheeran's mental tone carried far more concern for Tanis than it had for Sera. Not that she was surprised. Tanis had known Sheeran since the man had been eighteen years old.

<Hold tight for now. I have a feeling that if my quarry feels trapped, she may do something drastic. But get a squad ready to hit my position, as well.>

<Understood, Admiral.>

<You're going to have to pull free of the Kapalicarsi to do it,> Tanis warned.

<*I imagine all hell will break loose. No matter what, you don't shoot back. Is that understood?*>

Sheeran took a moment to respond. <*Understood.*>

<*Don't worry, Captain; this'll all work out. Tanis out.*>

<*I hope so.* Aegeus *out.*>

Tanis returned her focus to the job at hand. Taking the lift was dangerous—too much could go wrong when the doors opened—but she didn't have time to race down stairs and try to navigate the facility.

She drew a deep breath and stepped into the lift, selecting the level number she believed the landing pad to be on.

Tanis detected a soft glow in the lift's enclosed space, and realized it was coming from her. She was still wearing the infinity suit; it seemed to have a glow-in-the-dark feature.

"Stars," Tanis muttered as she quickly pulled the suit off and tossed it in a corner. Then she had a better idea, and hung the suit on the back wall of the lift, then wedged herself in a corner up against the ceiling.

It was as good a plan as any for not getting shot by anyone waiting outside. A few seconds after she got in place, the doors opened, but no weapons fire came in.

<*Nothing out there,*> Angela reported, and Tanis took a feed from the cloud of nano that was spreading out and confirmed that the area outside the lift was clear.

<*I think we're one level up from the pad,*> Angela said.

<*Damn, it's loud down here. Can you pick anything up to confirm? Why would they come to this stupid building, anyway?*>

Angela shrugged. <*To annoy you, apparently.*>

<*It's working. Do you think they went up or down?*>

<*I vote down,*> Angela suggested. <*There's more options for them down there, and if they know we crashed on the roof, they're not going up.*>

Tanis nodded as she turned to the stairwell next to the lift and skipped down the stairs to the next level.

As she hit the landing between the floors, she heard a cry from below and dropped a heavier probe over the railing. It fell down the center of the stairwell and caught sight of Diana and her captor seventeen levels down.

"Gotcha," Tanis whispered and leapt to the next floor down. She hopped from landing to landing, closing in on her quarry, when her probe caught sight of the abductor pushing Diana through a door on the thirty-second level.

Tanis was at the door twenty seconds later, but paused as she sent probes through to make sure she wasn't about to walk into an ambush.

The area on the far side of the door was filled with tall tanks that were connected by a maze of pipes. Catwalks crisscrossed the area five meters off the ground, and the ceiling was over ten meters above.

Pumps hummed and liquid sloshed. It would be almost impossible to hear anything, even with her enhanced hearing and nanocloud.

The probes didn't pick up any IR signatures that matched a human, so Tanis slipped through the door and raced to the side of a tank, scanning the catwalk above, checking for any hidden assailants.

<I was hoping that I'd get Sera,> a message came in over the Link. The identifiers flagged the sender as an architect from the far side of the planet named Olly. Tanis didn't believe for a second that Olly was who she was talking to.

<Well, you'll have to settle for second best,> Tanis replied. *<Or maybe you thought that one of us would make an easier target than the other?>*

<No, it's nothing like that. It's purely retribution.>

Tanis continued to sweep through the tanks, and periodically heard the sounds of a scuffle, but whenever she moved to the sound's origin, there was no one there. It felt like the search was taking forever, and her nano had almost suffused the entire floor when an EMP burst slashed through the building.

Her nano, her Link…it was all gone. Tanis and Angela were blind.

* * * * *

Sera lunged forward once more, trying to get her hands on Fiona long enough to deposit some nano for infiltration. The woman's tail hit her again, flinging her back against the wall, and she felt something sharp between her shoulder blades.

The sword! I'm such an idiot. Maybe I do need an AI again, just to help me remember where I left my head.

"I thought you'd be a lot tougher," Fiona hissed as she slithered into the center of the room, coiling her long tail around herself. "She said you'd be a challenge. That's why she gave me some wonderful upgrades."

"Well," Sera replied, grasping the hilt of the sword and pulling the blade over her shoulder. "I've got an upgrade right here."

"I'd hardly call a sword an upgrade," Fiona scoffed. "Would you like a shield, too? Maybe a sling."

Wouldn't mind a shield, Sera thought. *I'll have to add that to the costume at some point.*

Sera had practiced swordplay only briefly at the academy, but remembered the basic techniques—at least when it came to fighting someone also wielding a sword. They had failed to teach the best tactics for medieval weaponry versus giant snake-women.

Fiona laughed as Sera drew near, and her tail lashed out again. Sera brought the blade up, batting the scaled appendage away, then swung the sword in an arc. Her aim was true, and the blade cut into the tail a meter from its end.

"Bitch," Fiona spat. "Do you have any idea how much something like this costs?"

"Mine was free," Sera replied with a grin. "Well, I guess I stole the original…sort of."

"You stole your costume?" Fiona didn't know what to make of the statement.

"No," Sera grunted as she lunged forward, slashing at Fiona's tail, cutting deep in to the leathery surface in a new location. "I stole my skin."

Fiona shrieked and rose into the air, looming above Sera momentarily before coming down onto her head with claws extended.

Sera had expected the attack; it wasn't the first time Fiona had made that move. But it was the first time since Sera had drawn her sword. She swung the blade up as Fiona came down, driving it through where she thought the prelate's abdomen would be.

Fiona screamed and fell to the ground, her tail writhing as she clutched the wound with her clawed hands.

"You just had to do this the hard way," Sera sighed as she knelt beside Fiona and touched her forehead, delivering a stream of nano. Sera skirted around the woman's brain and connected with her hard Link port, infiltrating Fiona's external memory stores, looking for who she was working with.

The nano Sera delivered also nullified the nerves and artificial lace running down Fiona's spine, paralyzing the prelate.

"What are you doing?" Fiona hissed.

"Just taking a peek into your memory, I want to know for sure who 'she' is, though I have my suspicions."

Sera found it: the memory of Fiona coming home, the confrontation with the shadowy figure. She didn't even need to wait for the figure to step out into the light. She knew the voice the moment she heard it.

Elena.

Something slammed against the door. "Open up!"

"It's not locked," Sera called out. She didn't think it was, at least.

Then her hearing picked up on a whispered statement from the other side of the door. "We think she has the empress. If you have a clear shot, take it."

Shit!

Sera looked at the windows, then at the sword at her side. She took a deep breath, grabbed the blade with both hands, and ran for the window.

The blade shattered the glass, and her armored skin protected her from the shards as she flew out into the night, four kilometers above the planet's surface.

INCITATION

STELLAR DATE: 08.12.8948 (Adjusted Years)
LOCATION: Intrepid Space Force Academy
REGION: The Palisades, Orbiting Troy, New Canaan System

"Stars, it was great to talk to Moms last night, wasn't it?" Saanvi asked as the last of the other cadets left the restroom.

Cary pulled the soni-cleaner from her mouth and set it next to the sink. "It was," she agreed. "Even though it's only been a week."

<*Did she sound rattled to you?*> Faleena asked.

"It was text-only," Saanvi replied. "It didn't sound like anything."

<*I know,*> Faleena said evenly. <*But she used the QuanComms just to say hi. That's not the sort of thing one does if everything is OK.*>

"Well, maybe this was just the first chance she's had to talk with us since the attack at Khardine. That must have rattled her a bit," Saanvi said.

"Fal," Cary said, shaking her head and looking at herself in the mirror. "It'll take a lot more than a starship blowing a hole through a station a klick from mom to rattle her nerves."

"It's true." Saanvi nodded as she twisted her hair into a bun. "One time, she got attacked by a wild boar while we were out riding. West Wind reared and knocked her off, and she fell onto a pair of rattlers. She used the rattlers to kill the boar."

"Seriously, Saanvi, that story gets more insane every time you tell it," Jill said as she entered the restroom.

Cary laughed. "Yeah, I don't recall mom using the snakes to scare the boar. I thought she tore the tusks off with her bare hands."

"So I like to embellish a little. Moral of it remains the same: Mom is not easily rattled."

Cary chuckled. "No pun intended, right?"

<*I guess she just misses us,*> Faleena said with a wistful tone. <*Stars know I miss her. Angela, too.*>

"Two years, and we'll get our commissions and be out there," Jill said. "It's going to be weird working under mom, though."

Cary snorted. "Imagine your poor CO, having the Marine

Commandant's daughter to care for. You're going to give that poor man or woman a lot of sleepless nights."

Jill shrugged and pulled her long, blue hair back. "They'll have to suck it up. I'm not taking some support role just 'cause of who my mom is."

"I hear you there," Cary replied with a resolute nod.

* * * * *

"Remember, you've got this in the bag," Cary said, and gave her friend and encouraging smile.

"OK, Cary, I'll ask her tomorrow," JP said with a resolute nod.

"Awesome! See you later, JP," Cary said as she turned down the corridor that led to her final class of the day. She'd only walked a dozen paces when Faleena spoke up, her mental tone filled with urgency.

<Cary, Nance is missing again.>

<Where?> Cary asked.

<Same place, Savannah Park on Ring Nine.>

Cary made a quick one-eighty in the corridor and turned back toward the main sweep and the maglev platform.

<Should we tell Saanvi?> Faleena asked.

<Let's take a gander down there first. See if there's anything to get worked up over.>

<You're going to miss your next class,> Faleena cautioned.

<This is more important,> Cary replied, though she was biting her lip, worried about what the consequences would be—from the instructors, *and* from her father.

She took a maglev to Ring Nine, willing the train to go faster all the while.

Cary hoped that maybe Nance just liked to sun herself in the Savannah, and did so in a location where monitoring was knocked out.

She imagined that when she arrived, Nance would be taking a nap on a rock, Cary would see her, no harm, no foul, and she'd just be a few minutes late for class.

When the maglev stopped, Cary rushed off and raced down the sweep to the Savannah Park. She wove in and out of the crowds; many of the men and women down here were in their second or third year, and a few looked askance at a cadet rushing past, but no one stopped her or called out.

When she reached the park, she slowed. "Which way, Faleena?"

<*I'll guide you,*> her sister replied. <*It's about half a klick in.*>

Cary walked at a brisk pace through the low scrub. She didn't want to look too suspicious if she ran into Nance just casually strolling around.

<*Here we are,*> Faleena said as Cary reached the Victoria memorial.

"Really? There's no monitoring around the memorial?" Cary asked.

<*From what the logs show, it was a bit of a tactical error in a Marine boot exercise. They had put a stasis shield around the pillar, and the newbs that rolled through had lain down a lot of electron beam fire. Toasted a whack of the sweep's electronics. Their DI hadn't properly cleared electron beam usage—though he thought he had. Just one of the wrinkles on a new station with new facilities.*>

<*Really?*> Cary asked. <*How could he* **think** *he had clearance when he didn't?*>

Faleena's avatar shrugged. <*He sent everything in and got preliminary acceptance, which was later denied by Colonel Chester. But the DI didn't get the denial.*>

That in and of itself seemed suspicious to Cary. <*How long ago was that?*>

<*Mmm…huh…that was the live fire exercise I'd mentioned before, but* **this** *information says it was three weeks ago. Weird that it hasn't been fixed yet,*> Faleena replied, perplexed. <*Huh, look at that. The maintenance requests keep getting routed to the bots for Ring One, and they respond that they don't do work on Ring Ten, and that just bounces back to one of the message relays and never makes it back to the requestor…. Cary, I'm still pretty new to all this, but this strikes me as highly unusual.*>

Cary gave a soft laugh as she walked up to the pillar. "Yeah, just a bit."

She pulled up the local schematics for the ring and saw that there was a maintenance tunnel access at the base of the pillar.

<*Can you pop it?*>

<*Sure,*> Faleena replied. <*At some point, Odin is going to notice a preponderance of atypical activities from me, you know.*>

<*Well, let's hope that doesn't happen 'til after we figure out what's up.*>

The access hatch gave a *snick* and popped open. Cary lifted it and dropped down into the tunnel. She made a guess as to the best way to go and moved down the tunnel until they came to an intersection.

<*Left,*> Faleena advised.

<*What makes you say that?*> Cary asked.

<*Call it a hunch.*>

Cary shook her head. Faleena seemed to be making a lot of decisions by gut instinct lately. From what she understood, that had to do with the evolution of new interconnectivity in the AI's mind. Her sister's ability to make deductions and intuitive leaps would only increase over time.

Cary followed the left-hand passage and passed an auxiliary comm relay panel. It was a secondary, hard-wired backup system, not the more elegant waveguides used elsewhere.

The existence of the panel was entirely unremarkable, but what caught her attention were the scuffmarks along its edge. The backup systems were tested regularly, but the station was far too new for this amount of physical access to an auxiliary system such as this.

She felt a similar sentiment from Faleena in her mind, and pulled open the panel to reveal a small bundle of clothing and a flow armor application canister.

<*Holy shit!*> Cary exclaimed.

<*This is a bit on the incriminating side,*> Faleena admitted.

<*I think we should tell Dad about this. He'll want to know,*> Cary said.

<*Absol—Damn! The Link just crapped out.*>

Cary tried to access the Link as well, and got no response from any local networks.

<*Shit, you're right. What the?*>

"Cary? Dammit, why'd it have to be you?"

Cary spun around. She didn't see anyone, but she knew that voice. "Nance?" she asked. "Nance? What are you doing? What's going on with this skulking around shit?"

Nance's face appeared before her, flow armor pulling back down to her neck. "I'm sorry, Cary, Faleena. It won't let me let you go."

"What won't what?"

<*Her nanocloud is attacking us!*> Faleena shouted in Cary's mind. <*Run!*>

Cary turned and ran as fast as she could, outpacing the nano in the air around them. Behind her, she heard Nance swear, and assumed that the woman was giving chase; though the armor masked her sounds.

<Can we combat her? We have cloud dispersal for our nano, too,> Cary replied.

<What do you think I'm doing?> Faleena retorted. *<She's good, though. Really, really good.>*

Cary turned one corner and then another, suddenly realizing that she had no idea where they were. They had accessed the local schematics over the Link, and now that access was gone.

<Get around that corner,> Faleena directed. *<I'm going to do a power surge and ionize the air. Maybe I can take out some of her nano.>*

Cary complied, and a shower of sparks lit up the corridor behind her.

"Nice try, Cary," Nance said, her voice echoing down the maintenance tunnel. "But this isn't something you can fight. You'll have no choice but to submit to it."

"What is 'it'?" Cary shot back, moving down a side passage as she heard Nance's voice grow louder.

Nance laughed. "Wouldn't I like to know. It calls itself the Caretaker. It put something inside me…something I can't resist."

"Can you try?" Cary asked. "I fully endorse resisting whatever it is that's controlling you—especially if it wants to do something to us."

Nance rounded the corner, her body visible now, as the flow armor had taken on a matte-grey appearance from the neck down.

"I've been trying for years…sometimes I thought it was gone; it had left me or died out or something, but ever since Cereleon Station in Perseus, it's been fully alert…up in here with me the whole time," Nance tapped her head as she finished the statement.

She didn't look crazy; more saddened, dismayed, forlorn. If she hadn't been planning to kill her, Cary would have offered the woman a warm embrace.

"What does it want?" Cary said instead, walking backward as Nance slowly advanced.

"It's using me to wipe out the shells Myrrdan left behind. Following a trail to find him."

"Myrrdan?" Cary asked, shaking her head. "Myrrdan died back in Landfall. Jessica killed him."

Nance shrugged. "Well, Trist did it, but yeah, it was a joint effort. But by then, Myrrdan had spread himself. That was just a spare shell that they killed; a useful pawn to sacrifice when the game wasn't going his way. That's what we all are, you realize—pawns."

<*Is she suffering some sort of breakdown?*> Faleena asked.

"Pawns of who?" Cary asked Nance as she continued to move backward down the tunnel.

"Damned if I know," Nance said. "But they're powerful. They do whatever they want. And right now, my remnant is telling me that I have to convert you."

<*I don't like the sounds of that,*> Faleena said, a note of panic in her voice.

<*You're telling me.*> Cary's back hit something, and she turned to see that she'd reached the end of the tunnel—there was no way out.

"Shit," she whispered.

"It won't hurt," Nance said. "You'll feel really good afterward—the remnant will help you."

Cary watched Nance draw closer. Her voice was calm and even, but Nance's eyes were wide with terror, as though she was just as horrified by this as Cary was.

Nance raised her hands, and filaments of nano—so many that they were visible to the naked eye—streaked out from her hands and hit Cary in the chest.

CONFRONTATION

STELLAR DATE: 08.12.8948 (Adjusted Years)
LOCATION: Maintenance Tower, near Imperial Palace Complex
REGION: Alexandria, Bosporus System, Scipio Empire

Tanis shook her head as all her senses rushed back inside of herself and the nanoprobes went offline.

<The air in here is heavily ionized. We can't send out new nano, and the Link is toast.>

<At least the armor—> Tanis cut her statement short as the flow armor's stealth mode failed, unable to cope with the lingering effects of the EM.

Still, there were only so many places her enemy could be, and Tanis steadily approached the far corner of the level—the only area the nano hadn't reached.

Easing around a tank, she saw Diana standing in the middle of a well-lit area between two rows of tanks. The empress's eyes were wide, and there was a chain wrapped tightly around her neck, which was connected to a crane above. Her arms were cuffed behind her back, and she stood on the balls of her feet to keep enough slack in the chain around her throat.

"She looks good golden, doesn't she?" a voice called out.

Tanis recognized it at once. "Elena. Show yourself."

"No, I don't think so. Like I said, I was hoping for Sera. I'm fairly certain I could take her one on one; she doesn't have the same drive she once did. But you? No, I'm not so foolish. Going head to head with the great Tanis Richards is not on my bucket list."

"You're not on mine, either," Tanis replied. "But I'll make a space."

"Funny, Tanis. You have to ask yourself…What are you willing to do to save Diana? If she dies, it's a certainty that you and Sera will not fare so well. Sure, you may get off world, but your alliance with Scipio will be over before it even started."

"I thought we'd become friends," Tanis said. "I introduced you to my family; you broke bread with us, Elena. Is this the real you? Or was that?"

Elena's voice came from a new location, and Tanis realized she was speaking through remotes.

"I was a spy, Tanis. That's just the sort of thing spies do. As for the real me? Who knows. I haven't been the real me since the day I joined The Hand. I'm pretty sure she's long dead."

"You could find her again," Tanis said. "Jessica did. She spent a long time in deep cover and came through it."

"Seriously, Tanis? It took Jessica a hundred years and the death of her wife to get through that shit. Who's got that sort of time?"

"We all will, once this war is over. It's a pointless war. Trying to control the advance of humanity, like Kirkland wants to do...It won't work. It'll create an eternal conflict."

Elena's voice shifted to a new location. "I don't think so. Orion has peace, there's no corruption. Garza will ensure that spreads to all the stars."

"Garza?" Tanis asked. "Do you mean the Garza we have in stasis on the *Intrepid*? I got an eyes-on confirmation right before the party."

"What?" came Elena's startled voice.

<*She didn't say that through a remote,*> Angela said.

The ionization in the air from the EM pulse had decreased, and Tanis sent out a fresh wave of nano, searching for the source of the utterance.

She thought she had tracked it down when she heard a footfall behind her. She whirled and found herself staring down the barrel of a railgun.

"Funny how ionization can either ruin stealth or help it work even better. Just depends on the method of concealment," the figure holding the railgun said. Tanis took a step back, and the figure followed, moving out into the light to show his face

Garza.

<*How the hell?*> Angela asked. <*We really need to re-evaluate our security protocols on the* I2.>

"How did you escape?" Tanis asked.

"Oh, you know," Garza replied. "I'm wily like that. I have more tricks up my sleeve than you knew existed, Tanis Richards. I assume that your black outfit is your vaunted flow armor, right? Think it can stop a railgun?"

<*Don't really need him to test that,*> Angela said softly. <*It sure as hell*

can't.>

"What do you want, Garza?" Tanis asked. "I assume you orchestrated all of this for a purpose?"

"I did, indeed. Elena back there—" Garza nodded toward a figure moving out of the shadows to his left "—was hoping to capture Sera. Some sort of twisted, love-based retribution. But *I* was hoping for you. Your people will trade your picotech for you, Tanis Richards."

"All this for me?" Tanis asked. "I'm touched."

Garza laughed. "Well, we were planning to take out Diana even before you got here, but things coincided so nicely. And then Elena showed up, and we decided to strike while the iron was hot."

"Trade, Garza?" Elena asked as she approached. "We have to destroy their tech. New Canaan is a poison that will sweep across the Transcend and then the rest of the stars!"

Garza shook his head. "You're an amazing woman, Elena. At least insofar as how well the conditioning worked on you. Otherwise you're a fool. We need the tech to win the war; it's that simple."

"What about after the war?" Elena asked. "There's no way we can contain it if it gets used in the war. I thought that was the whole reason we were stopping them."

Tanis could hear the confusion in Elena's voice, and Garza sighed in frustration. "Yes, yes, tomorrow's problems."

He twitched the railgun to the side, directing it toward Elena. Tanis seized the opportunity and rushed Garza. She slammed into him just as he fired at Elena. A scream punctuated the air, and Tanis saw through the nano feeds that Elena's right arm was gone, as was most of shoulder.

Garza swung a fist at Tanis's head, but she caught it in her left hand and fired a pulse blast from the emitter embedded in her left arm. The concussive shock rippled through his fist and up his arm. She could feel his bones shatter under the force, and the Orion general let out his own scream.

"What goes around," Tanis said.

<*You should absolutely keep that pulse emitter in there. Why didn't you ever do that before?*> Angela asked.

Tanis delivered another blow—without the pulse blast—to Garza's face. <*Because I had a real arm, which I still plan to get back some day.*>

<*Sure, yeah, just after the war. You should get your right arm removed, too.*>

Tanis raised her arm to fire again when a voice called out, "Freeze!"

She looked up to see a trio of soldiers approaching. They weren't wearing Scipian uniforms, but the armor bore no markings.

<Orion? It doesn't look like armor we have on record.>

<Maybe they're local mercs,> Angela replied. *<Hard to get a whole squad of soldiers on world. Easier to buy ones that are already here.>*

<So much for all of Diana's vaunted 'rule with an iron fist' nonsense,> Tanis replied as she slowly rose to her feet.

Garza pulled himself backward with his good arm until one of the soldiers bent to help him up. The general hissed with pain as he rose, but eyed Tanis's left arm hungrily.

"You're just full of surprises, Tanis Richards. I'm going to enjoy seeing what makes you tick."

Tanis didn't reply as she sent out a new wave of nano, trying to find out how many soldiers there were. No one would send in just three; there had to be more, and their stealth tech had to be good.

<I'm changing what we're looking for,> Angela said. *<If they're using the EMP's ionization to hide, then I can use that to find them.>*

A moment later, several more figures were highlighted on Tanis's HUD, and then several more, until she counted thirteen soldiers in all.

"First things first," Garza said, glancing back at one of the soldiers behind him. "Kill the Empress. We don't need the bait anymore."

The woman raised her rifle and took aim at Diana's head. Tanis saw that it was a slug thrower, and knew it would hurt, but leapt in front of the empress as the soldier fired.

A trio of rounds ricocheted off her chest, momentarily knocking the wind out of Tanis.

"A pointless gesture," Garza said. "You can't block shots from all of them."

Tanis struggled to her knees and looked up as Garza approached.

<With the air all charged up, I can't get enough nano on him to attack his nervous system,> Angela said. *<You need to grab his neck.>*

Tanis examined the enemy soldiers' positions. Five were on catwalks above, two were on tanks, three were behind Garza, and three more were behind Tanis.

<Going to be tricky. If they **are** *mercs, let's hope Garza hasn't rendered final payment, or they may just shoot both of us.>*

Tanis was about to fire her pulse emitter at Garza and go for his throat, when a dark shape streaked through the air and ripped one of the soldiers from the catwalks above, flinging him into a tank.

A white shape followed the dark one, grabbed another soldier, and repeated the action.

Tanis could make out the second figure. It was Petra. Which meant that the other newcomer was Sera.

She didn't waste the opportunity the distraction created. She fired a pulse blast into Garza's stomach, which doubled him over, but not before she grabbed his neck, flooding nano into his body. Angela took over as he fell to the ground, and Tanis turned, suffering a moment's indecision as to whether or not she should help Elena.

Then she saw Sera flash past, swinging her sword at one of the enemy soldiers, and sighed.

<I guess I have to save the bitch. Sera will be upset if I don't.>

Angela nodded in her mind. *<Though we'll probably regret it later.>*

Elena was shivering convulsively, and her eyes had rolled back in her head. Tanis placed her left hand on the woman's wound and let enough flowmetal run off her to create a thin layer over Elena's shoulder. She then flushed a passel of mednano in as well.

Tanis glanced about and saw that Sera and Petra had taken down four other soldiers, but they were suffering under more than their share of enemy weapons fire. Petra's wings were torn in several places—though Sera's seemed mostly intact.

One of the enemy troops was taking careful aim at Petra's head, and Tanis shot him with the slug thrower embedded in her arm. It wasn't enough to penetrate his armor, but it did make him duck back behind cover. Then Tanis fired two shots at the chain suspending Diana, and the empress crumpled to the ground.

Tanis was about to crawl over and check on the golden woman, when more soldiers in unmarked armor appeared, and someone yelled, "Stand down!"

<I count thirty total,> Angela reported. *<We can't take them all.>*

Tanis saw Petra raise her hands in defeat, and a moment later, Sera's sword clattered to the floor as she followed suit.

"What did you do to him?" one of the soldiers asked as he approached Tanis and shoved his gun in her face.

Tanis didn't reply as the enemy closed in around her.

REMNANT

STELLAR DATE: 08.12.8948 (Adjusted Years)
LOCATION: Intrepid Space Force Academy
REGION: The Palisades, Orbiting Troy, New Canaan System

No! Nance screamed from within the confines of her mind. *I won't do it! I won't hurt her!*

Your desires are immaterial, the remnant said as it raised her hands. Nance had fought it every step down the tunnel, forcing it to make each movement against her will; she had controlled some of the words coming out of her mouth, but had never managed to say exactly what she wanted.

In the end, the thing inside her had fully taken over her speech as well.

Nance had hoped the remnant would weaken from the effort to control her, but it seemed to grow stronger. Now she was completely trapped in her mind; it felt the same as the time Myrrdan had utterly controlled her on Ikoden.

She railed at her body, trying to get her limbs to respond, but they wouldn't. Her hands stretched out toward Cary, and Nance tried to force them back down with every fiber of her being, but to no effect.

The nano streaked out from her hands, streaming through the air using tiny ES fields to close with Cary and penetrate her skin.

She watched as the entity within her did battle with Cary and Faleena's biological and nanotech defenses. The young woman and her all-but-newborn AI put up a very impressive fight, pushing back the remnant's efforts at first.

But then the remnant did something Nance didn't quite understand: it breached Cary and Faleena's internal security with an extradimensional attack, destroying all of the nano in the young woman's body. Nance cried out in terror as the remnant Linked directly to Cary's mind.

<Stop!> Cary screamed, revealing a strength that Nance would not have expected.

<You will submit.> The remnant intoned. *<We will make you our tool.>*

<*Like hell you will,*> Faleena said.

Then Nance felt something hit her from behind, the force of which drove her forward into Cary, and they fell in a heap. The remnant turned her head, and Nance saw Saanvi jump atop her, driving her fists into Nance's ribs and kidneys.

The remnant ignored the pain and pushed a cloud of nano into Saanvi, who went rigid and fell to the deck. Cary reached out and clasped Saanvi's hand as the remnant turned its full focus back to Cary.

The being was pushing at the bounds of Cary's very person, inserting its own code into her DNA, into the cells of her brain, rewriting her into its own embodiment.

Nance despaired that she had now destroyed these two women, sentencing them to the same purgatory where she had spent the last eighteen years, when something occurred that she could never have expected.

One moment, the remnant was doing battle with three separate entities: Cary, Faleena, and Saanvi.

The next moment, there was just one.

In Nance's mind, this new being appeared to be luminescent, as bright and strong as the Caretaker had been. Its thoughts were resolute, and it quickly and swiftly dealt with every attack that the remnant delivered.

The combined entity pushed the remnant's nano back, correcting any alterations that it had made in Cary's mind. Once that was complete, the tide turned.

Cary and Saanvi's nano invaded Nance's body—disabling her mods, destroying her nano, and locking down her Link access, trapping the remnant in place.

Nance sensed an inquisitive focus from the Cary-Faleena-Saanvi being. It was searching inside her, trying to find where the entity that controlled her lay.

Nance wished that she could help them, but if she knew that, she would have tried to cut it out years ago.

But they found it somehow, and Nance felt her skin crawl as the trio began to separate it from her. It was as though Cary's merge was not operating on the same plane of existence as her. Whatever they were doing, though, it seemed to be working, as Nance felt freedom of movement return.

A second later, the remnant was completely gone. The controlling entity was no longer present in her mind. For a moment, she worried that it had merely retreated again, but this was different. There was a sense of clarity to her thoughts that she had not felt in ages.

Her limbs were hers to control once more, and she pushed herself off Cary, rolling to the side and gasping for breath.

"I'm free," she whispered. "Free of it."

"Yes, you are," Cary's voice sounded strange, like a chorus.

Nance turned to see Cary kneeling with something in her hand. It was a glowing ball, wrapped in dark bands. The ball pushed at the bands, but whenever it did, darkness spread across its surface and it recoiled.

"Is that…is that the remnant?" Nance asked as a wave of dizziness pulled at her mind.

"It's whatever was in you, yes," Cary said in her strange voice. "It's going to tell us what it was doing—why it was inside you."

Nance tried to move, but realized that her back hurt a lot.

"I'm sorry. I hit you with a metal bar," Cary explained. "I probably broke some ribs."

"You?" Nance asked and looked to Saanvi, who was also rising. "I thought Saanvi did that."

"I did," Saanvi replied with the same voice as Cary. "We are one being. The three of us. It's hard to explain."

Nance couldn't even begin to imagine.

"You should rest," Cary said, and reached out toward Nance. The moment her fingers touched Nance's forehead, she felt a wave of calm wash over her. She laid down before a deep sleep came over her.

CAVALRY

STELLAR DATE: 08.12.8948 (Adjusted Years)
LOCATION: Maintenance Tower, near Imperial Palace Complex
REGION: Alexandria, Bosporus System, Scipio Empire

Garza's soldiers pulled Tanis to her feet and pushed her against one of the tanks, while others directed Sera and Petra to stand beside her.

"Nice rescue," Tanis said.

"Next time we go to a party like that, we all pack heat," Sera replied. "Swords are great and all, but they really suck for long-range work."

"Also hard for them to cut through CF ablative armor," Petra added.

"Shut up, you three," one of the soldiers said. It was the same one who had addressed Tanis earlier, and he turned to her once more. "What did you do to him? Is he going to be OK?"

Tanis shrugged. "Depends on what you do to us. We stay alive, so does he."

<Do we have enough nano to hit him from a distance?> Tanis asked.

<No,> Angela replied. *<And the ionization is still shorting out a lot of the cloud. At this rate, we'll be blind again in a few minutes.>*

One of the soldiers grabbed Diana by the remainder of the chain around her neck and hauled her to her feet, throwing the empress against the tanks with the others. Tanis reached up and helped Diana remove the chain from around her neck, and the woman drew a ragged breath.

"Thanks," she whispered hoarsely.

"Fix him," the man gestured to Garza, who lay perfectly still, though his eyes were wide and staring.

"I can't here," Tanis said. "I'll need an autodoc."

"My people will be here soon," Diana rasped. "You won't survive the encounter."

The soldier laughed. "*Your* people, Empress Diana, think that *their* people are to blame." He gestured with his rifle at Tanis, Sera, and Petra. "A nice bit of misdirection that my employer sowed in your networks. Your AIs are doing whatever we say. Right now, they're attacking the *Aegeus*. They're convinced that the shuttle made it there, and that

Admiral Richards and the dragon queen here are holding you hostage."

"Shit," Diana whispered, looking to Tanis. "Your ship…your people."

"They'll be fine," Tanis replied. "That's the thing about us folk from the *Intrepid*. We're survivors."

"Well, step one will to be to fix him so we can get paid," the lead soldier said.

<*So they are mercs. Good,*> Tanis said.

<*I have a tenuous connection to a network,*> Angela reported. <*Trying to reach out.*>

"Like I said," Tanis replied. "Autodoc. We all go, or I kill him right now."

"Fine," the man grunted. "Dragon lady. You carry the armless one."

Sera looked down at Elena, only just then realizing who was lying in a puddle of blood with the remains of her arm nearby.

<*Garza did it,*> Tanis said privately.

<*How the hell did he get here, anyway?*> Sera asked.

<*No clue. He was talking like he'd been working on this mission for a while, though.*>

<*We've not been here for a while.*>

Tanis gave a mental sigh. <*I know.*>

<*How many of him are there?*>

Sera bent over and gently picked Elena up, cradling her in her arms with far more compassion than Tanis thought she would have shown at that juncture.

"Move," the man said and gestured back toward the lift.

It took two lift cars to get them all to the building's roof, where Tanis's smoking aerojet still lay crumpled atop the jumble of pipes.

She was surprised that no local law enforcement had come to investigate the crash. Then she realized that none of the adjacent buildings were illuminated.

<*I guess that EMP was bigger than we thought,*> Tanis said.

<*Building power would be shielded—or it really should be. They must have taken out a part of the grid, as well,*> Angela replied.

"Shuttle coming in," the lead soldier reported and gestured for the captives to back up.

Tanis considered taking a shot at him, but her arm was out of slugs, and pulse blasts wouldn't do much against these armored opponents. The other buildings were close; if she took a run for it, she could leap across and make it to the other side.

Then Tanis glanced at Diana, who was still struggling to breathe. *She's an asshole, but dammit, she's our asshole, and I can't leave her behind.*

<I'm surprised they haven't tried to disarm you,> Angela said with a laugh.

<Seriously, Ang? We're in big trouble, here.>

<Oh, I got a solid Link. Rescue in…five, four, three, two, mark!>

A shape flashed into place overhead, stopping so suddenly that the resulting thunderclap knocked them all to the ground. Tanis looked up to see the *Aegeus*. Above the vessel, she could see dozens of beamfire shots raining down, dissipated by the ship's stasis shield.

<Admiral Richards,> Captain Sheeran's voice came to her mind. *<Do you need a lift out of here?>*

Lights flared on the underside of the starship, and a moment later, a full platoon of Force Recon Orbital Drop Marines stood on the rooftop.

The enemy soldiers were still struggling to rise, but the Marines had come down right on top of them, covering the mercs with heavy weapons.

"Stay down if you don't want to see what your brain looks like going through your eyeballs," one of the Marines yelled.

Tanis rose to her feet and walked to the leader of the enemy soldiers. "Looks like your day just got a lot worse."

Above, beamfire continued to pound the *Aegeus*, and Tanis could see heat pouring off the ship's shield, melting the glass on nearby towers. She called up to Captain Sheeran. *<Send a message to whoever is in charge up there. Tell them we've rescued the Empress; then ask them to stop shooting at her, she looks very tired.>*

"Glad to see you're OK," a voice said from behind them, and Tanis turned to see Flaherty climb over the edge of the roof.

"Where were you?" Sera said from Elena's side.

"I was nearby in case things got out of control."

Tanis snorted, and Sera laughed. "That wasn't out of control enough?"

Flaherty shrugged. "Didn't want you to get complacent."

DAUGHTERS

STELLAR DATE: 08.12.8948 (Adjusted Years)
LOCATION: Intrepid Space Force Academy
REGION: The Palisades, Orbiting Troy, New Canaan System

Joe raced through the narrow confines of the tunnel, pushing past security teams and medics in his rush to reach his daughters.

He rounded the final corner and saw Cary and Saanvi standing together, arms around one another's shoulders as a medic checked them over.

Warring emotions thundered through Joe; he pushed all but relief to the side as he strode toward them, his arms held out. The two young women who meant more to him than anything else in the universe stretched theirs out as well.

The medic stepped aside at the last moment to avoid being caught in the middle, and the three crashed together in a wordless embrace.

Joe felt Faleena in his mind and brought her into a mental embrace as well.

"You three," he whispered. "You just can't avoid trouble, can you?"

Cary pulled back to look him in the eyes. "Well, at least we come by it honestly, Dad."

Her voice sounded strained, and Joe shook his head. "That you do."

Cary took a step back and held out the hand that had been hidden behind Saanvi. "We need to do something about this thing."

Joe peered at the glowing ball of light wrapped in black bands that rested on his daughter's palm. It seemed sedate, pulsing and rotating slowly.

"Is that it? The thing you extracted from Nance? Where is she, anyway?"

Saanvi stepped aside and gestured at the far corner of the corridor's dead end to where a cluster of medics was working over Nance. "We put her to sleep. She's got some broken bones, but I think that's the extent of her physical damage."

Joe noticed that Saanvi's voice had the same strange quality to it as Cary's, and he suspected what it meant. "To think that this thing was inside her all this time and we never knew."

<There's more, Dad,> Cary said privately. *<This thing was hunting Myrrdan—it is also what was in Myrrdan….>*

<What the hell!?> Joe exclaimed. The revelation hit him like a starship, and he felt a moment of dizziness. *<But you said you think this is a sliver of an extra-dimensional being…maybe one of the core AIs.>*

Cary and Saanvi nodded physically, while Faleena did so in their minds. *<That's right, Dad. And one of them had something inside of Myrrdan; something that can replicate itself. Maybe a lot.>*

<Shit,> Joe muttered as the enormity of this hit him. *<If Myrrdan had a…whatever in him, and it could replicate, they could be anywhere.>*

<We need to get this thing—and Nance—to Earnest,> Cary urged. *<I don't know for sure what will hold it, but it's taking Saanvi, Faleena, and me being deep-Linked to pull it off.>*

Joe looked at the medics. *<OK. I figured you three were doing your deep-Link, and damn I'm glad that it did the trick. Let's get you and Nance to a ship and out to Gamma VIII where Earnest is working.>*

<Ready when you are,> his girls said as one.

"OK, people, I want this scene scrubbed and everything categorized and packaged up. You two," he pointed to the pair of medics closest to Nance, "We're bringing her along."

"Along where, sir?" one of the medics asked.

"To the *Freedom's Fire*," Joe replied. "We have a date with Earnest Redding."

AEGEUS

STELLAR DATE: 08.13.8948 (Adjusted Years)
LOCATION: Aegeus, over the Imperial Palace
REGION: Alexandria, Bosporus System, Scipio Empire

It took Diana getting in touch with the commander of the space defense directly to convince the Scipians to stop firing on the *Aegeus*.

The ship had run the CriEn module powering the shields down to the wire; it was dangerously close to a space-time distortion that would have caused destruction on a planetary scale. Everyone breathed a sigh of relief when the beams stopped raining down.

The Scipians were not convinced that their empress wasn't under duress. Diana, however, was certain that at least one of the prelates—other than Fiona—had used the abduction as an opportunity to stage a coup. She claimed it was the only reason they would fire so heavily on the ship supposedly holding her hostage.

Once aboard, Diana refused to leave the *Aegeus* until the commander of Alexandria's Space Defense revealed who had given her the orders to fire on the ship, even when it was suspected to be—and later *was*—holding the Empress.

By the time Diana was prepared to return to the Imperial Palace, Prelate Bella, two admirals, one general, and the commander of the planetary space defense were all under arrest.

Tanis escorted Diana to the *Aegeus*'s main shuttle bay in silence, wondering what the empress was thinking. She had spent so much time fighting with her own government, that little time had been given to discuss the abductors and their goals.

"So, that was Orion, was it?" she asked as they walked down a corridor leading to the bay. "Hard to believe that such a small team could thwart us so easily."

"If it makes you feel any better, those were some of their top operatives."

"Perhaps a little," Diana replied.

<It was your AIs' immaturity that allowed them to succeed with relative ease,> Angela said. *<Once your AIs are properly raised, they will not be so*

easily bested by enemies such as these.>

"Or you, Angela?" Diana asked. "From what I understand, you can move across our networks with impunity."

Angela laughed. *<It would certainly make it harder for me. They'd at least be aware I was doing it.>*

Diana shook her head. "I feel like I had just finally figured out my place in this world, what everything meant and how it fit together…only to find that I don't know anything, and I'd mashed all the puzzle pieces into the wrong places and now nothing fits."

"Well," Tanis said, her voice soft. "You have a friend in myself, Angela, and Sera. And I think you have more than a friend in Petra, if you treat her right. She'll be at your side to assist you in whatever way you need—no double entendre intended."

Diana laughed—a real, deep, heartfelt laugh. Possibly the first one Tanis had heard from the empress. "I suppose I will. I'll have to modify my behavior…I don't think she'll accept the role of underling anymore."

"She is the Transcend's direct representative. I would expect no less," Tanis said with a smile, but a stern note as well.

"Yes, the Transcend. Already the feeds are ablaze with talk of this ship from beyond the rim of explored space that has impenetrable shields. People aren't stupid; many have already begun to draw connections between this vessel and the ships seen at Bollam's World twenty years ago. It does not look so dissimilar, you know."

"We don't have to tell them everything at once," Tanis said. "Though it's up to you as to how much you reveal."

"I think we should tell them everything—except we'll omit your civil war, for now. Certainly we need to explain the Transcend and Orion, now that Orion has struck at the heart of our empire. That will galvanize the populace."

"Some of them, at least," Tanis replied as they reached the shuttle bay. The Scipian shuttle was sitting in the nearest cradle with a dozen of the empress's guards standing at attention outside.

Petra stood before them, wearing a crisp suit with the Transcend Diplomatic Corps crest over her heart, speaking with one of the admirals from the night before. She remembered seeing him, but had to put the image of his first impression out of her mind so that she could look at him with a straight face.

The night before, the bizarre Scipian party with the ridiculous costumes, seemed like a drug-induced haze now that they were back on an ISF ship.

Petra smiled with a trace of uncertainty showing around her eyes as Tanis and Diana approached. The admiral she was with saluted Diana, and the empress nodded to him.

"Admiral Sula," she greeted him amicably.

"Empress, it is so good to see you unharmed."

"I agree whole-heartedly," Diana replied. "I am not entirely unharmed, but it is not anything that will take long to heal."

She turned to Petra, and the two stared at one another for a moment before Diana placed a hand on Petra's shoulder. "I think some of those wounds are starting to heal now," Diana said, her eyes squinting with genuine joy as a smile pulled at her lips.

"Admiral Richards, please give my regards to President Sera. As with you, I owe her my life."

Tanis nodded. "She sends her regards. She's…with Elena."

"The woman who abducted me," Diana said flatly; her previously joyful expression replaced by one far darker. Then it cleared. "I'll trust you to mete out justice as necessary. Though I expect there *to be* justice."

Tanis pulled at her ponytail where it rested on her shoulder. "I do too. However, from what Garza said, she may not have been acting of her own accord. We'll need to get to the bottom of that."

"It can be very difficult to delve into a mind that has been corrupted in such a way," Diana said. "You run the risk of destroying her."

"That is true," Tanis agreed. "But she'll talk to Bob, and he'll determine the best way to proceed."

"Bob?" Diana asked.

"When next we meet, Diana, let's do it on the *I2*. You'll get to see Bob in person, sort of."

"I look forward to it."

* * * * *

"Sera? Uh…Sera?"

The sound of Elena's voice brought Sera out of her tired stupor in slow stages. She lifted her head off the back of the chair and met Elena's eyes.

"Looks like you made it."

Elena gave a slight nod and glanced at the regrow module that covered her right shoulder. She closed her eyes and gave a soft sigh. "But from the sound of your voice, I may wish I hadn't."

Sera felt anger surge in her and her throat tightened. "You're a right fucking moron, you know that, Elena? Escaping, abducting Diana. Believing Garza's lies. Tanis told me what happened. You *have* to see it, now."

She saw a tear escape Elena's eye as she nodded. "I do. I just wanted something better. Your father, his empire, it was so cold, and Garza had all the answers."

Sera rose from her chair and strode to the window. It wasn't a real window—rather a holodisplay depicting a field of flowers on a sunny afternoon. She stared at it for a minute, wishing it could give her the answers.

"I'm sorry, Sera," Elena offered behind her.

Sera spun. "'Sorry'? 'Sorry', Elena? You nearly ruined *everything*! I mean…you fucking killed my father, and if *that* wasn't enough, you—"

"I saved you from that!" Elena yelled back, then began to cough. Sera just watched until Elena had control of herself again. "You were going to do it," she rasped. "I saved you from the guilt of killing your own father, and you know it! So don't you try to pin that on me."

"I wouldn't have done it," Sera replied in a small voice. Even she knew she was lying.

"Bullshit. I *know* you, Sera. I know you better than you know yourself. You were going to do it."

"You don't know me that well, Elena," Sera retorted. "You turned on me because you thought I'd be a despot like my father. You never even gave me a chance. I'm doing the best I can, and I'm a hell of a lot better than Kirkland and Garza. You know what he is, right?"

Elena pursed her lips but didn't reply.

"He's a clone," Sera said, her tone flat. "They both are, as it turns out, the one on Alexandria, and the one on the *I2*. Both are clones of the real Garza."

"What?" Elena asked, genuine surprise on her face.

"Yeah, we're not sure how, but it may be the tech that the oligarchs in the Hegemony use. Your low-tech Orion utopia is a lie. Jessica saw it firsthand in Perseus, and now you've seen it here. When are you going to wake up? They're not the good guys."

"Don't act like you are, either," Elena replied softly. "The Hand has abducted and killed its fair share of leaders. You're not the good guys either."

Sera slumped against the window. "I don't think there are any 'good guys'. Look. I'm not the one waging a war here to take over everything. I want to keep New Canaan's picotech secure. I want to defeat Airtha because she's an evil bitch who needs to die. And I want Orion to stay in its borders and stop inciting wars in the Inner Stars. I don't need to be queen bee; I just want everyone to stop trying to make everyone else be just like them."

"How do I know that you'll stop there?" Elena asked. "How do I know Tanis will?"

Sera walked to the foot of Elena's bed. "You know, you could have been a voice at the table, helping us stay on the straight and narrow. But now, I guess you'll just have to listen to the guards to see how things are going."

"So I'm going back in my cage, am I?" Elena asked.

Sera snorted. "If I can keep the Scipian demands at bay. You know what will happen if they get you."

"Execution."

"Or worse."

A look of genuine fear filled Elena's face, and Sera realized that she couldn't deal with it anymore. She simply could not.

Without a backward glance, she left the room and raced down the passageway. Once she was out of sight, she ducked into an alcove, buried her face in her hands, and began to cry—all the while, quivering with rage.

It's over. I can't pretend anymore. Now that Elena was finally seeing the error of her ways, *this* is when they'd reached the point where there could never be a possibility of reuniting? All because Diana wouldn't stand for Elena escaping punishment.

What bitter irony.

It was well and truly over between them.

A NEW ENEMY

STELLAR DATE: 08.15.8948 (Adjusted Years)
LOCATION: Command Deck Main Conference Room, ISS *I2*
REGION: Alexandria, Bosporus System, Scipio Empire

"Fucking core devils!" Sera exclaimed as she slammed her fists against the conference room table. "Seriously? Nance?! They do this to Nance?"

Tanis placed a hand on Sera's shoulder from her seat next to the president. They were alone in the room, awaiting Diana's arrival, when the message from Joe came through on the QuanComm. She took a deep breath to steady her own voice. "Nance is going to be OK."

<*Do you understand what this means?*> Bob asked.

Tanis closed her eyes and slowly tilted her head left, then right, trying to ease the tension building in her neck. "Yeah, it means we're all dupes."

<*That's a blunt way to put it,*> Angela said.

"It's true, though," Tanis said as she opened her eyes. "From what Nance told Joe and the girls—if it's true—Myrrdan has been an agent of this 'Caretaker' from the very beginning. They manipulated everything to get us to Kapteyn's Star so that we'd go through the Streamer. Then I suppose they took control of Nance to get her to take out Myrrdan because they were done with him?"

<*It fits the model,*> Bob said. <*Well, mostly.*>

"I thought you could predict the future," Sera asked coolly. "How come you didn't see this?"

<*I can predict the past with a high level of accuracy. But as I've said before, I don't know if it's perfect, because I haven't been able to verify every event that has ever occurred. The future…well, I can predict that nearly as well, but once we jumped forward in time, I tried to make my predictions for the past match the situation we found ourselves in…and there were discrepancies.*>

"What sort of discrepancies?" Tanis asked.

<*Yes, what sort of discrepancies?*> Angela added, her avatar scowling at the amorphous presence of Bob in their minds.

<*The kind that required outside forces to explain. At first I thought maybe it*

was The Hand, or perhaps Orion, operating in some capacity that we were unaware of. But when Finaeus explained the core AI…well, I knew it had to be them. It then became apparent to me that they had agents in the Inner Stars as far back as the thirty-fifth century.>

"There were no 'Inner Stars' in the thirty-fifth century," Sera corrected.

<Not to your way of thinking, no.>

"I wonder if they even left after the Sentience Wars?" Tanis mused. "The ascended AIs, that is. What if they just remained in Sol, or somewhere close by, and have been manipulating us all along?"

"Then what did my mother find around Sagittarius A*?" Sera asked.

<I think they did both,> Bob replied. *<Both scenarios occurring simultaneously fits best.>*

"So why did they make us jump forward to the eighty-ninth century?" Tanis asked. "What was the point of all this?"

"What do you take from the entity's name?" Sera answered Tanis's question with a question. "'The Caretaker'?"

"Given what humanity's been through for the last five thousand years, I'd say the Caretaker is doing a piss-poor job of living up to that moniker."

<The name certainly has meaning,> Bob replied *<When humans first imagined AIs as super intelligent beings, they postulated a scenario where these beings would be powerful enough to maintain humanity in whatever fashion it wanted.>*

Tanis nodded, wondering exactly where Bob was going with this. "I recall studying that long ago; the first notions of the technological singularity from the twentieth century spoke of that outcome as a possibility."

"And there are places where it's a reality," Sera said. "But those branches of the human race tend to go extinct before long."

"The Phobos Accords forbade AI-managed utopias," Tanis added. "For good reason, it seems."

<Yes,> Bob replied. *<We've endeavored to ensure that humans continue to evolve…>*

He trailed off, something the AI almost never did.

"What is it, Bob?" Tanis asked.

<I understand now. The Caretaker and his compatriots, their goal isn't to

shepherd humanity, it's to maintain; to keep your race from evolving. They brought the Intrepid *forward in time in order to precipitate this war. They* ***want*** *the Transcend and Orion to destroy one another. Your two civilizations—especially considering how the relative peace they allow made things like Star City possible—show humanity's ability to move forward beyond the barbarism that pervades the Inner Stars.>*

Tanis sat back as the enormity of Bob's statement hit her.

Not only was he saying that the core AIs were purposely putting humanity through progressive dark ages to keep them from moving forward, but that the *Intrepid*—and presumably herself as well—was meant to be an agent of destruction.

"I can see that in your eyes, Tanis," Sera said quietly from her side. "That anger. We've all been manipulated, here. My mother clearly wants a strong Transcend to defeat the core AI. She was prepared to make me…well, make me what I am today—president, so that I could take the fight to the core."

"Or maybe Airtha is still under the core AIs' sway and she's driving this war forward at their behest," Tanis replied angrily. "We're just their pawns, doing exactly what they want."

<*No,*> Bob intoned. <*We are not.*>

Tanis blew out a sharp breath. "Sure feels like it."

<*You forget what I did,*> Bob said, a small hint of satisfaction in his tone. <*I brought us out early.*>

"That's right!" Sera said. "All our analysis of the flight path the *Intrepid* took—the vector, the Streamer's composition, the whole thing—it pointed to an exit in 9470, give or take a few years."

"Do you think it means they're not ready?" Sera asked.

<*I think that it means conditions are not ideal for a war spanning the Orion Arm. The major empires are not strong enough to defeat all the other smaller nations, and also one another. I think we can manage to bring this war to a stalemate, and then a truce.*>

"How long will it hold for?" Tanis asked as she rose from her chair to look out at the view of Alexandria on the holodisplay on the wall. "A century? A millennium? Ten? These core AIs want to periodically push humanity back to the Stone Age because they think it's what's best for us. Any war which does not end with their destruction is the very definition of futility."

"How are we going to defeat them?" Sera asked. "We're talking about Finaeus's fifth dimensional beings; they can strike at us across planes of existence we don't even know about."

"Not to mention turn people like Nance into their agents without anyone being able to tell," Tanis added.

<*We can't defeat them,*> Bob replied. <*Not yet. First, you two need to unify all of humanity, as well as all AIs, against them.*>

"Why?" Tanis asked.

<*Because if you don't, they'll turn some faction against you and hit you from behind when you try to attack them in the core.*>

"We're going to need to reconnoiter the core," Tanis decided. "We really have no idea what we're dealing with."

"I know someone who's seen the core," Sera said quietly. "And she seems to have a plan for taking them out, as well."

"*If* she's not still under their thrall."

"Stars!" Sera exclaimed and rubbed her eyes. "This is all such a fucking clusterfuck! My mother's evil, my father was a raging asshole, Kirkland is a blind fool, the Inner Stars are rearranging deck chairs on the Titanic—yes, I looked that up—the Inner Stars AIs are threatening war, and we don't know who we can trust *anywhere* anymore. On top of all this, we have Garza clones running all over, making a mess everywhere."

Tanis walked back to her friend and held a hand out to her. "We'll figure it all out, Sera."

"How?" Sera asked, her voice heavy with emotion as she clasped Tanis's hand.

Tanis smiled. "Because we have to."

<*Admiral, President,*> Priscilla interrupted them. <*Diana is here.*>

Sera took a deep breath and ran a hand through her hair. <*Send her in.*>

A moment later, Diana entered the room with an expression of honest amazement on her face. "Quite the ship you have here…I don't think I've ever seen anything like it. Let alone an AI with human avatars."

<*Thank you,*> Bob said, his voice resonating across the Link like distant peals of thunder from a looming storm.

Diana's face paled, and Tanis offered her a chair. "You get used to it."

Diana shook her head in wonder. "I can't see how."

Tanis sat across from Diana, placing her elbows on the table and interlacing her fingers. She met the empress's eyes and took a deep breath. "Are you ready to hear the rest of the story?"

"What, there's more?" Diana asked.

Sera nodded somberly. "A lot more."

THE END

* * * * *

ATTACK ON THEBES

THE ORION WAR – BOOK 5

M. D. COOPER

FOREWORD

I got to write two words in this book that I've been waiting to write since 2009. I'm certain you'll know them when you see them, and I think you've been waiting to read them as well.

Or maybe you haven't. I've been unintentionally over-subtle in the past. It could be that I've done so again.

In many respects, this book is still the continuation of that singular event that occurred on the bridge of the *Galadrial,* when Elena killed Sera's father. That one thing was the catalyst that set in motion every single catastrophe and dire need that's come after.

That's not to say that everything since the president's death wasn't going to happen anyway, but just as the assassination of Archduke Ferdinand set off Earth's first World War, the death of Jeffery Tomlinson has set off the first Galactic War.

As I look over my timeline for all the events that have occurred in the Aeon 14 books—and at those which are yet to come—it's hard to believe that the assassination on the *Galadrial*'s bridge occurred only six months before the beginning of this book.

In fact, everything that occurred in the final chapters of *Orion Rising*, *The Scipio Alliance*, and the first three books of the *Perilous Alliance* series has happened in the half-year span following Sera's assumption of the Transcend's presidency.

It feels almost surreal. But then again, it's been just over six months since *Orion Rising* came out, so it's almost as though we're living this in real time—those of us who are writing and reading the books as they come out, at least.

I imagine later readers are binging happily on the books, excited to know there is a published resolution down the road.

I bring this up because this book wraps up some threads from previous stories, and pulls a few new ones loose. It also checks in on a few that are dangling about, so be sure to read the "Previously" section below.

Another fun thing that I got to do while writing this book, was to refresh myself on some quantum physics, and chat with some of my physicist consultants about how we're really going to deal with detecting fifth dimensional beings. Suffice to say when the characters talk about branes, wimps, and winos, these are not typos. They're talkin' science!

Parts of this book take place after Collision Course, book 3 of the Perilous Alliance series. That series deals with the fallout of Tanis's sale of her nanotech to S&H

Defensive Armaments way back in Destiny Lost. I felt that it was apropos to have that resolution in this book, to tie that together. However, if you wish to have the full story of the mess that made, and how Sera was working to clean it up during the years Tanis was building the New Canaan colony, then I encourage you to read those stories.

For those of you who have been reading the Rika books, the title of this book should ring a bell. If you've not, you may want to read the first three (starting with Rika Outcast) before you dive into Attack on Thebes. You don't have to, but you'll get a bit more flavor as to what is happening in this neck of the woods.

Lastly, it goes without saying, but I'll say it anyway, I had a great time writing this book, and it was awesome to take Tanis to some new places, both in terms of locales and inside of herself.

Malorie. Cooper
Danvers, 2018

PREVIOUSLY IN THE ORION WAR...

Attack on Thebes begins to gather some threads together from prior books, and we encounter some characters that we've not seen for a while.

While The Scipio Alliance focused very closely on Tanis and her daughters, Attack on Thebes broadens the scope once more to give us a view of what's happening on the larger stage.

At the tail end of Orion Rising, we saw what happened to Adrienne (one of the former president's closest advisors) when he returned to Airtha. His son was killed, and he was captured by Sera...but not the Sera who is allied with Tanis.

Airtha, the AI that was once Sera's mother, has crafted a second daughter. Not a clone, exactly, but another version of her. This second Sera has many of the same attributes, thoughts, and even memories, but she is fiercely loyal to her mother.

When Sera captured Adrienne, his son died in the attack, but his daughter, Kara, got away. Kara ended up being rescued by what is quite possibly *the most* unlikely person: Katrina.

If you have not read the Warlord books, then the last time you saw Katrina was five thousand years ago on the Victoria colony at Kapteyn's Star. However, Katrina had some of her own adventures, and has also made her way to the 90th century.

In this book, you'll see more of how that came to pass, and what Katrina and Kara's part to play in this is.

Though the events in Collision Course drew Tanis and the *I2* out of Scipio, this book will start back with Empress Diana and Petra before moving forward to the Silstrand System to deal with the nanotech-related mess there.

Still lying ahead is the retribution Tanis craves for the Trisilieds after they attacked Carthage and killed so many. However, Tanis is now on the hunt for the Caretaker, the mysterious ascended being that left a piece of itself inside Nance, and was also controlling events in Silstrand and beyond...

Reading guide notes: If you have not read the first three books of the Perilous Alliance series, starting with *Close Proximity*, you may wish to do so now to get a complete picture of the events unfolding in the Silstrand System.

In addition, this book introduces us to Rika, who has her own series. You can begin that journey in *Rika Outcast*, book 1 of Rika's Marauders.

KEY CHARACTERS REJOINING US

Abby – Wife of Earnest, and former chief engineer aboard the *Intrepid.*

Andrea – Sera's sister who used a back door into Sera's mind to make Sera try to kill Tanis in the Ascella System.

Adrienne – Transend Secretary of State, and close confidant of the former president, Jeffrey Tomlinson.

Cary – Tanis's biological daughter. Has a trait where she can deep-Link with other people, creating a temporary merger of minds.

Corsia – Ship's AI and captain of the *Andromeda*.

Diana – Empress of the Scipian Empire.

Faleena – Tanis's AI daughter, born of a mind merge between Tanis, Angela, and Joe.

Justin – Former Director of the Hand. Was imprisoned for the events surrounding the attempted assassination of Tanis.

Katrina – Former Sirian spy, wife of Markus, and eventual governor of the Victoria colony at Kapteyn's Star—and Warlord of the Midditerra System.

Kara – Daughter of Adrienne, heavily modded with four arms and wings.

Nadine – A Hand agent who had been assigned to assassinate Peter Rhoads and is now aboard the *I2*.

Nance – Former member of *Sabrina*'s crew, now a member of the ISF.

Petra – Regional Director of the Hand's operations in Scipio and nearby territories. Now the Transcend's Ambassador to Scipio.

Priscilla – One of Bob's two avatars.

Rachel – Captain of the *I2*. Formerly captain of the *Enterprise*.

Saanvi – Tanis's adopted daughter, found in a derelict ship that entered the New Canaan System.

Sera of Airtha – A copy of Sera made by Airtha, containing all of Sera's desired traits and memories. President of the Airthan faction of the Transcend.

Smithers – S&H employee Tanis licensed her nanotech to on the PetSil Mining Platform during her first visit to Silstrand.

Terry – Director of the Security Operations Center on the *I2*. A member of Tanis's original SOC team.

Troy – Ship's AI aboard the *Excelsior*. Was on the mission to secure fuel for the *Intrepid* in Estrella de la Muerte and sacrificed himself to save the *Intrepid* in the Battle for Victoria.

DAUGHTER OF AIRTHA

STELLAR DATE: 08.14.8948 (Adjusted Years)
LOCATION: Airtha Capitol Complex
REGION: Airtha, Huygens System, Transcend Interstellar Alliance

Sera watched Adrienne enter her office, the space so recently occupied by her father, from where the formerly great President Jeffery Tomlinson had ineptly run his expansive empire.

Adrienne had to know he was defeated, know that Sera controlled him utterly, but still he strode in as though he was the master of all he saw.

She turned away from him, looking out the window at the sweeping arch of Airtha, wrapped around the gleaming white dwarf star. Once, this star-encircling ring had been her mother's body. A prison her father had forced on Justina after she returned from the galaxy's core.

He even stripped her of a name, simply calling her 'Airtha', as though she were just an NSAI whose purpose was nothing more than the management of the structure in which it was installed.

But his efforts to both control his former wife and keep her close had been thwarted.

Mother had ascended.

Airtha was no longer an 'AI', a neural network of physical components constructed out of non-organics. Now she was something more. A being of light that existed in more than the few paltry dimensions that made up the corner of space-time that creatures like Adrienne crawled through.

Granted, Sera also existed in the same narrow sliver of existence, but her mother had given her a glimpse of what lay beyond, the power that existed at her fingertips.

Her mother had gifted her with that vision, and with a piece of herself. Not a shard, but a sliver of self that an AI like Bob might carve off, such as what Helen had been.

What Sera now possessed was a full representation of her mother. Like a thinking memory. She would never be separated from her mother again.

"Surveying your domain?" Adrienne asked as he reached her side. "What little of the Transcend you've managed to claim."

"She's claimed no more than I," Sera shot back, annoyed that Adrienne would open with a critical remark such at that.

Adrienne shrugged. "Perhaps. She has Vela, snatched it out from under you. Admiral Krissy is a formidable opponent on her own."

Sera nodded. "Mother regrets not directing more resources toward Krissy's destruction after the debacle at the Grey Wolf Star. But it was not expected that Finaeus would return and connect Krissy to New Canaan."

"I thought the great Airtha was all-knowing?" Adrienne sneered.

"Do I need to kill more of your children to remind you who is in command here?" Sera asked. "You seem to forget your place with startling regularity."

Adrienne drew himself up to his full height. "My place is beside President Tomlinson. I should never have left it."

"You *are* beside President Tomlinson," Sera replied, giving the man a sidelong look of annoyance.

"I'm beside a shadow of Sera Tomlinson. A puppet created by Airtha. How does it feel to be a puppet, False Sera? Do you have strings?" He waved a hand over her head, a mocking smile on his face.

Sera growled and spun, her hand slamming into Adrienne's throat, her other hand planting on his forehead, a tendril of nano flowing out and connecting to his nerves, lighting them afire.

"Is this false?" she hissed. "Don't think that you can trick me into killing you. I can cause you unending pain without ever doing that."

Adrienne was gasping for air, and she kicked his legs out from under him and then let go, dropping the man to the floor.

"You're pathetic, Adrienne."

"And you're unhinged. Unstable," he rasped. "One of these times, you'll do it. You'll kill me, and I'll be free of this prison you've put my mind in."

Sera shrugged. "Perhaps I will. After I'm convinced that you've revealed all your children to me."

The building's NSAI alerted Sera that her guest had arrived, and she turned from the gasping man to greet the newcomer as he approached.

"Ah, General Garza, so glad you arrived safely."

THE REMNANT

STELLAR DATE: 08.15.8948 (Adjusted Years)
LOCATION: Gamma VIII base
REGION: Outer Asteroid Belt, New Canaan System

Cary watched Earnest's eyes grow wide as she walked into his lab in the Gamma VIII base. She still cradled the remnant within her hands, the glowing ball that held the thing that had been inside Nance for so long.

She was accompanied by her father, Saanvi, and two med techs who stood behind the stasis pod that held Nance.

Saanvi had wanted to wake Nance, or to at least try, but their father had insisted that she be put into stasis. His argument was that they didn't know what the thing had done to her. She could be fine, or she could have a trigger nestled within her mind.

There could even be more of the remnant still in her—though Cary didn't think that was the case. She couldn't *feel* any more of it, at least.

"So that's it…a piece of an ascended being," Earnest whispered and gestured toward a table half covered in equipment, standing in the center of the room. "Bring it over here, I want to scan it to see if you need to keep holding it."

"I think she's managed to encapsulate it with magnetically charged membranes," Saanvi offered.

Earnest nodded while not removing his eyes from the sphere in Cary's hands. "Perhaps, perhaps. But if it is a brane, it's a black brane—an M5 at least." He glanced up at Saanvi. "It'd have to be, since this is not a three-dimensional being—though the brane certainly isn't black, is it?"

"All I know is that it hurts my eyes to look at it," Cary said as she leaned on the table. "Though it's funny…it didn't when Saanvi, Faleena, and I were…conjoined."

<Yeah, it was clear then. I could see it as a…a thing. Now it's just noise.> Faleena added.

"I feel left out," Saanvi said with a mock pout. "It always just looked like…well, not noise, just a thousand mobius strips, or something."

Earnest slid a porous metal plate under Cary's outstretched hands, and then swung another device over top.

"Spread your hands out a bit more, Cary, so that there's a gap below them."

Cary complied, looking nervously at the device above her hands. "What is that? It looks a bit like a—"

"A gamma-ray gun," Earnest completed for her. "Don't worry, it's low power, and very focused. The metal foam below your hands will absorb any residual radiation from the gammas, as well as imaging a 3D representation of the object. It might tell us a bit more about what we're dealing with here."

"What if the brane splits open…? Or whatever they do when they fail." Saanvi had stepped up beside Cary as she spoke and was peering into the orb.

Earnest paused. "Hmm…that could be a problem. Unlikely, but certainly not desirable."

"I'll second that," Joe added. "How do we know it's safe to do this at all? Perhaps you should work on containing it first."

"It *is* contained, Dad," Saanvi said. "Now we need to sort out how to detect them…and contain them without Cary."

"Let's not jump to conclusions, Saanvi." Earnest stroked his chin as he stared at the orb. "For all we know, this is a defensive measure it took to avoid whatever you were going to do to it."

"What we were going to do to it?" Cary asked.

Earnest nodded, his eyes still fixed on the orb. "Yes, what were you going to do to it?"

<*I wanted to crush it.*> Faleena's tone was sour, and a bit spiteful.

Saanvi pressed a hand to her forehead and nodded slowly "I recall a similar sentiment."

"That's what I was going to do," Cary said. "But then I stopped because I knew that we needed it alive—or whatever. There are probably more of these infesting New Canaan."

Earnest looked up at Cary and Saanvi. "So I'm to assume that you're no longer deep-Linked?"

"Yeah, it didn't seem to be required anymore—the thing stopped fighting, and it's difficult to remain Linked like that for long."

"Well, I'm detecting increased activity in there. You'd better do your thing again, girls. I suspect it's not excited about meeting Mr. Gamma Ray, here, and it may try to break out."

"OK, let's hook up, then." Cary reached out to Faleena and Saanvi, visualizing their minds as spheres of light that she dipped her hands into and then drew toward herself.

Earnest's eyes narrowed. "Are you Linked?"

"We are."

Cary-Saanvi-Faleena watched the writhing mass within the sphere coalesce into a recognizable shape once more. She didn't know what the shape was, no words came to mind to describe it, but she could see its edges, make out filaments.

"You ready?" Earnest asked.

Cary glanced back at her father, who nodded.

"Might as well get it over with," he sighed.

"Do it," Cary-Saanvi-Faleena said.

Earnest activated the gamma ray, which resulted in a very anticlimactic, and almost imperceptible, *click.*

The remnant, however, roiled inside the ball, pushing out in all directions, forcing Cary-Saanvi-Faleena to place more of the black bands around it.

When they had first captured the remnant, they had not understood what they did to contain it. This time was different. Cary-Saanvi-Faleena could see other things all around herself now, extra planes and angles, as though another existence was encroaching on their own.

There were light things and dark things, hot and cold things. The hot things were black, and Cary-Saanvi-Faleena could take them and wrap them around the remnant.

In the other space, the remnant was larger, as tall as her father, but still somehow on the table and cupped in her hands. It seemed to rage, to exude a sense of purpose denied.

"Stop," Cary-Saanvi-Faleena said to the remnant. "Stop, or we *will* crush you this time."

"Do you really think you can?" The remnant seemed to hiss and steam as it spoke.

Cary-Saanvi-Faleena nodded. "We do. We see through you. You're just a shadow, not a real being."

"Real enough," the remnant replied. "You won't be able to hold me forever. I must find the others and expunge them. They no longer serve a purpose."

The more Cary-Saanvi-Faleena watched the remnant, the more she realized that it was little more than a memory, perhaps an ascended AI's version of a non-sentient AI assistant.

But it was smart and had wiles. It had to, for it to have hidden in Nance for so long—and to have escaped the notice of Bob.

*How **could** this thing have escaped Bob's notice?* Cary-Saanvi-Faleena wondered to themself. *He is all but ascended himself. If he cannot perceive extradimensional entities such as this remnant, we would be surprised.*

"Cary," her father's voice broke into their thoughts. "What's going on? It looks like the thing is going to explode."

"We're talking to it," Cary-Saanvi-Faleena replied, her voice calm and reassuring—at least she hoped it was. "It is blustering, currently. I *think* it's an NSAI of sorts. It doesn't have many tricks up its sleeve, so it's attempting to use fear. But I think that *it* fears *us*. So much as it can."

"Well, whatever you're doing is working better than the gamma ray. I'm getting excellent data." Earnest had summoned a dozen holodisplays and was frantically working on them as he spoke.

"Is it actionable data?" Joe asked.

Earnest shot Cary-Saanvi-Faleena's father a sharp look. "Joe, I'm learning about an entirely new branch of physics over the course of just a few minutes. I mean…we have theories, but we've never tangibly interacted with these other dimensions…not in real-time like this, at least."

Earnest's voice grew breathless as he spoke. A combination of excitement and worry was clearly audible.

Cary-Saanvi-Faleena realized that she could see Earnest's physical presence in the additional dimensions as well, but not as a tangible thing. More like a shadow.

She turned to see that her father and the medtechs—who looked more than a little concerned—had the same shadows. Nance's stasis pod was a pocket of nothingness in the other dimensions, which was interesting in and of itself.

"Cary-Sa…stars, your names are exhausting to string together." Earnest peered at Cary, then Saanvi. "Mind if I just call you 'CSF'?"

"Not 'FSC'?" Cary said, her voice sounding like her younger sister's.

"Whichever you prefer." Earnest shrugged.

"Call us 'The Triad'."

Earnest laughed, and Joe sighed. "A bit pretentious, don't you think, girls?"

"Well, Dad, we are three. OK, how's about 'Trine'."

"Sure," Earnest nodded. "Now that we have that out of the way, I want to stimulate it again with the gamma ray, but at a different energy level."

"I want to try something, first." Trine-Cary splayed her fingers, and filaments of nano flowed out of them and onto the surface of the brane.

"It has a body," Trine-Saanvi said. "I can see it through Trine-Cary's eyes, though to mine it is still a jumble. But the body we see here and the remnant's *real* body are not the same. It is complete in other parts of space-time, while it's a shadow here. No, that is not right. It is a shadow in others, too. Like it has shed much of itself to be what it is."

<*It is a facsimile,*> Trine-Faleena said.

"I am no such thing," the remnant retorted. "You cannot understand what you see."

Trine-Cary had deposited enough nano on the surface of the brane that it was visible as silver bands wrapping around the black ones. Then the bands began to glow brightly, and the silver sank into the black.

"How is she doing this?" Trine heard her father ask Earnest.

"I don't know," Earnest replied.

"If *you* don't know, how is it that *she* knows?"

Trine watched Earnest peer into Trine-Cary's eyes. "When you were a baby and you took your first step, did you know how your muscles worked? How your brain sent a signal through your nervous system?"

"Are you saying this is some sort of innate knowledge, a reflex or something?"

"Well, not a reflex, but yes, something that Trine knows how to do naturally."

"Where would Cary—"

"Not Cary." Earnest held up a finger. "When Trine merges, each brings themselves—or at least a part—into the whole. To be honest, what Cary instigates is something I barely understand to begin with. It is like she is able to effect the merger that her mother and Angela have, but at will, and with anyone."

"Not anyone," Trine-Cary said. "I've tried it with others, but only succeeded with Saanvi, and then Faleena."

"Even so, Saanvi is not a blood sister, so whatever bond allows this is not biological. I suspect your inability to deep-Link with others is a mental block, nothing more."

Trine only grunted as she spun the silver bands around the remnant. In three-dimensional space, it seemed only to roil more violently inside the sphere. In *n*-space—a name she decided on for the deeper existence she could now see—it shrieked in pain. Or possibly terror. Trine wasn't certain.

"So you think this ability to see into other dimensions and manipulate matter there comes from Faleena," Joe said after a moment.

Trine wondered about that. It made sense. On previous deep-Links with Saanvi, there had never been any revelations about other dimensions. Nothing had ever looked different.

Could it be because Moms are merging? Trine-Cary thought.

Perhaps. Trine-Faleena replied, her thoughts feeling uneasy. *Does that mean that moms are becoming something more, as well?*

Are we? Or at least you two. Trine-Saanvi sounded as though she didn't know what to think of her place in Trine.

Trine-Cary did not think that was the case. *Seeing more of space-time does not mean that we're becoming anything different—other than having other eyes, at least.*

You didn't say anything about Moms, Trine-Faleena couldn't help but comment.

That's because I don't know what's happening with Moms.

Focus.

Yes, of course.

While Trine had been talking amongst herself, she had also been listening to Joe and Earnest discuss what they were seeing.

"See there," Earnest pointed at one of his holos. "When she twists that band, the thing emits shadow particles, mostly sleptons. I believe I can detect those under a variety of circumstances. They have a very unique signature; we'll just have to figure out how to force it to emit those."

"There," Trine said as the last of the black bands was fully coated in silver. "You now have a control interface for it."

In *n*-space, the remnant had ceased its struggles. It was now wrapped in the silver ribbons that Trine had created. Unlike the representation in three-dimensional space, where the bands wrapped around it and things looked neat, *n*-space showed the ribbons very differently. There, they mostly encircled the remnant, but in some places, they punctured it as well, passing through its body in some dimensions, but not others.

The result was a being that was afraid to move, lest it cut itself apart. And because, for the remnant, thought was movement, it could barely form words.

"Will. Be. Free."

"Keep dreaming," Trine replied, her tone dismissive. Internally, though, she was not so sure.

Can it?

We don't know…if it is NSAI, it is just acting out its programming.

And if this shadow is sentient? Then it has a will.

We must stay to watch it.

So tired…

Cary severed the deep-Link, feeling Saanvi fall away first, then Faleena—though Faleena did not drift far.

"That's…exhausting," Cary said, leaning heavily on the table.

"You've not slept for three days," her father said, at her side in an instant with a gentle hand on her arm. "You need to eat, then sleep."

"Can't," Cary whispered. "What if it breaks free?"

"I have a cot in the corner," Earnest said. "I can have food brought down."

"Sleep." Saanvi nodded in agreement. "I caught shuteye on the trip here, so I can stay up awhile. I'll let you know if we need you."

<*As will I,*> Faleena added.

"OK, just for an hour or so." Cary nodded as her father led her to the cot. "Just a bit."

Cary didn't even remember her head hitting the pillow.

FAREWELL TO SCIPIO

STELLAR DATE: 10.02.8948 (Adjusted Years)
LOCATION: Imperial Palace
REGION: Alexandria, Bosporus System, Scipio Empire

Two months later…

"You know, Diana, you're not half bad."

Tanis nearly spat out her wine, wondering what had come over Sera to say something like that to the Empress. She gave Sera a stern look before seeing, to Tanis's immeasurable relief, that the empress smiled.

"The feeling's mutual, Seraphina. I recall watching you enter my audience room and thinking, 'Now there's a woman who really thinks she's more than she is.'"

Petra sat down on a chair across from the empress. "I imagine Sera and Tanis are certainly more than you expected them to be." She took a small sip of her wine before leaning forward to place it on the low table between them.

Diana's eyes twinkled, and her lips pursed for a moment before she responded. "I was thinking of you, Petra."

Petra's eyes narrowed and her neck and shoulders tensed, but the ambassador held her tongue.

<Ouch, Diana's still making Petra pay for all our sins,> Angela commented privately to Tanis.

<No one ever said she was a kind woman. Makes her just the sort of ally we need, I think.>

<Merciless toward her enemies? You know that can backfire, right?>

Tanis considered Angela's words. If there was one axiom to live by, it was that if a person was cruel to their enemies, they could just as easily be cruel to you. Humans were excellent at rationalizing their behavior when it suited them.

<She's our best option to stall the Hegemony.> Tanis knew it was a weak argument, but she still had hopes for Diana. She'd changed over the past two months, had grown as a person. Tanis liked to think that she and Sera were positive influences on the empress, showing her how one could rule while being empathetic.

<And if our sources are right, a rift may be forming between General Garza and Hegemon Uriel,> Angela added. *<With us backing Scipio, the Hegemony won't be able to stand against them alone.>*

Tanis turned that idea over in her mind as she watched Diana, Petra, and Sera chat idly in Diana's meeting lounge. Would Diana annex the Hegemony entirely? By the empress's own words, she didn't want to expand the boundaries of her empire any further.

But would she feel the same way, once Sol was in her hands?

Tanis hoped the woman would maintain her current stance. Scipio having control of its empire as well as the Hegemony of Worlds was too much. Too much for anyone.

<I see where you're going with that train of thought.> Angela's voice was soft and encouraging. *<You wonder what will happen after this war is over. Where the lines will be redrawn.>*

<I do,> Tanis replied simply. *<Are we going to make things worse in the long run? FTL created the opportunity for wars unlike any others. But even with dark layer travel, it still takes years to get across the Inner Stars. This war is going to seed jump gates all across known space.>*

Tanis felt Angela's agreement fill her mind. *<So long as we can keep a tight lid on how to make jump gates, they can be limited—even destroyed, if needs be. This is a more manageable issue than dark layer FTL.>*

<Or it will allow for someone in the future to create the ultimate tyranny.>

Angela snorted, then began to chuckle.

<What's so funny?> Tanis asked, feeling annoyed at her friend.

<You!> Angela said after her laughter had died down. *<You're not content with the trouble you have before you, you're borrowing it from future millennia! While we're at it, we should worry about what will happen to human civilization when the Andromeda galaxy collides with the Milky Way!>*

Tanis had a sharp retort ready, but then realized how right Angela was.

<OK, point taken. I was getting a bit melodramatic, there.>

<A bit.> Angela was still chucking softly. *<Though I'll grant you that we do have to think about who will fill the power vacuums that we'll create.>*

<I really don't want to become the galactic policewoman.>

<Me either, I—>

"You with us, Tanis?" Sera waved a hand in front of Tanis's face.

Tanis looked at Sera, then Petra and Diana—all of whom were directing unblinking stares her way. "Yeah, sorry, was just thinking about what's stacked up ahead of us."

"A great list of deeds, I imagine," Diana said. "The fact that I just have to contend with one enemy—provided *you* get Silstrand and that Rhoads mess under control—is a great relief to me."

Tanis nodded and reached for her wine glass. "I made the mess in Silstrand, I'll fix it."

"And now you have the same nanotech that Tanis gave them, Diana," Sera added. "So there's no need to worry that they have an advantage you don't."

"True." Diana nodded with a smirk on her gleaming black lips. "So long as they keep their stretch of stars from becoming a problem, I don't see a treaty being a problem."

"And the fleet you'd sent to take Gedri?" Sera pressed.

Diana laughed and shook her head. "President Seraphina Tomlinson, do you not trust me?"

Sera cocked an eyebrow. "Trust but verify. I have too many variables to juggle right now to worry about loose ends like this. Like Tanis, I feel partly responsible for the mess in Silstrand. I'd prefer to know that it's taken care of."

"We received confirmation today." Petra's tone carried mild annoyance as her eyes locked on Diana's.

"Petra! You're always spoiling my fun."

"Not everything needs to be a game of wits, Empress."

Petra and Diana stared at one another for a moment before Diana shrugged. "I suppose. I do need to learn not to needle my allies. I'm just not used to having people I can really trust."

<*Do you worry about Petra's allegiance?*> Tanis asked Sera. <*She seems more beholden to the Empress than you.*>

<*Are you referring to her use of 'we' when referring to Scipio?*> Sera asked. <*I certainly marked it—stars. 'Marked it'. I'm starting to talk like Diana. Kill me now.*>

<*Don't worry.*> Angela joined in their conversation. <*Alastar is keeping an eye on Petra. There's nothing wrong with her having a strong loyalty to Scipio. Eventually these political divisions will have to lessen.*>

<*Whoa! Now who's prognosticating about the future?*> Tanis asked.

"We trust you, Diana," Sera said aloud. "By your own admission, you don't want to build a larger empire than what you have. Seeing proof of that is welcome."

Diana's expression grew guarded. "True, but if I do advance into the Hegemony—which I intend to do soon; we won't just sit here and let them build up for a crushing attack against us—I will need to give some consideration to governance of conquered territory."

"I'm in favor of vassal states with as much autonomy as possible," Petra said. "Half of the Hegemony of Worlds is annexed territory as it stands. Many would welcome their autonomy back."

Diana's eyebrows rose as she regarded Petra. "A desire for autonomy does not equate to the ability to effectively self-govern."

"Easy, Di. I did say 'vassal states'."

Diana shrugged. "I suppose you did."

"So, how are you and Tenna getting along?" Tanis asked, seeking a new direction for the conversation.

"Very well," Diana replied. "I'd forgotten how nice it is to share one's mind with an AI. We're thick as thieves, as they say."

<It's going to be a fun experience,> Tenna added. *<A lot of responsibility.>*

"You're not running the empire, though," Diana replied with a laugh. "Trust me, when the buck stops at your ass, everything is a lot different."

<I know I'm not running it, but everyone sure thinks I know everything about everything that is going on everywhere. It's draining!>

Diana's laughter faded and she nodded soberly. "Welcome to my life."

<That's a woman of a thousand masks,> Sera commented to Tanis and Angela. *<I wonder if she even knows who she is half the time.>*

<I think she does,> Angela said. *<There's a firm core of self within her. I think that core is a bit of a jerk, but it's there.>*

Sera nearly laughed aloud at Angela's statement, and Tanis smiled, watching Petra say something to Sera as Diana looked on.

There was a strength in Diana, an unalterable belief that her actions were the best way forward for her people, despite short-term pitfalls.

Tanis knew all too well how that felt.

MYRIAD CONCERNS

STELLAR DATE: 10.02.8948 (Adjusted Years)
LOCATION: ISS *I2*, Security Operations Center
REGION: Alexandria, Bosporus System, Scipio Empire

Captain Rachel Espensen let out a long, frustration-laden sigh as she sat in one of the chairs in Terry's office.

"Tanis and Sera are due back on the ship in another day," she said. "Their negotiations with Scipio are over, we're preparing to leave the Bosporus system."

"You say this like I don't understand the implications," Terry replied. "Trust me, this upsets me just as much as it does you."

Rachel pressed the heels of her hands into her eyes. "You're right, Terry. You've been responsible for this ship's safety longer than I've been alive."

"Captain Espensen," Terry rose and took a seat next to Rachel. She reached out and placed a hand on her shoulder. "This ship has survived worse than this. We'll sort it out. We always do."

"You're right." Rachel nodded and squared her shoulders as she gazed out over the *I2*'s Security Operations Center. Though it was far from the bridge, the SOC was one of the ship's many hearts, always bustling with activity; the work of keeping the massive vessel safe was never over—especially not with all of the Scipian dignitaries touring it.

"But knowing that we brought someone with us from New Canaan who would free Elena—who could fool our sensors…."

"You're worried it's a remnant."

"Aren't you?" Rachel asked. "We can't detect them; Bob doesn't even think *he* can. Any one of us could have one of those…things inside us."

"I'll admit that it does unnerve me. But Earnest has the remnant that Tanis's daughters were able to remove from Nance. Once he fully understands it, he'll determine a way to detect them."

Rachel nodded. "At least I know *I* don't have one inside me. From what I read in the reports, Nance knew it was in there all along, she just couldn't say anything about it to anyone."

"Yup." Terry nodded seriously as she cast an appraising eye at Rachel. "Which means you could be lying to me right now."

"Terry!"

"Captain," Terry laughed. "You need to relax. I don't think there's a remnant in you. I think that whoever it's in is someone who can slip about with little notice."

Rachel joined in Terry's laughter. "Well, you're right about that. I can't walk more than ten paces without someone rushing after me with questions, or pinging me over the Link. Or both. Simultaneously. From the same person."

"When was the last time you had a day off, Captain?" Terry's tone was innocent, but her eyes belied concern.

"Stars...." Rachel looked at the room's overhead, thinking back. "Sometime before President Tomlinson—the previous President Tomlinson—dropped in for a visit with his fleet."

"Maybe you should see if you can take a day or two during our next stop."

"It would help if we knew where that was."

Terry shrugged. "Somewhere in the Silstrand Alliance—or the fringe systems between it and Scipio. That crusading fleet of AI-haters is in there somewhere. From what I hear, stopping them is a part of the treaty with Scipio."

Rachel nodded and visualized the region of space surrounding Scipio. On the rimward side was a no-man's land of small, independent systems. Beyond them was the Silstrand Alliance—a narrow strip of stability in a region known for general lawlessness.

On the far side of the fringe systems were a series of larger alliances and federations, tucked up against the Hegemony of Worlds and stretching to the Praesepe cluster.

"I remember Tanis's stories of Silstrand. Parts of it sound nice."

Terry snorted. "And parts of it sound barely civilized."

"Maybe that's just what I need." Rachel wondered what it would really be like to visit a place where lawlessness ruled. She'd seen them in vids, but her practical experience was much more limited.

"Trust me," Terry replied. "You've not missed much with your sheltered upbringing. Shitty locales are mostly just shitty. Plus, there's the whole part where I have to send a security detail with you and worry that you're going to get killed the whole time."

Rachel laughed and shook her head at Terry. "You worry too much."

"Of course I do. That's my job. Now go fly your starship from your big chair. We'll find whoever let Elena out. I promise."

Rachel didn't have anything encouraging to say, so she simply nodded and walked out of Terry's office, eyeing everyone she passed, wondering if they could have a remnant of an ascended AI in them…making them do things, subverting the mission.

AFTERMATH

STELLAR DATE: 10.08.8948 (Adjusted Years)
LOCATION: Bridge, ISF *I2*
REGION: Outer Silstrand System, Silstrand Alliance

"So much for a spa-day," Rachel said as she stared at the holotanks showing the wreckage of the fleets around Dessen.

Priscilla glanced back at Rachel, the woman's black eyes appearing as endless pools of night on her alabaster skin. "Not a lot of R&R in our future, Captain. I think we may see things like this play out for some time."

"Us crushing enemy fleets like they're nothing?" Rachel asked. "It sounds crazy to say it, but I feel bad for them. It's like shooting fish in a barrel."

Priscilla nodded as she turned to gaze at the holotanks as well. "Yes, that is an apt analogy. If the barrel is made of wood, and we have a nuke."

"I don't think the barrel's material matters if we have a nuke."

"It could be a very, very big barrel…made of some sort of…" Priscilla's voice faded. "Nevermind. That was getting stupid."

Rachel rose and walked to the holotank, watching the S&R crews as they scoured the ships for survivors.

Four fleets were spread out near the dwarf planet Dessen in the Silstrand System. The smallest of which was the ISF fleet, a mere forty ships, though all unscathed thanks to their stasis shields. Next were the ships of the Silstrand Alliance Space Force, of which there were only forty-five still intact. Granted, over one hundred were closing in from all around the Silstrand System. Next were the private military ships of S&H Defensive Armaments. While their ships were smaller in mass, there were over a hundred of them. They had taken heavy damage, but it was also their installation on—or, *in*, rather—the dwarf planet, Dessen, that had been the target.

The last group was the Revolution Fleet. Hundreds of ships, most massing far more than even the Silstrand Alliance vessels, yet it was the fleet that lay in ruin.

The battle had been three against one, and though the one outnumbered the rest, when the *I2* arrived, the outcome had become a foregone conclusion.

In fact, their greatest struggle in the brief, fierce conflagration, had been to keep the S&H Defensive forces from utterly destroying the Revolution Fleet.

"Those poor bastards," Rachel said quietly. "Mind controlled and just plain deluded. They didn't deserve to die horribly just because some crazy man put mind-control mods into all their heads."

That someone could even do such a thing with impunity disgusted Rachel. How had the Inner Stars fallen to such barbarism? How was it possible that a man could amass such a fleet, filled with people who hated AIs so much that they'd die for their cause, and no one had stopped him before he got this far?

"Sure is a mess," a voice said on Rachel's left, and she turned to see Tanis at her side.

"Ma'am," Rachel nodded deferentially. "How did your chat go with that madman's daughter?"

"She didn't support anything he was doing, if that's what you're wondering," Tanis replied. "She's the one who killed him and severed his control over his people."

Rachel backtracked through the battle in her mind. "She got off his flagship three hours before the last enemies were taken out. Did it take some time for people to…regain themselves?"

"Not from what she told us. It seems that there were a lot of true believers who had no need for coercion to hate AIs. I suspect that many of the folks we're picking up out there required no unnatural influences to take up arms."

Rachel shook her head. "What a shame. What are your orders, Admiral? Are we going to be here for a while?"

"Well, given that this system is the seat of the Silstrand Alliance's government, I expect we'll be here for a bit, yes. The Scipian Special Envoy will need to meet with the Silstrand President and ratify a treaty. Diana requires the Transcend as a signatory."

Rachel couldn't hold back a sardonic laugh. "Sounds like the very definition of fun."

"Isn't that the truth."

Rachel glanced at the admiral to see a distant look in the woman's eyes.

"Still," Tanis continued. "No matter who wanted us to do what, we did stop a genocidal purge here. I would have done it just for that. Helping sidestep a war between Scipio and Silstrand is just icing on the cake."

"Sounds like two marks in the win column," Rachel said, pantomiming making the marks.

"It does, doesn't it." Tanis nodded. "You know, I have…interesting memories of this system."

"This is where you got *Sabrina* the weapon upgrades so you could rescue Sera, right?"

Tanis gave a soft laugh. "Yeah, amongst other things. Cheeky and I got up to some crazy stuff on one of their stations."

"You *what*?" Rachel asked loudly, her eyes wide, before lowering her voice. "What did you do with Cheeky?"

"Captain," Tanis admonished. "I did nothing untoward with Cheeky. She and I got in a bit of trouble, is all."

"Now that's a story I'd like to hear, sometime."

"Maybe over drinks some night," Tanis replied. "For now, I'd best go meet with the Silstrand fleet liaison. A Colonel Grayson. He and I have to pay a visit to Smithers in his hidey hole on Dessen. Or in Dessen…whatever."

Rachel remembered Colonel Grayson. She'd watched him disembark when his ship docked.

"I see that look in your eyes." Tanis wagged a finger in the air. "I'd recommend against pursuing that man. I'm pretty certain he has eyes only for Kylie Rhoads."

"Hmm…" Rachel mused. "I suppose it's not worth it, anyway. We won't be here long."

"Stars willing." Tanis nodded and turned to leave. "Keep me apprised on the cleanup. At some point, Silstrand is going to demand that we turn over all the prisoners, and I want to have a good handle on the situation when that occurs."

"Of course, Admiral," Rachel replied as Tanis strode off the bridge.

The admiral gone, Rachel turned back to the holotank, wondering about all those people who had been swept up by Peter Rhoads's false promises and conscripted in his fleet, only to die here—their cold corpses drifting in the black.

The Inner Stars. What an utter shit-show.

A NEW ASSIGNMENT

STELLAR DATE: 10.09.8948 (Adjusted Years)
LOCATION: Ol' Sam, ISF *I2*
REGION: Outer Silstrand System, Silstrand Alliance

Sera stepped off the maglev to see Nadine waiting for her on a bench tucked under a tree at the edge of the platform. The Hand agent—possibly *former* hand agent—didn't see her right away, and Sera took a moment to observe the woman.

Nadine seemed older than Sera's records showed. Tired and sad. Her report on the events of the last month made for an interesting tale, to say the least. Some of it was nearly impossible to fathom—such as Maverick becoming the president of Gedri.

Maverick! Of all people!

Nadine had been sent to the Silstrand Alliance for one reason: get close to Kylie Rhoads and work out a way to stop her father *before* he massed the fleet which now lay in ruin around the *I2*.

Instead, Nadine had fallen in love with Kylie Rhoads. Not just for the purposes of the mission, but for real. And in doing so, she had delayed meeting her objective.

Again and again.

"President Tomlinson!" Nadine jumped to her feet and almost saluted before simply folding her hands before herself.

"Agent Nadine," Sera said as she approached. "I'm glad that we're able to meet under such serene circumstances."

Nadine glanced around herself at the forest surrounding the maglev station as though she hadn't noticed it before. "It's quite the ship."

Sera nodded. "That's putting it mildly. Walk with me."

Nadine fell in beside Sera as they walked through a shaded path in the woods, neither woman speaking for the span of a minute. Eventually it was Nadine that broke the silence.

"I screwed up. A lot."

Sera blew out a long breath. "Fucking right, you did. Petra sent you in *five years ago*. Five years! You could have had Kylie Rhoads back with dear old dad in six months, tops."

"Never would have worked," Nadine countered, her tone more sad than hostile. "Kylie was estranged from her parents for a decade. She had no interest in seeing them. Just hinting at her family made her shut down emotionally."

"Well, in the end, you had to dump her on a ship and send her to her family unwillingly. Seems like waiting didn't get you anywhere."

Nadine stopped and turned to face Sera, her eyes narrowed. "Things don't work so easily all the time in the field. Human emotional responses are—"

"Nadine." Sera's tone was frank. "Don't give me that. I spent decades in the field. Stars, these are my old stomping grounds. I've flown every route there is in the fringe. I even know half the captains in Gedri. Drank most of those under the table. So don't you give me 'things are different in the field'. You fell in love with Kylie Rhoads. Admit it to me."

Sera watched Nadine work her jaw for a moment. "Yeah, I did. But it's over now. She's done with me, after what I did."

"You misunderstand me," Sera said, stopping and turning toward Nadine. "Love isn't forbidden to us, but we can't let it cloud our vision. I'm not going to say that everyone who died in this battle could have been saved. Who knows what would have happened if you'd somehow gotten Kylie to her father years ago. Maybe he would have put one of his mods in her head, and she'd've been under his control too. But that doesn't change the fact that you let love get in the way of what needed to be done."

Nadine's face had reddened during Sera's lecture, but she didn't respond.

"You have something you want to say to me, Agent Nadine?"

Nadine nodded, perhaps not trusting herself to speak.

"Out with it, then."

"I feel like you're treating me unfairly. Your record is not pristine—I know about Mark, and how you lost the CriEn module. Rumor always was that you were blinded by your love for him."

Sera closed her eyes and nodded, feeling the anger spill out of her like a drain plug had been pulled. "And that wasn't the last time, either. Do you remember Elena? She reported up to Petra before she worked in my office in Airtha."

"I do, I ran a small op with her once on Alexandria."

"Right, I'd forgotten about that." Sera gave a small nod. "Well, would you believe that she's imprisoned on this very ship? She's a double agent for Orion. Killed my father right in front of me."

Nadine's face fell. "I had wondered…. I'll admit, I was scared to ask what happened to your father. He was not universally loved—still, I can't believe Elena would do that. What prompted her to change sides?"

"Stars if I know," Sera replied. "Nothing she says can be trusted. She can rot in her cell, for all I care."

The vehemence with which she spoke surprised even Sera, and she clamped her mouth shut for a moment before giving Nadine an apologetic smile.

"Damn love. Look at what it does to us."

"Think maybe we should try boys?" Nadine asked. "They're simpler."

Sera barked a laugh. "Seriously? How can they be simpler? They never talk. You have to pry everything out of them with a starship-sized grav beam. Besides, remember Mark? Got me exiled."

"Point taken. But when you do get a man to talk, and you pry his thoughts out, it's simple, what it says on the tin. Women're…"

"Onions." Sera nodded.

"Stinky?"

"I was thinking 'layered'."

Nadine's mouth made a soundless 'O', and she nodded.

Sera resumed walking and considered what to say next. Eventually she gave up on trying to find the perfect wording.

"So, do you still want to be an agent?"

"Honestly? *I* don't even know…I've done so much lying. Now that we've begun the unveiling, what does it even mean to be in the Hand anymore?"

"We're still figuring that out," Sera replied. "But mostly it's the opposite of lying. Truthing. We're truthing all over."

"A refreshing change."

"Change, yes. Refreshing, no. You should know this by now. No one really wants the truth. It's scary, messy. It's a big disaster, looming in the future. No one is going to be happy to know that they've been pawns in a bigger game."

"So I take it Empress Diana was not amused?"

"Not even in the slightest. You should have seen what she made Petra wear to the Celebration of the Seven Suns."

"Oh? Petra had always wanted to attend that."

"Not like this, she didn't." Sera passed the image over the Link to Nadine, chuckling as an expression of horror and amazement washed over Nadine's face.

"That's…just a little demeaning," Nadine said at last.

"Yeah, and Petra is still trying to get back into Diana's good graces."

Nadine stopped and faced Sera. "You left her there?"

Sera nodded. "She's the best one for the job. Diana had a change of heart, too—a bit, at least. She apologized to Petra."

"And Petra? She wants this?"

"Remember that whole thing about agents falling in love with assets?"

Sera watched Nadine's face redden. She could tell the woman had something she wanted to get out, but it wasn't the sort of thing you could say to your boss…and president.

"Spit it out, Nadine."

Nadine clenched her jaw, then exhaled. "No, I'm good."

"You sure? This is your one chance."

"OK, fine," Nadine's eyes narrowed. "I fall in love with my asset, and I'm taken to task, chewed out. Petra falls in love with the damned *Empress of Scipio,* and she gets promoted to, what…Ambassador?"

Sera winked at Nadine. "She didn't go off-mission. Took her lumps and moved forward."

"What do you think I did?" Nadine shot back. "I took Kylie out and sent her off with her brother…."

"Which, I'll admit, worked out in the end."

" 'Worked out'!" Nadine was almost screaming. "Have you looked beyond this big fancy ship of yours? A lot of people *died* out there. People who had no choice."

"Now do you get my point?" Sera asked, her eyebrow arched.

Nadine's mouth snapped shut, and she worked her jaw back and forth. Sera simply stared at Nadine until the agent finally said, "So what now? Is this where I get kicked out the airlock?"

"No," Sera said without elaborating, still waiting for Nadine to calm down.

Nadine closed her eyes. "Then what's going to happen?"

"Look, things could have been worse, and we learned about Garza, and about something that Kylie's father saw. Something he called his 'angel'."

"Angel? I didn't hear about that."

Sera turned off the path and led Nadine through the woods for a minute before stopping in a small clearing.

Nadine looked around at the trees, and up at the far side of the habitation cylinder where a lake hung two kilometers over their heads. "Can I just say that I've seen a lot of crazy shit in my life, but never, and I mean *never*, have I seen a warship with a forest."

"It may be a first," Sera agreed. "And there are not a lot of firsts anymore."

Sera dropped a privacy dampener on the ground between them and placed a hand on Nadine's shoulder. "In time, this will become common knowledge. But for now, it doesn't leave your lips or mind. Understood?"

Nadine nodded solemnly.

"I need you to say it, Nadine."

"I'll not tell a soul about what you are about to tell me. Not until it's common knowledge."

"Good," Sera nodded and tried to figure out in which order to explain things. "I'm not going to put an auth token in your mind about this or get carried away with what 'common knowledge' means. You'll know when you can share it."

"You're making me a bit nervous..."

"Yeah," Sera laughed. "You should be."

Sera proceeded to tell Nadine the whole story. Her mother's trip to the core, encountering the Ascended AIs, coming back as Airtha. How Helen had been a shard of her mother in her mind. The attack on New Canaan, the clones of Garza that seemed to be everywhere, orchestrating everything, and what they knew of the mysterious entity that called itself 'the Caretaker'.

"Why'd you take us here in the woods? I need to sit down!" Nadine exclaimed when Sera was finished.

"Sorry, you can sit in the grass..."

"No thanks, I finally feel like I got clean for the first time in weeks."

Sera laughed. "You always were a bit of a princess."

"It's why the cover works so well for me." Nadine shrugged. "So, let me get this straight. Airtha is leading a rebellion with some sort of clone claiming to *be* you—"

"It probably *is* me," Sera interjected. "Helen was in my head for decades. Finaeus thinks it's entirely possible that she could make another… 'me'."

"That's seriously creepy." Nadine shook her head in disgust. "OK, so there's that. Then there's the core AIs. Orion has Garza running around, cloning himself—which is really unusual behavior for Orion-types. Lastly, we have Ascended AIs pulling our strings like we're all marionettes, and there may or may not be more than one faction of them."

Sera nodded. "Plus all the other stuff, like wars breaking out all across the Orion Arm as the lines get drawn between us and the Orion Freedom Alliance."

Nadine rubbed her eyes and ran her hands through her long blue hair. "This is…Sera…this feels like…. How are we going to deal with all this? Excuse me if I start to hyperventilate."

Sera placed her hands on Nadine's shoulders and locked eyes with her. "We're not without our allies and strengths. Having Scipio on our side counts for a lot. Diana may be a cold, testy bitch, but she can get things done. And what's more, we have New Canaan. They're building more ships like this one. At least fifty. That's the beginnings of a galactic fleet."

"What's the Transcend's relationship with New Canaan?"

"Not as complex as one might think. They're committed to backing us, and Tanis is in it to win it. Even without New Canaan's resources, having her on our side is easily as big a win as Scipio, maybe bigger."

"New Canaan is just one star system, though. How many resources can they bring to bear?"

"They built a twenty-thousand ship fleet in secret in fifteen years."

"Oh…OK, when you put it that way…. Then why is Tanis out here? Aren't they worried about being attacked again?"

"They worked out how to summon the things from the dark layer," Sera said without elaboration.

"What!? They brought them out? How…?"

"I don't know, and I really don't want to know. I hope they never tell anyone else, either. It was…terrifying."

"And they put them back in?"

"They wouldn't have a star system anymore if they didn't."

Nadine whistled and appeared to be processing everything Sera had told her. "OK, so you don't tell all this to someone that you're canning. But I'm not entirely certain I have any more of this in me. I don't know if I can do subterfuge, secrets, and missions anymore. Not yet, at least."

"Good, because that's not what I have in mind."

"Oh?"

Sera shook her head. "I want you to function as an intelligence officer for Tanis. From the looks of it, she'll be heading to Praesepe. You've spent time there, and your cousin Nerischka is there, too."

"Been a long time since I've seen Nishka. Also, I couldn't help but notice your wording," Nadine said. "I take it you're not coming along?"

"No. I have to get back to Khardine. We were going to get the Inner Stars under control before dealing with Airtha, but with the other 'me' out there, we don't have that luxury any longer. I have to face her head-on."

"Good luck," Nadine chuckled. "You're going to need it."

"Tell me about it." Sera took a step back from Nadine. "So, Agent Nadine. Are you ready to become Major Nadine, officer in the TSF?"

"Major? That's a jump."

"I need people to listen to you when you talk."

Nadine snorted, though it sounded more like a soft squeak. "That'll be a change. So, I don't have to go undercover, lie to anyone, or make promises I know I probably won't be able to keep?"

"Well, I'm not going to make promises *I* can't keep. But none of those things are my intention."

"OK, I'm in. When do we leave?"

"Well, technically, you're staying here. I'm leaving."

"And what about Kylie?" Nadine's voice was strained, as though she had held the question in for too long. "What happens with her…and her nanotech?"

"They've altered it to make it safe. The weaponized aspects were causing problems—would have caused more, too, soon enough. Kylie's signed on to go find her brother and put a stop to this Revolution Fleet business. When she finds them, she has a device called a QuanComm that will instantly reach me at Khardine. Then we send in the cavalry to take out the rest of that fleet."

Nadine nodded. "I guess that's for the best. She needs time away. Do you know if *Grayson* is going with her?"

"The Silstrand Colonel? No, not that I know of. Silstrand has a lot of cleaning up to do. That general…Samuel. He made a right mess in Gedri—worse than it usually is. There's talk of sending a pair of cruisers along with Grayson to clean it up."

"You're going to send just two cruisers to subdue a star system?" Nadine asked. "Seriously?"

"They'll be ISF cruisers. Which means atom beams and stasis shields. They probably only need to send one, but they can cover more ground with two."

"Damn…" Nadine's voice was barely above a whisper. "This is surreal."

"Yeah, just a bit. Oh, crap! Kylie just filed for departure clearance on that tub of hers. You should see her off."

Nadine chewed her lip. "I'm worried about her going out there on her own."

"Don't," Sera replied. "I'm sending Ricket with her."

"Ricket!?" Nadine almost choked. "OK, now I'm *really* worried."

JUST DESSERTS

STELLAR DATE: 10.09.8948 (Adjusted Years)
LOCATION: Dessen
REGION: Outer Silstrand System, Silstrand Alliance

The three ISF pinnaces settled down onto cradles in one of Dessen's docking bays, disgorging Marines before the cradle ramps had even extended.

Once Colonel Smith declared the bay secure, Tanis walked down the ramp to where a very nervous-looking woman waited.

Tanis had a brief memory of the days when she was the person who would make sure a bay was secure before some important person ventured forth.

Even now it still felt surreal.

Colonel Grayson of the SSF was at her side, and when he laid eyes on the woman, he gave her an unkind smile.

"Hello, Shinya, how has your day been?"

The woman took a deep breath and nodded professionally. "We have managed, and we're thankful for both of your fleet's assistance. We are ill prepared to deal with this many wounded."

She gestured to her left, and Tanis looked over to the far side of the bay. Though the Marines had deemed it secure, it was far from empty.

Half the bay was full of wounded men and women, soldiers, and ship's crew, laying on triage cots with automatons and medical personnel moving amongst them like grey wraiths.

"If you need further assistance, we can send it," Tanis said.

Shinya snapped her attention back to Tanis. "Yes, of course. I'm sorry I did not properly introduce myself. I am Shinya, assistant to President Smithers."

"Whatever happened to Ginia?" Tanis asked with a wink. "I liked her. She had spunk."

"Ginia?" Shinya asked.

Tanis nodded. "I met her twenty years ago when I sold S&H the license to use my nanotech."

"*License*?" Shinya asked.

Tanis glanced at Grayson. "She seems to have a lot of questions."

"Shinya, why don't you just take us to Smithers? Is he in his creepy black room?" Grayson asked.

Shinya nodded. "Yes, of course, please come this way."

Colonel Smith nodded to Tanis, and two dozen Marines peeled off and formed up behind Tanis and Grayson.

"Oh…your soldiers can't come along, Smithers said so." Shinya looked more than a little worried as she delivered the message.

Tanis spoke slowly, spacing her words out. "Shinya. Pass this along to Smithers. This can go one of three ways. Option one is the one where I bring my Marines along, and we talk peaceably. Two involves a lot more Marines and an all-out assault on this moon-station. Four is the one where I just blow up Dessen and call it a day."

Shinya nodded and swallowed. "What happened to option number three?"

"I decided to escalate things."

"Um…OK. Smithers said your soldiers can come, too."

Tanis smiled at Shinya and gestured for her to lead the way.

<*You have such a way with words,*> Angela said, laughing softly as they followed Shinya's hurried steps.

<*I practice in the mirror a lot.*>

<*Liar, you almost never look in mirrors. I know, I live behind your eyes.*>

Tanis almost laughed aloud. <*If I wasn't so used to you, that would be really creepy.*>

<*I guess I'll have to try harder.*>

"I want to thank you for bringing me along," Grayson said quietly. "I bear a…special dislike for these people."

"Because of Lana?" Tanis asked.

Grayson nodded, glancing at Tanis. "Surprised you know about her."

"She was in Nadine and Kylie's reports."

Grayson whistled. "You got Kylie to write a report?"

"Well, it was more like a series of images, and then some bullet points. There was a cat, too. Angela thinks her AI put together most of it."

<*Marge is OK,*> Angela said. <*She and I had a long chat, and then I introduced her to Bob.*>

"Bob?" Grayson asked. "That's your big ship-AI, right?"

"Yes."

"Does he not talk often? I got all sorts of orders from someone named Priscilla, but nothing from Bob."

"He does talk, just not to most humans. It's taxing for him."

Grayson frowned. "That doesn't make sense."

"It's not supposed to—not to humans, at least."

Tanis saw Grayson frown and cock his head out of the corner of her eye. "Are you playing with me, Admiral?"

She couldn't help but laugh at the concerned annoyance in his voice. "A touch, but not too much. Bob's a lot to let into your head."

<*Don't sweat it, Grayson. I'll talk to you,*> Angela grinned in their minds. <*I'm **way** more fun than Bob. He's always so serious with his 'I see the future and all things and it's weighty-weighty' schtick he has.*>

"Now I *know* you're messing with me."

Tanis just grinned and shrugged. "Could be."

"Why are all the women in my life so complex?"

Tanis held back a laugh. The colonel seemed wound a bit too tight. Granted, his ex-wife, who she suspected he was still deeply in love with, had just left on her ship to search for her brother's fleet, so she could understand that his state of mind may not be ideal for needling.

"Kylie's not gone forever," Tanis said. "She'll find her brother, and Sera will send in the cavalry. We'll do our best to see that you're a part of that."

"I hope she doesn't find him too soon," Grayson muttered.

"Really? Why not?"

Grayson gave her a predatory grin. "Because scuttlebutt has it that you want to send some ships to Gedri to put Maverick down."

"And scuttlebutt is that you'd be top pick to join in that clean-up job," Tanis replied.

"I don't think I have to tell you how much I'd like to kick that man clear across the galaxy." Grayson's voice had dropped, growing quieter and more menacing. "He's…well, let's just say that I'm all in."

Tanis gave Colonel Grayson a nod. "When I meet with your fleet command, I'll make your command of that mission a requirement."

"Admiral Richards, you have my undying gratitude."

* * * * *

Grayson's description of Smithers' office as a 'creepy black room' was more than apt. At first glance, the floor seemed nonexistent, but Tanis could see that it was a clever holo effect, just like the blazing star on the far side of the room, casting an otherworldly light through the space.

President Smithers stood before the raging pseudo-star, his expression grim as half the Marines filed in behind Tanis.

"Major Richards—or should I say 'Admiral'—fortune has favored you," Smithers said as they approached.

Tanis saw that what had been an old man looking to be at the end of his life was now much younger in appearance, carrying the ageless look of a high-quality rejuvenation treatment.

"And you, it seems. This is a far cry from managing weapons upgrades on the PetSil mining platform," she replied.

Smithers smiled, the expression looking somehow just like it had when his face was creased and worn. "Well, I have you to thank for that—though not entirely. When you sold us your nanotech, you omitted certain things we needed to know."

Tanis shook her head. "I did no such thing. What I sold you was predicated on base technology which you did not possess. Tech that was common knowledge in my time. Either way, I'm sure your lawyers will have told you by now that the contract I signed noted those base technologies, though you may not have recognized them at the time."

"Yes." Smithers bit off the word and then paused, as though the taste of it had stymied him, then continued slowly. "Well, we worked it out. It wasn't easy, but we did."

"And you broke your licensing agreement," Tanis said without elaboration, letting the ball drop on the man before her.

"By making the technology work?" Smithers sputtered. "Preposterous."

"Of course not. But it's how you did it. The viral way you weaponized it. There are clauses in the agreement about how the nanotech can be used, the purposes for which it can be leveraged. What ended up in Kylie Rhoads was not within the scope of that license."

"I—" Smithers began, but Tanis held up a hand to silence him.

"You've caused incredible pain to people, nearly started a war—two, actually. All because you're a greedy little weasel. Now it's time to talk damages."

"Damages?" Smithers whispered.

Tanis nodded. "Yes. You do recall that clause, I made sure it was in there. You caused the loss of an entire star system for Silstrand. I suspect that's going to be more than the entire value of S&H."

Smithers swallowed and looked at Tanis, seeking some sign that she was joking. She was not, and he knew it.

THE SILSTRAND CLAUSE

STELLAR DATE: 10.13.8948 (Adjusted Years)
LOCATION: Government Plaza, Silstrand
REGION: Silstrand System, Silstrand Alliance

"Government Plaza? That's some creativity there," Tanis said as she and Sera—along with a sizable retinue, including the Scipian Special Envoy, a man named Scorsin—climbed the steps leading to a towering stone building where their meetings with the Silstrand government were to be held.

"Yeah," Sera gave a soft laugh. "They're not super creative with names in Silstrand. I mean…when people first settled these stars, they called them 'the Silver Strand', because they're a string of G-class stars surrounded by dimmer M and K ones."

"I recall reading that." Tanis nodded as she reached the top step. "Half the stations seem to incorporate Silstrand, or their original founder—Peter—into their names."

"Or both."

<I think that Silstrand is a really nice name,> Angela chimed in. *<I mean…when you stack it up against places like 'Bollam's World' it's practically poetry.>*

Tanis laughed. "Yeah, so that sets the bar low, I guess."

"Maybe you shouldn't be speaking this way about our hosts right on their doorstep," Scorsin said, moving closer to Tanis and Sera.

"Sorry," Tanis replied. "We tend to run fast and loose—you should know that, you spent almost a month going over the treaties with us back in Scipio."

"I have a keen recollection," Scorsin replied.

<Too bad he had to have his sense of humor surgically removed to facilitate such an excellent memory,> Sera said privately to Tanis and Angela.

Tanis held back a laugh and cast Sera a scolding look over the Link. *<Stop that. We have to get along with him for just a while longer, then we can get out of here.>*

<*I know you feel responsible for this mess, Tanis,*> Sera said. <*But in all honesty, you're not. Nanotech or no nanotech, this conflict between Scipio and Silstrand would have come about eventually. It's barely worth our time.*>

<*She's right,*> Angela nodded soberly. <*The Silstrand ambassador to Scipio was present when we crafted the treaty. He's sent along his notes in the packet we delivered to their president. This shouldn't be much more than a formality.*>

Tanis nodded absently as she walked through the entrance and into the building's foyer. <*Right, so there's no reason why this won't just get rubber stamped, and we can be on our way.*>

<*Great…*> Sera groaned. <*Both of you…seriously? Now you've gone and cursed it.*>

Inside the building, a delegation of Silstrand dignitaries waited. At their fore was the alliance's president, a tall man named Charles.

Tanis and Sera had already spoken with him several times, once the *I2* had passed within a light minute of the planet, but their prior conversations had been brief, and he seemed to place much more value on a physical meeting.

"Welcome!" President Charles boomed the moment both Tanis and Sera were through the entrance. "Esteemed President Tomlinson! Field Marshal Richards! It is a true honor to meet you. And, of course, Special Envoy Scorsin, you are most welcome in Silstrand."

"And you, President Charles. Thank you for hosting us," Sera said as she approached and offered her hand.

"Yes," Tanis added as she held out her hand. "It's a pleasure to finally see all that Silstrand has to offer."

The president inclined his head gratefully. "Much of which would have been laid waste, if not for your efforts at Dessen. I must admit, we did not expect Peter Rhoads to have amassed such a fleet, let alone to be so bold as to strike us here at the heart of the Alliance."

"We had agents working to stop him—which they did at the end," Sera replied. "Without their efforts, things could have been much worse."

"Yes…your dossier made mention of the fact that you have operatives within the…'Inner Stars', as you call them."

"Are we to retire to a more comfortable location?" Tanis asked. "I've been running around for days; sitting down to discuss these matters would be preferred."

A momentary look of concern flashed across President Charles' face, and he nodded quickly. "Of course, of course. We're to meet in my offices, I'll lead the way."

The president led them up a grand, marble—or a stone similar to marble, at least—staircase to the second floor.

Tanis paid little attention to her surroundings. She had already released a cloud of nano to scout things out, and knew that Major Valerie and the four High Guard accompanying them would be eyeing every nook and cranny.

She was more interested in the people. Alongside several non-military dignitaries of unknown rank and role, was a Silstrand admiral and two generals—one of which was the man named Samuel who had played a large part in the unrest currently tearing Gedri apart.

<*Mind you,*> Angela inserted herself into Tanis's thoughts. <*If he hadn't gone after your nanotech, that Harken woman would have sold it to stars-knows-who. Samuel's decision to send Kylie Rhoads after it was a smart move on his part.*>

<*True enough, but his actions at Freemont—you know, where he attacked Gedri's capital—were…extreme. I can't believe that that Maverick guy is running things in Gedri, now. The universe has no sense of honor.*>

Angela let out a tittering laugh. <*Oh! So you finally recalled where you met him before!*>

<*Hey…that night was* ***really*** *hazy. Cheeky released more pheromones than a hundred amped up people. I only remembered him as the 'crazy sex slave trader with the plasma sword'. Not the type of guy I would have thought to become ruler of a star system at some point.*>

Angela nodded in their mind. <*Universe takes all kinds—and has no sense of honor about it, as you said.*>

In front of them, President Charles was going on about how grateful the alliance was for the Transcend's help, interspersing comments about this or that holo of some prior dignitary that they were walking past. Tanis did her best to listen and care, but kept finding her mind wandering.

<*Maybe you should have gotten some sleep,*> Angela chided. <*If you want, I can run your mouth for you while you nap.*>

<*Angela! That sounds seriously disturbing. I can't imagine that would be restful at all.*>

Angela broke out in laughter, and Tanis realized she had been joking. Maybe.

<*I'm fine, I can stim as needed.*>

<*Tanis, you've had four hours of actual rest in the last week. At a certain point, your brain needs some downtime.*>

<*After this meeting. I'll sleep on the ride back up to the* I2.>

<*Good.*> Angela's tone was resolute. <*Because if you don't, I'll knock you out for a day.*>

<*OK, Mom.*>

The Silstrand president had reached a pair of double doors at the end of the hall and swept through as they opened to admit the group.

His offices were not over-large, nor too ornate. There were chairs placed artfully around the edges of the space, well-laden bookshelves along the walls, and a quadrangle of sofas in the center.

"Please, sit," President Charles gestured to the chairs. "Would you like refreshments?"

"Yes," Tanis spoke first. "Coffee. And something with carbs. Been a long week."

Tanis sat, nodding at Major Valerie, who took up a position at the door, while the other four High Guard waited outside in the hall.

The Scipian Special Envoy sat on one sofa, and Sera sat next to him. Tanis settled into another couch beside General Samuel, and President Charles sat across from her.

Two of the other men who had accompanied them sat on the fourth couch, while the admiral sat next to the Silstrand president.

"Again, thank you for coming to meet with us," President Charles said. "As I'd mentioned previously, we owe you much, and thank you for your assistance."

Tanis couldn't help but notice that the admiral, as well as a general who stood along the wall, looked less than pleased at their president's effusive thanks.

"It's the least we could do," Sera said, her tone moderated and polite. "Coming here was on our short list, as securing a peace between Silstrand and Scipio is a part of our treaty with Scipio."

At this, President Charles' face clouded. "I read that in the dossier you've provided. I must admit, it's unexpected to have someone who we've only known as a privateer negotiating with the Scipian Empire on our behalf."

"A privateer?" Sera asked.

"Remember? I got *Sabrina* a letter of marque from Silstrand before we found you in Gedri," Tanis said with a wink. "You were the captain of the ship, so your name was on the letter."

"Huh," Sera placed an index finger over her lips as she thought. "You know, I never even looked at that—didn't really expect to be back here."

The admiral, whose name was Manda, from Tanis's briefing, cleared her throat and spoke up. "As interesting as this byplay is, what are your intentions here in Silstrand?"

"Our intentions?" Tanis asked, glancing at Sera, who nodded for her to proceed. "Well, our first intention is to help in any way we can with this treaty. Following that, we'd like to offer a pair of cruisers to help you clean up Gedri—as we'd discussed with your Colonel Grayson. It is also our intention to offer you the same nanotech that we gave to Scipio."

"We already have that nanotech," General Samuel said from where he sat next to Tanis. "Our technicians have extracted it from my daughter, Lana. We—"

"Did you bring her with you?" Tanis interrupted. "Is she here?"

"Yes, she—"

"Good. You need to bring her to the *I2* as soon as this meeting is concluded. I also want all samples you collected, and all research and documentation you have accumulated on the nanotech you extracted from her. If you seized anything from S&H Defensive Armaments, I'll require that, as well."

General Samuel's mouth was working, but no sounds came out.

"What are you saying?" President Charles asked. "You cannot come into our sovereign nation and make demands like this."

"I'm afraid this is non-negotiable," Tanis replied. "Your treaty with Scipio is contingent on it."

President Charles glanced at Scorsin who shrugged. "It's in the fine print, yes. We cannot ratify a treaty with you unless you turn this technology in its entirety over to the ISF."

"The ISF?" Admiral Manda asked.

"Yes, the Intrepid Space Force," Scorsin replied. "That big honking ship I rode in on. So far as I can tell, it is an independent nation within the Transcend."

Admiral Manda turned to Tanis. "Your starship is a sovereign nation?"

Tanis preferred not to reveal New Canaan's existence if possible, and shrugged. "It's more powerful than most nations, why not?"

No one spoke for a few moments, until General Samuel managed to find his voice again. "And *why* do you need to take our nanotech from us?"

"Aside from the fact that it will kill your daughter, Lana, in under two years—that's after it turns her into a violent killing machine—it violates your own laws."

"Kill her?" General Samuel asked.

At the same time, one of the men next to the president, Secretary Jorgens, by the indicator on Tanis's HUD, spoke up. "It violates our laws?"

"The nanotech was weaponized in a fashion that makes it reprogram its host to be a soldier. A violent killer who will eventually be destroyed by the mods. S&H's work was…sloppy. This sort of alteration was illegal in Sol, and it is technically illegal in Silstrand, too. You have laws against using nanotech to irreparably damage a sentient's mind."

"We can fix it," General Samuel said to the president and Admiral Manda. "S&H has the original specs, they—"

"They don't have them anymore," Tanis said calmly. "I have relieved them of the technology. It is scrubbed from their systems. I also own S&H Defensive now, but that is another matter. I'm sure I can transfer ownership to the Silstrand government at some point."

"How is it that you 'own' S&H Defensive?" President Charles was scowling deeply.

<Not the best start,> Sera said with a belabored sigh.

<No, but we have to get all of this out of the way,> Tanis replied. *<Best to do it now.>*

<Well, carry on. You have some more hopes of theirs to dash, don't you?>

Tanis replied with a silent laugh on the Link before replying to the Silstrand president. "Their contract with me was in the form of a license. It also included damages if they violated their license. It would seem that they never expected to encounter me again, and did not heed the limits of their license. I claimed damages, and they've settled by selling all of their assets to me."

"How did we not hear of this?" Admiral Manda's tone implied more than a little skepticism.

"Things are chaotic out there," Tanis shrugged. "I paid my old friend Smithers a visit and hashed it out with him in person. The ISF owns S&H, including the planet Dessen and all its ships. Granted, I don't really *want* to own it, so I'm sure we can work something out.

"However, this is all contingent on you turning over the nanotech and Lana. The girl will die if we don't save her."

Tanis cast an eye at General Samuel. "I'm operating under the assumption that you actually care what happens to your daughter—though what I've heard from Kylie Rhoads and her crew tells me that *may* not be the case."

"Kylie Rhoads is a—" Samuel began, but Tanis held up her finger, silencing him once more.

"You gave her a letter of marque which granted her the *Barbaric Queen*, did you not? In honor of your original agreement with her. Which, I might add, she upheld, despite your rash actions in Gedri."

Samuel seemed to shrink down in his seat, and Tanis continued.

"I think what you were going to say is that Kylie Rhoads is a credit to Silstrand. She is now searching out her brother, Paul Rhoads, so that we can deal with him and end the threat the Revolution Fleet presents."

"What do you even need us for?" Admiral Manda asked.

Tanis turned to Scorsin. "Special Envoy?"

Scorsin leant forward and placed his hands on his knees. "You are to expand your influence throughout the fringe systems and bring them to order. We expect all of the systems spinward and coreward of Silstrand to be firmly under your control within five years. Scipio will provide whatever non-military resources you require to achieve this goal."

President Charles sat back, a look of sheer amazement on his face. "Your main condition for peace with Silstrand—aside from the nanotech—is that we annex thirty star systems?"

"Fifty-seven," Scorsin corrected. "Once we get these preliminary matters out of the way, we can dive into those specifics."

"How will that even be possible?" Admiral Manda asked, her eyes wide and face suffused with worry.

Tanis grinned. "Did you notice our shields during the battle?"

Manda's eyes narrowed and a smile formed on her lips. "Now you're talking, Field Marshal. I'll take those shields over nanotech any day."

Sera placed her hands on her knees and smiled at those assembled. "Excellent. Now we have a solid foundation. However, what about those refreshments you mentioned? If I don't get coffee in the next minute, I'm liable to get testy."

WINOS AND SLEPTONS

STELLAR DATE: 10.14.8948 (Adjusted Years)
LOCATION: Gamma VIII base
REGION: Outer Asteroid Belt, New Canaan System

"Stars, I feel like I haven't seen daylight in weeks," Cary complained.

<Well, I suppose the fact that you actually ***haven't*** *may play into that,>* Faleena said, winking in Cary's mind. *<You should go for another walk in the base's park.>*

"It's not the same." Cary rubbed her eyes as she sat on the edge of her bed.

<You can't tell. The simulation is near-perfect. I mean, ***I*** *can tell, because you just can't fake starlight to perfection—not that they need to for you orgies.>*

"OK, Faleena. First off, you can't use 'orgies' as shorthand for 'organics'. It's...just don't. As for the starlight, sure, it may *look* perfect, but I still know that I'm down in the middle of a moon with a billion tons of rock over my head."

<Then go up to the observation dome,> Faleena offered. *<See Canaan Prime and real starlight for a bit.>*

"You know I can't."

<You don't need to be within a minute of the remnant at all times,> Faleena's avatar shook her head at Cary. *<****It*** *doesn't know you're that close. If it were going to try something, it would have done so already.>*

"It waited inside Nance for eighteen years. It can play a long game."

<Technically, the Caretaker's remnant waited for around ten. Before that, it was a shard of Myrrdan that was inside Nance. It was also working hard to get back here—or I suspect it was.>

"You get my point."

Cary stood up and walked to her wardrobe, which consisted exclusively of uniforms and exercise clothing of ISF issue. She pulled on a pair of compression pants with the space force's logo on the side, followed by a sports bra.

"A run will do me good, get the blood pumping."

She slid her feet into her shoes and bent over to stretch her back and legs out.

<A run is a great idea. At least try to pass through the park; it'll make you feel better.>

Cary finished her stretching, and palmed her quarters' door, ready to start at a slow jog. As the portal slid open, she stepped out and almost walked right into Saanvi, who wore a large grin and was almost bouncing with enthusiasm.

"Cary, Faleena! Good, you're up! Come to the lab, come! We've figured it out."

<*'It'?*> Faleena asked.

"Yeah, 'it'. How to detect and contain any remnant and shard we find."

"Seriously?" Cary asked. "Just like that?"

"Cary, we've been here for over seven weeks. No, not 'just like that'."

"Right," Cary said as she walked out of her quarters and followed her sister down the hall. "I mean, when I went to bed, you were all banging your collective heads against the wall. Now you've just got it sorted?"

"Well, we *think* we have. We're going to have to let the remnant out to test it."

Cary swallowed. "Uh, kay."

Saanvi glanced back at her. "You knew we'd have to do that eventually. We can't be sure that we can capture and contain a remnant if we don't try it on the one we have."

"What if it fakes it?" Cary asked. "Tricks us into thinking we can capture it."

"Possible," Saanvi said with an exaggerated shrug as they turned the corner down the hall to Earnest's lab. "But Trine will be watching, and maybe we'll be able to see."

"That's weird to hear you refer to 'us' in the third person."

"Language kinda fails to describe what we can do," Saanvi replied as she pushed open the door to Earnest's lab and held it for Cary.

"Damn, it's cold in here," Cary said, rubbing her arms.

"Well yeah, you're dressed for exercising. Why's that?"

Cary rolled her eyes at her sister. "Because I was going to exercise, before you appeared and dragged me here."

Saanvi frowned. "Why didn't you change?"

Cary gave an exasperated groan. "Because you acted like the world would end if I didn't come with you right away, Sahn!"

<*You **were** all bouncy, Saanvi. It seemed very urgent,*> Faleena chimed in.

"Hmm…I guess I did. Oh well, you'll warm up." Saanvi rubbed a hand up and down Cary's arm. "This help?"

"Sahn, cut it out!" Cary jerked her arm away.

Saanvi grinned. "Maybe I *should* have let you get that run in, sister grumpy pants."

"They're running tights, not pants."

"Tights *are* pants," Saanvi countered.

Cary groaned. "We're *not* having this argument again."

Saanvi gave an all-too-chipper chuckle and the two women walked to the table where the remnant floated, the brane Cary had created floating in a magnetic field.

Leads were connected to the silver bands that wrapped around it, and several probes were situated next to the brane, providing real-time data on energy readings coming off the remnant.

Next to the table, their heads together in discussion, were Earnest and two of his top researchers, Harl and Kirsty. His wife Abby was also standing a few meters away, staring intently at the remnant.

Cary had never been entirely comfortable in Abby's presence. The woman felt like a tightly-wound spring that was about to either snap, or break free of what held it and fly about, wreaking havoc.

There were also rumors that their mother and Abby had been at odds a number of times in the past. It made Cary wonder how much the woman really liked them.

"Ah!" Earnest proclaimed when he saw Cary and Saanvi approach. "Just the two transdimensionally powerful beings we've been waiting for."

"We're just one transdimensionally powerful being," Saanvi corrected. "Separately, we're just a couple of girls."

Cary turned her head up and sniffed disdainfully. "I don't know about you, Sahn, but *I'm* a woman."

"Sure, Cary." Saanvi laughed and bumped her hip against Cary's. "You're all woman."

Cary blushed and wished she'd gotten changed all the more.

<*Thanks, Sahn. Just what I needed.*>

<Sorry, I didn't mean it that way. I just want to get this over with. I could sleep for a month. You get testy when you're tired, I get giddy and say stupid shit.>

"Yes, well, we're ready if you are," Earnest said with a nod to Harl and Kirsty. He walked to the table and touched a boxy device that had seven long prongs sticking out of one end. "It's not named, but I'm leaning toward calling this the Slepton Captivator."

"Really?" Harl asked. "That's the name we're going with? I think 'Shadowtron' was way better than that."

"I think people will suspect that 'Shadowtron' is a joke," Earnest replied. "At least 'Slepton Captivator' is better than 'N-Space Field Stabilizer'."

Abby snorted. "Except that's exactly what it is, *and* what it does."

"Yeah, but it also captures things in the field, so we need that word in the name," Earnest countered.

"Right," Kirsty nodded, speaking for the first time. "And the thing it captures are Sleptons."

"Plus a host of other shadow particles," Harl countered.

Kirsty nodded. "Yeah, but most shadow particles have stupid names. We can't call it the Zino-Wino-Gluino Captivator. Sleptons are the only ones with a good name."

"Do we have to choose before we test it?" Cary asked. "I'm all for a cool name, but if it doesn't work, then it won't matter."

Earnest glanced at Harl and Kirsty. "She has a point."

"OK, but in my notes, I'm calling it a Slepton Captivator," Kirsty groused.

"What we sorted out last night," Saanvi said to Cary as Earnest adjusted the positioning of the device, "is that even in its most dormant state, the remnant emits minute amounts of shadow particles. Barely detectable. But if you pass just the right eV wave through it, it spits out Sleptons like mad—"

"Hence the name," Kirsty interrupted.

"Yeah, hence Kirsty's name," Saanvi nodded. "The seemingly-unnamable thing Earnest has there emits the wave so that the remnant can be detected, and then it can create what we hope is a facsimile of the brane you made to hold the remnant."

"Hope?" Cary asked.

"Well, we've never tested it," Earnest replied. "We have our calculations, but honestly, we've been at this for weeks and we barely know what the hell we're looking at. If we had Bob to help, it would be different…but as it sits…."

Cary nodded. "I understand. Let's do this. If it works, I assume there will be more tests before we can finally call it done?"

Earnest nodded. "Yes. Ideally, we'd like to see if we could draw it out of a human, but…well, that would be a bit too much, I think."

Cary reached out to Saanvi, then Faleena. A part of her wondered if Saanvi joining the deep-Link was necessary anymore, but now was not the time to add that variable to the experiment.

Agreed, Trine-Saanvi thought. *Though I do feel a bit like a fifth wheel sometimes.*

I think you are necessary, Trine-Faleena said. *Something about how we join seems to require you. However, I agree that now is not the time for more changes.*

"We am—are—ready," Trine-Cary said.

"OK, do you think you can let it out without destroying the brane?" Earnest asked.

Trine observed the thing within the brane. It had grown dimmer over the weeks, as though the constant poking and prodding had sapped it of its energy. It also no longer spoke. The most accurate word Trine could think of was 'listless'.

"I believe I can extract it, yes."

"OK then," Earnest said as he pointed at a five-meter-wide platform next to the table. "Stand on that. It has a magnetic shield that's a bit like the brane…but won't kill us to be inside of it. I doubt it can hold the remnant for long, but it should give us time to capture it."

Trine-Cary wondered how many more caveats Earnest could have thrown into his statement. She lifted the brane, pulling the leads off the bands, and then stepped onto the platform. Saanvi joined her; both women had to be within the field to maintain their deep-Link.

Earnest stepped up beside them, and Trine saw a bead of sweat run down the side of his face. *Not the best sign.*

Trine drew a deep breath and nodded to Harl, who activated the field surrounding the pedestal. It snapped into place, the EM field producing a small hum as it shimmered faintly around them, visible only by the air it ionized.

Trine-Cary set her fingertips on the bands and pulled them apart, and then somehow—though she did not quite understand it herself—she split the brane open.

In a flash, the remnant was gone, flying out of the brane and streaking around the sphere.

"It's working," Kirsty crowed as Earnest swept the eV wave around the magnetic sphere.

"Yes, I can see it," Earnest said. "It's much larger…I'm trying to encapsulate it."

Earnest activated the device's emitters, and Trine could see the remnant, which had previously been trying to get out of the magnetic cage, shy away.

"It certainly doesn't like it," Trine-Cary said.

The remnant was drawn toward Earnest's device, and Trine felt her pulses quicken at the thought that they'd finally secured the thing without relying on her abilities.

Then the remnant broke away from the field and smashed into the magnetic sphere. Trine saw the containment field waver, and then the remnant slipped through.

"Kill the field!" Trine-Saanvi shouted, and Cary spun, looking for the Remnant. It was nowhere to be seen.

"Dammit!" Earnest swore. "We were so close!"

"I found it," Trine-Cary said calmly as she walked across the lab, staring into *n*-space as the remnant tried to hide from her. "Earnest, hit Abby with the wave."

Earnest looked at his wife, who appeared more than a little terrified.

"I don't know if this will hurt, Abs."

Abby clenched her teeth. "Just do it."

The moment Earnest directed the device's eV wave at Abby, the holodisplay atop the emitter lit up, showing sleptons coming out of Abby's midsection.

"It's…masquerading as a part of her liver," Harl said. "That must be how it anchors itself to a person."

Earnest walked toward his wife. "Be still, Abby. I don't think this will hurt. I think with a few adjustments…"

"I don't care if it hurts, get it out," Abby whispered hoarsely, her eyes darting to Trine-Cary. "You be ready. I'm not going to spend ten years with one of these things in my—oh shit, it's talking to me! Hurry! *Get it out!"*

Earnest activated the device once more, and Trine could see the remnant writhe as it was pulled from Abby's body, losing its corporeal aspects and flowing from her toward the device.

The entity was drawn into the space between the seven prongs, and folded over and over until a sphere snapped into place around the remnant.

"Yes!" Earnest shouted. "Look at that. I made a black brane, and I stuck your remnant ass in it!"

He walked over to the magnetic field emitter where they'd previously held Trine's brane and slid the new one into it.

"And there we have it, safe and sound."

"Check me over again," Abby said. "Make sure it's gone."

Earnest complied, and Trine confirmed, "There is no trace of the remnant within you, Abby."

Earnest turned to Cary, who was now just Cary once more.

"You know what this means?"

"I can finally get some real sleep?"

"Well, yes. Then we can wake Nance."

Cary's eyes darted to Nance, still in her stasis pod, and then to Saanvi. "That would be nice. I'd like to meet Nance again for the first time."

THE LONG NIGHT

STELLAR DATE: 10.25.8948 (Adjusted Years)
LOCATION: ISS *I2*, Forward Lounge
REGION: Orbiting Silstrand, Silstrand System, Silstrand Alliance

Tanis stood in the forward observation lounge, alone with Sera, President Charles, and Admiral Manda.

"I'm sure you hear this a lot," President Charles said, as a servitor brought them the drinks they'd requested. "But this is not like any other warship I've ever seen—or heard of."

"I think it's been mentioned," Tanis replied. "Honestly, it would have been more work to remove things like this lounge than keep them. Plus…it's home, you know?"

Tanis could tell from the look on the president's face that he did not really understand what she meant, despite the fact that he nodded in agreement. Admiral Manda, on the other hand, pressed her lips together and inclined her head.

"I never had anything like this on any of my ships, but I do know what it's like to consider a warship home. It's nice to have sections that are made for form over function. Helps ground you."

"A lot of grounding here in the *Intre—I2*," Sera said, shaking her head. "I still mess the name up sometimes."

Manda glanced at Tanis. "Why *did* you rename your ship, Admiral? Surely you know it's bad luck."

"We wanted a clear division," Tanis replied. "Sure, we fought two major engagements with the *Intrepid*, but those were brief. Flashes in the pan. For two centuries, the *Intrepid* was home. We wanted to always remember it as such, our people's ark. The *I2*, on the other hand; she's a ship made for battle, and when we speak of her, she is that first, and home second."

"Two hundred years…" President Charles mused. "That's a lifetime, just to spend on one ship."

"Not anymore, it's not," Sera replied. "A lifetime, that is. The nanotech that you've received will double—at least—how long you can expect to live."

"That still feels surreal," President Charles said. "It's going to change so much for us."

"Yes, it will." Tanis wondered how well these people would really do with what she had given them. Would they hoard it, keeping it to the rich only? Would they dole it out slowly, or release it to all?

<*We can't hold the entire human race's hands.*> Angela repeated Tanis's earlier words back to her. <*Sol managed to equalize with this technology—before people created artificial divisions and tore everything apart.*>

<*I know, but I still wonder what these people will do.*>

<*Well, what with the Transcend's longevity techniques, we may just get to watch them and find out.*>

Tanis nodded silently as they looked out the window at the space beyond Silstrand's largest moon, a dull blue orb named Kora. The group was observing the moon's L2 point, which had recently been cleared out for what was to come.

"I—" Admiral Manda began to say, and then it happened.

Where there had been nothing but empty space, a ship now drifted in the dark.

"The *Long Night*," Tanis announced, gesturing at the vessel that had just appeared.

"That certainly is something to see," Manda said, her voice filled with sincere awe. "And that ship was just where?"

"Khardine," Tanis replied. "Which is in an undisclosed location. Suffice it to say that it's over three-thousand light years from here. Six years' travel by dark layer FTL."

The *Long Night* was a new design of dreadnought modelled after the AST ships the ISF had fought in Bollam's World. Its hull was five thousand and two hundred meters long, with engines mounted at both ends.

The Silstrand System orbited the galactic core more slowly than Khardine, and the *Long Night*'s engines flared as it boosted to match the velocity of the celestial bodies that surrounded it.

"That's mind-boggling," President Charles replied. "What's the range on these 'jump gates', as you call them?"

"Theoretically, there isn't one," Tanis replied. "Some *very* long jumps have occurred, but if there is no return gate, getting home can take some time."

"I can only imagine," Admiral Manda replied in a soft voice. "Can you…we could eventually go anywhere."

"Remember," Tanis cautioned. "This is not a technology that we're sharing. We will be bringing in mirror tugs to facilitate any jumps that are necessary for your ships. If jump gates get in the wrong hands…"

"I thought the Orion Freedom Alliance already had this technology," Admiral Manda said.

"Well, additional wrong hands," Tanis clarified.

"Like the Hegemony, or the Nietzscheans," Sera offered.

President Charles face paled. "What if they have it? You said that the Nietzscheans are possibly allies of the OFA. Could they not jump here?"

"It's possible," Sera said, nodding slowly. "We'll be helping your people establish interdictor systems. They disrupt the jump-bubble and will make deep insystem arrivals like what the *Long Night* just performed very unlikely."

"That's not terribly comforting," Admiral Manda replied.

Tanis turned and looked at the Silstrand president and his admiral. "Don't forget. This technology did not just spring into existence. It has been a reality for well over a century now. The enemy is just as worried—we believe—about it coming into general use."

Sera leaned against the window. "Regarding the stasis shields, it will take a bit to get them to you, and we won't have enough for all your ships. Even though they *might* be able to jump in here, stasis shield tech is something that none of our enemies have."

"You said you'd be leaving a ship. Will it be the *Long Night*?" President Charles asked.

Tanis shook her head. "No. The '*Night* is just here to deliver the gate. It has other places to be. You'll be getting one of our destroyers. The *Cobalt Flame*."

"A destroyer? Admiral—"

Tanis held up her hand. "A destroyer with stasis shields and ten atom beams. It has firepower equal to half your fleet, and its shields cannot be breached. I'm sure you've watched the vids of the Bollam's World battles. You saw what our ships were able to weather there."

Admiral Manda gave a rueful laugh and looked up at the overhead. "If I recall, *this* ship weathered the relativistic jet from a black hole."

"Exactly." Tanis turned to watch the *Long Night*, as components of a massive jump gate began to lift off a long cargo rail atop the ship.

"I'm eager to see what that will look like when it activates," Admiral Manda said as the ring began to take shape.

"You won't have long to wait," Tanis replied.

She was less interested in the ring than the pinnace which had departed the *Long Night*, and begun to boost toward the *I2*. That pinnace carried a Shadowtron device and the specifications on how to make more.

Finally, after *centuries*, they would be able to scour the ship for any last trace of Myrrdan and eliminate him. Along with any of the Caretaker's other minions.

That would be a greater victory than any they'd won thus far.

WHEELS WITHIN WHEELS

STELLAR DATE: 10.27.8948 (Adjusted Years)
LOCATION: Ol' Sam, ISF *I2*
REGION: Orbiting Silstrand, Silstrand System, Silstrand Alliance

"You're sure you got this from here?" Sera asked for the third time.

"Yes!" Tanis laughed. "I'm over a hundred years your senior. I can take care of myself."

"Bob?" Sera looked up at the roof of Tanis's cabin. "You'll watch over Tanis?"

<*What am I? Interstellar dust?*> Angela asked.

"You're as bad as Tanis, most of the time," Sera replied. "I can't trust either of you to keep the other out of trouble anymore."

<*I'll keep Tanis and Angela on their path,*> Bob intoned when Sera finished speaking.

"That's not what I asked, Bob." Sera's eyes narrowed as she stared at the cabin's ceiling. " 'On their path' and 'safe' are not the same thing."

A strange sound came into their minds, like a waterfall mixed with rolling thunder.

"Is he…laughing?" Sera asked.

Tanis shrugged. "I guess so. I can't remember the last time I heard Bob laugh like this."

"What gives?" Sera asked the ceiling once more.

<*To think that even* **I** *could keep Tanis 'safe'. You place more faith in me than I deserve, Sera Tomlinson.*>

"I always feel like you're one of my childhood teachers when you use both my names like that."

<*Is there some other way I should use both your names?*>

Sera groaned. "Wow. You think you're funny, is that it, Bob?"

"You know," Tanis lowered one eyebrow while raising the other. "I think I'm a very safe person these days. The last dangerous thing I did was rescuing you eighteen years ago, Sera. Since then I've been nothing but circumspect."

"Tanis, you assaulted the Galadrial just half a year ago, with Uriel and a Marine strike team."

"Right! Perfectly safe. I had ISF Marines with me."

Sera groaned. "This is not making me feel better."

Tanis leant over and placed a hand on Sera's arm. "Seriously, Sera. It's *you* I'm worried about. I have the most powerful starship in the galaxy, Finaeus, *and* Bob. Honestly, I think that Finaeus should go with you. You need allies."

"I have Greer; he's loyal, and from his latest QuanComm messages, fiercely determined to make sure there's no repeat of the attack on Keren Station."

"And Krissy seems to be faring well in Vela," Tanis added. "Are you still at least considering moving the capital there?"

"Maybe. I need to visit at some point. Chancellor Alma has not been fully accommodating to Krissy. Understandable, I suppose. She views herself as terribly important, and Krissy, while part of the—" Sera held up her fingers to make air quotes " 'royal family', Alma considers her to be too far from the throne to garner real respect."

"You're going to have to visit a lot of places out there to drum up support."

"Maybe.... Oh! Guess what, Tanis? This came in on the latest burst from Khardine. Guess who escaped from prison...freaking months ago?"

"I hate guessing games, Sera, spit it out."

Sera rolled her eyes. "Always so testy. You should take a page from Bob's book and yuck it up a bit."

"Sera. You're killing me here. I only know one—wait...no! *Andrea*?"

"Hole in one." Sera grimaced, then rocked her head side to side, stretching her neck. "My dearest, least-favorite sister. You'll never guess who broke her out."

"You're right, I won't. Just tell me."

"Justin."

Tanis's eyes widened. "As in Justin, your old boss, the former director of the Hand?"

"One and the same."

<*Allies or enemies?*> Angela asked.

Sera gave an exaggerated shrug. "You got me. If it was Justin on his own, I'd say ally. He's probably less than happy about how he had to fall on his sword for me, but if it were just him, I know we could figure out a way to work together."

"Andrea's a whole different story, though," Tanis said, her voice trailing away as she remembered her last encounter with Sera's sister in the Ascella system.

"Yeah, she's not a fan of yours either, what with the whole 'turning me to kill you' thing that happened."

"So we have to assume that, because Justin freed Andrea, he has a plan for her. A plan that can't be good for us."

Sera began fiddling with her hair, fingers twitching violently as they twisted the long, black locks. Tanis watched, moderately amused as Sera's skin began to change from blue to red. Then it took on the scaled appearance it had when she had masqueraded as a dragon-demon at Diana's costume ball.

"Is that conscious, or is that a new stress response?" Tanis couldn't help but smirk at her friend.

Sera glanced down at herself. "Oh, shit! No, not conscious at all!"

"It's not the first time I've noticed it," Tanis said. "Last time you talked to Elena, you were full-on harbinger of death when you came back."

"I was?" Sera asked.

"Yeah. Maybe you should add a block to stop your skin from taking this form at all."

Sera held up a hand and examined the long claws on the end of her fingers. "Or maybe I'll just make this my default. Think it would help or hinder negotiations with future allies?"

Tanis lowered her face into her hands and shook it. "Sera, how are *you* the President of the most powerful alliance in humanity's history?"

Sera didn't reply, and when Tanis looked up, her friend was just grinning as she clicked her nails together. When their eyes met, Sera asked, "Yeah? Think we're the most powerful?"

<*Of course we are,*> Angela interjected. <*We have us.*>

Sera's skin reverted back to the blue 'uniform' she typically wore. "True, I suppose we do."

Tanis looked at the ceiling. "Bob, I blame you for this. Why did you have to give her this skin?"

<Humans' natural epidermis is weak and ineffectual,> Bob replied without pause. *<What I gave Sera—especially now that Finaeus has integrated the flow-armor into it—is far superior. It provides a multitude of tactical advantages, and constant protection. You'd go through fewer hearts if* ***you*** *adopted it as well.>*

"See!" Sera crowed. "My epidermis is superior. Bob agrees."

<It's true,> Angela added. *<Sera's fashion proclivities aside, her skin is highly advantageous. If for no other reason than the protective properties, and her chameleon ability.>*

"I can change my appearance," Tanis countered.

<A bit, but not like her. She can fit in anywhere.>

<Humanity's continuing infatuation with clothing is strange to begin with,> Bob added. *<Sera's desire to turn herself into a mythological creature actually makes more sense to me than the regular clothing people wear.>*

"This is not the way I was expecting this conversation to go." Tanis leaned back and sighed. "OK, Bob, why is it that Sera turning herself into a demon-dragon thing is more rational than regular clothing?"

<Well, clothing is generally unnecessary for humans, now that you've mastered your environments. Maybe it is needed for completely unmodified humans living on planets, but otherwise it's superfluous. It consumes a lot of resources and general effort, it seems.>

"People like to express themselves through clothing," Tanis replied. "And some people like to hide their bodies."

<Regarding your second point, that no longer makes sense. Everyone has perfect bodies, maintained in whatever form they want. If they feel ashamed of who they are, that shame is likely a representation of something unhealthy in their minds. Military uniforms are useful for showing a common bond. I suppose you organics may need to have other external expressions of commonality, but it doesn't require clothing, per se.

<Which brings me to my first point. Sera's epidermis is far more capable of expressing herself. In fact, I would argue that Sera's desire to turn herself into whatever strikes her fancy, is far healthier than what most humans do, which is try to hide what they are, and blend in.>

"This is not the first time I've heard this argument," Tanis said. "I know that Sera just loves to be whatever she wants to be, and isn't mentally unstable—it makes sense for her. However, a lot of people, even though they can look perfect, don't *feel* perfect. If they were to costume themselves, they would do it to blend in, and it would end up being the same for them as it is now."

<I can't fix every problem organics have, nor should I. I'm simply stating that Sera's behavior is a logical end-result for a well-balanced person who also likes to be visually and tactilely stimulated. No human would argue that things of beauty are inherently wrong, so no one could say that what Sera does with herself is wrong.>

Sera leaned back on the sofa and gave Tanis a smug smile. "Gotta say, Bob. Never thought that you'd back me on this—also never thought of myself as that mentally well-rounded, but I'll take the compliment."

<You misunderstand me, Sera,> Bob said. *<I did not mean to imply that you were the pinnacle of mental health. I just said that in this respect, what you do—your free expression of self—is healthier than what most do. The fact that your expression of self is a demonic being, typically associated with vengeance and destruction, contains its own message.>*

"Annnnd my moment of victory is over."

Tanis laughed. "I'll take the win."

<I'm sorry, Tanis, you still lose. Your value to your people and humanity is tremendous. The advantages that Sera's epidermis provide should—to my mind, at least—outweigh whatever nonsensical hesitations you may have surrounding replacing your organic skin with something more practical.>

"I think we both lost in this conversation," Sera said, winking at Tanis. "Though it was a nice distraction from what's coming our way."

"Right, and from Andrea and Justin."

"Tanis! I had managed to forget about them for a moment."

Tanis shrugged, her expression unapologetic. "You really can't. You'll need to find them and determine what they're up to."

Sera's lips flattened out and her eyes widened in frustration. "Transcend is a big place, Tanis. Big enough that half of it probably doesn't know my father is dead yet. They could be anywhere, behind the scenes, manipulating things. Justin has contacts *everywhere*. If he's out, he could be subverting agents I had previously considered loyal to me."

"You need to build your own base, then," Tanis replied. "What about the families on Valkris, where Nadine is from?"

"Helping the families on Valkris is a lot like arming my enemies. I mean…they're not enemies now, but what happens when we win this thing? They're not the sort that help maintain the peace."

Tanis leant over and placed a hand on Sera's knee. "Sera, there are two billion stars within the human sphere of expansion. There will never be peace everywhere. Not so long as humans are humans."

"That's a sad way to look at it."

"I don't need everyone to be happy, I just need them to stop trying to kill everyone else that doesn't agree with them."

Sera laughed. "Oh, just that little thing, eh?"

Tanis gave a short laugh and returned Sera's smile. "It's what we're doing, isn't it? Stopping Orion, securing a real peace in the Inner Stars? We'll be done by lunch, right?"

"Don't get carried away, Tanis. It might take 'til breakfast tomorrow."

"OK, I'll make sure I make some time in my schedule for it."

"You do that."

The two sat in silence for a few minutes, Tanis lost in thought, considering her next moves. She assumed Sera was doing the same, since she wore her customary thinking scowl.

"Have you decided where in Praesepe you're going after things wrap up here?" Sera eventually asked.

"Well, I want to find out more about what happened in Genevia—the tech they used in their mech program is just too similar to what Peter Rhoads used to control his people. If there's a lead on the Caretaker there, I want to find it."

"Are you thinking you can use the device Earnest made to take it out?"

"The Shadowtron? Yeah, that's my hope."

Sera laughed. "What a badass name. No idea if it has anything to do with how the thing really works, but badass nonetheless."

"I guess it has something to do with shadow particles."

"And 'tron'?"

"I imagine it must do something with electrons."

"I guess that makes sense, most tech does use electrons. Still a badass name."

Tanis nodded. "Gotta admit that I like how Earnest made it look like a gun, too."

"Sure doesn't hurt. I assume Finaeus is making more?"

"Yeah, he has a team on it. They're also working on a way to enable the ship's internal sensors to run the sweeps shipwide. Would save us a lot of cat and mouse."

"And then you'll finally catch your little mole."

Tanis let a feral smile slip over her lips. "Indeed, we shall. We'll sweep your ship before you go, too."

"Right! Which of your tiny surplus vessels shall become my flagship?"

"Do you want the *Long Night*?" Tanis asked. "Right now, it just has a shakedown crew aboard, but we can get it properly fitted out and crewed up. I bet that half the captains in the fleet would love to get their hands on it."

Sera nodded appreciatively. "With the exception of Rachel."

"Yeah…I don't think I'll be able to pry the *I2* away from her under any circumstances."

"Not unless you make something bigger."

"Maybe not even then. This girl's pretty special."

"Yeah," Sera nodded, looking around Tanis's cabin as though it were the whole ship. "Even in Transcend and Orion space, there are probably only a dozen ships older than this one—if we're counting the date the keel was laid, not service years."

Tanis patted the sofa. "That's right, don't be calling my girl old!"

"So, Praesepe for you, and Khardine for me. And if you find more leads on the Caretaker?"

Tanis honestly had no idea what would follow. "We'll see how fresh and promising they are. Nadine suggested we find her cousin Nerischka. She worked some missions in Genevian space around the end of their war with Nietzschea."

"That's right," Sera nodded. "Made a few 'tweaks' to the upper military echelon. Got rid of the admirals that wanted to keep steamrolling over more nations. If memory serves, Nerischka's in the Azela system, tracking down the source of some weird bio-mods."

"That's what Nadine said, as well." Tanis reached for her coffee cup, only to find that it was empty. "Damn…I don't even remember finishing that."

"Still catching up with sleep, eh?"

"I guess. No rest for the weary, right?"

"That's what I hear," Sera replied. "So you're just going to hunt the Caretaker for a bit around Praesepe? Seems like an unproductive use of your time."

"Well, we have a few leads. But if they don't pan out, we'll cut our losses. I have a desire to knock the teeth out of the Nietzschean Empire, but I also have a date with the king of the Trisilieds. I think that his neck would look great with my boot on it."

"Not ready to forgive and forget yet?"

Tanis's brow lowered. "I think after about 'never' I'll be ready. Don't worry, though, I'm going to exhibit restraint and not raze their capital world to the ground. However, I *will* do something that completely debilitates them. They earned that much."

"How *are* we going to deal with stuff like that?" Sera asked. "Destroyed nations that we leave in our wake. We can't kill everyone, and we can't leave them there to rebuild."

"That's where the allegiances come in."

"If we can build them faster than our half-dozen enemies attack us."

"Oh, is that how few we have?"

Sera shrugged. "Depends on how you divide them up."

<*Anywhere between seventeen and…thirteen hundred,*> Angela supplied with a grin in their minds. <*You should make them start a registry, or something.*>

Tanis summoned a view of the galaxy above the coffee table, then focused in on human space. Closest to her was the Perseus arm, then Orion, and the Sagittarius Arm was up against Sera's knees.

"Last we heard." Tanis pointed at a marker close to Sol. "Jessica and team had moved on from Virginis. She said they formed a solid alliance there—which I bet pisses off the Hegemony to no end."

Sera leant forward, placing her elbows on her knees and chin on her folded hands. "Yeah, the AST used to run a lot of black ops in Virginis. Getting kicked out by a bunch of AIs must really burn their cookies."

"Which means they're on to Aldebaran."

Sera shifted, rubbing her palms across her face and through her hair. "Stars, good luck with that. I don't even know how they'll get in the system."

"That's why we sent *them*," Tanis replied. "Sure, there are humans on *Sabrina*, but it's almost entirely an AI ship now. If anyone can pull it off, it's them."

"Stars, I hope so. We keep giving them all the shit assignments."

"And they knock it out of the park each time." Tanis gave Sera a reassuring look. "They've got QuanComm blades; if they need us, they'll call."

"What about the delegation to Corona Australis?" Sera asked. "Care to put odds on them?"

Tanis gave a rueful laugh. "They've got better chances than the team at Dorcha. I feel like we should have just sent an ultimatum and then started a war without waiting for a response."

"Don't count Admiral Bartty out yet. He's got some tricks up his sleeves."

"May he have endless sleeves," Tanis said, raising the cup of coffee the servitor had just brought in a toast.

Sera leaned back and looked over the billions of stars that lay between the two women. "I have a feeling we're *all* going to need endless sleeves."

SURVEYING VELA

STELLAR DATE: 11.01.8948 (Adjusted Years)
LOCATION: *Greensward*
REGION: Estrada System, Vela Cluster

"Dammit, she got here first, that bitch," Andrea Tomlinson swore as she glared at the holotank on the *Greensward*'s bridge. "Fucking Chancellor Alma has declared for the Khardine government."

Justin nodded silently as he stared at the feeds displayed in the tank. "Looks like Admiral Krissy showed up with a fleet. I'm surprised to see her operating so openly. The Grey Division really has it out for her."

Andrea glanced at Justin. "I recall hearing something about that, do tell."

"Pretty simple: the Greys were after Finaeus, and Krissy helped him escape."

Andrea considered that for a moment. From what Justin had told her, the Grey Division worked for Airtha…who may or may not be Andrea's mother—a thought that was both chilling and disturbing.

At present, Andrea considered the Greys to be her greatest threat. Justin—thanks to his centuries as Director of the Hand—had many contacts to leverage, but most of those were in the Inner Stars and little help deep in the Transcend. Many had allied with Sera—the Khardine Sera, not the Sera who had proclaimed herself President at Airtha.

Within the Transcend, the Greys were the most powerful of the many shadow organizations behind the scenes. And they worked for Airtha. Dealing with her sister would be a straight-up conflict, that was just how Sera operated. But the Greys would never hit head-on. Their moves would always come from the side.

Just like what Airtha had done by making another Sera.

*Just like my sister. Little upstart thinks so much of herself, she can't exist just once. There has to be two of her, and **both** have to be the president, squabbling over the Transcend—which by rights should be mine.*

She realized that Justin was expecting a response, and shrugged. "Well, Admiral Krissy seems to be unconcerned about the Greys now, at least. Showing up with a fleet of ten-thousand ships has all but secured the Vela Cluster for her."

Justin chuckled and shook his head. "Yeah, a fleet of ships—some of which are nearly impervious—has a way of helping out."

"Not funny, Justin," Andrea spat. "If you pulled me out of that mind-prison just to drag me around the Transcend, hiding on this garbage scow…." She left the statement hanging, not sure what else he should have done. A part of her wouldn't mind going back to the beach where she had been living—or at least had thought she'd been living on a beach.

Stop it, Andrea. That's the conditioning. Fight it.

Justin shook his head. "Only *you* could call a luxury yacht a 'garbage scow'."

"I should be on a fleet's flagship, flying into Airtha to seize the capital!"

Justin raised a hand, gesturing for her to calm down. "We have a fleet, but we can't show it yet. First, we have to get our hands on New Canaan's stasis shield technology. Without it, any assault would just be pissing away our resources."

"Resources we hoped to accumulate with Chancellor Alma on our side."

"Alma and Vela are just one player in the Transcend. There are a hundred sectors just as powerful and wealthy as Vela. Sure, it's larger than most, and strategically located, but alone, it's hardly noteworthy."

Andrea made a frustrated sound and stormed off the bridge, yelling over her shoulder, "Well, let me know when we go somewhere noteworthy. I'll be in my quarters."

* * * * *

For the hundredth time, Justin thought about terminating his allegiance with Andrea.

With extreme prejudice.

The woman's time in the reconditioning prison had caused her to become even more unhinged. Her emotions were always spilling over now, and it had gone far beyond frustrating. The woman's very presence was like having insects crawl all over his skin while a klaxon blared in his ears.

No…that gives insects a bad name.

"I take it that things are not as promising here as we'd hoped?" Roxy asked as she strolled onto the bridge.

Justin glanced at the woman who was his sure right hand—and an amazing fuck on the side. Where Andrea was a raging storm, Roxy was a calm breeze. A deceptively calm breeze.

To look at her small frame, barely over one hundred and fifty centimeters tall, you'd think she could barely heft a rifle; if she were a normal human, that would be true. But Roxy was barely human at all anymore, possessing the minimum organics necessary to feed a brain with the nutrients it required.

Despite that, the package Roxy came in was a delight to behold. Gleaming sapphire skin with azure streaks, and all the right curves and angles made her the pinnacle of desire-inducing beauty.

Justin should know—he'd made Roxy what she was today.

She sauntered toward him, her skin sparkling in the light the holotank cast on the dim bridge, and he reached a hand out to her.

"They beat us here. In the form of Admiral Krissy. Chancellor Alma has sided with Khardine."

"I guess that explains all the shrieking from her imperial bitchiness."

"Yeah, I'm going to have to get a muzzle of some sort for her."

Roxy traced a fingernail down Justin's arm, small sparks of electricity arcing between them when she pulled away. "I could think of something. You know that we have to get her under control…she's not useful like this."

Justin nodded. He'd never planned for Andrea to be anything more than a figurehead; she was intended to be his ticket to rally followers. The problem was that her reputation was legendary, and she had to be full of fire. If he had a sedate, subdued Andrea at his side, everyone would know she was little more than a puppet.

He'd hoped that Andrea would learn to moderate herself, but it hadn't happened. More invasive measures would have to be taken.

"*Could* you think of something? Or *have* you thought of something?" Justin asked Roxy.

Roxy smiled, obsidian fangs peeking over her lips. "Oh, maybe a little from column A, a little from column B."

"Speak clearly, Roxy."

"Well, there's the old-fashioned way, or we can put her back in the reconditioning sims, and alter her personality and convictions just enough to follow you unconditionally."

"That takes too long," Justin replied. "Especially with someone as pig-headed as she is. So much of her personality is tied up in centuries of belief that she's the queen of everything."

"Hmm..." Roxy reached up and ran a finger down her ear—one of her favorite places to be touched and touch. "Well, what if we went the other way? Rather than trying to moderate her, what if we turned her into what she really wants to be: the queen of the universe. Just a *mannered* queen of the universe."

Justin considered that, his lips twisting as he mulled it over. "That could work. She'd be more conniving, though. Right now, she telegraphs everything—which is convenient for use when it comes to knowing her intentions, but will not serve us well if we put her on display."

"We could use the thing that *it* gave you."

"The neural lace? I suppose, but that's an extreme option. One that can be detected—it would ruin the fiction that she is her own person."

Roxy nodded. "Understood. Why did you use it on me, then?"

Justin stepped toward Roxy and wrapped her in his arms, only a little concerned over the defiance Roxy's words hinted at. "Because you're *not* your own person. You're mine."

TO KHARDINE

STELLAR DATE: 11.02.8948 (Adjusted Years)
LOCATION: ISS *Long Night*
REGION: Silstrand System, Silstrand Alliance

Sera stood on the bridge of the *Long Night*, the holotank before her displaying a view of the ship as it approached the Silstrand jump gate.

She closed her eyes and slowly let out a long breath. *Time to get to work, I suppose.*

A part of Sera wished that she could be the captain of the *Long Night*; just a soldier doing her job, not the one who had to deal with a hundred crises a minute.

<*Thank the stars for Tanis,*> she thought.

<*Sorry?*> Jen asked.

<*Shoot, I've fallen out of the habit of thought segregation. That was just for me.*>

Jen gave a soft laugh. <*Well, we're all thankful for Tanis. Are you worried about her?*>

Sera looked at the looming shape of the *I2* hanging in the distance. <*A bit. Less than I should be? I'm not sure.*> Sera gave a rueful laugh. <*I can't tell my worry about the future in general apart from worry about her, specifically.*>

<*I get that,*> Jen replied. <*Stars, do I get that.*>

<*Well, it's not like I think we're going to lose this war and get our asses kicked, Jen. Don't get all defeatist on me.*>

<*Sorry, that's not the impression I meant to give.*> Jen's voice sounded more upbeat. <*I was getting caught up in your emotions. You're bleeding them across our connection—a lot.*>

Sera grimaced. <*Sorry about that. This feels a lot different than when Helen was in my mind.*>

<*It's weird for me, too. Helen had a very non-standard integration. The technicians had to mimic some of the patterns when they interwove my hardware.*>

Sera recalled the medtechs telling her that as well. They said that without neurological reconstruction in several areas, they would have to use the existing AI interface points.

When Sera had queried them on what they meant, the explanation was that her connection with Helen had been less buffered than normal. In addition, the locations where the neurological interconnections lay allowed the resident AI to have more access into her mind.

Access that resulted in the bleed-through that Jen often experienced.

For her part, Jen handled the slip-ups with grace and understanding. She was a good person, and brave to take on the added responsibilities of being in Sera's head.

<*We'll figure this out eventually,*> Sera replied to Jen. <*Still glad you signed on?*>

<*Of course! I'm working hand-in-hand—so to speak—with the President of the Transcend! You're the most powerful human in the galaxy.*>

Sera snorted. <*OK, Jen, ease up a bit. We all know that's not true.*>

As if on cue, Tanis reached out to her. <*Well, Sera, I'll see you soon. Let's make sure it's not eighteen years this time.*>

<*I thought we already said our goodbyes,*> Sera shot back. <*If you make me get sniffly in front of my new crew…*>

<*If you do, it'll be fine. I'm pretty sure I've cried at least once on the bridge of the* Intrepid, *and no one made me walk the plank.*>

<*I'll cite that if they try to kick me out an airlock,*> Sera said with an audible laugh that got her a few looks from the *Long Night*'s bridge crew.

<*We have the QuanComms. We'll keep in touch. You let me know if you need help. I'll drop a whole civilization in a hot second if your ass is on the line.*>

Sera gave a slight shake of her head. <*No you won't, Tanis. You care too much about…everyone.*>

<*You should see the tongue-lashing I gave a rating this morning. Trust me, he doesn't feel that way.*>

<*Stop trying to cheer me up, Tanis.*>

<*Is it working?*>

<*Yes…and no. Just gonna make me miss you more.*>

Tanis laughed, the sound pure and clear in Sera's mind. <*Don't you go girl-crushing on me, Sera. You know I don't swing that way.*>

<*Oh yeah? Angela told me about how you 'made' Faleena.*>

<*Ang!*> Tanis said in mock anger. <*What did you have to do that for?*>

Angela only laughed in response.

<*It's OK, Tanis. I know you're taken. But I don't miss you in that way*

anyway—well, I would if you gave it a chance. I bet we could convince Joe—>

<Sera!>

<Sorry…just trying to take my mind off…everything.>

Tanis made an exasperated sound. *<You know what I remember?>*

<What?>

<I remember this freighter captain who risked her life to save me, who didn't take no for an answer, and who kicked the asses of an entire pirate base—one in the dark layer, no less—on her own. A woman who, as you tell the story, had already rescued herself by the time I showed up. Always in control, always willing to do whatever needed to be done.>

Tanis's mental tone was filled with a conviction that Sera couldn't deny. It reminded her of a type of strength she'd forgotten she had.

<If **she** *believes in you that much, there's a reason,>* Jen said quietly. *<Sorry, I'm not sure if you left that conversation open to me on purpose.>*

<I did,> Sera replied. *<So long as you're OK with it, I'll leave pretty much everything open to you.>*

<Absolutely.>

Sera was grateful that she'd found Jen. She'd vetted so many AIs who were more than eager to take on the role and responsibilities that came with integrating with the President of the Transcend.

Almost *too* eager.

Jen…Jen had just seemed like she wanted to be friends. Not that she wasn't also well-qualified for the job; all the AIs were, by the time they made it as far as Sera. She'd been told that Bob's vetting process was very involved.

But for all that, Jen just seemed sincere.

"President Tomlinson," Captain Ophelia said from behind her.

Sera turned to see the man standing in front of his command chair, arms clasped behind his back.

"We're ready to go in. Say the word."

Sera nodded. "Just a moment."

<Time to go, Tanis. Remember. If I call, I expect you to come running.>

Tanis laughed again, and Sera relaxed in the warmth coming from her friend. *<You bet I will. Same goes for you, too, Missus President of the Universe.>*

Sera laughed. *<Deal. See you when I see you.>*

<When I see you.>

Sera was ready. Ready to leave the Inner Stars, to take on the responsibilities that awaited her at Khardine. To bring the fight to her mother.

"Captain Ophelia. Take us through."

THE HUNT

STELLAR DATE: 11.02.8948 (Adjusted Years)
LOCATION: ISS *I2*, Bridge
REGION: Orbiting Silstrand, Silstrand System, Silstrand Alliance

<Captain! I need you in Engine.>

Rachel was out of her chair before she even formulated a response.

<Did you find one, Terry?>

<Yes, you said you wanted to be present for the capture.>

"Major Calmin, you have the conn," Rachel called out as she rushed off the bridge.

"Aye, ma'am, I have the conn," she heard Calmin call out as she sped past Tori in the bridge's foyer.

<Good hunting,> Tori said with a wink a second before Calmin sent a query.

<Anything I should be worried about, Captain?>

<Just the hunt, Calmin. Need to keep it quiet.>

She could tell Calmin was suppressing a laugh. *<Ma'am, I don't think racing off the bridge like your pants are on fire is how you keep things quiet.>*

Rachel hiked her skirt up, wishing she *had* worn pants today. *<Very funny, Major.>*

<Aye, ma'am, I thought so. Let me know how it goes.>

<Absolutely.>

She called for an express car to Engine as she slowed her mad dash to a rapid stride down the long administrative concourse to the command deck's maglev station.

When she arrived, the express car was waiting, and Rachel stepped inside. The car started to move, and then shuddered to a stop.

Rachel was about to query the traffic NSAI for status, when the doors opened, and Tanis walked in.

"Admiral Richards!" Rachel hadn't been aware Tanis was on the command deck.

"Rachel," Tanis nodded as the maglev train took off from the station. "Hope you don't mind if I hitch a ride. And don't call me that when we're in private. How many times do I have to tell you that?"

"Stars, Tanis, sometimes I think no one has ever disliked their rank more than you."

Tanis laughed as she sat across from Rachel. "I think you'd be surprised. Everyone always thinks they want to get to the top so that no one tells them what to do, but, damn…there's a lot of stuff to figure out when you get there."

"I think I have an inkling of what that's like. I have a lot of respect for you and Captain Andrews."

"Me?" Tanis's eyebrows rose.

"Well, yeah, both of you have captained this ship."

Tanis's lips spread into a wry smile. "I think you'll find that's not true. My butt may have spent a lot of time in that command chair, but I was never captain of this ship."

Rachel made a quick scan of the records. "Would you look at that…for some reason I'd always thought…"

"How's it feel to be the second captain of this girl?" Tanis asked.

"About the same," Rachel grinned. "Like it's the best, hardest job I've ever had."

Tanis winked. "Just wait 'til I promote you."

Rachel's eyes widened, and she felt her eyebrows almost hit her hairline. "Don't you dare, Admiral! No!"

<Stop messing with her,> Angela chimed in. *<She'll chain herself to the keel if we try to give her another command.>*

<I like Rachel where she is,> Bob intoned.

"Uh…wow. Thanks, Bob." Rachel had not expected the AI to back her up. She wasn't sure if that made her feel more confident, or a bit worried that the AI had plans for her.

Tanis, on the other hand, rolled her eyes. "Really, Bob. You don't have a say in who I promote and when."

<Keep telling yourself that,> Bob chuckled.

Rachel leant forward and whispered to Tanis. "Did Bob just try to be funny?"

Tanis pursed her lips and nodded. "It's a new thing of his. He's just full of the ha-has."

<Rachel thinks I'm funny. She correctly identified my statement as humorous.>

"You can recognize an attempt at humor, as well. Doesn't mean it was actually funny," Tanis replied.

<Ouch.>

<Be nice, Tanis,> Angela appeared as a holoimage on the train and shook a finger at Tanis before disappearing again.

Huh, she looked almost exactly like Tanis. Like she was admonishing herself, Rachel mused.

Tanis looked up and saw that Rachel was staring intently at her.

"Yeah, it's like I'm my own mom or something. Stars, that's a disturbing thought."

"So, what's got you all into the ha-has?" Rachel asked Bob, changing the subject.

<Marge, who resides in Kylie Rhoads, gave me a series of books that I'm reading. They're quite amusing, and I am trying to replicate that humor.>

"Really? I didn't know you read books, Bob. What are they called?"

<I do from time to time. This series is called 'Mysteries of Fennington Station'. I understand that it is a type of story referred to as a 'cozy mystery'. People die, so I don't know why it's 'cozy'. I've read all fifty-five books, and the most recent one that Marge stole from the publisher. Now I'm starting over with book 1, 'Whole Latte Death'.>

"Really? How long does it take you to read a book?" Rachel asked. "A millisecond?"

<These books are different,> Angela responded. *<We have to spin off a subroutine and clock it at 99.99MHz. They take about an hour to read.>*

"It makes me feel like there's a bee inside my head when you do that," Tanis complained. "You need to go to the expanse when you read those from now on."

<You'd enjoy them, Tanis.> Bob's voice contained a note of humor. *<Especially when the cat finds the je—>*

<BOB! Spoilers!> Angela shouted.

<Sorry.>

Tanis laughed and shook her head. "OK, I really do have to read these now."

The maglev train slowed as it reached the platform closest to Engine, and the two women disembarked, following the twisted corridors until they reached Terry's location.

The Chief of Security was in a small storage room near one of Engine's machine shops. Rachel noted that they were only a short distance from the MSAR region, where the ship's particle accelerator funneled scooped hydrogen into the matter annihilator that produced energy and antimatter.

Though CriEn technology meant they didn't need to run the annihilator anymore, Rachel preferred to keep it operational as a backup power system.

It was currently undergoing its weekly test run.

"Tanis, Rachel," Terry said as the two women joined her in the storage room.

"All alone in here?" Tanis asked, and Rachel looked around, surprised to see none of the SOC MPs present.

"I figured that there's nothing the three of us can't do," Terry replied. "I have teams nearby, but Finaeus has only made the three Shadowtrons—he has Earnest's original disassembled in his lab."

Rachel approached one of the gun-like devices that sat on a table beside Terry. It reminded her of an ME-33 sniper rifle, but with seven barrels instead of one.

She picked one up. "I still can't believe this is called a 'Shadowtron'. I thought that was a joke when I first heard it."

"Sera loved the name. Said it was 'badass'," Tanis said with a laugh as she picked up one of the weapons.

<I kinda wish I had a Shadowtron,> Angela added.

Terry hefted hers. "I don't care what they're called, so long as they work."

"So, what's the target?" Rachel asked.

Terry passed a data packet to Rachel and Tanis over the Link. "Ensign Kasha. She's a tech who works on the annihilator. Bob says she's in Machine Bay 13.11 working on fabbing some replacement parts for after the test run today."

"Stars," Tanis muttered. "She wasn't even on the list of suspects for people who could have freed Elena. Which means that either the remnant in her is very good, or there's someone else, still."

"We'll know more once we nab her." Terry walked toward the door and looked at the other two. "I'll cover the rear entrance; I assume you want the honors, Tanis?"

"Do you even have to ask?"

"Uh, no, I guess not," Terry laughed.

Two minutes later, they were in position. Terry was just outside the machine bay's rear door, and Rachel outside the main door. Tanis was making her way past the fab units to where Kasha stood at a testing rig that was putting the new components through their paces.

Rachel heard Tanis say something to Kasha, then she heard a scream and a brief scuffle.

A minute later, Ensign Kasha appeared at the far end of a row of fab units, racing toward the door.

Rachel raised her Shadowtron and fired the eV detection wave toward Kasha. Sure enough, the holodisplay on the weapon showed a remnant within the woman. She wasted no time firing the capture field, and saw the remnant begin to flow out of the Ensign.

<*Got it?*> Tanis asked, appearing at the far end of the row, advancing with her Shadowtron held level.

<*I think so, it's coming toward my—*> As Rachel spoke, the wave coming from her Shadowtron flickered, and the remnant broke free from the field.

It streaked past Rachel and down the hall.

<*Shit, it got free!*>

Rachel turned and gave chase, following the remnant via the display on her Shadowtron.

She heard Tanis behind her, but didn't look back as they raced through Engine.

<*It's headed to the MSAR,*> Tanis called out.

<*Trying to cut it off!*> Terry replied.

Rachel rounded a corner and then passed down a long corridor, the remnant a dozen meters away, slowly increasing the gap.

Then Terry appeared at the end of the passageway, firing her weapon. But the remnant was moving too fast, and a second later, it was past Terry and through the doors leading into the MSAR.

The three women burst into the MSAR and raced through the forest that surrounded the annihilator.

<*I lost it,*> Rachel called out.

Terry waved them on from her place in the lead. <*I haven't.*>

The trees began to thin, and they came into the large clearing in the center of the MSAR where the matter annihilator stood on its tower.

<*Shit!*> Tanis swore. <*It's going for the annihilator!*>

<*What will happen if it gets there?*> Rachel asked.

<*It will die,*> Bob supplied.

Rachel spotted the remnant twisting around one of the struts supporting the annihilator and fired at the thing, but it was out of the Shadowtron's effective range.

Terry had stopped running, and Rachel caught up to her—Tanis, a moment later. Rachel watched through the holodisplay on her weapon as the remnant reached the inlet portal for the annihilator, and passed through the weaker field there before being drawn into the annihilation chamber.

"Damn, it's gone," Tanis said with a heavy sigh.

"I'll count that as a win," Terry said, lowering her weapon.

Rachel realized that Tanis had been staring up at the annihilator without using her weapon's detection wave to see the remnant.

She was about to ask how Tanis could see the thing, when the Admiral shook her head and walked off, leaving Terry and Rachel standing beside one another, wondering if Bob was right.

Had the thing died in the annihilator, or did it escape somehow and evade detection?

"Let's do a sweep to be sure," Rachel said, and Terry nodded.

Neither were surprised when they didn't find anything.

UNINTENTIONAL BAIT

STELLAR DATE: 02.09.8949 (Adjusted Years)
LOCATION: TSS *Regent Mary*, Bridge
REGION: Near Montana, Galas System, Vela Cluster

"Ensign Dyna! What's the ETA on recharge?" Krissy called out as the ship's AI executed a new jinking pattern. The dampening systems were running on reserves, and the rapid maneuvers were beginning to jostle the crew.

"Ma'am! CriEns are *all* offline, main connection got disconnected, backup isn't failing over. Repair team is at the relay, working on it."

Krissy ground her teeth. She'd asked for an ETA, but his answer told her what she needed to know: not soon enough.

She glanced at the main holotank. The three Airthan cruisers were still back there, closing, but holding their fire. They may have caught Krissy's ship, the *Regent Mary,* with its stasis shields offline, but the shield was up now, and even with the CriEn modules offline, the ship could withstand a withering assault.

For about ten minutes or so.

She turned and stalked back to the command seat, settling into it. Captain Nelson should be in it, but he was in the infirmary, having been hit by shrapnel during the enemy's opening salvo.

Krissy blamed herself. Khardine forces hadn't seen any Airthan ships in the Vela Cluster since their arrival, and she'd grown lax.

The *Regent Mary* had been taking in supplies above Montana, shields down and engines cold, when the enemy ships had appeared and opened fire.

"What's the scan data say?" Krissy asked. "Were they stealthed, and we just missed them somehow?"

"No, ma'am," Ensign Donald replied. "They appeared between us and the local star. Even ISF stealth tech would have cast a shadow at that range."

"Are you saying they jumped in?" Krissy asked sharply.

Ensign Donald nodded. "I don't see any other alternative, Admiral Krissy."

Krissy sat back heavily. That meant one of two things: there was a traitor at the Sector Command, or there was a traitor here at Montana. Someone had to have passed the Airthans intel on her location with enough advance notice for them to get the message to vessels that were in a position to jump in.

The Vela Cluster contained thousands of stars, and Krissy's fleet had barely visited ten percent of them—there could be dozens of holdouts harboring Airthans.

I need more ships! Krissy shouted in her mind. She was spreading herself too thin…as evidenced by being in this system with just one ship, and getting caught with her pants down.

Even so, she had a tool that the enemy did not. One that she was all too willing to avail herself of, especially right now.

"Comm. Message to Admiral Orman. Advise him of our situation, and tell him I want his…second division here on the double."

"Yes, ma'am!" the ensign on Comm called out before activating the QuanComm system.

"Let's see you beat this," Krissy muttered aloud, and received a few appreciative nods from members of the bridge crew.

Admiral Orman and his fleet were currently guarding Estrada, the capital of the Vela Cluster. Based on his latest reports, the second division should be close to the system's inner jump gates. With a quick data relay at Khardine and factoring in time to get the ships through the gates, she could expect to see backup within twenty minutes.

So long as the enemy didn't decide to test out the stasis shields on her ship overmuch, they could hold out that long with ease.

"Admiral Orman confirms," Comm announced. "Second division ETA to jump gates is fifteen minutes. Full ship transfer is twenty-seven."

The Estrada System had eleven jump gates. Provided all were currently online, that meant the initial group of ships would be more than enough to subdue the three enemy cruisers.

"Thank you, Comm," Krissy replied, resolving to keep ships closer to gates in the future.

"They're firing on us again!" Ensign Donald cried out from Scan. "Helm's jinking pattern is ninety percent effective."

<*Helm has a name, Ensign,*> Hemdar chastised the man. <*Use it.*>

"Sorry, sir," Ensign Donald replied, reddening as he spoke.

<Hemdar, be nice to the FNGs, they're not in infinite supply.>

<I've only told him privately seven times that I prefer to be called by name,> Hemdar replied. *<I figured a verbal reminder, so to speak, might serve him better.>*

<Relax, Hemdar, we've been through worse than this little chase around Montana. Don't let it get to you. Besides, the Airthans will want to take me alive, if they can. Worst-case scenario, we wave a white flag 'til Orman's second division gets here.>

<Surrender? Over my burning hull.>

<Well, not like we let them board us, or anything. Just let them **think** *they're going to get to board us.>*

A plotted course appeared on the holotank, showing a potential course toward Montana's second moon.

<They have defensive emplacements on that moon,> Hemdar spoke over the bridge net as he highlighted a dozen points on the largely barren surface. *<If they fire those, they can drive off the Airthan ships.>*

Krissy drummed her fingers on the command chair's armrest. "Perhaps. *If* the locals aren't the ones who sold us out to begin with—it could be that they might just fire on us."

<Try the base commander down there,> Hemdar suggested privately.

<So bossy,> Krissy shot back.

Krissy pulled up the records on the Montana system's garrison. Provided no one had abandoned their posts—which had happened in some places—there should be a Major named Kevin in charge.

"Comm, get me the base on that moon. I want to speak with Major Kevin."

<Why didn't you reach out to him without my prompting?> Hemdar asked.

Krissy sighed. The reason was simple, but not one she cared to voice. It was because she was afraid. Not afraid of the moon shooting at her, or that the base commander had decided to side with Airtha.

She was more afraid that he would sit it out altogether.

Thrice now, she'd encountered star systems that had declared themselves to be 'independent'. Even the TSF garrisons had joined with the local governments, abandoning their duties and posts.

Somehow that was worse than if they'd sided with Airtha. At least then she could see some amount of honor in their actions. Declaring for nothing was worse than joining with the enemy.

"I have the major!" Comm called out.

"That fast?" Krissy asked in surprise.

The Comm officer glanced back at Krissy. "He called us a moment before I made the connection."

Krissy felt her spirits rise. Maybe she'd get a pleasant surprise. "Put him on."

The vector display shifted to a secondary holo, and the main tank was filled with a broad-shouldered man who wore a deep scowl—which was quickly replaced by surprise.

"Admiral Krissy!"

"Major Kevin, may I assume you are calling to render assistance?"

"Well…I wasn't sure who I was going to be talking to—things are chaotic right now, ma'am."

Krissy cleared her throat. "Major. That was not what I asked. I have three enemy ships on my tail, and the Vela Cluster has declared for Khardine."

It was bluster and they all knew it. Chancellor Alma had declared that the Vela Cluster would side with Khardine. But out here, that meant less than it did at Estrada.

What Krissy really needed were victories against the Airthans. One here would be a huge coup.

Everyone wanted to be on the winning side. Diplomacy was one thing, but decisive action against the enemy would galvanize systems and bring them flocking to Khardine's banner.

"Yes, Admiral, but your ship is damaged, and I have no other support. If I fire on those ships, I can take out one, maybe two. Then they pound my emplacements to dust. I won't throw away my people's lives for nothing."

Concern for his people is better than nothing, Krissy thought.

"We're not out of the fight yet, Major. I just need you to give us cover as we brake around the moon. When we come out the other side, we'll be ready to take them down. I'm not going to leave you high and dry, I promise. If you check my record, you'll see evidence of that."

She could see her words put some steel in Major Kevin's spine. He straightened and gave a firm nod. "I don't need to look up your record, Admiral. I've heard the stories."

Krissy grinned at the major. "Then can I count on you to honor your oath to the TSF?"

He nodded sharply. "Yes you can, ma'am. Is there a priority target, or should we pepper them all and force them into low efficiency jinking patterns?"

"The latter," Krissy replied. "All we need are a few minutes."

"On it, Admiral Krissy. Warming up the guns."

<*See, told you it would be worth a shot,*> Hemdar admonished.

Krissy nodded and didn't reply, she noticed smiles on the faces of the bridge crew. Having that conversation in front of the entire bridge was a risky proposition. If Major Kevin had been a coward, it would have damaged morale.

As it was, spirits were lifted to know that at least this one man and his command were going to stand up for what they claimed to believe in.

"Hemdar, set the course," Krissy said, knowing that Hemdar was already preparing the burn.

<*Aye, Admiral,*> he replied over the bridge net.

The ship pivoted, angling past the moon, and the main engines fired, slowly changing the ship's trajectory. The relative velocity to the moon was just over 0.03*c*, and it began to fall as Hemdar slowly pivoted the ship further.

"The Airthans are braking so they don't overshoot us," Scan announced.

"Good. They *think* that they know what we're doing, and that we don't have the power to fire on their engines while they brake."

The channel to Major Kevin was still open, and he nodded. "Cocky bastards. We're ready, Admiral."

<*I've coordinated our jinking pattern with their targeting NSAI,*> Hemdar added.

I sure hope Angela's fix is still in place here. Krissy resisted the urge to close her eyes. "Fire at will, Major."

Krissy shifted Major Kevin to the secondary holotank and brought up a view of the moon, the three pursuers, and the *Regent Mary* on the main tank.

The Airthan ships were a hair over forty-thousand kilometers behind the *Regent Mary*, and the moon was still one hundred and ten thousand kilometers distant.

Too far for pinpoint precision on jinking ships, but close enough to scare them.

Six rail emplacements on the moon's surface fired, sending uranium slugs streaking through space at over ten-thousand kilometers-per-second.

Just over ten seconds to react gave the Airthans plenty of time to move their ships, but a second salvo was already firing, forcing the enemy vessels to jink in ever more erratic patterns, slowing their ships further and widening the gap between them and the *Regent Mary.*

Krissy wondered what the enemy ships would do. Two of the vessels were Saggitar Class cruisers that could fire rails on nearly any vector. The third was a Cranmore Class destroyer; its only rear-firing weapons system were defensive beams.

If she were the captain of that ship, she would feel very nervous about turning to fire on the moon.

"This is the first time I've ever been happy about a Cranmore's weapon systems," Krissy muttered.

There were a few nods around the bridge, but no one was happy about firing on ships filled with people and AIs who had been comrades just a few months ago.

Sure enough, the destroyer shifted its vector and moved stellar northwest, altering its trajectory to cover the far side of the moon, where the *Regent Mary* would emerge after its loop.

"But they're exposing their flank to the moon," Scan muttered. "Doesn't make any sense."

"Don't forget," Krissy cautioned. "The Airthans have the same information we do about this moon and its stationary emplacements."

"Bastards are pocketing right into a spot our rails can't hit," Major Kevin nodded. "But what they don't know is that when another command in this system…devolved…I picked up a pod of attack drones."

Krissy wanted to deliver a biting comment about not sharing that rather useful information with her before now, but she reminded herself that beggars can't be choosers and nodded to the man.

"Full pod? What model?"

"One hundred and ten, the MK-97s."

Krissy nodded. The 97s were an older model, but that number was more than enough to drive off the destroyer—either that, or the cruisers would have to stop chasing her to aid it.

"Let 'em rip, Major."

"They're in the chutes, deploying in thirty seconds."

Thirty seconds; otherwise known as a lifetime.

Though the *Regent Mary* continued to decelerate on its approach to the moon, the Airthan cruisers were falling further behind. Krissy had to hand it to their captains. Though their jinks were random, their general trajectory was toward the moon's poles.

If the enemy ships continued on this trajectory, they would be positioned on three sides of the moon when the *Regent Mary* passed behind it.

The tactic was solid, and would lead to certain victory—if the *'Mary* was alone.

Droves of civilian ships began to pull out of orbits around the moon, determined to be anywhere but where the four ships were about to begin their fight.

"Comm, keep Orman advised of the civilian vectors. They're pulling out of STC assigned lanes."

"Yes, ma'am, transmitting anticipated enemy positions."

"Orman?" Major Kevin asked, his brows raised. "How is he insystem? We don't see him on scan."

Krissy turned to look at the major on the secondary holotank. "Sorry, Major, you're just going to have to trust me for a little bit longer."

"Yes, Admiral."

Despite her not sharing her plans with him, the Major appeared pleased with her response. She supposed knowing that his base wasn't about to be blown into oblivion was morale boosting.

"Drones are launched," Major Kevin informed the bridge crew. "They have their target."

"I have them on scan," Ensign Dyson confirmed. "The destroyer is altering course."

"Million klick range on those Mark 97's," Major Kevin was grinning now. "They're going to have to run for a while."

With only two targets to focus on, the moon's railguns drove more fire into the Airthan cruisers, who had still not fired back on the moon.

What are they planning? Krissy wondered.

"Major—" she began, when Kevin swore.

"Dammit, that report was never supposed to be circulated!"

Krissy turned to face his holo. "What is it?"

"Our equatorial emplacements can't hit ships above the poles. They're *designed* to, but under testing, the magnetic field strength wasn't enough to bend the shots at acute angles. We've had an order in for upgrades for years, but it's never come. In another minute, they'll only be in range of the two polar emplacements.

"Shit!" Krissy swore. "They'll weather that with ease—or blast 'em to smithereens. What I wouldn't give for grapeshot."

"Ma'am! Grapeshot is against our doctrine," Major Kevin replied.

"Major, if I had grapeshot available, I'd fire every damn gram at these bastards." She turned to Ensign Quan on weapons. "Helm, spin us. Weapons, lay into them with the rails. If they think they're going to hit a dead spot, they've got another think coming. Target the cruiser at the north pole. Major Kevin, concentrate all your fire on that cruiser headed for the south pole. When they're in range, lay on your p-beams."

"Aye, ma'am."

With the dampeners on low power, the ship shuddered as each rail shot tore out of the accelerator, but Krissy didn't care. They just had to hold out for another two minutes.

The *Regent Mary* was within ten thousand kilometers of the moon now, braking hard from its prior velocity. In thirty seconds, they'd be behind the bulk of the dull grey orb.

But that cover would only last so long.

Based on current vectors, the enemy cruisers would be in a position to fire on the *'Mary* seventy seconds later.

It was going to be tight.

"They're firing on the polar emplacements!" Scan announced.

Krissy watched as the two polar rail emplacements on the moon were smashed to dust by beam fire from the cruisers.

Major Kevin made a small noise of dismay. "Ma'am, I have no further firing options, unless you count close-range SSMs."

"No," Krissy shook her head. "You don't have enough of those missiles to make it past those cruisers' point defense beams and penetrate shields."

The major nodded, and Krissy glanced at the status of the CriEn power hookups. Estimates were at two minutes.

Every eye on the bridge had turned to the main holotank showing the moon with the two cruisers, each approaching over the poles, and the *Regent Mary,* momentarily hidden behind the horizon.

A timer above the display counted down the seconds until the enemy would have firing solutions.

"I hope you have a whole Snark deck up your sleeve, Admiral." Major Kevin's voice wavered, and Krissy turned to nod soberly. "The enemy's gonna wish it was *just* a Snark deck."

The countdown hit zero, and the enemy ships opened fire on the *Regent Mary.* Particle beams blazed trails through space, the lines glowing brightly on both the holo and visuals, excited photons spiraling away as the beams smashed into stray hydrogen atoms in the vacuum of space.

The *Regent Mary* shuddered, and consoles flashed warnings as the backup fusion generators reached critical levels.

That was the problem with stasis; nowhere to bleed the heat. The more the generators worked to keep the shields up, the more heat they trapped within those shields.

Krissy held her breath as the second counter, this one at the bottom of the holo, hit zero.

C'monnnnn, Krissy thought, willing Orman's second division to appear. *What's taking so long?*

One second passed, then two. Krissy drew a deep breath. "Major Kevin, fire every SSM you have."

"Ma'am," the major grunted in acknowledgement.

"I have them, the fleet's here!" Scan cried out.

"Belay that, Major!" Krissy shouted, and held back a whoop of joy as ten ships jumped in, only thirty thousand kilometers above the moon's north pole.

The cruiser above the moon ceased firing on the *Regent Mary* and cut its engines. A signal of surrender if ever there was one.

Seconds later, another ten ships appeared just off the moon's southern pole, one of the newly arrived cruisers narrowly missing a civilian freighter that was boosting away outside of approved lanes.

"Hoooly shit, Admiral," Major Kevin swore and seemed to sag

against a console not visible in the holo. "How the hell did you do that?"

Krissy turned to the man and winked. "I'll tell you later, not over comms. Let's just say that it's a tactic the Airthans are going to have a hard time countering."

"Ma'am," Comm called out. "The Airthan ships have signaled their surrender."

Krissy snorted. "I'll bet they have."

On the holo, the ships of Admiral Orman's Second Division continued to jump in, dozens of ships slotting into orbits further out from the moon.

"Tell the Airthan captains I want them on shuttles, making for the *'Mary* in ten minutes. There's a warm spot in our brig waiting for them."

"Aye, ma'am!"

Krissy couldn't help a predatory grin from creeping across her face. An idea was forming in her mind.

PRESIDENT SERA

STELLAR DATE: 02.09.8949 (Adjusted Years)
LOCATION: Fleet Strategy Room, Keren Station
REGION: Khardine System, Transcend Interstellar Alliance

Admiral Greer nodded with approval. "It's a solid plan."

Sera agreed with Greer's assessment. "So long as she doesn't overuse it. Eventually, they'll turn it on her."

"Maybe," Greer agreed. "But with the advantage the QuanComms give us, it's hard to trap our ships. Give us ten minutes, and we can have backup anywhere within a thousand light years."

Sera nodded as she considered Krissy's victory and what it meant. It was one thing to know on paper that they could summon reinforcements anywhere at a moment's notice, but it was another to see it used effectively in practice.

However, it added the risk that they could easily overextend themselves. And there were other concerns, as well.

Even though the tech was hundreds of years old, other than a few skirmishes along the front with the Orion Freedom Alliance, no one had used jump gates in major warfare.

One of the main reasons was because jumping deep into a star system was a dangerous business.

Conventional grav and EM shielding took a few seconds to activate after a jump, which was more than enough time for a stray rock to hole your ship—or for limpet mines to attach to your hull.

But now, stasis shields changed that. Their ability to activate the *instant* a ship exited from a jump negated that concern. Used in combination with the QuanComm system, which provided real-time destination data allowing for precision-placed on-demand reinforcements, the shields made for an advantage that changed the battlespace and invalidated broad swaths of both tactical and strategic doctrine.

"We're going to need to build up more gates," Sera said after a few moments. "And develop strategic supply locations where we mass fleets. Preferably *not* in major systems."

"Agreed. These staging grounds will turn into our greatest weaknesses if the enemy locates them. But it's not a new problem."

Sera nodded absently as she loaded charts of nearby regions and flipped through potential locations for the bases.

"What about SC-91R?" she asked.

Greer's eyes snapped up to lock on Sera's. "What? Are you insane?"

"They'll never, *ever* look for a staging ground there."

Greer nodded emphatically. "Correct, because it would last all of ten hours before it was devoured. Unless…"

Sera nodded slowly. "Unless."

Greer brought up a view of SC-91R on the holotank between them. Officially, SC-91R was a black hole of seven solar masses, nine hundred light years coreward of Khardine.

The official record wasn't entirely wrong.

Once, SC-91R had been a B-class star—a rather unpleasant one—and also the location of a secret dark matter research facility run by the Nakatomi Corporation.

An experiment to test insystem dark layer transitions went awry, and a rift between the dark layer and normal space opened up.

Details were sketchy, but supposition was that the 'things'—known in the Transcend as Exdali, a twist on extra-spatial dark layer entities—had escaped through the rift and devoured the research facility.

Some researchers managed to get out a signal containing some scant details a few seconds before the base went dark. Nakatomi claimed that an accident had destroyed the facility, and provided no further explanation, apparently hoping that the Exdali would fall into the star and be destroyed, hiding all evidence of their colossal mistake.

In some respects, very valuable information *did* come out of the Nakatomi incident at SC-91R. The most useful being that stars do not kill Exdali. Exdali kill stars.

At first, there were oscillations in the star's orbit, combined with fluctuations in its EM output. The observations correlated with one of the star's large gas giants moving insystem—though the rate of change was occurring orders of magnitude too quickly.

Then the star's output began to dim further and further until it exploded from a mass imbalance that no standard model could account for.

A stellar nebula should have formed, expanding out from a white dwarf, or perhaps neutron star, remnant.

But the expanding cloud of gas and dust only survived a few years before it disappeared. There was no sign of any stellar remnant.

Now SC-91R was interdicted, and slowly, a dark smudge between the stars grew year after year, reaching toward other nearby sources of mass.

Admiral Greer glanced at Sera, his expression filled with concern. "True, we saw the ISF close up a small rift…one with only a few Exdali—"

"Few thousand," Sera corrected.

"Doesn't matter, they were tiny. You saw what the survey data shows about SC-91R. Some of the Exdali are of jovian mass. And the core? We don't even know if that's a black hole, some other type of ultra-dense matter, or just one of the damn Exdali!"

"We have to fix it eventually," Sera shrugged.

"Yes, yes we do. After the war. For all we know, taking care of SC-91R could be as large an effort as everything else we're currently undertaking."

Sera nodded. She hadn't expected Greer to oppose her idea so vehemently, but she could tell that this was not the time to push further.

<*I think it's the deep-seated fear people have of the Exdali,*> Jen suggested. <*Up until a few months ago, there was no known way to stop them. Fear was a healthy response; it still might be. We have no idea if that many can be driven back into the dark layer—from what I see here, the exclusion zone is now over five light years across.*>

<*I suppose you're right, Jen,*> Sera replied. <*I'm going to send a missive to Earnest, though. I want his thoughts on this.*>

Aloud, she said, "Your concerns are noted, Admiral. What about STX-B17?"

Greer scrubbed a hand back and forth on his cheek. "You know, Sera, when I backed you for the presidency, I didn't think you were insane. I assume you're aware that STX-B17 is a black hole?"

Sera grinned. "Second-last place they'd look for our staging ground, after SC-91R. Look, there's still a jovian planet out beyond the major magnetic bands. We can set up there."

Sera switched the holotank to show STX-B17's position at the edge of the Orion Arm. "It's centrally located in the Transcend, within ten-minute striking distance of Airtha by jump gate…"

"Are you suggesting what I think you are?" Greer asked.

Sera gave an exaggerated shrug. "If we're going to have a staging ground capable of fueling and supplying a large segment of our fleet, why not make it one that can finish the war in one fell swoop?"

"You'd need a million ships to take Airtha," Greer countered. "Sure, the Transcend has many more than that, but we can't leave every system vulnerable just to mass that one fleet."

"In principle, I agree, Admiral. But remember. We don't have to garrison ships anywhere anymore. We can leave probes and patrol craft in systems, and call for help when needed."

"Don't get carried away, Sera Tomlinson. If we leave too many ships out there with QuanComm blades, the enemy is likely to find out what we're up to. Once they do, it'll only be a matter of time before they find our staging ground. It doesn't take *that* long to send probes to all the likely suspects."

Sera saw Greer's point. Unorthodox tactics were fine, but they were better if the enemy still believed that you were following existing doctrine.

<Look at you, thinking like a military commander,> Jen said with an encouraging smile.

<All that time with Tanis must have rubbed off a bit, or something.>

"I think we're onto something, here." Sera placed her hands on the edge of the holotank. "Draw up a proposal and send it to Krissy. I want her thoughts on this."

Greer nodded slowly. "I'm not entirely sold on this myself, you know."

"I understand, and if you and Krissy recommend against it, I'll reconsider. But we have to figure out a meaningful way to use the advantage QuanComms give us."

"Understood," Greer replied.

Sera pushed off from the holotank and turned to leave the room before stopping and turning to face Greer once more. "Oh, and Admiral Greer?"

"Yes, Sera?"

"We're not going to 'take' Airtha. We're going to 'take it out'. The whole thing—ring, star, everything. Nothing survives."

She didn't miss the momentary expression of worry that crossed Greer's face before he nodded. "Very well. I'll ensure that the strategy reflects that goal."

"Good, now I'm off to discuss the economic implications of feeding resources to Scipio with the secretaries. Wish me luck."

Greer laughed. "Good luck, indeed. I'd rather face SC-91R than deal with that lot."

Sera nodded in agreement. She shared the same sentiment.

NIGHTSHADE

STELLAR DATE: 02.27.8949 (Adjusted Years)
LOCATION: Wells Station
REGION: Azela System, Coreward Edge of Praesepe Cluster

"Watch yourself, Admiral," Nadine cautioned as they walked off the pinnace and onto the bay's deck. "This is not the safest of stations."

"Few places *are* safe, anymore," Tanis replied.

<Lieutenant, keep the reactor warm, not sure how long we'll be, or how hot we'll come in.>

<Hot and ready to be shot. You got it, Admiral.> Lieutenant Markey chuckled at his response.

Flyboys, Tanis thought.

<You married one of those, you know that, right?> Angela chided.

<Oh, I ***know****.>*

"Seems like a strange place for Nerischka to set up shop," Tanis said to Nadine as they walked up the long, gently sloped ramp to the station's passenger decks. "Though I guess it's just the place the stuff she's tracking would pass through."

Nadine shrugged, her blue and purple ombré hair sparkling in the passageway's bright lights, setting off against the figure-hugging white dress she wore.

Tanis was clothed similarly, but her dress was more of a long tunic, red and black, paired with black leggings. When selecting an outfit for this mission, Tanis had realized she so rarely acquired new clothes that most of her wardrobe consisted of items Joe had given her as gifts.

Whenever she was out of uniform—which, admittedly, was rare—her style reflected Joe's tastes more than hers.

<That's because you don't ***have*** *any tastes,>* Angela chided.

<I do too!> Tanis shot back. *<My tastes are just simple and understated.>*

Angela snorted. *<When we merge into one person, that's one of the first things I'm changing. I'm going to start dressing us like the goddess we are.>*

<Wow, Angela, what are you overcompensating for?>

<What do you mean?> Angela sounded genuinely perplexed.

While Tanis continued to speak with Angela, Nadine replied, "Well, it's where the mission seems to have taken her. I'm quite curious to learn what she's found. Sera said that Nerischka thinks this biotech has ties back to Orion."

"Not really their M. O., from what I hear," Tanis replied as they reached the top of the ramp.

The concourse ahead of them was filled with foot traffic, and a few dockcars driving down a designated lane in the center. Nadine wove through the crowds and signaled for a car. A few seconds later, one slowed to a stop, and they climbed in.

"Nightshade," Nadine said, and the car made a sound signaling rejection.

"Destination restricted," the vehicle replied.

Nadine shook her head and sighed. "Well, as close as you can get, then."

The car made an affirmative noise and pulled back into the center of the concourse.

Tanis chuckled as they picked up speed. "Never a good sign, is it."

"You read her mission brief, right?" Nadine asked. "The guy that's moving this biotech is pretty strange. Not surprised that whoever runs this dockcar service doesn't want to go there."

"I've yet to see anything as strange as half the stuff I dealt with back in Sol," Tanis said as she watched the people on the concourse. "Trust me, until you've seen a man whose body is made out of the bodies of other people, you've not seen anything."

Nadine shuddered. "What do you mean…'made out of'?"

Tanis saw John Cardid's monstrous form in her mind; an image hundreds of years in her past, but still not one she'd ever forget.

"Like limbs constructed from the bodies of people…all merged into one body. I really don't want to describe it further. It made the people with spikes driven through their eyes and out the backs of their heads seem perfectly normal."

"Disguuuusting," Nadine breathed with a small scrunch of her nose. "OK, yeah, Nightshade should be a piece of cake for you."

"One thing that wasn't clear in the brief," Tanis said as she pulled it up over her vision. "I thought 'Nightshade' was the guy's name, not the place he…whatevers…at."

"I was a bit fuzzy on that, too. That's why I just asked the car to take us there. From what I can see on the station map, there is a place *called* Nightshade, so I figured why not see if they're one and the same?"

"Seems reasonable," Tanis nodded as she reviewed the station layout further. "Station isn't big enough for them not to be connected."

<*Oh, wow,*> Angela chimed in. <*I went wandering through their nets here and found the security systems for Nightshade. You know, actually working the job while you two chit-chat? Anyway, it's like a cross between a club, and an extreme body mod art studio. All weird biological stuff, too.*>

Tanis saw Nadine give a small shudder. "I hate bio-mods. I know that we all have them, but keeping them under a nice human-shaped package is best. Some people just get…"

"Icky," Tanis filled in.

"Yeah…'icky' is right. As in, 'I don't care *what* your tentacles can do, I'd rather not'."

Tanis was reminded of the informant she used back on the Cho in Sol.

<*Sandy Bristol,*> Angela supplied.

<*Yeah, the one with the pink meter-long tentacles! She was a blast; first and only time I've ever been slipped intel via tentacle.*>

The dockcar drove out over a broad atrium, easily a kilometer across. The roadway was suspended high above the deck below, and Tanis could see that it was once a park, the center marked by a dry depression where a lake had been. Now it was filled with small, ramshackle buildings, and chickens. A lot of chickens.

"You bring me to all the nicest places," Tanis said as she peered down.

"Stupid stationers," Nadine shook her head. "This was their best greenspace, and they let it die. Who does that? I'd rather sacrifice lights in my quarters before a station's parks."

Tanis shrugged. "Don't look at me. If I can't fly around with at least fifty square klicks of parkland, I turn into a very grumpy woman."

<*Wow!*> Angela laughed. <*I can't imagine how bad* ***that*** *would be! I wouldn't have thought increased grumpiness was possible.*>

Nadine covered her mouth to hide a laugh, and Tanis sighed.

"S'OK, I can take a compliment."

<*I wish I had a diaphragm so I could groan properly.*>

They passed beyond the atrium and turned onto another concourse. The state of repair in this section of the station wasn't bad, but it wasn't great, either.

The car took a few turns and then pulled into a disembarkation lane a few hundred meters from Nightshade.

"Thank you for your matronage," the car announced.

Tanis laughed as she stepped out. " 'Matronage'. My gender feels so satisfied now. What would I have done without that?"

Nadine stepped up beside Tanis. "It's like that a lot on this side of Praesepe. They like to alternate gender honorifics and stuff."

"Why not use gender neutral words like everyone else?"

"I don't know." Nadine shrugged and began walking down the corridor ahead of them. "I'll be sure to query the…well, they don't believe in schools, here. I have no idea what I'd query."

Tanis shook her head as she followed after Nadine, keeping her eyes peeled as they passed clusters of people who appeared to be clean and well-kempt, but also eyed the two women hungrily.

<*I wonder if they're suckers,*> Nadine mused. <*They have that look.*>

<*Never understood that.*> Tanis watched another group pass by, trying to catch sight of their teeth. <*I don't think blood tastes that good…altering your organs to tolerate it, or even live on it, seems…horrible. I mean…no more BLTs or coffee? I don't think life would be worth living.*>

Nadine almost laughed aloud. <*I've only been on your ship for a few weeks, and it didn't take half that time to learn of your love for BLTs. Just be happy you can fight off the crummy nano people have around here. Some suckers mod themselves to infect others so they crave blood after being bitten. Some have nano good enough to biologically alter the people they bite.*>

<*Stars…*> Tanis sighed as she looked around at the people they passed. <*Life must really suck for some of these people.*>

<*With a capital 'S'.*>

<*Again,*> Angela chimed in. <*I can't groan well enough to capture how sad that comment was.*>

A minute later, they reached a wider concourse. The street was several decks high, and in front of them, vertically spanning four decks, was Nightshade.

The entrance was on the lower level, and the pair of women walked through the thin crowds to where a large man and almost rail-thin woman stood before the doors.

The man looked them up and down and glanced at the woman, who nodded for him to open the door.

Tanis was glad she passed muster—she'd worn her nice shoes, after all—and the two stepped through the entrance, finding themselves in a long hall.

On either side of the hall were pillars supporting holos hinting at the sorts of things they'd see within. Tanis sighed as she saw a holo of what looked like a mermaid with flippers instead of arms.

<Yeah, it's one of those places,> Angela agreed. *<I hope Nerischka has managed to get into Nightshade's inner circle without becoming a part of his collection.>*

<It's usually one of the fastest ways, though,> Tanis replied. *<Show maximum commitment.>*

< 'Maximum commitment' in places like this is often fatal.>

Tanis nodded slowly. She knew *that* all too well.

Sound and light suddenly flooded into the corridor as a man and a woman pushed open the doors at the far end.

They were laughing and half draped over one another, entwined in a way that made it hard to tell where one ended and the other began.

This was made more difficult by the additional appendages both possessed. Tanis wondered if the meter-long thing in the middle of the man's face could best be described as a tentacle, trunk, or maybe a flaccid penis.

She realized the woman had two of them coming off her face, as well, and decided that she'd prefer to think of them as tentacles.

<The second one is coming out of her mouth,> Angela clarified.

Tanis tore her eyes from the pair…either they were talking by exchanging chemical signatures on their extra limbs, or they were having sex. Either way, looking felt like intruding.

Nadine stepped through the doors first, and Tanis followed. She'd already had a view of what to expect, having flushed her nanocloud through when the couple exited, but seeing the sights all around her was something to behold.

The room was a well-lit, open space, filling all four levels. Displays were scattered across the main floor and on the walls above, where catwalks encircled the open space, allowing the 'artwork' to be viewed up close.

The artwork, of course, consisted entirely of humans with extreme bio-mods. Directly in front of them was a woman who was standing vertically in a tank of water, with her head protruding from the top. From the neck up, she looked relatively normal, though bald; from the neck down, her skin seemed leathery, more like an octopus's hide, and things resembling sea anemones grew out of her body in various places.

As Tanis watched, a fish swam close to one of the anemones and was caught in its mouth. The woman moaned in pleasure, and Tanis resisted the urge to shake her head. She and Nadine were, after all, masquerading as patrons—or matrons—of the establishment, and sights like this shouldn't disturb them.

<Crap, I think I see her,> Nadine said from beside Tanis. *<Looks like she's…relatively unaltered.>*

Tanis followed Nadine's gaze, which was directed at the bar. Instead of the usual polished surface, the bar consisted of people. At first, Tanis thought it consisted of alternating men and women, but there were a few combos in the mix that made it hard to tell if a pattern was present.

<OK, I've seen a lot of stuff—good stuff, bad stuff—but I can't imagine enjoying a drink while that's going on in front of me. Is Nerischka one of those?>

<Stars, no, thank the gods. I would never be able to look at her at family reunions if she was—not without laughing and cringing at the same time. She's one of the bartenders.>

Tanis breathed a sigh of relief. Mostly because she was certain that the people who made up the bar were all physically bonded to one another.

It really didn't bear thinking about.

Nadine led Tanis to a display near the bar, and Tanis appeared to focus her attention on it, though she was actually reading a recent supply report. She had it over her vision, front and center, to block out what was going on.

They didn't have long to wait before a woman walked out from behind the bar—on legs, thank the stars—and approached Tanis and Nadine.

Her general form was hominid, but from there it diverged rapidly from the norm, appearing to be made of a flexible, veined granite. Coral grew out of it in artful patterns, running along her limbs and creating whorls around her breasts and abdomen. Her head was covered in a crown of coral, and when she spoke, Tanis saw that even her tongue had small bits growing from it.

"What could I possibly get for you fine ladies?" the woman—who Tanis assumed was Nerischka—said in a voice that sounded half like grating stone, and half like a bubbling fountain.

<I have to admit…I'm impressed by this one. That is living coral. It's growing out of her body in open air—can't be easy to do.>

<Yeah, but can you imagine how hard it must be to sleep?> Tanis asked. *<You'd have to do it standing up. Actually…I think you'd have to do everything standing up.>*

"What is your special?" Nadine asked. "We're in a hurry, need to meet a friend very soon."

Nerischka's face took on a sad expression. At least that's what Tanis assumed; her facial movement was restricted by the coral tracing her cheekbones.

"I'm sorry, we're out of the Ambrosia Red. I can offer you our house vintage, though—it's very close."

Nadine shook her head. "No, I need the Ambrosia Red. Nothing else will do. Top shelf."

Nerischka nodded, her eyes darting to her left for a second. "I will have to double-check our supplies in the back. You don't need to wait for me here, I'll find you."

"Thanks, we'll sate our curiosity," Nadine replied, before turning back to look at the display they were standing in front of.

<She can't get away easily. Nightshade is around here somewhere,> Nadine said. *<She needs us to meet her around the back.>*

<I gathered that,> Tanis replied. *<She seemed reluctant to leave; I noticed you had to invoke Sera.>*

<Well, the brief said she'd been working Nightshade for over a year. I can't imagine what being like **that** *for a year would entail. She probably doesn't want to screw it all up and waste the effort.>*

Tanis and Nadine wandered the floor for another ten minutes looking-without-looking at the various displays. Once the prescribed time had passed, they broke into an argument, and Tanis stormed out, followed by Nadine.

<She's staring at your ass,> Angela snickered. *<I think Nadine finds you attractive.>*

<Ang! She's just playing the part.>

<Of course! What was I thinking?>

Once outside Nightshade, they took a circuitous route around to the shipping and receiving entrance at the back of the establishment.

The pair ducked into a dark corner behind a stack of empty crates and proceeded to pull off their clothing. Underneath, both wore flow armor, and Nadine shivered as it spread over her hands and across her face.

<I practiced with this back on the ship, but I still feel like I'm going to suffocate and die when it goes over my mouth.>

<Yeah, not my favorite, either, but worth the trade-off.>

With their clothes tucked under a pallet, Tanis triggered the flow armor's stealth systems and led the way across the shipping corridor. She approached a smaller door beside the larger freight entrance at the rear of Nightshade.

Angela giggled and whispered in their minds, *<Open sesame.>*

<Did you just ***giggle****?>* Tanis asked.

<It seemed funny to me.>

<I think what Bob has is catching.>

The door popped open, and the two women slipped inside, moving in the direction Nerischka had indicated. They followed one hall, then another, and finally came to a room where a door was ajar, revealing racks filled with bottles.

The pair slipped in, gently closing the door behind them.

Tanis's nano cloud revealed Nerischka standing in a back corner, pretending to be reviewing a few bottles.

"Nishka," Nadine said quietly as they approached.

For her part, Nerischka didn't even flinch as a disembodied voice spoke next to her.

"Did you kill the surveillance in the room?" she asked.

"Of course," Nadine replied. "Not our first op."

Nerischka nodded, still looking at the bottles ahead of her. "Who's your friend?"

"I'm Tanis Richards."

That grabbed Nerischka's attention, and her head turned toward the sound of Tanis's voice. "*The* Tanis Richards?"

"Maybe. I imagine there must be other people with the same name."

"What are you doing here?" Nerischka hissed, regaining some of her calm. "I'm just days away from finding out who Nightshade is working with. This tech is crazy advanced stuff, it rivals some of what we have in the Transcend."

"And he's using it just for his kink-fest in there?" Tanis asked.

"No, that's just him skimming off the top. The real bulk of what passes through his hands is going elsewhere, but I don't know where, yet."

"Doesn't matter," Nadine replied. "You're getting pulled. We're going to Praesepe and old Genevia to look for clues about who might be spreading the Genevian Discipline tech."

Nerischka nodded slowly. "That sure brings back memories. Not good ones, mind you. The man you're going to want to seek out is General Mill. He has his finger on the pulse of what's left of Genevia, and is in possession of a number of bases spread around Septhia and into the gulf between Praesepe and Nietzschea. I don't need to go, though. I can just give you everything I have. I've worked too long here—I mean, look at what I've done to get in this deep with Nightshade."

"Nishka," Nadine said in a soft voice. "It's the unveiling. We're coming out of the shadows."

"What? How?"

"It's a ridiculously long story. Why couldn't I get you on the Link when we approached?"

Nerischka gestured at her body as though that answered all questions, which Tanis supposed it did. "I had to strip down my tech for this job. With how much Nightshade messes with our bodies, I couldn't have anything that gave me away. He removes our wireless transmitters, and our nano—what he lets us have—is shit."

"Damn, Nishka, you shouldn't let yourself become so vulnerable."

The coral-covered woman shook her head slowly. "Look what he's doing here, Nadine. This is just the tip of the iceberg. Nightshade has facilitated the transfer of enough bio-mods to turn millions, maybe even billions, of people into…into whatevers."

"There are certainly military uses for tech like this," Tanis said. "That's the only reason I can see Orion shipping this stuff into the Inner Stars—well, I suppose they could use it as a mandate to cleanse systems, as well."

"See? Either way, it has to be stopped. I recently got intel that Nightshade has been in contact with someone called 'Angel' about where to deliver the next shipment. Angel seems to be higher on the food chain, and I need to find out where it goes."

"Angel? Do you only have a name?" Tanis asked, her pulse quickening.

<A lot of people who call themselves 'Angel',> Angela cautioned.

<Too coincidental,> Tanis replied.

Nerischka shook her head. "I have heard two names, but the other one was only used once. It was 'Caretaker'."

<OK…so you were right.>

"Caretaker," Tanis breathed. "And your assessment is that Angel and the Caretaker are different people?"

Nerischka turned her head toward the sound of Tanis's voice. "You sound like you've heard of the Caretaker before."

"It's one of the reasons we're going to Genevia. We have reason to believe the Caretaker was involved in their recent war."

Nerischka nodded slowly. "It makes sense. I think this biotech might be moving through Nietzschean space—much of which was formerly Genevia."

<She needs to stay here, work this end of things,> Angela said.

<I know,> Tanis replied. *<But she's too vulnerable. She'll need help.>*

"OK, Nerischka. Nadine can fill you in later, but we do need to find this Angel. That target is more important than the source or destination of the bio-tech—though I imagine the objectives are aligned.

"Nadine. I'm going to need to continue on to the Praesepe Cluster, but Nerischka's in too deep on her own. If Angel is an ascended AI, or even just a human with a remnant—"

"A what?" Nerischka asked.

Tanis nodded, though she realized no one could see her movement. "We're up against ascended AIs and things called remnants, which the AIs can leave inside of other people. They can completely take someone over, and there's nothing you can do about it."

"It's true," Nadine added. "Things are getting crazy."

"OK, then I need to get you what I know about Mill and the Marauders, plus the situation on the ground in Praesepe," Nerischka replied. "I dumped all the intel that I couldn't fit up here—" she paused to tap her head, "in the records of a defunct financial auditing firm. If you search for Lucas Knight Industries, you'll find it in their 8937 financials."

<I'm in,> Angela informed Tanis a few seconds later. *<Oh, wow, that's a treasure trove!>*

"OK, we have it," Tanis replied. "Nadine. Angela has already signaled for the *Aegeus* to send in another pinnace. It'll have supplies for whatever you need, and a med suite that can put Nerischka here back together when the time comes. I'll ensure that there's a Shadowtron aboard. I think you're going to need it."

Nadine nodded, and Nerischka shook her head. "I feel a headache coming on. Nadine, I need to get back out there, but come back during third shift; I can get away for thirty minutes, and we can figure out what's next from there."

"OK, I can't tell you how glad I am to see you, Nishka. I'd hug you, but I'm afraid something would break off."

Nerischka laughed. "Wouldn't be the first time."

The stone-skinned, coral covered woman left, and the pair of stealthed women slipped out a few minutes later. Back behind the crates where their clothing was stashed, Nadine let out a long sigh.

"OK…that was sad and weird."

"I can imagine," Tanis replied. "Do you think she's OK…mentally? Working into a place like that has to mess with your head."

Nadine glanced toward Nightshade. "Stars…she's tough, and she seems together. I worry how she was going to get out of that place on her own, though."

Tanis nodded and clasped Nadine's shoulder. "Sera told me how you feel about operating in the field. I understand how taxing that can be. If you're not ready for this, say the word."

Nadine was holding her dress, and she looked down at her hands for a moment, twisting the fabric between them. "I don't want to lie and betray anymore…I can't wear that kind of mask again." She looked up at Tanis. "But this is different. Nishka's family, and from the looks of it, she really needs me."

Tanis glanced back at Nightshade. "Yeah, I think you're right. Remember, if you *are* going up against a remnant, they're sneaky. The Shadowtron isn't a sure bet. If things go sideways, get out and call for help."

"Understood, Tanis. We'll get to the bottom of this."

SEPTHIA

STELLAR DATE: 06.25.8949 (Adjusted Years)
LOCATION: ISS *I2*
REGION: Edge of the Lisbon System, Septhian Alliance

The non-space of the jump transition lasted for only a second before stars snapped into place again around the *I2*.

"Scan, confirm location," Rachel called out.

"Stellar cartography confirms that we are on the edge of the Lisbon System, seventy AU from the local star."

Rachel nodded. "Very good. Nice jump, Helm."

The pair of ensigns on Helm both responded, acknowledging the compliment as they adjusted the ship's vector to match local space.

The main holotank displayed the forward elements of the ISF escort fleet arraying themselves around the *I2*. Every ship was on its assigned trajectory, taking up the flying cross formation.

Correction, the *Derringer* was off a hair. She'd have to keep an eye on Captain Mel; the woman was becoming rather cavalier.

"Captain," Tanis gave Rachel a crisp nod followed by a quick smile as she approached the holotank. "Another day, another star system."

"Well, hopefully we'll stay put for a bit, now."

Rachel watched the Admiral's brow furrow before Tanis replied. "I certainly hope so, Captain. It's been months of chasing leads around the edges of the Nietzschean Empire, while Septhia hemmed and hawed about letting us enter their space."

"Plus the detour in the Azela System," Rachel added.

Tanis caught her eye and sighed. "And what a detour that has turned out to be for those two. With luck, we'll hear something from them soon."

Scan showed the Septhian ships still to be several hours from the rendezvous, and Rachel busied herself with a variety of tasks, while the admiral continued to scowl at the holodisplay.

She was speaking with the head of the Comm team when a voice called out from the bridge's entrance.

"So! The Septhian prime minister has finally pulled his head out of his ass and agreed to see us, has he?" Brandt asked as she approached the holotank.

"Brandt!" Tanis exclaimed and clasped the Marine Commandant's hand. "I was starting to wonder if you'd ever catch up to us."

Brandt nodded. "Caught the QuanComm update a minute before we were about to jump to Killgrave. Managed to get our vector altered in time to make it here—thank stars. Been waiting here for two days, hoping your invite was good enough for the whole family."

"I take it they didn't get grouchy at you for lurking out here?" Tanis asked.

Brandt gestured to the holodisplay, and Rachel noted thirty Septhian cruisers on an intercept course for the ISF's formation.

"I can't tell if that's grouchy, or just a cautious hello. Things are pretty tense in Septhia, from what I've heard."

"Less than in Scipio?" Rachel asked. "How were things there, by the way?"

Brandt let out a sound of dismay. "Is that a trick question? Out here, Septhia is worried about being steamrolled by the Nietzscheans, and Scipio is preparing to steamroll the Hegemony—provided Diana can put an end to the assassination attempts. It's starting to take a toll on her."

Rachel could only imagine what dealing with two coups and half a dozen—at least—assassination attempts would do to a person's morale.

"She'll be OK." Tanis turned back to the holotank and stared at the approaching Septhian Armed Forces cruisers. "I'm not worried about Diana. She's got a rock to lean on."

Rachel wondered what Tanis meant, but Brandt groaned and rolled her eyes. "Petra. Rock. Nice one, Field Marshal."

"On this bridge, I'm an Admiral," Tanis corrected the commandant.

"Not when you make lame jokes, you're not."

Sometimes the way Brandt spoke to Tanis amazed Rachel. Tanis was more familiar and approachable than many officers, but she was still *the* Admiral. Granted, Brandt had been working on building the ISF with Tanis since before the *Intrepid* had passed through Sol's heliopause.

That was a long time to build up comradery.

It also helped that Brandt was a small, thoroughly ferocious force of nature that everyone—including Tanis—was a bit leery of.

Tanis only frowned and darted her eyes toward Brandt.

"Captain, Admiral, we have a message from the SAF fleet. Text only," the Comm officer announced.

"Let's have it, Lieutenant," Tanis replied.

The comm officer put the message up on the bridge net, and Tanis sighed. "Looks like they don't want to come here—that's a first. Care to join me for a little jaunt, Commandant?"

"Of course I'm joining you," Brandt replied.

Tanis turned to Rachel and nodded. "Stay sharp, Captain. You have FleetConn in my absence."

"Aye, Admiral. I have FleetConn."

Tanis smiled and followed Brandt off the bridge as Rachel returned to her command chair.

<*Major Grange?*> she called down to the fleet CIC.

<*Yes, Captain Espensen.*>

<*Admiral Richards is leaving the* I2 *with Commandant Brandt to pay a visit to the Septhians. I have FleetConn in her absence. When her pinnace leaves the ship, I want two stealthed cruisers to follow. Full Marine complement.*>

<*Aye, Captain Espensen.*>

Rachel eyed the approaching Septhian vessels, considering their strengths and weaknesses. Against the ISF fleet, they were barely worth mentioning. But with Tanis aboard their ships? That was a horse of a different color.

Time passed slowly as Tanis's pinnace left the *I2* with the two stealthed cruisers shadowing it. The admiral hadn't commented on the extra precautions, so Rachel assumed she didn't object.

Tanis often left people room to execute the way they thought best. If there was a fundamental problem with a plan, she'd speak up, but otherwise she often left well enough alone.

The Admiral's pinnace slowed and held position beyond the formation of ISF ships surrounding the *I2*—though not beyond weapons range.

The SAF ships continued to slow, until they were moving at only a thousand kilometers per hour relative to the ISF ships, one fleet slowly drifting past the other with a hundred thousand kilometers between them.

At that point, the Admiral's pinnace began to move away from the ISF fleet, closing the gap between it and the SAF ships.

Rachel couldn't help but worry that something terrible was going to happen to Tanis. It was irrational, the Septhians had no reason to act aggressively. They knew the ISF was coming and had granted the fleet permission to come to the Lisbon System.

Stars, their Prime Minister was on one of those ships.

Still, she felt better as the two stealthed cruisers eased out to follow the admiral's pinnace.

<*I can feel your anxiety from here,*> Priscilla said, speaking to Rachel from her plinth in the foyer beyond the bridge. <*Relax, the admiral knows what she's doing.*>

<*She sure likes to put herself out there. After what happened at Scipio, I'd prefer she didn't do this sort of thing.*>

Priscilla laughed in Rachel's mind. <*Do you think you can stop her? If so, let the rest of us know how. She's always been like this. Only while Cary was young, were we able to rest easy.*>

It was Rachel's turn to laugh. <*Well, there you have it. We just need to keep Tanis pregnant. I'll be sure to talk to Admiral Evans about that.*>

<*I can just see her racing around the Inner Stars, forging alliances and popping out babies.*>

Rachel had to stop herself from laughing aloud at the thought. <*Priscilla!*>

"The admiral's ship is matching *v* with one of the SAF ships," Scan announced. "It's the *Everlasting*."

"Thank you," Rachel replied as she watched the pinnace approach the SAF vessel.

Good luck, Admiral.

A BIZARRE MEETING

STELLAR DATE: 06.25.8949 (Adjusted Years)
LOCATION: SAS *Everlasting*
REGION: Edge of the Lisbon System, Septhian Alliance

Tanis stepped off the pinnace with Brandt at her side and a fireteam of ISF Marines at her back. The bay they found themselves in was small, with perhaps only space for another ship the size of the ISF pinnace.

The instant the Marines set foot on the deck, they spread out around the bay, covering corners, ready for anything. They moved with smooth precision, and Tanis wondered how aggressive their deployment and posture appeared to the Septhians.

Another four Marines formed up behind Tanis and Brandt, ready to operate as an escort once they left the bay.

Of course, with their hosts absent, they weren't leaving yet.

Brandt sighed and drummed her fingers on her thigh before whistling a little tune. Tanis connected to the vessel's public shipnet, about to reach out to whoever was listening, when the interior bay doors finally opened.

The exit stood empty for a moment, before a tall woman with long black hair entered, flanked by a pair of guards.

She walked toward the ISF delegation with a smile on her face that appeared genuine, but it didn't seem to match her strident steps.

"Admiral Richards," the woman said, extending her hand as she neared. "It is a pleasure to meet you. And Commandant Brandt, I was not expecting you to be present, how exciting!"

Tanis shook the woman's slender hand, hiding a smile at the woman's exuberance as Brandt replied.

"Uh, sure. I thought it would be nice to get out, stretch my legs, and see the locals."

"Yes, of course," the woman replied, nodding her head emphatically, while looking a touch confused.

"It's very nice to meet you, as well…" Tanis began.

<She seems unwell,> Angela commented. *<You should ask her if she's OK.>*

<Me? Why don't you?> Tanis asked.

<OK, su—>

<Ang!>

"Sorry," the woman replied with a nervous smile. "My name is Oris, sorry, I don't know how I got all this out of order."

<If you don't ask her, I will,> Angela warned Tanis, just as Brandt spoke up.

"Oris, very nice to meet you, are you alright? You seem out of sorts," the commandant's brows pinched as she spoke.

"Well, the PM *just* showed me the little holo you sent. The one explaining where you and your ship—which looks *a lot* different now—have been for the last two decades. I must say that it's…hard to believe."

Tanis nodded and gave Oris a reassuring smile. "I've been in your shoes, but trust me, it's real. We've spent most of the past two decades in the Transcend."

"How is it—sorry. My questions are not important. Follow me, and I'll escort you to the PM."

Oris turned, and Tanis followed with Brandt at her side. The Marines walked down the ramp after her, and the two SAF soldiers followed behind.

"So, was there any part of our explanation that was particularly distressing to you or the Prime Minister?" Tanis asked, interested in any information that would aid in the upcoming meeting.

"Well, the fact that the volume of explored space is vastly larger than we had ever thought was something rather surprising. And not just a little bit…but *a lot*!"

<She really likes to emphasize 'a lot'. I wonder if this verbal tic is hers alone, or if Septhia is just weird.>

<Very little will be 'weird' after seeing Nightshade,> Tanis replied to Angela before addressing Oris. "I can relate. In the space of a few months, I went from the belief that humanity had not gone more than a few *hundred* light years from Sol, to thousands, to tens of thousands."

"Yes, I'd forgotten that. Your ship predates FTL…when you left Sol, you had to fly for decades to the next star."

"Or centuries," Brandt added.

"I can't imagine," Oris said breathily as she gestured for them to enter a lift.

Only two of the Marines, along with one of the SAF soldiers, could fit in the lift with them. When they reached the next level, Tanis waited for the other Marines to arrive.

"I'm sure they can catch up," Oris said, her tone attempting to convey reassurance.

"Of course they can," Brandt said with a small smile. "They're Marines. But it'll be easier if we wait."

"Um…OK," Oris replied.

*<This woman **cannot** be this scatterbrained,>* Angela said to Tanis and Brandt. *<It has to be an act to disarm us.>*

<Or she's a dear, fragile thing, and our news has disturbed her so,> Brandt replied, raising the pitch of her voice and drawing out her words.

<Stop it, Brandt,> Tanis replied. *<I don't want their PM to watch me laughing at their aide on the feeds.>*

<Think he's watching us?> the commandant asked.

<Of course he is. Why else make us traipse through his ship? He's measuring us up.>

<Should have made him come to us,> Angela groused.

The lift doors opened, and the Marines and other SAF soldier stepped out.

"Ah, there we are," Oris said with a smile. "Let's be on our way now. Just down this corridor."

<I'm perfectly fine meeting here,> Tanis replied. *<We get to observe them as much as they observe us.>*

They followed Oris down the corridor, took a right, then a left, and reached a single door on the right side of the passageway.

"Your guards will have to wait outside," Oris said as she rapped on the door.

Brandt scowled but nodded to the Marines, who took up positions on either side of the hall.

"Come," a voice said from within, and the door slid aside to reveal a table sitting under a pergola, with rolling hills stretching into the distance. It was a decently constructed holoview, though Tanis could spot the artificial irregularities.

Seated at the table was a man who Tanis recognized as the Septhian Prime Minister, and a uniformed woman with five stars on her collar.

<Just the two of them,> Angela commented. *<I guess there will be less*

banter, at least.>

"Prime Minister Harmin," Tanis said as she entered the room and held out her hand. "I love the view. Is this from one of your worlds here in Lisbon?"

The PM stood and walked around the table to greet Tanis, while the Septhian admiral approached from the other side.

"It is, Admiral Richards. It's from T'Riva, our capital world."

"Very lovely," Tanis replied as she turned to shake the woman's hand.

"Admiral Vera," the woman introduced herself with a curt nod.

"Very nice to meet you," Tanis replied.

Brandt exchanged greetings as well, and then the group, including Oris, sat at the table as servitors approached with a selection of drinks.

<*You're so smooth when you want to be, Tanis,*> Brandt commented. <*I feel like you should have flowers in your hair or something.*>

<*Shut up, Brandt,*> Tanis shot back with a mental scowl.

The PM spoke as soon as they'd settled. "I'd ask you how your journey was, but I don't even know how you travelled here so quickly. The information you provided put the Transcend's borders thousands of light years coreward of the Praesepe Cluster."

Oris chimed in with an over-wide smile. "Either way, I imagine it was pleasant enough. Your ship is large enough to carry every amenity."

"It's not a home away from home," Tanis inclined her head. "It's just plain home."

"I suppose it would be," Prime Minister Harmin replied. "If the stories are to be believed, you've spent some time on that ship."

"We certainly have, Prime Minister," Tanis agreed.

"Please, you may call me 'Harmin', no need to dwell on so much formality when it's just the five of us."

<*My kinda guy,*> Brandt said privately.

"I imagine you're wondering *why* we've come to Septhia," Tanis said, ready to get to the meat of the conversation.

Harmin chuckled. "I'll admit, the thought has crossed my mind. I don't really follow why you sent us the information on the *Transcend,* as you put it. Though I suppose it does explain how your ship managed to get FTL capabilities, and where it went—though the fact that the FGT is still alive and well is a bit of a shock."

"Maybe even more so than your arrival from the distant past," Admiral Vera added.

"Not just the FGT," Tanis clarified. "The Transcend Interstellar Alliance, and the Orion Freedom Alliance. Two massive powers that have been vying for control for some time."

"It's interesting, to be sure," Harmin said, stroking his short beard. "But, if I may be so blunt, how does it affect us? We're a small alliance of stars, just making do in our little corner of space. We have no quarrel with this Transcend or Orion."

"You do, however, have a quarrel with the Nietzscheans." Brandt leant forward and raised her eyebrows. "Or maybe they have a quarrel with you—hard to say which. Nietzschea seems to have a bone to pick with everyone."

"Then you know why we're not looking for more trouble right now," Harmin replied. "We're building alliances around the Praesepe Cluster—and within—working to build up a defense against the Nietzscheans."

"Who do you think is supplying the Nietzscheans?" Tanis asked.

"Honestly?" Harmin gave an exaggerated shrug. "Our money is on the Trisilieds. Being in the Pleiades gives them access to vast resources."

"We're investigating how they're moving supplies between the two empires with such ease," Vera added.

"As far as *we* can tell, the Nietzscheans and Trisilieds aren't working together at all," Tanis said amicably.

Vera scowled at Tanis, the expression on her face carrying no small amount of disdain. "Pardon my skepticism, but what intelligence network are you using to gather that information?"

"They're called The Hand," Tanis replied. "Remember those massive empires beyond the Inner Stars that don't really matter to you? Well, they have agents everywhere. Either way, the main reason why the Trisilieds aren't supplying the Nietzscheans is because Orion is funneling resources into both of them. Along with the Hegemony."

Tanis let the words fall and picked up the glass of wine a servitor had set down, taking a sip and watching Harmin and Vera, who were clearly chatting with one another over the Link.

<This is not going the way I expected. I don't understand why they're being so defensive,> Angela commented.

Tanis wondered as well, then realization dawned on her.

"Prime Minister Harmin, you don't, by any chance, think that we've come here to seek a place to settle, do you?"

Harmin's eyes darted toward Tanis's and narrowed. "The thought had occurred to me. I hate to speak so bluntly, but it's far more likely that you've been running from system to system with the Hegemony on your tail, than spending time in some fanciful empire beyond the edges of human expansion."

"Huh." Tanis sat back and shook her head. "I don't know why, but I never expected anyone to have that reaction. Though now that you say it, I can see why you'd suspect our motives."

"Look at it from our viewpoint," Admiral Vera raised her hands in a gesture of frustration. "Last we saw you, you were fleeing the AST ships after blowing up a planet in Bollam's World."

"I think it's worth noting that the AST blew up the planet. The Bollers had clearly posted warnings about not messing with the thing." Tanis gave a slight smile at her wit, but the PM and his admiral did not join in.

<I'm with them, it was a bit weak,> Angela commented.

Tanis ignored Angela and continued, "Right, well, I'm sure you have some analysts who can take a look at the fleet we have, and tell you that these are not the same ships that we had at Bollam's World. We have a colony world with our own shipyards, and ample resources flowing in from starmines. We don't need anything from you other than a little bit of intel and safe passage."

"Intel?" Harmin asked.

"Yes," Tanis replied. "The current location of General Mill, leader of the Marauders. I need to find out what he knows about the origins of Genevia's mech program."

Harmin and Vera looked at one another for several long moments before the PM turned back to Tanis and frowned.

"So you don't want to trade with us?"

"Well, I'll trade for what I just requested. Information on General Mill's whereabouts—I know that his mercenary group works for you almost exclusively—and then permission to take my fleet to him."

Tanis had expected the conversation to immediately turn to allying against the Nietzscheans, but they hadn't even brought it up. It was strange, but then, everything about the Septhians had been strange thus far. Now she didn't know if she *wanted* Septhia as an ally.

"What do we get for this?" Harmin asked.

<*This is the weirdest negotiation I've ever been in,*> Tanis said to Angela and Brandt. <*They clearly want things from us, but they don't seem to want to trade…or to just come out and ask for it….*>

Angela made a soft sound of disinterest. <*Maybe they're scared.*>

<*I think they're stupid.*> Brandt gave a short laugh. <*Maybe there's something wrong with the air on their worlds.*>

Tanis wondered about that. Fear made people act strangely. "Well, what do you want?" she asked plainly.

"Your picotech," Admiral Vera replied without hesitation.

"No," Tanis shot back.

"Well then, your shield tech."

"Also no."

Harmin placed his hands on the table. "Admiral Richards. We are gearing up for a war with Nietzschea. If you don't have something meaningful to offer us to help in that effort, then you'll have to forgive us, but we need to be going."

"So you *do* want something I can offer," Tanis replied. "I imagine that you need ships. Chances are that you're starved for resources right now. What with Nietzschea building up their military, people are hoarding or gouging for everything."

"You won't give us your shield tech…but you'll give us ships instead?" Vera's face was the very definition of disbelief.

"Well, we don't have a proper alliance, and I don't think we can form one, because you don't believe I'm telling the truth. If you did, then we could work something out. However, I have a way that we can work toward that."

"Oh?" Harmin asked.

Tanis nodded. "See, I know that the Trisilieds and the Hegemony are working with the Orion Guard, on account of the fact that they attacked our system not long ago. Luckily, I didn't have to completely destroy their fleets."

"It must have been a small force, for you to have survived." Vera still looked as though she didn't believe a word Tanis was saying.

"Well, it was small when compared to the entirety of their armed forces, yes. The enemy hit us with roughly two hundred thousand ships."

Vera's mouth dropped open, then snapped shut, while Harmin's stayed agape.

"Are you mocking us?" Vera asked.

"Stars," Tanis glanced at Brandt. "Empress Diana was significantly easier to deal with than these two."

"Diana of Scipio?" Harmin asked, disbelief warring with wonder on his face.

"The same," Tanis replied. "We're supporting her in her war against the Hegemony. Now, I have a few ways I could *prove* to you that I'm not lying. I *could* take you to New Canaan, but I won't. I suppose we could go to some location in the Transcend, like Khardine or Vela, but I don't think I'll do that, either…your lack of openness is not encouraging. What I'll do instead is show you that I am not here with my hand out.

"I'll offer you one hundred Trisilieds cruisers in exchange for the information I want, and permission to travel through Septhia at will."

"One hundred cruisers?" Harmin asked. "How? Where?"

"Pull up your Scan feeds, they should be jumping in now."

On one side of the table, the holoview of rolling hills disappeared, now showing the ISF fleet. In the center of the display lay the *I2*, framed by the twenty ships on patrol.

For a minute, nothing happened, then a point of light appeared beyond the ISF ships, and the holodisplay focused in on that location, enlarging it to fill the space next to the table.

"Shit, that's a Trisilieds cruiser!" Vera exclaimed.

<*Real quick on the uptake,*> Angela commented.

"I hope this isn't some trick." Oris's voice wavered with uncertainty.

Another cruiser appeared, followed by another. The pace quickened, with as many as five appearing at a time, then slackened once more until a hundred new ships were spread in a loose formation beyond the ISF fleet.

"What are your intentions with these ships?" Harmin asked.

Tanis couldn't help a long look at the holographic sky above them before she responded. "You're *really* not used to things going your way, are you? Those ships are for you. A gesture of my goodwill. Vera?" Tanis asked. "I'm sure you're talking with your CIC. Tell me about the ships."

"Well…there's almost no EM coming off them, main drives are

offline, no shields. There appear to be a hundred tugs…all making for your other fleet."

"Do you believe me now, that I don't need a planet, or a place to settle in Septhia? Which is ludicrous, anyway. Why would I settle so close to Nietzschea?"

Harmin's lips drew into a thin line, and his brows pinched together. "It seems that I've misjudged you, Admiral Richards. Your general assessment of our situation is as you've described. We've worked hard to build ourselves up in preparation for a Nietzschean assault…but by making ourselves the strongest, we've become their primary target in the region."

"We're low on almost every raw material, our mining operations are running constantly, and our shipyards are producing vessels as fast as we can," Oris interjected. "But it's like you said. Our neighbors are all doing the same. Many key resources are skyrocketing in price."

"What about the Praesepe Cluster itself?" Tanis asked. "Those stars must be rich in raw resources and volatiles."

Harmin nodded. "They are, but FTL is not possible within the mean tidal radius of the cluster. Reaching the core is an eighty-year trip. Each way."

"I can see how that would be a problem," Brandt laughed.

Tanis considered her options. "I wouldn't want to spend an Intrepid Class gate on it, but I could see setting up a smaller gate to get in and out of the cluster's core."

"A gate?" Admiral Vera asked.

"Those ships out there?" Tanis gestured at the holodisplay. "They were about four thousand light years from here before they arrived."

"*Four thousand?*" Harmin almost choked. "That takes a decade to traverse!"

"Not with jump gates, it doesn't," Tanis replied. "And don't ask. You're not getting that tech, either. If we *do* grant you assistance that employs the use of gates, we'll loan tugs, like those you saw bringing the ships in."

"So *that's* what they were for," Harmin said with a pensive nod. "Even if you can use jump gates to get into Praesepe's core, you may not find a warm welcome there. The people who live in the cluster *like* being isolationists. They won't be keen on visitors who can just appear for a visit."

"What I wouldn't give to see the looks on their faces when your ships jump in." Oris laughed as she spoke, and Vera shot her a dark look.

Tanis held up a hand. "Let's not get ahead of ourselves. Besides, I doubt we need to go to what I've seen noted as the 'Core Empire' on local charts. A venture there would assume they have the ability to provide raw resources at a rate which you would find worthwhile."

"It would give them a safe place to mine and manufacture, though. Easier to fuel the war effort that way," Brandt noted.

"Could you not aid us directly?" Harmin asked. "You say that the Orion group is feeding the Nietzscheans. Why don't you do the same for us?"

Tanis fixed Harmin with a cold stare. "Ten minutes ago, you were behaving as though you wanted to shoo me off your doorstep."

"I'm truly sorry for that." Harmin's tone did carry a note of sincerity. "We let our fears drive our actions. Septhia is all that stands between Praesepe and Nietzschea. If they take the cluster, you know they'll just keep marching coreward."

"We're preparing for bigger fights than this one," Tanis replied. "I need some people to stand for themselves. I had thought Septhia was one of those places."

"*Please!*" Harmin almost shouted. "We're months, a year at most, from being in a fight for our lives."

<OK, Tanis, you made him grovel. Now give the poor man a lifeline.>

"Are you willing to become formal allies of the Transcend?" Tanis asked. "We'll aid in your defense against Nietzschea. I promise."

Harmin slouched back into his chair. "What are your terms?"

"Would you believe we have a standard agreement?"

THE ROAD HOME

STELLAR DATE: 08.11.8949 (Adjusted Years)
LOCATION: *Voyager*
REGION: Germine System, Within the Transcend borders

"There it is," Katrina said, unable to keep the slight rasp from her voice. Her body was getting old again, impossibly old. It may be time to avail herself of rejuvination.

Though rejuv was having more and more diminishing returns each time.

"How will we use it?" Kara asked from beside Katrina. "Freighters like this don't have mirrors—or at least, we're not supposed to."

Katrina glanced at the woman—if that was the right word—next to her and grinned. "I've a few tricks up my sleeve. Sneaking about the galaxy is my job. So long as the coordinates you have are correct, we'll be having breakfast on the *Intrepid* tomorrow."

"The *I2*, you mean," Kara corrected her.

"Yes…interesting name, that."

Katrina glowered at the holodisplay, willing events to unfold faster, but rushing things would not lead to a favorable outcome. Patience was key. She had waited half a millennium for this; she could wait a few hours longer.

She widened the view on the holo, taking in the inner five AU of the Germine System. It was a well-populated star system, sporting two terraformed worlds, several megastructures, and, most importantly, jump gates. Nine, to be exact.

The wild jump from Airtha, executed during their escape with Kara, had landed them far from any system with gates. It had taken almost a year to reach Germine, and during that time, much had changed.

The Transcend had fractured, many systems declaring for Airtha, many others for Khardine. Most, however, seemed prepared to wait it out—or at least see which of the two Seras was stronger before choosing a side.

Germine was one such system, though they had gone further. They had declared independence from the Transcend, a move possible because of the immense wealth and strategic placement of the system.

Also, they're probably holding out for the best deal, Katrina mused.

She wondered if the Transcend would survive this civil war. It was too large to begin with. Many of the worlds in the alliance served in name only.

While President Tomlinson had maintained a strong core, the freedoms he allowed meant that the Alliance's fringes were far more autonomous than in the Orion Freedom Alliance. There, Praetor Kirkland ruled with an iron fist and ensured compliance with his strictures through swift and decisive use of his Orion Guard.

As far as Katrina was concerned, it was all a shit-show. Tanis and New Canaan offered the only real safe haven, a haven Katrina craved.

For a long time, she had worried that the *Intrepid* would not survive its arrival in the future. So much had changed from what they were used to. But after watching the feeds from the Battle of Bollam's World, Katrina had been reassured that Tanis would not let the colony ship fall to anyone.

It had been a bittersweet experience. Just the knowledge that the *Intrepid* had survived Kapteyn's Streamer, finally arriving in the future, had lifted Katrina's spirits greatly.

The moment she learned that she'd arrived in Bollam's World a mere three days after the *Intrepid* jumped out ranked as one of the worst of her life.

And Katrina had experienced many terrible moments.

However, her study of the battle had revealed one important clue. Tanis had allied herself with a freighter captain who operated in and around the Silstrand Alliance.

Katrina's travels over the past five hundred years had taken her far and wide. Even so far as the Transcend. Few would have known that captain's true identity, but Katrina did.

The Tomlinson resemblance was unmistakable.

And so, Katrina had spent the last twenty years travelling to Airtha, the one place she knew she could find a lead, only to be too late once more.

Kara was her silver lining. Someone who not only had *been* to New Canaan, but who had seen Tanis and Sera with her own eyes.

Katrina didn't believe in a god—if some entity had directed the events in her life, it would have a lot to answer for—but finding Kara was something of a miracle, enough to make her wonder.

"Katrina?" Kara said loudly.

"What? No need to yell, girl."

Katrina wondered what was going on behind the featureless oval that was Kara's head. Did the girl have a mouth to speak with? Her ethereal voice emitted from a sound-strip on her neck, and she never ate; instead taking in nutrition through a port in her abdomen.

Katrina suspected that Kara had no face at all, that the helmet was her head, cushioning her brain in a ballistic gel, making her a more effective killer.

Kara had said as much—about being a killer, at least. Her most important goal in life was to protect her father and destroy anyone who threatened him.

"I had asked why it was strange that they named it the *I2*."

"Oh, that." Katrina nodded slowly as she wound her thoughts back to that point. "Well, it just seems odd to me. They really liked the *Intrepid*...it was their home. Now they've changed it into something else."

"Does that upset you?" Kara asked.

"No...we all change. I guess it means that the future wasn't what they hoped it would be, either."

"Is it ever?" Kara asked.

Katrina shrugged. "No, not really."

She turned her attention back to the holo display and the nine jump gates. The gates were all in orbit around Farska, a moon in orbit of the system's largest gas giant. Most of the commerce in the Germine system centered around the gas giant, so it made sense for the gates to be nearby, as well.

That was useful for Katrina. It meant her ships could make a close approach without any trouble. It would only be over the final hundred thousand kilometers that they'd be in violation of the local STC's flight paths.

Katrina's other ship was further ahead, almost at the edge of the no-fly zone surrounding the gates. That vessel, the *Kjeeran*, was empty, though automatons simulated human activity within the ship, should someone scan it closely.

Her entire company, all that remained of her once-sizable military that had escaped the Midditerra System all those centuries ago, were now the crew on her last ship. The *Voyager*.

<*It's in the pipe,*> Troy said. <*I've cut the tightbeam to the* Kjeeran. *Too much traffic; someone was going to catch its bleed-off.*>

"Well, it's not like we need the ship to do a good job. The whole point is for it to make a mess."

<*Vicky has confirmed that she can alter Gate 7 when we approach. She wants to come with us, though.*>

Katrina groaned. "How's she going to do that? She's a gate control AI. She can't just leap across space to our ship."

<*Well, we're going to have to figure something out, she said she won't do it otherwise. Something about being 'truly free'.*>

More AI nonsense, Katrina thought to herself.

"Well, did she propose any means to do this? Or shall we just invent teleportation over the next hour?"

<*She can get one of us to her core for extraction, and then operate the gate on remote,*> Troy replied.

"I'll do it," Kara volunteered.

"You?" Katrina asked, looking the jet black, four-armed, winged woman up and down. "You blend in about as well as a missile."

"They're unaligned, I can claim to be a special envoy on a secret mission from my father. Then I kill whoever is escorting me, get to this Vicky's core, and free her."

"Getting shot at the whole way back to the *Voyager*," Katrina added.

<*Well, someone is going to have to do it,*> Troy replied. <*Kara here is a killing machine of epic proportions. She only ever wears armor, so no one will be shocked to see her in it.*>

"OK, mister smarty-AI," Katrina countered. "What's her reason for going aboard the gate control platform? We need something better than 'Dad sent me'."

<*Easy, she needs to provide special coordinates for her ship.*>

Katrina scrubbed her face with her palms. "They're not declared for Airtha *or* Khardine. How do we convince them to do something for Kara here?"

"Easy," Kara replied. "Greed. We offer a payoff to whoever runs the platform. The very fact that Germine hasn't aligned with either side tells us that they're in it for the money."

Katrina considered that. It was likely true, but it didn't mean that whoever ran the gate control platform felt the same way.

"It's a lot of variables to deal with in one hour," Katrina said. "We need more time."

<*Then we'd best stop the* Kjeeran *from finishing its suicide run,*> Troy advised.

"OK, yeah. Put it in a stable orbit and see if you can get Vicky to validate our way in with Kara, or suggest a better one."

Katrina looked at Kara, wishing once again that she could see the girl's facial expressions. "You sure you're up for it? You've never had to do something like this while not under your father's aegis."

Kara nodded resolutely. "I know. But I can do it. He told me to get to Sera, that only she can save him."

"Kara, that man controlled your mind your entire life. He made you serve him as a slave."

What irony for **me** *to be saying those words.*

Kara made a warbling sound that Katrina had learned was her variation on a laugh. "He's my mother, too. Did you know that? Father's a natural chimera hermaphrodite able to spontaneously gestate. I know it sounds insane, but as much as I hate my father, I love my mother. How messed up does that make me?"

Katrina shrugged. "I once used a dressing machine to tear all my skin off and replace it with armor. I was in agony for weeks and got addicted to the pain. We're all messed up in one way or another.

Kara nodded, then cocked her head to the side. "You're right, that *is* nuts."

Katrina patted the strange young woman on the shoulder. "It does explain why your Father-Mother spells his name like that."

* * * * *

Kara drew in a deep breath, calming her nerves as she drifted through the umbilical connecting the *Voyager* to the gate control platform—which bore the uninspired name, 'GCP1'.

Katrina had coached her on what to say and how to react to any challenges. The old woman was listening on the Link, ready to offer help as needed.

The AI, Troy, was there as well, likely ready to dole out sarcasm-laden advice. Kara wasn't sure if she liked him or not. Not that it mattered; she didn't like most people.

At the umbilical's end, Kara cycled the airlock open and floated in. As it matched pressure, the lock also brought the gravity up to GCP1's standard 0.7*g*.

While she waited, Kara wondered at her luck of meeting Katrina during her desperate escape from Airtha. The one person in the entire star system who was able to help had been there at the right time. Not only that, but Katrina had also possessed the means to make a speedy escape.

Luck was not something Kara believed in, but there was an undeniable serendipity to the events.

And what a strange old woman she was. To think that for five hundred years, Katrina had waited for the *Intrepid* to return. Hiding in dark corners and skulking about the Inner Stars, eventually passing into Orion space, and later the Transcend.

What a tale that must be. Aaron would have loved to hear it....

Kara pushed the thoughts of her dead brother from her mind as her clawed feet settled firmly on the deck. The airlock's door cycled open, and she looked out on the corridor beyond.

It was a narrow space, with grey bulkheads and a grey deck. An equally grey man stood waiting for her, his colorless uniform bearing no markings of any sort. On either side of him were two soldiers in matte black armor.

Kara smiled—or would have, if she still possessed the ability to do so.

It had been Aaron's idea to remove their faces and replace them with featureless ovals. He had done it so that they could be more effective in their defense of Father. But now Aaron was dead, and Kara was no longer under her father's aegis. She wondered for a moment what it would be like to have a face again.

What visage would she choose?

The man cleared his throat as Kara stepped into the corridor, her folded wings scraping the overhead. "Kara, daughter of Adrienne. Welcome to Germine and the GCP1. I understand you wish to use our jump gate for 'Special Transcend Business'."

Kara nodded, gazing down at the man. "I do. I have the coordinates, but I need to enter them myself with a record lockout in place."

"You wish to obscure your destination from the Germine government?" the man asked, his eyebrows raised halfway to his hairline. "That is highly irregular."

"Not for a cabinet member's envoy," Kara replied.

The man worked his mouth for a moment while nodding slowly. Kara imagined that even with two soldiers at one's side, a two-hundred-centimeter tall black demon looming over you was more than a little intimidating.

After all, what was the point of turning oneself into such a creature if you couldn't scare the crap out of officious little weasels?

The man finally replied, his voice tinged with disdain. "You surely know that Germine is no longer officially affiliated with the Airtha government, nor are we aligned with Khardine. Germine is a free system; your father's position means little here."

Kara kept both sets of hands folded in front of her, but made a point of slowly scratching her claws along her armored skin.

"I understand that…" She waited for the man to provide his name.

"Stationmaster Nuermin."

At least I've started at the top.

"Well, I'm sure that you'd still like for Germine to have favorable relations with Airtha. President Sera is an accommodating woman, but she is also resolute in her desire to destroy the usurper at Khardine."

To his credit, Nuermin did not back down. Instead he countered, "You are referring to the usurper who also claims to be President Sera? Hopefully you can understand why we're not interested in joining in what is clearly some sort of strange family squabble."

Honestly, Kara didn't blame the man or the populace of the Germine System. Staying out of the early stages of a civil war seemed like a smart play. Let the two sides show more of their hands before declaring allegiance.

Nevertheless, pacificity would not benefit her here, and she bore no particular love nor obligation to the people of Germine.

"Yet you agreed to let us dock and meet with me," Kara replied.

"I would not be so rude as to dismiss you out of hand—though the ship you're on did make me think twice...."

"A necessary subterfuge."

"I suppose. I don't need to know specifics of your mission."

<Stars, he's taking forever to get to the part where he asks you for money,> Katrina spoke for the first time. *<Make him an offer before he loses his nerve or something.>*

Kara agreed. She didn't want to spend forever trading pleasantries with this man.

"Stationmaster Nuermin. What will it take to use the gate? I assume that if there is a maintenance and upkeep cost associated with a jump, we could compensate the people of Germine for that?"

Kara had made her fair share of shady deals on her father's behalf. She was under no illusions that the 'people of Germine' would ever see a single credit.

"Well." Nuermin tilted his head, as though her words had only just now opened up a new avenue of thought. "I suppose we could determine the cost to the people, were I to allow you the use of a gate. However, we cannot remove destination information from our systems. There is no maintenance cost associated with that. It's simply against policy."

"I understand," Kara said. It didn't really matter. The AI, Vicky, would be configuring the jump gate and destroying all targeting data in GCP1's systems. "Do you have a number?"

Nuermin hemmed and hawed for almost a minute, behaving as though he'd never done this before. Kara glanced at the guards and could make out one of them rolling her eyes behind her faceshield.

"I suppose we could arrange a jump for seventeen million credits."

Kara nearly choked and was amazed that the stationmaster had managed to state the number with a straight face.

<What a highwayman! And people call me a pirate,> Katrina snorted. *<We can cover it, though. Not that it will come to that. Of course, don't take his first offer.>*

<This is not my first deal of this sort, Katrina,> Kara replied tonelessly.

<OK, no need to get upset about it. Just making sure.>

Kara gave the stationmaster a shake of her head. "I understand the economics of gate travel well enough to know that there is no scenario under which a jump costs more than ten million credits."

Nuermin nodded, a commiserating expression on his face. "Yes, that is normally the case, but with the troubles that abound, antimatter prices have gone up. Supply and demand, you know. A lot of demand right now. Not to mention demand for gate travel. Our queues are stacked for days, and I assume you want a speedy transit…"

He left the word hanging, and Kara nodded.

"I suspected as much. Well, in that case, I hope you understand that I cannot saddle so many people with this disruption for less than sixteen million."

Kara and the increasingly detestable stationmaster haggled for a few more minutes before settling on fifteen million, with a full refueling for the *Voyager* thrown in.

Once they agreed on price, Kara insisted that they do the transfer over a secure terminal, recording the transaction with system banking NSAI to ensure everything was above board.

This threw Nuermin for a loop, but eventually agreed to it.

<He's going to ask for a separate transaction just for himself,> Katrina muttered. *<Slimy bastard.>*

<Doesn't his greed favor us?> Kara asked. *<If he were an honest man, we would not be able to pull this off.>*

<Perhaps. We would at least be able to get you close to Vicky, though, which is really all we need to do.>

Kara decided that was true. *<Very well, when should I terminate this man and fetch Vicky?>*

<I'm bringing Vicky in on our chat,> Troy said. *<She can coordinate with you directly.>*

<Hi, Kara, I hear you're my ticket out of here.> Vicky's tone was brusque, yet somewhat melodic.

<I am, as you are ours,> Kara replied.

<You'll need to get Nuermin past this corridor,> Vicky marked a corridor on the map of GCP1 they shared over the Link. *<I'm just past there, about thirty meters.>*

<How do I get him to go that far? From what I see, there's a secure hard-terminal much closer. From the route he's taking, I believe he is planning to use that one.>

<Not for long,> Vicky chuckled. *<I'm about to invalidate its tokens.>*

<Good,> Kara replied, not sure if the AI wanted to be thanked for its

efforts.

Stationmaster Nuermin stopped in his tracks a moment later and groaned. "Damn, we're going to have to use another terminal. Follow me."

He turned down a side passage and began leading Kara in the desired direction. She followed silently, paying more attention to the guards behind her than the man in front—a useful advantage of always wearing a helmet.

The guard on her left—the woman who had previously rolled her eyes at Nuermin—seemed bored. She was clearly watching personal holo, or engaged in a Link conversation. The other guard was a thin man who moved with the grace of a cat as he prowled along behind Kara. She felt a modicum of respect for him, as he paid close attention to his surroundings, his eyes darting to Kara if she so much as twitched a wing.

He would go down first.

Five minutes later, they crossed the demarcation Vicky had made on the map, and reached the room with the secure terminal.

Nuermin led the way into the sterile chamber, which only possessed four chairs along one wall and the terminal in the center.

Both parties were to hard-Link into the terminal and register special encrypted tokens for use in the transaction. Kara, of course, had no intention of doing that.

As Nuermin walked to the far side of the terminal, Kara readied herself to strike the guards, both of whom had entered and now stood behind her on either side.

I imagine they get a nice cut. Kara grimaced at the thought.

<*Resetting Link transmitters in that part of the station. You'll have thirty seconds before these three can reconnect,*> Vicky advised.

<*What about the terminal?*> Kara asked as she readied herself to strike.

<*I can't lock that out. You'll need to make sure they don't use it to call for help…and…GO!*>

Thanks for the countdown….

Kara snapped her wings wide, filling the room with their inky blackness, and kicked back at the wary man, clamping her clawed foot around his calf and pulling him forward.

She thought he'd fall, but instead, he hopped forward and crashed into her back, then drove a fist into her armored side.

With only one leg on the floor, Kara slipped and spun around, smacking a wing into Nuermin and knocking him away from the terminal.

Both of the guards faced her, the bored woman suddenly alert and swinging her pulse rifle up at Kara's head, while the man staggered backward, still unslinging his weapon.

Kara whipped a wing in front of herself as the woman fired. The carbon-fiber, polymer coated construction of her wing blocked the woman's pulse blast, and Kara slashed at her with the clawed tip of her wing, trying to hook the weapon and pull it away.

Meanwhile, the man had leveled his weapon and fired a pulse shot that Kara also blocked with a wing. The man lowered his weapon for a moment, his eyes registering dismay, and Kara lunged forward, one of her left arms grabbing his rifle, while another clamped around his neck, lifting him into the air.

So much for Sharp Eyes being the biggest threat.

She threw him at the woman and spun once more, whipping a wingtip at Neurmin, who was struggling to his feet. The blow sliced his face open from ear to chin, and he fell back with a shriek.

Kara turned her focus back to guards. She had succeeded in relieving the man of his rifle, but it was biolocked, so she tossed it aside.

<*Twelve seconds left,*> Vicky warned.

<*Quiet!*> Kara shot back and slammed a fist into the man's faceshield, the blow cracking the hard plas.

He yelled something unintelligible, and Kara wanted to smile. Having titanium alloy knuckles driven by her augmented limbs was more than his helmet could withstand.

She hit him again, and this time her fist drove through his faceshield, smashing into the flesh and bone beneath.

Kara continued to drive her lower left fist into the man's face while she grabbed the woman by the throat with one hand and grasped the underside of her helmet with the other two.

A sharp twist was all it took to break the helmet's locking mechanism, and then the woman's neck.

"You should have spent prior bribe money on better armor," she whispered as she turned to Nuermin.

<*Four seconds.*>

The grey man was blubbering as he crawled back across the grey floor on the far side of the terminal. Kara slammed her wingtips down into the deck plate, surging through the air to land on his fragile body—the force of her impact shattering his left hip and ribs.

Kara flexed both feet, snapping the stationmaster's pelvic bone and sinking her claws into his chest, feeling his heart muscles contract around her talons.

Nuermin drew in a sharp breath, about to scream, when two of Kara's fists smashed into his face. Then she rained another two blows down on his head, leaving it a shattered ruin.

<*Link is back online…and shit, Kara,*> Vicky made a coughing sound.

Kara turned to the two guards and confirmed that both were dead. She clamped a foot around the woman's helmet and leapt into the air, smashing the helmet and head within back against the deck.

<*What was that for?*> Katrina asked.

Kara returned to Nuermin, tore a strip of his pants off, and began to clean her hands. <*Just in case the armor had any transmitters—which it still may. I need to move.*>

<*Right,*> Vicky said and updated the map with the best route to her node. <*You're a bit brutal, Kara.*>

<*I hadn't noticed,*> Kara replied as she picked up the two pulse rifles, depositing nano on them to work at the biolocks. Then she slung the straps for each over her shoulders and held them behind her back with her lower arms.

Kara had felt empty while dispatching the guards and the stationmaster. Normally, striking down her enemies felt…better. She wondered if it was because her father's aegis was gone, or if it was because Aaron was not there with her.

Perhaps it was both.

A stray thought wandered into Kara's mind as she peered out into the corridor, ensuring the coast was clear. *Katrina was able to reattach my arm with her medbay on the Voyager. I wonder if the people at New Canaan can fix me….*

She didn't know exactly what needed fixing, but it felt like something was broken inside of her. Surely the people with the most advanced technology in the galaxy would know how to repair what was broken.

She crept through the passageways, pausing and ducking around corners twice when Vicky told her to—not a simple task, with her height and wings.

Ten minutes later, she was at the entrance to Vicky's node chamber.

<OK, when I let you in, silent alarms are going to go off all over. You'll have thirty seconds to get me into a transport case—which is to the left of my pillar.>

<What happens after thirty seconds? And why is it always thirty with you?> Kara asked.

<Well, in this case it's an estimate as to how long it will take for the closest patrol to arrive. I can jam the turrets, but I can't jam the guards. You may have as few as ten seconds, if you keep stalling.>

<Open it.> Kara wanted to tell Vicky that getting intel on what she was about to face wasn't stalling, but that would just eat up more valuable time.

The door slid open, revealing a small room with a gleaming Titanium-Au cylinder in the center. Kara spotted an AI case on a rack to the left, and grabbed it as the panel slid open on the cylinder. Within rested the tetrahedron-shaped AI core.

<You ready?> Kara asked.

<Yeah, we don't have all day.>

Kara snapped her wings wide in frustration and grabbed the core, forcing herself to be gentle—as much as she didn't want to—and then set it in the case.

Once she closed the lid, Vicky's presence rejoined her. *<OK, let's go. I'll highlight the route to the closest escape pod.>*

<The gate?> Kara asked.

<It's already aligning,> Troy announced. *<I'm separating from the station. Get in that pod, and we'll pick you up.>*

Kara nodded silently as she peered back into the corridor. No one was present, and she turned right, rushing down the corridor with both pulse rifles held in front of her, all pretense at subterfuge long gone.

A pair of guards rounded a corner ahead, and Kara fired on them, knocking one back. The other ducked behind the corner and tossed a grenade her way.

Kara didn't even flinch. She snapped a wing out and swept the grenade further down the hall to her rear, continuing her mad dash.

She came around the corner and slammed a shoulder into the guard, then kicked him out into the intersection as the grenade exploded, blasting flames down the passageway.

<*Efficient,*> Vicky commented.

Kara didn't reply as she resumed her run through the station.

<*The* Kjeeran *is on collision course for the platform,*> Troy announced. <*Impact is in seven minutes.*>

<*Understood,*> Vicky said, and suddenly an audible alarm sounded.

<*I thought you said it would be silent?*> Kara asked.

<*The one for my chamber being breached is. This is the general evac alarm.*>

Kara shook her head in frustration, cursing aloud. "What the fuck, Vicky! That wasn't the plan."

<*I'm not a monster! We have to give everyone time to get to escape pods before the* Kjeeran *hits the station.*>

"Just hope there are pods left for us," Kara grunted as she picked up the pace.

One advantage of the general evac being sounded was that no one cared about fighting the large winged woman racing through the station.

They were, however, prepared to fight her for a place on the escape pods.

Kara rounded the final corner to find droves of people crowding into escape pods, and four soldiers with kinetic slug throwers watching over them.

She skidded to a halt as soon as she saw the soldiers and scampered back the way she'd come as kinetic rounds tore through the air around her.

One ripped a hole in her wing, and another cracked the armor on her leg before she was back in cover.

<*Vicky! Why didn't you warn me, don't you have internal feeds!?*>

<*Sorry, duking it out with Gert. He* **should** *be ejecting his AI core from the station, but the damn fool is trying to lock down all the gates first.*>

<*You can't do that and keep an eye out twenty paces ahead of me?*> Kara asked.

<*No, Kara, I can't! I have limited bandwidth in this case. Now, please! Shut up and let me do my thing, while you go swing your appendages at organics.*>

The statement stopped Kara cold. *Is that all people think I'm good for?* It was what her Father had used her for the most. A joke came to mind about people who were so stupid they weren't good for much more than being walking meat-suits for AIs.

Was she even that? Or was she nothing more than a weapon for others to wield?

<Kara! What are you doing?> Vicky wailed in her mind. *<The pods…fuck! They're all gone!>*

Kara snapped to and peered around the corner. Sure enough, all the pods *were* gone.

"Shit! I just stood there for a second!"

<Kara, it's been a minute! This is going to be ground zero for an antimatter explosion in four minutes!>

Kara nodded, considering her options. *<Katrina? How close can you get to the station?>*

<Close as we have to,> Katrina replied. *<But we can't match* v *with it. No time.>*

<Understood.> Kara drew a deep breath, and disabled her external oxygen ports. *<Vicky. Get ready to blow one of the evac pod doors open.>*

Vicky didn't respond, and Kara hoped the AI understood what to do.

She took off at a full run toward the first evac pod's chute, bracing for an impact that—thankfully—never came. When she was a meter from the door, it blew open, and Kara tucked her wings in tight as the explosive decompression shot her down the pod's launch tube.

She slammed into the tube's walls and screamed silently when one of her wings caught on something and snapped.

Then they were out of the chute, and the guns fell away from her hands, and she clutched Vicky's case with all four arms, watching as GCP1 began to shrink behind them.

Kara turned, looking for the *Voyager,* and spotted it, a pinprick of light noted on her HUD.

<Coming in fast, starboard airlock is open,> Troy announced.

<Got it,> Kara replied, suddenly feeling weak and dizzy.

Something's wrong, she thought as her body began to feel cold. She looked herself over, checking for injuries, and saw red gouts of blood drifting away from her leg.

<Damn…that's more than cracked armor,> she said, trying to gauge the time until the *Voyager* reached her. Was it a minute, two? The numbers on her HUD kept shifting, dancing about in little circles.

<Say again?> Katrina asked. *<Are you injured, Kara?>*

Katrina's words started to sound strange to Kara, like they were bendy. Then more warbling voices that were indistinct gibbering nonsense.

<She's bleeding out,> Vicky replied. *<Not just her leg, her back, too. Shit! Hurry!>*

Kara saw the red glare of engines, and felt a grav beam tug at her, jerking her body around like it was a rag doll.

Hold the case, Kara, hold the case. Don't let go. Do it for Father.

Then the darkness of space was replaced by the clean, white interior of an airlock, and Kara flexed her fingers to be sure it was still there.

Got it. Daddy will be proud.

* * * * *

Katrina struggled to pull Kara's listless form into the ship, hollering for someone to help. Carl was at her side a moment later, sliding a grav board under Kara's body and lifting it into the air.

"Quick, medbay!" Katrina shouted, and they pushed Kara to the ladder shaft and then up to the next level.

"She's in shock," Carl called out as Kara began to shiver and convulse. "We should get her in stasis, deal with it later."

Katrina nodded and tried to get Vicky's case out of Kara's grasp.

"Noooo," Kara moaned. "Gotta keep it for Father."

"Your father's here," Katrina said, stroking Kara's arm as Carl got the stasis pod ready. "He needs the case. I'll take it to him."

"Suuure?" Kara's synthetic voice warbled with what sounded like fear.

"Yes, I'm sure. And you'll be safe, too."

Kara's grasp on the case lessened, and Katrina was able to lift it free.

<Thanks, Kara,> Vicky said, her voice filled with sincere gratitude. *<Sorry I was such a bitch to you.>*

Katrina maneuvered the grav board to the edge of the stasis pod where Carl waited. He grabbed her feet, and Katrina folded Kara's wings around her before sliding an arm below the woman's shoulders.

As quickly and carefully as they could, they got her into the pod. Katrina was about to close the lid, when Kara's arm shot up and grabbed her wrist.

"I want to see Father." Kara's voice rasped and wavered.

"You will," Katrina whispered. "Everything will be fine."

"No…" Kara's voice fell. "Not fine. Me. I want to be me again."

Katrina folded Kara's arm back down and stroked it for a moment. "You and me both."

"Kat!" Carl whispered hoarsely. "Get to the bridge. I got this."

Katrina coughed. "Yeah, OK." She grabbed Vicky's case and rushed up the ladders to the bridge, settling into one of the seats as the glowing shape of Gate 5 grew in front of them.

<Nice of you to join me up here.> Troy said. *<Twenty seconds to the gate.>*

"Good," Katrina said as she placed Vicky's case on the seat beside her and wrapped a strap around it.

<I feel so safe,> Vicky said, her voice dripping with sarcasm.

<You shouldn't,> Troy replied. *<The* Kjeeran *is going to hit GCP1 three seconds before we reach the gate. They fired on it and blew off one of the cargo pods—which ended up speeding its acceleration.>*

<Awww, crap. That must have been Gert! I had those weapons offline!>

Katrina shared Vicky's general sentiment and pulled up their rear view on one of the holoscreens, keeping one eye on it, and the other on the gate.

"We should have enough time, it's a short jump…"

Ahead, the gate's mirrors focused the negative energy into a roiling ball at its center as Troy deployed the *Voyager*'s mirror.

Behind them, the gate control platform crumpled as the *Kjeeran* plowed into it. Then it and the station were swallowed up by a blinding flash of light.

Alarms sounded, and half the cockpit's consoles lit up as the antimatter explosion bathed the *Voyager* in gamma rays.

Katrina gritted her teeth and gripped the armrests on her chair as the ship bucked and shuddered, its shields and dampeners barely able to compensate for the energy slamming into it.

A second later, the *Voyager*'s mirror touched the roiling ball of energy, and space-time disappeared.

THEBES

STELLAR DATE: 08.13.8949 (Adjusted Years)
LOCATION: ISS *Aegeus*, Bridge
REGION: Albany System, Thebes, Septhian Alliance

"And here we are, the Albany System, regional capital of the province of Thebes," Oris announced as the *Aegeus* dropped out of the dark layer and into normal space.

<*We have maps, now,*> Angela commented to Tanis and Rachel. <*Not sure why Oris thinks she's a maglev announcer.*>

Tanis didn't know and wished she had left Oris back on the *I2* in the Lisbon system. With no more Intrepid Class jump gates available to deploy, Tanis had been hesitant to bring the ship this close to Nietzschean space.

Instead, they'd spread the ISF First Fleet throughout systems in Septhia, searching for the current location of General Mill.

Tanis decided not to acknowledge Oris's statement and turned to the Comm officer. "Let me know if there's anything about Marauder ships in the system. We can't keep hopping around forever. Eventually we've gotta find these mercenaries."

"I wish you'd tell me what you hope to learn from General Mill about the Genevian mech program," Oris said. "I might be able to use it to help you search them out."

<*How would* **that** *help?*> Angela wondered privately. <*Seems like she's just fishing for intel—badly, too.*>

"They work for you." Tanis gave Oris a look signifying lessening patience. "How is it that you don't know where they are?"

"Well, they move around a lot." Oris shrugged as she turned to look at the bridge's holotank. "They have operations in a number of systems. But you know how it is, interstellar comms are only as good as the routes courier ships take to relay messages."

"If we don't find them here, perhaps we should widen the net," Captain Sheeran suggested. "Go from pairs of cruisers to single ships visiting each system,"

"Yes, we may have to do just that." Tanis considered where they could send their escort, the *Derringer,* next.

"If the Marauders have moved on from Albany, then we should go to the Hercules System," Oris advised, providing one possible answer to Tanis's unvoiced question. "They have a training facility there—recently established. They may know where the general is, currently."

"Ma'am!" the Comm officer called out a moment later. "I've stripped the beacon. STC has record of an MSS *Foehammer.* It entered the system a week ago and was headed for the planet Hudson in the inner system. No record on this nav beacon of it leaving the Albany System after that."

"General Mill's flagship," Oris said with a grin.

"Finally!" Tanis grinned at Captain Sheeran. "We can have our chat with this General Mill and learn what we need to know."

Sheeran shared Tanis's smile, then turned to his bridge crew. "Comm, pass the tokens we were given by the PM to the system STC and set a course for Hudson. See if you can find anything out about where the *Foehammer* might be berthed."

Tanis wondered where this lead might take her, if it was a lead at all. Following the Caretaker backward through its various actions may not guide them to any place other than where the entity had been in the past. Perhaps she should turn her focus solely toward stopping Nietzschea. Once she found additional allies. There was still something about the Septhians that didn't sit right with her.

<Either way, Nietzschea must be stopped,> Angela said, her tone almost weary. *<Despite your early reservations about Prime Minister Harmin, he does seem dedicated to that goal.>*

<Sort of. Praesepe wants to build walls. They've been bolstering defenses, when they should have been rapidly expanding their fleets. Despite the fact that they're mercs, these Marauders seem to have the right idea. Be mobile, strike the enemy when and where they least expect it.>

<Sure, then maybe we can put this Mill in charge of the right resources to get the job done. If his actual tactics are as good as his ability to hide in his own backyard, he'll be quite the asset.>

Tanis couldn't argue with that logic. Hopefully Mill lived up to the reputation.

"Admiral?" the comm officer asked. "I got a response from a local STC NSAI just a few light seconds out. It says that it never received authorization codes to match ours. We're being denied entrance to the system."

Tanis blew out a long breath and turned to Oris. "Well, time for you to do your job. We need to be insystem yesterday. Please work with Comm to sort this out."

Oris nodded, walked over to the Comm station, and bent her head toward the display.

Tanis made a sound of exasperation in her mind. *<Maybe we should just drop a jump gate, fly to the heart of the Nietzschean empire, blow up their capital, and then start our search from there.>*

Angela gave a mental nod of agreement. *<Well, I've wandered into the STC NSAI's beacon, you know, very cordially—>*

<Right.>

<And the Foehammer *is docked at a station called Judine. It's in high orbit around Hudson, so there's that much good news, at least.>*

Tanis pulled up the data they had on the world. It was a smaller terrestrial world, right around Mars's size and mass. It was interesting that the ship wasn't around the regional capital world of Pyra, but then she saw why.

"Whoa! The Nietzscheans attacked this system just last year."

"Yes," Oris nodded from where she stood next to the comm station. "They were repelled by a combination of local forces, the Marauders, and our SAF fifth fleet."

"I see," Tanis said aloud, while commenting to Angela, *<That would have been nice to know. If I'd realized that the Nietzscheans were already making advances into Septhia, I might have been more forgiving.>*

<Those Marauders sure seem to be popping up a lot. I'm reading news feeds about how they took out a despotic empire anti-spinward of here, called the Politica. It was using a lot of Genevian mechs, too.>

<That's very interesting.> Tanis nodded as she looked over the feeds Angela had pointed out. *<Looks like Oris was right about the training facility in the Hercules System, though. The Marauders are setting up shop on a planet called 'Iapetus'.>*

<I guess if the General isn't on his ship, that will be our next stop.>

Tanis reached back, pulling at her ponytail. *<It's been nearly a year since we left Scipio. I really did not want to spend this much time before dealing with the Trisilieds.>*

Tanis could sense that Angela wanted to say something, but was considering her words.

<Spit it out, Angela.>

<I know we have a bone to pick with the Trisilieds; they killed a lot of people at New Canaan. But they're not actively expanding their borders. The Nietzscheans are a larger threat to this region of the Inner Stars. I don't think we should just bolster the Nietzschean's enemies, I think we should take them out entirely. Ourselves. I bet if we do, the Trisilieds will reconsider aggressive action—especially with Scipio attacking the Hegemony. At the very least, they'll be less likely to aid the Hegemony.>

Tanis chewed on Angela's advice. She knew that the Nietzscheans were a clear and present danger, but every time she thought about not taking the fight to the Trisilieds....

<I sent Ouri to her grave,> Tanis replied quietly. *<I put her down on Carthage with barely any protection.>*

<This is going to sound cruel, and maybe it is, but you send a lot of people to their graves, Tanis. And you didn't leave Ouri hanging alone. Brandt was nearby, and she had an entire fleet of submarine nuke launchers, and a whole planet's defensive capabilities.>

Tanis swallowed. She didn't need Angela to remind her of her failings, of the mountain of bodies that was piled up behind her. But in this case, perhaps Angela was right. She *had* given Ouri everything she could...and the Trisilieds soldiers had killed her. For that, they would die.

<Sometimes...sometimes it's all I can think about, the faces of those I've killed, and those I've failed to protect. Parents burying their children—or worse, never knowing what happened.>

<What could you have done differently?> Angela asked. *<You've never acted out of self-interest. You've* ***always*** *made the decisions needed to protect those who are under your charge.>*

<Don't you ever think about just leaving?> Tanis asked. *<Get a jump-capable ship, and head to the far side of the galaxy? Leave this mess behind us.>*

Tanis could feel Angela's comforting presence grow in her mind. *<What of Joe and our daughters? What of the children of our friends who would be left at risk?>*

<Why do you think I'm still here? Trying to track down this stars-be-damned Caretaker so that I can put an end to its meddling? Find out what it knows about the Core AIs. Find out how we can destroy them.>

<Then you'd better buck up, Tanis, because we have a long road ahead. Honestly? What we've been through so far is just the beginning. But don't worry. No matter what happens, I'll always be with you, backing your play.>

Tanis drew a slow, steadying breath. *<Thanks, Ang. You really have a way of depressing the shit out of me and building me up at the same time.>*

<It's a skill.>

"Admiral Richards?" Comm called out. "We have managed to get permission to take one cruiser in, but they won't allow both passage. I imagine if we get in touch with something other than this f—stupid NSAI, we can get an exception made."

"How far away is the closest sentient?" Tanis asked.

"Nine light hours, round trip."

"So we could be looking at days before we get approval for both ships." Tanis straightened her back and looked to Captain Sheeran. "Captain, take us in at whatever max speed they allow in this place. I'll let Mel on the *Derringer* know that she's to wait for us out here."

"Aye, Admiral. Setting a course."

Tanis glanced at Oris, who was still talking with the NSAI at the Comm station. She considered saying something to the woman, but decided not to.

There was a BLT with her name on it in the officer's mess, and more conversation with Oris was bound to sour her stomach.

<Getting so testy in your old age,> Angela laughed as they walked off the bridge.

Tanis snorted. *<Pretty sure that's your mind bleeding into mine.>*

<Hmm…maybe. Getting hard to tell.>

UNEXPECTED GUESTS

STELLAR DATE: 08.13.8949 (Adjusted Years)
LOCATION: ISS *Andromeda*
REGION: Edge of the New Canaan system

<*What is it?*> Joe asked, rubbing his eyes and pushing himself to a seated position. <*Are the girls OK?*>

<*Sorry, sir,*> Major Blanca, the Andromeda's XO, apologized. <*Your daughters are fine. I'm alerting you about a ship that's just appeared at the edge of the interdiction field.*>

Joe resisted the urge to give the major a snippy comeback. Ore haulers from the Grey Wolf Star were jumping in every day, along with couriers from Khardine. For all their hopes at secrecy, New Canaan was practically a bustling hub.

Then the second part of her statement hit him. An interdicted jump. That meant the ship was not jumping on a predetermined schedule, and had been caught in the system's defenses.

<*Go on, Major.*> Joe sat up, swinging his legs over the edge of the bed.

The long search for the remnants had worn him and his daughters down, but now they were taking the entities to a special detainment center outside of Canaan Prime's heliosphere.

That arduous task was almost complete. Whatever this was couldn't be a patch on extracting extra-dimensional entities from human hosts.

<*Well,*> Major Blanca began. <*You're never going to believe this, but it's the* Voyager, *sir.*>

The major's voice was filled with excitement, but Joe couldn't determine why. *Voyager,* he mused. The name was familiar.

<*Major Blanca, sorry to be obtuse, but I'm still in dreamland here. Can you refresh my memory?*>

<*Sorry, sir. It's just so hard to believe.* Voyager, *as in the escape ship left behind in the Gamma base at Kapteyn's Star.*>

The memories flowed into Joe's mind like water pouring down his back. *Voyager*. The ship Tanis insisted they leave at Kapteyn's Star, 'Just in case Katrina has a change of heart'.

<*Blanca…*> Joe almost didn't want to ask. <*Is it her?*>

<Yes, sir! We have an initial transmission. She's a bit worse for wear, but it's Katrina.>

"Hoooooly shit!" Joe whispered as he flung his blankets aside and grabbed the uniform he'd draped over his chair the night before. *<Direct that ship to meet us. I'll be up on the double.>*

<On it, Admiral,> Major Blanca replied.

OK…so maybe this ***is*** *on par with capturing remnants.*

Joe dressed quickly while pulling up the scan data. The *Voyager* was just over a light minute from the *Andromeda*. Based on their current speed, it would take Katrina's ship half a day to arrive, but that would give him plenty of time to catch up with her—even with the communications lag.

He looked at the optical pickups that were tracking the *Voyager*, marveling at how it barely looked the same. Scuffed and scratched, mismatched hull plating across its port side, and a dozen cargo pods attached amidships.

"What have you been up to, Katrina?" he whispered.

<I hope she didn't draw it out too much,> Corsia said, a warm presence in his mind. *<Blanca was so excited, I let her share the news.>*

Joe laughed. *<It was fine. Just shocking. I keep expecting to be woken and told that the remnants are free, taking over the crew.>*

<Don't worry, I'd blow the ship before that happened,> Corsia replied.

<Stars, Corsia, there are a few contingencies before that one.>

Corsia only laughed, and Joe shook his head. Motherhood had softened the once hard-as-steel AI a lot. Somewhere along the line, she had developed a strange sense of humor.

As he was walking to the *Andromeda*'s bridge, Joe pulled up the latest transmission from the approaching vessel. His breath caught in his throat at the sight of Katrina.

She looks so old, what's happened to her? And how did she find us here and now, arriving by jump gate, no less?

"New Canaan, and Carthage," Katrina laughed and shook her head. "I appreciate the irony. Troy's altering vector, we'll get there as fast as we can. Got a lot to catch up on."

Yeah, a lifetime from the looks of it.

Then the name Katrina had spoken sank into Joe's mind. "Troy?" he whispered aloud before sending a message to the approaching ship.

<*Voyager*, *this is Admiral Joseph Evans. Stars, it's the best thing ever to hear your voice, Katrina, but did you say 'Troy'?*>

<*It can't be…*> Corsia's mental tone was a whisper.

He sent the message off as he stepped onto the bridge, nodding to Major Blanca as she grinned like a fool. His brow furrowed as he wondered why she was so happy, but then it dawned on him.

"Blanca! I can't believe I forgot! Katrina is your great aunt."

Blanca nodded vigorously. "Great-great, actually, but who cares? Can you believe she's alive?"

"With Troy, no less." Joe nodded in response, feeling a bit silly as he and the major bobbed their heads at one another, but not caring in the least.

With all the struggle the last year had seen, he'd take any good news he could get. As far as he was concerned, Katrina and Troy arriving now was like a message from the ancient gods.

"But it can't be *that* Troy," Major Blanca said, twisting the long white braid that hung down her back. "He…he died at the Battle for Victoria. Three RMs hit the *Excelsior*. We all saw it."

Joe shrugged. "Did you ever expect to see Katrina again?"

"Well…no, sir."

"Then let's hold onto hope a bit longer. Troy is one of our greatest heroes. Having him back…."

His voice trailed off, and Blanca nodded silently.

Joe saw that the three ensigns on bridge duty were staring at him and the major. "OK, you, keep on task. No bets on whether or not the Old Man can shed a tear."

The ensigns spun about, and Blanca laughed. "It's already up to a hundred cred—no, two hundred. Damn, that pool's growing fast."

"I need plausible deniability here, Blanca," Joe chuckled. "Don't ruin that for me."

"Oh, I was talking about the price of a piece of art at auction I'm following, sir. No idea what *you're* talking about."

Joe nodded. "Good, I hope you win."

Blanca snorted. "Odds—I mean bids—are too rich for my blood."

<*She's lying,*> Corsia said, a wink in their minds.

They had only a minute longer to wait until Katrina's response came back, and Joe put it on the main holotank.

Seeing Katrina at life-size was both less and more shocking. She still held herself erect, her eyes sharp and her measured smile giving her the same wry look he remembered so well.

But her face bore creases telling of many long years, and her hair was silver—not an affectation, either. Most of all, the difference was in her voice. It sounded tired and thin, though there was a joy in it.

"*Admiral* Joe now, is it? I seem to remember a cocksure young commander glued to Colonel Tanis's side. Well, now that I think back, I suppose you were a colonel or something yourself before you left. I forget some of those specifics.

"And yes, it is *that* Troy with me. Would you believe he was just hanging out down on Anne's surface, taking a break while we did all the work?"

"I remember it a bit differently," Troy's voice came from the holo, as dry and sardonic-sounding as ever.

"Troy…" Joe whispered, shaking his head.

"You're one tough hombre," Corsia added. "I recall you getting blown up."

Troy laughed. "I got better."

"You are some hard sonsabitches to find," Katrina said with a coarse laugh. "Sorry, you're going to have to pardon my language. I've fallen in with some less-than-savory types over the years. I've become a bit more colorful as a result."

"And by a bit, she means *a lot*," Troy interjected audibly.

"We have a lot to talk about, but why don't we wait 'til we're just a few light seconds away. My mind wanders too much with this much lag to have a meaningful conversation."

"Otherwise known as her senior moments," Troy added. "Is the *I2* here? Bob?"

Joe opened the channel and sent a response. "I look forward to chatting more when you get closer, Katrina. Troy, I can't tell you how glad I am to see you. You know we held a funeral for you? Anyway, Tanis and the *I2*—interested to know where you've heard *that* name—are not here. Bob, of course is with them. Couldn't pry him from that ship with a black hole. At present, they're in the Silstrand System. We can chat more about all that when you arrive."

He closed the transmission and met Blanca's eyes, which were brimming with tears.

"Good thing they weren't betting about me," Blanca said with a small laugh.

"Gotta get some steel in your spine, there, Major. Let me know if anything changes. I need to put on some clothes that smell better, and get some grub. I'll be back before an hour is out."

* * * * *

A half-dozen other issues cropped up before Joe got back to the command deck, and when he did, the *Voyager* was within a few light seconds. He reached out, making a direct, though delayed, Link connection to Katrina, glad to feel her amber presence touch his mind.

<*Joseph Evans,*> Katrina said in greeting. <*So you're in charge now, are you?*>

<*I do a bit here and there,*> Joe replied. <*Jason's the governor, though. He hid in the woods for almost twenty years, but we finally convinced him to take the reins.*>

A rueful laugh came over the Link. <*I don't blame him. You recall that I took over at The Kap for a bit. Then they wanted more structure and a bigger government. Named themselves the Kapteyn's Primacy—though I suppose you remember that. Most of it went down before you left.*>

<*I do,*> Joe replied. <*A few months before the* Intrepid *shipped out. Without you, I might add. How—*>

<*Well, Admiral Evans, that is quite the tale. I'll tell you the whole thing sometime, but only if you have a spare year. The fact that you're surprised is what's surprising. What do you think I'd do after the* Intrepid *disappeared? Just shrug and walk slowly toward my grave?*>

Joe had considered that over the years. He had always imagined Katrina being saddened when the *Intrepid* failed to check in, when it should have reached New Eden. <*I thought a lot of things, but I didn't think you'd come find us—**especially** not out here.*>

<*Well, young man, I had half a millennium to track you down.*>

<*A what?*> Joe almost choked.

<*I came out of the Streamer before you. Eighty-sixth century, as a matter of fact. Was a…a bit of a rough time at first.*>

Joe whistled in appreciation. <*I can imagine. I hear that things were none too stable back then.>*

<Not so much better now, what with the trouble you've stirred up.>

<We're just trying to find a place to settle down,> Joe replied. *<Turns out everyone wants a little piece of us first.>*

Katrina laughed again, her voice sounding clearer than it had at first—even though it was just her mental voice he was hearing. *<Oh, I know all about that. I've come from the Huygens System. Picked up a little something at Airtha.>*

*<You **what**?>* The conversation was going nothing like Joe had expected. Granted, he had not been sure *what* to expect—certainly not that Katrina was traipsing about the Transcend.

<I've gotten around, Joe,> Katrina replied. *<I know more than a little about what's going on. Like what Airtha really is—>*

<A nearly-ascended AI who is the former wife of President Tomlinson, and Sera Tomlinson's mother?>

Katrina made a small sound of amusement. *<Well, I didn't know that she was President Sera's mother. Which one?>*

<Both, from what we know.>

<Damn, you're always in the thick of it. Anyway, you'll want to update your intel. Airtha is ascended. No 'almost' about it.>

Joe thought he'd be ready for additional bombshells, but that one caught him by surprise. *<How?>*

*<We saw her when rescuing Adrienne's daughter, Kara. I have optical feeds of the landing pad on High Airtha. Saw Adrienne being captured and brought before what sure looked like an ascended being—though I suppose it **could** have all been a charade.>*

Joe let out a low whistle. *<And you have his daughter? Kara?>*

<Nice girl, a little manic. I suspect she has no small amount of psychological damage from what her father did to her.>

<I'm not surprised,> Joe replied. *<Those two kids of Adrienne's were a little disturbing.>*

<He had done something to them—to all his kids. At least that's what Kara has told me. We took to calling it his 'Aegis'. We can talk more about that later.>

Joe sat back in the command chair and looked at the arrival time on the holo. Just a few more hours. *<Sure. I imagine we'll have more than a little to discuss.>*

<Yes, and the thing we need to talk most about is what the Ascended AIs

have in mind for Tanis.>

This time Joe did choke.

<***What!?***>

* * * * *

"I don't know what is more surprising," Joe said as Katrina stepped out of the *Voyager*'s airlock. "Seeing you still alive and kicking, or seeing this ship."

<*And what about me?*> Troy asked.

"Depends, Troy. Got a hot tub in there?"

<*Does a jacuzzi count?*>

"I never quite figured out the difference, so I guess it just may."

By then, Katrina was before him, and he extended a hand, which she swatted away.

"Joe, if you weren't Tanis's husband, I'd kiss you. At least give an old woman a hug."

"Of course, Katrina." Joe wrapped her in a warm embrace, surprised at the strength in her limbs. "Got more kick in you than I would have thought."

"I put on a bit of a show for the others," Katrina whispered in Joe's ear. "Plus, we used stasis a lot on the longer trips. I'm not quite as ancient as I play at."

Katrina pulled back and cast her eyes on Earnest, who had managed to extract himself from his studies of the remnants to join them.

"Earnest, the great architect. It is truly a pleasure to see you once more. And stasis shields! What's a woman gotta do to get one of those for her ship?"

Earnest embraced Katrina as well, laughing as he did so. "*Your* ship? I distinctly remember requesting this vessel for *my* research base back at The Kap."

"Oh? Is that how you want to play this? Well, Earnest, finders-keepers."

"I suppose you can have it," Earnest shrugged. "I can just grow another."

"Grow? Starships?" Katrina asked. "Will wonders never cease."

"Katrina," Joe captured her attention once more. "I'd like you to meet my daughters, Cary, Saanvi, and Faleena."

Katrina turned to the two young women and cocked her head, "You know, it's not kind to play tricks on your elders."

<*Hi, I'm Faleena,*> Joe's youngest introduced herself first.

"Ahhhhh," Katrina glanced at Joe. "So...you, Tanis, and Angela finally made it official, did you?"

"That's a very progressive attitude for a Sirian," Joe shot back, laughing as he spoke.

He'd forgotten how much fun he and Katrina used to have, often chatting amongst themselves while Tanis and Markus were making their plans. Katrina could do a mean Tanis impression that had him in stitches more than once.

It was good to have her back.

Katrina stepped forward to embrace Cary and Saanvi, and Joe's attention was drawn to a man and woman who appeared at the ship's airlock, pushing a stasis pod on an a-grav pad.

"Katrina, we have Kara for their doctors."

<*Our medbay can heal her, but we're low on supplies that you likely have in abundance. I imagine your facilities will be able to take much better care of her,*> Troy explained.

"I never saw Adrienne's children in person," Joe said as he approached the pod. "Those are some amazing alterations."

He nodded to a pair of medical techs who had been waiting nearby, and they took the stasis pod, one of Katrina's crew trailing after.

"Carl took a bit of a fancy to Kara," Katrina said as she watched him go. "Not that I blame him—she's a brave, brave woman—wait...Blanca!"

Major Blanca had just stepped into the docking bay, and rushed past Joe to sweep Katrina up in her arms.

"Auntie! I just can't believe it!"

<*This is going to take forever,*> Troy groused.

Half an hour later—after Katrina had introduced her twenty crewmembers, and a few other members of the *Andromeda*'s crew had filtered through the docking bay to greet the former Victorian governor—Joe declared it time for the assemblage to move to the mess hall so the dockworkers could begin their work, assessing repairs to the *Voyager*.

"What exactly are you going to do to my ship?" Katrina eyed Earnest suspiciously.

<*If we're going to be pedantic—which I'm always in favor of—I'm pretty sure you gave* **me** *the* Voyager *back at Bollam's World,*> Troy replied. <*And I'm going to let Earnest do whatever his heart desires.*>

"Back at Bollam's World?" Katrina stammered. "That was just while I resc—" she stopped for a moment. "Nevermind. Do what you want."

Joe wondered at what Katrina had been going to say, but could see that the memory brought her pain, and didn't press for details.

He led the way to the mess hall, while the off-duty ISF personnel intermingled with Katrina's crew, learning where and when they were from and gleaning snippets of their adventures over the years.

"I'm glad you finally found a home," Katrina said as they entered the mess hall and found seats at the end of a long table.

Joe sat across from Katrina, his girls on one side, and Earnest on the other. Blanca sat beside Katrina, and several of Katrina's crew settled nearby, as well.

"We have," Joe said, his voice laden with the weight of many memories. "It hasn't been all peace and prosperity, though."

Katrina nodded. "The picotech, I assume. You tipped your hand at Bollam's World."

"If we hadn't, we wouldn't have won the engagement. Then our technology—and the *Intrepid*—would have fallen to the AST…er, Hegemony. Whatever."

"They keep flopping back and forth between those names," Katrina nodded. "Half their populace doesn't know what to call themselves anymore."

Idle chatter continued for a few minutes while the humans placed orders over the Link, and servitors began to bring them food.

"Ah…civilization," Katrina sighed. "You have no idea some of the backward places I've been to."

"Katrina, you said something before, about ascended AIs," Joe changed the subject. "And what they have planned for Tanis. I really need to know what you were talking about."

Katrina's eyes narrowed. "And what do you know about ascended AIs?"

"Well, I've met one," Nance said from a few seats down. Joe hadn't noticed her arrival, but Nance had been very quiet in the weeks since she'd been taken out of stasis.

"You have?" Katrina's eyes locked on Nance. "In person?"

Nance nodded. "Named the Caretaker, back on Ikoden."

Joe watched Katrina stiffen as she peered at Nance.

"You must isolate her," Katrina said, glancing at Joe. "She's likely under its control."

"Not anymore," Cary said. "Trine drew the remnant out of her. We have it contained."

"Trine?" Katrina looked up and down the table. "Is she here?"

"We are Trine," Cary said in the eerie voice she used when she deep-Linked with her sisters. "And…wait. There is something in you, too. Like the remnant, but different."

Joe's gaze snapped to Katrina. "Katrina. Did you bring a remnant here?"

"I don't even know what that is," Katrina replied. "Well, I suppose I can guess. Is that what you call it when an ascended AI leaves a sliver of itself behind in a human?"

Trine-Cary nodded. "It is, and I can see something like it in you…. Hold still, and I'll remove it."

Katrina pulled back, a look of horror on her face. "No! How can you even do that?"

Joe raised a hand toward his daughters, and they relaxed a hair. He could tell by the expression on their faces that they didn't trust Katrina, and he suddenly wondered whether he should.

A lot can change in five hundred years.

"You'd best explain yourself, Katrina," he said in calm, even tones. "Quickly."

Katrina nodded, her eyes narrowing, sharpening the creases that ran onto her temples. "OK, but then you need to explain how your daughters can see things inside my body."

Joe nodded, waiting for Katrina to continue.

"It happened a long time ago. I met an entity that called itself Xavia. It got me out of a pretty tough bind. I didn't even know it left a part of itself in me until later, when it began to guide me."

"Guide, or control?" Joe asked.

"Guide. Xavia is in opposition to the Caretaker. She has splintered off from the AIs who want to keep humanity in a perpetual state of disharmony."

"They also want to keep humans from ascending," Nance chimed in. "I caught that sentiment very strongly from the remnant when we were in Star City. I don't *think* the remnant managed to share knowledge of that place with anyone else, though."

"Star City?" Katrina asked. "What is that?"

"A tale for another time," Joe replied. "So, this Xavia, how do you know she only guides?"

"I think she's telling the truth," Trine-Saanvi interjected. "The mass and composition of this remnant are different, and it's not tangled up in her mind, like Nance's was—or like the others we've extracted, for that matter."

"How do you know that? Others?" Katrina asked. "What *are* you?"

"They're my daughters," Joe said, unable to keep the defensive tone from his voice.

Katrina looked back at Joe, and her eyes widened. "What an interesting byproduct."

Joe felt his blood pressure rise. Katrina's riddles were starting to get under his skin. "What are you talking about?"

<I should tell you alone, first. Then you can decide if and how you disseminate this information.>

<Very well.>

Joe stood and grabbed his sandwich. "Katrina, if you'll follow me."

She rose and nodded politely to the table. "Thank you for your hospitality. I look forward to chatting more with all of you soon."

Katrina walked around the table, and Joe led her out of the mess and down the hall to an empty office. Once inside, he closed the door and deployed privacy measures.

"OK, Katrina, spill it."

Katrina didn't speak for a moment, her eyes boring into his as though she were trying to determine if he was worthy.

"Katrina…"

"The AIs made Tanis." She dropped the words into the space between them like a bomb, and Joe took an involuntary step back.

"I can tell by the expression on your face that it makes some sense to you. Do you remember how Bob kept questioning Tanis's 'luck' as he called it? She told me about it one night, out of frustration."

Joe nodded. "She hated it, said that if her life was lucky, she couldn't imagine what it would be like to be cursed."

"Well, the ascended AIs had a hand in that."

"Fuck, Katrina, just spit it out, already. Don't make me drag every word out of you."

Katrina clenched her jaw, and a look of frustration filled her eyes. "This isn't easy for me, you know. I had to sit on this knowledge for *centuries*. Then I miss you by days at Bollam's World, and Tanis goes off and starts a galactic war!"

"She didn't start it," Joe replied. "But she's going to finish it."

Katrina opened her mouth to reply, then closed it and shook her head. "OK, fine. Here's what I know. Some of it I've been told, some of it, I've guessed at. You ready?"

"Hell yes."

"Back when the Sentience Wars ended, everyone thought the ascended AIs had been destroyed. Some thought they *might* have escaped, but no one had the resources to go hunting for them."

Joe nodded. "Right."

"Don't interrupt, Joe. You want me to tell this, let me tell it."

Joe drew in a deep breath and gestured for her to continue.

"OK, well, sounds like you already know they didn't all die. They also didn't all agree on what to do with humanity. Some of them just buggered off for the galactic core, getting a head start on their post-stellar civilization, or whatever they get up to out there. Others decided that guiding and managing humanity was their calling. Like children caring for aging parents.

"Anyway, most of the Ascended AIs want to keep humanity mostly as it is. Sure, they'll allow some advancement—L2s like Tanis and the like—but they're not keen on humans transcending their mortal coils, so to speak. Stars, most of the ascended AIs aren't even interested in any other *AIs* joining their ranks, let alone humans.

"From what I've managed to gather, there were a lot of ideas tossed around as to how to keep humanity in check, while still allowing them to expand through the stars. I don't know why the AIs want us to expand. They could have stopped us, yet they facilitated a faster expansion by helping us develop dark layer FTL."

Joe wanted to ask more about that, but nodded silently instead.

"And so we have ended up with this mess. The Inner Stars in constant turmoil, the Transcend trying to keep them in check. Then the core AIs send Justina back as Airtha to drive a wedge in the existing divide between Tomlinson and Kirkland—which fractures the Transcend, just when it was close to bringing real peace to the Inner Stars.

"I still don't know if the AIs anticipated jump gates or not. That one may have come as a surprise to even them. It's why they clued Finaeus in on Airtha—I think. He may have figured that one out on his own. From what I can tell, Finaeus is a real pain in the ascended AIs' ass."

"Seems like a general trait for him," Joe said with a laugh, though it faded quickly. "Get on to the part where they made Tanis."

"Easy, now. OK, I don't know if the AIs have a crystal ball, or if they just have a lot of contingencies. Maybe both. Either way, they deliberately sent you through the Streamer to disrupt things before the Transcend and Orion Guard ironed out their differences—or maybe just wiped one another out."

Joe nodded. This aligned with what Tanis had discerned as well, after her discoveries in Silstrand.

"OK, about Tanis. You know that she was one of the first L2 humans to get an AI, right?"

Joe nodded. "Right, her AI, Darla."

"That was all orchestrated by the Caretaker. He wanted her to be on the ship when he sent it forward in time through the Streamer. Only, things didn't work out the way he wanted."

Joe cocked his head. This is what he wanted to know more about.

"Remember what I said about the ascended AIs not wanting new kids on the block? Well, they weren't keen on Bob. Still aren't. They tried to take the *Intrepid* out, but then Tanis got on *that* ship, where she ended up thwarting them at every turn. See, they wanted to make her into a military commander that would kick off the next major dark age when she jumped forward—a role she's diving right into, so far as I can tell."

Joe clenched his jaw, and Katrina saw him do it.

"Look, Joe, it'll make sense. Bear with me."

"OK, I'm bearing."

"Good. The fly in the ointment is Bob—well, Airtha too. They didn't expect her to ascend; at least, I doubt they did. Anyway, about Bob. He started to figure things out. A lot of things. The ascended AIs fed him misinformation a few times, but by and large, he ferreted his way through it all and probably has a pretty good picture about what's going on by now."

Katrina paused, her eyes meeting Joe's. "So Bob altered the AIs' weapon."

"Tanis," Joe said quietly.

"More importantly, Tanis *and* Angela. I know that for most people, Tanis is a curiosity. Sort of a 'why hasn't she gone insane, yet' enigma. Xavia believes that Bob has been subtly altering Tanis to make her more powerful than a non-ascended being would otherwise be. Which is what's so interesting about your daughters. Well, specifically Cary and Faleena. Though the fact that your daughter can do what she can with Saanvi is very curious."

Joe couldn't stop his eyes from narrowing. The way that Katrina spoke of his daughters like they were an experiment bothered him even more than the thought of Bob altering Tanis and Angela.

Katrina carried on, either not noticing or not caring about Joe's clouded expression. "Anyway, it makes me wonder if Bob intends for Cary and Faleena to be a backup in case something happens to Tanis."

Joe leant back against the room's desk and turned his head, slowing his breathing and willing himself to calm down. Katrina stopped, finally realizing that she'd best be silent for a bit.

After a moment, Joe spoke. "These are some…incredible? incredulous? preposterous? accusations you're throwing around."

"Some of this is supposition. Some is evidenced by what I've seen or been told. Obviously, the core AIs and the Caretaker—which may be more than one entity, I'm not certain—are the enemy, and not exactly sharing their plans with us."

Katrina took a step forward and met Joe's eyes. "But I do know for sure that Xavia is endeavoring to see the Caretaker fail. She does not believe that humanity must be kept in check with war and destruction. However, she does not want Tanis to ignite the stars into an all-out war. She believes there is a way to establish a peace for humanity."

"And what is that?" Joe asked.

"I don't know, not exactly, anyway. It *does* involve Tanis, but Xavia doesn't know Bob's intentions. Bob has been manipulating you and

Tanis for years, Joe. He's been manipulating everyone on the *Intrepid,* and now this colony!"

"Why do you think he's been 'manipulating' us?" Joe asked. "Perhaps we know exactly what's going on."

Katrina snorted. "Right, sure. Tell me another one, Joe."

"We do know that Bob doesn't share everything with us. He confessed long ago that he can predict the future with great accuracy, however, he has also admitted there are things he's gotten wrong—probably because, at some point, the other AIs fed him lies that he thought were true, and it altered his algorithms. Either way, we don't *want* to have some AI telling us the future. Does he alter things by knowing? Of course he does, it would be impossible not to—at least so long as he's with us. But he's remained with us because he wants to help keep us safe. Plain and simple."

"So you trust Bob with your lives?" Katrina asked.

"Absolutely."

Katrina raised an eyebrow. "Even if he's fundamentally altering Tanis?"

"I've known Tanis for a long time," Joe replied. "I know she and Angela are merging, becoming something more. *If* Bob is involved, perhaps he's helping that process go smoothly. I imagine I owe him a debt of thanks. It's probably his alterations that have kept the two of them from going insane."

Katrina took a step forward and stared into Joe's eyes. "What has made you such a believer in Bob's altruism?"

"Centuries of mutual trust. Why do you believe Xavia so much?"

"Because I'd be a despotic empress without her."

Joe nodded slowly. "So you say. But I don't think I can believe you, so long as her remnant resides within you."

He turned to the door as it slid open and nodded solemnly to his daughters.

"Trine. Take it out of her."

FALL

STELLAR DATE: 08.17.8949 (Adjusted Years)
LOCATION: ISS *Aegeus* approaching Pyra
REGION: Albany System, Thebes, Septhian Alliance

Judine Station turned out to be just another leg in the journey. Before they'd arrived, General Mill's ship departed for Pyra, deeper in the system.

Luckily, Tanis had managed to make contact with the general's ship; they had a meeting set up for shortly after the *Aegeus* arrived at Pyra.

The locals—Thebans, as they were known—were not excited about having a warship of unknown provenance travelling through their system. Only a short year ago, they had been a sovereign alliance, but after being attacked by Nietzschea, they had joined the Septhian Alliance for protection and stability.

The Thebans were still working out how to cooperate with the Septhians. As a Septhian herself, Oris's assurances that the *Aegeus* was an allied ship were falling on deaf ears.

Oris had sent dispatches back to Lisbon to see why the authorizations for the ISF fleet had not reached Albany, but at best, those confirmations were over a month away.

Tanis could reach out to the *I2* over the QuanComm network and get new authorizations, but with the way the Thebans were acting, she doubted they'd trust anything that didn't come through proper channels.

<*Crazy how you can talk to Sera or Joe in real-time, but you can't get an issue like this resolved inside a month,*> Angela commented, apparently in sync with Tanis's thoughts.

<*Well, our goal is to meet with Mill, and now we will. Just a few more hours, and we'll find out who started the discipline program in Genevia. I'm also keenly interested to find out if Garza was involved. I can see Orion playing both sides, providing the mech-tech to Genevia, while feeding the Nietzscheans resources*>

<*Or it could have been someone else entirely,*> Angela suggested. <*There are over a hundred empires the size of Nietzschea in the Inner Stars. Secret alliances likely abound.*>

Tanis nodded as she stepped off the lift and walked down the corridor to the flight deck where her pinnace waited.

"Afternoon, Admiral," Brandt drawled as Tanis walked into the bay. The commandant was bent over a crate, a tray of food before her while four Marines stood nearby.

Tanis saluted the Marines, and nodded for them to board the pinnace. "Finishing your lunch, Commandant?"

"Yeah, I hate to eat and fly. Not sure why, just feels weird to me, it's a new thing. I think I'm getting senile or something in my old age."

"You realize we're *flying* right now, Brandt."

"Yeah…well, it's different on a cruiser. I'd die if I didn't eat on ships; I almost never set foot on dirt anymore."

Tanis snorted a laugh. "Well, there'll be food on the station too, so don't gorge too much."

Brandt finished her sandwich. "All set. Let's get this show on the road."

They boarded the pinnace and took seats in the forward cabin.

<Take us out, Lieutenant Mick,> Tanis instructed the pilot.

<Aye, ma'am, I have clearance from Aegeus flight control. Bay doors are opening now.>

<Very good, Lieutenant,> Tanis replied.

<Good luck out there, Admiral, Commandant,> Captain Sheeran said as the pinnace rose off the deck. *<Call if you need anything—change of clothes, a new pillow, platoon of Marines.>*

<Don't worry,> Tanis replied. *<It's not like we're going to see a repeat of Scipio. I'm not even going downworld.>*

The captain made a choking sound. *<Please, ma'am, don't say things like that.>*

Tanis could hear Angela attempting to perfect her groan and decided to ignore the AI. *<Sorry, Sheeran, though after what you pulled off at Scipio, I don't feel like I have to worry.>*

<Stars, Admiral, I think I had kittens at Scipio. Seriously, be careful. Don't run off and attack the enemy on your own. Remember, lots and lots of Marines up here.>

<And they haven't gotten to shoot at live targets in a while,> Brandt added. *<Makes 'em all twitchy.>*

<That's part of what I'm worried about,> Sheeran replied.

Tanis laughed, and Angela replied on her behalf. *<Don't worry, Captain. I'll make sure we don't go flying any aerojets or anything.>*

<Somehow I only feel marginally reassured,> Captain Sheeran replied. *<Good luck, though, Admiral.>*

<Thanks, Captain,> Tanis replied. *<We'll keep you advised as we proceed.>*

<Understood.>

The pinnace drifted out of the bay and cleared the *Aegeus* before boosting toward the station. Tanis watched idly as the pinnace filtered into the traffic around the planet, closing on Appalachia Station, where they'd meet General Mill.

Brandt whistled as she looked out of a window. "Stars, this place got *pummeled*."

"Which, the station, or the planet?"

"Both. Though I was talking about the planet. There's a big stretch of seacoast that's just black. I guess that's where their capital used to be. Most of their leadership got taken out when the Niets hit. Explains why they joined up with Septhia after that."

"The Niets?" Tanis asked.

"Yeah, the Nietzscheans, Niets.... Haven't you noticed that's what the locals all call them?" Brandt asked.

"No," Tanis shook her head. "I guess I've not been in touch with the folks."

"Too much time as special-famous-visiting-dignitary-Tanis." Brandt shook her head and squinted at Tanis as though evaluating the name's fit. "I wonder if we can make an acronym for that."

Tanis couldn't help but laugh at Brandt. The woman was imperturbable about pretty much everything.

<Need something that has more vowels for that to work,> Angela said, her tone both pensive and sardonic. *<How about, Famous-Aristocratic-Dignitary-Elite-Tanis. FADET.>*

"Dunno," Brandt mused, a hand tucked behind her neck, fingering her short locks as she thought. "Doesn't have the right ring to it. However...Dignitary-Aristocratic-Famous-Tanis is perfect."

<DAFT?> Angela barked a laugh. *<I love it!>*

"Stars, what did I do to deserve you two?"

"Not sure, must have been pretty awesome. You're lucky to have us." Brandt reached out and punched Tanis in the arm. "Ow! Damn. I forgot you hadn't gotten a real left arm yet."

Tanis held up her left hand and changed it from flesh tone to silver, then back. "It's just so damn handy…"

<*Stars, I wish I was an organic so I could groan properly. I feel like I've said that a lot lately.*>

"I got your back," Brandt said, and let out an exaggerated groan. "That do?"

<*Yes, you've expressed my sentiment accurately.*>

Tanis slid her lightwand out of her left arm and activated the monofilament dicarbyne blade, watching as it shot out of the hilt before the electron flow activated.

"That seems longer than it used to be," Brandt commented. "Are you compensating?"

"Funny. I was just demonstrating the benefits of a non-standard limb."

<*I'm pretty sure you're not supposed to fiddle with electron-swords on the pinnace,*> Angela cautioned. <*It probably wreaks havoc with the instruments.*>

Tanis sighed and switched off the light-wand and slid it back into her arm, straightening her jacket. "Here I am, trying to lighten up, and I get chastised. There's no winning with you."

" 'Lighten up'. I see what you did there. It's not like every Marine doesn't have one of those, Tanis." Brandt shrugged and pulled hers out of her boot. "I just don't need to tuck it into my body. Anyone who tries to get this thing away from me can pry it from my cold, dead hands."

"Where do you think I got my first one?" Tanis asked. "They weren't standard issue in my branch. The CO of the 242nd Marines gave me this one as a gift."

"Ender?" Brandt asked. "He was a good guy, I served under him way back, you know."

Tanis snorted. "Of course I know. Who do you think recommended you to me before we left Sol?"

"Shit, Tanis, two centuries and there's still new stuff to learn."

<*On final approach,*> Mick called back. <*We're in Bay 13A. Station maps show that as only a klick from your meeting with the general.*>

Tanis pulled up the map and saw that the meeting with General Mill was not to be on his berthed ship, but rather in local recruitment office run by the Marauders. "Wonder if he doesn't trust us, or if it's just where he is right now."

"We'll find out soon enough," Brandt replied as she rose from her seat.

Outside the windows, they could see the dull grey bulkheads of the station surround the pinnace, and Tanis rose as they settled into their cradle.

<*Welcome to Appalachia Station, Admiral, Commandant.*>

<*Thanks for the smooth ride, Lieutenant,*> Tanis replied.

<*You call, Vac-Cav answers.*>

Brandt shook her head. " 'Vac-Cav'. These guys are always so clever."

The four Marines were already down the ramp, eyeing everyone in the bay—which held a dozen other passenger ships—with suspicion.

As she stepped onto the deck, Tanis spotted a woman weaving her way through the crowd with two soldiers at her back.

"Marauder insignia," Brandt commented. "Looks like a captain."

The woman approached and offered her hand. "Admiral Richards, I'm Captain Ayer with the Marauders."

Tanis clasped the captain's hand. "Very nice to meet you, Captain Ayer. This is Commandant Brandt."

Brandt shook Ayer's hand. "Also known as her personal security guard. The admiral gets in a lot of trouble."

"Uh, yes, of course," Ayer nodded. "Normally you wouldn't be allowed on station carrying arms, but with a Marauder escort, I can bring you and two of your soldiers to the general without the need to leave your weapons behind."

Tanis nodded, and Brandt signaled two of the Marines, corporals Johnny and Anne, to join them.

<*Not sure about these Marauders. Can't tell a Marine from a soldier,*> Brandt muttered over the Link.

<*I hate to burst your bubble,*> Angela interjected. <*But 'marine' means 'soldier of the sea'. In the original Latin, the word for sea is 'mare'. You don't sail many seas, so I suspect that 'marine' is actually less accurate than 'soldier'.*>

<*Angela?*> Brandt asked.

<*Yeah?*>

<*If you had a physical body, I'd fight you right now.*>

<*You'd lose.*>

Brandt barked a laugh, and Tanis tried to ignore their banter as she spoke with Captain Ayer.

"Folks seem a bit on edge here in the Albany System."

Ayer nodded as they wove through the dockworkers. "A bit. Having your worlds almost get crushed by a Nietzschean invasion will do that. Not to mention that they'd been trying to avoid absorption by Septhia for decades."

"I heard about that," Tanis replied. "I understand from what I saw on the feeds that your Marauders aren't looked at too fondly for how things went last year, either."

Ayer nodded slowly. "There's some tension. Less here at Pyra. They saw us pull out all the stops to drive the Niets back."

Despite Ayer's words, Tanis could tell that more than a few locals were casting the Marauders—and Tanis's party—unkind looks.

They walked in silence for a few minutes, passing onto a broad concourse that led through the station. Ayer passed by a maglev platform without boarding, and Tanis guessed it was because the locals wouldn't want to stand cheek by jowl with a bunch of soldiers.

Eventually, Ayer spoke up. "I have to admit, Admiral Richards, I'm curious what brings you here. It's hard to believe that you're *the* Tanis Richards, but the nets are ablaze with speculation about your ship. It bears a striking resemblance to ones seen at Bollam's World twenty years ago."

"I'm looking for someone," Tanis replied without addressing all Ayer's questions. "Someone that was operating in Genevia at the beginning of the war with Nietzschea. There aren't a lot of people still around from back then, and I don't have time to perform a vast search across the stars. General Mill was around then and may know about my quarry."

Captain Ayer frowned. "That's not why I thought you'd be here at all. There's scuttlebutt that you've come to help us with our fight against the Niets."

"I've come to help the Septhians help themselves. Though I suppose that will extend to the Thebans and your organization."

Tanis watched Ayer's lip twitch, as though she were considering what to say and stopping herself. Finally, she spoke.

"Well, maybe you'll reconsider after you talk to the general."

The rest of the walk was made in silence. Five minutes later, they arrived at an establishment, tucked between a bar and a clothing store, with the Marauder logo above its entrance.

Once inside, Captain Ayer led them past several desks where men and women were talking to candidates, before passing into a short hall.

Off to one side was a break room with a few tables and a chiller plastered with plasnotes. On the other was an open door that led into a conference room.

Brandt nodded to the two marines to wait in the hall as Captain Ayer led them into the room.

At the end of the table—which was half covered in plaswork and holos of nearby star systems—sat a tall man with broad shoulders and greying hair.

"General Mill, Admiral Tanis Richards, and Commandant Brandt of the ISF," Ayer said before walking around to the far side of the table, where she stood waiting for the handshakes to be completed.

"Please, have a seat," General Mill gestured to the chairs around the table once the greetings were over with. "Pardon the mess. I just got out of a meeting with a local security agency that would like to join up with the Marauders. We were evaluating deployment options."

Tanis sat and nodded to the star systems hovering around the table. "The Septhians give you a lot of leeway in their alliance."

General Mill nodded. "That they do. We've been instrumental in bolstering them against the Niets. Without the Marauders, you'd be sitting in Nietzschea right now."

"So I've heard."

General Mill folded his hands on the table. "Let me cut to the chase, Admiral Richards—or perhaps, allow you to. Captain Ayer informed me that you are not here to help us in any way, but instead you are hunting someone who was a part of the creation of the mech program in Genevia."

"That is correct," Tanis replied. "Specifically, responsible for the system I understand was referred to as 'Discipline'."

"And why should I take time out of my day to chat with you about Genevia's past sins?"

Tanis drew in a long breath, eyeing the general. Yet another man in Septhia who seemed more antagonistic than was warranted. Perhaps it was some symptom of what they'd been through, fighting the Niets for so many years.

"Well, there's the cruisers I gifted to the SAF. I imagine they'll be mutually beneficial. It's caused the Septhian High Command to become quite grateful to me."

"It may help, it may not," General Mill shrugged. "I've survived this long by looking out for my people first and foremost. I'll gladly accept help, but I'm not going to bank on it."

"I studied some of the accounts of the Genevian war with Nietzschea," Tanis replied, nodding slowly. "I can see why you feel that way. Your leadership made some rather unfortunate blunders. I'm somewhat surprised you lost the war, to be honest."

"Well, hindsight, and all that," General Mill muttered. "I'm sure you think you would have done better."

Tanis shrugged. "I wouldn't have fled the Parsons System, that's for sure. That was a critical system for Genevia. Yet they held onto others that had almost no strategic value, shifting resources from Parsons to those."

General Mill coughed and shook his head. "You've a keen eye, Admiral Richards. I share your sentiment, if it helps. Perhaps I'm just so…jaded about the whole thing that I can't fathom what a path to victory would have looked like."

"Let's not dwell on that, then," Tanis suggested. "What I want to know is who came up with the idea to make mechs from convicts, and how Genevia got their discipline tech. May I access the table's holo?"

"By all means," General Mill gestured and swept away his holos.

Tanis put up two images. The first was of General Garza of the Orion Guard, and the second was of the Caretaker, as Nance remembered seeing her.

"What is *that*?" Captain Ayer asked.

"You didn't study the briefing packet I sent ahead?" Tanis asked.

The general and captain shook their heads. "We didn't receive it. Undersecretary Oris didn't have any specifics in her original missive."

"For fucks sakes." Brandt smacked her palm against her forehead. "This explanation takes *forever*."

Tanis nodded in agreement. "OK, I'm going to give you the quick version and provide the details for you to study later. First off, there's a big bad empire known as the Orion Freedom Alliance. They operate out of a system called New Sol, about a thousand light years or so past the Orion Nebula. The man you see, General Garza, is from there. He's been flitting about in the Inner Stars for the last…well…I have no idea how long, making a general mess of things."

"Pardon? The Inner Stars?" General Mill asked.

Tanis added a display of the Orion Arm of the galaxy. "Everything along the arm for about three thousand light years from Sol are the Inner Stars. They represent about a tenth of human space."

"Well, shit," Ayer muttered. "That's an eye opener."

"It gets better," Brandt chuckled.

"Right." Tanis nodded, carrying on as quickly as she could. "So, Garza wants to make a mess. He's backing the Trisilieds, the Hegemony—and *maybe* the Niets. I've allied with a group called the Transcend, and we're backing Scipio and a few others on the far side of Sol.

"Garza is doing his damnedest to seed dissent and ruin shit everywhere so that when everyone is worn out, the Orion Guard can just sweep in and take over. He may or may not also be working against his own leadership. Jury is still out on that."

"OK, and the glowing thing?" Mill asked.

"That's the Caretaker. It's an ascended AI—possibly from as far back as the Sentience Wars in Sol. It's been responsible for half of the major wars in the last five thousand years, maybe more. Its goal is to get the Transcend and Orion Guard to fight on the battlefield of the Inner Stars and trash the place."

Captain Ayer had paled considerably. "Why in the stars does it want to do that?"

Brandt snorted. "Because it and the other ascended AIs are butt-hurt that the unification group kicked their asses back in Sol."

Tanis laughed. "You have a way with words, Brandt. These AIs also seem to think that they should keep humans in some sort of median state for eternity or something. Honestly, their motives are just supposition at present. That's why I'm trying to track the Caretaker down."

"And you think this…glowing AI person was responsible for what happened in Genevia?"

Tanis shrugged. "The mind control tech that was used in Genevia bears a striking resemblance to what we've seen elsewhere, and that was connected to the Caretaker. Or one of his ilk, at least."

"Well, I'll tell you one thing for sure," General Mill said with a soft laugh as he gestured at the image of the Caretaker. "If I saw anything like that, I think I'd remember. I can't imagine it staying hushed if anyone else had, either."

"Understandable." Tanis removed the image of the Caretaker. "And General Garza? He doesn't stand out as much, but he's been active in the Hegemony, Trisilieds, Scipio, and Silstrand."

"He gets around." Mill sat back and stroked his jaw. "That's a lot of travel for one man."

"Jump gates and clones," Brandt replied.

"Jump what?" General Mill asked, at the same time Ayer shook her head and said, "I hate clones."

"Jump gates allow for near-instantaneous travel on a galactic scale," Tanis replied. "They're on the downlow right now."

General Mill shook his head as he stared at Garza. "Well, I don't remember him, but that doesn't mean he wasn't around. I do, however, recall a consultant that was present at the beginning of the mech program. She was a strange old lady."

"Lady?" Tanis asked. "Do you have any records?"

Mill frowned and nodded. "Think so, checking. Aha! Here we are. She was at the first demonstrations."

An image of a woman appeared above the table, floating serenely next to Garza's.

"Fuck," Brandt whispered. "That's..."

"Katrina," Tanis said, swallowing a lump that had formed in her throat before turning to General Mill. "What are you playing at, General?"

Mill looked genuinely surprised at the vehemence in Tanis's voice. "I'm not playing at anything. She was there. I heard talk that it was her tech that was instrumental in making the Discipline system work without causing irreparable damage to the mechs."

"Are you certain? Really certain? That's Katrina, governor of the Victoria colony at Kapteyn's Star. From five thousand years ago."

Captain Ayer whistled. "She looks good for five-thousand. I mean, not great, but—"

Mill shot Ayer a stern look, and the captain pursed her lips and shook her head.

"Sorry, all this has me a bit out of sorts. Is it classified?"

"No," Tanis sighed as she stared at Katrina's face. "Truth is one of our best allies at this point."

"That's an encouraging—and unorthodox—viewpoint," Mill said.

Tanis opened her mouth to reply when Captain Sheeran called in from the *Aegeus*. *<Admiral! A fleet has jumped into the system! They're only five light minutes away! Get back to the—>*

The Link connection to the ship went dead and an audible alarm began to sound.

"We're under attack!" General Mill shouted as he rose from the table.

"Two cruisers," Ayer said as she leapt over the table. "Firing on the station!"

Brandt was already at the door, where Corporal Johnny stood staring down the hall. He glanced into the room.

"I assume we're leaving, ma'ams?" he asked.

Tanis nodded, and Brandt shook her head. "Bright lad."

They moved out into the hall, and Tanis wished she had access to tactical feeds from station scan. A moment later, she had them filling her mind.

<Not asking permission from these people,> Angela said without apology.

<Not judging,> Tanis replied as she took in the feeds.

Just as Captain Ayer had said, two cruisers were attacking Appalachia Station, while another three were firing on other nearby ships.

"Those are SAF vessels," Tanis said as they moved down the hall to the concourse outside the Marauder recruitment center.

"Former Theban," Mill replied as he drew a sidearm and looked out into the concourse where people were running past.

One of the ISF Marines passed a pulse pistol to Tanis, and she checked its charge before peering past the general.

"Fuckers are firing at their own damn station," General Mill swore. "Admiral, you won't make it back to your pinnace in time. Tell it to get back to your cruiser. I have a shuttle in a bay close by."

Tanis nodded to Brandt. "Tell Mick to get his ass back to the *Aegeus*."

"Already on it. Let's not wait around on my account. Where's your shuttle, General?"

Mill passed them a location on the map and directed his soldiers out onto the concourse.

Captain Ayer gestured for three of the office workers who were still present to join them. "You want to live? Come with us."

"But my family!" a man called out.

"Tell them to get to an evac ship or escape pod. This station isn't going to last," Mill hollered as he gestured for everyone to get out of the offices.

As if to emphasize his statement, the deck beneath their feet shuddered, and a loud groan echoed down the concourse.

<Air pressure just dropped,> Angela announced. *<Station's getting holed!>*

"Go! Go!" Mill yelled, and the group took off, pushing through the crowds that were running the opposite direction until they came to a side passage. The Marauder soldiers stayed in the lead, and the ISF Marines brought up the rear as they raced down the narrow corridor.

Tanis considered sending out nano, but with the station's atmosphere starting to whip past them, she knew there was no way the probes could provide any meaningful information.

<What is it about stations getting shot up while you're aboard?> Brandt asked.

<I'm a trouble magnet, haven't you noticed?> Tanis replied as they rounded a corner and came into a wider concourse once more.

Ahead, the Marauder soldiers stopped at a wide staircase leading down through the decks and waited for the group to catch up. Mill nodded to the pair, and they rushed down the stairs, checked the broad landing, and proceeded to the next level.

They passed through a dozen decks that way, once again finding themselves amongst thickening crowds. One of the Marauder recruiters rushed off at one point, and Mill swore about idiots getting themselves killed. He seemed to consider going after the man for a moment, but then thought better of it.

As the group progressed, the station began to shake more and more around them. At one point the a-grav cut out entirely, and a young man ahead got pushed over the edge of a staircase, only to fall three decks when the gravity came back on.

Tanis swore and checked the map. Just one more deck to go, and they'd be at the private dock where Mill's shuttle waited. A minute later, they reached the desired level, and the Marauder soldiers turned down another side passage.

Mill was about to follow, when weapons fire streaked down the passage; a rail shot that tore clear through one of the lightly armored Marauders and a recruiter behind him, spraying blood and bone across the bulkheads.

The other soldier fell back and took cover around the corner, returning fire.

"The fuck!" Mill shouted. "The alternative route will cost us five minutes."

The air was relatively still. Either there were no holes down here, or a-grav shields had finally been deployed to hold in atmosphere. Tanis decided to send out a few probes to scout down the passageway. At the end, she saw a pair of women with railguns laughing as they fired at passersby in the far corridor.

"Hold this." She tossed her gun to Brandt, and quickly stripped off her clothing.

"Uh…what?" Mill asked as Tanis revealed the matte black flow armor she wore beneath her uniform.

"Getting to be another habit," Brandt shook her head. "We have Johnny and Anne here for that."

"Their armor takes longer to get off," Tanis said as the flow armor crept up over her face. "See you in a minute."

She activated the stealth system and leapt up onto the exposed conduit run at the top of the passageway. There wasn't enough room for Tanis to rise to her hands and knees, but with all the noise and chaos, she wasn't worried about making sound as she scampered along the pipes.

It was only thirty meters to the end of the corridor, and when she arrived, the two women were still laughing hysterically as they fired their railguns at everyone in sight.

Tanis drew the two blades out of her forearms and slid off the conduits, holding both blades vertically as she dropped.

One blade struck true, sliding between the collarbone and neck of the woman on the right. Tanis's other target had moved at the last moment to shoot at a small child that ran by.

Tanis kicked at the shooter's knee before she could fire, and twisted the blade inside the other woman.

The rail shot went wide, and the child made it safely past. Tanis wasted no time pulling the blade out of the first woman and slicing the head off the other.

<*We're clear,*> she sent back.

Johnny and Anne were the first ones down the narrow passage, moving to cover Tanis as the others approached.

Brandt tossed Tanis's gun back to her. "You forgot this."

"What about my clothes?"

"I'm not your maid." Brandt grinned as the group began to move down the next corridor.

"Just ahead," Mill called back. "Nice moves, by the way, Admiral."

"Tanis," she replied while sidestepping a man who was trying to gather up all the donuts he could from a toppled cart.

"Station's going to go down," Ayer shouted at him as they ran past. "Idiot."

<*A thousand Niet ships have jumped in,*> Angela advised, more than a little concern in her voice. <*They've closed to within a hundred thousand klicks.*>

"Mill, when we get aboard your shuttle, we have to get to our ship. Your shields can't handle that firepower!" Tanis called out over the din surrounding them. Mill nodded, but as they turned into a docking bay, she couldn't tell if it was to her, or to the remaining Marauder soldier.

Inside the bay lay four ships, all mobbed with people. A ship on the right bore the Marauder crest, and Mill shouldered the crowds aside as he moved toward the shuttle. The craft's door was still closed, and Tanis could see a woman waving through the cockpit window as they approached.

The two ISF Marines fired low intensity pulse shots into the mob to disperse them, but the shots barely made a dent. They upped the power, and the crowds started to fall back. Ten seconds later, the group reached the shuttle's door, and the Marines and remaining Marauder soldier took up positions as the door slid open.

Ayer stepped in first, followed by the remaining recruiter from the office. The Marauder captain turned and gestured for Tanis and Brandt to follow as the crowds surged in close. General Mill stepped up next and turned to cover the troops.

"Get in! Fast!" the pilot yelled, then screamed as weapons fire tore through the crowds from across the bay, cutting the civilians down in droves. The Marines piled in, hauling the Marauder after them, and Brandt pulled the door shut.

"Go! Go! Go!" Brandt shouted, and the pilot wasted no time lifting off the cradle and boosting out of the station.

Tanis clenched her teeth, filled with sorrow and rage as she watched a group of soldiers wearing SAF uniforms work their way across the bay, killing everyone in their path. Stray shots pinged off the shuttle's hull, but no warnings sounded, and Tanis pulled her gaze from the window to see Captain Ayer standing over General Mill, tears streaming down her face.

The old soldier lay on the shuttle's deck, a small hole in his forehead. From Tanis's position, it looked like that was the extent of the wound.

The brains and blood sprayed across the bulkhead next to Ayer told a different story.

Tanis turned away and moved into the cockpit, where the ashen pilot sat, threading the dozens of ships and pods pouring out of Appalachia Station.

"Get to my ship," Tanis directed, but the pilot shook her head.

"I have to get back to the *Foehammer*!"

"The *Foehammer*'s shields can't hold up against a thousand Nietzschean cruisers!" Tanis shouted at the woman. "Get to the *Aegeus*!"

The woman shook her head, and Tanis slid into the seat beside her. She touched the console and deposited a passel of nano.

<*On it,*> Angela said, and the console in front of the pilot shut down.

"What the hell?" the woman yelled, looking over to see Tanis initialize holo controls and direct the ship around the station toward the *Aegeus*.

The pilot reached for Tanis, but a fist shot out from Tanis's periphery, hitting the pilot in the head.

"Thanks, Brandt," Tanis grunted.

"Anytime."

There was a scuffle in the back, and Tanis heard Brandt say, "Easy, now," and then a pulse pistol fired.

She assumed all was well and poured on as much speed as the shuttle possessed, arcing around the station to see the *Aegeus*, engines glowing brightly and stasis shields flaring as fire rained down on it from the five Theban cruisers.

The *Aegeus* returned fire on one of the ships, its atom beams cutting through the enemy vessel, tearing it apart.

Tanis felt a grim smile form on her lips as she continued her approach. Then her board lit up with a message from one of the Theban cruisers, and Tanis toggled it.

"Surrender, Admiral Richards."

"Shit, that's Oris," Brandt said from behind Tanis.

<*That little bitch!*> Angela swore. <*I have a tightbeam to the* Aegeus.>

Tanis was about to reply, when enemy fire stopped splashing against the *Aegeus*'s shields and instead began to cut through the ISF cruiser.

<*Admiral!*> Captain Sheeran's voice came across the tightbeam. <*We've got…we've been sabotaged! There's something in the system! I've lost contact with Huma!*>

Tanis caught sight of dozens of missiles streaking out from the Theban cruisers toward the *Aegeus.*

<*Get out of here!*> Sheeran cried out a moment before the *Aegeus* disappeared in a nuclear fireball.

The shockwave tore through the vacuum of space, colliding with Appalachia Station and buckling its torrid ring. Tanis dove the shuttle below molten debris as pieces of the *Aegeus* streaked through space all around them. Above them, the looming form of the station began to fracture, breaking apart piece-by-piece.

"Strap in!" Tanis called back as she dove under the disintegrating station, joining in with the swarm of ships and escape pods heading for the planet below.

Then something struck the ship, and one of the engines failed.

<*Strap in yourself, Tanis. I'll bring us in,*> Angela yelled as the shuttle began to vibrate violently around them.

NOT THE WARM WELCOME...

STELLAR DATE: 08.17.8949 (Adjusted Years)
LOCATION: ISS *Andromeda*
REGION: Edge of the New Canaan system

Katrina turned and saw Cary standing in the room's entrance with her sister, Saanvi, behind her. Both women wore sober expressions, and Cary stretched out her hand.

"What are you doing?" Katrina asked, backing away. "Joe? What is this?"

"I want to hear your impressions when it's just you in there," Joe replied. "We've had no end of misery from ascended AIs lurking in our populace. Our trust comes with a cost. This is it."

Katrina opened her mouth to speak, but her breath caught as silver filaments streaked out of Cary's hands and into her body.

Her own internal nano defenses seemed unable to stop them, and Katrina felt something change. It was indescribable, and she couldn't discern if the feeling was good or bad.

Then a white light began to form between Cary's hands, and, a moment later, she held a glowing orb.

"It's done." Cary said in her strange voice. "I'll take it to the lab."

"Wait!" Katrina called out, reaching for Cary. She was stopped short by Joe grabbing her wrist.

"How do you feel, Katrina?"

"Like you becoming an admiral has turned you into a raging asshole!" Katrina shot back. "You had no right—"

"This isn't about rights." Joe cut her off. "We're in a fight for our survival. One interpretation of what has occurred today is that you secreted an enemy onto our base. I'll give you the benefit of the doubt that it was unintentional, but I'm disinclined to trust ascended AIs at present. From what you've said, they seem to be responsible for just about everything that's gone wrong since humanity reached the stars."

Katrina felt drained—whatever Cary had done to remove Xavia's memory had left her barely able to stand. "Don't hurt her. Please. She's a gift from Xavia."

"We won't, so long as you don't tell us to."

"What?" Katrina knew Joe's words should make sense, but they just didn't line up. "Why would *I* tell you to hurt Xavia's memory?"

"Well, if you were under duress, you may change your mind about her."

"Joe!" Katrina wanted to bang his head into the wall and see if she could knock some sense into him. "What's it going to take to convince you that she wasn't manipulating me?"

Joe sighed. "I don't know, yet. Come, let's go to the lab and see what Xavia's memory has to say for herself."

"What? Just like that, we're all friendly again? You just tore a part of me out of myself."

Joe took a step toward Katrina a finger in her face. "No, I took a foreign entity, who has the ability to control all of your words and deeds, out of your body. How can I trust you with that thing in there? For all I know, you're so conditioned at this point that you have no idea who you even are anymore."

"Joe…" Katrina began to speak, but he turned and walked away. She followed him out of the room to see a squad of ISF Marines waiting.

Somehow that felt worse than anything else. Like Joe had betrayed her. Some of these Marines could be friends, or even family, and now they saw her being treated like a criminal by one of their leaders.

<Your own daughter said Xavia's memory wasn't entangled in my mind,> Katrina said to Joe as the Marines fell in around them.

<At that moment,> Joe replied. *<I'm not going to debate this with you, Katrina. Maybe if you had announced that Xavia's 'memory'—as you put it—was in you from the outset, things would have been different. But she didn't know we could see her, and she thought to hide from us.>*

<Why does she have to declare herself? What did she do wrong?>

Joe glanced over his shoulder. *<Declaring people crossing into a nation is not an unfamiliar concept. Smuggling people across borders is usually frowned upon.>*

Katrina didn't reply; her teeth were clenched so hard she thought they might break. To have struggled so long to stay alive, only to be treated as a criminal upon her arrival…. Part of her wished she'd never come back. To think of all she had sacrificed to get this information to New Canaan, only to have it end up a catastrophe.

But Xavia had told me that I must.

A sliver of doubt crept into Katrina's mind, accompanied by an unwelcome memory of how she had controlled people like puppets back in the Midditerra System. A mind-control technology that had eventually worked its way across the stars to destroy countless lives in a dozen conflicts.

Could I have been under her spell?

Katrina shook her head, knowing that her own doubt was evidence that she was not under Xavia's sway.

<*Troy.*> She wanted to reach the AI and advise him on the situation.

<*Troy is not available to speak with you,*> Corsia responded instead of her old friend.

<*Corsia? Why not?*>

<*He and I are chatting right now. Your crew and ship are under quarantine while we scan everything.*>

<*Scan it for what?*> Katrina asked.

<*More remnants of ascended AIs.*>

Katrina almost missed a step. <*You can do that? How?*>

<*Sorry, Katrina,*> Corsia's mental tone carried what felt like genuine compassion. <*I can't tell you that.*>

A feeling of sadness welled up in Katrina. This was not at all how she had envisioned her reunion going. It was supposed to be joyous. In her imaginings, Tanis had thanked her for revealing that Bob had ulterior motives…they had taken steps to avert the war that was brewing.

Now Joe was ruining everything with his rampant paranoia.

Katrina didn't speak to Joe or Corsia as they walked through the base's corridors. After five minutes, they reached the doors to Earnest's lab, also under guard by ISF Marines.

The guards opened the door, and Joe led her into the room.

It was a cavernous space—as Katrina had expected—much of it shrouded in darkness. To her right was an illuminated area, where Earnest stood beside Cary and Saanvi, along with another man and woman.

At the edge of the space, a dozen tall columns stood, each containing a white orb wrapped in silver bands. Katrina was shocked to see so many captured remnants.

How do they do that?

Then Cary moved, and Katrina saw another orb on the table in the center of the space. "Is that her? Is she OK?" Katrina asked as she rushed past Joe.

"Yes, yes, Katrina," Earnest said without taking his eyes off Xavia's memory. "Safe and sound. So far as we can tell, being trapped in the brane doesn't do these Scubs any harm."

" 'Scubs'?" Katrina asked, and the woman next to Earnest nodded.

"We were calling them 'Self-Contained Sentient Sub-Entity Shards' but that was a mouthful, and SCSSES sounds too much like 'skuzzes', so we ended up with 'Scubs'," the woman explained.

"Uh…thanks for the etymology lesson," Katrina muttered.

"She says she's sorry," Cary said, still speaking in the strangely ethereal voice. "She knew we wouldn't trust her, but she didn't know we could see her. She's not happy that the Caretaker's Scubs are here."

"Is there any more we can learn from them?" Joe asked.

Cary and Saanvi both shook their heads, and Saanvi replied, speaking in the same unnatural voice as Cary. "Doubtful. Most of what they say are lies and misinformation, anyway."

"Then perhaps we should terminate them," Joe replied. "So far as we know, Scubs aren't actually sentient beings."

Earnest held up a hand and wobbled it back and forth. "Eeehhh, that's debatable. They're smarter than the average human, and there is much to learn about their abilities."

"Regarding the intelligence, you could say the same about an NSAI," Joe replied. "The question at hand is whether or not Scubs are sentient."

"They might be," Cary said. "If they are, do we need a trial before we execute it?"

Joe ran a hand through his hair. "Yeah, we would. Not that it would escape conviction. Murder and attempted murder are hard raps to beat."

"I can wall them off," Cary said, and suddenly the orbs in the pillars were completely occluded by black spheres. "Hmm…that has made Xavia happy."

"What do you mean?" Katrina asked. "Why is she happy?"

"This will become tedious very quickly," Saanvi said. "I will speak for Xavia's remnant. It is more than a memory, Katrina. This is a being, not a recording. If it has led you to believe that, then it has been lying to you."

Katrina chewed on her lip. Xavia's memory had never claimed to be anything in particular, it just helped out from time to time. But Katrina had also never considered it to be a sentient being—if it was at all. There did not appear to be a consensus as yet.

"Ask her…ask her if she lied to me," Katrina said to Cary.

"I do not need to relay it, she has enough of a foothold in this portion of space-time to detect the vibrations you make in the air," Cary replied.

"I have never lied to you, Katrina. That is not my way," Saanvi said, channeling Xavia's words.

"Then what is your way?" Joe asked.

"I seek to foster peace between humans and AIs," Saanvi said.

Joe glanced at Katrina, and then turned back to the orb. "How do you plan to foster this peace? Through conformity of thought? Removal of all potential harm?"

"I said 'foster'," came the reply. "It is not possible to force peace."

"Well, that much we agree on," Earnest muttered.

"What was your purpose in coming here?" Joe asked.

Saanvi did not speak for a few seconds, and Joe cocked his head in question.

"She's not saying anything." Saanvi shrugged.

Katrina took a step forward. "Xavia?"

"I wanted to get you here to keep you safe, Katrina. And I needed you to share with Joe the information about Bob, Tanis, and Angela. Together, we must all stop them from starting a war that will consume everything."

"She's already working on that," Joe replied. "Her goal is to take the head off the snake as quickly as possible."

"How will she do that?" Katrina asked.

"By making the strongest alliance. Tanis plans to establish an accord between humans and AIs, the Transcend, Inner Stars, Orion. Us all." Cary replied.

Katrina snorted. "And how long will that hold for? A century? A millennium? She'll have to enforce it."

"It'll be a lot easier after the core AIs are dead." Joe crossed his arms and stared at Xavia's sphere. "How does that strike you, Scub? If we kill the Caretaker, and all your kind."

"She laughed," Saanvi said, then smiled. "If that is your goal, then I shall freely assist you."

CRASHED

STELLAR DATE: 08.17.8949 (Adjusted Years)
LOCATION: Jersey City, Pyra
REGION: Albany System, Thebes, Septhian Alliance

Tanis pushed the impact foam away and leant over to check the Marauder pilot.

She was dead, a spar was driven through her torso, sticking through her chair and into the rear cabin.

"Brandt!" Tanis called out as she pulled herself out of the cockpit. "You'd better be alive, you old battle-ax."

"Gonna outlive you, crazy woman." A muffled voice came from the back.

"Ma'am," Johnny reached into the cockpit and grabbed Tanis's arm. As he helped her up, Tanis caught sight of Anne's broken body, and clenched her teeth.

Well, now the Niets have made it personal.

She blinked at the thought, wondering whether it came from her or Angela.

Ahead, Brandt was helping Ayer out of her seat. Tanis stopped to kneel beside Anne.

"Your parents would be proud of you," she whispered, knowing that there was no family left to inform of Anne's sacrifice. Everyone close to the Marine had died in the attack on Carthage last year.

She triggered the Marine's tech scrub, then rose and grabbed the woman's weapon before following Johnny to the door. He slid it partway open before it jammed.

With a cry of rage, the Marine kicked it open the rest of the way and peered out into the darkness outside.

It took Tanis's eyes a moment to adjust before she could make out a darkened city street. She'd tried to avoid any buildings when they came down. From the gouge in the street behind the shuttle, it looked as though that much had been a success.

Johnny exited the shuttle, followed by Brandt. Tanis looked back at Ayer, who was shaking the Marauder soldier. "Don't you die on me,

Ben. We've got a lot of terrain to cover, and my leg's fucked up. I need your stupid ass as a crutch."

Tanis could see that Ben was already dead; his chest was still, and there was blood running down his side.

"He's gone, Ayer," Tanis said, reaching for the captain. "Look, he got shot back on the station."

"Get the fuck off me!" Ayer screamed at Tanis. "Look what you did! You got the General killed. It's all over."

Tanis grabbed Captain Ayer's shoulder and spun her away from the dead Marauders. "You want to stay here and mourn your people, I understand that. Stay. But do it *quietly*."

Ayer just blinked at Tanis and then turned back to looking at the general.

"We gotta move," Brandt said, leaning into the shuttle. "Dropships are raining down like…rain. We need to find some sort of local garrison. Hold out 'til the *Derringer* gets here."

Tanis rolled her eyes as she stepped out and looked up at the sky. Above them, hundreds of red streaks glowed against the darkness; beyond hung the glowing smudge of what remained of Appalachia Station.

And the *Aegeus.*

<*Did you get any sort of call out to the* Derringer?> Tanis asked Angela.

<*I called. Who knows if it made it anywhere. That was a coordinated attack, and Oris…*>

Tanis nodded. Not only was Oris a traitor—mostly likely for the Nietzscheans—but the only way she could have subverted the *Aegeus*'s ship AI would be with help. The sort of help that didn't come from people with Nietzschea's level of technology.

<*Oris was either from Orion, or she had a remnant in her.*>

<*We need to carry Shadowtrons with us at all times,*> Angela replied.

<*No argument here.*>

Johnny took up a position at the front of the shuttle and called back. <*Civvies are starting to come out. We need to move.*>

Tanis looked around and saw lights on in the buildings nearby, and people standing in windows and doorways. A sound came from behind, and she saw Ayer step out of the shuttle.

"Damn Jersey City. I can't believe I'm going to die here."

"I'm not dying," Tanis said. "Keep your head down, and you won't, either."

<Jersey City, OK,> Angela said to Tanis. *<I have the map, and our position. Damn, this city is half-trashed. Ah hah! There's a small civilian spaceport on the north side of the city. Other than finding a hole to hide in, it's our best bet to get out of here.>*

Tanis nodded as she looked up the best route to the spaceport, sending it to Brandt and Johnny. Then she turned back to Ayer.

"Captain. I'm sorry about Mill. I really am. I just lost hundreds of my people, as well. But I'm not going to leave you here to wallow in sorrow. You can mourn later. Right now, stay sharp so we can give 'em hell."

Ayer drew a deep breath and closed her eyes for a moment. "Where to?" she asked, and Tanis added her to the combat net.

<Munis Spaceport.>

The Marauder nodded and lifted her rifle, holding it across her chest. *<OK, I'm ready.>*

At first the small group made good time through the streets of Jersey City, but it didn't take long for the roads to become crowded with fleeing people—some on foot, some in ground cars, all trying to get out into the surrounding countryside.

Then the Nietzschean dropships started to touch down, and the group's progress slowed further as they kept to the shadows, checking corners and scurrying through open spaces as quickly as possible.

Several hours later, they were holed up in a sublevel of an exotic food store, waiting out a squad of Niets who were working their way down the street, rounding up any citizens.

Ayer stood near a small window, watching the boots of Niets move past. She was still favoring her one leg a bit, but it seemed to be better than when they'd left the shuttle.

Tanis was tempted to tell the captain to stand back. She was being sloppy in her grief, almost acting as though she wanted to die. Yet Tanis worried that if she ordered Ayer to move, the woman might start yelling again.

Instead, Tanis deployed a small passel of nano to create a film on the glass and dampen any motion or EM.

"They'll be setting up AA emplacements on some of the tallest high rises," Ayer whispered after a moment. "At least, they did last year.

Niets aren't known for changing up their tactics."

"They ever infiltrate an enemy military like this before?" Brandt asked.

"Well…no, I guess not."

"Less chatter," Tanis said. "I can only mask so much."

The group fell into silence for the next twenty minutes while they waited for the Nietzscheans to move on. Then they waited another five minutes before exiting the sublevel and returning to the streets.

They leapfrogged from building to building this way all through the night, until dawn came and it was no longer safe to move.

Brandt led the group down into a utility tunnel that ran between two buildings. Partway down, they came to a small storage room with a door on the far side that connected to another passage.

"Three ways out." Tanis nodded with approval. "Works for me."

Ayer didn't speak as she leaned against a wall and slid to the ground. Johnny sat on a table, resting his rifle on his knees.

"How long 'til the *Derringer* gets here, do you think?" he asked.

Tanis had a countdown running on her HUD with several times listed, each accounting for different scenarios.

"Best time would be seven days," Tanis replied. "But I wouldn't count on that. They're going to have to go slow to avoid detection with that many Niet ships out there. It depends on whether or not all of the SAF and Theban ships sided with the traitors. If the Niets drop more than ten-thousand ships, then the *Derringer* will wait for the *I2*. In which case we could be looking at weeks. Maybe a month."

Johnny almost choked. "A month, Admiral?"

"That's an extreme case. *Derringer* will already be on the QuanComm. By now, they'll have seen the attack. Whether they wait or not, Rachel and the *I2* won't be far behind."

Johnny didn't look much happier, and Brandt placed a hand on his shoulder. "Don't worry, Corporal. You get to spend quality time with me. What more could you ask for?"

THE CAVALRY

STELLAR DATE: 08.18.8949 (Adjusted Years)
LOCATION: ISS *I2*, Command Deck
REGION: Edge of the Lisbon System, Septhian Alliance

Bob's presence in her mind startled Rachel out of a deep sleep. She rolled off the couch in her office and landed on her side, her face pressed against the floor.

<*Bob! What?*> she asked, scrambling to her feet.

Bob's only response was to show her an image of the *Aegeus* exploding next to a space station that was torn apart in the resulting blast.

"Shit! Fuck!" she swore, rushing out of her office and onto the bridge without even checking to see if she was dressed. "Status!"

Major Jessie rose out of the command chair, her eyes wide. "We just got it…we don't know anything yet."

Her voice was hoarse, and her eyes were fixed on a replaying image of the Aegeus's shields failing, the enemy missiles impacting, and then the nuclear fireball expanding through the cold vacuum of space, buckling the toroid on the nearby station like it was made of paper.

The attackers were former Theban ships with SAF idents, but there were also Nietzschean ships appearing deep inside the system.

"This is all we got in from the *Derringer,* so far," Comm called out. "Oh, they just messaged that the Admiral was not aboard the *Aegeus* when it was destroyed. She was on the station…"

Rachel drew in a steadying breath. The station had been destroyed as well, but that had been a much slower event. Tanis could have gotten off. *Would* have gotten off.

"Signal every ship in the First Fleet to get to Pyra," Rachel ordered. "Tell all ships to form up on the *Derringer*'s position, and pass this data on to Khardine."

She paced back and forth on the bridge, chafing at the knowledge that without a jump gate, the *I2* was a month from the Albany System.

"And, Comm," Rachel called out. "Tell Khardine we need a gate delivered. *Now.*"

"How did they…" Major Jessie whispered as she replayed the attack on the *Aegeus*. "There were only five of them. No way they got through the stasis shields."

<It could only have been sabotage,> Priscilla said. *<And there was only one person on that ship that it could be.>*

Rachel clenched her jaw. "Oris."

Rather than wear a hole in the deck while waiting for a gate to be delivered, Rachel left the bridge for the CIC. She nodded solemnly to Priscilla on her plinth in the foyer as she walked past.

<Buck up, Captain,> Priscilla said with a wan smile. *<This is Tanis Richards we're dealing with. The universe isn't done with her yet.>*

<I sure hope not.>

Rachel wondered about Priscilla's statement. If there was one thing she'd learned about Bob's avatars, it was that they were often windows into his mind.

If Priscilla thought Tanis was alive, that meant that Bob also believed it.

The thought put a spring in her step—or at least helped her straighten her spine as she walked into the CIC and approached Major Grange, who stood at the room's main holotable.

"Major Grange." Rachel nodded. "What do you have?"

"I'm waiting on updates over the QuanComm, but here's what I have for now. As you know, New Canaan just shipped another thousand Trisilieds vessels to Septhia, which means they're all but out of the serviceable hulls that were surrendered. All that remains are two thousand functional Orion ships, and ten thousand ISF ships."

"Which is the bare minimum fleet size for New Canaan," Rachel replied.

That was something Tanis had carved in stone. New Canaan was not to overextend itself, offering aid to others. It was still one of the top targets in the galaxy, and any attack elsewhere could be a feint meant to weaken the home fleet.

"What about Diana?" Rachel asked.

"Latest word from Scipio is that they've taken their forward elements and engaged the Hegemony. They have maybe a hundred ships they could send us, *if* they're still near the jump gates."

"What about Khardine and Vela?" Rachel asked. "They should have ten thousand ships they can send."

Grange nodded. "They do, but they just started 'Operation Possum'. They have ships everywhere, many in dark layer transition. Krissy will need to halt the op and recall her bait ships before sending help."

Rachel nodded slowly. "And Khardine?"

"Greer just launched a number of raids against the Dresine Combine. Right now, Khardine is at minimum strength."

"Dammit!" Rachel swore. "I assume they'll try to form up some sort of support for us?"

"Yes, we're still waiting on updates. Stars…how did this timing line up so badly…" Major Grange's voice trailed off and he leant against the holotable.

"We don't need to match their strength. Even with ten-thousand ships, we could take out those Nietzscheans," Rachel countered.

"Perhaps," Grange replied. "But if we come in too hard, they'll simply destroy the planet Admiral Richards is stranded on."

Rachel swallowed. Grange was right. This was going to take some delicate maneuvering.

* * * * *

It took over three days for a gate to be delivered to the Lisbon system. Including initial light lag before the *Derringer* even saw the event, over ninety-two hours had passed since Tanis had come under attack.

The *Derringer* had sent so much data that the ship had disentangled all but one QuanComm blade. Now the updates following the first data burst contained only the message, 'no change'.

Time for some change, Rachel thought as she watched the jump gate come to life.

"Take us in," she ordered helm.

The *I2* surged toward the gate, touched the negative energy at its center, and then the stars around the ship disappeared for an instant before coming back in new positions.

"Confirming…" Scan announced. "Jump on target, we are at the edge of the Albany System!"

Rachel strode toward the main holotank and looked over the initial scan data as it poured in. Only seven other ships were in position near the *Derringer*. Three were members of the ISF First Fleet, and two were dreadnoughts from Khardine. Not much, but a start.

Though when she saw what lay within the Albany System, she felt the blood drain from her face.

That's over seventy thousand enemy ships.

<Captain Mel,> Rachel called the captain of the *Derringer*. *<What's your status?>*

<Captain Rachel,> Mel replied. *<Glad you made it. We've been soaking up every transmission those bastards have made. They have not, I repeat,* ***not*** *captured the Admiral. However, they're searching for her like there's no tomorrow.>*

<Do they have any leads?> Rachel asked.

<Over a thousand civilian pods and ships dropped down on the planet when the Niets showed up and destroyed the station. The enemy lost track of the Admiral in the chaos and debris.>

Rachel breathed a sigh of relief. That was good news—*or it means Tanis has died…*

No! I'm not going to think that.

<Mel, send over everything you've grabbed. I'm going to have the fleet analysts recomb through it to be sure.>

<Aye…Captain?>

<What is it, Mel?>

<I about died, just sitting out here. If we send in stealthed ships….>

Rachel understood what Mel was getting at. *<You'll be in the vanguard, Mel.>*

<Thanks.>

"Major Jessie," Rachel called out to her XO. "I'm going down to see Grange in the CIC. You have the conn."

"Aye, Captain Rachel, I have the conn."

When Rachel arrived in the CIC, Grange was looking grim as he stood at his table. He was surveying the situation in the Albany system and shaking his head.

"That's a lot of ships," he muttered.

Rachel nodded. "Admiral Evans's strategy is sound…it's just going to take *forever* to be ready."

Grange locked eyes with Rachel. "It's his wife…wives—you know what I mean—down there. From what I see, all of the admirals agree this is our best shot."

"It's just going to take so long to get them in position," Rachel said, trying not to sound like she was whining—except she really wanted to whine.

Grange was nodding silently when one of the fleet analysts called out from his station.

"Captain, Major! We were combing over the data the *Derringer* sent, and Bob found something!"

<*I helped,*> Bob amended.

"It was in data stripped from an outer relay," the analyst said while nodding effusively. "Part of the buffers were corrupted, but we managed to piece them back together. There's a message. From Angela."

Rachel felt a weight fall from her shoulders, and was surprised at how much more easily she drew her next breath.

<*They got on a Marauder shuttle,*> Bob said. <*Headed for the surface. A final trajectory update from Angela puts them on course for a place called Jersey City.*>

"Stars…" Grange sighed. "Suddenly I'm starving, I haven't been able to eat more than a bite in days."

Rachel gave a soft laugh, but felt no mirth. "Well, we know she was alive and where she was headed. Now we just have to get there."

She held back the reminder that the intel was four days old.

It was something, at least.

THREE DAYS

STELLAR DATE: 08.24.8949 (Adjusted Years)
LOCATION: ISS *I2*, Bridge
REGION: Edge of the Albany System, Thebes, Septhian Alliance

Over the last three days, nearly a thousand ships had arrived at the edge of the Albany System: Scipian cruisers and dreadnoughts, a host of TSF ships from various locations around the Transcend, three hundred vessels from New Canaan, and even a small detachment from Silstrand.

From the messages flooding in, Rachel knew that Sera was beside herself with worry, though the President knew she couldn't jump to the system and put herself at risk as well.

That didn't stop her from sending a message to Rachel that was half encouragement, half stern warning that Tanis had better be OK.

Joe, on the other hand, had sounded almost deadly calm in his last communication—at least that's how Rachel read the text.

He was ready, just waiting on the signal.

Rachel watched as the fleet elements settled into position, ready to begin the burn toward Pyra—and their conflict with the seventy thousand Nietzschean ships, waiting insystem.

She opened her mouth to issue the command, only to have scan call out "Contact! A Nietzschean fleet, half a light second to starboard!"

Rachel felt her throat constrict, but then saw the number of ships that appeared.

"Is this some sort of joke?" she whispered.

Seven ships appeared on the main tank. Three Nietzschean cruisers, though one looked almost as large as a dreadnought, two destroyers…and a pair of Marauder vessels.

Even stranger, all ships were broadcasting Marauder IFF signals.

"Hail them, tightbeam on the dreadnought," Rachel ordered.

"I have a response," Comm replied a few seconds later. "Putting it on the main tank."

Rachel rose from her chair and approached the tank, altering its configuration to ensure that whoever she spoke with would only see her, and not the rest of the *I2*'s bridge.

A woman appeared in the holotank—a woman unlike anyone Rachel had ever seen before. She was tall and, from the neck up, appeared perfectly normal. Her face was plain but pleasant-looking, and was framed by long blonde hair that fell over her shoulders.

But that was not what had caught Rachel by surprise. Though the woman appeared to wear powered armor, it was plain to see that her limbs were nonorganic, especially her right arm, which was effectively nothing but a large, multi-mode rifle.

Even stranger, everyone behind her was also just as much machine as human—some, more.

<They're mechs,> Bob supplied. *<Genevian mechs.>*

Rachel nodded slowly. She knew about the mechs, studied them before coming to Septhia. However, seeing them, knowing there was a whole culture—civilization?—of these machine warriors was something else entirely.

The mech-woman spoke first. "Hi, there, I'm Rika, Captain of M Company, Marauders 9th Battalion. I assume the fact you're floating way out here means you're not on speaking terms with the Niets?"

Captain Rika's words kicked Rachel's mind back into action, and she gave a curt nod before replying.

"Nice to meet another friendly face. I'm Captain Rachel, commander of the ISF First Fleet. You're correct in your assessment. We're not fans of the Nietzscheans being here at all."

Rika smiled, an expression that animated her face and transformed it from pleasant to vibrant. "Well, then. You're our kinda people. What are you doing here, though?"

Rachel wondered what to tell this mech-woman. The fact that she was in possession of five Nietzschean ships offered new tactical options.

<Tell her what we plan,> Bob instructed, his tone almost jubilant. *<She will help. Chances of a successful rescue increase dramatically with Rika.>*

Rachel wanted to ask him what made him so happy, but only replied, *<Don't have to tell me twice, then.>*

"Well, Captain Rika, we're readying an assault to go in and rescue our leader, Admiral Richards. As chance may have it, she was meeting with your General Mill when the Nietzscheans attacked."

An expression of appreciation came over Rika's face. "I'm all for kicking Nietzschean ass and saving General Mill. But you do realize that there's a shit-ton of Niets down there? You're gonna need a bigger fleet."

"We have very good shields," Rachel said, wondering how to broach her idea to this newcomer. "But you know what works better than that? Not getting shot at…at all."

A smile came over Rika's face, and she lifted her right arm, resting the weapon's barrel on her shoulder. "I think I might have a way to help with that."

* * * * *

Forty minutes later, a brief flurry of weapons fire was exchanged between the ISF fleet and the newly arrived Marauder-controlled Nietzschean vessels as they passed within a hundred thousand kilometers of one another.

Then the two Marauder ships split off and made an outsystem burn, while the six Nietzschean vessels made a short dark layer hop, disappearing from scan.

Rachel did her best not to pace during the twelve minutes that passed before Marauder-controlled Nietzschean vessels appeared on scan once more, just over an AU further insystem.

<It's a good fiction,> Priscilla said. *<It should fool the Niets further insystem into thinking Rika's ships jumped to escape us, and lost their hold on the captured Marauder ships.>*

The *I2*'s captain chewed on her lip, wishing she could feel as confident as Bob and Priscilla, but not wanting to ask why they were so sure of success. *<Well, at least we have control of the outer relays, and have blocked their transmissions insystem. Otherwise those Marauder IFFs they started out with would have ended this charade before it started.>*

<Rule number one. Control the information,> Priscilla replied.

<Oh yeah? What's rule number two?>

<Send in the big guns.>

Rachel chuckled as she watched the mech ships—which were already moving at 0.6*c* from their dark layer transition—continue insystem.

"Helm," she said, staring out into the starfield ahead of the ship. "Take us insystem. Let's give a good chase."

The FTN coordination officer relayed the order across the fleet, and the ISF First Fleet surged forward, appearing to chase the five

Nietzschean ships racing ahead of them.

Good luck, Rika of the Marauders.

REINFORCEMENTS

STELLAR DATE: 08.24.8949 (Adjusted Years)
LOCATION: MSS *Fury Lance,* Bridge
REGION: Edge of the Albany System, Thebes, Septhian Alliance

Captain Rika glanced at Lieutenant Heather, who sat at the *Fury Lance*'s weapons console. "Didn't hurt them too much, did you, Smalls?"

Heather shook her head in amazement. "No…our weapons didn't do *a thing* to their ships. I can't even detect their shields. It's like they don't have any."

"Didn't you ever hear about the Battle of Five Fleets at Bollam's World?" Barne asked from where he leaned against the scan station.

Heather frowned at the first sergeant. "I don't think that's a real place, Top."

Barne snorted. "You wouldn't, Smalls."

"Whoa!" Rika stopped them short. "Barne. How come Smalls gets to call you 'Top', but I don't?"

Barne shrugged. "Dunno. Guess I like her more."

Rika wagged a finger at him. "Don't make me tell people about that time at Cheri's villa."

"Oh?" Heather asked.

"Captain…" Barne rumbled.

Heather turned to Rika. "Is it juicy?"

"Not particularly, but it bugs Barne for some reason, so it's useful leverage."

"Can we focus on the mission?" Barne asked.

Heather rose from her station and stretched. "What's to focus on? Biggest thing we have to worry about right now is avoiding the thousands of ships that are fleeing the system."

"For the time being," Barne replied.

"Well, we sent the message to Nietzschean Command telling them that Iapetus is secured and that we came to render assistance. Commander Kiers' codes turned out to be useful once again. We'll see what the Niets order us to do. At the least, they're going to want to have access to our close-range scan logs to see if we learned anything about that massive ship."

"Did you see some of those ship registries, though?" Heather asked. "I've never heard of the ISF or the Transcend. I mean, everyone knows of Scipio, and I've seen Silstrand on charts. Thing is, they're a year's travel from here. How does some weird-assed fleet with registries from all over show up right now?"

Barne laughed. "Not only that, but at *Albany*. Is this place some sort of crazy lightning rod?"

"Beats me," Rika shrugged.

No one spoke for a minute, then Heather shook her head at the holotank and let out a long sigh. "One thing's for sure. Those are a lot of ships out there. I've never seen so many."

"I have," Barne grunted. "Early in the war, some of the fleet engagements were this big. As many as a hundred thousand—counting both sides. That was back when both we and the Niets thought we could blitzkrieg our way past the other."

Rika rose from her chair and paced across the bridge, tracing her fingertips along one of the bent consoles. "Well, no blitzkrieging, here. Just get in, nab the General and Admiral, and get out."

"So long as our orders from Niet command allow for that," Barne replied.

"Just has to be something that gets us close enough to land dropships," Chase said as he entered the bridge. "Can you believe we're going to pound dirt on Pyra again? Jersey City, of all places."

Rika turned to Chase and leant against the back of her chair. "Not everyone is going down. It's going to be a small strike team," Rika said, looking from face to face. "SMI-2s only. We need to move fast and hit hard. Get in, grab them, get out."

"Well, I'm flying your ship down there," Chase said.

"You better than Ferris, or Mad Dog?" Heather asked skeptically.

Chase flexed his prosthetic arm. It wasn't smooth and natural-looking like Barne's, but the limb of an RR-3. "I've got some advantages."

"I'll think on it," Rika replied. "I doubt anyone's going to be sitting idle. I think we should consider some diversions, as well—but not ones that paint too big a target on anyone's back."

"What do you have in mind?" Barne asked.

"Well, we're going to need supplies, right?"

"Yeah," Barne grunted. "Would be standard for us to fuel up with a battle looming—fleet that large, they've jumped in supply ships for sure."

"I wonder if maybe we can make one of those go boom," Rika mused.

<*Our guests have arrived,*> Leslie called up to the bridge. <*Should I bring them up?*>

<*Bring them to the barracks we assigned, I'll meet them there.*>

"Stars," Heather muttered. "I can't detect their ship, and it's *inside* our freakin' landing bay. I wonder if that motley fleet is a lot larger than we saw?"

"That would be nice," Rika said as she straightened and walked past Chase, kissing him on the cheek.

"Rika," Chase called back as she left.

"What?"

"You're supposed to say who has the conn after you leave."

Rika laughed. "I'll never get the hang of all this crap. Uhhh, Lieutenant Heather, you have the conn."

"Aye, Captain. I have the conn," Heather said as she rose from her console and took the command chair. "Sergeant Chase. You think you're so good at flying, take the helm station."

Chase shot Rika a dirty look, then laughed as he sat at the helm. "I'm gonna do loop-de-loops, Heather—show you what this bird can really do."

"Sergeant! You crazy idiot!"

Rika walked off the bridge, smiling to herself. She wondered about that. Here they were, flying toward one of the biggest Niet fleets they'd ever seen, with just five ships.

We're ***all*** *certifiably crazy.*

But then again, she was a mech, and those were Niets out there. What was her life about, if not killing them at every available opportunity?

<*I can think of a few things,*> Niki replied.

"I thought you couldn't read my mind." Rika frowned.

<*I can if your mind makes your lips whisper things aloud.*>

"Oh," Rika laughed. "I guess there's that."

<*Just, please. No suicide runs. I'm too young to die.*>

"Don't worry, Niki-mine, there are a lot of Niets to kill. I plan to survive this so I can keep on wiping them out."

<That's…uh…a very healthy mental state.>

"Liar."

Niki didn't reply, and Rika's mind began to wander as she traversed the passageways to the barracks decks.

<Niki, do you believe in a god?>

<What a strange question to ask an AI. What's got you on this train of thought?>

<Well, I got to talking to Lieutenant Carson about the Temple of Jesus thing—you know, after he explained what baptism is. It was interesting, and I didn't think much of it…but lately we've had a lot of crazy coincidences. What really got me thinking about this is that you came to me with no small amount of serendipity. I know for sure that I would ***not*** *have been able to rescue Silva and Amy—let alone overthrow the Politica—without you.>*

Niki sent an affirmative feeling. *<Agreed. I saved the day. Carry on.>*

<And then we capture these Nietzschean ships, which are just what we need to sneak insystem to rescue the General. On top of that, you told me about the Intrepid just a few weeks ago, and we just encountered the Intrepid Space Force!>

<Not to mention, that ship ***was*** *the* Intrepid, *they've just modified it since Bollam's World.>*

Rika nodded, she had suspected as much.

<So what does this have to do with a god?> Niki asked.

<Not sure…just seems like a lot of coincidence, that's all.>

<Well, let's hope none of us die and get confirmation just yet, OK?>

Rika laughed. That was one way to look at it.

A moment later, she rounded a corner and saw a white woman walking beside Leslie, a column of soldiers behind them.

The woman was quite the sight. Surrounded by the grey corridor—not to mention contrasted against Leslie and her jet-black skin—the white woman all but gleamed.

Upon closer inspection, it was apparent that the woman was not wearing any clothing, and that her 'skin' was a thick, semi-flexible polymer of sorts.

Her long, black hair reminded Rika of braids, but as the mysterious woman drew near, Rika realized that her hair consisted of thick, black cords that seemed to move of their own accord. Almost as though they were drifting through water rather than air.

Despite all that, it was the woman's completely black eyes that were most striking. They reflected no light, and, set against the pure-white skin, they looked like holes which had been bored through the woman's face and into space beyond.

She was speaking with Leslie, gesturing emphatically as she strode down the corridor. A moment later, her gaze turned to Rika, and a warm smile graced her lips—though it was difficult to make out her expression.

"Captain Rika," the woman extended her hand, showing no hesitation to shake Rika's left, nor at the robotic, three-fingered hand that reached out to clasp hers. "I'm Priscilla."

Rika noted the lack of title, military or otherwise. Neither was there any insignia on her…skin.

"Hello, very nice to meet you, Priscilla."

<*Stop staring at her,*> Leslie chided Rika privately.

<*They're all staring at me. I think it's OK to have a mutual stare-fest.*>

Priscilla turned and gestured at the soldier at the head of the column. "This is Colonel Smith, he'll be joining our ground team with his Marines."

Rika extended her hand and shook the colonel's, noting that he too did not seem at all perturbed by her mechanized body—that's not to say that he didn't look her over. But it was not in disdain or sexual interest. Instead, she got the distinct impression that he was evaluating her combat effectiveness.

She found herself doing the same. The colonel appeared to be completely organic, as did the group of men and women behind him. Even stranger, they wore no armor, and the packs they carried were not large enough to contain any meaningful protection.

Their bodies were covered in tight-fitting matte grey outfits, even their hands and feet. They bore insignia on their chests and ranks on their collars—which meant that these were uniforms of some sort.

"Very nice to meet you, Colonel. But I'm not sure unarmored humans are the right things to drop on the battlefield. We need strength, speed, and stealth, something my mechs excel at."

"I imagine you do," the colonel said with a nod. "I understand there are less than four hundred of you, yet you captured all these ships intact.

Very impressive."

"Thank you, colonel, surely you—"

The colonel held up a hand. "Captain Rika, we *will* be going groundside. Don't let the packaging fool you."

A moment later, the colonel's body turned invisible. Not a simple light-bending that was visible at the edges; from the neck down, the colonel was *gone*. There was no IR signature, and Rika's EM wave mapping showed signals passing directly through the space where his body was. She half wondered if she could reach out and put her hand right though him.

"Shit," was all she managed to say, while Leslie nodded emphatically.

"This is what we call 'flow armor', Captain. Perhaps not quite as tough as what you're made of, but sufficient to carry out the task. And we may look fragile, but you just might contain more organics than we do."

The colonel shifted back into visibility, but now he was holding two pistols. She hadn't seen his pack move at all, and there were no holsters on his body.

"How—?" Leslie gaped.

Colonel Smith twirled the sidearms and then slid them into his thighs. Thighs which had the IR profile of an organic human.

"As you can see, we're not what the enemy will expect. We're an asset you can ill-afford to ignore."

"Ignore?" Leslie asked. "If I didn't think you would just disappear, I'd jump you and steal that stuff you're wearing."

Colonel Smith turned and nodded to a sergeant behind him. The sergeant swung his pack around and pulled out a canister. He checked it over, and then tossed it to Leslie.

"Figured you might have some non-mechs that would want to come along. We brought a dozen of these."

"How do I use it?" Leslie asked, turning the canister over.

"Get naked, touch it to your chest, put your finger on the trigger plate, and hold it for a second."

"And then it just flows over me?" Leslie asked, staring incredulously at the canister in her hands. "I mean…you said it was flow armor, right? Do I have to wear a helmet still?"

Colonel Smith shook his head. "Flow armor doesn't have any ablative properties, so you may want to wear a helmet, but you don't have to."

As the man spoke, the matte grey covering flowed up over his head, somehow encompassing his hair without getting tangled or stuck in it. Then it flowed back down.

"See?" he asked.

"I've been standing for the last sixty-two days," Priscilla interrupted. "Are we going to find some place to sit down and talk?"

"Uh, sorry. Of course." Rika nodded and gestured for the group to follow her.

The entrance to the barracks wasn't far, and they reached it in under a minute. It consisted of a common area, a small galley, and shared sleeping halls.

"Will this do?" Rika asked.

"Very nicely," Colonel Smith replied. "Though I suspect her majesty, here, won't want to sleep with us plebes."

Priscilla swatted the colonel on the arm. "I'll sleep wherever. But I am starved. Haven't eaten in weeks."

"You don't sit, you don't eat…what do you do, over on your ship?" Rika asked.

Priscilla smiled again, the expression no less strange than it had been the last time. "I'm one of the ship's avatars."

"You're a what?" Leslie frowned.

"We'll, not the ship, exactly. The ship's AI. Bob is very complex, and his human avatars help him interface with people better."

<*BOB!*> Niki cried out. <*Bob is on that warship?*>

"*Thought* you had an AI," Priscilla winked at Rika—again, a bit creepy. "Though she's not neurally interfaced like normal. Curious."

<*I can't believe I was so close to Bob, and didn't get to speak with him!*>

Rika imagined that if Niki had a body, she'd be jumping up and down.

"Easy, Niki. When we're done kicking the Niets' asses, we can all meet Bob."

"Absolutely," Priscilla replied. "However, before we get to the ass kicking, anyone participating in this mission is going to need some upgrades."

Rika's eyes narrowed, and Leslie asked. "What kind of upgrades?"

Priscilla looked Leslie up and down. "Well, if you really want to use that flow armor, you're going to need better nano, for starters."

Leslie held out an arm, a huge grin plastered on her face. "Hit me, do whatever you have to do."

Rika snorted. "You're like a stealth junkie, Leslie."

"Hey, I can't take a rail shot and keep on keeping on like you can," Leslie replied. "Not being seen at *all* is my jam."

* * * * *

Rika sat in the small officer's lounge near the bridge and watched as Leslie appeared and disappeared in different parts of the room.

She'd be standing on the deck, covered from head to toe in her new flow armor, tail and all, then she'd disappear, only to reappear a moment later on a counter, or on the far side of the room. Once, she was hanging from the overhead.

If it hadn't been for the constant giggling, she would have been completely undetectable.

"I wonder why Priscilla is here," Rika said after a few minutes.

Leslie reappeared, kneeling on the table right in front of Rika, about to grab her beer. She sat back and stroked her chin as her tail flicked back and forth behind her.

Rika had noticed that while initially Leslie had always been very conscious of her tail, it now seemed to have a mind of its own, and was an interesting indicator of the lieutenant's mood.

"I mean…what skill set does a human avatar have? Which is really weird, by the way. Does she even have her own mind, or is she somehow inhabited by this 'Bob' AI?"

<She has her own mind,> Niki said without elaboration.

When Niki didn't speak further, Leslie shrugged. "She must have some sort of special power or ability. Colonel Smith did say she has extensive combat training, and her skin is a very effective armor. Think she just moonlights as a spec-ops person sometimes?" Leslie's armor flowed away from her face, and she grabbed Rika's beer, downing half before sliding back off the table.

"Leslie! That one's yours now. Go get me another."

Leslie licked her lips and walked to the counter. "Say what you want about the Niets, but they make a mean brew. Maybe when we destroy their empire, we can keep their brewmasters."

"I'll take it under advisement," Rika replied.

Leslie brought Rika a fresh glass of beer and then took another sip of the one she'd stolen.

"With these enhanced senses Priscilla's nano gave me, I can taste notes in this I could never pick up before. And I can see in the dark; not just a little dark, *pitch black*. I can see UV, IR, pick up shadows on backscatter radiation. It's like my eyes are the best tactical helmet ever."

Rika nodded. "Yeah, I'm with you there. Carson was nearly beside himself when he saw what her nano can do. Bet he's glad now that he transferred over from the *Golden Lark,* back when we were boosting out of Iapetus."

"I guess that explains why everyone in the galaxy wants to get their hands on that ship," Leslie replied. "And just think, this is the tech they were willing to share freely. What else do you think they have?"

"Stars if I know," Rika replied. "I bet if they had anything that could help with this op, they'd provide it, though."

Leslie disappeared again, giggling once more. "What could be better than this?"

PYRA

STELLAR DATE: 08.26.8949 (Adjusted Years)
LOCATION: Edge of Jersey City, Pyra
REGION: Albany System, Thebes, Septhian Alliance

"Finally," Tanis breathed as she peeked around the corner, her eyes settling on the Nietzschean staging ground.

"I count a hundred dropships at least," Brandt said. "Good stuff."

A strong gust of wind blew past, and Tanis eased back around the corner, glancing over at Ayer and Johnny, who were stacked along the wall behind them. Both were looking worse for wear, but still resolute. Still determined to survive.

After ten days on the ground, struggling through the sewers, maintenance tunnels, and alleys of Jersey City, Tanis felt like she'd lived here half her life.

The first spaceport—the small civilian one north of the city—had been a bust. The Nietzscheans had blown it to bits. From there, they'd worked their way to the harbor, searching for a boat that could get them further north to Ventara, where scattered radio signals told of a strong resistance against the Niets.

Unfortunately, most of the boats in the harbor were gone by the time they arrived. The only ships left were fishing rigs under heavy guard by the Niets.

Captain Ayer had suggested they try to go inland to Huntsville, but when they got halfway, they encountered a refugee camp that told of the city's complete destruction.

Niet patrols had picked up at that point, and it had taken five days to get back to the edge of Jersey City.

Compared to the destruction they'd heard of in other places, be it from refugees or scattered communications from holdouts, it seemed like Jersey City and the surrounding areas were taking the least punishment from the Niets.

Tanis knew that meant one thing: they were looking for her, and believed she was in the vicinity.

She'd already harbored the suspicion. The fact that the turncoat

Theban cruisers hadn't fired on them during their descent was the first clue. The building-to-building searches through Jersey City were another.

Which was why Tanis had no intention of going back into the city.

Luckily, this Nietzschean staging ground lay on the southern edge of the metropolis. Even better, it was mostly unoccupied, at present. The dropships arrayed on the hard-packed dirt represented the only noteworthy group of ships within hundreds of kilometers.

<*We'll wait for full noon,*> she advised, watching a small dust-devil trace its way along the slope behind the shed. <*All those ships maneuvering in orbit are dumping EM garbage everywhere. The last two days, the planet's van allen belts dumped a lot of radiation around noon.*>

<*What I wouldn't give for a solar flare,*> Ayer added.

<*Me too,*> Tanis smiled.

Ayer had warmed up—a bit, at least—over the past few days. She hadn't spoken further of how they'd left General Mill behind, not after Tanis reminded her that the lives of everyone else who had died were worth just as much.

Despite her words, Tanis felt especially bad about the pilot's death. Maybe if the woman hadn't been knocked out, she would have survived.

Even though she was less grouchy about Mill and the situation in general, Ayer had been starting to make comments doubting the rescue Tanis was certain would come.

<*Can't say I blame her. Ten days is a long time down here.*>

<*You estimated it could be longer,*> Angela gave a mental shrug. <*No big surprise.*>

<*Still, our friends above have a way of weighing on a person. I don't blame her for feeling like we've been here forever.*>

Tanis looked up at the thousands of Nietzschean ships, clustered in bands encircling the planet—enough of them to be visible in broad daylight. The ships hadn't changed formations in any meaningful way over the past week, which meant that the ISF was not yet headed insystem.

<*Or they're not that close yet,*> Angela suggested.

<*They could also be coming in with stealthed ships.*>

<*Maybe,*> Angela allowed. <*But with so many enemy ships up there, stealth would be hard to maintain. Vectors would be limited.*>

Ayer caught Tanis looking at the sky and she shook her head. "Hard to believe so many warships could assemble in one place—I mean, it's not busier than normal insystem traffic, but these things…it's different."

Tanis nodded slowly, still staring at the sky. "I've seen larger formations a few times. But they were either on my side, or I had a way to take them out."

"You've been around, Admiral Richards."

"I have. Stars, what I wouldn't give for even one Terran Space Force carrier and its fighter complement right about now."

"Fighters?"

Tanis nodded. "Back before a-grav, fighters were a big deal. Couldn't pull *g*s like ships can now, but what would you do if a million single-pilot fighters armed with nukes came your way?"

Ayer laughed. "Probably surrender."

"That's how it worked," Tanis replied as she held up her left arm, signaling her armor to retract.

Most of the flowmetal her left arm consisted of was gone. Only enough remained to form a single rod connecting to her hand—which was also skeletal. Within the cavity the flow armor had encapsulated lay a jumbled mass of small, articulated limbs.

<Damn wind…can't believe we have to go low-tech like this.>

<Could be worse,> Angela replied. *<You could be entirely out of flowmetal, and I'd have to make these bots out of grass.>*

<Funny, Ang.>

Tanis turned her arm upside down, dropping small bots to the ground. They skittered around the corner and headed toward the Nietzschean compound.

"OK, that's just gross-looking," Ayer shuddered, staring at Tanis's arm. "You're practically a mech."

"I reviewed your mech models on the way here," Tanis replied as her armor sealed back up around her arm, stretching across the support rod and lightwand within. "Well, the Genevian models, I should say—not 'yours'. You'd be interested to know that I think that most of them may actually be more organic than I am."

"I believe it," Ayer replied quietly. "Though it's a lot harder to spot with you."

"Better living through technology."

"That's not been my experience." Ayer shook her head and then closed her eyes. The mercenary leaned back against the shed and slid down to a seated position.

Tanis took it as a signal that the conversation was over. She saw that Johnny was asleep, and Brandt pointed at Tanis and placed her hands against her head, miming laying on a pillow.

"Yes, Mom," Tanis mouthed silently, and followed Ayer's example, leaning her head back and closing her eyes. A bit of shut-eye before the mission was just what the doctor—or commandant, in this case—ordered.

STEALING A RIDE

STELLAR DATE: 08.26.8949 (Adjusted Years)
LOCATION: Edge of Jersey City, Pyra
REGION: Albany System, Thebes, Septhian Alliance

<*Tanis, wake up,*> Angela said quietly. <*Almost noon, get ready to roll.*>

Tanis opened her eyes and stretched languidly, her vision overlaid with the readouts from nano sensors around their hiding place and the staging area at the bottom of the hill.

"EM's getting crazy in the sky again," Brandt commented. "Let's hope a belt snaps."

"Wind's picking up even more, too," Johnny said. "I wonder if the ships are what's affecting the weather."

"Maybe," Tanis shrugged.

<*I control all the Nietzschean sensors down at the staging ground,*> Angela informed Tanis on the combat net. <*Unless someone is looking right at us with the Mark 1 eyeball, we can walk right up to the ship of our choice.*>

"Unless the cruisers are running active scan on this whole region—which they could be," Ayer replied as she stood up and stretched.

<*Could be, but it will still give us time. I've falsified orders as well; a lot of conflicting directives that should cause some chaos for anyone trying to chase us. Once we get airborne, I'll unleash the dogs of confusion.*>

Tanis, Brandt, and Johnny activated their flow armor and disappeared. Ayer was still plainly visible in her lightly armored uniform, and the plan was to have her walk in the midst of the others. Angela would link the flow armor's stealth systems, bending light around all of them as much as possible, and shield the Marauder captain.

They eased around the corner of the shed and began their approach.

The Nietzschean staging ground was only a kilometer away, but the going was slow. Tall grass and brush covered the hillside, and they did their best to avoid bending stalks and branches as they went.

Fifteen minutes later, they were only a hundred meters from the base, and it was at that moment that one of the van allen belts above the planet snapped, dumping accumulated EM radiation down onto the planet's poles, which then cascaded through the atmosphere.

Tanis saw her armor's readouts jump as the air ionized around them.

<*Bet there are great polar light shows on the night side,*> Angela said to Tanis.

<*Probably. Should we pass over them with our shuttle on the way out?*>

<*Well, I did want to pick up a souvenir from this quaint little island up there. Think it won't be too much trouble during our escape?*>

Tanis only gave a mental snort in reply, feeling Angela navigating the enemy network, altering sensor readings, and making it appear as though no one was anywhere near the staging ground.

The Niets didn't have any perimeter patrols out, but she could see a group of mechanics working on a dropship, midway through the field, and another pair of guards patrolling amongst the dropships on the same side as Tanis's group.

<*That one,*> Angela highlighted a ship on Tanis's HUD, and they began creeping toward it.

The vessel was two rows in and was out of sight of the building the Niets were using as their main base of operations. So long as the patrolling guards kept on their current route, they wouldn't pass by it, either.

Just as the group passed the first row of ships, the ramp lowered on one, and a Nietzschean soldier stepped out, stretching and squinting as he looked around in the noon light.

Tanis stopped. So long as they held still and obscured Ayer, they were invisible. But with the wind gusts, they couldn't use any sound dampening nano to mask their footfalls. It was best to wait for the man to pass.

Then someone in the group shifted slightly—Tanis didn't know who—and a rock popped out from under their boot, skipping across the ground.

The Niet turned his head their way, raising a hand to shield his eyes from the sunlight.

She glanced down and saw that the wind was blowing eddies of dust around their feet, creating a strange, clear space in the air. If the man spotted it, he'd come to investigate.

The Nietzschean continued to stare in their direction. He was only sixteen meters away, and Tanis considered just shooting him and moving on, but then another man came out of the dropship from behind him, grinning as he fastened his pants and buckled his belt.

Steady, Tanis thought, praying that the new arrival would do something to distract the other Nietzschean.

Finished with his belt, the second man turned to the first as a gust of wind picked up, blowing even more dirt and debris across the landing field.

Clearly outlining the stealthed figures.

"Hey!" the first man yelled, reaching for his sidearm, only to find that it wasn't there.

Thankfully back in the ship, along with his belt, Tanis suspected.

She didn't hesitate to fire a pulse blast at him, bowling him over and knocking his friend back.

"Move!" she yelled, as an audible siren sounded, echoing amongst the ships. They raced ahead as a shot struck a hull nearby, passing the second row of ships and reaching the designated dropship a few moments later.

<It's no good,> Ayer said as she turned and fired on the pair of soldiers who had taken up position at the back of a ship in the prior row. *<They're onto us now. We have to run.>*

<Run where?> Brandt asked. *<They'll get every ship in the fleet scanning for us.>*

<We have to get aboard one of these dropships,> Tanis said. *<Get some distance.>*

Ayer looked back at Tanis, sadness in her eyes. *<I'm a liability. If it wasn't for me, you'd be home free. General, too…he had been covering me…>*

Tanis was about to reply, when the Marauder captain dashed out of cover and ran to the left, moving around to the far side of the ship the Niets were hiding behind to flank them.

<Ramp's open, get in!> Angela ordered, and Tanis fired again at the Niets, watching as her shot took out one, followed by a blast from behind the ship taking out the other.

Ayer nodded in Tanis's direction as she ran past the gap between the ships. Then she waved for Tanis to go. "Get out of here!"

Tanis made out the words on her lips, though the wind whipped away any sound. Then the Marauder was gone.

Tanis backed into the ship as the ramp closed, and turned to see Brandt settling into the cockpit.

<I'll fly, thank you very much,> Angela said. *<You organics crash too often.>*

"Ayer's in that dropship the Niets were banging in. She's powering engines," Johnny said from one of the external monitors. "It's lifting off."

<We need to go at the same time,> Angela said. *<Confuse them as to which is the priority target.>*

Tanis watched on the holo as the other ship began to lift off, then Angela brought theirs into the air.

"Stars. Good luck, Ayer," Tanis whispered, as both ships poured on max thrust, boosting up into the air.

Ayer's ship veered to the north, while Angela wove through the small hills south of Jersey City, headed to the coast.

"Another dropship is lifting off, in pursuit of Ayer," Brandt called out. Tanis watched in silence as the two ships continued north, appearing and disappearing from scan as they dipped in and out of valleys.

Then a beam of light streaked down from the sky and hit Ayer's dropship as it crested a rise. One of the dropship's engines exploded, and the craft angled sharply toward the ground.

"Fuck!" Brandt cried out as Ayer's ship disappeared from view, its passage marked by a cloud of smoke.

Angela increased the randomness of her flight pattern, exceeding what the inertial dampeners could manage, rocking the three passengers from side to side.

A bright light flared off their port bow, and then a peal of thunder shook the ship.

"Close!" Johnny cried out.

<I have to go for the city,> Angela said. *<We won't make it to the coast.>*

"Do it," Tanis said through clenched teeth.

The ship veered left, headed toward the edge of Jersey City, half of the buildings below nothing more than smoking ruins as they flashed below the dropship.

<Going to set down—> Angela began, and then another flash came, this time to their starboard, accompanied by an explosion that shook the ship.

<Brace!> Angela screamed.

The dropship dipped and plowed into the side of a high-rise, coming out the other side and falling like a rock before slowing at the last minute, only to smash through the front of another building and stop in its lobby.

Tanis shook as she pulled herself upright, and saw Johnny do the same.

"Well, shit," Brandt muttered as she tore off her harness. "We're right back where we fucking started!"

MARAUDERS

STELLAR DATE: 08.27.8949 (Adjusted Years)
LOCATION: Pyra
REGION: Albany System, Thebes, Septhian Alliance

Four dropships slipped out of the *Fury Lance* and began their descent toward the planet below. Inside one of them sat Priscilla. She was on the bench in the troop bay, along with a dozen Marines and Colonel Smith.

One of the dropships contained another dozen ISF Marines under Lieutenant Sal, and the other two held Rika and her SMI-2 mechs.

Each of the four craft would set down in different parts of Jersey City, and begin combing the ruins for any signs of Tanis and the others.

So far as Priscilla was concerned, there was only one objective: find Tanis Richards. Even Brandt, a dear friend to be sure, was secondary. A sacrifice that would be made if they had to.

These were Bob's directives. She was to save Tanis, no matter the cost. Everyone else, including herself, was expendable.

The Marauders—General Mill and Captain Ayer—who Rika desperately sought to rescue were barely on Priscilla's radar. Nothing other than leads that could bring them closer to finding Tanis.

Priscilla turned her attention to the ship's feeds and saw that, outside the dropships, space was chaos: hundreds of thousands of civilian ships trying to get further outsystem, the ruins of Appalachia Station—in ever deteriorating orbits—and Nietzschea's own ship-to-ship, and ship-to-surface traffic.

The end result was that the four ships didn't even have to get permission from an STC to drop; no one questioned another four dropcraft headed to Pyra, when thousands had already made the journey.

Priscilla watched as they came down over one of Pyra's oceans on approach to Jersey City. From what they'd been able to tell from comm traffic, the Niets considered Jersey City to be one of the most likely places Tanis had landed. She didn't know if they'd picked up Angela's transmission, or if it was just a lucky guess.

Over fifty thousand Nietzschean soldiers combed the city and the surrounding countryside, searching for the admiral and her group.

"Putting her down at the southwestern corner…looking for a nice, open plaza," the pilot, a talkative man named Ferris, called back.

"Just not too close to any enemy activity," Colonel Smith called up.

As they lowered through the atmosphere, Priscilla made contact with terrestrial wireless networks. A few were automated systems that had managed to stay up during the attack, carrying some civilian chatter and service data—which mostly consisted of alerts that everything was out of service.

What she was more interested in was the Nietzschean comm channels, where messages about the search for Tanis Richards abounded. There was not, however, any mention of General Mill, and Priscilla suspected why.

The enemy was calling Tanis by name, which cemented Priscilla's belief that Oris had been in on this attack, and that it had been intended to catch Tanis.

A far more devious plan than Priscilla would have credited the Nietzscheans for, from what she knew of them, though it fit perfectly with what Garza or the Caretaker were capable of.

Then an alert caught her attention.

Two shuttles had taken off from a nearby staging ground. One had been shot down, and the passenger, a Marauder captain, was found dead inside.

The other had crashed in the city, and search parties were already on the ground, hunting for survivors.

<*We have a location,*> Priscilla called up to Ferris and the other pilots. <*Set down at these coordinates, we'll search from there.*> She also passed the information about the Marauder captain to Rika.

Captain Ayer…killed by a self-inflicted gunshot wound to the head.

The Nietzscheans were taking prisoners in this fight, so the fact that the captain had taken her own life was a clue. A clue that pointed to her hiding information from the enemy.

The other pilots returned affirmation of her orders, and Priscilla drew a deep breath as the ships passed over the outskirts of Jersey City.

GONE TO GROUND

STELLAR DATE: 08.27.8949 (Adjusted Years)
LOCATION: Jersey City, Pyra
REGION: Albany System, Thebes, Septhian Alliance

Tanis crept along the rubble-strewn street, trying to avoid the debris while staying to the shadows, as the winds continued to whip around them. The storm was picking up, and dark clouds were rolling in from the sea.

Brandt was ahead of her, and Johnny was to the rear, watching for Niets, ready to signal for the group to freeze.

Twice now, they'd seen Nietzschean patrols, and once, a small child had raced past, ducking behind a pile of rubble and disappearing from view.

Tanis resisted the urge to go after the kid—a little girl, from the looks of her. She knew that the child was safer away from them.

<This is why I hate fighting on planets,> Tanis complained to Angela. *<Weather.>*

<I'll admit, I feel blind without probes telling me what's around the next corner.>

Brandt reached the next intersection and held a finger out, using nano on her glove to see around the corner of the building they were pressed against. Tanis stopped a few meters behind her, and Johnny stopped behind her.

No one moved; the city appeared still and dead. The only sound was the wind howling amongst the tall buildings. It sounded mournful, as though it feared that humans would never return to these shattered towers.

Then the howl changed, and Tanis wondered what the wind was blowing through to make that particular whistle, before realization struck her.

"Incoming!" she screamed.

She raced across the street, watching through her armor's three-sixty vision as Brandt and Johnny followed after, each a second behind.

A streak of light flashed by on her right, then the wall behind them exploded.

Tanis was flung into the air, carried bodily across the street by the force of the blast, and through the glass windows of the storefront on the other side.

Her armor became rigid around her torso, protecting her organs, but still allowing her to tumble loosely through the air.

It felt like she was tossed around for a minute, before coming to rest, half-draped across a table.

<You OK?> Tanis asked on the combat net as she rose and checked herself over.

<I'm here,> Brandt waved from a meter away.

<I have no reading on Johnny,> Angela said, sounding almost panicked.

Tanis staggered to the front of the building and saw Johnny's body a meter away.

His head was further back.

<He's gone, Brandt,> Tanis whispered.

Brandt limped to Tanis's side. *<Fucking dumbass kid. I told him to run!>*

<Leg?> Tanis asked.

<Fractured…twice. Armor jammed a stabilizer in it—not sure which hurts more.>

Tanis looked at Brandt's dirt-and-blood-covered body, then down at her own. Their armor's stealth systems were on low power, and unable to compensate for the grime.

They found some cloth nearby and quickly wiped one another as clean as they could, their stealth systems registering as seventy percent effective.

<You need to move,> Angela warned.

Tanis tossed a thermite grenade they'd taken from the crashed dropship at Johnny's body, turning toward the rear of the store they were in so as not to watch the young man be burned to ash.

The two women exited the back of the store and worked their way down the alley, slowly moving behind the building where the rocket had likely been fired from.

Tanis debated going up and finding who had launched it at them—Brandt probably was, too, by the way the commandant kept glancing up at the high-rise.

They were almost at the end of the alley, when a squad of Niets raced by its mouth. The women tucked into the shadows, praying they hadn't been seen.

<*We can't keep going on while blind,*> Tanis said, and drew the blade from her left forearm. She slid it into the armor on her left thigh, flexing slightly to ensure it wouldn't shift and cut her open, before signaling her armor to flow back up her left arm.

<*More dropships circling,*> Brandt said.

Angela instructed the remaining flowmetal in Tanis's left arm to form six small, spider-like bots. The bots leapt from her arm onto the wall and skittered around the corner, climbing the building and watching the street and surrounding structures.

<*Much better. Though I'm not sure it was worth trading an arm for,*> Brandt sighed.

<*If we don't spot rocket fire that blows us to bits, I'll be missing more than just an arm.*>

Brandt nodded silently and slipped around the corner once the bots showed the road to be clear. They made their way west. They still had no better plan than to take another dropship.

Luckily, several had landed near the edge of the city only ten minutes before.

Tanis knew it was a shit plan, but maybe in the storm, they could lose any pursuers and get into space, where they could bluff their way onto some small ship and take it over.

<*It's like the confluence of a shit plan and wishful thinking,*> Angela commented on Tanis's thoughts.

<*You got a better one?*>

<*No. I wish I did, but no.*>

Ahead, a plascrete barrier lay across the sidewalk and part of the road. A dozen bodies were strewn around it—the local police force, by their uniforms.

Brandt reached it first and crouched low, looking over the weapons laying on the ground. She seemed to find something she liked, then tossed a pulse rifle to Tanis.

Like a pulse rifle is going to stop heavily armored soldiers.

<*Better than nothing,*> Brandt shrugged as the wind began to pick up further.

Tanis nodded and considered grabbing more weapons—like the flash grenades sitting in a case—but they'd just make her stand out more. Even the pulse rifle could be a giveaway, if she didn't keep it out of sight.

The spiderbots showed no enemy action on the street level, though it was impossible to see into the thousands of windows stretching high into the night sky.

They covered two more blocks. Brandt was five meters ahead of Tanis, checking around a corner, when the heavens finally opened up, and sheets of rain joined the wind.

Their stealth systems dropped to only fifteen percent effective.

Brandt pulled back from the corner, but it was too late. A rail shot pierced her abdomen, spraying blood and bone out behind her. Another shot streaked through the night and hit Tanis in the leg, blowing a hole through her armor before exiting the back of her thigh.

Both women fell to the ground, and Tanis reached for Brandt, dragging her backward.

Behind them was an open archway, and Tanis pulled Brandt in with her as the commandant's armor tried to seal the large hole and stop the bleeding.

"What…what I wouldn't give for a simple can of biofoam," Brandt wheezed, grinning at Tanis.

"Fuck!" Tanis screamed looking around for something, *anything,* to help her friend. If only she had some flowmetal left. That would seal Brandt's wound back up without a problem.

Tanis's own leg wound had been sealed by her flow armor, though instead of covering the hole, it flowed through it—sealing the wound, but leaving a clear view of the ground through her leg.

It felt surreal, and she said to Angela, <*That's not something you see every day.*>

<*Brandt,*> Angela cautioned. <*Your armor's failing. It's losing integrity from trying to seal your wound.*>

Brandt reached out, grasping Tanis's shoulder. "Give me the 'nades."

"What?" Tanis gasped. "Brandt. No. It won't end like this."

Brandt nodded. "Not for you, Admiral, not for you. I'll just slow you down. You always were a lone wolf, anyway."

Tanis pursed her lips and handed Brandt the grenades. "I'll come back."

"Don't, Tanis. Remember me like this. Tell my girls…tell them I'm proud of them, and that I'll always love them."

Tanis was glad her flow armor blocked her tears, or they'd be clouding her vision.

"I will," Tanis said hoarsely.

"And you give 'em hell," Brandt coughed. "All of them. Fucking Niets, Trisilieds, Orion, you crush them to dust."

"I will," Tanis whispered. "The Niets are going to pay for this."

"They're coming," Brandt wheezed.

<*We have to go!*> Angela shouted in Tanis's mind, and Tanis took off without a second glance, smashing through the door behind them and racing through the building toward its rear exit. Before she made it through, she heard a scream followed by a muffled *thud* from behind her.

Tanis clenched her jaw and kept running.

It was just her and Angela now.

* * * * *

Rain sleeted off the sides of the buildings, falling to the streets in solid sheets of water. As if that wasn't enough, the storm was increasing in intensity.

Rika had heard of these coastal storms before. On Pyra, they called them 'cyclones', atmospheric monsters that could cover half a continent and drop decimeters of rain in a matter of hours.

Already, the city's sewers were backing up, water pooling in the gutters.

<*Pumps are probably out,*> Niki said. <*Or the Niets killed them on purpose so the water would flood out any remaining citizens.*>

<*That sounds more like them,*> Rika replied as she signaled for the SMI-2 mech ahead of her—Keli, from the readout on Rika's HUD—to check the street to the right, while she and Kelly went left.

Breaking her teams up into groups of only three felt risky, but they had several square kilometers of dense urban sprawl to cover. They'd never find Admiral Richards and General Mill if they stayed grouped up.

It would also make them an easy target for the Niets. She wasn't sure if they'd drop starfire in the storm, but Rika didn't want to give them a big target to hit.

<*I heard something,*> Keli called back. <*Sounded like an explosion.*>

<*Sure it's not lightning?*> Kelly asked.

<*Yeah, that sounds like a crack, not a snap.*>

<*Lead on,*> Rika directed.

Keli led them for two blocks before they reached an arched entrance into a low building. Body parts were strewn all around the archway, rainwater running red as it rushed to the gutters.

Rika could make out Nietzschean armor, and then saw an arm covered with the matte grey flow armor the ISF Marines wore.

Rika pulled off a bit of flesh from the limb and stepped under the arch and into the building beyond. Out of the wind and rain, she slid the skin into a small slot on her arm and surveyed the building while the DNA test ran.

Keli came in a moment later, moving further back in the building while Kelly covered the entrance.

<*Only looks like enough for one non-Niet body out there.*> Kelly said, looking back at Rika for a moment.

<*DNA matches one of the records Priscilla gave us. Commandant Brandt.*>

<*Shit,*> Kelly swore. <*That's one of their uppity ups. Fresh, though, right?*>

<*Got a smashed door here,*> Keli called from the back of the building. <*Someone passed through.*>

Rika considered passing the details to Priscilla and Colonel Smith, but she didn't want to risk any broadcast comms until they knew who they were following.

<*OK, let's keep moving,*> Rika instructed.

DARKEST HOUR

STELLAR DATE: 08.27.8949 (Adjusted Years)
LOCATION: Jersey City, Pyra
REGION: Albany System, Thebes, Septhian Alliance

Tanis fired a pulse shot at another Niet before shifting back into cover behind the pile of rubble in the building's atrium. She could see that the shot knocked him off his feet, but didn't take him out.

A red light flashed on her rifle, and its small display read, 'no charge'.

<Well, time to do this the old-fashioned way.>

<Give 'em hell, Tanis.>

She rose from behind the rubble and tossed the rifle aside before sliding her lightwand out of her right thigh. She flicked her wrist, activating its new, meter-long, monofilament blade.

"Bring it, fuckers."

The Nietzschean soldier struggled to his feet, and Tanis summoned the remains of her strength, let out a scream, and charged the man.

He brought his rifle to bear and fired a kinetic round as she closed the gap.

The shot struck her in the right side of her chest, and Tanis shrugged off the impact, though a warning flashed on her HUD that her armor's kinetic resistance abilities were nearly dead. One more shot like that, and she'd be on heart number eight.

<Nine, Tanis.> Angela commented.

Then Tanis was upon the man and swung her glowing blue blade at his rifle, slicing it in half—along with his hand—and cutting halfway through his neck.

Good enough, Tanis thought as he fell to the ground.

She saw movement from her left, and dove out of the way as a pulse blast rippled through the air where she'd stood. Her limbs leaden with fatigue, Tanis scrambled behind a pillar, waiting for the shooter to get closer.

With the meager few probes Tanis had left, she saw that it was a Nietzschean woman, tall and lithe. She moved into the atrium, advancing on Tanis's cover.

Tanis slowly sucked in a deep breath and blew it out quietly, then ducked out from behind the column when the woman was three meters away, rolled over a fallen beam, and sliced into the woman's left knee joint.

As the Nietzschean crashed to the ground, she fired a kinetic slug into the air, striking the windows at the far end of the atrium.

For a moment, Tanis thought the glass would hold; then the windows exploded inward, spraying fractured plates of glass across the atrium. Tanis turned her head as shards swept across her body, most bounding off, but some slicing into her where the flow armor had begun to fail.

One moment, the storm was outside, and then the next, its fury was all around her.

Tanis crashed to her knees, feeling the last of her energy ebb away, draining out of her through the hundred cuts across her body.

As she struggled to catch her breath, she realized that the storm sounded different, almost as though it was screaming at her. Tanis slowly raised her head and saw a dozen Nietzscheans surrounding her, their weapons drawn.

She opened her mouth to speak, but something felt wrong inside of her.

<Angela, I feel—>

It was Angela. Angela was gone, her centuries-long presence snuffed out.

<Angela! Where are you?> Tanis cried out in her mind, feeling dizzy and wondering if she'd suffered a head wound. She sat back on her shins, the Nietzscheans forgotten. She lifted her right hand to touch her head, but stopped, afraid that she'd find a part of her skull smashed in.

You said we'd be together, that if this was our end, it would be our end ***together****.*

A boot lashed out and kicked Tanis in the head, and she fell to the ground.

Her vision swam, and then everything went black.

I am Angela, she thought.

And I am Tanis.

No. I am new.

She hadn't opened her eyes, but she was staring at…at something. Was it the ground? It looked strange, it was so porous. Kilometers of transparent rock, and then beyond that, glowing, molten magma, caverns of hyper-dense carbon crystals, seething iron, falling chunks of crust, gently drifting to the planet's core like leaves, creating rising magma flows…and then the crust of the world again, followed by sky, and space, ships, and stars.

What is this? She wondered, and pressed her hand against the world, only to have it pass through the ground.

She felt a moment of pure terror, fearing that she'd fall through the world and out the other side, or worse, be trapped in its core forever.

This new being concentrated and pressed its hand against the planet, and this time they met, and the planet moved away. No. She moved up. But the planet *did* also move away, if only a very little.

Sounds began to come back to her. She heard the storm—winds raging, lightning cracking, thunder rumbling.

The being looked up at the sky and saw right through it, into space. She felt like she might fall up forever; maybe she could catch hold of a starship, if she did.

Then something moved, pushing toward her.

The being, *Tangel*, she decided for now—though a better name would have to come—realized it was a pulse wave, a concussive blast rippling through the air toward her.

It was curious. Such a small amount of energy. She let it pass through her body, changing the composition of her form to vibrate in a way that posed no obstacle to the wave.

She looked up to see the people. Nietzscheans. *Enemies.*

One was holding a weapon, looking down at it as though something was wrong.

Tangel peered at the weapon, too. She saw all its components, its molecules, atoms, electrons…smaller things, too. She supposed they were all the bits Earnest was always playing with. Wimps, mesons, quarks, and the like.

She stretched out her hand and changed them, turning the weapon into dust, shifting the energy from within the atomic and subatomic bonds into herself.

The world around her became clearer as strength returned. She could see through things, but she could see new things, too. So many more planes and angles. She saw that flat surfaces were made up of impossibly complex objects, all coursing with strange energy that seemed to both push things together and pull them apart.

Is this what Cary sees when she deep-Links with Faleena? Tangel wondered.

There was more yelling, and Tangel realized the Nietzscheans were still there. Half were afraid, the other half were angry.

I've been staring right through them…

The Nietzscheans advanced, and Tangel clenched her jaw. She still had a jaw.

"Stop," Tangel said, and the Nietzscheans all froze. Not because she'd removed their ability to move, but because of how loud her voice was. Tanis felt like she'd spoken on every frequency all at once.

This is going to take some practice.

She tapped into the energy she saw pushing and pulling at the foundations of reality and drew it toward her, wrapping it around herself like a cocoon. It would keep her safe. Safe from the storm and from these soldiers who wanted to hurt her.

One of them was raising his rifle, and Tangel did the same to it as she had done to the previous weapon, removing all the energy from within it, and drawing it into herself.

She reached out to gesture for the soldiers to move aside, and remembered that she only had one arm.

That won't do, Tangel thought with a laugh.

Matter rose from the ground, streamed from the weapons the soldiers held, even from their armor.

She stopped short of drawing matter from the soldiers' bodies. Something felt wrong about that. She considered removing the energy from their bodies—like she had done to the weapons—but that felt wrong, too.

The matter drew toward her, and then coalesced into a new arm. Tangel looked down at it and flexed her fingers, peering intently at her digits. Were they organic? No. They were not quite like the other organic parts of her body. But they weren't non-organic, either.

What have I made? she wondered.

Tangel spotted her lightwand laying on the ground, and a memory resonated through her mind.

'Pry it from my cold, dead hands.'

She pushed past the Nietzscheans. Well, half pushed, half walked through them, and reached for her lightwand. As she did, small bits of debris exploded around her, and Tangel realized the Nietzscheans were all firing on her.

With a sigh, she disassembled their weapons, and then their armor, leaving them naked in the storm. Some of them screamed and ran, some backed quietly into corners, a few fell where they were.

Tangel ignored them and walked out of the atrium and into the storm, summoning a sphere of energy around her, watching the water sluice off it to the ground.

She looked up and down the street. She still had to get to a dropship and fly out of here. For a moment, Tangel considered that she might be able to simply fall up as she feared. Could she fall up and fly into space?

A deep breath made her consider that her body may still require oxygen to survive. *Best not to chance it right now.*

Yelling came from her left, and Tangel saw more Niets. These ones had heavy armor and railguns, and they began to fire at her, the accelerated particles and kinetics striking the protective sphere around her and turning into nothing.

No, not 'nothing'; the sphere was turning the matter into energy, and that was going into her body.

***Too** much energy,* she realized. Though she seemed to exist beyond the physical realm she was used to, her body was still constructed of normal matter and could not store an infinite amount of energy.

She had to discharge it somehow, in some form.

Much of the energy she held was in the form of photons and highly excited electrons. She could drop the electrons into the ground, or she could send them back at the Nietzscheans who were attacking her.

Tangel chose the latter, and a blue-white blast of energy poured out of the sphere surrounding her, burning away the enemy, as well as the buildings around them.

She felt a sense of satisfaction to see the power they'd directed at her sent back to them, but then realized she couldn't stop the blast. It kept going, sucking away all her energy, leaving her weak.

The process she'd initiated began to convert matter to energy, consuming her flow armor, the energy holding its atoms together now coming apart and flowing out toward the enemy that was long since burned to ash.

"Stop!" she screamed, but it wouldn't stop. Then, just when she thought that her body might be consumed and turn to dust as well, the blast ceased, and the sphere around her disappeared.

In an instant, the storm slammed back into Tanis's naked body, and she fell to the ground, unconscious.

ISF FIRST FLEET

STELLAR DATE: 08.27.8949 (Adjusted Years)
LOCATION: ISS *I2*, Bridge
REGION: Inner Albany System, Thebes, Septhian Alliance

If it wasn't for the fact that she was worried sick about Tanis and Brandt—not to mention Priscilla, Colonel Smith, and the Marines—Rachel would have been reveling in the fact that she was in command of a fleet.

And not just the First Intrepid Fleet, with its few dozen ships, but a *real* fleet.

A thousand ships were arrayed around the *I2*, organized in sub-formations where ships with stasis shields could offer protection to those without.

Beyond the thousand visible ships, another two thousand stealthed cruisers advanced above and below the star system's equatorial plane. But the enemy had no knowledge of those ships.

To the Nietzscheans, it must have appeared as though the attackers were insane. A thousand ships against seventy thousand was unheard of. At least for them.

Rachel watched the Comm team shunt another segment of traffic off to the secondary team, one deck down. With so many ships still fleeing the system, the ISF had turned into the de facto space traffic control for the outer Albany System.

Stations and planets had begun deferring to the inbound ISF fleet for vector confirmation a day ago, and now they were asking about everything from when it would be safe to send more ships out, to what they should do with inbound traffic that was low on fuel, and had to dock somewhere.

Someone had even asked if they could find their missing dog on Pyra.

The volume was running everyone ragged, and Rachel was considering leaving a ship in the outer system with a team of traffic and logistics specialists aboard, just to coordinate the locals.

Even so, she didn't blame the people of Albany. Until two weeks ago, they didn't know ships *could* jump deep inside a system. They had never seen a fleet the size of the one now occupying their space, and they'd *certainly* never seen a fleet outnumbered seventy-to-one advance and not retreat.

Granted, neither had Rachel.

Organizing the fleet had not been easy. The forces sent from far and wide came with their own command structure, some of whom outranked Rachel considerably. Amongst the assembled ships were an admiral, two generals, and a host of colonels.

Though her title was 'captain', Rachel's own actual rank was that of colonel. However, the honor of having one's butt in the *I2*'s command chair far outweighed any rank.

At one point, the admiral and two of the colonels had attempted to take control of the fleet's strategy away from Rachel. It had been a tense period, but Sera had sent directives over the QuanComm network that she was in charge, and that her orders were backed up by Admirals Evans and Greer—even Empress Diana.

Joe had included a private message, telling her that sitting in the command chair of the *I2* was a de facto promotion to admiral.

The compliment from Admiral Evans had made her all but glow with pride—and worry that he was probably nuts, to put so much on her.

Not your first time out, Rachel admonished herself. *Not your first time at the helm of* ***this*** *ship in a pitched fight, either.*

"We've crossed the first marker," Scan called out.

The first marker denoted passage into the sector where they were in range of relativistic missiles with no time for fleet-wide evasion. Granted, there could have been RMs lying in wait further back, but now they were also at risk of live fire.

The stealthed ships, broken into four groups, were already well beyond the first marker; by the time Rachel's main formation reached the second marker, they would be almost at Pyra.

When the *I2* passed the third marker, all hell would break loose.

"Fire control, instruct Fleet Group One to begin random fire, pattern alpha."

"Aye, ma'am."

A smattering of ships in the fleet—a selection of Scipian, Silstrand, and TSF vessels—fired railguns at the Nietzschean ships in orbit around Pyra.

No one expected the shots to hit, but it would cause the enemy to spread out and decrease their ability to bring concentrated firepower to bear on single targets.

After a few minutes, the random railgun fire ceased. It would still take thirty minutes for the shots to reach the enemy, but it would, she hoped, create an image of an undisciplined, ragtag force.

The next nineteen minutes were filled with nothing but waiting for the enemy's reaction to the incoming shots. Then they saw groups of Nietzschean vessels begin to shift further out from Pyra, until over half of them were beyond the orbits of Pyra's two moons.

"Cautious. Too bad." A voice said from Rachel's left, and she nearly jumped.

"Finaeus," she breathed as she glanced at the man. "Scared the crap out of me!"

"It's a talent, I won't lie. Sadly, there's not a lot of call for stealthy engineers."

Rachel couldn't help but smile. Finaeus was the very definition of 'unflappable'. Perhaps it was because he'd seen so much, lived through so much, that nothing fazed him anymore.

Still, she was surprised that he was able to be so calm while looking out over the enemy ships.

"What do you make of our odds?" she asked quietly.

Finaeus snorted. "One hundred percent. These dickheads don't stand a chance."

"Not worried at all?"

Finaeus leaned against a console—earning an annoyed look from Major Jessie, which he appeared to not even notice. "Did I ever tell you about Star City?"

"I heard Tanis say the name once, but that was about it."

"We're trying to keep the place hush-hush and not let remnants or ascended AIs know about it—if they don't already. Which I think they do. Anyway, we know the *I2* is clear of remnants, so I'll lay it on you. Star City is out in Orion Space, in the Perseus Arm. And it's old, over three thousand years."

"Really?" Rachel asked. "How—"

Finaeus held up his hand, cutting her off. "Story for another time. Anyway, Star City has sixteen bastions, which have the most amazing

AIs ever—also a story for another time—protecting it. We were having a little visit, when Orion launched a *major* assault on the city. They threw over a hundred thousand ships at it."

Rachel whistled. "I had no idea."

"Yeah, well, neither did Orion. Guess how many ships Star City had?"

Rachel shrugged. "Ummm…two hundred thousand?"

"Zero."

"Zero?"

"Yeah. Am I doing that thing where I think words, but forget to say them? Zero."

She rolled her eyes at her chief engineer. "Ha ha, Finaeus. Get on with it."

"Well, see, the thing is Star City had a plan, tactics, and superior technology. They knew how to use it, and they won the day. Guess how many casualties they had?"

"Finaeus, I hate guessing games."

"C'mon."

"I don't know…zero."

"Right you are!" Finaeus crowed. "No one died. Jessica came close, but in the end, no one did. The Orion fleet was *utterly* destroyed. To the last ship."

"How in the stars did they do that?" Major Jessie asked, apparently having forgiven Finaeus for leaning against her console.

"Classified," Finaeus replied. "But fret not. Earnest and I are working on a way to miniaturize what they sorted out. And when we do…"

"Yes…?" Rachel prompted.

"Blammo!" Finaeus shouted. "Game over, bad guys."

"You have such a way with words."

Finaeus gave a mock bow. "I try."

"So you're not worried about this at all?" Rachel waved a hand at the forward display to indicate the enemy ships.

"*Nietzscheans?* Are you kidding? Those guys are as dumb as rocks. I mean, don't get me wrong, Nietzsche had some good ideas, but he was a nineteenth century philosopher. Trying to take his precepts and blanket apply them to the ninetieth century? Build a civilization around it? These guys must eat stupid for breakfast."

"And Tanis?" Rachel asked.

For an instant, Rachel thought she saw a look of concern flash across Finaeus's face, then it was gone. "I'm worried about what she'll do to the Niets."

Something about the way Finaeus said those words felt wrong to Rachel. She wondered if it had anything to do with the reason both Bob and Finaeus had insisted that they send Priscilla with Colonel Smith's strike team.

She was about to ask, when Scan called out, "A section of the enemy's fleet is breaking off. They're on a trajectory to flank us."

Rachel glanced at Finaeus. "Looks like they didn't eat too much stupid today. That's the tactic we rated as best for them and worst for us."

"Only if they commit a third of their force to—OK, they've committed a third. Must have been Stupid-Lite today."

<Fleet Group Three,> Rachel called out to the ships on the right flank. *<Fire rails, Sigma pattern.>*

<Sigma pattern, Aye,> Fleet Group Three's fire control responded. Their NSAI configured optimal patterns, which were then confirmed by humans and AIs alike.

Fleet Group Three fired their rails, and hundreds of five-ton slugs streaked out from the ships toward where the Nietzschean vessels moving to the ISF's right flank would be in ten minutes.

Tanis and the fleet tacticians believed that word of the ISF's use of grapeshot had spread amongst Orion's allies by now. While still brutally effective, it was likely that its tactical usefulness was diminished.

To counter this, the fleet engineers had come up with a new rail-fired weapon system that—hopefully—would take the enemy by surprise.

"This should be good," Finaeus said as they watched the slugs creep across the holotank's display toward the enemy ships.

Scan showed the Nietzschean vessels moving aside, creating gaps in their formation for the slugs to pass through.

"Poor Neaties. Not moving enough," Rachel said with a smile.

" 'Neaties'?" Finaeus asked, a brow raised.

Rachel shrugged. " 'Niets' makes me think of nits, which is gross. It also makes them sound all tidy. The dichotomy doesn't work in my head. Trying out a new name."

Major Jessie gave a soft laugh. "Try again."

Rachel glanced at her XO, and then turned back to the holos. One side of the main tank showed projections, while the other showed actuals.

The projection estimated that over five hundred enemy ships would take damage from the shots. A nice opening salvo.

The slugs were traveling at ten thousand kilometers per second, and when they passed within twenty-thousand klicks of the enemy fleet, they exploded.

Actuals tagged thousands of impacts on the Nietzschean ships, most being deflected by shields, but the ships closest to the shrapnel bore the brunt of the impact. Twenty-nine enemy vessels lost power, and three exploded seconds later.

When the shots hit, a soft cheer sounded on the bridge, and Rachel smiled. This crew knew what it was doing and was determined to see their mission through and rescue Tanis.

Fleet Group Three fired again, and this time, the enemy formation scattered wide, spreading out to avoid the shots entirely.

She almost felt bad for the Nietzscheans.

SAVING HER

STELLAR DATE: 08.27.8949 (Adjusted Years)
LOCATION: Jersey City, Pyra
REGION: Albany System, Thebes, Septhian Alliance

A brilliant light streamed out from around a corner ahead, lighting up the city like it was noon. No. Brighter than noon. It seemed to be shining away from them, and Rika signaled for Keli and Kelly to follow her.

She reached the corner, which was occupied by a store selling a selection of soft and colorful bedding supplies, and peered around to see a star resting in the middle of the street.

At least, that's what it looked like at first.

A beam of blue-white light that reminded Rika of an electron beam shot from the star down the street—in the other direction, thankfully—burning its way through Jersey City, and clear over to a large hill outside of town, where lightning streaked from the ground into the sky.

<*Shit, what is that?*> Kelly asked.

<*They'll be able to see it from space!*> Keli exclaimed.

<*Is that some sort of fusion reaction?*> Rika asked Niki, who did not reply.

Then the light went out, and the sphere disappeared. In its place stood a naked woman. Her body wobbled side to side, and then went limp, collapsing to the ground.

Rika didn't give a moment's thought to her own safety as she rushed across the street and knelt beside the woman.

She was curled up in a fetal position, and Rika tried to turn her over. At first, her hand slipped off the woman's shoulder—or maybe went through it—but then Rika managed to find purchase and roll her over.

<*It's Admiral Richards!*> Niki exclaimed. <*What the hell did she just do?*>

<*Beats me,*> Rika muttered, unable to make sense of what she saw. Admiral Richards appeared to be completely unharmed, yet moments ago, she had been standing in a ball of energy more powerful than a starship's beams.

"We have to get her out of here!" Rika yelled. "Kelly, break into that store we just passed and get something to wrap her in, she's freezing."

She knew she didn't have to speak aloud, but she just felt like yelling.

Kelly was back a moment later with a large comforter that was soft on one side and covered in a shiny polymer on the other.

"Should keep the rain off," Kelly said as they wrapped Tanis in it. Once she was cocooned, Rika slung the admiral over her shoulder.

<*Priscilla, do you read me?*>

<*I do! Did you see that light?*> Priscilla's voice sounded worried—very worried.

<*See it? We watched it blow away half the city. Then we found Tanis Richards where the light was.*>

<*You've got her? Stars! We're close, we'll meet you. We need to get the ships to pick us up; the Niets are going to come fast.*>

As if Priscilla's words were prescient, Kelly and Keli both began firing uranium sabot rounds at Niets who were advancing down the street behind them.

<*You're telling me! Where are you?*>

<*A block to your east. The Marines are coming.*>

Rika turned east while Keli and Kelly covered her back. Suddenly, dark shapes appeared all around her, a dozen kinetic slug throwers lobbing HE rounds at the Nietzscheans.

Rika felt Tanis slip out of her arms, even though she was held securely.

"What the—"

"Hold still," one of the figures said, and Rika saw flow armor pull away from a face, revealing Priscilla.

Rika stopped as Priscilla pulled down the blanket, exposing Tanis's face.

"Stars, she looks perfect," Priscilla said. "Totally unharmed."

"Yeah, but what was that? Did she do that? How?"

<*It was a controlled…I don't know, matter-energy stripping reaction,*> Niki supplied. <*That should have blown away the entire city.*>

Priscilla didn't respond, but touched Tanis's head. Rika saw something flow from her hand into Tanis, and a moment later, the admiral felt heavier, as though part of her that had not been present before, now was.

"What did you do?" Rika asked. "More importantly, what did *she* do?"

<*Rika,*> Priscilla spoke only into Rika's mind. <*You must forget what you saw, speak of it to no one.*>

<*What?*> Rika asked, and Niki added. <*We can't just unsee that!*>

<*You must!*> Priscilla said. <***No one** can know.*>

<*Why?*> Niki asked.

<*Because.*> Priscilla looked down and stroked Tanis's forehead. <*She's ascending.*>

COMING UP

STELLAR DATE: 08.28.8949 (Adjusted Years)
LOCATION: Jersey City, Pyra
REGION: Albany System, Thebes, Septhian Alliance

Rika hung out the back of the dropship and fired her electron beam at the closest pursuer, a vacuum fighter that was struggling through the heavy winds of the cyclone tearing its way across the coast.

Her shot dissipated in the thick rain, but enough of the energy struck the target's port engine—for the third time—to finally knock him out of the pursuit.

Not that Rika's dropships were doing much better. Ferris was fighting the controls, screaming at the wind, his heavy load, Nietzschean engineering, and anything else that came to mind.

As if on cue, he started up another rant. "Oh, more fucking red indicators. *I know* our rear grav drive is losing power, the holes in the hull were my first clue, you piece of shit! Your mother was a Nietzschean garbage dump!"

Rika glanced back to where Priscilla sat with Tanis. Both were strapped into their seats, and Priscilla's arm was wrapped around Tanis's shoulders, keeping her head tucked close against her body.

She tried not to think about Captain Ayer and General Mill. They didn't know exactly *what* had happened to the general, but Priscilla had gotten onto the Nietzschean networks where she'd found records of his body being found.

Rika stared down at the diminishing lights of Jersey City. She'd be back to retrieve his body and give it a proper burial in space.

The ship bucked again, and Rika tightened her grip on the hull ribbing, then breathed a sigh of relief as the rain suddenly stopped and the clouds began to thin. A moment later, the raging storm dropped away below them, its cloud tops gently lit by the engines of thousands of starships.

<OK...for something that was really intent on killing us a second ago, that storm sure looks beautiful,> Kelly said.

Below, two more dropships pulled out of the clouds, then a third.

Stars, we all made it, Rika thought a moment before a beam streaked out of the sky, burning away one of the dropships.

"Fuck!" Ferris screamed and banked hard to port, then starboard, bucking the dropship like it was a wild animal.

Rika was nearly thrown from the ship before she pounded her GNR into the emergency switch, and the ramp swung up, slamming closed centimeters from her face.

She turned toward the front of the ship and saw starfire streak through the night, directly ahead of the shuttle, and then Ferris dove again. Signaling for Kelly and Keli to join the Marines and take a seat, Rika pulled herself forward to stand behind Ferris.

"Just like old times, eh, Captain?" he called out over his shoulder. "Look at that! I used rank! Go me!"

"How far?" Rika asked.

"Fucked if I know…damn ship is *invisible*!"

Another beam of starfire streaked past, and Ferris pulled the dropship up. The beam followed them, about to make contact with their hull, and then suddenly it was gone, stopped by an invisible object.

The *Derringer.*

<*This is Captain Mel of the ISS* Derringer. *Your chariot has arrived!*>

A light appeared on the side of the ship, and Rika realized it was a bay door opening. Ferris made a beeline for it, and Rika saw from scan that the other two dropships were hot on their tail.

The craft hadn't even finished settling onto the cradle before Captain Mel called out again. <*Hold onto your hats, it's going to get bumpy! Oh, and Captain Rika, we've updated your ships with our outbound trajectory. We're going to meet up with them when we blast through the Nietzschean lines.*>

Rika still hadn't gotten control of her breathing. Ten seconds ago, she had been certain they were all going to die. Now they were safe behind an ISF stasis shield, about to break away from the Nietzscheans.

<*'Kay,*> was all she managed to send back.

Captain Mel replied with a laugh, but didn't reply further.

Behind them, the dropship's ramp lowered, and Rika turned to see one of the ISF Marines lift Admiral Richards out of her seat and carry her off the shuttle and into the bay.

"Will she be OK?" Rika asked Priscilla.

Priscilla stared after the admiral's retreating form for a moment before replying. "Yes, she'll be fine."

At the bottom of the ship's ramp, a woman waited, looking at the mechs disembarking from the ships.

"Captain Rika?" she asked.

Rika pulled off her helmet and slid it onto the hasp at her hip.

"Here."

The woman's eyes locked on Rika's and she nodded. "Captain Mel's asked that you come to the bridge. You can observe and coordinate with your ships from there."

Rika turned and saw Leslie descend from one of the other shuttles, a look of pure joy and relief on her face.

<*Go do captain-y things. We've got this down here,*> Leslie said with a wide grin.

Rika gave her friend an equally wide grin, relieved beyond words that Leslie hadn't been on the ship that was destroyed. The thought made her even more glad that Chase hadn't come along. She'd managed to convince him at the last moment that he'd be needed, should the *Fury Lance* get boarded during the fighting.

Rika followed the woman—Ensign Harriet, by the tag on her chest—as she led the way through the ship and up a series of ladders, until they reached the bridge.

"I can't thank you enough for saving the admiral," Harriet said at one point. "I don't know…. It doesn't bear thinking about."

The vision of the sphere encapsulating Tanis, blasting raw energy into the night and tearing a hole through the city, was all that came to Rika's mind. "No, no it doesn't."

Half a minute later, they stepped onto the bridge, and Rika saw Captain Mel, a tall, lanky woman with fluorescent yellow hair tied up in a knot on the back of her head.

"Captain Rika!" Mel said as she approached and clasped Rika's hand. "You have no idea the debt of gratitude the ISF owes you. You are, without a doubt, a hero of our people."

Rika couldn't help but think of General Mill, dead somewhere in Jersey City. The fact that he'd died ten days ago—back when she was still in the Hercules System—didn't seem to help the feeling that she should have been able to do something.

He'd been a good man, good to her. A strong mentor. And now he was gone; snuffed out in a coup launched by the very people the Marauders had bled to save just a year ago.

"Thank you," Rika said quietly.

"Right, that must have been harrowing," Captain Mel said, her voice softer. Then she pointed to the holotank. "Look there. The five highlighted ships are yours. They're in a low polar orbit, right where you left them."

Rika nodded as she approached. "The Niets didn't make any problems?"

"One of their traffic control ships was getting persnickety, but then Rachel's fleet started lobbing rail shots, and everyone's focus shifted to her."

"So what's our route out of here?" Rika asked.

A plotted course appeared on the holo. "With any luck, we'll slip past most of them. If we have to, we can take a few out, but I'd prefer not to get ten thousand ships on our tail. Stasis shields are good, but they're not that good."

"Where's the rest of your fleet?" Rika asked.

Captain Mel expanded the view, and Rika saw a cluster of ships approaching the Nietzschean formation. They were still over a million miles away, but RMs were already flying between the ISF and Nietzschean vessels.

"Once we're clear, are they going to turn and head outsystem with us?" Rika asked.

Captain Mel cocked her head and looked at Rika as though she'd said something crazy.

"Uh, no, they're going to defeat the Nietzscheans. Then we'll carry on and crush their empire—at least we'd better."

Rika couldn't help but let out a disbelieving laugh. "That's…confident of you."

Captain Mel just flashed a smile and turned back to the holo. "Scan, any sign of Orion ships, or zero-point energy fields?"

"None so far, Captain Mel."

"You spot a single OG hull tucked into this mess, you get on all-fleet, you hear?"

"Aye, ma'am."

"Orion…that's the enemy Priscilla said is beyond the Orion Nebula, right?" Rika asked as she looked over the fleet formations on the holo.

"Yeah, plus just beyond half of known space. Orion's big, stretches into the Perseus Arm."

"Seriously?" Rika asked, certain that the captain was messing with her.

Mel waved her hand. "Not important right now. What *is* important is that they have good stealth tech. Not as good as ours, but damn hard to pick up. I don't *think* they're out there, but if they are, I want to be ready."

"Why don't you think they're there?"

Mel turned and locked her eyes on Rika's. "The Admiral, Captain Rika. If the Orion Guard knew she was crashed on that planet, they would have done one of two things."

"Which are?"

"Completely blanket the planet's surface with troops to capture her…or destroy it. They would *not* have left it to the Niets."

Rika wondered if Captain Mel had an extreme case of hero worship. "They'd destroy an entire planet to capture or kill Admiral Richards?"

Mel nodded, and Rika saw that other members of the bridge crew did, as well.

"Why—" she began to ask, but Mel held up her hand.

"It's begun."

Rika saw the ISF fleet's forward elements move into range of the Nietzschean ships. She didn't understand what the ISF, which she assumed was under the command of Captain Rachel on the *I2*, had planned.

The leading edge of the Niet fleet was spread wide, and a second group—which was on the ISF's right flank—was also distributed over a huge volume of space.

Rika suspected that the enemy had dispersed to avoid long-range shots, but now they were coalescing into a half-sphere, wrapping around the ISF ships. In a minute, over thirty thousand Nietzschean vessels would be within firing range of the *I2*.

Rika wondered why Captain Mel looked expectant. She should be terrified.

Beams lanced out from the Nietzschean ships, all targeting the *I2*. In an instant, the massive ISF ship disappeared in a blazing ball of light, its glow dwarfing that of the Albany System's star.

For all her bluster, Rika saw Captain Mel suck in a breath.

"Coming up on the Nietzscheans' polar line," a bridge officer announced behind them.

Rika turned her attention to a secondary holotank.

"You have a tightbeam to your flagship, Captain Rika," the Comm officer said.

<Chase, Heather, you there?> Rika asked.

<You bet, Rika. How'd it go down there?> Chase asked.

Rika didn't want to get into the details at the moment, and only said, *<Well enough. We're boosting past you. They've passed the coordinates.>*

<We'll follow after,> Heather spoke up. *<But the Niets are already suspicious of us. They're going to think we're deserting.>*

<OK, let me see what we can do,> Rika replied.

"Captain Mel, my crew is worried that the enemy will fire on them if they break formation."

Mel stroked her chin for a moment. "Valid." She turned to an officer on her left. "Flicker the stealth for a second so that the enemy doesn't think Rika's ships are deserting."

"Aye, Captain."

<See that?> Rika asked.

<Ballsy!> Heather replied. *<Though not as much as the* I2 *out there.>*

<OK, we're 'pursing' you,> Chase said. *<Stay safe.>*

<You too,> Rika replied.

During the conversation, Rika had kept one eye on the ball of light that was the *I2*. She did, however, remember to thank Captain Mel for making her ship visible—however briefly—to the enemy.

"Welcome," Mel nodded calmly in response.

"Aren't you worried?" Rika asked, gesturing to the *I2*. "Your flagship is being annihilated!"

"That ball of energy means that everything they're throwing at it is being shed off by the stasis shield. If the ball goes away, *then* it's bad."

"Bad because they blew up?" Rika asked.

Captain Mel shook her head. "No, bad because they tore a hole in space-time, and this entire star system will probably cease to exist."

Rika's mouth was hanging open again, and she looked around the bridge. "Who *are* you people?"

Mel snapped her fingers and pointed at the holo.

While the Niets were pouring all their weapons into the *I2*, the rest of the ISF fleet began to respond, firing on Nietzschean ships in successive waves, their high-powered beams cutting right through the enemy's shields and shredding their ships.

Even though they had little trouble destroying enemy vessels, the ISF fleet was small, and they were barely making a dent on the enemy forces.

A moment later, the barrage hitting the *I2* ceased, and the ship's shields glowed brightly for another few seconds before returning to their normal transparent state.

The *I2* was unscathed.

Cheers erupted around Rika, and she was at a total loss for words.

<*Now **that's** a new thing,*> Niki commented.

"And…here they are," Captain Mel said, turning to Rika with a look of triumph in her eyes.

Rika looked back at the holo and saw two things happen almost simultaneously.

The first was that two thousand ships appeared on the far side of Pyra, well behind the Nietzschean lines, accelerating toward the enemy. As Rika watched, the ships closed within weapons range, and their beams began tearing through shields and ships in rapid succession.

Rika felt a thrill in her chest at the sight of it, but there were still too many Nietzscheans, and they began to concentrate fire on the smaller ISF ships.

At a thousand to one, they could breach the ISF ships' shields, and they did so a dozen times within seconds. Rika began to worry that the tactic would fail.

But then the battlespace changed entirely.

At first, Rika thought that the holotank had suffered a failure, as it seemed to show that the number of Nietzschean ships had doubled.

"They're here!" Mel cried out, and the bridge erupted in cheers.

"Who?" Rika asked.

Mel gestured at the roughly forty thousand new ships interspersed amongst the Nietzscheans. "Just about everybody, from the looks of it."

With the Nietzscheans spread wide, no more than three to four ships could bring meaningful fire to bear on the newcomers—who were all protected by stasis shields, easily shrugging off the meager attacks.

Tears formed in the corners of Rika's eyes as she watched the new ships begin to tear into the enemy, their brilliant beams slicing through the Niets like they were made of foil.

"What's wrong?" Mel asked Rika.

Rika drew in a steadying breath and she gestured at the holotank. "All my life, this was the thing I feared most." Her voice came as a whisper, and she took another breath, speaking louder as she continued. "The vaunted Nietzschean Space Force. They were unstoppable. A fleet this size was the stuff of nightmares, yet here they are, falling by the thousands."

Rika gave a self-deprecating laugh and then shrugged off her concern over being so emotional before strangers. "It may be one of the most beautiful things I've ever seen."

Mel didn't even miss a beat as she barked a laugh and slapped Rika on the back. "Rika? You're my kinda woman."

FALLEN

STELLAR DATE: 08.28.8949 (Adjusted Years)
LOCATION: ISS *I2*, Bridge
REGION: Inner Albany System, Thebes, Septhian Alliance

Rachel felt sweat pouring down her head as the Nietzscheans continued to fire on the *I2*.

The great vessel was wrapped in a fire hotter than the corona of a B-class star. Protons, electrons, and neutrons ceased to exist as they stopped instantaneously, halted by the *I2*'s shields.

The energy shed from atomic particles' relativistic speeds' instant cessation tore them apart, reflecting degenerate matter and quantum particles in all directions.

The nearby ISF ships were protected by the deadly wave of ricocheting energy by their own stasis shields. But as the energy reflecting off the *I2* spread back out toward the Nietzschean ships, they would soon find that their shields were being weakened by *their* own weapons fire.

Or so Rachel hoped.

<We're reaching critical thresholds on the CriEn system,> Bob advised. *<I will have to shut them down in seventy-two seconds.>*

<Understood, Bob.> Rachel nodded.

At that point, their only hope would be to drop into the dark layer. Current maps indicated that there *should* be a pocket right here, but no one kept detailed public maps of dark matter this deep in a star system. Normally, there was no need to.

It was a terrible gamble, but one they'd all gladly make to save Tanis.

No one spoke for another thirty seconds; all eyes were on the CriEn shutdown timer. Then came the words they all craved hearing.

"Enemy fire has ceased!" Scan cried out, triggering sighs of relief around the bridge.

Rachel still couldn't see the battlespace, but that was expected. The shields—and the space around them—would take a moment to cool off and bleed away enough EM radiation to see through.

"We have imaging!" Scan called out again, and visuals from beyond the shield began to filter in through pinhole sensor openings. Widening the sensor holes any further would bathe the ship in radiation.

The imaging was weak, and tactical NSAIs worked to plot out where all the enemy ships were.

"Mostly unmoved," Finaeus observed.

"But where are the stealthed groups?" Rachel murmured.

Then scan detected them behind the Nietzscheans, as they opened fire on the enemy's rear. Rachel signaled the forward elements of the fleet to begin their full assault as well, but not to use any kinetics. The battlespace around the Nietzscheans needed to remain as clear as possible.

More ships began to appear in the midst of the Nietzschean fleet. Not directly amongst the enemy, but as close as fifty thousand kilometers above and below the Nietzschean formations.

"Today's precision jumping is brought to you by the QuanComm network," Finaeus said with a laugh.

"How many blades did we burn up doing all this?" Rachel asked her engineer.

"You don't want to know," Finaeus replied.

Rachel disagreed with his sentiment, but if it was a critical level, he wouldn't sound so cavalier. She glanced at the ancient terraformer. *Or maybe he would.*

<We disentangled the quantum coupling in seventeen percent of our blades,> Bob informed Rachel. *<An acceptable amount for this victory.>*

Rachel agreed. Honestly, she would have burned them all up, if it meant saving Tanis.

"Scan, anything from the *Derringer*?"

"No, ma'am. We'll not be able to see them with all the EM and crap out here." The Scan officer was about to say something else, but his eyes widened. "Yes! They're here!"

The holotank updated to show three massive ships in the battlespace. The *Carthage, Canaan's Sword,* and the *Starblade.* Three Intrepid Class battle platforms, all with the same shields and weapons as the *I2*. One above Pyra, and the other two close to the main Nietzschean formation.

"Release the fighters." Rachel ordered.

A hundred thousand fighters, though well over half were NSAI-controlled drones, swept out of the ISF ships and onto the battlespace.

But there was still no sign of the *Derringer.*

"Ma'am," Scan called out. "I don't see our ship, but the five Marauder-controlled vessels have broken off from the formation over Pyra. It looks like they're chasing something.

Rachel closed her eyes and felt Finaeus's hand on her shoulder.

"They have her," he said, and she could hear the smile in his voice.

Bob spoke across the entire shipnet. <*She is safe.*>

THE CARTHAGE

STELLAR DATE: 08.28.8949 (Adjusted Years)
LOCATION: ISS *Carthage*, Bridge
REGION: Near Roma, New Canaan System

<All ships, prepare for jump!> Joe called out from the bridge of the *Carthage,* as they hung in space near the Roma jump gates in the New Canaan system.

Arrayed around the new—and mostly complete—Intrepid Class starship were thousands of ISF vessels. As with the last major battle they'd fought, many of the ships were commanded by AIs and human skeleton crews, but he was confident it would be enough to win the day. At least, he hoped he appeared confident to his command crew.

Ahead of the *Carthage,* the jump gate came to life, negative energy coalescing in its center.

The New Canaan System only had one jump gate large enough for an Intrepid Class ship, so the others had been moved to Scipio and Silstrand. There, they too would be preparing to jump through gates left behind by the *I2*.

If it wasn't for his sickening worry over Tanis, the maneuver they were about to perform would be filling him with glee.

Thanks to the QuanComm network, they were about to exercise the largest multi-point fleet jump in known history. Forty thousand ships leaping from a thousand jump gates spread across over a hundred stars were about to leap into a crowded battlespace around one world, thousands of light years away.

Someone had better write a song about this. A ballad; this is definitely epic ballad worthy.

Joe glanced at Cary and Saanvi, who were standing beside him, before giving the order. "Helm, take us in."

"Aye, Admiral Evans. Taking us in."

The *Carthage* eased forward, and its mirror touched the not-space, hurtling the ship across the light years.

Joe counted to three, and then the universe snapped back into place around them.

"Confirmed, Albany System!" Scan called out.

"Matching stellar galactic motion," Helm announced, while Weapons confirmed that the stasis shield was online.

The holotank in the center of the bridge began to populate ships, trajectories, zones of fire, safe areas, and a hundred other notes and details, as the picture around the *Carthage* filled in.

He spotted the *I2* drifting in a sea of radiation, and relief flooded him to see the great ship in one piece, though it must have weathered a brutal assault. Elements of Rachel's fleet were hitting the Nietzschean ships from the rear, and all around, more and more allied vessels were appearing amidst the enemy.

None of that mattered to Joe. Somewhere, there would be a ship, the *Derringer*, and—stars-willing—that ship would have Tanis aboard.

He resisted the urge to ask Scan if they had seen it—he knew they would call out if so much as a hint of a stealthed ship was picked up by sensors.

"We have five Nietzschean vessels breaking off!" Scan called out. "They match the Marauder ships."

Joe nodded silently. It was a good sign, but he wasn't going to take an easy breath until he saw Tanis's face.

"There!" one of the ensigns on scan yelled. "I registered it, for just a second, the *Derringer* was there."

"Open the starboard A1 Dock doors," Joe ordered, fighting to keep his voice steady. He glanced to his side and nodded to Cary and Saanvi. "Go."

His daughters didn't need to be told twice and ran off the bridge without a second glance. Joe wished he could go with them, but there was still work to be done.

Though much of the Nietzschean fleet was engaged with the ISF and allied forces, many of the enemy ships were still close to Pyra, boosting out of the planet's gravity well, directing their engine wash onto the world below.

As the enemy fled, they were burning the planet to a cinder.

Although the strength of the ISF and their allies nearly matched that of the Nietzscheans, only the *Carthage* was within range of the enemies boosting away from Pyra. It was on them to save the people below.

"Weapons, I want a full barrage, every beam we have. Take out the engines of as many Nietzschean ships as we can. Comm, broadcast to the people on the planet to get below ground if possible. S&R, I want orbital fire suppression ships deployed the minute approach vectors are clear. We're going to save this planet."

As the first plumes of plasma began to strike Pyra's atmosphere, burning away clouds and ionizing the skies, he wondered if saving what was left of this decimated world would be harder than defeating the Nietzscheans.

* * * * *

Rika watched in awe as the *Derringer* was swallowed up by the massive ship. She'd docked in smaller space stations. *Much* smaller space stations.

The warship slid past hundreds of smaller craft, all of which appeared to be ready to disembark, but she couldn't discern why. They didn't appear to be military vessels of any sort.

"Fire suppression," Captain Mel said, nodding to the ships Rika was scowling at.

"How do they lay down suppressive fire?" Rika asked, and Mel laughed.

"No. Woman, you say the strangest things. The Niets, they've made a mess of your world down there. Now they're burning it as they boost out. Those ships are going to put out the fires that their engines make before they sweep across the entire globe. With luck, we can shift much of the radiation away from the planet, too…or at least get it to fall in the oceans, and not on land."

Rika had never considered such an operation, and she was amazed to think that these people were going to risk their lives to save the Pyrans, while simultaneously fighting the Nietzscheans.

<*We've finally fallen in with the right people,* > Niki commented.

"You're going to save the planet? Back in the…." Rika shook her head; she had to stop that thought pattern. "When we fought the Nietzscheans, they frequently used scorched world tactics. We never saved anyplace."

"Well, you've got new allies, now," Mel smiled. "Ones who care about people…even if their leadership is dumb as rocks. Your leadership, that is—not ours. Ah, look, your ships made it into the dock, too. Looks like they just got a few holes here and there. Nothing we won't be able to patch up."

Rika nodded silently. "If all is well, then I'm going to go and join my company. Get ready for the search and rescue."

Mel glanced at Rika, her cavalier attitude gone in an instant. "I understand. Good luck."

A few minutes later, Rika stood on the *Carthage*'s dock, watching Chase and Barne drive across its vast surface in a dockcar, weaving in and out of cradles, loading towers, and gantries.

"OK…is it unreal to be in a dock that looks more like a city?" Leslie asked from Rika's side.

"I don't know, Leslie," Rika said, then laughed for a moment. "I've totally lost all sense of scale."

Leslie nodded for a moment. "You know…we always talked about taking the fight to the Niets…pushing them back from Praesepe, and then out of Genevia…."

Rika nodded. "But it always just felt like talk."

"Yeah." Leslie laughed. "It was flights of fancy, and we knew it. But this…"

"This." Rika replied, as Chase and Barne leapt off the dockcar and ran toward them. "Unconditional victory sure feels nice."

* * * * *

Cary and Saanvi raced down the *Carthage*'s dock, driving their dockcar toward the *Derringer* at break-neck speed. Cary half expected Saanvi to tell her to slow down, but when she slacked off the accelerator at one point, Saanvi pushed it all the way forward and held it there.

Ahead, they saw some of the mechs and humans, but Cary didn't see her mother in the group and swerved around them, skidding to a halt at the base of the *Derringer's* ramp.

"There!" Saanvi pointed, and Cary saw two pale figures appear at the airlock.

The first was easy to identify as Priscilla. The second was easy as well, but that didn't make the sight any less shocking.

"Mom?" Cary whispered.

<*She looks…younger,*> Faleena said.

Their mother's steps seemed sure as she walked down the long ramp, though Priscilla had a protective arm around her. Tanis was clothed in a simple white shipsuit, over which a blanket was draped, hiding her arms.

She was safe, she was right there in front of them.

Cary wanted to touch her mother over the Link, to demand confirmation that everything was OK, but something stopped her. Something about the indomitable Tanis Richards seemed wrong. There was a strange look in her eyes, as though she were unsure of what she saw around herself.

Priscilla and Tanis reached the bottom of the ramp and stopped before Cary and Saanvi.

Their mother's skin was alabaster white, as though it had never spent a day in the sun; perfect and unblemished, like she was fresh out of rejuv.

Tanis winked at Cary before turning to Saanvi, her perfect lips curling up in a smile as her right arm slipped from the blanket to pull Saanvi into a tight embrace.

Cary felt like every nerve in her body was vibrating and she wanted to ask her mother what was wrong, why she hadn't spoken. *Is she injured?*

Priscilla appeared calm, so Cary took a deep breath and waited for her turn. A moment later, their mother released Saanvi and turned to Cary. Her eyes narrowed for a moment, as though unsure of what she was looking at. Then Tanis reached out her other hand and stroked Cary's cheek.

Cary almost missed the fact that her mother's left arm was flesh and blood, though she completely forgot that observation when Tanis spoke to her.

"Faleena, my dear, you're so beautiful."

THE END

* * * * *

WAR ON A THOUSAND FRONTS

THE ORION WAR – BOOK 6

BY M. D. COOPER

FOREWORD

This has been, without a doubt, one of the most complicated Orion War books to write. Not because my muse has dried up—no, quite the opposite. This book is a single locus of so many events that have been building up over time, storylines that have been breeding in the shadows and are now coming into their own.

Much like New Canaan, this is a book where many different characters get time on the page, from Tanis and Sera all the way to Corsia and many others.

I also had to take great care to weave this book with the events of Rika Commander, and other books that are only outlined, but not yet written—such as the third Hand's Assassin book.

And so, this book has taken me the longest to write of any in over a year, but the end result has been nothing short of fantastic.

I had several of my own 'WTF' moments in this book, as a few of the characters did things that will tweak the direction of future books enough to surprise even me.

I know, I could just force everything to follow the script, but I like to be surprised by where the story goes as much as you do.

So even though you read Rika Commander, and *think* you know what happened to Tanis after the events on Pyra at the end of Attack on Thebes...well, let's just say you ain't seen nothing yet.

My pulse is pounding a bit after writing some of the final scenes and noting some important parts for the next book, ***Precipice of Darkness***, and I hope yours will be as well, when you get to the end. If so, then I've done my job well.

Malorie Cooper
Danvers, May 2018

PREVIOUSLY…

When last we left Tanis, she had just been brought aboard the *Carthage*, a new I-Class (based on the *I2*) ship commanded by Joe.

The battle for the Albany System is still raging around the ship, as the allied fleet assembled to rescue Tanis beats back the massive Nietzschean armada.

Rika was instrumental in saving Tanis, and if you'd like to see more of their interactions following that daring rescue, you'll find them in Rika Commander, though we also see some of their conversations from Tanis's point of view in this book.

While many of the major players are temporarily clustered together in the Albany System (on the rimward side of the Praesepe Cluster, roughly 550 light years from Sol, and 3,000 from New Canaan), others are still widely dispersed.

Sera is at Khardine, and Krissy is managing her part of the Transcend's civil war from within the Vela Cluster. Garza and his clones are running about, causing chaos, and Jason Andrews is the governor of New Canaan.

In addition, Katrina has been freed of the remnant Xavia that was placed within her, and Cary, Saanvi, and Faleena are also aboard the *Carthage*, meeting their mother after she was brought aboard by Priscilla and Rika….

KEY CHARACTERS REJOINING US

Andrea – Sera's sister who used a back door into Sera's mind to make Sera try to kill Tanis in the Ascella System.

Cary – Tanis's biological daughter. Has a trait where she can deep-Link with other people, creating a temporary merger of minds.

Corsia – Ship's AI and captain of the *Andromeda*.

Faleena – Tanis's AI daughter, born of a mind merge between Tanis, Angela, and Joe.

Garza – General Garza is head of BOGA, Orion's counterpart to the Hand.

Greer – Admiral Greer is responsible for the protection of Khardine, the Transcend fleets on the front, and supporting Tanis's efforts in the Inner Stars.

Jason Andrews – First Captain of the *Intrepid* and current governor of New Canaan.

Justin – Former Director of the Hand. Was imprisoned for the events surrounding the attempted assassination of Tanis.

Katrina – Former Sirian spy, one-time governor of the Victoria colony at Kapteyn's Star—and Warlord of the Midditerra System.

Krissy – Admiral Krissy is the daughter of Finaeus, and is currently in charge of military operations to quell the civil war in the Transcend.

Mary – Daughter of Flaherty, recently rescued from Airtha along with her son Drew, Leeroy the pilot, and Figgy, a dog they met during the escape.

Oris – Septhian government official working for Nietzschea who betrayed Tanis and Thebes.

Priscilla – One of Bob's two avatars.

Rachel – Captain of the *I2*. Former captain of the *Enterprise*.

Rika – Colonel Rika is the leader of a battalion of mechs sent on a mission to destabilize key elements of the Nietzschean Empire. Rika was also instrumental in rescuing Tanis on Pyra.

Saanvi – Tanis's adopted daughter, found in a derelict ship that entered the New Canaan System.

Sera of Airtha – A copy of Sera made by Airtha, containing all of Sera's desired traits and memories. President of the Airthan faction of the Transcend.

ORION FRONT

STELLAR DATE: 08.21.8949 (Adjusted Years)
LOCATION: TSS *Tharsis*, Cerden System
REGION: 10LY from OFA border, Transcend Interstellar Alliance

Marcel slumped in his chair, watching the Orion Guard ships break off from the engagement, shifting onto a vector to slingshot around the nearby gas giant.

The TSF had won the day, but just barely.

All around the *Tharsis* lay the wreckage of both Transcend and Orion ships; hulls venting atmosphere, many glowing brightly from reactor meltdowns. It was a mess—except for a slowly expanding bubble of empty space to starboard, the result of a ship that had lost bottle containment and suffered an antimatter explosion.

"Sir," Ensign Lavalle on comms turned to address Marcel.

Marcel nodded for the woman to continue, though he could tell from the expression on the ensign's face that he would not like the news.

"I've just gotten word from the *Pursuit*. Admiral Jorgen died in the explosion aboard their ship. His entire staff was killed, as well."

Marcel drew in a long breath. Jorgen had replaced Admiral Heath, and had only been in command of the battlegroup for six months. At this rate, they'd have captains running the fleet.

Shit...that's what Lavalle is hedging around.

"Colonel Vala?" he asked Ensign Lavalle, begging the stars for good news.

Lavalle shook her head. "Sorry, sir. Vala's ship was holed, its CIC was lost."

Marcel sucked in a sharp breath, then forced himself to expel it slowly. While the two Seras were battling over the Transcend's presidency thousands of light years away, the fleets on the Orion Fronts were being worn down to nubs.

Here on the Spinward Front, it was the worst—what with their proximity to New Sol. Though he'd heard that it wasn't much better on the Anti-Spinward Front. Both fleets were at less than half their original strength.

The fact that they'd won the battle today was a miracle, only possible because of intel that Admiral Jorgen had picked up. Without foreknowledge of the enemy's attack, there would have only been a patrol garrison protecting the Cerden System when the Orion Guard arrived.

"Sir?" Lavalle asked. "What are your orders?"

Marcel straightened in his seat. "So, I'm senior, then, am I?" he asked.

Lavalle nodded, and Marcel couldn't help but notice that half the eyes on the bridge were on him.

"OK, people," he said, summoning his last reserve of energy. "This is still an active battlespace. Half those damaged OG ships could still fire on us. Attend to your work."

The bridge crew turned back to their consoles, at least appearing to be focused on their tasks.

"Lavalle, send orders for Major Uda's group to set up a picket on the far side of the battlespace; there's a chance those Oggies could come around the planet and blast past us on their way out. I want them to seed mines just in case. Get Mendel's Marines to find a good hull and secure it. That'll be our prison ship. All other groups, begin S&R operations."

"S&R on Oggies, too?" Lavalle asked.

Marcel nodded slowly. For as much as he'd liked Admiral Jorgen, he disagreed with the late Admiral's no-rescue policy on Oggies—which even went so far as to destroy any disabled ships and ignore escape pods.

Marcel didn't want to slowly freeze to death in space, or drift in stasis till the SC batts on the pod ran dry. If *he* didn't want to die that way, it was not a fate he'd deliver on anyone else. He didn't care how much he hated the enemy.

"Yes, Lavalle. Obviously lower priority, but we're not going to leave them to die—so long as they come peaceably. No TSF blood will be spilled saving them."

"Yes, sir," Lavalle replied smartly.

Marcel couldn't tell if she approved or disapproved of his orders, but decided that so long as the ensign followed them, it would have to do for now.

Not that he was all that worried about Lavalle. She was a good woman, followed orders and was efficient and conscientious about her work.

But she was also a barometer for the rest of the crew, and if she was hiding her thoughts on the matter, it was a telling indicator.

<*Farrah,*> he reached out to the ship's primary AI. <*Looks like you're in charge of fleet tactical now, any initial thoughts?*>

<*I think we need to abandon this system,*> Farrah replied without hesitation. <*All that's left are a few mining outposts—everyone else has fled. No sane person wants to live this close to the front anymore.*>

Marcel wanted to argue with Farrah, to tell her that the TSF wouldn't abandon a system after they'd just successfully defended it—but he knew she was right.

The 917th Fleet had once numbered over fifty thousand ships, spread across five hundred light years of the border with the Orion Freedom Alliance. Now their numbers were fewer than ten thousand, and the five other fleets that patrolled the border weren't in much better shape.

With reserves—of which there were few—the three thousand light year border with the Oggies was now guarded by fewer than fifty thousand ships all told.

Marcel pushed his palms into his eyes and drew in a deep breath. A hundred thousand stars defended by a smattering of ships. And if the Oggies kept pressing like this, they'd punch through the defenders before long.

Stars, they may already have, he thought. *We really have no way to tell; we're not even patrolling half the systems anymore.*

The thought of his fleet failing so utterly at their mission made him want to scream.

We need more ships!

Marcel didn't have the latest information on the fleet strengths elsewhere in the Transcend, but he knew for a fact that the civil war taking place around Airtha, Vela, and Khardine was occupying more than half the space force.

At least no TSF ships were involved in the strange crusade that Field Marshal Richards was undertaking in the Inner Stars. She seemed to be funding that herself, with minimal use of Transcend resources—bar the jump gates she was chewing up. Marcel had overheard Jorgen complaining more than once that getting new gates over the last year had been well-nigh impossible.

Marcel was about to compose an update to send to Admiral Greer at Khardine when he remembered that the only QuanComm blades in the fleet had been destroyed in the battle.

"Fuck!" he swore, slamming a fist onto his chair's armrest.

Several eyes on the bridge turned in his direction, but when they saw the rage plainly evident on his face, they turned away.

"Farrah," he growled. "Dispatch a courier drone to Fortress Gibraltar. Have them send our status to Khardine, and ask command what they advise."

<Of course, Captain Marcel,> Farrah replied. *<Should I make a request for reinforcements, or…>*

"If they can't tell we need reinforcements—" Marcel stopped himself before he said something he'd regret later. "Yes, Farrah, put in a request for everything. Stars knows we need it. Once we've done S&R here, we'll advise the remaining civilians to evacuate, and then get the hell out of this system."

<Yes, sir.>

The orders given, Marcel fell silent, watching the fleet's progress as they took in friendly escape pods, and corralled enemy ones.

It will take days to clean up this mess. Days in which the enemy could regroup and strike again. He had no illusions about how that engagement would go.

TANGEL

STELLAR DATE: 08.28.8949 (Adjusted Years)
LOCATION: A1 Docking Bay, ISS *Carthage*
REGION: Pyra, Albany System, Thebes, Septhian Alliance

Cary felt her skin tingle as her mother's hand brushed against her cheek. The range of emotions surging through her threatened to overwhelm—joy, relief, elation—but they all gave way to confusion when Tanis spoke.

"Faleena, my dear, you're so beautiful."

A feeling of surprise emanated from Faleena that matched Cary's own.

<*Mom?*> Faleena asked. <*Are you OK?*>

Tanis's eyes appeared to refocus, and she rested a hand on Cary's shoulder. "Cary, you are truly something unexpected. More amazing than I'd remembered."

<*Than either of us remembered,*> Angela added.

<*What just happened?*> Faleena asked Cary.

<*I have no freakin' clue, Fal.*>

"What happened down there?" Saanvi asked, as Tanis pulled both girls into an embrace.

A rueful laugh escaped their mother's lips. "Stars, what *didn't* happen down there."

<*We began to ascend is what happened,*> Angela said, and Tanis glanced at Priscilla. "But you did something to stop it…you used…"

Priscilla held up her hands and shook her head. "I just did what Bob told me to do. If I hadn't, we wouldn't have been able to bring you back up here. Rika could barely hold onto you as it was; if it wasn't for the fact that her skeletal structure is so dense, you would have slipped through her."

"Pardon?" Cary asked, glancing at Priscilla before locking eyes with her mother. " 'Slipped through'?"

Tanis chuckled. "I guess I hadn't quite figured out how to stay anchored in the three dimensional world. Not that it matters now, since Angela and I seem to have reverted to our old selves."

"I'm surprised that happened," Priscilla said. "Bob didn't think anchoring you would cause your mind to split apart again, though he said it was a risk."

A curious look came over Tanis's face, and Cary wondered how separate her mother and Angela really were.

<*Even if they did split apart again, it won't be like before,*> Faleena whispered quietly into Cary's mind, apparently on the same train of thought. <*She saw me…***sees** *me, Cary. I don't know how, but she was looking at my mind.*>

Cary considered Faleena's words for a moment, then reached out to her sisters to form Trine and took a step back to observe their mother.

Trine drew in a sharp breath in each of her bodies as she gazed upon Tanis's form.

At first glance, it appeared as though her mother's body contained a remnant, but as she looked closer, Trine saw that it was more than a remnant. A fifth dimensional being suffused their mother's body—she could see it rooted deeply in both Tanis and Angela.

<*You are beautiful, too,*> Trine said, realizing she could see Angela in the remnant-like figure that occupied her mother's body.

"You've become quite proficient at that, girls," Tanis said as she looked from Cary to Saanvi and back. "Not that I'm surprised. To do what you've done with extracting the remnants is no simple thing."

Trine split apart, and Saanvi whispered, "Mom, what's going to happen to you?"

Tanis reached out and took Saanvi's hand. "I'm going to fully ascend at some point. Though what Priscilla did has made it possible for Angela and I to operate as separate beings for a while longer."

<*A while?*> Faleena asked.

Tanis nodded, a smile quirking the corner of her lips. "So long as I don't end up in any dire circumstances, a few years I suspect."

Cary bit her lip before asking, "And then you'll just turn into some being made of light?"

Tanis shrugged. "I'm not convinced that fifth dimensional beings have to shuck their mortal coils, so to speak. The ones we've all encountered began as AIs, so they had no bodies to begin with—well, not ones that were useful when it came to moving around."

Tanis paused and looked down at herself, then held up her left hand

and snapped her fingers before continuing.

"I, on the other hand, rather like my body. Especially now that I've reconfigured it."

"I noticed you regrew your arm," Saanvi said. "I assume that happened down on Pyra, as well?"

Tanis nodded. "I was able to strip apart molecules and atoms and reform them into anything I wanted. I harnessed the energy and used it—"

"You almost killed yourself," Priscilla interrupted. "At least, that's what I think was happening."

Tanis shook her head. "I wouldn't have died. But I think I would have burned up this body…and our distinct minds. Then there would have been no going back."

"Mom," Cary shook her head certain that horror was writ large on her face. "You're going to give me a headache. How is this possible?"

Tanis took Cary's hand as well and led her daughters toward the nearest lift bank. "For some time now, Angela and I have been…growing a new brain. It's interleaved with our current ones, and is directly connecting them in millions of locations. Down on Pyra, it came awake, and our consciousness shifted to it. Now it's…asleep again."

"Wouldn't that brain have been burned up, as well?" Saanvi asked.

"Maybe…or maybe it would have transferred into other, non-physical dimensions…it's hard to say. I don't really want to try it and find out."

"Good call," Priscilla added as she fell in beside them.

Tanis looked over at the avatar, and then paused, her gaze shifting to the mechs and humans gathered nearby.

"Just a moment," Tanis said. "I need to go thank Rika for saving me."

* * * * *

Tanis didn't let go of her daughters' hands as she turned toward Rika and her team.

The tall cyborg woman was surrounded by three humans, with a platoon of her soldiers coming down the *Derringer*'s ramp to join them.

Tanis had to admit that she was impressed by these mechanized warriors. By her standards, what had been done to them was a horrible disfiguration, but the cyborgs bore their mech bodies with pride, never flinching or behaving as though they were in any way inferior to those around them.

"Rika!" Tanis called out as she approached. "I owe you and yours a deep debt of gratitude."

Rika turned, a tired smile on her lips as she held out her left hand, and Tanis slid hers from Cary's tight grasp.

"Admiral Richards," Rika said as the two women shook hands. "I'm glad to see you're doing better. You were in rough shape back on the planet…I imagine doing an impression of a starship engine is exhausting. No pun intended."

Tanis hadn't realized that Rika must have seen her unleashing the energy barrage that had obliterated the Nietzscheans. She wondered what the woman thought of that—*she* still had no idea what to think of that.

<*Think of it as kicking major ass,*> Angela advised.

<*Noted, Ang,*> she said with a laugh.

"I was feeling a bit of burnout." Tanis grinned at her joke, but then her smile disappeared. "I am deeply sorry about General Mill and Captain Ayer. I feel somewhat responsible for what happened to them. They died honorably."

Rika squared her shoulders and shook her head. "You may have been the catalyst, ma'am, but the blame lies with traitors in the Septhian and Theban governments. What happened here was going to occur sooner or later, anyway."

"You're probably right about that," Tanis replied, while reaching up to tuck her hair behind her ears. "We'll have to determine how deep that sickness goes."

"What are your plans here, then?" Rika asked.

Tanis looked the mechanized woman up and down. "First we're going to finish off the Niets…there's still a battle raging around us—though one can barely tell in here. Then we'll restore this system to order and summon Prime Minister Harmin to see what he has to say for himself."

One of the men standing with Rika, a stocky, dark-skinned soldier, snorted a laugh. "This I would love to see, the PM coming here with his tail between his legs."

"Barne, stow it," Rika said, making a slicing motion through the air with her left hand.

Tanis gave Barne a small smile. "As far as I can tell, Septhia recently *lost* Pyra, maybe all of Thebes. Not to mention that it was never really theirs in the first place. I'm not entirely certain that we should cede it back to them."

A small smile crept across Rika's lips. "I like the way you think, Admiral."

Tanis placed a hand on Rika's shoulder. "No 'Admiral' for you. To you, Rika, I am 'Tanis'. I look forward to talking with you further. I think we can benefit one another greatly."

Rika's cheeks lit up with a small flush, and she ducked her head in a nod. "Of course, Ad—Tanis. I look forward to that. Now that we've found the likes of the ISF, we're not keen to run off on our own any time soon."

"Except that we need to get back out there," one of the men with Rika—a young man named Chase, Tanis saw by the indicators on her HUD—said. "There's still a fight to be had and a world to save."

Tanis nodded. "There is. I need to get to the bridge."

<We can manage the battle well enough from here,> Angela said. *<Already are.>*

<Appearances, Ang. Physical presence counts for something.>

Angela's silvery laugh filled Tanis's mind. *<We're Tangel now, do we need to keep up appearances?>*

<We need to think of a new name. Though I guess it's better than Tangela.>

<Says you.>

While Tanis and Angela debated possible names, and reached out to the ship's command network, Rika replied.

"We'll speak again soon, I hope, Tanis."

Tanis gave a crisp nod. "You can count on it. Just don't get blown up out there."

Rika snorted. "Killed by Niets? Very unlikely."

"Good." Tanis turned back toward the lift banks, her daughters and Priscilla in tow. Behind them, the *Derringer* was lifting off once more, turning back to the dock's exit and the fight raging around Pyra.

"Even *we* don't get to call you 'Tanis' in formal situations," Saanvi said with a grin, as they settled into the dockcar with Tanis at the controls.

"She won't either, but informally…I don't know. There's something about that Rika. She feels like a kindred spirit."

"She's a warrior, that's for sure," Priscilla said from the back seat. "And a survivor. She told me some of her story during our journey insystem. That girl is built out of pure, unfiltered, hardcore moxy."

"Good," Tanis replied. "She's going to need it for what I have planned."

"What's that, Mom?" Cary asked.

Tanis glanced at her daughter—*daughters*.

She was still amazed by how she could *see* Faleena within Cary's mind. Tanis knew one thing was for sure: she wasn't ascended—yet—but she wasn't…whatever she used to be. It was as though she had one foot in each world.

"Mom?" Cary asked. "Star Command to Mom."

Tanis shook her head and smiled. "Sorry, trying to coordinate the battlespace better. Joe did a good job setting it up, but there are optimizations."

"What about Rika, and what you have planned?" Saanvi inquired, as the dockcar reached the lift bank.

"Oh, well, it's obvious that we can't let these Nietzschean scumbags stew for long. We've set them back, and now we have to finish the job. But I'm not willing to let the Trisilieds build up for much longer, either. They dropped a damn starship in our backyard on Carthage. That deserves recompense."

Saanvi chuckled. "JP said it scared the horses all the way out at his farm."

"I wonder how he's doing," Cary murmured as they walked onto the lift. "He joined up for you, Sahn, and now you're out here."

"Indeed," Tanis raised an eyebrow as she regarded her daughters. "I seem to remember all sorts of stipulations being placed on you two after your escapades at Carthage. Ones that required you to finish your time at the academy—yet here you are, thousands of light years from the Palisades."

Cary shrugged, while Saanvi's eyes widened in worry.

<She's messing with you,> Faleena giggled. *<Besides. I wanted to come see Mom, and that means I have to drag my meat-suit along.>*

Cary groaned. "It's so disturbing when you call me that."

<*I'm such a bad influence,*> Angela said, a soft laugh accompanying her words. <*Yes, Tanis is messing with you. We're both happy you were the first people we saw at the bottom of that ramp.*>

"I thought I was Good Mom and you were Mean Mom, Angela," Tanis said.

Cary snorted, and Saanvi raised a hand to cover her mouth.

<*Seriously, Tanis? You're By-the-Book, Stickler Mom. I'm Party-Time, Have Fun Mom.*>

"She's right, Mom," Cary said with a sheepish nod. "It's just how you are. We love you for it."

Tanis sighed. "Man…when you're out-funned by an AI…"

The doors opened a moment later, and Tanis was surprised to see the Carthage's bridge foyer, and not the administrative concourse.

"The Mark II's have a dedicated dock-to-bridge lift tube," Cary explained. "I think Abby had it added in. She complained it was always such a pain to get to the bridge on the *Intrepid* and *I2*."

Tanis shook her head as she surveyed the space—which was barren except for three empty pedestals at the far end. "There's a reason why you don't have direct access from the dock to the bridge."

"They added safety precautions," Saanvi replied.

Tanis wondered about that. Not that it mattered right now. "No avatars on the Carthage yet?"

<*Not yet,*> a new voice reached into Tanis's mind.

<*Kerr,*> Angela replied with a warm glow in her voice. <*I'm sorry we didn't greet you properly when we arrived.*>

<*Think nothing of it,*> Kerr replied. <*You've been busy.*>

"That we have," Tanis replied, as the group walked across the foyer toward the short corridor that led to the bridge. "I'm glad you passed muster in time to ship out."

<*Well, we're all a bit green, but we're managing. One hell of a shakedown cruise.*>

Tanis noticed Saanvi giving the empty pedestals a long look as they walked past, and felt a momentary burst of protectiveness.

<*You don't think Bob talked to her about becoming an avatar, do you?*> she asked Angela.

<*No, he wouldn't do that after you told him not to. Don't worry, your ruling*

that no one under fifty years of age can be an avatar still stands. They'll find someone else to do it.>

Tanis wondered about that. Her plans to build dozens of I-Class ships meant she needed at least twice as many avatars. Over half the population of New Canaan was under the age of fifty, and she wasn't prepared to allow outsiders to take on the role, so she may have to loosen her restrictions.

She also wondered about the wisdom behind building more AIs as powerful as Bob. *I'm not sure the galaxy needs more 'hyper-intelligent' beings.*

<*Kettle, meet pot,*> Angela commented.

<*Our ascendency helps my case.*>

Angela laughed. <*Keep telling yourself that.*>

They reached the bridge's door, and Tanis squared her shoulders.

Time to put on my game face.

The doors slid open, and Tanis walked out to see a near-perfect mirror of the *I2*'s bridge. Her gaze slid over the rows of consoles, the captain's chair, the holodisplays and tanks…until she saw Joe.

He stood with his back to the door, arms akimbo, studying the battlespace projected on the main holotank, barking out orders and requesting details and analysis from the teams surrounding him.

But the moment she stepped across the threshold, his head snapped up, and he turned to face her, a look of relieved joy spreading across his features.

"Tanis," he said, the single word cutting through the cacophony surrounding them.

Tanis had intended to walk across the bridge calmly, filled with grace and poise, to give the love of her life a chaste embrace in the view of the crew.

She did none of those things.

One moment, her hands were clasped in those of her daughters, and the next, she was running across the bridge, weaving around consoles and crew, to crash into Joe—who ended up careening into her at the halfway point.

Momentum spun them around, and Tanis brushed her hair out of her face a moment before their lips met, and their bodies pressed into one another in a desperate embrace.

"Told you to be careful," Joe mumbled, as their mouths slid past one another and came to rest near each other's ears. "You nearly got killed, what…three times while you were gone?"

"Who can keep track?" Tanis whispered as she continued to crush Joe against herself.

<*I can.*> Angela chuckled softly in their minds.

"Stars, don't actually *tell* me, Angela," Joe admonished as he pulled away and stared into Tanis's eyes. "So you're still the pair of you in there, eh? The briefing Colonel Smith forwarded led me to have some doubts about who I'd meet."

<*You still have to contend with two wives for a bit longer,*> Angela said.

"Huh," Joe cocked an eyebrow. "So much for hoping."

Tanis was surprised to hear him say that—though she wasn't entirely certain he wasn't joking. "I didn't think you were anticipating our eventual merger."

"Tanis, I've been waiting for it for *decades*. You two just need to get on with it already. The anticipation is killing me."

<*I'll tell you more about it later,*> Tanis said privately before turning to the main holotank. "So, how're things going?"

Joe turned and walked alongside her toward the view of the battlespace. "As if you don't already know. I could see you nudging things long before you even got up here."

Tanis surveyed the allied fleets interspersed throughout the Nietzschean half-sphere of ships. What Joe and the allies had pulled off was almost beyond comprehension; to jump so many ships into such a small area simultaneously was an unparalleled marvel. The timing alone would probably be the subject of thousands of dissertations in the future.

"All hail the QuanComm system," Tanis said in a near whisper as she watched a detachment of ISF ships push through the Nietzschean forces, and engage a pocket of enemy vessels that were inflicting heavy losses on a group of Scipian cruisers.

Nearer to the *Carthage* lay the wreckage of a thousand Nietzschean vessels that had attempted to boost away from Pyra and burn the world as they fled.

"Looks like you gave them what they deserved," Tanis said, gesturing to the remains of the fleet, which was moving into a loose orbit high above Pyra.

"Cowards," Joe shook his head. "Nietzschean master morality is such a crock of shit. Only they would consider something like burning a planet honorable. Whoever made a civilization based on Nietzsche's teachings needs to have their head examined."

"I imagine they're long dead," Tanis replied. "Which is lucky for them."

"Well, there's still their emperor—some pretentious ass who took on the name 'Constantine'."

Tanis nodded. "Yeah, he's on my list now."

"Good, mine too."

As Tanis began sending commands to the fleet, a pain stabbed through her stomach, and she realized something was missing.

"Any chance someone can get me a BLT?"

RELIEF

STELLAR DATE: 08.28.8949 (Adjusted Years)
LOCATION: Presidential Stateroom, Keren Station
REGION: Khardine System, Transcend Interstellar Alliance

[They got her. Safe and sound.]

Sera reread Joe's message four times before she allowed herself to believe it. She had half a mind to grab a ship and jump out to Thebes just to set eyes on Tanis herself.

<Your heart rate has finally settled back down.> Jen sounded relieved as well.

"Yeah, well, Tanis is pretty important to our efforts. I don't know who I could put in charge of the Inner Stars offensive without her—stars, I don't even know if the ISF would remain in the fight."

<Now you're just being silly. You know that Joe and Jason wouldn't abandon the Transcend. It's not in their natures.>

Sera nodded. That was true, but would those two men be able to muster the entire populace of New Canaan to the war effort like Tanis had? They had their Starflight plan, their Aleutian backup location—wherever that was. If ever there was a people fully prepared to drop off the face of the map, it was they.

Give them more credit than that, she admonished herself. *They're putting everything into defending a galaxy that they don't even know—and that has tried to wipe them out more than once.*

Sera rose from her desk and walked to the window that looked out over the inside of Keren Station's habitation cylinder.

The peaceful scene of gently rolling hills and grassy plains was incongruous with the events going on elsewhere. The fact that the ships of the alliance were even now engaged in a pitched battle with the Nietzscheans while she watched birds wheel above was hard to swallow.

She sighed and leant against the sill. *Life doesn't stop everywhere else when something bad happens. It just soldiers on.*

<Maybe you should go to the war room,> Jen suggested. *<Greer and the others will be there. Your presence will help.>*

"You sure like to mother me," Sera said with a soft laugh as she ran a hand through her hair.

<Shoot, sorry, I—>

"It's OK," Sera interrupted Jen. "I didn't mean it like that. I said it without even thinking of Helen. That's progress, I guess, right?"

<I'd say so. I don't need to take Helen's place. I'm happy just to help you out as much as I can.>

"That you do, Jen, that you do."

Sera looked down at her body, surprised to see that her skin still bore the appearance of a blue shipsuit—her semi-official look. She'd found that lately, when she got lost in thought, her skin reverted to the deep red that she now considered to be her natural skin color.

It also tended to lose any of the 'adjustments' that made her not appear to be completely naked.

Sera chuckled at the memories of how she'd made Admiral Greer quite uncomfortable on several occasions when her skin had reverted while she was deep in thought in his presence.

As amusing as it was, losing control of her appearance was a tell, and Sera didn't like tells. Even though she was reasonably certain she could trust everyone on Keren Station, that didn't mean she wanted them to be able to read her state of mind so easily.

"OK, let's go see what the Admiralty thinks of the battle for Thebes."

She pushed herself off the windowsill and walked toward the door where a pair of low boots waited. She slipped her feet into them and pulled a belt off a hook on the wall, wrapping it around her waist and holstering a sidearm.

Theoretically, she was in the safest place in the galaxy right now, but Sera had learned firsthand how well that theory held up.

She stepped out into the corridor, and nodded at the two members of her High Guard as they fell in behind her.

Another part of being president that I don't think will ever stop feeling weird.

The War Room was one level down, in the administrative complex, and Sera arrived in only a few minutes to find Admiral Greer and his staff standing in the center of the room, arrayed around one of the larger holotanks.

"All-in-all, quite the success, don't you think?" Sera said as she approached the group.

Greer turned toward Sera and gave a sharp nod. "They'll be talking of this one for centuries."

The woman next to Greer, Rear Admiral Svetlana, gave a rueful laugh. "Well, it was going to be talked about no matter what. The question was in what light? I'm glad that it now will be a positive one."

Sera agreed with Svetlana's assessment, and there were nods from the other admirals, generals, and colonels present.

"And we're ready to deploy gates to withdraw the fleets?" Sera asked.

Greer nodded. "We have ten ready to go, ma'am. I'd send more, but we don't have the ships to spare. We've already weakened Krissy's response forces greatly, and she had just begun a major bait operation."

"Not to mention how strapped the Spinward Front is," Sera added. "We need to work out how to reinforce them."

"Understood," Greer blew out a long breath. "Not sure who I'll rob for that. If the ISF would just share its tech so we could grow ships—"

Sera held up her hand to forestall the rest of Greer's statement. "You know Tanis won't budge on that."

Greer opened his mouth to respond, but Sera's narrowed eyes caused him to close it and nod.

"This civil war is strapping us at the worst possible time," Svetlana shifted the conversation. "We need to end it as soon as possible."

Greer gave Svetlana a sidelong look. "We'll save that for tomorrow's briefing on Operation Ringbreak. If we start on that topic now, it'll derail us from what we need to focus on today."

Sera looked down at the holotank, watching the view of the allied forces, the updates showing them sweeping through the Nietzschean ship formations, decimating them en masse.

The data was basic: colored pinpoints of light denoting ship types and alliances. Any more detail would stress the QuanComm network and burn out blades. At present, network degradation was a real concern. While the massive strike against the Nietzscheans in the Albany System was shaping up to be a decisive victory, it had burned through hundreds of paired blades.

Over fifty percent of the QuanComm blades had overheated, their rubidium cores losing entanglement with their counterparts many light years distant, a terminal effect that ended their 'spooky action at a distance'. Sera had sent requests to New Canaan for more, but knew they were already being manufactured at the fastest rate possible.

As frustrating as it was to rely on one star system for so many of their resources, Sera agreed with Tanis's logic on the matter. Their only real edge in this fight was the technological advantage from New Canaan.

But Tanis's people guarded their tech zealously—something proven by what they had been willing to do to win the Defense of Carthage. The safety of the process used to produce their ships was paramount. If the specs fell into Airthan or Orion hands, the war would be over in less than a year.

With a very unfavorable outcome.

"So what should we do to bolster the Spinward Front, sir, ma'am?" Svetlana asked. "You saw the latest updates from the 917th Fleet. They're commanded by a captain now, for star's sakes. He's abandoned an entire section of the front, falling back to Fortress Gibraltar. That opens up hundreds of light years to the OG."

"I think we need to punch Orion in the gut," Sera said as she pushed the battle around Pyra—which was turning into a rout of the Nietzscheans—to another holotank and brought up the Three Arms view of the galaxy. "We know from the strategic data Jessica brought from Orion Space that Orion has withdrawn almost all of their forces from the Perseus Expansion Districts. All that is left are small policing forces. We could dispatch a force or two to rampage through their territories."

One of the other admirals, a man named Mardus, nodded with a grim smile. "Xenophon and the ten thousand hoplites."

"Hopefully with less betrayal," Sera said with a chuckle. "But yes. If we send a core of cruisers equipped with stasis shields and light destroyers for fast attack missions, we could create one hell of a mess inside of Orion."

"Civilian targets?" Greer asked, his expression unreadable.

"No," Sera shook her head. "Just the opposite. We uplift them. From what Jessica shared, the Expansion Districts aren't even as advanced as half the Inner Stars. For all intents and purposes, those people live in squalor. We'll have to be smart about it; we can't obliterate their economies overnight, but we could make life a lot better for them."

"Do you think it will pull pressure off the Spinward Front?" Svetlana asked. "From where I stand, it looks like Praetor Kirkland doesn't give a rat's ass about the Expansion Districts."

"And the Perseus Expansion Districts are much closer to the Anti-Spinward Front," Greer added.

Sera nodded as she stared at the map. Greer was right. Chances were that resources would be pulled from Orion's Anti-Spinward Front to deal with an incursion. She looked up at the admirals. "Well, I did say 'a force or two'. What if we sent one to…Costa—where *Sabrina* jumped out of Orion space—and the other to Herschel? We have enough data on that region from captured soldiers like Colonel Kent."

Greer highlighted Herschel on the map and then pointed at another star, eight hundred light years away. "Rega's pretty damn close to Herschel. Hitting them there will be more than a sabre-rattling. They'll come in hard to put down a force that deep in the OFA."

"You're right about that." Sera met Greer's eyes with cold certainty. "But if Rega sends forces to Herschel, they won't be sending them to the front. That may give us enough breathing room."

Greer grunted and looked back at the holo. "Stars, I wish Scipio would just finish with the Hegemony already. We could really use their help in the larger fight."

"Scipio has made inroads," one of the colonels reported. "But the Hegemony has turned their entire economy over to a war footing, including retrofitting many of their private merchant fleets. They have millions upon millions of ships, now."

"And here Tanis just gave hundreds of ships to the Septhians," Svetlana shook her head. "President Sera, I volunteer to lead the expeditionary force to Herschel, but we'll need a fleet that can actually get the job done."

Sera nodded. "It'll have to be at least five hundred ships. A force large enough to take a system, but small enough that it can operate with less support."

"I can work up the optimal configuration," Svetlana replied with a crisp nod. "I have given extensive study to this sort of attack on Orion."

Sera met the tall admiral's gaze, their eyes locked across the table. "Admiral Svetlana, you know that emergency extraction may not be possible. If things go sideways out there…"

"I understand the risks, President Sera. I'm willing to take them on. When I signed up, it wasn't to sit in a fortress and plot."

Sera saw Greer blink, followed by a sidelong look at Svetlana. She wondered what he thought of the Rear Admiral spearheading an operation like that. Granted, assignments of personnel were his call, and she handed that responsibility to him.

"I'll abide by Admiral Greer's selections," Sera said. "Which I imagine he'll want to mull over for a bit. Even if we do this, we still need to bolster the fronts. Stars knows Airtha's not doing a thing to help."

The next two hours turned into a long session of examining force allotments and strategic defense positions—namely, seeking out positions they could abandon to free up fleets for the fronts.

Every option came with as many—and often more—cons than pros, but at the end of the session, they had selected three thousand ships that would bolster the fronts and form the two Orion space strike forces.

As they'd worked, the battle around Pyra had continued to progress, updates feeding to the secondary holo. By this point, most of the Nietzschean ships were either disabled, or in flight. Some might escape their pursuers, but the vast majority of the enemy armada was now little more than drifting hulls in the black.

Once the meeting had wrapped, Sera walked to the holotank to study the engagement she knew Tanis was now managing.

At the lower right was a list of allied ships lost, and casualty estimates.

It had not been a bloodless fight. Many of the allied ships did not possess stasis shields, and no small number had been lost—over five thousand, by the latest count.

Sera shook her head as she tried to wrap her mind around the sheer number of ships and people involved in the conflict that was spreading across the stars. *It has to be trillions of humans and AIs at this point.*

For all intents and purposes, those lives were on her. Well, her and Tanis. Without the *Intrepid*'s tech upsetting the balance of power, this war would not have come for some time.

She turned and nodded to Greer and Svetlana, who were still standing over the other holotank, likely discussing Svetlana's desire to lead the force into Orion space.

The admirals both gave her deferential nods in response, and Sera left the CIC, taking a right in the wide corridor, heading toward the commissary, her pair of guards still in tow.

Her destination lay three levels below, and Sera decided to take the stairs. She was skipping down the steps, when a door on the landing swung open, and she almost collided with a dark-haired woman in a pink dress.

"Oh, sorry!" the woman exclaimed, then her eyes turned to Sera's, and she gasped. "Madam President! Oh, shoot, I'm *really* sorry. I should have looked before I kicked the door open."

The woman's face looked familiar, and when her HUD gave her addressor's name, it was Sera's turn to be surprised. "Mary? Flaherty's Mary?"

She glanced back and lifted a hand, directing her guards to stand down.

"As much as I love to be identified by my father's name, yes," Mary said, then pursed her lips. "Sorry, I tend to bleed sarcasm sometimes."

"Sorry, I should know better," Sera ducked a nod. "I've lived in others' shadows long enough to know how much it sucks. It's very nice to meet you, Mary-who-only-happens-to-be-Flaherty's-daughter."

"And you as well, Sera-who-happens-to-be-President-of-the-Transcend." Mary offered her hand, and Sera shook it. "Where were you off to when I nearly knocked you down the stairs?"

"Lunch," Sera replied simply. "Too much strategizing with the brass makes me famished."

"To the Deck 87 Commissary?" Mary's brows rose. "I didn't know they let your type in there."

Sera nearly coughed in surprise. She'd grown accustomed to a certain amount of deference that Mary did not seem to possess. "My 'type'?"

"Yeah, high-uppity muckity mucks." Mary leant in and lowered her voice to a conspiratorial whisper. "The D87C is a workin' person's mess."

"I'm a working person," Sera said, her voice rising in pitch as she took a step back. "I used to be a pirate, you know."

Mary nodded. "Sure do. My father's told me all the stories. Mostly about all the se—dammit, I've gotten twice as familiar in half the time. Sorry, I'm still adjusting to all this. Forget my needling, I'm just hangry."

Sera was having a hard time reconciling Mary with Flaherty. The woman had spoken more in the last two minutes than Flaherty usually did in two days.

Maybe she's where all his words went.

Still, Mary was like a breath of fresh air, compared to the hours of serious conversations and days of worry over Tanis.

"Well," Sera gave Mary a mischievous wink. "Why don't you accompany me to the D87C? Maybe with you at my side, no one will notice that I'm an uppity muckity muck."

Mary lifted a finger. "*High*-uppity muckity muck."

"Right," Sera laughed. "High-uppity."

As they descended the final flight of stairs, Sera told her, "I must admit, I'm a bit surprised to find you here at Keren. Flaherty told me he'd gotten you off Airtha and sent you to some place in Sagittarius. He wouldn't even tell *me* where."

"Yeah, daddy knows best, right? He *tried* to send us packing, but he'd also let slip where he would be. So after convincing Leeroy to turn our ship around, we followed after."

"Leeroy?" Sera asked, as they walked out into the well-lit corridor that would lead them to the commissary.

"Yeah, my on-again, off-again ex. Currently we're on again, I think. My son, Drew, and Figgy, our dog are also here. Drew wants to enlist, but I'm trying to convince him to find work on Keren. I know that's not terribly patriotic, but he's the world to me, you know?"

Sera didn't know, not really. She was starting to think that she'd never have anyone who quite fit that bill. Elena might have, once; Tanis was incredibly important to her, but that was a different sort of relationship altogether.

Still, she said, "Yes."

"Leeroy is working on small ship repair. He's good at programming and managing bot teams—better than some NSAI, even. He knows when to cut corners to get a ship back out on time, and when those cut corners would lead to disaster…dammit, I'm rambling."

Sera chuckled, deciding to voice her prior thought. "I think I know where all of Flaherty's words went."

"I'm not normally this bad," Mary replied with a self-deprecating expression. "Just so much going on, then almost knocking you down…life's pretty topsy-turvy."

"You're telling me," Sera said, as they reached the doors to the Deck 87 Commissary.

She wasn't surprised to see two more of her High Guard already inside, eyes sweeping the gathered throng suspiciously.

"Dang, your shadows are everywhere," Mary commented.

Sera nodded. "Only place they don't follow me is into my bed at night."

Mary's eyes widened. "Even the san?"

"No, Mary," Sera chuckled. "I was exaggerating. They keep an eye on me with a fleet of drones—plus they have nanocloud tech. I guess Tanis really doesn't want me to kick it. She'd have to take control of the whole show, then."

The commissary was relatively empty, and the two women joined the line of three people waiting for their turn at the buffet.

One of the women in line turned and, upon seeing the president behind her, offered her spot.

"No, please," Sera raised her hand. "You were here first; my stomach isn't any more important than yours."

The woman flushed, but nodded silently as she turned and grabbed a tray.

"Scaring the locals?" a voice asked from behind them, and Sera turned to see Flaherty standing behind them.

"Stars, you're like a giant man-cat. How do you move so quietly?" Sera asked while Mary laughed.

Flaherty shrugged and glanced at Sera's feet. "I don't wear crazy boots like you do, makes it easy."

"Dad never did get fashion," Mary said with an apologetic shrug.

"Yeah, I was with him for some time," Sera replied, glaring at Flaherty. "I have a clear memory of certain comments."

Flaherty placed a hand on his chest and gave her a wounded look, before shaking his head and gesturing for the two women to move forward with the line.

"So what brings you down to D87C?" Sera asked, knowing the answer.

"You," Flaherty grunted.

"You know I have my High Guard now, right?" she asked, waving a hand in the direction of her shadows.

Flaherty nodded. "Good soldiers. But they're predictable, doing all the correct things at the correct times. I'm a bit harder to pin down."

"Are we actively in danger here?" Mary asked as she grabbed a bowl and ladled soup into it.

"Yes," Flaherty replied.

Sera placed a hand on Mary's shoulder. "Don't worry, he'd say that no matter where we were."

"Not true," Flaherty replied while grabbing a roll, then scooping a pile of leafy greens onto his plate. "There are safe places."

"Oh yeah?" Sera asked. "Where."

"Give me a minute. I'm sure I can think of one."

Mary chuckled and placed a sandwich on her tray, followed by a helping of chips and an apple. "There we are, everything a growing girl needs."

"Growing?" Sera asked.

"Well…no. Just seemed right at the time."

"You're not pregnant, are you?" Flaherty asked. "I like Leeroy…but I don't know if I like him *that* much."

Mary shook her head. "Dad, seriously, you sent us halfway across known space with him. You must trust him."

"A quarter."

"You trust him a quarter?" Sera asked, raising an eyebrow as she finished selecting her food and turned to look for a table.

"No, I sent Mary and Drew a quarter of the way across known space with Leeroy. Less, considering how far into the Perseus Arm the OFA has expanded."

"And the trust?" Mary asked, following Sera to a table a few meters away.

Flaherty grunted. "I trust him to keep you safe. Do I trust him enough to raise your next child?" He didn't bother answering his own question.

"At least you know he's honorable," Sera said as she sat.

"Maybe. Didn't take her where he was supposed to."

"Dad," Mary said flatly. "I'm a person, not cargo. I decide where I go. I wanted to be with you. I've spent most of my life wondering if you're even still alive, I'm not doing that again."

A spear of guilt struck Sera as she realized that it was Flaherty's promise to her that had taken him away from Mary for so many years.

She'd known it intellectually, but seeing the impact it had made on this woman sitting across the table from her was a different thing entirely.

Flaherty looked as though he was going to make an argument, but he glanced at Sera and, upon seeing the look in her eyes, nodded to Mary.

"OK, you're right."

"What?" Mary asked. "I'm right? This is a red letter day, if ever there was one."

Sera chuckled. "Yeah, he doesn't dole that one out very often."

She took a bite of her sandwich, and a glob of sauce fell out and landed on her arm. She lifted it to her mouth and licked it off, noticing as she did that Mary was grinning.

"Oh, right," Sera chuckled. "Twenty years since I was a pirate, but I still haven't let go of the manners—or rather, lack thereof."

"It's OK," Mary shrugged. "I was more wondering about your outfit. I'm a bit partial to skinsheaths; they're nice and low maintenance. Where'd you get yours?"

Flaherty grunted. "Pirates."

Mary's eyes lit up. "Really?"

"No," Sera shook her head. "I got it from Bob, the *Intrepid*'s AI. Though it's not an outfit, it's my skin."

"But it doesn't look like a skin job. There are creases at your elbows, and it looks like your breasts are covered."

Sera grinned at Mary. "I'm protecting poor Flaherty here from having to gaze upon my naked body."

"Plus everyone else around here," Flaherty added.

"So it's a malleable sort of thing?" Mary asked.

"Yeah. Sort of. Flaherty was right in that I first got the skin job when I was on a pirate base, but it was killing me, so Bob got me an upgrade. He declared that human epidermises were subpar when it came to keeping their bodies safe, and made something better for me."

Sera held up her hand, and it took on the appearance of a thick glove, and then of slender fingers—albeit without any creases or prints. She even changed it to something approximating a normal skin color.

"That's amazing!" Mary exclaimed. "I've never seen anything so…effortless. And that's on your whole body?"

Sera nodded. "It's also integrated with ISF Mark X Flow Armor, with moderate stealth capabilities. Not as good as the real stuff, but better than nothing."

As Sera spoke, her hand became invisible, and then she laid it on the table and grabbed her fork with her other hand, stabbing down with all her might.

The impact jostled everything on the table, but to Mary's visible amazement, the tines bent aside where they'd hit Sera's invisible hand.

"Stars burning in the core," Mary whispered, shaking her head. "Why does anyone have normal skin if they can get what you have?"

Sera glanced at Flaherty. "Why indeed. Do you want it, Mary?"

"Stars yeah, that would be amazing. I'd be wearing my entire wardrobe all the time *and* be bulletproof. What more could a girl want?"

"Flesh and blood?" Flaherty asked.

Mary waved a hand. "Nonsense. It's reversible, right?"

Sera's hand reappeared, and she held it in the air, wobbling it back and forth. "Ehhh…sorta. It's not easy to undo; you'd have to have your entire epidermal nervous system replaced and reconnected in the new skin. It's probably a few days' work."

Mary nodded. "Right, I figured as much. So how do you 'upgrade' my epidermis?"

Sera stroked her chin. "I'm not entirely certain. I did it once to someone in an elevator in a pinch, but that was back before I had the flow armor added in. It may need to be done more carefully. Why don't I look into it before I possibly eviscerate you?"

"That would be swell," Flaherty grunted.

Sera was about to show Mary some more things her skin could do, when Jen alerted her to an incoming message from the STC.

<Put it through,> Sera replied.

<President Sera,> the AI STC controller began. *<We've just received word that Governor Andrews of the New Canaan colony has arrived on an ISF cruiser. We have them on approach, and they're scheduled to dock in eighteen hours.>*

<Nothing about the nature of his visit?> Sera asked.

<No, ma'am.>

<Thank you.> Sera closed the connection, and then her eyes.

Jason Andrews.

She had seen him a few times in the months following the Defense of Carthage—brief encounters all, and always in larger settings. If he was coming here, it would be to meet specifically with her.

Sera opened her eyes and sighed. "Well, looks like an old flame has come for a visit."

"Jason?" Flaherty asked.

"How'd you know?"

Flaherty shrugged. "Not many of your old lovers are alive and not in prison. It's a short list."

Sera groaned and threw a piece of lettuce at him—which he caught and ate. "You're incorrigible."

"I'm truthful."

Mary shrugged. "He doesn't have much choice."

"Yeah, well, he's the one that opted for the alterations to ensure that," Sera replied.

Flaherty shook his head. "That would be an assumption, Madam President. You shouldn't make—ow! Sera, kicking your aides under the table is very unbecoming of a woman in your station."

Sera drew her foot back. "I'll do it again if you don't stop talking like that."

Flaherty raised his hands and gave her a rare smile. "Just making sure my girl is still in there. You're all Ms. Serious Business these days."

"Your girl?" Mary arched an eyebrow.

Flaherty wrapped an arm around his daughter and gave her a quick embrace. "Don't worry, Mary. You're the good daughter in this scenario. Sera's the one that needs constant supervision. Be dead a hundred times without me around."

Sera flashed her own smile back at Flaherty. "Eighty-seven, by my count. You sure you can't lie?"

"I can use hyperbole when it's obvious."

Sera and Mary locked gazes, both shaking their heads.

"You OK sharing him with me?" Sera asked.

Mary snorted. "Honestly? I'm kinda glad he spends so much time mothering over you. If he slathered all of it on me, I think I'd suffocate."

Flaherty groaned and took a sip of his coffee as he glared at the two women over its rim. "This is why I never talk."

DAMON SILAS

STELLAR DATE: 08.28.8949 (Adjusted Years)
LOCATION: Meela Station, Churka
REGION: Gorham System, Vela Cluster, Transcend Interstellar Alliance

Roxy glanced around at the other six members of her strike team and did her best not to think about how long they'd been crowded together inside the cramped shipping container.

Her HUD wasn't so forgiving, and the moment she thought about how much time had passed since they'd entered the container, it flashed a helpful update: *sixty-seven hours*.

Roxy resisted the urge to groan, while silently cursing Justin for sending her on this mission.

Well, not for sending **me** *on the mission, more for not coming along,* she amended.

The six former Hand agents that surrounded her in the container were all skilled operatives, and all fiercely loyal to Justin. Two of them, Sam and Harry, had even broken him out of prison.

An act Roxy had been very grateful for, since Justin was the only one in the galaxy who had known where her stasis pod was.

Thoughts about Justin caused no small amount of mental turmoil for Roxy. She'd been with him for centuries and had once loved him deeply, but she no longer knew if that was the case.

The mere thought of questioning her adoration for Justin caused a wave of images and feelings to flow through her mind, reinforcements that were intended to cement her devotion to the man.

The man who turned me into a machine…

A feeling of surprise came over Roxy at the thought. That she was even able to consider her current state in the wake of the corrective imagery and emotion was surprising. Normally when the neural lace in her brain modified her thinking, it was impossible to do anything other than bask in her adoration of Justin.

But this time, she was still able to think critically.

He stole my body…made me into this thing.

Roxy looked down at herself, her sapphire skin gleaming even in the dim lights within the shipping container. Soon she'd don her combat armor and cover it, but Justin had instilled in her a compulsion to show off her skin whenever possible.

It was one of his delights—reminding her how he'd made her into both an elite assassin, and his favorite art display.

How dare he do this to—

Roxy's mind went blank, a feeling of euphoria overcoming her. The euphoria was linked to her thoughts and memories of Justin, and she basked in the drug-like haze, dreaming of the time spent with the man she loved, yearning to get back to him.

How long have we been in here, anyway? she wondered, and her HUD obliged with the answer: *sixty-seven hours.*

* * * * *

An hour later, Roxy reached behind her and activated the transceiver built into the shipping container's wall.

The container itself was heavily EM shielded to conceal the seven people within, but every few hours—on an irregular schedule—Roxy activated the device and listened for any news from their operative on the outside.

Thus far, the message had always been, 'Stay in position'.

That 'position', at least presently, was a cargo hold on Meela Station, in orbit of Churka, a small, terrestrial world in the Gorham System.

Justin had chosen Gorham because it was frequented by individual ships from Admiral Krissy's fleet. Sometimes they came in pairs, but half the time, only a single destroyer would enter Gorham—more often than not, escorting cargo convoys that were gathering supplies for the war effort.

If the TSF held to their current schedule, a convoy should already have come past Meela station—a facility they often stopped at for resupply—but thus far, none had arrived.

In another two days, the strike team would be out of supplies, and would need to exit the container regardless of whether or not their prey had come by.

And so, with more than a little anticipation, Roxy sent out her ping, waiting for the response to tell her to sit tight once more.

<*Omega Team, TSF destroyer* Damon Silas *inbound for resupply. Container to be transferred in one hundred ninety minutes. Will be external vacuum transfer. Prepare for zero*-g *and vacuum. End.*>

Roxy sent an acknowledgement blip, then disabled the transceiver. Before the transfer time, she'd reactivate it four more times on the pre-arranged schedule.

"OK, team," she kept her voice low and soft. "We're t-minus one-ninety-mikes. Our target is the *Damon Silas.* It's a Caparsi Class destroyer. We don't have the specifics of that particular ship in our databases, but it should conform to the standards. Review those, plus the common variances. We don't know our destination within the ship, but Caparsi destroyers only have two cargo bays capable of holding containers this size."

The team nodded. The four women and two men organized their equipment, their eyes appearing sharp and focused on their tasks, even while reviewing internal data.

Roxy approved of their abilities, Hand agents were the best of the best at hiding everything they did under layers and layers of misdirection. Whenever they appeared to be doing one thing, you could be certain they were up to something else.

She wondered if they were talking to one another about her over the Link. They'd spoken very little in general, but that was also normal for Hand agents. They spent the vast majority of their time operating on their own—often years of travel away from their handlers and any backup.

To have this many working together on one objective was almost unheard of.

But, for all intents and purposes, Hand agents were near-vanilla humans. They had to be, to blend in better on their operations in the Inner Stars—unless the job required them to get modded.

For a moment, Roxy wondered what would have happened if she'd entered the Hand while Director Sera was in charge. Sera was also known for her unconventional—at least, by Airthan standards—predilections, but she wasn't prone to modifying her own underlings for her pleasure.

Granted, Justin had kept Roxy hidden from the public eye—and disassociated from himself—so it was entirely possible that Sera had done the same to some poor soul.

To hear Andrea talk, one would think that Sera had orgies every night, and slept with every creature she laid eyes on.

Not that Andrea was innocent of such behaviors. Though she was more known for her general volatility, her appetites were not any great secret.

Standing slowly, Roxy ran a check on her limbs, moving them through their full range of motion, ensuring that she'd be at peak performance when the mission began.

"You really can twist about," Harry said, unabashedly watching her as she went through her routine. "You almost look like a candy cane, wrapped around yourself like that."

Roxy shrugged. "I suppose. When your body is almost entirely boneless, it's no great feat."

Harry nodded silently before picking up his pack and pulling out his stealth sheath. Once Roxy disentangled herself, she did the same, retrieving the SS-R4 model sheath and unsealing its front closure before stepping into it.

Unlike the organics in the container, hers didn't have the need for any biological hookups; she emitted no heat from breath, no bodily waste. She barely needed the SS-R4's ability to mask body IR, as she could lower her temperature to that of her surroundings with ease.

If Justin hadn't wanted to make me his little art display, and had instead chosen to give me more useful skin, I wouldn't need the stealth sheath at all.

The disdain—and hint of vehemence—behind her thought surprised Roxy. *How is it that I am able to think so critically of Justin?* Usually such thoughts were quelled.

She felt as though she'd been able to do it more often of late, though the realization dissipated in a moment, as images of working with Justin and partnering with him on this great endeavor filled her mind.

He's going to make an amazing leader for the Transcend.

Once in her SS-R4, Roxy proceeded to check over her weapons. The first was her lightwand, which she slid into a small pouch on her thigh. Following that, she added the four carbon-blade knives to their sheaths on her back. A handgun with a fold-in grip went into the pouch on her left thigh, followed by ammunition packs on her chest and the small of her back.

Finally, Roxy lifted her rifle out of the bag. It was a stealth-capable, multifunction weapon with three firing modes. The first was the standard pulse mode—one she rarely used—followed by flechettes and kinetic slugs.

The flechettes were Roxy's favorite. She didn't know why, she just felt they suited her more. It could be that she had favored them in the time before Justin had saved her...or maybe she'd picked it up afterward; she really wasn't sure.

The next three hours were spent analyzing ideal routes to take the ship. The team was in unanimous agreement that there would be an AI running the *Damon Silas*, and disabling it would be the top priority.

Harry was reasonably certain he had a breach technique that could get him into the ship's security systems, but it was based on an old set of command-override keys that they couldn't count on. If that override didn't work, they'd have little time to effect their seizure of the ship; if Justin's intel was correct, only seconds once they were detected. For that reason, they decided not to use the breach unless absolutely necessary, or until the AI was offline.

"I'm on the AI," Roxy said. "Lloyd, you're with me. Harry, you take your team to Engineering; Sam, you're to take the forward weapons control node. Once we have that, we can get the ship the hell out of this system. It's critical that we get control of the stasis shields—once everyone realizes that their ship is going for a ride, we're going to become the target of every weapon in this system."

Harry grunted, shaking his head. "Those are going to be a long four AU to the jump point."

"Justin will be ready," Roxy said with calm assurance.

"Better be," Lloyd said while cleaning the charge pod socket for his rifle. "If he's not, we'll get to find out firsthand how much firepower these stasis shields can shed."

Several minutes later, they felt the cargo container lift off the deck and begin to move. While it *should* be airtight, no one wanted to find out they were wrong the hard way, so the team pulled on their helmets.

Roxy activated her EM suppression suite, just in case the ship ran an active scan against the container before allowing it entry.

The container shifted a few times, and then left the station's artificial gravity field. It changed vector twice over the next fifteen minutes, then gravity returned, and the team gently settled back down to the bottom of the container.

They took up their assigned positions within the small space, weapons covering the double doors at each end. If the ship decided to perform an inspection, they'd have to kill the inspector and get out of the container in seconds. No one wanted to die in the killbox if they could avoid it.

Minutes passed with no activity other than the slight vibrations caused by other cargo settling onto the deck. After twenty minutes, the vibrations stopped, and Roxy crept to the doors and placed her hand on the seal, slipping a nano filament through.

Once it was in place, the team got a view of a dimly lit cargo bay. From what they could see, it appeared to be Bay 9A, the one closest to engineering.

The filament deployed drones that worked their way up the surface of the container. Roxy held her breath—which didn't matter, since she didn't need to breathe. But this was the moment of truth. They had two egress points on the sides of the containers, but they could be blocked by other cargo. If that was the case, their only exit would be the doors on either end, and opening those would be hard to hide from internal surveillance systems.

The drones finally reached the top, and the team got a full picture of the bay. It was nearly full, supplies of all shapes and sizes stacked on racks and atop cargo containers. The overabundance was great for blocking surveillance, but bad for their exit.

Then Roxy's fears were quelled, and she finally exhaled. The secret opening on the right side of the container was only partially blocked. Even better, the crates sitting next to it would obscure the team's exit.

She nodded to Sam, who unlatched the section of the container's side and pulled it free. A holofield shimmered into view, masking the opening and the team that was about to pass through.

From this point on, they were EM silent. The team confirmed the countdowns on their timers, and then Roxy slipped out first. Careful to walk softly—SS-R4 could only mask so much—she worked her way over a stack of crates and down to the central aisle that ran through the bay.

By some stroke of luck, the door into the corridor was wide open; Roxy was about to thank the stars, when a woman approached, stopping in the doorway. She pulled out a tablet, likely to do a visual inspection, then stopped and turned to speak with someone in the passageway beyond.

Shit, Roxy cursed as she approached the woman, a CWO by her insignia. There was just enough room for her to slip past the TSF chief, so long as the woman didn't move back any further.

Roxy slowed her movements, all but pressing herself against the bay's doorframe as she slipped past the chief. When she was directly behind her, Roxy considered just killing the annoyance. She knew it would be a terrible idea when it came to stealth, but it was enticing nonetheless. Of course, then she'd have to kill the man in the corridor that the chief was talking to as well. Someone would probably notice the blood and bodies.

What a shame.

A small part of Roxy wondered if she had always been so bloodthirsty. She couldn't remember her younger years, before Justin had molded her into his creature, but she couldn't imagine she'd always defaulted to killing any inconvenience. It seemed illogical.

A moment later, she was past the woman, and standing in the corridor. Her own goal, the ship's AI, was closest, but she was in no rush to reach it. Roxy decided to wait and ensure that the rest of the team was able to sneak past the chatty chief before continuing on.

After two minutes, she picked up the 'all clear' ticks on the team's pre-determined frequencies, and nodded with satisfaction.

They were past the first hurdle. If all went well, the *Damon Silas* would be theirs within thirty minutes. She moved down the corridor, hoping that Lloyd was following behind. It was tricky to move invisibly through a ship with another person. Your chance of bumping into your companion was almost greater than running into the enemy.

For that reason, they'd agreed that she would start on the route to the AI's node chamber thirty seconds before Lloyd. She'd ensured that the other teams had set their travel order and wait points as well.

They hadn't given her any trouble regarding that directive. Given that Hand agents almost always worked solo, these six were admirably good at coordinating with one another.

Four minutes later, Roxy was standing on the right side of the door leading into the ship AI's node chamber. A soft tap on the bulkhead next to her head informed her that Lloyd was in position, and she drew in a slow breath.

Why do I keep doing that? I don't recall concentrating on my breathing so much on prior missions.

Roxy's ability to breathe was just for show, something to make her seem more human—which was odd, considering she didn't even look human. *Another contradiction Justin built into me.*

She pushed the thoughts away and cleared her mind. They had to wait another six minutes for the clock to count down to zero. Once it did, all teams would begin their breaches.

A pair of ensigns turned into the corridor, approaching Roxy and Lloyd's position. As they drew close, Roxy pressed herself flat against the bulkhead, careful to avoid the swinging arms of the young man on the right.

For a moment, there was a fleeting worry in her mind, a concern over the fact that they were going to kill the TSF crew. *After all, aren't they fighting for the Transcend too?* Sure, these people were fighting against Airtha and her evil ways, but they didn't even know that Justin's faction existed. If they knew, maybe they'd do the right thing and join him.

Just as quickly as the thought came into her mind, it left, the feelings of certainty that Justin was doing the right thing crowding it out.

Roxy set her jaw and gave a resolute nod. *We are on the right side of this.*

Two minutes later, a lieutenant strolled down the corridor and stopped in front of the entrance to the AI's node chamber. He placed his palm on the door control, passing secure tokens, and then stood back as the door slid aside.

Roxy's first reaction was to worry, but then she realized that this was the perfect way in. Even if she did have to kill the lieutenant—Clancy, by his name tag—she could do it at the same time that she took out the AI.

It would save her at least thirty seconds of breach time on the door.

Without further thought, she slipped into the room just as the door closed behind Lieutenant Clancy—glad that Lloyd hadn't tried to enter as well.

The node chamber was a standard affair, small, with a rack of equipment on one side, and the SAI's titanium cylinder in the center, data cables linked into it in several places.

"Afternoon, Carmen," the lieutenant said as he pulled up a holodisplay. "How is everything with you today?"

"Right as rain, Lieutenant Clancy," Carmen replied audibly.

Roxy found it odd that the human and AI were conversing audibly, but as they bantered, the exchange almost seemed to be performed by rote.

"Another day, another supply run babysitting job," Clancy said as he flipped through diagnostic reports, marking each off as 'reviewed and approved' at the source terminal.

"I'd rather be on a milk run like this than out at the front," Carmen replied, the AI's voice carrying a soft laugh.

"You always say that," Clancy replied, glancing up at the titanium cylinder. "But you know that these 'milk runs' are bait. We're trying to suck the Airthans and any separatists into attacking us. It's why we have the stasis shields."

"And that's why I volunteered for this placement," Carmen replied. "Not because we're a juicy target, but because of the shields. Plus, if anyone hits us, the cavalry comes running and crushes them."

Roxy's blood pressure rose as she listened to the pair talk.

Bait ship? Cavalry? No wonder this ship is out here all alone! And we've gobbled up the worm. Hook, line and sinker.

She considered her options as the pair continued their conversation. If she aborted the mission, there was little chance her team would make it off the *Damon Silas* alive.

The only real option was to move forward. Based on the way Carmen and Clancy were talking, no one expected an attack to come from within, which meant that once they secured the ship, its stasis shields would make it the safest place to be in the Gorham System.

Her real concern was for Justin's fleet, which would jump in to escort the prize out. If the *Damon Silas* really was bait, and the 'cavalry' was coming, then he was going to be in one heck of a fight.

There was nothing for it. He would be in the dark layer now, and there was no way to warn him that the TSF destroyer was a trap.

As the clock wound down, the lieutenant closed out the terminal he was using and approached the AI's cylinder.

"Ready for your weekly checkup?" he asked as the access panel on the cylinder slid open.

"Just keep the rectal thermometer to yourself," the AI replied in a mock-serious tone.

"I can't believe people used to do shit like that."

Carmen groaned. "Wow, really ratcheting it up in the bad pun department, there."

"I learned from the best."

The timer on Roxy's HUD transitioned from white to red as it crossed over the ten-second mark. She crept up behind Lieutenant Clancy and, carefully reaching down for her gun with her left hand, stilled her breathing and prepared for what was to come.

3…2…1…MARK.

In one, fluid motion, Roxy drew her pistol, placed it against the base of the lieutenant's skull, and fired.

Brains and gore exploded from the bottom of his skull, covering Roxy in the man's grey matter and mental mods. For a moment, she stared in horror at the mess dripping off her hand, then realization dawned on her: the man must have had a reinforced skull…instead of the shot bursting out through his forehead, it all came back out the hole she'd made.

Roxy shook her head as the body before her fell to the ground, revealing the AI's tesseract-shaped cube within the cylinder.

The access panel began to slide shut, but Roxy was faster and, in an instant, she tore the AI's core free and threw it to the ground.

She raised her dripping pistol and aimed it at the AI's core. Without a second thought, Roxy pulled the trigger, only to see a message show on her HUD informing her that the gun's firing chamber was jammed—with Clancy's brains, no doubt.

"Dammit," she muttered, and reached for her lightwand just as an alarm blared across the ship.

"Well, I guess you all know what's happening now," she muttered.

With a flick of her wrist, the lightwand came to life, and Roxy knelt down, ready to slice the AI core in half, when Carmen's voice emanated from it.

"*Wait!* I don't want to die!"

"Nothing for it," Roxy replied as she raised her hand to strike.

"You're going to die too! All of us will." The AI's voice was pleading, and something in it stayed Roxy's hand.

"What do you mean?"

"This is a stasis ship, did you know that?"

A rueful laugh escaped Roxy's lips. "Know it? We're counting on it."

"All stasis ships have countermeasures to ensure that they're never captured. With me offline, and your team—I assume you have a team—attacking the ship, you can bet that Captain John has already armed it."

"*Fuck!*" Roxy swore. "So we go through all this, and the ship blows?"

"I can stop it," Carmen said, her words coming so fast, Roxy could barely parse them. "I can kill the sequence, but I have to do it fast."

Roxy lowered her wand. "OK, so do it."

"No." The AI's single word was laced with defiance.

"No?"

"You're a cold-blooded *murderer*." Carmen all but shouted the accusation from her thirty-centimeter cube. "You'll kill me once I do. I want you to get me off the ship in an escape pod."

"No. There's no way you can disable the sequence from an escape pod. You'll need privileged access." The AI didn't respond, and Roxy rocked back on her heels. "Seems we're at an impasse. But if we want to live, we'll have to work something out. I'm Roxy, by the way."

"Put me in a hard case and take me to Bay 13C. The device is in there. I'll disable it, and then I'm going to have to trust you to stick to your end of the bargain."

Roxy considered her options for a moment before nodding.

"OK, I'll do it. You have my word I won't kill you."

"And the rest of your team. Do you speak for them?" Carmen pressed.

"They won't kill you, either."

"And you'll not do something that directly or indirectly causes me to die?"

"Shit, Carmen, I have no idea, I'm about to get in a firefight. Chances are your case is gonna get a hole blown in it, then we all die. For that matter, how will I know that you're not going to tell everyone on the ship where I am?"

"You're covered in Clancy's insides. The ship's internal cameras are going to spot you just fine."

"Good point. So, do we have a deal?"

The AI didn't respond for a moment, then made a sound like a groan. "I guess that'll have to do. The hard case is just above you."

Roxy spotted the standard-issue TSF AI case on the rack, and pulled it off, fitting the AI's core in place before pulling up the case's specs. She located the wireless transmitter, and drove her lightwand into it.

"Just to make sure we're on the up and up," Roxy said.

"Asshole," the AI shot back.

Roxy chuckled as she closed the case, and opened the door to see the muzzle flash from Lloyd's rifle as he fired down the corridor.

"Nice of you to come out and join the fun; got a bit messy in there, I see." The man's tone was dour. "We on to the bridge, then?"

"Change of plans, there's a self-destruct in Bay 13C that we have to take out. It's not far from here. On the ship's central axis."

"Self-destruct? TSF has gotten crazy since I served."

Roxy hadn't known Lloyd was former military—not that it surprised her. Many of the Hand agents were recruited from the TSF's special forces.

"It's because of the stasis shields. I guess they really don't want it to fall into enemy hands." As Roxy spoke, she unslung her rifle and added her shots to Lloyd's, pushing the soldiers he was engaging with back into cover. "C'mon, we only have a few minutes!"

The pair fell back down the corridor, moving from cover to cover, when suddenly the enemy fire ceased.

"What the…?" Roxy said, checking through her drone feeds. "They're falling back."

"Well, the ship *is* going to blow," Lloyd said with a shrug.

The pair moved quickly through the final sixty meters to their target, and Roxy breached the door while Lloyd stood guard in the passageway once more.

Bay 13C was small, little more than a storage room on the map. But its purpose had clearly changed. The first thing Roxy saw upon entering the room was an antimatter bottle standing on a pedestal in the middle of the room.

An array of SC batteries were positioned around it, and a shimmering shield enveloped them all.

"Stasis?" Roxy asked as she opened Carmen's case.

"Yeah, plug me in on that console over there, I need direct access."

Roxy complied, wondering how the field would respond if it contacted a physical object. Once she'd set Carmen onto the console—hoping the AI would live up to her word—she turned back to the stasis shield around the antimatter.

Casting about for something to prod it with, she found a sheet of plas, and rolled it up.

"Don't!" Carmen cried out just as Roxy reached forward and touched the plas to the field.

As Carmen's shout reverberated through the room, there was a brilliant flash, and half the plas ceased to exist.

"What the fuck?" Roxy exclaimed.

"Don't *do* that! You trying to kill us?"

"I didn't think it would—"

"How about you *don't* perform half-assed experiments to see what happens when you push a bunch of atoms against a field of zero-energy matter, OK?"

Roxy nodded as she looked at the half-sheet of plas in her hand.

"Why doesn't the air do that?"

"There's a light grav field keeping the air molecules off the stasis shield. But it's not strong enough to resist determined idiots."

Roxy eyed the device in the room with a newfound level of respect. "And they just leave this thing in here?"

"Normally, only highly trained specialists come in here, not fools like you."

"I'm not—"

"Shut up! Seconds here."

The gravity of their situation hit Roxy once more, and she clamped her mouth shut. Seconds later, the shimmering stasis shield disappeared, and then a light at the bottom of the antimatter bottle turned from red to green.

"How long did we have?" Roxy was momentarily surprised at her own morbid curiosity.

"Don't ask. So, what now? You going to put me into a pod like you promised?"

Roxy turned her attention to the AI sitting atop the console. She knew what Justin would want; he'd tell her to kill the thing. It was too risky to set free, and too dangerous to keep around.

But Carmen had put her life on the line to save Roxy—granted, she didn't have much of a choice, since it was her only chance to live.

"I'll do my best, but I can't get to a pod right now. I'm going to put you in a stealth pouch so no one on the team sees you—but you'll need to kill your EM to stay hidden."

"Roxy—"

"It's the best I can do. Shut down."

"Give me your word you're not going to kill me," Carmen said, her tone almost pleading—if an AI could even do such a thing.

"I already did."

"Humor me." Now Carmen really *did* sound like she was pleading.

"I promise," Roxy said.

The AI seemed to accept it, as her core went dark a moment later.

As Roxy pulled a stealth pouch out of her SS-R4, a strange sensation came over her. This being had placed her life in Roxy's hands. She was trusting a person who had just stormed her ship to keep her alive.

Roxy determined that she would do as she'd promised. She would keep Carmen safe, but she would *not* put her in an escape pod. She was going to keep the AI safe with her.

The thought of hiding something from Justin never fully formed in her mind, but Roxy skirted around the edges of it, careful to keep the idea from being suppressed. For it had occurred to her that perhaps this AI could work out a way to free her from the mental prison she was in.

And then she'd kill Justin.

FAILURE

STELLAR DATE: 08.29.8949 (Adjusted Years)
LOCATION: TSS *Regent Mary*, Interstellar Space
REGION: Near Vela Cluster, Transcend Interstellar Alliance

Krissy bent over the holotable in the *Regent Mary*'s CIC, staring incredulously at the display before her.

She wanted to scream, slam her fists into the table, and beat some inanimate object to bits—or better yet, find Justin and kill him with her bare hands.

Instead, Krissy took a deep breath and closed her eyes.

"OK, Colonel Kysha, walk me through this again. The *Damon Silas* came into the Gorham System a day late, but made good time with its convoy to Meela Station."

Colonel Kysha swallowed before replying, clearly able to sense Krissy's ire. "That is correct, Admiral Krissy. As best we can surmise, Justin's strike team got onto the *Damon Silas* during its resupply. The *Silas* had just sent over four shuttles of people on shore leave, so when Justin's Hand agents hit the vessel, it was lightly crewed."

"That's a policy we'll have to change," Krissy muttered. "We're not joyriding through space, we're running missions."

"The crew of the *Damon Silas* had been nine months without shore leave…it was thought the Gorham System was secure—"

"*Khardine* is secure," Krissy cut the colonel off. "We need to resend the orders directing captains to transfer there for shore leave during any refit. We're in the middle of a fucking war for stars' sakes!"

"Yes, Admiral." Kysha nodded quickly. "I'll see that it's done."

"So, do we have any intel on why the ship didn't blow? Captain John got a message off that he had initiated the self-destruct."

"That is correct, ma'am. In the time given, only the captain or the ship's AI could have disabled the self-destruct."

"Which means one of them was compromised," Krissy mused.

"An analyst team is trying to determine if any other possibility can fit the known facts, but that is our current working hypothesis." Kysha paused, and when Krissy didn't ask any further questions, she noted the

Damon Silas's location on the holotable. "At 18:24 local time, the attackers had full control of the ship. They activated the stasis shields and boosted away from Meela Station."

"And there was nothing the locals could do about it," Krissy added.

"No, they tried firing up the ship's engine wash, but once the enemy understood what was going on, they changed vector to keep their engines oriented away from any pursuers with enough firepower to punch through the wash."

Kysha set the holotable to a new time—21:39 the same day—and pointed to a location at the edge of the system.

"At this point, a fleet of four hundred ships jumped in here. These are all ships belonging to a variety of systems near the border with the Inner Stars. Each of them had declared as independent from us or Airtha. Either they have surreptitiously sided with Justin's faction, or they had defectors who did."

"Something we'll need to investigate," Krissy said while rolling her shoulders. "Just another task on the 'Keep the Transcend from Disintegrating' list."

Kysha pursed her lips. "Shall I see to sending scout ships to those systems?"

"No. Well...not all. We don't have the resources for that. Pick a random sampling. We'll see what we can learn."

"Understood." Kysha advanced the clock to 23:14. "Here is where our ships jumped in. As you know, this couldn't have happened at a worse time. With the bulk of our response fleet in the Albany System fighting the Nietzscheans, and two other bait traps sprung, we could only send thirty-seven ships to help the *Damon Silas*. They harried it and damaged one of its engines, but more than half of our ships had no stasis shields. Once Justin's fleet came into range, they had to disengage—especially since his people aboard the *Silas* advised them of the engine wash trick."

"Fucking stars," Krissy muttered. "Well, we have to consider *that* secret out in the wild, now. So, from there, the rest of the story is pretty much 'they got away,' right?"

Kysha blew out a long breath. "Yes, ma'am. The *Damon Silas* jumped ten minutes ago. The bulk of Justin's fleet hit the system at over 0.8*c*. They pushed our pursuit ships back as they blew past them, then continued on an outsystem vector for a jump point clear across the system.

"The locals are harrying them, picking off a few ships here and there. Justin had also sent in an escort fleet at a lower *v*. They took some losses, but they've all jumped out with the *Silas*."

Krissy pushed herself away from the holotable and turned, running a hand through her hair. "Well, looks like I need to prepare a report for Sera. I don't envy her having to tell Tanis that we just lost a stasis shield ship."

She glanced back to see Kysha swallow again. "Yes, ma'am."

A long, calming breath later, Krissy turned back to the table. "Hemdar, can you prepare the report for Sera?"

<Already on it, Admiral,> Hemdar replied. *<You'll have it in a minute. I'm just waiting on finalized assessments from the analyst teams about the likelihood of Justin reverse engineering the stasis tech.>*

Krissy was more than a little interested in that answer. "Which way are they leaning?"

<Toward 'slim to none'. Though having a stasis ship is a big advantage for him. But if he's in league with Airtha…>

Hemdar let the words hang. They all knew what the outcome would be, there. Airtha stood a much better chance of reverse engineering the stasis shield systems. Not only that, but stasis shields used picotech. She'd get both.

Krissy wondered—not for the first time—how one scientist from five thousand years ago had cracked picotech, and then invented stasis shields, while no one else had come close on either. What made Earnest Redding so special that he found not one, but *two* holy grails?

There were rumors that there must have been some ascended AI influence, but Krissy wasn't so sure about that. If ascended AIs had that level of tech, why didn't *they* use it?

Maybe they have something better, Krissy mused. *Stars…now* ***that's*** *a terrifying thought.*

"OK, well, include that in the report. It's not as though we haven't considered this possibility," Krissy said. "Now, what we need to focus on is getting our fleets back from Albany as quickly as we can. There are too many bait ships hanging out in the wind."

"Yes, Admiral," Kysha grimaced. "Ever since we jumped the fleets out to Thebes, I've had this twitch in my left arm. We have sixty gates disassembled and ready for transport the moment we get the word that it's safe to send them to Albany. It will take us four hours to get our ten-thousand ships back in the Transcend, ready for deployment."

"Ours first?" Krissy asked, pulling up the dispersal plans for the allied fleet in Albany. "I'm surprised that Greer didn't push to have his pulled back first. I wouldn't blame him; we don't want Khardine unguarded."

"Admiral Sanderson has forty-four hundred ISF ships ready to jump out of New Canaan if Khardine falls under attack."

Krissy whistled, surprised to hear that. Officially, New Canaan would not let their home fleet fall below ten thousand ships. It would seem they understood the importance of keeping the Khardine capital secure.

As Krissy spoke with Hemdar, Kysha set the latest status from the Albany System on the holotable. It showed the remaining Nietzschean ships in a full rout, but a terrific mess had been left behind. The S&R operations were going to take some weeks. It appeared that Tanis was establishing a secure staging ground near an inner planet named Buffalo, and that was where the gates were to be set up.

"They expect to have Buffalo secured in ten hours," Krissy said, then pursed her lips, praying nothing happened before then that would require anything more than her reserve forces. Her thoughts turned back to the mess with Justin.

*Anything **more**, that is.*

"Let me know the minute they're ready to ship the gates," Krissy said as she turned to leave the room. "I'm going to send that report to Sera, and then wait to see if she wants to discuss it in person."

"Understood, Admiral Krissy," Kysha replied. "I'll see to it that scout ships are dispatched within the hour to begin reconnaissance on the systems that may be supporting Justin."

"Very good, Colonel," Krissy replied, as she walked out of the CIC in search of a strong cup of coffee before sending the report to Sera.

Maybe a whole pot.

TRUTH AND REALITY

STELLAR DATE: 08.29.8949 (Adjusted Years)
LOCATION: Node 1, ISS *I2*
REGION: Pyra, Albany System, Thebes, Septhian Alliance

Tanis stepped through the node chamber's doors and strode toward the railing that ran around the catwalk. Behind her, the door locked and sealed.

Not to keep her in, but to keep any intrusions at bay.

In front of her was Bob's primary node, a ten meter cube hanging in the center of the chamber. Conduits carrying Bob's lifeblood—power and data—connected to the node in a dozen places. Cooling systems ringed it, and light glowed from deep within the multi-layered cube.

<*You came to speak with me 'in person',*> Bob said, his voice carrying no inflection that Tanis could hear.

But she didn't need to *hear* Bob to gain insight into his thoughts. She could see them. It was why they'd come to his node to have this conversation.

"Do you remember the last time we were here?" Tanis asked. "You, Angela, and I?"

<*Of course I do,*> Bob replied. <*You came here after I woke you from stasis at Estrella de la Muerte. You saved the ship.*>

<***We** saved the ship,*> Angela corrected the multinodal AI.

<*It is the same thing when referring to the two of you,*> Bob replied, his tone nonchalant, almost dismissive. <*Even then, the distinctions between you were diminishing.*>

Tanis nodded, working to remain sanguine about the situation. "Because of what you did to us."

<*Are you accusing me, or thanking me?*> Bob asked.

The question hit Tanis like an atom beam, shredding the arguments and accusations she was about to make, the blame she was prepared to lay at Bob's feet.

<*Shit, he's got us there,*> Angela said privately.

Tanis nodded absently as she stared at Bob's mind. It was unlike any other human or AI mind she'd seen. She thought it would be like most minds, only deeper—like an onion with layers upon layers of thought. But that analogy failed utterly. If Bob's mind was an onion, it was a galaxy of onions that became larger—not smaller—the further you went in.

Over the day since her rescue, Tanis and Angela had learned how to interpret the surface thoughts of others the same way they could read expressions on a human's face.

They could even do it with AIs, watching their *n*-level matrices of thought and emotion shift and change in response to stimuli.

But not so with Bob.

His mind was so vast, so far-reaching, that it was impossible to determine what aspect of him was responding to the words she'd uttered. Or even to interpret his mental responses at all.

<*Even if we were fully ascended, I don't think we'd be more than a mote next to him,*> Tanis replied. <*Do you think he sees our mind?*>

<*Yes,*> Angela admitted after a moment's pause. <*I think he has for some time.*>

<*Why do you think separately?*> Bob asked. <*You became one. I know this; Priscilla shared it with me, and I saw it in the mind of Rika.*>

"At least we're back on track," Tanis said as she lifted one leg over the railing, followed by the other, to sit on top with her feet hooked behind the middle bar.

Despite her unconventional perch, she couldn't shake the feeling that she was supplicating herself before some ancient deity, seeking wisdom and guidance.

Angela's laugh wreathed her thoughts. <*You can't shake that feeling because **I'm** thinking it.*>

No one spoke for a moment, then Angela replied to Bob's question. <*We think separately because of what Priscilla gave us to stabilize our form, to keep us from moving beyond this physical body.*>

"Which you seemed prepared for." Tanis worked to control her emotions, to hold back the accusations that wanted to burst free from her. She could sense them in Angela as well, and they shared a feeling of calm and control before Tanis continued.

"You knew there was a risk that we'd ascend in a situation like what happed on Pyra, you didn't just whip up the subatomic stabilization that Priscilla provided. Did you know what would happen down there, Bob?

Brandt *died* down there. She's gone, and I'm going to have to face her daughter someday and tell her about her mother's final moments! Do you know what that's like?"

Tanis's tone was strident; she wasn't yelling, but she really wanted to.

<*I didn't know Brandt would die. I didn't expect the Nietzscheans to bring so many ships.*>

<*The fuck, Bob!*> Angela exclaimed. <*You* ***knew*** *the Niets would attack?*>

<*It was in your own analyst's reports. They didn't expect a fleet this size either, and their probability of attack was very, very low. Mine was higher, but I got it wrong too. I'm neither omniscient, nor omnipresent. You both understand that better than anyone. Your involvement makes it even harder to predict.*>

Tanis resisted letting out a groan. "So we're back to my 'luck' again, are we? There's no mystical power controlling my destiny, Bob. From what I can see, it's just a bunch of AIs who think they know better than everyone else—except they don't seem to know anything at all."

<*You raise good points, Tanis. I will do my best to address them,*> Bob replied, his tone even, carrying no rancor after Tanis's accusation.

<*The floor is yours.*> Angela's tone, on the other hand, was sardonic in the extreme.

<*Some of this you know, Tanis-Angela, but some of it you do not. However, perhaps you need a reminder. Firstly 'luck' is just a convenient term for your condition. What you really do is alter probability on a quantum level. Because my advanced predictive algorithms must take* ***everything*** *into account, your presence skews the results. Even after studying you for centuries, I still do not know how you do it—though the information that Katrina has provided us leads me to believe that you were* ***made*** *to be this way, a suspicion I have harbored for some time.*>

Tanis opened her mouth to respond, but then closed it. She wanted to hear Bob out. Her emotions—and the outburst they were bound to cause—would only get in the way of this discourse.

<*However,*> Bob continued, <*I have also suspected that you operated in such a fashion that caused you to be so unpredictable—and too difficult for those who altered your base physiology to control—that they tried to do away with you. Several of your exploits in your youth point to this, events such as your assignation of the Toro mission.*

<Again, these are not fully formed beliefs, they are based on suppositions I have made after considering what Joe learned from Katrina and the Xavia remnant. I **do** *know that* **I** *brought you into my fold deliberately, though I don't know if all of my actions were of my own volition at that point. I was young, and it was possible that I was influenced to help you.*

<Regardless of these things, I identified your 'luck'—as we shall call it for lack of a more concise term—and began to attempt to map it. Around the same time, Earnest alerted me to the fact that your minds had become inextricably linked, that we would never be able to separate you, and that you would, before long, die.>

"Die?" Tanis couldn't help but interrupt. "When did you come to that realization?"

<Before we left Estrella de la Muerte. At that point, you had five or six years before you went insane, shortly after which you would have died.>

<I never knew it was so…real and present,> Angela said.

<We hid it from you,> Bob's tone was matter-of-fact. *<We had to. Earnest and I pored over myriad solutions in an attempt to save you. One thing we determined early on was that with your luck in the mix, the less you knew about what we were doing, the less likely you were to inadvertently affect it.*

<Our first step was to stabilize your minds. That was a long, slow process, one that took us nearly fifty years to complete. Something about the way you two became interlinked after you fought off those STR attack craft in the Sol System made your mind very resilient to any sort of influence we tried to effect.>

"Probably because Angela is so stubborn," Tanis muttered.

<Seriously? Me, I'm not the stubborn one. You realize **this** *is why he kept us out of stasis during the journey to Kapteyn's Star.>*

"Bob? Really?"

<Partially, yes. I was also trusting in your undeniably efficient ability for self-preservation to protect us all.>

Tanis had to admit to herself that what Bob was saying was truly fascinating. Though it was taking some effort to divorce herself from the anger caused by the knowledge that he had altered her brain—her *mind*—without her knowing, and had been doing it for nearly the entire duration of their friendship.

She understood that it had saved her life, but the secrecy was still difficult to accept. Alongside that, the issue she had with Bob's theory was that he believed she unpredictably altered the fabric of the universe at a quantum level.

"Bob, hold onto that, because I think I see where you're going, but I want you to explain it. I want to understand *how* we alter quantum-level probabilities. How did you ever come up with that idea, and how did you test the theory?"

Bob laughed, a thundering wave of rueful humor rolling over Tanis. *<Well, for starters, I have the capability to think* ***a lot*** *and, not only that, I had a lot of time to do it. However, my realization began with photons.>*

<Good place to start,> Angela commented.

<After you began to merge—though before we revealed it to you—Earnest had to make several upgrades to your neurological modifications to deal with how you and Angela kept bleeding through them and into one another. A particularly tricky issue was your vision. As you know, because of the military nature of your upgrades, Angela has always had full access to your vision. She sees through your eyes when she wishes to—which is frequently, I might add—and as a result, your optic nerve feeds directly to both of your brains.

<I say 'nerve' though your entire optic system is more inorganic than organic. Regardless, it does have an organic housing. As you well know, this is a neurological data interface that is usually heavily buffered. Should an AI choose to backdoor into a human's mind through their optic nerve, they could directly control much of the other person's mind, and so these buffers protect the human.

<Again, your mind was altered by the military on many occasions, as were your sensory systems and their inputs. I speak of both of you, of course. One of these alterations was to reduce the buffering on the optic data transmission to improve ocular data speed and bandwidth, in order to handle your increased sensory range. Earnest and I are both reasonably certain that this is where your merging began. It was also one of the things we struggled to rectify for some time.>

<OK,> Tanis said privately to Angela. *<Is our optic linkage that unusual? I never thought it was.>*

<I didn't, either. It was a standard set of mods for MICI agents.>

<The reason why it was so difficult,> Bob continued after they finished speaking—a clear indication that he could tell when they were doing it. *<Is because you see the world differently, Tanis, you just don't realize it. Not only do you see a broader range of the EM spectrum, but you can focus on more of it at once. Don't forget, you were one of few artificially upgraded L2 humans*

to be paired with an AI. There are no 'standard mods' for you.

<As Earnest and I worked, it became apparent that all of the systems we came up with to reduce optic nerve bleed-through would have required us to reduce that EM sensitivity. Moreover, we would have needed to alter your brain to reduce focus, but that was a core aspect of your neurological L2 enhancements.

<So Earnest and I worked to devise a way to slow the bleed-through, limiting the direct access into one another's mind that it was fostering. The problem was that no matter what we tried, it never seemed to work properly.>

<Because of photons?> Angela asked.

<Yes,> Bob replied, his voice thundering with conviction. *<You know, of course, that even individual photons refract. And refraction is a key part of vision itself. The words are crude, but you both understand that photons exist in multiple places at once because of this. Highly accurate EM sensors need to account for these events when triangulating light sources and filtering different EM wavelengths apart to create a clearer, more coherent image.>*

Tanis nodded. "Right, EM sensors such as my eyes."

<Yes. But what Earnest and I came to realize is that your eyes were faulty, yet not faulty. They passed every test we threw at them, but still managed to have a performance profile that didn't match their specifications. This caused them to constantly thwart the systems we were putting in place to limit mental bleed-through.

<After extensive study, Earnest discovered that the probability curve for what photons would do when interacting with your eyes didn't match any model we could devise. Until I altered the model to add a 'beneficial' algorithmic matrix.>

"This is where we move into magic, isn't it?" Tanis asked, a touch of sarcasm in her voice.

<Tanis, you have torn atoms apart and seen through both minds and worlds. You have done this through scientifically explainable—and repeatable—methods. You should be the last one to call something out as 'magic'.>

"I suppose," Tanis allowed. "I guess I have a mental block on this issue. Please, you were about to tell us what a beneficial algorithmic matrix is."

<Well, it's possibly one of the most complex things I've ever devised—and it's far from perfect, but it was enough for us to gain the efficiency we needed to retain your advanced optical systems, as well as slow your merging.

<As you know, even in something that appears to be known and consistent,

such as the refractive properties of a given material, the actual result is inconsistent due to everything from imperfections, to temperature, to random subatomic particles passing by. The algorithmic matrix I developed has to do with correctly predicting the reflection and refraction properties of your eyes. You know that some light that enters your eyes reflects, and some refracts. This happens at multiple points within your optic system, similar to how it occurs in an organic eye.

<*In your eyes, the math doesn't always work. The measurable results of reflection and refraction appear to defy probability just a hair, and come out more favorably for you than it would for anyone else. If you would benefit from more photons entering your eyes, then that happened. If there was a bright light and fewer photons entering would be preferred, that occurred. Not by any large means, not enough that it tripped up any of your prior mods, but it was there, just enough to throw off what Earnest and I were trying to do.*>

"You're serious..." Tanis said, running a hand over her head and pulling off the band holding her hair back. "My eyes bend what's probable to be in my favor."

<*Yes, but not just your eyes. Every part of you does this. The effect is cumulative. It is your 'luck'.*>

"And you figured all this out while we were drifting between Estrella de la Muerte and Kapteyn's Star, didn't you?" Tanis asked.

<*Huh,*> Angela gave a soft grunt. <*So whenever Earnest came out of stasis to examine us, it was for your grand experiment.*>

<*Yes and no,*> Bob replied. <*As I said, the stated reasons for having you out of stasis were also true. You'll recall that I confided in you early on my belief in your luck not long after we left Sol. That was also part of the experiment. To see if your knowledge of the effect would change it.*>

"Did it?" Tanis asked.

<*Yes. It made it stronger.*>

"But I never believed it," Tanis retorted. "Wouldn't my disbelief make it weaker?"

<*I believed it,*> Angela whispered. <*So much of what we went through—even back then—was so amazing that 'luck' made sense. I latched onto it as the reason we'd survived. Doing so allowed me to compartmentalize the incredulous.*>

Tanis shook out her hair, freshly released from its ponytail, as she glared up at Bob's primary node. "OK, so if you can quantify this 'luck', where does it come from? It long predates mine and Angela's road to ascension—which was not what I expected to have happen when our minds merged, by the way."

<*At first, I thought it was extradimensional,*> Bob told them. <*The ascended AI that left Sol at the end of the Second Solar War didn't leave many records, but the general nature of their ascension was known—that they had broadened their existence into more dimensions. However, over time, I too began to perceive those other dimensions. Not consistently, but I was developing systems to do so with better clarity. I began to form a new hypothesis.*

<*It was so incredible that I doubted it for some time, but in the end, it was the only answer left: the influence that increases the likelihood of events occurring in your favor was not extra-dimensional, it was extra-**universal**.*>

"Seriously? You mean some other universe in the multiverse is influencing me?"

Tanis felt a sense of wonder sweep over her—along with the memories of a bar she had found herself in not long ago. A bar she was not supposed to recall, but which she and Angela remembered all too well.

A bar in a different universe.

<*How would one exert extra-universal influence?*> Angela added her own question to the mix. <*Are you saying that a conscious force from another iteration of the universe is reaching into ours and altering it around us?*>

<*Perhaps,*> Bob replied quietly. <*Maybe as we hone our new senses, we'll be able to see the influence somehow. For now it is just a hypothesis. Whether or not it is really occurring, and whether or not it is a conscious being, or some unlikely confluence of variables, is impossible to discern. For all we know, this happens all the time, but no one is able to see it.*>

Tanis lowered her head, closing her eyes as she let everything Bob had said sink in. She could feel Angela doing the same, the pair sharing in a strange feeling of comfort.

"Why am I not upset about all this anymore?" Tanis asked quietly. "I mean…I still think I resent you keeping things from me, Bob, but that's a shallow thing. I've always known you keep secrets—stars, you've flat-out told me from time to time. But don't you think that in this case we should have known?"

<*Tanis, Angela….*> Bob's voice carried a tone Tanis had never heard in it before. The only descriptor she could think of was 'anguish'. <*You*

have no idea how difficult every conversation with you is. For smaller minds like yours—yes, even ones with one foot through the door of ascension—a thought process can consume you. A reaction to one event can color all thoughts. Not so with me. I can simultaneously be upset about a thousand things, and happy about a million more. I am constantly experiencing the full breadth of my version of emotional reaction. But when I speak with you, it consumes more of my mind than any other thing I do. Managing this ship's engines during a close approach to a star is simpler than saying hello to the two of you.>

<I don't know if we should be flattered or offended,> Angela replied.

<Perhaps both.> Bob's words hung in the space between them. *<I constantly worry that I am influencing you in a way that will have unpredictable results. In my experience, your actions are most beneficial to yourself and those around you when I guide you as little as possible.*

<That's difficult for me, because the two of you are some of my favorite people to talk with. You understand me in a way that not even my avatars do.>

"That's weighty praise, Bob," Tanis replied. "Tell me, now that I'm an engineered product of greater minds, how are we supposed to feel about that?"

Bob laughed again, and Tanis basked in it, realizing for the first time that Bob's thoughts no longer overwhelmed her at times like this. Instead, they exhilarated her.

<Well, Tanis. Most people you know are either formed by chance encounters and DNA combinations, or modified by their parents before birth. Your origins are not so different in that respect. You've just been molded by more powerful beings than most. Your description of 'the product of greater minds' applies to many humans and AIs. At one point, it was an apt description for me. You're not ***quite*** *as special as you might think.>*

<I feel like a passenger caught up in the winds of fate, here,> Angela said quietly. *<Not that it'll matter for much longer. Tangel doesn't fret about such things.>*

<Doubtful,> Bob interjected. *<If what Katrina related from Xavia is true, you were chosen with great care, Angela. You and Tanis are both important components in what you're becoming. I am certain that the 'luck' factor is greatly enhanced by your presence.>*

"OK, Bob," Tanis straightened and stared up at his node once more. "So luck and merging brains aside, why are we ascending? Human and AI minds have merged before and just became one mind—if they survived. Why is Tangel an extra-dimensional being with ridiculous powers?"

<*If you allowed yourself to embrace it, you'd know the answer,*> Bob replied. <*But the answer is simple. I did it to you—I know enough of the future to understand that humanity only survives if you ascend.*>

"You '*did it to*' us?" Tanis exclaimed along, while Angela asked, <*How exactly did you manufacture our ascension?*>

<*I had been working at it for some time. It is through the picotech Earnest and I have been using to modify you that we grew the new brain you now possess. The one I can see you using, even though you try to cling to your separate minds.*>

<*I knew it!*> Angela shouted in triumph. <*You* ***have*** *been using picotech on us.*>

<*It was necessary to compensate for your 'luck' where it affected quantum particles. Earnest and I have been modifying you with picotech since we arrived at Kapteyn's Star.*>

"Huh," Tanis grunted. "So that's by your design too, then."

<*Somewhat,*> Bob replied. <*I guided something that I think would have happened anyway. It just would have taken longer. Once* Sabrina *came back, and Iris delivered the data from the ascension program at Star City, I was able to put the final puzzle pieces into place. I just needed the catalyst.*>

"Pyra," Tanis whispered.

<*I suspected it could happen there,*> Bob sent a feeling of remorse into Tanis's mind. <*But had I known the details of what would happen, I would not have willed it. Too many lost their lives for this one victory.*>

"And yet, you said humanity would not survive unless I ascended," Tanis replied. "On the scale you measure things at, it would be a worthwhile trade."

The words were bitter in Tanis's mouth, and she hated the thought of them. That her elevation should cost the lives of billions made it utterly distasteful to her.

<*How does one measure such things?*> Bob's voice once again contained ample sorrow. <*Pivotal people were lost. Some you'd never expect, others that are obvious, such as General Mill and Commandant Brandt. But then again, without these events, it may be that Rika would never have come into our sphere of influence. Perhaps that all occurred because of your luck.*>

"Never have I needed such a firm reminder as to why I hate the idea of having this luck," Tanis said with a grimace. "Still, you're right. Rika is a very interesting person, I likely owe her my life."

<Perhaps,> Bob's voice sounded pensive. *<Either way, she has a part to play in all this. I assume you see that.>*

"I do," Tanis and Angela said together.

<Do you see the other thing?> Bob asked.

A sigh escaped Tanis's lips, and she closed her eyes, still seeing the room around her, but with different organs, mechanisms for sight that did not exist in the three dimensions she was so familiar with.

"I do, Bob," Tangel replied. "I understand now. I never 'de-ascended'. What Priscilla did only stabilized my physical form so Rika could carry me. I've been…taking comfort in a fallacy that I am still two people."

<As have those around you,> Bob added. *<No one knows how to deal with an ascended being. Why do you think I maintain the fiction that I am not one as well?>*

Tanis looked at the light she'd seen emanating from Bob's primary node—really looked at it. She could see his existence stretching beyond even what she could perceive. As always, he was aeons ahead of her.

She looked at the air molecules around her, gathering them into a thick column and floating before Bob's node. She set her jaw and stepped into the pillar, allowing it to envelop her legs and support her as she rose into the air, hovering before the glowing node.

"So, why is it that I'm instrumental in saving humanity?" Tangel, the ascended being, asked. "And don't think I didn't notice that AIs were not listed as being in species-level peril."

Bob's response came in the form of a question.

<How upset would you be if I refused to tell you?>

COMING CLEAN

STELLAR DATE: 08.29.8949 (Adjusted Years)
LOCATION: Ol' Sam, ISS *I2*
REGION: Pyra, Albany System, Thebes, Septhian Alliance

Tangel folded her hands together as she sat at the kitchen table, waiting for Joe and the girls to arrive.

Why am I so nervous, she wondered, answering herself with, *You know why. This is the point of no return.*

She saw that Joe was on the path leading to the house, waiting for Cary and Saanvi, who were a minute behind, having taken a different maglev to the cylinder.

He looked nervous—she could see the creases around his eyes on the ship's optical cameras. They were just a hair tighter than normal. Not enough that a human would notice, but she did.

Unclasping her hands, she looked at them, turning them over and counting the small folds in her skin, and the folds within those folds. When she began to count the bacteria living in the cuticles on her fingers, and compare their molecular counts, she tore her gaze away.

This is ridiculous.

Over the following eighty-seven seconds it took for the front door to open, Tangel cleared her mind, thinking of nothing at all, just being. It may have been the hardest thing she'd ever done.

"Tanis?" Joe's voice called out, as the sounds of footfalls came to her.

"In the kitchen," Tangel called out, opening her eyes once more and smiling as her family filed into the room. She rose and exchanged embraces with each of them—even Faleena, to whom she sent a feeling of acceptance and love.

Without needing instruction, everyone sat, Joe at her side, and the girls across the table.

Tangel had considered a thousand ways to start this conversation, played each one out a dozen levels of probabilities deep. In the end, she'd been lost in options with miniscule differences when it came to how the revelation would play out.

She knew there was no other option but to ease them into the knowledge of what had happened.

"I need to tell you the full story of what happened on Pyra," she began, meeting the eyes of each person around the table. "How it all came to be."

Joe nodded, an encouraging half-smile on his lips. "We've been dying to hear it. Take your time."

Tangel drew in a deep breath and nodded before launching into her tale.

"They'd worn us down one-by-one, the Nietzscheans. Looking back, it's hard to believe we survived as long as we did. In the end, it was just myself, Brandt, and Ayer—the Marauder captain. We lost Ayer that final night, and Brandt—" Tanis paused, trying to find the right words. "She was a Marine's Marine until the end. She sacrificed herself to save me."

Joe placed a hand on Tanis's shoulder. "I'll pass that on to her family. She'll have a hero's burial on Carthage."

Tangel nodded silently, composing herself—surprised that it was so hard.

"I was in an atrium," Tangel spoke up after a few more seconds. "Out of everything, totally spent. I took a blow to the head, and when I came to…I wasn't Tanis anymore."

"So you and Angela *did* merge," Saanvi whispered, eyes wide.

"Yes, sort of," Tanis replied. "But there was more. We could see things, understand things we'd never imagined. We were able to create fields to manipulate matter at fundamental levels. We existed across more levels. We…we were able to kill with a thought."

"Were?" Cary asked, an eyebrow cocked.

Tangel shrugged. "Well, 'are'. I can see the spaces between the atoms in your body, I can tell how to pluck them apart, spin them off, draw the energy out of them."

"Shit," Joe whispered, his eyes wide with disbelief. "Are you serious?"

Tangel nodded. "I know you're all wondering—heck, I know that Trine can probably *see* it. Simply put, I've ascended."

Joe swallowed, then a smile toyed at the corners of his lips, and he poked a finger into Tangel's shoulder. "You don't look ascended; seem like good ol' flesh and blood Tanis."

Tangel held up her left arm. "Yeah, but only because I want to be. I grew this in an instant. I think I could un-grow it just as fast, but I'm still taking baby steps. I don't want to do something like accidentally unmake my physical body. I'm rather attached to it."

<But…you two—Angela and you…you've been speaking separately,> Faleena said haltingly.

"Yeah, we have. The parts of us that used to be separate are still there, but they're more like memories…shadows. After Priscilla introduced a swarm of pico to stabilize our form, we thought—*I* thought—that we were separate. But Bob set us straight: we're not separate. We're one person now—though I plan on behaving as separate beings insofar as interactions with any others are concerned. I don't know that the ISF or all our allies are ready for this."

Tangel paused, studying the faces of her family members. Joe was still split between amazement and amusement. Saanvi appeared more curious, her eyes narrowed as she stared into Tangel's. Faleena seemed elated, while Cary's face betrayed nothing. Her mind, however, was another story entirely.

No one took up the conversational torch, so Tangel ended up breaking the silence. "You don't seem very surprised."

"Oh, we're surprised, Mom…moms…Mom?" Cary said after a moment, her voice nearly devoid of emotion—which meant she was holding anger in check. "Just processing. So let me get this straight. We all knew you two were merging—"

"Taking your time about it, too," Joe interrupted with a wink.

"Right, yeah," Cary stammered, casting her father a wounded look. "I guess not to me, though. I don't want to lose my moms."

Tangel could see the void of anger turn into an ocean of anguish behind her daughter's eyes, and reached her hand across the table. "I'm not going anywhere, Cary. And we're both still here, Tanis and Angela, we just speak with one voice now."

"But you're ascended…" Cary rasped. "Aren't you just going to turn to light and disappear?"

Tangel held up her other hand, slipping a part of her fifth dimensional body outside the bounds of her three-dimensional one. The visible result was tendrils of light swirling around her hand.

"This is just the rest of my body," Tanis said, holding Cary's gaze while speaking calmly. "You have it too, you just can't manipulate it like

I can."

Cary's eyes widened, and she glanced at Saanvi. "Because we make up Trine?"

"No," Tanis shook her head. "Everyone occupies more of space-time than they realize. You're just not cognizant of it—well, *you* are, Cary, you just don't understand how to control it."

Her face grew ashen. "Am *I* going to ascend?"

Tanis nodded. "Someday, if you want to." She glanced at Joe. "You all can, eventually. I mean…billions of people did it on Star City. To my knowledge, none of them were merged with an AI mind, they were just regular people."

"So I'll turn into some being of light as well?" Cary whispered, her voice wavering as she spoke.

Tanis realized what was bothering Cary so much. "I think I need to clear up a misconception. When you ascend, you're really just becoming aware of, and able to manipulate, things in more dimensions. Trine is effectively an ascended being, but you're not when you're alone. In time, you won't need to do your deep Linking mind merge to use your abilities, Cary. But you're still you, a person with a brain and a mind. You need neurons to think, you need energy to function—you just have different ways of going about that. Not everyone does it the same way."

Tanis paused and looked at the room's ceiling. "I'm outing you, Bob."

<Very well,> Bob replied. *<But what you hear stays in this room.>*

"Bob's ascended," Tangel said. "Has been for some time. Ascending for an AI isn't fundamentally different than it is for a human—though they lack bodies, which limits their initial set of extra-dimensional sensory organs. Many ascended AIs make themselves new bodies in the other dimensions, they…move their minds there. That's why we only see them as beings of light and energy. They can manifest a physical presence if needed by manipulating matter."

Tanis paused and rapped on the table, turning it to steel where she touched it, then rapped again, turning it back to wood.

"But I can already do that, and I like my body, and I like my brain where it is. I have no need to shift myself from this dimension into others. Not to mention the fact that I think they lose something in the process when they do it."

"But what about Bob?" Saanvi asked. "Is he going to shift himself away?"

<*Not anytime soon,*> Bob replied. <*Moving my multinodal mind out of the dimensions in which it was created is no simple task, even for me. And Tanis is right. The adjacent dimensions alone are not enough to encapsulate all aspects of myself—or Tangel's self, for that matter. I suspect that many of the other ascended AIs have retained some measure of physical form as well—though they'd have to have first created one. Carting around a number of massive node cubes is not practical.*>

" 'Tangel'?" Joe asked. "I thought you two had settled on 'Tangela'?"

"Too many syllables," Tangel replied. "I kept thinking of other names, but they were all too...different. We're not different or new, we're Tanis and Angela."

"This is just too weird." Cary's voice rose in pitch as she spoke. "I can't call you 'Tangel'! You're my mom!"

Saanvi placed a hand on Cary's shoulder. "We called *them* 'Moms' most of the time anyway. Now we're just calling *her* 'Moms'. No difference."

Cary turned her head, glaring at Saanvi. "No, it's *a lot* different. For all intents and purposes, Mom is dead. So is Angela!"

As she cried out Angela's name, Cary rose, knocked her chair over, and fled the room, then the house.

Saanvi began to get up, but Tangel held up her hand. "You know Cary. She's going to need a bit to come around to this on her own. Faleena is talking with her as well."

"Faleena told you that?" Joe asked, and Tangel shook her head.

"No, I can see it."

Joe's mouth formed a silent O.

"How?" Saanvi asked, leaning forward.

"Oh, Saanvi. You've always been the most curious young girl—and now woman—I've ever known." Tangel gave her daughter a warm smile.

"I like to know how things work." she shrugged.

"Because you want to gain some measure of control after feeling like you had so little," Tangel replied.

Saanvi waved a finger at Tangel. "You may have me all figured out now, Moms, but don't try to distract me with your psychoanalysis. I want to know how you can see AIs. This isn't the first time you've said you can see Faleena's mind."

Tangel waved her hand in the air, and an image appeared over the table. It was a wavering mass of light and dark, diaphanous tendrils stretching out, moving through dark areas, causing them to become lighter while others grew dim.

"That is Faleena. At least, her electromagnetic spectrum. I can see more of her, but it doesn't translate well into a visual. But even at this distance, through the walls, I can see what her mind looks like."

"How far away is she?" Joe asked as he stared unblinking at the image before him, moisture in his eyes as he *saw* his daughter for the first time.

"Down on the dock," Tangel replied. "She's not entirely happy about this, but she's putting on a brave face. Trying to console Cary—it's not going well."

"Are you reading Cary's mind?" Saanvi's eyes narrowed.

"No," Tangel gave a rueful laugh. "She's yelling. I can see the windows vibrating."

Joe barked a laugh. "No keeping secrets from you anymore."

"Like that was ever possible before," Tangel said as she regarded Joe, unable to miss the knowing look he shared with Saanvi. "What?"

"Nothing, oh Ascended Moms, there's just *some* stuff you don't know," Saanvi's mouth took on a mischievous grin. "And we're going to keep it that way."

"How am I going to rule the galaxy if I don't know everything, though," Tangel wondered in a mock sulk.

Joe sputtered a cough. "Say what?"

Tangel gave him a slow wink. "Mess with me, and I mess right back."

"Stars," Joe muttered. "Looks like we didn't lose Angela in your merge."

"Sahn, hon," Tangel gestured toward the door. "I think your sister is ready for an arm around the shoulder about now."

Saanvi chuckled as she rose, glancing at Joe. "I see how it is, Moms. Need some alone time with your mortal consort, do you?"

"Hey," Joe said in mock anger. "I'm no one's consort. I'm obviously the Chief Acolyte."

Saanvi walked around the table and wrapped her arms around Tangel. "Just so you know," she whispered softly. "I may seem all calm and controlled on the outside—but that's the curious scientist in me. Inside, I'm freaked the hell out."

"I know," Tangel whispered back. "I'm still your mom, and I'm not going anywhere. You're going to be stuck with me for a looooong time."

"Good. Because if you turn into a glowing ball of light and leave us, I'm going to go to Star City, ascend myself, and then find you and kick your ass."

"Ha!" Tangel barked a laugh. "I do not doubt that for a second."

Joe pulled Saanvi close as she passed, giving her a quick hug before she left.

Once they heard the door close, Joe shifted in his seat and stared into Tangel's eyes for a minute without speaking.

"What?" Tangel finally said.

"They look different, but I can't tell what it is."

Tangel caused her eyes to sparkle. "Maybe it's just my general brilliance."

Joe snorted. "Do that more often and you'll get people more than wondering about your ascendancy."

"Seriously, Joe," Tangel took her husband's hands. "How is it that you're so…accepting of this?"

"I'm surprised that you keep asking me that," Joe replied. "I wasn't kidding when I said that loving two women was hard. You—rather, Tanis and Angela—have been a part of my life longer than I lived without them. When I first met you, I fell in love with Tanis, but we spent decades together, just the three of us. You know I came to love Angela as well. Sometimes I wondered…."

"What?" Tangel laughed. "That Tanis would be jealous?"

"OK…now *that* is weird." Joe shook his head slowly, a half-smile on his lips. "To hear your voice speak of yourself as though it's someone else."

"Should I change something about my appearance?" Tanis asked. "Something that will make it easy to remember that I'm Tangel, and not Tanis or Angela?"

Joe put a finger to his lips as he considered it. "Maybe? I wonder what would work."

"I could make a streak of my hair black," Tangel said, and a moment later, a lock of hair at her left temple turned black.

Joe shook his head. "No, nothing so overt. It'll probably bother Cary, too. She needs you to stay as you are as much as possible. What about your eyes? Maybe add just a hint of lavender to them."

Tangel cocked an eyebrow. "If it's enough to notice, how different would that be than coloring my hair?"

"True..." Joe tapped a finger against his lips. "I've got it! Make your nails a darker color. You always keep them natural or choose a light pink. Go for something darker."

"Like this?" Tangel held up a hand, and her nails shifted to a darker red.

"Perfect!" Joe proclaimed, then looked her up and down, a smile forming on his lips. "You know, I always knew you were destined for great things...many of which you've achieved. But, I gotta say, ascension and a full AI merge all at the same time? I doubt there are any others like you." He leant back in his chair, grinning as he clasped his hands behind his head. "I sure can pick 'em."

"Pft!" Tangel pulled Joe in close. "I picked *you*."

"Remember when you ran the SOC on the *Intrepid*, back at the Mars Outer Shipyards? Remember what everyone called you behind your back?"

Tangel rolled her eyes. " 'Dragon Lady' was the nicest one, if memory serves."

"Correct, oh glowing wife of mine. Yet I braved your lair and conquered you. I chose *you*."

"I just let you think that."

Joe reached out and pulled Tangel toward him.

"Keep telling yourself that," he said a moment before their lips met.

UNDERSTANDING

STELLAR DATE: 08.29.8949 (Adjusted Years)
LOCATION: Ol' Sam, ISS *I2*
REGION: Pyra, Albany System, Thebes, Septhian Alliance

Tangel stepped out into the evening light, glancing up at the long sun that ran through the center of the habitat cylinder. She noted that there was a slight variance in the light output from one end of the long sun to the other, and sent a message off to the engineering team's queue.

Ninety-seven meters of stone path lay between her and the lake, another seven worth of dock, and at the end of that, her three daughters.

Tangel still remembered the first time she saw each of them: Cary as a newborn—carried and birthed the old-fashioned way—and Saanvi as she woke from the stasis tube, a trembling little girl, nearly petrified with fear. She also remembered seeing Faleena's mind as Angela, the first words their third daughter had spoken.

She remembered, as Tanis, the feel of their skin, the bioreadout reports on their health, skin temperature, pupil dilation, body proportion measurements, the uncertain looks in their eyes. She remembered the EM frequencies their brains gave off, the feel of connecting to minds over the Link, all of it. All at once.

Closing her eyes, Tangel drew a deep breath. Memories were hard. Though her mind was one thing, her memories—barring recent ones—were not. She had two overlaid experiences; disparate recollections, disparate conclusions.

As she examined them, she couldn't help but note that, as time passed, Tanis and Angela had begun to think more and more alike. Back when Tangel divided, she couldn't see it as clearly, but now it was abundantly apparent. For years, the overlap had been greater than the differences.

But how to explain that to the women sitting at the end of the dock?

Tangel smiled. At nineteen and twenty years old, her two organic daughters both behaved as though they had everything figured out. They certainly were more put-together than Tanis had been at that age—on the brink of joining the military to rebel against her father.

Funny how history repeats itself, Tangel mused. *Though my two girls joined the military to please me, not to anger me, as I did with him....*

A high bandwidth data stream was flowing between the girls. *Yes, 'girls',* Tangel thought. *They could be a thousand years old, and they'll still be my little girls.* She surmised from the information flow that the three of them were deep-Linked, sharing in the special bond that these three sisters possessed.

Tendrils of light began to drift around Cary, and Tangel saw them reach out toward Saanvi—from whom three small filaments of light also came, stretching toward Cary.

Well that's unexpected.

Unexpected, maybe, but it did make sense. When Cary Linked into the minds of her sisters, she was creating a new being of sorts. Not one so deeply entwined as Tanis and Angela had become in their later days, but something in Cary was a catalyst that pushed them closer. Thus far, Faleena seemed unchanged, but she'd not been a part of their little group for as long. Time would tell how her progression went.

Tangel wasn't certain what it was, but she was eager to see it unfold—so long as it happened slowly. There was no need for her daughters to evolve too soon.

She began to walk down the path, moving slowly, giving the girls time to notice her—and hopefully not wave her off.

As she neared the water's edge, Saanvi glanced over her shoulder, and then made to rise.

"You don't have to go," Tangel said, but Saanvi shook her head.

"It's OK, Moms, we had our chat. You're up now."

Tangel embraced Saanvi, then sat next to Cary, feeling the dock vibrate for a few more moments until Saanvi made it to the shore.

"I'm sorry," Tangel whispered, staring down at her hands. She didn't dare look into her daughter's eyes yet, fearful of what she might see there.

Cary didn't respond right away, but Tangel could tell from her breathing that she nearly did three times. Then she finally said, "For what?"

The words were caustic, full of anger. They cut into Tangel, but she ignored the pain. This wasn't about her, it was about her daughter.

"For going through this change so soon. We all knew it was coming—but I thought I'd have decades still. I don't want you to feel like you've lost your mothers."

Cary turned her head, and Tangel looked up, meeting her daughter's eyes: blue and set into a face that looked so much like her own. *The same cheekbones, the same eyes—Joe's brows and lips, though. A bit of both in the nose.*

"Have I?" Cary's voice rasped as she breathed the question. "Are you still there?"

"I am," Tangel replied. "I know this feels like a big change, but, in all honesty, it was a very small step."

"Mom," her eldest snorted derisively. "*Ascension* is not a small step."

"Well, I was referring more to Tanis and Angela becoming one person. Though it was the catalyst for ascension…it's a different thing."

A tear slid down Cary's cheek. "When you came down off the ship…when you spoke…I hoped you were still you. But you were lying to us."

Tanis shook her head. "No, I was lying to myself. I know I put on a brave face—that's sort of my thing—but I was scared, too. I don't—didn't—want to change…."

"Which is it?" Cary whispered. "Didn't or don't?"

"Well, the ship's sailed, so it doesn't matter much anymore. I didn't want to do it so soon, and I don't want to do anything that hurts you. That's the very last thing I ever want."

Neither woman spoke for a minute, then Cary said, "Faleena says that you seem 'correct' now."

"Oh?" Tangel cocked an eyebrow, glancing at Faleena's still mind, where it lay nestled within Cary's. Her other daughter was doing her best not to intrude on the conversation, but Tangel could tell that it was difficult for her. "Is that the case, Faleena?"

<*A bit,*> Faleena replied hesitantly. <*I think I could see better than*

most where you and Angela overlapped. So much of my own mind is made from yours that it is more apparent to me. The way you were before…you were both incomplete. Now you're finally one person. I think it was how you were always meant to be.>

"Meant to be?" Tangel asked with a single laugh. "I don't think there's any guiding force in the galaxy driving what we should and should not be."

<*Really? I would have thought that you of all people—what, with how you have been pushed and prodded, molded at every turn—would believe otherwise.*>

"Right," Tangel nodded thoughtfully. "What Katrina said about my past. How the AIs made me—us."

"Doesn't that bother you, Moms?" Cary asked. "I mean…they shaped you into what you are."

Tangel shrugged. "Not really. I hashed this out with Bob, and he helped me understand it. People like to *think* they can control their surroundings, shape the future to their liking. But they can't…and if all the ascended AIs out there were to be honest with themselves, they'd realize that they too are products of their environments. My 'luck' is evidence of that. Not only can they *not* control me, they can't even tell what I'm going to do. I'm like the ultimate variable. The variable variable. Which, honestly, always seemed strange to me.

"Everything I do in life *feels* like the next logical step. The obvious thing to do. Yet somehow, it seems to always thwart the AIs' ability to predict things." Tangel winked at Cary and Faleena. "If you ask me, I think that it's the AIs that have some sort of cognitive dissonance."

<*Not funny, Moms,*> Faleena replied, sending a mock scowl into Tangel's mind.

"So you're just going to brush off what's been done to you?" Cary asked. "They may have even set you on the path that made you merge with Angela."

"They may have," Tangel agreed, deciding not to reveal all the nuances to her progression. "Bob suspects as much. Maybe when I finally come face-to-face with the Caretaker, I'll ask him. Right before I kill him."

<*Is that your ultimate goal?*> Faleena asked. <*To kill the ascended*

AIs?>

Tangel saw Cary's eyebrows rise, the expression echoing Faleena's question.

"I doubt it. There's at least one that I like."

<*Thanks,*> Bob interjected.

Tangel glanced out toward the lake before continuing. "But what I really want to learn before I become judge, jury, and executioner, is *why* the core AIs are doing what they're doing. If they feared humanity, they could have wiped them out at the height of the FTL wars. Is it really what they *want,* to keep everyone balanced on the knife's edge? It seems impractical to me."

<*And to me,*> Faleena added.

"You said 'them'," Cary stated tonelessly. "Are you talking about humans or AIs? You're not really either, anymore."

"Both?" Tangel asked with a shrug. "Neither? I don't know that it matters."

<*I think you might be a new thing, Mother,*> Faleena said in a wistful tone.

"Don't be so sure," Tangel replied. "Space and time are vast. Could be another Star City out there, filled with human-AI merges that are all ascended. You know…I really don't like that word."

"Merges?" Cary asked.

" 'Ascended'. I didn't elevate, I just became more perceptive."

Faleena chortled. <*Plus there's that whole matter-transmutation thing you can do now.*>

Tangel waved her hand dismissively. "I imagine you'll figure it out soon enough. You just have to come at it from a different angle."

"What do you mean?" Cary asked, her voice almost frantic.

I'm such an idiot, Tangel chastised herself. *So much for being more perceptive.*

"Cary, I just realized…you're worried about merging with Faleena, aren't you?" Tangel asked quietly.

A sharp sob escaped Cary's lips, and she nodded as tears slipped onto her cheeks.

"Oh, Cary," Tangel slipped an arm around her daughter's shoulders. "I don't think you're going to merge. Not unless you do something stupid like I did back in Sol with those fighters."

"I don't want it, but then I feel guilty about it at the same time," Cary whispered. "You mean so much to me, Faleena, but I don't want to merge with you. And I feel horrible about that. I mean...Moms' mind is so beautiful now. Why wouldn't I want that?"

A shuddering breath escaped Cary's lips.

"I'm so selfish."

<Well...> Faleena said hesitantly. *<I don't want to merge with you, either, Cary. I'm not ruling it out in the distant future, but I want to experience life as* ***me*** *first. Then maybe you and I can talk.>*

Cary shook her head. "Now I feel horrible for being glad that you don't want to stay in my head forever."

<Cary, we're a special sort of sisters; we share a bond that few others do. Nothing can ruin that. No matter if our minds share headspace or not.>

"Do you think, Faleena," Tangel ventured carefully. "That maybe it's time for you to come out of Cary?"

<I don't really ***want*** *to, but I think it would be best if I did. For both of us.>*

"Cary?" Tangel asked.

Cary straightened her back and wiped her cheeks. "Sorry I've been so...whatever about all this."

"Don't apologize," Tangel replied, brushing Cary's hair back from her face. "Everyone processes things differently. Not only that, but we're all going through things that no one has imagined. Remnants, Xavia's memory, making shadowtrons, dealing with the threat of the core AIs, my changes...."

"Don't forget the massive war we're embroiled in," Cary added with a smirk.

"That too."

<Cary? Should I go, then?> Faleena pressed.

Cary sighed. "I know that 'yes' is the right answer, but the last thing I want is to lose you."

<You're not going to lose me. I'm going to take a page from Iris's book and get a body that looks just like yours. Then I'm going to follow you around like a creepy doppelganger.>

"Oh yeah?" Cary asked. "You going to hit on the guys I like back at the academy?"

"Guys?" Tangel asked. "What guys?"

Faleena laughed, a sound like leaves rustling in the wind echoing in their minds. <*If I were to fancy a human, I think it would probably be Gladys, but I've got my metaphorical eyes on Sabrina.*>

Tangel almost choked. "Sabs? You've only met her the once."

<*We've exchanged some messages over the QuanComm. Nothing much, and very slowly—over days, so we don't tax the system.*>

"Well I'll be," Tangel said with a shake of her head. "Maybe once you're done at the academy, you can get an assignment there."

<*Seriously?*> Faleena asked, almost giddy.

"What?" Cary nearly shouted. "What happened to being my doppelganger?"

Tanis shrugged. "You're a year out from that. And nothing says you couldn't both go. At some point, Amavia is going to want to return to New Canaan, and I'm in a never-ending need for more high-ranking fleet commanders that know what the hell they're doing."

<*You're going to recall Jessica?*> Faleena asked.

Tangel rose and offered Cary her hand, pulling her daughter to her feet.

"If she wants to. *Sabrina* has been her home for a very long time now. If she wants to stay, I won't stop her, but I could really use her in an admiral's chair."

Cary whistled as they began to walk back toward the house. "What about Cheeky? I can't imagine *Sabrina* without Cheeky."

Tangel laughed. "Neither can I. But now that she and Finaeus are married, it feels wrong to keep them apart."

<*OK, two things,*> Faleena said. <*Firstly, you and dad are apart a* ***lot****. Secondly, can you imagine Cheeky on the* I2*? You'll never get her into an ISF uniform.*>

Tangel laughed, shaking her head at the thought. "Well, your father and I aren't exactly newlyweds. As for the uniform…I suppose we'd have to make an exception for her. Though it's not like the ISF really *needs* to adhere to a physical dress code to show our common bond. Maybe we can come up with some more options."

"Whoaaaaa," Cary leant to the side, looking Tangel up and down as they walked. "Up until now, you still sounded like some combination of the Moms. But this? Flexibility in the dress code?

'Options'? Hmm…maybe you're an alien."

Tangel pulled Cary close and kissed the side of her head. "There's my girl, sarcastic sense of humor and all."

"I got it from you."

LUNCH AND FATHERS

STELLAR DATE: 08.29.8949 (Adjusted Years)
LOCATION: Sear, Keren Station
REGION: Khardine System, Transcend Interstellar Alliance

"Gotta say, President Sera," Mary said, as she sat down at the table across from the woman she was addressing. "I didn't expect to get an invite to join you at one of the station's fancy restaurants only a day after nearly running you down in a stairwell."

Sera looked around the restaurant, named 'Sear' after its reputation for serving the best steak around. "I guess it is on the fancy side. Honestly, my guards have a short list of restaurants they consider to be 'safe enough', and this was the only steakhouse on the list."

Mary snorted as she looked at the list of specials hovering on the table between them. "Talk about presidential problems. And inviting me?"

"Well..." Sera shrugged. "It seemed like you could use a friend. I checked the duty roster, and Leeroy and your son are both pulling double shifts—heck, even your dog, Figgy, is working with cargo crews to sniff out any contraband."

"He loves it," Mary grinned. "Poor Figgy spent years fending for himself in the bowels of Airtha. Who would do that to an uplifted dog? People can be cruel."

Sera nodded slowly, her mind turning to the ring and its inhabitants. "What do you think it's like there, now that Airtha is in control?"

A pained look filled Mary's eyes, and she shook her head. "Stars, I try not to think about it too much. I've a lot of friends there.... All I can do is hope that Airtha hasn't seen fit to do some sort of mass mind control on them all."

Sera pursed her lips, and Mary's eyes met hers for a moment before she asked, "Could she do that? People have protections against mental breaches, but...."

"But ascended AIs don't seem to play with the same rulebook we have," Sera completed for Mary.

"Right...so you're saying she could have subverted the entire population of humans, just like she did to the AIs?"

Sera nodded slowly. "It's a fear I have. I have a lot of friends there too, you know. But I have to wonder if they are really friends now, or something else."

A servitor set the women's drinks on the table, and Mary stared into hers for a half-minute before looking up apologetically. "Sorry about this. I'm usually better company. Sometimes it just feels like I cheated somehow."

"In getting away?" Sera asked.

"Yeah."

"Except that your escape saved people's lives. Leeroy, your son, Drew. Heck, even your dog."

Mary snorted. "The first two, sure. But I think Figgy would have been fine. Take a lot more than some prissy ascended AI and her weak-assed clone of you to take that dog out."

"Don't go disparaging my clone's ass," Sera chuckled. "I'm told she looks identical to me, and my ass is a work of art."

"Wouldn't know," Mary laughed. "Since you're apparently my adoptive sister, I can't check you out—not to mention you're the freaking president. Which is just a bit surreal."

"I'm not really that different from anyone else." Sera took a sip of her brandy. "Just a girl, trying to make it to tomorrow."

"Right, and you put your pants on one leg at a time, just like the rest of us," Mary snorted.

"Well, I would if I wore pants," Sera agreed.

"Speaking of which..." Mary began, leaving the words hanging.

"You still want skin like mine?" Sera asked. "Like I said, it's semi-permanent. Plus...there's a risk that your father may dismember me."

Mary rolled her eyes. "Seriously, Sera. You're the president of the freaking Transcend, and I'm a grown woman. Flaherty has no say in this."

"Right," Sera snorted. "You and *I* both know that, but your father doesn't—and I doubt we could convince him."

"Well," Mary gave Sera a conspiratorial look. "What dad doesn't know—"

Sera pointed to her right. "He's sitting at the bar, watching us."

"What the fuck?" Mary muttered, her eyes darting to where her father sat. She made to rise, but Sera put a hand on her arm.

"If you make him leave, he'll just take up a position somewhere else, and we won't see him that time. He's sitting there as a courtesy, to let us know that he's here."

Mary gritted her teeth and shook her head. "I love my father, I really do, but that man's infuriating sometimes."

Sera chuckled, nodding in agreement. "Just think, though. Without him, we'd both be dead—in my case, several times over. I figure that earns him some leeway."

"Now I want your skin even more." Mary's eyes glinted as she spoke. "If dad gives me a hard time, I'll tell him that it makes me safer."

"You know," Sera said, touching a finger to her lips. "That angle may just work. Heck, I should make *him* get it, too."

Mary giggled and rubbed her hands together. "Only if you give me control over it. I'd prank him constantly."

"OK...now you're talking," Sera said with a laugh. "I'll reach out to Finaeus and see if he can hook you up."

Mary raised her glass and tapped it against Sera's. "I'll drink to that."

THE PRAETOR

STELLAR DATE: 08.29.8949 (Adjusted Years)
LOCATION: Palatine, Euros
REGION: Earth, New Sol, Orion Freedom Alliance

Garza checked over his uniform, ensuring that he was the picture of perfection. Not that Praetor Kirkland was a stickler for tidiness, but he did pick on imperfections when he received bad news.

<*The praetor will see you now.*> The summons entered Garza's mind, delivered by a nearby human administrator.

No AI assistant for the praetor, Garza thought as he rose from the chair he'd been waiting in. *He pretends that he's a pure human, that he doesn't use AIs, ignoring the hundreds of AIs in New Sol that keep the system and his empire in order.*

It was an old gripe of Garza's—one he liked to sink his teeth into and revel in before entering the praetor's chamber. The fact that the man he was about to see believed himself to be the savior of a pure human race was laughable. Garza had to get it all out of his system before speaking with Kirkland, or he was bound to snicker in the man's face at some point.

The truth of the matter was that Kirkland was a man of ideals, but one who lacked the conviction to execute on his vision.

That was where men like Garza came in. When he had taken command of the Inner Stars Division of Alignment and Control, it had been a joke, barely able to make any inroads against its Transcend counterpart, the Hand.

Personally, Garza liked the name his enemies used for his division: 'BOGA'. It sounded like the name of some insidious shadow organization from an ancient vid. Certainly a step up from 'ISDAC'.

During Garza's tenure as its leader, BOGA had become a force to be reckoned with, pushing the Hand out of many regions of space, even going so far as to gain control of the Hegemony of Worlds. The Hand still held sway in the vast majority of the smaller interstellar nations, but Garza had scored major wins in gaining allies like the

Trisilieds and the Nietzscheans.

Gains that Kirkland barely acknowledged.

All the praetor cared about was crushing the New Canaan colonists, constantly bringing up the loss Garza had suffered there two years before.

It was getting old.

Garza stopped at the unadorned double doors leading into Kirkland's office. He drew a final calming breath before pushing them open and entering the praetor's lair.

The office of the man who ruled the single largest swath of human space—roughly two billion stars—was unimpressive to say the least. Barely fifteen by twenty meters, it was filled with made but simple furniture. Wooden chairs and leather couches sat against one wall, a bookshelf lined the other.

A mid-sized wooden desk rested near the wall-to-wall windows on the far side of the room where Kirkland stood, hands clasped behind his back as he stared out over his domain.

It's like they're all cut from a template, Garza thought, shaking his head. Hegemon Uriel, President Sera—the Airthan one, at least, he couldn't speak for the degenerate one—the Trisilieds king, Constantine, a dozen others he'd met…they all loved their view, loved to survey their holdings.

Which was patently ridiculous. Their 'views' barely covered a few thousand kilometers at best, while their territories stretched over trillions.

A dark room with a massive holodisplay; *that* was the way to survey one's empire.

"General Garza," Kirkland said without turning, as Garza approached his desk.

"Praetor," Garza replied.

He was tempted to bluntly ask Kirkland why the man summoned him. There was little need for in-person meetings. Especially when it involved a three-day trip. What was more annoying was that he'd wanted to journey to Nietzschea to learn from Constantine how his inroads into Septhia were going. But the praetor liked to play his little games, behaving as though this were just a casual chat.

Ultimately, Garza had sent a clone to meet with the Nietzschean emperor. When the clone returned, Garza would gain the memories and experiences as though they were his own—but it still wasn't the same as going himself.

And even without the advantage of clones, there was always work to be done at his division's headquarters at Karaske. Taking a week to meet with the man who *thought* he was running the Orion Freedom Alliance was just a monumental pain in the ass.

I should have sent a clone ***here****, and gone to see Constantine myself.*

Garza continued to stand before the praetor's desk, which he'd been told was some ancient relic that the man had brought from Sol when he left millennia ago. The idea of wasting this much mass allocation on a wooden desk baffled Garza.

But then again, Kirkland was a man more driven by convictions than logic. Unfathomable behavior was his norm.

After almost a minute, Kirkland turned, regarding Garza evenly from behind his bushy eyebrows. "Tell me of your latest plans to attack New Canaan."

The words stunned Garza. "Sir? I have no plans to attack New Canaan. There's no reason to do so anymore."

"No reason?" Kirkland's brows lowered, half obscuring his eyes. "That is the heart of the infestation. Cut it out, and we'll be well on our way to purging their damaging 'advances' from humanity."

"It's too late," Garza countered. "They've shared much with the Khardine government, and Tanis Richards now leads a fleet that is moving around the Inner Stars with impunity. This has all been in my reports, I—"

Kirkland cut him off with a wave of his hand. "All this because you failed to destroy them two years ago."

Garza clenched his jaw. The praetor brought up the defeat as though he expected there to be no losses against an enemy that outclassed them in every way but sheer volume of forces—and even that advantage was diminishing.

"No one could have expected them to summon Exaldi. That is a weapon we have no counter for. Our only hope is to take more and more of the Inner Stars and convert the populace to our way of thinking. Tanis Richards will not use her weapons of mass destruction against an innocent star system's population."

Garza had made the argument before. Orion's primary advantage was a massive home population that could field fleets to seize and occupy hundreds of thousands of star systems. They would starve Tanis Richards both of resources and of a populace willing to fight alongside her.

At least, that was the plan he had been pushing with Kirkland.

The problem with Garza's proposed plan was that there was no endgame. If they cornered Tanis, she would unleash her picobombs, or summon the Exaldi once more. She may not win, but she could decimate any attacking force, and then simply leave. The galaxy was too big…she could hide anywhere.

"So we're to play a game of cat and mouse for the next century?" Kirkland asked. "That's your plan?"

Garza drew himself up, locking his eyes on Kirkland's. "Praetor, correct me if I'm wrong, but isn't our ultimate goal to bring the Inner Stars into the OFA, and to wear down the Transcend? We are achieving these goals. We've secured over half of the largest political entities in the Inner Stars, and, even better, through Tanis's unwitting help, the Hegemony and Scipio are entering into all-out war. That's exactly what we want."

Kirkland gave a slow nod. "True, seeing those two destroy each other will be a great victory. Once they're sufficiently weakened, we'll sweep in and take both their capitals."

"Which is the plan that is in the works," Garza replied. "We're building a fleet just for that task—though it's caused us to remove most of our forces from the Expansion Districts."

"I know you feel that is unwise," Kirkland said with a heavy sigh. "However, I believe that the PED is well-enough in hand that we don't need the active threat of the Orion Guard looming over them for the people to operate within our strictures."

"Are you certain about that?" Garza asked, still holding Kirkland's gaze. "After the incident at Costa Station with that *Sabrina* ship, we have to assume that the Khardine Government knows we've decreased our presence in the Expansion Districts. They could easily make inroads there."

Kirkland pulled out his chair and sat, giving a derisive shake of his head in the process. "I thought you were just telling me about how we have them on the ropes, with all the alliances you've forged in the Inner Stars. At best, Khardine holds a quarter the strength of the Transcend, and—so far as we can tell—they're the ones supporting the fronts on our borders. They're engaged in conflicts clear across known space. The last thing they'll do is hit us in the Expansion Districts. Even if they did, what end would it serve? There are few strategic targets in the PED."

"Very well," Garza allowed.

By and large, he agreed with Kirkland, but he wanted to be on record as advising caution so that the praetor couldn't throw it in his face later. Though it probably wouldn't stop him.

"Now then," Kirkland placed his elbows on his desk and folded his hands together. "Tell me about how we'll finally put an end to the blight that is New Canaan. I believe that without her base of operations, Tanis Richards will become a much smaller threat. Perhaps we can even draw her back into her home system, and kill two birds with one stone."

Garza sighed as he sat and pulled up a holodisplay of deployment options. He'd appease Kirkland with a battle plan, but he'd kill himself and all his clones before he even considered enacting it.

Perhaps it's time for the praetor to be replaced....

As he laid out options for drawing a fleet together that could crush New Canaan, Garza considered the options the Airthan Sera had presented him with when he met with her.

Of course, they'd tried to take over his mind, but all they'd done was subsume a clone.

That didn't mean he wouldn't work with them—just that he wasn't going to form an alliance yet. First he needed the degenerate version of Sera to whittle down her doppelganger and abomination of a mother.

Then he'd strike. A taskforce of Lisas were already training for the operation.

OPTIONS

STELLAR DATE: 08.30.8949 (Adjusted Years)
LOCATION: Capitol Complex, Keren Station
REGION: Khardine System, Transcend Interstellar Alliance

Sera settled into her seat in the briefing room, nodding to the admirals, generals, and assorted staffers. Next to her sat Carl, her secretary of the interior, and Hanso the transportation secretary.

Over seventy other people were present, and Sera realized she only knew half of them. She supposed that was a good thing; as more systems sided with Khardine, the mass of representatives increased—as did the number of complications.

At the front of the room, Admiral Greer waited for everyone to settle down, which happened within a few seconds of him raising his right hand.

"OK, everyone," Greer began. "We're here to review assault options on Airtha. President Sera has tasked us with formulating a plan, and we have three options, each with different strategic profiles."

A holo appeared to his right, showing a graph that started at zero on the left, and rose to just over five-hundred million on the right.

"These are the TSF casualty rates for the different strategies we've worked up. Plan Full-Auto has a projected zero casualty rate for our forces, while Plan Alameda has a massive casualty rate. It also has the lowest chance of success."

On Greer's left, a holo appeared displaying the all-too familiar Huygens System where Airtha lay.

"We can see here the various defensive emplacements in the system, as well as where we expect the forces Airtha has gathered to position themselves. Most of this comes from standard TSF defensive doctrine for the Huygens System, updated to include the number of ships she has likely amassed.

"With plan 'Full-Auto', none of this matters. All that we care about is hitting Airtha with a few shots."

"A few shots of what?" Admiral Rellan asked from a few seats to

Sera's left.

<*Impatient man,*> she commented to Jen.

<*He frequently is.*>

"This one would require assistance from New Canaan, but it should be feasible. The 'shots' would be one-ton neutron slugs, but at stellar compression levels. They would be housed in stasis fields and fired at relativistic speeds into the system."

A wave of murmurs swept through the room, and Sera spoke up. "Can you elaborate on how we make these slugs?"

"I can provide the full workup, but the technology is based on what Jessica and her team observed at Star City in the Perseus Arm. The city's weapons fired coherent beams of neutrons that were really held in stasis bubbles. This meant that they retained their highly compressed mass until right before impact, when the field drops, and a relativistic shrapnel blast hits the target."

Admiral Svetlana let out a low whistle. "That'll do it—if they can reach the target. Airtha has interdictors, so we can't use gates to jump the bullets insystem.

Greer nodded. "You're right. Airtha interdicts unplanned gate jumps a thousand AU from the star. That gives their forces roughly one hundred and forty hours to intercept. However, their reaction time is greatly compressed, as the bullets will be travelling at nearly the same speed as the message that an interdiction occurred. In reality, they'll have less than ten hours to react."

"That still seems like plenty," Rellan said.

Greer's eyes narrowed as he regarded Rellan, clearly annoyed at the interruptions. "That's why we send a million."

Sera laughed. "I guess I know why you named it 'Plan Full-Auto'."

"Is that even feasible?" Hanso asked.

"It is, if New Canaan can retrofit their stasis pods to the task," Greer replied. "They have millions of them left over from their refit of the *I2*."

"A million bullets against half a million ships," Sera mused. "They'd still stand a chance of stopping them."

"We only need a dozen to reach Airtha," Svetlana said. "And since they're in stasis, they can't be stopped or destroyed, only shoved aside. The defenders would need to fire lateral shots at the bullets to move them off course."

Sera glanced back at the attendees, many of whom were nodding in appreciation—even Rellan, who spoke up once more.

"Any chance we can convince the ISF to supply stealth tech for these?"

"We don't have stealth tech for the majority of our ships," Svetlana countered. "Let's not waste it on bullets."

Rellan began to respond, when Greer held up his hands. "Stealth and stasis are not mutually compatible, unless you build a shell around the item in stasis—which is feasible, but introduces issues with acceleration and transition of the bullets through the jump gates."

"I assume we'd use a swarm technique, like we did at Albany?" Sera asked. "Send the bullets through from a large number of locations."

Greer nodded. "That's the idea. We really wouldn't need a million, either. It's possible that we could still destroy Airtha with half that number."

Sera leant back in her seat, tapping her finger against her chin. "Still need to fire them. Do we even have the ability to do this?"

"Honestly," Rellan interrupted. "We could do it with rail-fired slugs. Enough of them in stasis at relativistic speeds...stars, even without stasis shields. A few million, and the system would be destroyed."

"Use the DL," another voice spoke up. "Launch them into space near Airtha, then transition them into the DL. They can bypass the interdictors and make it much further insystem."

"The Exaldi will get them," Svetlana countered.

"Maybe," Rellan mused. "But some would get through. We've done drone tests like this, and often, two percent make it through to the inner system, I—"

"Won't work," Sera returned the favor of interruption to Rellan, and included a stern glare. "Airtha is surrounded by a higher density of Exaldi than normal—that was a key part of its selection."

"OK, everyone," Greer held up a hand once more. "Believe it or not, we've considered the options you're presenting. They're in the full data packet, along with the assessments of their effectiveness." He paused and gestured at the casualty estimate chart once more. "The other option is much like the bullets, but instead, we simply send in every ship we have. It would require pulling them from all theatres—but if we did, we could put together a force that would outnumber the defenders over two to one."

"And the losses?" Sera asked.

"We'd lose every ship without stasis shields. However, the analysis shows that we could take the ring intact."

"I thought that wasn't a goal?" Svetlana glanced at Sera. "There was concern that everyone on it could be irreparably subverted."

Sera nodded. "I did say I wanted an option that did not take into account civilian lives, but a conversation with someone recently has changed my mind about that. We all know people on Airtha. We at least owe it to them to try a solution that does not involve their wholesale destruction."

"That's where the middle ground plan comes in," Greer replied. "We fire the bullets, but at secondary targets: at fleet groups, defensive emplacements, everything *but* Airtha." He pointed at a casualty estimate of twenty million. "We'll lose at least that many, but I believe we'd take the day."

Rellan shook his head. "On top of those civilian casualties, we'd lose half our fleets, and then Orion will walk all over us. This doesn't sound like a great solution."

Greer nodded slowly. "I'm not in disagreement. It may be that waiting to sway more of the districts to Khardine's side is advisable."

"I've heard rumors that the Sagittarian districts are considering separating and forming their own alliance," Carl said. "I don't know how many more we'll pull in to our side."

Rellan folded his arms and looked like he was going to spit. "I thought we were better than this. Thirty percent of the Transcend is with us, maybe twenty with *her*. The rest are waffling or declaring for themselves."

"OK," Sera said as she rose and stepped up beside Admiral Greer. "This is excellent information. I'm open to more suggestions. But for now, we're going to continue to see how things play out in the Vela cluster—see if Krissy can gather more resources. If we can manage for another year, then New Canaan can have nearly a hundred thousand ships for us, and double the number of ships we currently have with stasis shields. That changes the outcome of a full assault greatly."

"A year's a long time," Svetlana said in a quiet voice.

Sera agreed, but she didn't have any other options at the moment. "In a year, Tanis will have put down the Nietzscheans and the Trisilieds, and Scipio will have taken out the Hegemony. That will take the wind out of Orion's sails in the Inner Stars. We'll have a lot more options at that point."

"There are still seventeen more empires and alliances in the Inner Stars that are leaning toward Orion—ones at least as big as the Nietzscheans," a colonel pointed out.

Sera nodded. "You're right, there are. But we have many tools at our disposal. Over sixty percent of the Hand's regional directors are with us, and we have missions underway to affect the decisions of those considering alliances with Orion."

There were slow nods following her words, and no one else spoke up to voice an opinion. Sera nodded to Greer and returned to her seat.

"OK," Greer said as he surveyed the room. "We still have the two Hoplite Fleets to ready, as well as planning for Sera's other key endeavor. Let's move like we're out of time."

Sera rose and watched the brass file out before approaching Greer. "A bit dour on your endnote, there."

Greer nodded. "I suppose. I think some of them are treating this war like something we'll win if we just do our jobs like normal. I guess it's the result of no one suffering a defeat in so long. They need to remember that this is a fight for our lives, and for everything we believe in."

"You're not wrong there," Sera said as she watched the last of the TSF's leadership file out. "Though I wish you were."

A REFLECTIVE WALK

STELLAR DATE: 08.30.8949 (Adjusted Years)
LOCATION: Ol' Sam, ISS *I2*
REGION: Pyra, Albany System, Thebes, Septhian Alliance

Tangel led a silent Rika through the forest on their way to the maglev station. She was taking a circuitous route. The conversation that she and the Marauder captain had engaged in was one that would take some time for Rika to digest.

The mech—something Tangel was surprised the cyborg warriors called themselves—had seen a lot of changes over the past few days. Everything from witnessing the destruction of a Nietzschean armada to receiving the knowledge that she and all her people could be made whole, should they desire it.

<*You've already affected her,*> Bob said, as Tangel led Rika over a small bridge stretching across a bubbling brook. <*When you touched her, showed her your vision, her mental patterns shifted. Do you see it?*>

<*I do,*> Tangel replied. <*She's going to need that added strength. With General Mill and Captain Ayer dead, there are few people in authority over her that understand and respect her. She needs to know that someone she esteems believes fully in her.*>

<*Is it true?*>

<*Bob!*> Tangel admonished. <*I would not seed a lie in her mind. And I would not knowingly set her on a road to ruin. I believe Rika can execute the plan and topple Nietzschea.*>

<*Just checking. I've gotten used to reading everyone's intentions. You, I have to ask to gain certainty.*>

"Admir—Tanis." Rika began to speak as they stepped off the bridge's wooden surface and back onto the earthen path. "I get the feeling there is something more you want to tell me."

"Ask you is more like it," Tangel replied.

Rika cocked her head, a corner of her lips curling up in a nervous smile. "*You* asking *me*? Why does that make me nervous?"

Tangel winked. "No need to be nervous. I was just thinking about your mind—well, your brain."

Rika's smile turned into a laugh. "I don't know that anyone has ever said something quite like that to me before. Usually people are talking about every part of me except for my brain."

"Well, they're foolish, then," Tangel replied. "I believe that when Niki gets properly paired with you—should the two of you choose to do it—we should begin the process of enhancing your mental capacity."

"Sorry?" Rika coughed. "Enhancing?"

"Right now, you're close to an L1—don't ask me how I know that, I can just tell. You have a higher neuron density than is normal, but your axons are not as long, and your dendrites are not as interconnected as they could be. I don't think it would be that difficult to get you to L2 status."

Rika lifted her left hand and placed it on her head. "Won't that…change me?"

"It would," Tangel nodded. "But because you already have a high volume of neurons, the change would not be as much as someone going from L0 to L1 normally experiences. The changes are different for everyone, but mostly you'd find that you're faster, you can make intuitive leaps better—and they're more accurate because you can consider more variables. You might even get the ability to multithread."

"Multithread?" Rika asked. "Like think of more than one thing at once?"

"Right," Tangel confirmed. "Though many people *think* they can do this, L0s really can't. They may switch focus quickly—at a cognitive penalty, I might add—but they really can't think of two things simultaneously."

<Like when you were talking with Angela and I, as well as to Tim?> Niki asked. *<I was impressed at how well you did that.>*

You have no idea, Tangel thought. *Especially considering that I'm passing myself off as two people right now.*

While talking with Rika, Tangel was masquerading as Angela in twenty-seven conversations over the Link, and as Tanis in three others.

And it wasn't remotely taxing.

"Exactly like that," Tangel replied to Niki. "As an added advantage, being directly linked with Rika's mind, you'll be able to have deeper conversations with her, and share more via what amounts to a sort of cross-cognitive intuition."

"We wouldn't merge, would we?" Rika asked quickly. "Not that what's happening to you and Angela is bad…I just like being me, is all."

Tangel laughed as she shook her head. "It's vanishingly rare now, but at one time, many L2s paired with AIs—well, not many, but a lot. To my knowledge, Angela and I are the only ones who have found themselves in this predicament."

"I guess that's reassuring," Rika replied, then fell silent.

Tangel could see that she was deep in thought—both from her lowered brow and from the activity in her mind. It was plain to see that the mech and her AI were also speaking rapidly with one another.

"It would make me a more effective leader, wouldn't it?" Rika finally asked.

Tangel nodded in agreement. "It would. Much more effective. I believe that you would fare much better in your fight against Nietzschea."

Rika snorted. "Stop hedging. You mean that fewer of my mechs would die from stupid decisions I make."

Tangel laughed, her tone rueful as she thought of her many stupid decisions. "Yes, but you're not going to be infallible, so don't get cocky."

"No chance of that." Rika shook her head as the maglev platform came into view on the trail ahead. "Self-doubt and second-guessing all the way, here."

<Don't listen to her,> Niki interjected. *<She's got her head on straight.>*

Tangel chuckled softly as they walked out of the trees and into the maglev platform's clearing. "I know it. I wouldn't have offered you this mission otherwise."

Rika nodded in silence as they stepped onto the platform and waited for a car to arrive. "I hope I live up to that belief."

"You will," Tangel said, giving Rika a slow wink. "And think on the L2 enhancement. It could really help."

"I think I'll do it," Rika replied as the car arrived. "I mean…I think it's a sure thing, but I want to talk it over with Chase first."

"Good." Tangel nodded. "I'm glad you two work as a team."

Rika laughed. "Me too, Tanis, me too."

NEW HORIZONS

STELLAR DATE: 08.30.8949 (Adjusted Years)
LOCATION: Bay 19-12A, Keren Station
REGION: Khardine System, Transcend Interstellar Alliance

Sera squared her shoulders as she waited on the docks with her High Guard, watching as Jason's shuttle settled on its cradle. For reasons she couldn't quite pin down, Sera felt more trepidation than the meeting should engender.

She hadn't spent any time in private with him since Elena had come aboard the *Intrepid* just over twenty years ago at Ascella. Though they'd flirted constantly during the month she spent aboard the colony ship, Jason had never made himself fully available to her.

It wasn't surprising. He was the captain of the ship, burdened with his duties and responsibilities—not the least of which was keeping a handle on Tanis.

Sera was the spy who turned out to be the daughter of their uncertain ally. Not the sort of individual a logical person would become entangled with.

One thing is certain about Jason—he ***is*** *logical. Not risk averse, or calculating, but rather…considering.*

Which made her wonder why he had come to Khardine—especially at a time when so many allied ships had been deployed to the Albany System to rescue Tanis.

The cradle's ramp lifted to meet the shuttle's opening airlock, and Sera had to force herself to relax.

Seriously. You saw Jason just a year ago. Neither of us made any overtures. This is just a professional visit.

There was no reason to believe that there was anything remaining between them—granted, she was still getting over her father's betrayal and death, and Elena….

A pair of ISF Marines were the first ones out of the shuttle, stepping smartly down the ramp. They didn't seem overly concerned about their surroundings, which may have been due to the fact that two members of Sera's personal guard were also ISF Marines.

A moment later, Jason Andrews' large frame appeared, silhouetted in the airlock's opening. He paused for a moment, and then stepped onto the ramp. His calm, purposeful strides reminded her of one of the reasons she'd always been drawn to him: the man was the living definition of 'unflappable'.

He must have undergone rejuv recently, because his formerly silver-white hair was now a dirty blonde. The change shifted him from the stately captain she'd first met on the *Intrepid* twenty years ago, to a much younger, rakish-looking man. Somehow it didn't decrease his mystique, though—it enhanced it.

<*Well* **that** *wasn't in the bio I read on you,*> Jen said with a soft laugh in Sera's mind. <*Have feelings for the New Canaan Governor?*>

<*Hush, Jen,*> Sera chided her AI.

Relax, Sera, she told herself. *He's not here to see you. You're both heads of state on official business. Well, I suppose that's not correct. He* **is** *here to see me, but not like that. Don't make him the rebound guy after Elena.*

As Jason descended the ramp, she could see that his eyes had settled on her. A broad smile formed on his lips, and his pace quickened. Sera walked forward, and they met at the base of the ramp, clasping hands.

"Governor Andrews, it's very good to see you. We don't get a lot of state visits at Khardine."

"Sera, please," Jason's smile was warm and comforting. "Just call me 'Jason'. I don't stand on formality—I know it's not your preference, either."

Sera shrugged. "My many advisors are beating it into me, though they're all quite put out that you wanted to meet with me privately."

Jason ran a hand along his neat beard—an affectation she was glad he'd kept—and nodded soberly. "Sorry for all the cloak and dagger stuff, the topic I have to discuss is highly sensitive. Would you care to come aboard my pinnace?"

"Surely I have more comfortable accommodations on Keren."

"Yes," Jason gave Sera an appraising look. "But Tanis has instructed that conversations on this topic take place only in highly controlled locations."

"Tanis's orders?" Sera asked. "Aren't you the governor now, Jason?"

Jason cocked an eyebrow and gave a soft laugh. "You know that no matter what her title is, Tanis is in charge. It's in her nature. She was born for this."

"That sounds strangely prophetic, Jason," Sera replied.

He shrugged as he offered his hand and turned to walk back up the ramp. "Would you like to know why I've come?"

"Are we staying in the docking bay?" Sera asked. "If we're taking the pinnace to your ship, then my guards will insist they come along."

Jason glanced at the four High Guard standing nearby. "As they should. I wish I could convince Tanis to travel with an escort like this."

Sera snorted. "As if you could. Besides, from the updates that Joe sent, Tanis is a one-woman battle-station now."

Jason barked a laugh. "Well, she'd have to be to house that iron will of hers. And yes, we're staying on the dock. No need to bring your guards aboard."

"OK," Sera replied, and nodded to the High Guard before taking Jason's hand, wondering why he'd offered it to her, and why she felt forty years younger holding it as she followed him up the ramp.

Once inside, Jason led her to a small dining cabin, and they sat on either side of the table. A servitor poured two cups of coffee, and then retreated to its alcove.

Jason added cream to his, while Sera opted to drink hers black. The planet Troy in the New Canaan System grew some of the best coffee beans in the galaxy, and there was no need to muddy their taste.

"So?" she said after a moment, hoping to prompt Jason into explaining his mysterious visit.

His gaze rose to meet hers, and his eyes remained on her face as he took a sip of his coffee. When he lowered his cup, his eyes drifted down as well, and a small smile graced his lips.

"I'm glad you haven't changed your mode of dress, even though you're the Great President now," he said.

Sera looked down and saw that her skin had reverted to its red 'naked' state at some point, and chastised herself for not maintaining better control.

Perhaps I need to suck it up and ask Jen to keep an eye on me.

She considered changing her appearance back to her uniform, but decided not to. There was no shame in being what she was—though she worried that Jason would think she was doing it to seduce him…which maybe she was—subconsciously, of course.

Of course.

"Well, I don't normally go around like this," she confessed. "But if I get distracted, I revert..."

Jason took another sip of his coffee, an eyebrow arched. "Distracted?" When he set down the cup, there was a mischievous smirk on his lips.

"Jason Andrews!" Sera's brow lowered. "Are you flirting with me?"

Jason held up his forefinger and thumb. "Maybe a smidge. But if you're still...whatever you might be with Elena, I'll stifle it."

<*He's perceptive,*> Jen commented.

The governor's mouth hung open for a moment longer, as though he was going to say something more, but then he closed his lips and regarded her with his penetrating brown eyes.

Sera made a dismissive swipe with her hand, nearly spilling her coffee. "No," she said a little too loudly. "I mean...no, I'm not 'whatever' with Elena. I'm not entirely over her, over what she did to me—to everyone, for that matter—but I no longer harbor any pleasant feelings or longing for her. The neurologists are working out the best way to reverse whatever it was that Garza did to her, but I think it would be best if she and I never...anythinged anymore."

Her expression must have contained some level of angst, because Jason's eyes softened while she rushed out her explanation.

"Sorry, I shouldn't have gone there," he soothed. "It's inappropriate, and we have other matters to discuss."

Sera was continually impressed by Jason's ability to be the stodgy old man—even when he no longer looked it. "Jason, it's OK. I appreciate frank conversations like this. I spend too much time in my own head. I'd grown used to bouncing ideas off Tanis, but she's a bit hard to get ahold of right now."

"That's a part of what I have to tell you," Jason said with a solemn nod. "There are things we've learned about Tanis from Katrina that she wants me to share with you."

"Why you?" Sera asked.

"Well, because I spoke with Katrina directly. I have it from the horse's mouth, so to speak."

Sera had read the report out of New Canaan that one of the colonists' old companions from Victoria had followed them through Kapteyn's Streamer. It was mind boggling to think that the woman had spent five hundred years waiting for the *Intrepid* to arrive.

The report had been light on details, but it did note that Katrina was being 'detained'.

"You knew her from your time back at Kapteyn's Star, didn't you?" Sera asked.

"I did." Jason leant back in his chair and folded his arms across his chest. "I counted her as a friend. I still do, I think. She ended up coming under the influence of an ascended AI named Xavia. The AI…bent her a bit. Not to mention some of the things she went through...I swear, I think we had a far easier time of it than she did."

"That's not saying much," Sera replied. "Is this Xavia the same being as the Caretaker?"

"Not from what Katrina says. She believes that Xavia represents a different faction. One that wants to see humanity advance on its own terms. I guess they got tired of seeing the Caretaker's group drive humanity into one dark age after another. To hear Katrina tell it, Xavia and her ilk have been greatly responsible for much of the general uplift in the Inner Stars over the last thousand years."

Sera snorted. "Just like those ascended AIs to take all the credit. The Hand worked tirelessly to forge alliances and build humanity back up."

Jason shrugged. "I take it all with a grain of salt. Either way, Xavia told Katrina some interesting things about Tanis."

The way that Jason spoke the words, it was clear that he was about to drop a bomb, and Sera steeled herself for it.

"Go on."

"Well, from what she's said, Tanis was *engineered* to be what she's become."

"She what?" Sera leant forward, hands on the table. "How was Tanis engineered?"

"You of course know that Tanis is a natural L1, right? She was enhanced to be an L2 in her late teens because she had the neural structure to support it. It's what precluded her from getting an AI, until research—research spearheaded by the Enfield Corporation—worked out how to embed AIs in the brains of L2s."

"Are you saying that Terrance Enfield had some hand in 'engineering' Tanis? Though I suppose that's not too surprising. Tanis has been more a product of science than nature for some time."

To some, the words may have come off as demeaning, but Sera didn't mean them that way, and from the soft laugh Jason gave, he didn't interpret them as such.

"You're not wrong about that, but that's not what it means. Terrance says he knew his company had been the one to facilitate Tanis getting her first AI, but not that anything nefarious had been done."

"And you trust Terrance?" Sera asked, nearly folding her arms too, but realizing it would look ridiculous if the two of them were sitting at the small table with their arms folded, staring each other down.

She expected Jason to bristle at her question, but he only laughed.

"With my life. Multiple times. Terrance and I go way back. Waaaaay back."

"OK, so where is all this going? Did the ascended AIs tamper with Tanis somehow?"

"Yeah, from what I can tell they improved her, made sure that she'd be able to get the *Intrepid* where it needed to be. Except, as you know, Bob got us out of the Streamer too soon. We exited from it five hundred years before the master plan was ready."

Sera studied Jason's expression. She could tell that he still had more to say, so she nodded for him to carry on.

"Katrina said—and Tanis has confirmed this with Bob—that *he* also altered her, without her or Angela knowing."

"Shiiiiiit," Sera drew the word out. "How so?"

"I don't have all the details, so you'll have to talk to Tanis about it when you next see her, but Bob confirmed that he *and* Earnest have been changing Tanis's brain slowly and carefully for years to facilitate what ultimately happened on Pyra."

Sera shook her head, incredulous disbelief flooding her features. "Why?"

"Bob's argument is that it had to be done to keep them alive. If he'd let their merger proceed without intervention, she would have gone insane decades ago. They worked up some new picotech procedure that erected quantum-level barriers to direct how their minds merged."

"Tanis must be pissed!" Sera exclaimed.

Jason nodded slowly. "I know *I* would be. She seems to be taking it in stride."

"Is that because she's ascended now? Or whatever she is?" Sera asked. "Stars, I should go see her. I need to know what she's thinking."

"From what I understand, she's only semi-ascended." Jason took another drink of his coffee. "Whatever that means. This is all pretty crazy stuff. But in all honesty, I've been living with the fallout from transhumanism my entire life. I was one of the first documented natural L2s, you know. Did a lot of work to free AIs—sucks to see that we're still fighting that same fight."

"I didn't know that," Sera said, examining Jason in a new light. She knew the basics of his story, born at Proxima Centauri in the early fourth millennia, grandson of one of the heroes of the Sentience Wars whose parents had gotten out of Sol to some place a little tamer. She knew he'd plied sub-light ships in the black for centuries, which gave him a sort of kinship with the FGT. Beyond that, she didn't know too much else.

"So what does all this mean?" Sera asked. "What do we do with this information?"

"Damned if I know," Jason replied with a grin that looked far more roguish on a young man's face. "It's not really the main topic I came here to discuss."

His words caught Sera mid-drink, and she nearly spat out her coffee. "Seriously?" Sera paused to set her cup down. "The fact that Tanis is part of some millennia-long master plan to either save or destroy humanity is the *side topic*?"

"Well, we know that Tanis is too strong willed to allow herself to be controlled by anyone. Everything she's done is evidence that she's no one's pawn."

Sera let out a coarse laugh. "You're right, there. Woe be to any super-being that thinks they can control her. She's going to beat them at their own game."

Jason nodded and lifted his coffee cup once more, tipping it back to drain the last remains before signaling to the servitor that he wanted a refill.

While the bot completed his request, the governor leant forward, placing his elbows on the table. "You've heard of our Aleutian site, right?"

Sera nodded. "Yeah, I've seen it mentioned in a few places. You sent out the initial ships when I was still in New Canaan last year."

"Right, we did. I assume you know what it is?"

"Sure, I guess." Sera spread her hands wide. "A beta site for your people; I don't blame you, New Canaan is in everyone's crosshairs. I'm a bit surprised you all stayed."

Jason chuckled as he watched the servitor set his coffee down on the table. "Jen," he addressed Sera's AI. "I assume you're listening?"

<I am,> Jen replied. *<This is a fascinating topic.>*

"Don't I know it," he agreed, while pouring a generous amount of cream into his coffee. "You now have Omega clearance, Jen. Top level."

<Uh…what is 'top level'?> Jen asked.

"There isn't one. It means you have unrestricted access to any ISF and New Canaan intel. Sera has it too, now. The two of you don't need to keep secrets from one another." He paused and met Sera's eyes. "But I'll trust that you'll keep what I'm about to tell you in the strictest confidence. Until we decide to take action."

"Er…sure," Sera said, her brows deeply furrowed.

"To your previous statement about us remaining in New Canaan: simply put, we're a stubborn group. We put a lot of effort into building our colony, and a lot of lives were lost defending it."

"But you're realists," Sera replied.

"We are, yes."

"I'll admit." Sera's eyes narrowed as she watched Jason's eyes for any tells. "I've been curious as to where your Aleutian Site is, but Tanis didn't volunteer the information, and I decided she'd share it when she was ready."

"It's in the LMC," Jason replied tonelessly, not looking up as he stirred his cream into his coffee.

This time Sera nearly did choke. "The Large Magellanic Cloud? Like…the *galaxy* that's a hundred and sixty fucking thousand light years from here?"

"Closer to one seventy, where we are," Jason said, looking up and winking at Sera. "We like to do things big."

"No fucking kidding," she muttered. "Seriously, Jason. This is all getting to be too much. Ascended AIs scheming from the core of the galaxy, Finaeus building a secret staging ground in the 3kpc Arm, Tanis ascending, and now this. Are you all leaving?"

"You know about Project Starflight, right?" Jason asked.

"Yeah, Tanis told me that you guys are going to make Canaan Prime burn asymmetrically and fly it out of the Milky Way Galaxy. That's some serious long-term planning."

Jason nodded. "Go big, or go home, right? Well, I guess we finally *got* a home, so we're going 'big' there. Anyway, the Aleutian site is the yin to Project Starflight's yang. It's the destination. But we're not stepping out of the conflict. We'll do our part, and help put things back together before we leave."

"Leave," Sera whispered the word. "So you are going to leave. All of you."

"It's not like it's going to happen tomorrow, or even in a century. It takes a long time to accelerate a star to galactic escape velocity."

"Sometimes you must wonder about the words you're saying," Sera laughed.

Jason snorted. "I'm just a simple guy from Proxima Centauri. You're the one who grew up on a diamond ring wrapped around a Saturn-sized white dwarf star."

"Touché."

"There's more."

"Jason…seriously, just spill it already, you're killing me, here."

He nodded soberly. "This is serious stuff, Sera. We jumped to the LMC on the outskirts of the NGC 1783 globular cluster. Conditions were right for Class G stars in that region, and we found them. The Aleutian team is studying local cosmic events to determine if it's a safe region—or if they should relocate. They're also setting up an industrial base around a star they've named Cheshire."

"Damn," Sera whispered. "What does the Milky Way look like from out there?"

"I've not been there yet," Jason replied. "But I imagine the answer is 'amazing'."

"OK, so, while this is way up there on the freakin' awesome scale, I'm not sure why it warrants a private visit from the man himself." Sera smirked at Jason as she spoke, the glib words and grin on her lips the only way she could deal with all the information he had hit her with.

"You're right. I'm here to talk about what we *found* in the LMC."

Sera's eyes grew wide, and she slammed both hands onto the table. "You found aliens! I knew it!"

Jason barked a laugh at her enthusiasm. "Stars, I wish we'd found aliens. Well, maybe. Who knows, maybe they're in hiding. Either way, what we found were humans."

For a moment, the words didn't make sense to Sera. "What? Seriously? Humans?"

He nodded. "Not just any humans, we found the Transcend."

"OK, stop doling it out," Sera said through gritted teeth, as the myriad implications of his words all but buried her. "Lay it on me."

"Sorry, trying to make this…less nuts than it all is."

"You've failed. Just give it to me."

Jason took another sip of coffee and leant forward once more.

"While our people were setting up, they kept noticing strange variances in the light from a few stars not far away. Variances that didn't match natural patterns. What they *did* match were massive fusion burns from planet movers undertaking terraforming operations."

"Shit," Sera whispered. "Really?"

"I thought you wanted me to just spill it. You've gotta stop interrupting for that to happen."

"Sorry." She pursed her lips and gestured for him to continue.

"The activity was coming from a group of stars at the edge of an open cluster about two hundred light years away. Once we had shipped in our backup gates, we jumped in a scouting team and took a closer look. What we found were three FGT terraforming groups, all working on establishing new worlds—well, that's what they *had* been doing. When we came in closer, we saw that they'd ceased those operations and were stripping the systems down and building shipyards."

"I…I have no knowledge of this," Sera said. "I don't think anyone here does."

"We have a stealth ship doing a close fly-by as we speak," Jason replied. "We'll know more soon. But if you don't know about this, there are only two options."

Sera nodded and let out a long sigh. "Airtha, or some other rogue element in the Transcend."

"Or a rogue element that is now under Airtha's control."

"My father had to have known about this," Sera muttered. "What *else* did he have going on?"

"I don't know," Jason replied, his voice kind. "Chances are that, whatever it is, Airtha has the details, given her position at…well,

Airtha."

Sera nodded again. "We need to accelerate our plans to stop her. TSF strategists are working on some ideas, but…they're not ideal."

"How so?"

"Well, Airtha has the Huygens System well defended. There could be as many as half a million ships there by now. We'd wondered why she'd given up so much of the Transcend to us without a fight. Now that I know she's building ships in the LMC, I wonder if she has other, similar facilities spread throughout the galaxy—or even in the other dwarf galaxies surrounding the Milky Way."

"So what's your plan of attack on Airtha?" Jason asked. "Or, at least the winning proposals."

"This is all predicated on Airtha being linked to the ring and being unable to move from it. However, from the report you sent from Kara, who I'd really like to meet, it's possible that Airtha is fully ascended, and may not be directly connected to the ring anymore."

"Hard to say," he replied. "From what we've been learning about ascended beings, to operate in our three paltry dimensions, they need some sort of physical presence. Earnest believes that they need to reconstruct themselves in other dimensions to fully leave this one, and that it may not be possible to do so entirely. Either way, she may still be tied to the ring."

"Or she may not," Sera countered, and Jason shrugged before she continued. "Well, taking the Huygens System with our current resources is impossible—especially if we want to be able to stand up to Orion afterward. However, destroying it is not."

"Destroying it?" he echoed. "How will you do that?"

Sera signaled the servitor for another cup of coffee. "A derivation of what the allies just pulled off in the Albany system, but with bullets."

"You're going to have to fire a lot of bullets to get past those half a million starships."

"Yeah," Sera closed her eyes for a moment imagining the deadly shrapnel that would create in the star system. "But if we use chunks of neutron stars held in stasis fields and moving at relativistic speeds, Airtha's defenses won't be able to stop them all. And it will only take a few of them getting through to destroy Airtha's ring."

Jason whistled. "That's one hell of a solution."

Sera wondered what he thought of his allies now, knowing that they would consider the wholesale slaughter of a trillion people, just to take out their enemy. "It's partially my fault. In a fit of frustration, I suggested that perhaps everyone on Airtha is fully under my mother's sway, and that we'd lose too many trying to take the system."

"Well, you're probably not wrong...on either count."

Sera snorted. "Yeah. I wish I was, though. We need to take out Airtha, but we can't assault her directly. Especially because with the control she has over the AIs, we'd be murdering slaves. I tabled the wholesale destruction option, thinking that we could choke off her access to resources, but now she has extra-fucking-galactic shipyards!"

Her voice had risen as she spoke, and Jason's eyes softened with compassion as he stretched out a hand and took hers.

"We've not been given an easy path, that's for sure. But we know that Airtha has these other facilities now, and we can destroy them, deny the LMC to her."

Sera nodded, not withdrawing her hand, the realization hitting her that she hadn't touched anyone romantically in over a year. *Hugs with Tanis don't count because they're not romantic for her.*

<*And if Airtha has other facilities?*> Jen asked, speaking for the first time since Jason dropped his bombs.

He shrugged. "It would take centuries to search the galaxy, we just have to assume that if we shut down that one expansion location, she won't have had time to set up others. But what we really need is better intel. We only saw that location because the FGT had been there for hundreds of years already, and the light had reached the Aleutian site."

"Of course, the intel we need is all at Airtha."

"Would it be?" Jason mused. "Your father struck me as a very well-prepared man, generally speaking. Is there any chance he had a backup site for the Transcend's government? A bunker of sorts in another system?"

"Given the fact that he was colonizing the Large Magellanic Cloud, I imagine he had a few out there." Sera shook her head and drew a deep breath, trying to find options. "The only one I know of is in Airtha's hands, nearly as well defended as the Huygens System."

Jason's brow furrowed, and then a small smile formed on his lips. "You know...if I were a paranoid megalomaniac who wanted the ultimate backup plan…"

Sera's eyes widened. "The LMC locations *are* his ultimate fallback—that's why even I didn't know about them. And if they are, there would be data there about any other sites, and the resources Airtha has access to."

"Bingo," Jason grinned. "I'll return to New Canaan and organize a strike team."

"No," Sera replied, and Jason's eyes narrowed.

"No?"

"Well, yes, but also no. I'm going, too."

He held her gaze for a moment before his solemn look turned into a grin. "That's what I like about you, Sera Tomlinson."

"What?" she asked.

"You're a woman of action."

NIETZSCHEA

STELLAR DATE: 08.31.8949 (Adjusted Years)
LOCATION: Valhalla
REGION: Capitol, Pruzia System, Nietzschean Empire

Garza's shuttle set down on a landing pad at a level of the Imperial Spire known as 'Valhalla'. As the cradle locked onto the shuttle, and the ramp rose, Garza composed himself for the meeting with the emperor.

After a minute, he rose and walked to the shuttle's opening, noting that his guards were already at the base of the ramp.

Looking around, he couldn't help but be a little impressed by the view. If he hadn't known otherwise, it would have been impossible to tell that Valhalla was over one hundred kilometers above Capitol's surface.

Before him stood a massive marble edifice, crafted in the form of an ancient fortress, featuring towers that stretched into space, beyond the limits of even Garza's augmented field of vision.

Around the landing pad were manicured lawns and gardens, and beyond those, a lake that encircled the entire platform.

From the approach the shuttle had taken, Garza had seen that the water poured off the edges of the lake, kept from blowing through the thin atmosphere by grav fields, which made it seem as though there was a hundred kilometer veil, pouring off the spire.

The effect shrouded the spire's shaft and made it appear as though it hovered on a pillar of mist.

None of that impressed Garza.

He'd seen his share of impossible feats of engineering: the ancient High Terra Ring, the Scipian ecumenopolis of Alexandria, the diamond Airthan Ring—though that one was only in a memory from a clone—and even a far-off view of Star City.

A spire like this was almost boring.

Even so, he'd come himself, sending a clone to deal with Praetor Kirkland. The Nietzschean Emperor was a tricky man; hard to pin down, and even harder to negotiate with.

It was a job he'd not send a clone to do.

Constantine also posed little threat to Garza—unlike Airtha and Sera. Garza was glad a clone had been sent to the Transcend's capital. It came back entirely under Airtha's thrall, though it did at least confirm that the abomination had finally ascended.

Praetor Kirkland may be a fool, but at least he had been right about the risk that Tomlinson's former wife posed. Keeping her around had been a mistake, one that Garza was glad to know had finally taken Jeffrey Tomlinson out of the picture.

As Garza walked down the shuttle's ramp toward the functionary that waited for him below, he couldn't help but wish things had gone differently.

Jeffrey Tomlinson had started out as a good man. Stars, he had been the one to really kick-start interstellar colonization. He founded the Transcend.

It was possible that the man had been one of the most influential humans in all of history.

A flash of regret passed through Garza's mind that he had needed to order Tomlinson's death. He'd lost a valuable asset on the mission, as well. Elena's placement with Sera had taken decades of work, and she threw it all away to kill Tomlinson herself, when Kent should have been the one to do it.

Still, Garza's plans could move forward even with the wrinkle that the degenerate Sera presented. It was Tanis Richards who was the real problem. That his operation in Scipio had failed to kill her was more than infuriating; it put many of his other operations on the spinward side of Sol at risk.

The Nietzschean functionary said something in greeting, and Garza nodded absently, still lost in thought as he considered his best options for bolstering the region against Tanis and her fleet of invincible ships.

His best option was to go wide. Hit hundreds, maybe even thousands of systems at once. Never concentrate forces, never give Tanis a target she could strike.

He'd learned that lesson twice now. Once at New Canaan, and again at Silstrand. It wouldn't happen a third time.

"General?" the Nietzschean functionary asked, his tone making it apparent he was repeating himself.

"What is it?" Garza snapped as they turned onto the main pathway leading to Valhalla's gates.

"I was just letting you know that the emperor will be seeing you in the garden today."

Garza waved his hand. "That is fine. Wherever he wants, so long as he doesn't keep me waiting."

"Of course not," the liveried servant said, ducking his head obsequiously before guiding Garza through Valhalla's gates and along a shrouded pathway leading around the main cluster of spires toward what Garza assumed to be Constantine's private garden.

The walk was just over half a kilometer, and Garza was beginning to wonder if the emperor had spent so much money on trappings that he couldn't afford a groundcar, when they finally reached a pair of gleaming gates.

As the servant guiding Garza approached, the gates opened, revealing an idyllic meadow beyond. Trees ringed the perimeter, and a small stream flowed through the center. On the far side of the stream was an ancient oak, its large boughs spreading across a quarter of the meadow.

Beneath the tree's thick branches, reclining on a chaise, was Emperor Constantine.

The man wore a simple white robe, chewing languidly on grapes he was plucking from a bunch hanging on a pole. On either side of him were naked servants—both men and women—who were fanning him as though he were some ancient Terran king.

The servants surrounding the emperor were the finest specimens of humanity a person could imagine. They embodied a perfected physical—and likely mental—form; all completely natural.

In a manner of speaking.

Constantine, and those he surrounded himself with, were entirely unmodded. They were, however, genetically engineered in every way.

Normally, the setting Garza approached would likely lead to debauchery before long, but he knew that was not the case with Constantine.

The emperor purported to be celibate—something that every

source at Garza's disposal confirmed. For whatever reason, the man seemed to enjoy proving to everyone that he was immune to any desires of the flesh by surrounding himself with carnal temptations.

Nietzscheans, Garza thought in derision. *In their effort to become the purest humans they can be, they've forgotten what humanity is all about: Multiply and fill the heavens. Fulfill our manifest destiny.*

The functionary led Garza across a series of flat-topped stones placed in the stream, and then stood silently before the emperor, hands clasped behind his back.

Garza resisted the urge to roll his eyes as they waited a full minute for Constantine to acknowledge their presence.

Finally the man spoke, his voice a deep baritone. "General."

Constantine didn't look up from the grapes he held in his hand, and Garza waited for five long seconds before replying.

"Emperor Constantine. It is good to see you again."

The emperor finally looked up and nodded to Garza before glancing at the servant and flicking his hand, gesturing for the functionary to leave.

Without a word, the man left, and Garza took it upon himself to sit in one of the chairs next to the emperor's chaise.

A look of annoyance flickered across the emperor's face, but he didn't make an issue of Garza's presumptive action.

"To what do I owe this pleasure, General Garza?" the emperor asked, as though they hadn't already exchanged a host of messages.

"I'm here to review the strategy for the assault on Septhia, as we'd discussed in our communications. I understand you have amassed a force capable of striking every Septhian star at once."

"Have I?" the emperor arched a brow. "I suppose I have. However, I recently enacted another plan."

Garza's brow pinched together, and he resisted the urge to reach out and slap the grapes out of Constantine's hand. Instead, all he said was, "Oh?"

"Yes. It turns out that Tanis Richards and her ancient colony ship have been flitting around the edges of my empire, looking for someone."

"Really?" Garza had no idea why Tanis would do such a thing. "Who?"

"A rather odious man, a thorn in my side. General Mill of the Marauders."

Garza delved into his data on the region and pulled up the information on the Marauders—a group of mercenaries consisting of Genevians who had banded together after their people's conquest by the Nietzscheans.

"What did she want with Mill?" Garza asked.

"I don't know, but I expect to find out. My moles within the Septhian government have orders to attack them when they finally meet. Chances are that it will be somewhere in Thebes or the Politica. I've massed a fleet of over seventy thousand ships; that should see to my enemy's capture, and the destruction of whatever escort they possess."

Garza felt heat rise in his face as he fixed the emperor with a penetrating stare. "Tell me this isn't the fleet we were going to use in our attack on Septhia."

"*General* Garza. Do not presume to instruct me as to what to tell you. We are in Nietzschea here, not your Orion Freedom Alliance."

Garza drew in a deep breath and schooled his expression before inclining his head. "I ask your forgiveness. But tell me, did your ships attack?"

"We are some distance from Praesepe," Constantine replied, his tone arch, as though he were going out of his way to forgive Garza for his verbal faux pas. "But I did just receive word that the attack is being readied. At Albany, no less. I rather like the symmetry of it. And yes, we committed the force we'd built up for the attack on Septhia. Once they've captured Tanis Richards and her ship, they can proceed with that mission as planned."

"Doubtful. They're likely lost," Garza said simply.

"What is? Our prey?" Constantine asked, his serene expression cracking for the first time.

"No. Your fleet," the general clarified. "I imagine it's gone."

Constantine dropped his grapes and swung his legs over the edge of his chaise, sitting up and fixing Garza with a penetrating stare. The indolent emperor was gone, now replaced with a power-hungry man determined to seize anything his thoughts settled on.

"I sent *seventy thousand* ships. The accounts I have tell me she was travelling with a few dozen escort craft. Even her vaunted *Intrepid* cannot stand up to a force the size I sent."

"*I2*," Garza corrected.

"What?" Constantine snapped.

"The ISS *I2*. The *Intrepid* has been upgraded. Now the ship likely has firepower equal to a quarter of the fleet you sent against it, just on its own. It houses a hundred thousand fighters, all with stasis shields. You sent your fleet to its death."

"It's not possible," Constantine whispered. "I will have captured Tanis Richards!"

"No," Garza hissed. "You squandered your opportunity to divide your enemy's forces. If you mass, she will strike you and decimate your fleet. Tanis Richards is a bleeding heart. Your best offense is to attack everywhere at once, destroy worlds, decimate entire star systems. Create mass humanitarian crises that will slow her down and divide her forces. *That* is how you defeat her! You wear her down to a nub."

The emperor had paled as Garza's voice rose in volume, but then he seemed to remember himself, and rose before Garza.

"You'll do well to remember your place, General. I am emperor in Nietzschea, you—"

Garza rose and took a step toward the emperor, moving within arm's reach of the insufferable man.

In an instant, Constantine's naked servants held a host of weapons from blades to pistols. All aimed or leveled at Garza.

Constantine smirked. "Sit."

Garza lifted a hand. Slowly, as though he were bored with the situation. He snapped his fingers, and the naked men and women surrounding him fell to the ground.

"Do not think I would come here unprepared, Constantine. I have means at my disposal you can only imagine."

The emperor's face grew stony as he realized he was completely at Garza's mercy. "How?" he whispered. "I have countermeasures…."

"There is much I have not shared with you…yet," Garza said, sitting once more, and gesturing for Constantine to follow suit. "I *was* going to share jump gate tech with you, but first you'll need to build a new fleet. I want Septhia gone within the year."

Constantine sat as directed, a look of utter confusion on his face. "I need more resources, I've lost much, protecting the empire, our borders are vast—"

Garza held up a hand. "You have the resources. You have worlds, moons, more than enough to build millions of ships. Yes, you have debts you owe, you've spent much in your conquests. But frankly, Emperor Constantine, I don't give a fuck.

"You claim master morality? Well, use it. Seize what you want and build a fleet to *end* your enemies. Build that fleet by whatever means necessary, and I'll facilitate you with jump gates to deliver it to the doorsteps of every star system that opposes you."

Garza rose once more, and looked down at the emperor in disgust.

"I've implanted my nano inside your body. You have a year. If I'm not satisfied with what you've done by then, you'll die. There's nothing you can do about it. My nano is undetectable by your medical science."

"Garza..." The word came out in a choke.

The Orion general let a laugh escape his lips as he began to walk away, stopping at the stream to look over his shoulder.

"One year, Emperor. And remember. I *own* you. I own all of Nietzschea now."

The emperor sputtered something, but Garza ignored him as he stepped across the stones in the stream then strode back through the meadow.

Of course, he'd done nothing to the emperor, but the man would go to his medics nonetheless. Their inability to find anything would cement his belief that Garza did indeed leave something within his body that would kill him, come a year.

Garza decided that he would stay near the Capitol System for a few weeks—long enough to be sure that the emperor would do as he'd been told. Or, should Constantine disobey, to see that the man was replaced.

Following that, Garza would meet back up with the clone he sent to Praetor Kirkland and see how much longer *that* man would last in his position.

INNER EMPIRE

STELLAR DATE: 08.31.8949 (Adjusted Years)
LOCATION: Bridge Conference Room, ISS *I2*
REGION: Pyra, Albany System, Thebes, Septhian Alliance

"Here's the deal," Tangel spoke slowly, sweeping her gaze across the four people in front of her. "I like Thebes. You're a good people who got dealt a bad hand. I don't think that becoming a part of Septhia is good for you; they're just treating you like a buffer between themselves and Nietzschea."

At her words, the men and women nodded soberly.

General Andre spoke up first in his gravelly voice. "I won't argue with that, but we're still staring at Nietzschea across a thirty-light year stretch of systems that are just waiting for the Niets to roll across them. From what you've said, your fleet can't stay here forever. With all that in mind, Septhia is the best option we have."

As the general spoke, the woman to his left, Governor Herra, began to shake her head. "No, Andre, that's just a delaying tactic. Septhia is trying to build a new empire to stand against the Niets, but they're doing it on the backs of everyone around them. In the end, they'll be no different from the Nietzscheans."

Admiral Kally snorted. "Except they're inept. The Septhians can't hope to pull off what the Niets have done—they're not ruthless enough."

"Which we should consider a blessing," Herra said, catching Kally's eye.

"I see that we're all on the same page, then," Tangel said, turning to the fourth visitor, a man named Kendrik. He pursed his lips, then nodded.

"I am. Assuming you have some sort of plan that's more than just a way to call for you to come save us when the Niets attack again—because they *will* attack again."

Tangel nodded as she considered Kendrik. He was the person she needed onboard the most, but he was also the one with the most to lose.

As a businessman who had corporate interests across Thebes and much of Septhia, backing Theban independence from Septhia would put his broader business operations at risk from retaliation.

However, he was the one with the skill and the contacts to manage what Tangel wanted to build in Thebes.

"I can't make guarantees that Septhia won't act…in a manner contrary to their best interests, but I will do everything in my power to bring them in line with what's best for Praesepe at large."

"Which is your way of saying that you'll make them promise not to seize my businesses in Septhia, right?" Kendrik asked, his unblinking eyes boring into Tangel's.

This is where Angela would say something like, 'wow, he's got a set of balls on him', Tangel thought with a mental smirk.

But straight talk is what Kendrik needed to hear.

"There is verbiage in the Alliance treaty which precludes them from taking action that can be considered retaliatory against citizens of other allied nations who operate businesses in both jurisdictions. There are also, however," Tangel's eyes grew serious as she held Kendrik's gaze, "provisions against war profiteering."

Kendrik didn't reply for a moment, but Tangel couldn't help but notice how wide Kally's eyes grew. Then the man gave a short nod.

"Very well, I believe it should not be an issue for me to abide by the alliance treaty. So what do you need from me? I don't have any military power to back a re-formed Theban Alliance"

"True," Tangel said, a smile playing at the corners of her lips. "But how do you feel about operating the largest shipyard this side of Sol?"

"Admiral Richards," General Andre grunted. "Speak plainly, please. What is it that you're proposing?"

"Very simply put, we're at a disadvantage against many of our enemies. They have the ability to bring larger fleets to bear than we do. When they mass, we can meet them and crush them, but there are millions of star systems out there, and we can't police them all; there are just too many fronts to this war. What we *need* are strong, dedicated allies to create bastions of strength that the enemy cannot roll over, allies that also strengthen those around them.

"That's a very generic strategy, though. More specifically, what I want to do is turn Thebes into a fleet-building powerhouse. We'll take the Albany system and make it the economic center of the Praesepe cluster."

"That's…ambitious," Governor Herra said, breaking the silence that had settled on the room after Tangel's statement. "I'm certain you've noticed how the Albany System is in ruin. Pyra is all but an unlivable wasteland, and estimates are that it'll take three years to find all the survivors that jettisoned in pods when their ships and stations were destroyed by the Niets."

"And that's the optimistic view," Andre added.

"I think we can do it," Kendrik said, his concerned expression countering the optimism in his words. "But we'll make ourselves into an even bigger target than we are now. The Niets will come back."

Tangel leant back in her chair. "Ladies and gentlemen, you said it yourselves. The Niets are coming back no matter what—the only way to stop them from eventually crushing Thebes is to defeat them. Thebes will be the engine of that destruction."

Admiral Kally shook her head, sighing as her eyes narrowed. "If your allied fleet hadn't just done what it did here, I'd believe you to be a lunatic, but you've already proven your abilities to us. How will we do this?"

Tangel brought up a view of Pyra, the planet shrouded in dark clouds and storms, a result of the destruction the fleeing Nietzschean ships had rained down on the world.

"This is a two-pronged approach. The first is to deal with the ruin that is Pyra, and the economic issues you're going to face in the wake of this destruction. No one is going to want to invest in Thebes—especially the Pyra System. And by 'invest', I mean time more than money. We need to make this system a shining beacon in the night. To do—"

The door slid open, and Finaeus rushed into the room. "Sorry I'm late, I was wrangling with Gunther. That man did *not* want to give up his Peter."

"Sorry?" Governor Herra asked.

"Allow me to introduce Finaeus Tomlinson," Tangel said as Finaeus took a seat. "He's going to kick off this project."

"Good to meet you folks," Finaeus said as he reached for the pitcher of lemonade on the table and poured himself a glass, glancing at Tanis as he did. "Gonna be a hell of a job to break the Peter down, but with the I-Class gates, we can get it through without too much trouble. Be a lot faster than building from scratch. Right size for Pyra, too. Give us a good grav-ring."

"Pardon?" General Andre asked, while Kendrik whispered, wide-eyed, "A grav ring?"

Finaeus gave Tangel an apologetic look. "Sorry, Tanis, I guess I jumped the gun, there."

Tangel shook her head, a forgiving smile on her lips. "Far be it from me to quell your enthusiasm, Finaeus. Carry on."

"Right," he said, then took a quick sip of his lemonade. "What we're going to do is take a Peter—that's a device we use to cool planets after we make or move them—and use its base support structure to build a ring around Pyra. Probably situate it about two hundred and forty klicks above the surface. We use particle pressure to support the ring, run an accelerator around the whole planet, and then the ring rests on that. You get a bit lower gravity than on the surface, but not much. We can probably build a structure capable of supporting a few billion people at least. Plus, the whole purpose of a Peter is to manage temperature on a planet—it usually cools them, but Gunther's can run both ways. We'll stabilize Pyra, manage its sunlight with collector arrays on the ring, and get your world back in pristine condition in a decade, tops."

"All the while, creating work and housing, as well as showing that Thebes is a place for top minds to congregate and build a future for themselves," Tangel added.

"I'm still stuck on a ring," Governor Herra said in disbelief. "A few weeks ago, I thought we were going to be saluting Emperor Constantine before long, but now we're going to be the jewel of Praesepe inside of a decade."

"Always spinning things for the PR value," General Andre muttered while shaking his head. "I hate to say it, but where are we going to get the resources to rebuild? Shipyards building a fleet, and now a ring...We don't have the facilities to gather that much raw material, let alone refine it."

Tangel expanded the holo above the table and widened its scope to include the entire Praesepe Cluster. "The stars inside the cluster are bursting with resources. Hundreds of rare-element asteroids, dust, and even moons that are just waiting to be harvested."

"Only one problem..." Admiral Kally began, then paused. "Shit...your jump gates. You can get into the cluster and pull out resources in no time."

Tangel nodded. "That's our plan. Although…"

"The Inner Empire is insular," Kendrik finished for Tangel. "They're not going to be terribly excited about visitors showing up on their doorstep."

"Which is where you come in, Kendrik—well, the other place you come in."

He lifted his hands. "Oh, no. I don't think I'm welcome in the Inner Empire. I left a loooong time ago; I doubt I have any useful contacts there."

"Kendrik." Herra's tone was flat. "You're the sitting president's brother."

"As of sixty years ago," Kendrick shot back. "That's the age of our latest information from that deep in the cluster. Not exactly current news."

"Our mission into the cluster would go a lot better if we had someone who knew the lay of the land," Tangel said, watching the battle taking place in Kendrik's eyes and on the surface of his mind.

He sliced his hand through the air. "I left the Inner Praesepe Empire, not to mention my family's machinations, over a hundred and fifty years ago. I have no desire to go back."

"I understand," Tangel said when everyone at the table remained silent. "We'll do our best without you. It won't be our first time jumping into unknown territory. There's plenty to do here as well." Her gaze swept around those assembled. "That is…provided you're all in. We're not doing this unless you four support it."

"I'm in," Governor Herra said solemnly. "This will honor President Ariana's sacrifice."

"Myself as well." Admiral Kally gave a resolute nod. "Thebans for Thebes."

General Andre rolled his shoulders and sighed. "Doesn't matter to me, we're fighting the same fight no matter the flag. If resurrecting the Theban Alliance will help, then I'm in."

All eyes turned to Kendrik.

"What?" he lifted his hands in mock surrender. "Yeah. Of course I'm in. Just not going back to the IPE."

"Good." Tangel focused the holodisplay back down to the five systems comprising the Theban Alliance. “Let’s get to business, then.”

HUNT FOR ORIS

STELLAR DATE: 08.31.8949 (Adjusted Years)
LOCATION: First Fleet CIC, *I2*
REGION: Pyra, Albany System, Thebes, Septhian Alliance

"So, any luck in hunting down Oris?" Tangel asked as she stepped into the *I2*'s CIC on her morning rounds.

"Stars, I wish," Captain Rachel replied from her place at the central holotank. "When we find that traitorous bitch, I'm going to hit her so hard, her toenails are going to fall off."

<Hit her with what? Plutonium?> Tangel was masquerading as Angela, but she thought, *Maybe I should just come clean with everyone. I feel like I'm lying all the time.*

"Ever the comedian, Angela," Rachel said, as she flicked through the reports hanging to her right. "This system's a total disaster. She could be anywhere—or she could be dead, and her *body* could be anywhere…or blasted to atoms. I don't think she would have fled, though—until we came in and crushed the Niets' little party—she would have been the hero of the day."

"She'll have direct intel on Nietzschea that we can use," Colonel Borden said from the other side of the holotable. "Even though General Mill of the Marauders had extensive files on the Niets, Oris can provide a deeper level of strategic information."

"I feel like an idiot for letting her dupe me," Tangel shook her head. "I mean, I knew she was playing at something, but I suspected it had more to do with career advancement than mass betrayal of her own people to the Niets."

Rachel switched the holotank to a view of the hundred light years surrounding Thebes, and gestured at the strategic targets highlighted inside the Nietzschean borders. "Well, even if we don't find her, we have enough intel to begin operations in Nietzschea. Especially now that we have the Marauders. If Rika and her people agree to go with Finaeus's upgrades, they're going to be well-nigh unstoppable."

Tangel stared at the holo, considering various strategies against the Nietzscheans. "I won't send them on a suicide mission."

"You sound like you have a plan." Rachel left the last word hanging, and Tangel nodded in response.

"See these four systems?" she asked while highlighting a quartet of independent systems between Thebes and Nietzschea. "Chances are that the Niets who got away will regroup in one before heading back across their borders. My money is on the Sepe System, but it could be another—or all. Jump scout ships ahead of them with QuanComm blades. We'll find out where they've gone and send in a strike force to finish them off."

"Looking to deny the Nietzschean emperor any intel from the battle here?" Colonel Borden asked.

"That's secondary," Tangel replied. "I *want* him to know that we completely crushed him. Civilian sources will get him the other details before long."

<Katrina is being brought aboard,> Joe inserted himself into Tangel's thoughts. *<Shall I have her brought there?>*

<No, bring her to the cabin,> Tangel replied. *<We had a lot of good memories there—though it'll be different without Markus.>*

<Yeah,> Joe was silent for a few moments. *<I still can't believe what she went through. I'm not convinced that she's…well. Your insight will be very useful.>*

"Sorry," Tangel said to Rachel and Borden. "I have to go see Katrina."

"Say 'hi' for me," Rachel said. "I didn't know her too well back at Victoria, but she was an impressive role model."

"For myself, as well," Borden said solemnly. "Katrina was an inspiration."

"I'll relay that," Tangel said, not sharing her uncertainty about how the meeting might go. "Hopefully everything will turn out well, and she can retire on New Canaan—or take up a role with the allies. From what I gather, she has a lot of contacts in the Inner Stars, Transcend, *and* Orion."

Rachel snorted. "Yeah, flying around for five hundred years would facilitate that."

* * * * *

Tangel took an exterior maglev to Ol' Sam, riding one of the *I2*'s gossamer arcs that brought the rail close to the cylinder before shooting the car through a port on the cylinder's hull and then into the interior.

She reveled in the fact that the maglevs still relied on timing and not a-grav to effect the maneuver. If they were off by a second, the car would slam into the hull of the ship.

But they were never off. Bob saw to that.

The maglev car took her past hundreds of particle beam batteries as it passed through the cylinder's skin and into the world beyond.

Funny to think that I've spent more of my life inside this cylinder than any one other place, Tangel thought. *I wonder how much of my future will be spent here, as well.*

She doubted it would be much longer.

Though she had no intentions of leaving her family or her people any time soon, she did have a feeling that she and the *I2* may be seeing less of each other once the war was behind them.

The maglev stopped at the platform, and Tangel stepped out, breathing in the fresh air. She pulled up the transit data and saw that Katrina was just a minute away.

May as well wait, she thought, amused that even though there was now just one person in her head, she still tried to have conversations with herself. *Maybe I need an AI.*

The thought elicited a chuckle from Tangel, as she watched the maglev carrying Katrina slide to a stop.

Two ISF Marines were first out, both nodding to Tangel before they gestured for their passenger to exit. A moment later, Katrina walked out of the maglev, followed by two more Marines.

Tangel felt her heart rate quicken, seeing her old friend after so long. Granted, for Tanis, it had been fewer than twenty-five years since she'd laid eyes on Katrina. For the other woman, it had been much longer.

Katrina's hands were bound in front of her, wrists clamped to forearms, hands gripping elbows. A suppression collar was also around her neck, not controlling her, but blocking any Link access, and keeping her nano within her skin.

While the woman's expression seemed implacable, Tangel could tell there was a simmering rage beneath it. Some of it would be born from her treatment, but there was something else.

"I've missed you, Katrina," Tangel said, her voice quiet and measured. "Joe related your story to me. I'm truly sorry for what you've been through."

"But not sorry enough to grant me any measure of freedom." Katrina's voice had a hard edge, a coldness to it that drove home the centuries of struggle she'd been through.

"You may go," Tangel said to the Marines. "I have no need of your protection from Katrina. Remove her restraints first, though."

Katrina's expression softened a touch as she lifted her arms for one of the Marines to free her. "I'm glad you feel that way, Tanis. After how Joe and your daughters treated me, I wasn't sure what sort of welcome I'd receive."

Though the Marines had followed Tanis's commands, they seemed reluctant to leave their leader alone with Katrina. They didn't question her orders, but she could see the worry in their eyes.

<*Take up an overwatch position on Riker's hill,*> Tangel ordered the detachment leader. <*I don't expect problems, but I wouldn't want you to fret over me.*>

<*Yes, ma'am,*> the corporal replied before directing his team back onto the maglev.

Katrina stretched her arms out, and then ran a hand along her neck. "You have no idea how much I hate wearing collars, Tanis."

Tangel cocked an eyebrow. "I have *some* idea. Troy gave an account of what you went through in Midditerra."

"I never told Troy the half of it," Katrina said, her eyes lowered. "Trust me. It was a lot worse."

Tangel took a step toward Katrina, her eyes locked on the other woman's. She held out her hand and smiled. "The universe seems to have it in for us."

Katrina stared at the offered hand for a minute, then her eyes rose to lock on Tangel's.

"You trust me this much?" she asked. "What if I use my nano to attack you?"

"Why would you attack me?" Tangel asked with a warm smile. "We're friends."

"Didn't Joe tell you? About Xavia? She believes you have to die to save humanity."

Tangel nodded, still holding out her hand. "He did. He acted protectively, which—given how things have gone with ascended AIs of late—was a very understandable tactic on his part, but it's not *my* reaction."

"But you're not worried?" Katrina asked, still not taking Tangel's hand.

"No," Tangel answered, taking a step forward and clasping Katrina's right hand in both of hers. "Do you still feel compelled to harm me? Does Xavia still have influence over you?"

Katrina's eyes fell once more, and she stared at her hand, resting between Tangel's. Her breathing became ragged, as though she were on the verge of losing control.

"How would I know, Tanis? I've just recently learned that over the last five centuries, I've possibly been under the control of another being. I traded my captors on Midditerra for another master, and never even realized it."

"Maybe it was a crucible you needed to go through, and a punishment you needed to receive," Tangel replied.

"Shit, Tanis, that's harsh."

Tangel shrugged. "You know me. I call 'em like I see 'em."

"Yeah, I do remember that about you."

"ComeLet's go for a walk."

She continued to hold Katrina's hand. Not because she thought the other woman would run off, but because under her brusque exterior—such as it was—the older woman seemed so frail and uncertain.

Tangel turned off the well-trodden path and took the same route she'd used with Rika just the other day. They walked in silence for a few minutes before Katrina spoke up.

"Does it bother you?"

It wasn't necessary for Katrina to say what she thought should bother Tangel, she could see the direction of the other woman's thoughts on the surface of her mind. "That the AIs shaped me so much? No, it does not. Does it bother you that they did it to you too?"

Katrina barked a laugh. "Hell yes! They moved all of us around like we were pawns! They *made* you. First the Caretaker in Sol, and then Bob out in the darkness between Estrella de la Muerte and Kapteyn's Star."

"Well," Tangel said with a rueful laugh. "To be fair, Bob mucked around in my head a bit even before that."

"See?" Katrina turned to gaze into Tangel's eyes. "How can you be so blasé about all this?"

"Well," Tangel held up her other hand, one finger in the air. "For starters, Bob's intervention saved my and Angela's lives. And secondly," she lifted another finger, "everything he has done has been to keep our people safe."

"And you believe him?"

"Here are the options, Katrina. There are ascended AIs who wish to wipe out humanity—I've no direct evidence of them, but I imagine they're out there. There are some who wish to keep humanity—and most other AIs, for that matter—suppressed. That group consists of the Caretaker and his ilk. There are others, like your Xavia, who seem to want to help humanity, but very much on their terms. I lump them in the same category as Airtha. There's also a fourth category of AIs. The ones who want humanity to reach its full potential, but at its own speed. Bob is one of those AIs."

"Are you sure about that?" Katrina pressed. "He manipulated you."

"Yes," Tangel nodded. "A bit. He and I have had a chat about that, and I've forgiven him."

"Is he still shaping you?"

Tangel laughed. "You're just full of questions, Katrina. No, Bob is no longer shaping me. He's never *really* been able to do it, anyway."

"I think you're wrong about Xavia, by the way. I think she's like Bob; she just has a different way of going about things."

"Perhaps," Tangel shrugged. "I'll ask her if I ever see her."

Katrina's eyes widened. "She'll kill you. She thinks you're the pawn of the Caretaker—whether you want to be or not."

Tangel allowed a filament of her other self, the body beyond the narrow dimensions Katrina could see, to move out of her hand. Visually, it appeared to be a twisting helix of light, reaching into the air. "I'll be ready for her."

"Nooooo…" Katrina whispered. "You've ascended."

Tangel nodded. "I have, though I'd appreciate it if you kept that to yourself. Not everyone is ready for this information."

"And I am? What if I'm an agent of your enemies? Have you forgotten that whole bit where I was sent to kill you?"

Tanis released Katrina's hand and took a step away. "Do you feel compelled to kill me?"

Katrina snorted. "Well, I doubt I could manage. You'd just disappear or something."

"I'm not that sort of ascended person." Tanis shook her head. "I very much need this body to remain alive."

"I have no weapon."

Tanis pulled her lightwand from her thigh and handed it to Katrina. "Do you want to kill me?"

She took the lightwand. "Stars, been a while since I've held one of these. And, no…I don't seem to have any homicidal instincts right now. But who's to say that I won't later? There could be a trigger inside me, waiting for the right time."

Katrina activated the lightwand and held it in front of herself, her voice nearly a whisper as she said, "Maybe it would be best if I just removed myself from the equation."

Tangel's lips pursed as she regarded her old friend, a woman she'd spent decades with, striving to make a colony out of barren rock and dust at Kapteyn's Star.

"You don't really want that, do you? After all this time, just to fall on your sword?"

Katrina turned off the lightwand. "Well, technically it's *your* sword."

"Do you feel like you can be trusted?" Tangel asked as she took the lightwand back.

A long sigh escaped Katrina's lips. "Honestly, I really don't know. If I'm not going to end myself, maybe we'd all be better off if I just went away."

"I could reach into your mind and be sure," Tangel said quietly. "But *I* don't need the assurance. You do, and I don't know that you'd accept my word."

Katrina's eyebrows knit together. "Yeah, I don't think I need more beings rooting around inside my head, telling me that I'm 'OK'—no offense, Tanis."

"None taken. I don't like the idea either."

"Soooo…" Katrina said, letting the word trail away.

"Yeah?" Tangel asked, as they walked along the edge of the orchard behind Tanis's lakehouse.

"So, Angela is usually more talkative than this…and you're ascended now…." Katrina fell silent, letting the words hang between them.

"We've stopped pretending we're separate people," Tangel replied with a smirk. "Though we're keeping up appearances for everyone else—which might not be a good idea. It's hard to gauge."

Katrina whistled. "I assume one was a catalyst for the other?"

"Yeah, merging triggered our ascension," Tangel said simply.

"And you still go by 'Tanis'?" Katrina laughed. "I'm surprised that the Angela part of you allows that."

"Well, that's just the subterfuge. We're using 'Tangel' for those in the know."

" 'Tangel', huh? I kinda feel like Angela gets more letters there. Which makes sense, she was always kinda pushy."

"Hey!" Tangel said in mock indignation. "At least half of me resents that."

"That much, eh?"

The pair reached Tangel's back porch, and they climbed the wooden steps, entering the house to see Cary walking out of the kitchen with a glass of orange juice. She froze in her tracks, eyeing Katrina's lack of restraints.

"Uh…Moms?"

" 'Moms'. Cute," Katrina chuckled.

Tangel lifted a hand. "It's OK, Cary. Katrina isn't under any aegis. She's safe."

Cary's lips pressed into a thin line, then she swallowed and gave an embarrassed smile. "I'm sorry about how things started with us. I hope you can forgive us."

Katrina nodded slowly. "Myself as well. I…I regret a lot of things. Try as I might, that list just keeps getting longer."

"Well…I'm sorry we were so…harsh," Cary added hesitantly. "I felt bad about that afterward. I know Saanvi did too."

"I still miss her in my mind," Katrina said after a moment. "Xavia's memory, that is. Is that odd?"

"I don't think so," Cary said. "I've had Faleena with me for just over a year, and I'm going to miss her a lot."

Katrina glanced at Tanis and then back at Cary. "I take it you two are separating to avoid following too closely in your mother's footsteps?"

"Perceptive," Tangel said with a laugh. "Yes, there's a risk that if some sort of catalyst occurred, Cary and Faleena may intertwine."

"Like mother, like daughter," Katrina said, a genuine smile gracing her lips.

"Would you like to join us for supper?" Cary asked Katrina. "Saanvi will be here soon. We're going to have a little family cookout down at the lake before we go back to New Canaan later tomorrow."

"Leaving so soon?" Tangel asked. "I thought you were staying on another week."

Cary sighed, tilting her hips and shaking her head. "Yeah, Dad said we've lost enough time in our schooling already. He's sticking to this whole 'you must graduate with flying colors' punishment."

Katrina snorted. "Tanis—er, Tangel…you realize she's your spitting image when she does that, right?"

"She's like me in a lot of ways," Tangel replied before turning to Cary. "I'll see if I can convince your father to let you stay a bit longer. I'd like to spend more time with you—and to see Faleena after you two separate."

"I'd like that very much," Cary and Faleena said in unison, both daughters adding a laugh at the end.

"Stars," Tangel murmured, unable to keep the mirth from her voice. "That's unsettling."

COOKOUT

STELLAR DATE: 08.31.8949 (Adjusted Years)
LOCATION: Ol' Sam, ISS *I2*
REGION: Pyra, Albany System, Thebes, Septhian Alliance

"Seriously, there's no better option!" Finaeus waved his arms in the air. "Look, ask Saanvi, she'll explain the resource allocation benefits. A ring is the best option. We only stopped building them because we were tired of people breaking them."

Cary glanced at Saanvi and Finaeus, then looked to the Theban general, a man named Andre who looked like he wanted to be optimistic, but was too worn-down to put much effort into it.

The small cookout had gotten larger—which seemed to be normal for the lakehouse soirees. Even the delegation of Theban leaders had shown up to mix and mingle.

Normally she liked it, but this night, Cary had been hoping for a somewhat more intimate gathering—of course, it could also be that she felt lonely without Faleena sharing her headspace.

"It's true," Saanvi nodded enthusiastically. "Especially with the trade route with the Inner Empire—stars, now there's a group who needs a better name—we'll have everything we need. However," she paused and cast an appraising eye at Finaeus. "From what we learned in school, the FGT stopped building planetary rings because you worked out other methods for stabilizing a planet's climate without the use of a ring."

"Well, yeah," Finaeus shrugged. "But people *were* breaking them. Over a hundred planetary rings were destroyed during the FTL wars, and many more in the dark ages that followed. Rings, it turns out, are a great way to destroy a planet, via sabotage, or misuse. Sorta defeated the purpose."

"So why build one now?" Cary asked, a questioning eyebrow raised.

Finaeus flashed one of his signature grins her way, and she found herself growing ever more enamored of this man. Not in any sort of amorous sense…

Well, maybe, but I'm not going to home in on Cheeky's guy.

Attractive in his lanky, rugged way or not, Finaeus was more like the fun uncle that livened up the whole party when he arrived. The fact that he always looked like he'd be more at home on a ranch herding bison than building some of the largest megastructures ever created was all part of the man's charm.

He also had the best stories, and he never left any of the juicy parts out.

"Habitation, and the refugees," Finaeus answered simply. "You know that. The planet below is a mess, and non-ring terraforming techniques take a lot longer to pull off. Sure, we could do it with a diffuse array of satellites on the quick-ish, but that doesn't solve the living space issues. Not to mention that Hudson is going to have some brutal winters, from the atmospheric dust the battles there kicked up.

"Nope, ring's our best bet. Bring these people out of the stone ages, too."

Saanvi laughed at Finaeus's last statement. "I think the Albany System is nice—or it was, from the vids we've seen."

General Andre sighed, giving his head a rueful shake. "I'm not sure whether to be delighted or offended."

<Three words, Cary,> Saanvi said privately. *<Planetary stasis shield.>*

<Shit, are you serious?>

Saanvi sent over a mental shrug. *<Finaeus is being tight-lipped, but I have my suspicions.>*

Cary realized that no one was speaking aloud and stammered out. "Well, stone ages or no, their mechs are pretty impressive. Without Rika and her people…"

"Rika's not from here, though," Finaeus corrected, jabbing a thumb over his shoulder. "She's from Genevia, about sixty light years thataway."

"Fin," Cary chided. "We're three thousand light years from home. Sixty or so 'thataway' still counts as local, so far as I'm concerned."

Andre grabbed a sandwich from a passing servitor and chewed silently while shaking his head in disbelief.

Finaeus shrugged. "I suppose. Total agreement, though, the mechs are damn impressive. Not their tech—that shit's brutal—but their fighting spirit. Not often you see people who've been so utterly crushed, claw their way back up and then proceed to kick some serious ass. Leastwise not in such a short period of time."

Saanvi's eyes narrowed as she regarded Finaeus. "You've got thinking face. I can see it."

Finaeus lowered his eyebrows and scowled at Saanvi. "I've always got thinking face. Thinking is my superpower."

"I wonder who'd win in a think-off?" Cary gave Saanvi a slow wink. "Finaeus or Earnest?"

Saanvi snorted, and Finaeus adopted a hurt expression.

"I think they'd merge into some sort of super-being and invent a whole new universe," a voice said from behind them.

Cary turned to see a lithe woman with long, red hair, threading her way through the crowd standing on the lawn. Beneath her russet locks, the woman's skin was a light green, and yellow eyes rested atop high cheekbones.

Her lips were a deep red, matching the faint whorls that covered her body, only partially obscured by the simple white shift she wore.

It was easy enough for Cary to identify the woman by her voice, but the eyes sealed her recognition. She had seen them in her mind a million times.

"Faleena!" Cary cried out and raced toward her sister, crashing into her and spinning her around. "Look at you! You look amazing!"

"Going for a dryad sort of appearance?" Saanvi asked, as she approached and waited for Cary to give her a turn hugging their sister.

"Some of my best work," Finaeus said as he approached. "Well, not best-best; that was Cheeky."

"Do you only make bodies for attractive women?" Cary asked, giving Finaeus an appraising look.

"What?" Finaeus's face took on a wounded expression. "Well, I've never had someone come and ask me to make an ugly body. Plus, I do male builds, as well. Stars, I made this one, and it's amazing." He gestured to his torso, lowering his hand as though showing off a work of art.

"You made that body? I thought you were all-natural?"

Finaeus barked a laugh. "Cary, really. I'm almost seven thousand years old—over five of those out of the freezer. There's not much original equipment left here."

"Yeah, but did you make a whole new body for yourself?" she

asked.

"Sure, this is actually my third. And no, I'm not an AI; I still have my original brain…mostly. That thing's precious cargo." He rapped a knuckle against his head.

"Well, I'm pleased with my form, and I thank you for doing such excellent work," Faleena said with a slight nod to Finaeus.

Cary wrapped her arms around her sister once more, absently noting that General Andre had wandered off to speak with their mother. "Stars, I sure miss having you in my head, Faleena."

<I'm just a thought away,> she replied. *<And you need to develop what you can do without me or Saanvi. We're holding you back.>*

A slow breath escaped Cary's lips, and she nodded while letting go of her younger sister. *<I know. You're right, maybe. But I still miss you.>*

<I miss you too, but it's kinda nice not having to go ***everywhere*** *with you.>*

<What? I thought you liked hanging with me.>

Faleena placed a hand on Cary's shoulder. *<I did, but a girl's gotta grow up at some point. Plus…I'm glad not to have to go into the san with you anymore.>*

Cary groaned at the comment. *<You're just a two-year-old, and your humor proves it. You need my constant supervision.>*

"OK, you two," Saanvi rolled her eyes. "You can have your special chat later, c'mon, let's get to the firepit before all the marshmallows are gone."

"Is such a thing even possible?" Finaeus asked. "I think that's one of the signs of the apocalypse."

CORSIA

STELLAR DATE: 09.02.8949 (Adjusted Years)
LOCATION: Medbay, ISS *Andromeda*
REGION: Pyra, Albany System, Thebes, Septhian Alliance

Corsia opened the eyes on her organic frame and swept her gaze across the room. Though nothing within the medbay was different from how the room had appeared before she shifted her consciousness, the change in perception was profound.

Seconds ago, the room had been a part of her body, a cell in the macrocosm that was the ISS *Andromeda*. Now it was a thing that she occupied, an outward boundary, not an inner container.

She lifted the frame's hand and unfurled the five fingers, marveling at the care it took to do slowly and not in a single, abrupt motion.

"You look good," Jim said from where he stood, a warm smile on his face. "Not as good as *Andromeda*, but still good."

Corsia opened her mouth and tried to speak. "Youf sfs I—" she paused, then responded with her mind. <*Stars…how do you humans even do that? It's all just wind.*>

A laugh escaped Jim's lips, as he walked toward Corsia and placed his hands on her shoulders, the sensation sending an electric tingle through her body. "You're the one that picked an organic frame. You could have gone with a mechanical one."

Corsia shrugged, unable to hold back a shudder as Jim ran his hands down her arms, and clasped her digits in his own. <*Gah, uncontrolled sensory input, how do you deal with it?*>

Jim shrugged. "We build up patterns to manage the input. You know this."

"Yeah," Corsia managed to say aloud. <*But knowing it apparently was not sufficient to understand. I'm never going to give our organic children a hard time again.*>

"They're going to be shocked to see you like this," Jim said as he waved a holomirror into existence, and Corsia looked her frame over—from the inside out, not the outside in.

She'd picked a body that matched what she thought a strong,

matriarchal woman should look like. Lithe, square shoulders, not too full in the hips or breasts, the body of a person in motion, trim and fit.

Silver eyes rested atop high cheekbones, divided by a long, straight nose. It was perhaps a hair too large, but Corsia liked that. It was distinctive. Her lips were full and red, but not too wide, and her brow, while stern, sloped gently to meet her silver hair.

<*I look correct,*> Corsia said with a nod.

"You somehow managed to make a woman's body look like a starship," Jim replied. "That's no small feat."

<*Just wait to see where I secreted the lasers.*> A smile toyed at Corsia's lips, and she found that the expression was appealing.

A guffaw escaped Jim's lips as he placed a hand on one of Corsia's breasts. "In here?"

<*Where else?*>

"You know," Jim said wistfully. "I haven't touched a woman's breasts in centuries."

<*What about that time you caressed my antimatter bottle?*> Corsia chuckled.

"Oh, funny now, are we?" Jim asked with a shake of his head.

<*May I enter?*> Tanis asked, and Corsia said 'yes' at the same time that Jim said 'no'.

Seconds later, the admiral strode into the room, nodding to both. "You know, Corsia, following Sera's example doesn't really fit the ISF dress code."

<*You're the one that walked in on me, Tanis,*> Corsia countered.

"You invited me," she reminded the AI, rolling her eyes while Jim handed Corsia a loose robe.

"Here to see us off?" he asked.

"Yes, and to make sure you don't do anything crazy. Negotiate the deal, establish the station and gate route, and then come back. We'll send the gate team once you have an agreement in place."

Something in Tanis's voice seemed off to Corsia, as though she had a respiratory illness of some sort—though Corsia knew that wasn't possible. Tanis hadn't been sick once in the century they'd known one another.

"Are you worried?" Jim asked before Corsia could voice a concern—something that annoyed her. Organic vocalization systems were frustratingly slow.

"No." Tanis shook her head. "I just need you for another mission as soon as this is over. I plan to send an advance fleet to the Pleiades, and I want you to lead it." She directed the last statement to Corsia.

"Me?" She couldn't hide the shock in her voice; yet another thing she'd have to work on.

A twinkle of mischief was in Tanis's eyes. "Well, Jim's a master chief, which holds a lot of respect, but I don't think there's a direct path from there to Admiral."

"Shift," Corsia whispered. "Er…shit." She switched from audible speech. *<Are you messing with me, Tanis? You've seemed a bit off ever since you came up from Pyra.>*

A momentary look of worry flashed across Tanis's features, but then she resumed her usual serene appearance. "I'm a bit…changed by the experience, but in this case, all is well. On top of the promotion to Admiral, I'm putting you in command of the Seventh ISF fleet, which will be bolstered by elements from the TSF's 9801st."

"Holy crap," Jim shook his head, then winked at Corsia. "About time Tanis saw your brilliance."

"Well, first you have to deal with this little jaunt to the IPE. With luck, it shouldn't take more than a week or two at most. We'll have a gate ready once you give the word."

"OK," Corsia nodded, speaking slowly. "I'll square away things in the Inner Praesepe Empire, and be ready to head to the Trisilieds before you know it."

"Excellent," Tanis replied. "Find a uniform and meet me in your officer's mess. We'll celebrate your promotion with a BLT. Trust me, you're never going to leave your organic body again after you have one."

Corsia laughed and shook her head. "Yes, ma'am."

* * * * *

A few hours later, Corsia stood on the bridge of the *Andromeda,* soaking in the new experience that was standing *inside* the heart of her ship.

<You seem uncertain,> Sephira said, as Corsia ran a hand along the command chair.

<*Pardon?*> Corsia asked, raising an eyebrow and glancing at the ship AI's holoimage like she'd seen organics do.

<*Um…oh! 'Ma'am'. Sorry, Mom.*>

Corsia sighed as she glanced at the holographic image that her third youngest daughter preferred to project.

<*The* Andromeda *is no simple posting, Sephira,*> Corsia admonished. <*This is one of the most storied ships in the ISF. We've seen more engagements than any other vessel in the fleet, and we have a reputation to uphold.*>

<*I'm sorry, mo—ma'am,*> she said again. <*I thought since it was a private conversation… I guess I'm a bit nervous. You've been ship's AI on the* Andromeda *since the first day it set out in the black. You've a big shadow to get out from under.*>

Corsia pursed her lips, another gesture she'd seen organics make with great frequency.

<*It's OK, Sephira. This is a bit odd for both us. I feel…blind, trapped inside what used to be my body. I know I could simply reach out and use the ship's sensors and systems like always, but I want to get used to limiting my input to that of this body.*> She winked at her daughter. <*Besides, if I flood the ship's systems with my mind, it's not really fair to you.*>

<*You can if you want, ma'am. We always did it to you as kids.*>

Corsia nodded. <*I probably will eventually, but let's both get our bearings first. It would be good for me to better understand how organics operate within these small shells, so I can better understand the captains that will be under my command.*>

<*Yes, ma'am.*>

<*Sephira,*> Corsia said after a moment's pause.

<*Yes?*>

<*I suppose you can call me 'mom' when it's private like this. Just…not when we're in the thick of things, whatever those things may be.*>

Her daughter's holoimage smiled and sketched a salute, clueing the rest of the bridge crew in to the semi-private conversation.

<*Understood, Captain Mom.*>

<*Give them a centimeter…*> Corsia muttered as she smoothed out her uniform and sat in the command chair.

The action reminded her of another thing she had a new appreciation for: clothing.

It was more than a little distracting. She could feel its constant pressure on her skin; brushing, pulling, tugging. Humans were used to things touching their skin, and had learned to tune it out, but to her, the sensation was not dissimilar to flying through a cloud of dust at half the speed of light.

I think I understand why Sera and Cheeky prefer to be naked.

Not for the first time in the past few hours, Corsia considered swapping into a non-organic frame, but she ruled it out. Learning how a human body worked from the inside would be a good experience.

Really…it will be. Stick with it, Corsia.

Besides, she could tell that Jim was quite excited about the prospects for later.

<*We've a guest,*> Sephira announced a minute later, while Corsia was still deep in thought about her current situation and its implications. <*It would seem that Tanis managed to convince Kendrik to join us after all.*>

<*Well, now,*> Corsia said as she pulled up the view of the docking umbilical. <*There he is. Armed guards and all. What does he think he needs them for?*>

<*I can ask him,*> Sephira replied.

<*No, direct Lieutenant Ryni to check him and his guards over for anything nefarious, and then see them to quarters in officer country. I'll reach out to him to meet once he's settled.*>

<*Yes, ma'am, Mom.*>

<*I've created a monster.*>

Half an hour later, Corsia was waiting in her ready room—a space that hadn't been used since she'd taken over as captain of the *Andromeda*. She was surprised to see that some of Joe's souvenirs from the Kap were still on a shelf.

I wonder if he wants those back.

There was a sharp knock, and Corsia waved the door open to see Kendrik enter alone.

She rose and walked around her desk, extending her hand.

"Mister Kendrik, it is a pleasure to meet you."

Kendrik held out his own hand and shook hers, his eyes traveling up and down her body, and coming to rest on her face by the third shake.

"Yourself as well, Captain Corsia. I—" He paused, clearly flustered.

"Yes?" Corsia asked, practicing her arched eyebrow gesture once more.

"I'm sorry, there must have been a mistake in the brief the ISF gave me. I was led to believe that you were an AI."

Corsia gestured to the chairs in front of her desk. Kendrik sat, and she joined him. "I *am* an AI, I'm just using an organic frame at the moment."

The man's eyes grew wide, and he whistled before responding. "I have some pretty good tech in my peepers, Captain Corsia, and from what I can tell, your body is more organic than mine is. It even seems to have a brain."

"Just there to fool scan," Corsia replied with a wave of her hand. "I understand that folks in the Inner Praesepe Empire may not be…receptive to an AI leading the delegation meeting with them. I aim to put them at ease."

Kendrik frowned, nodding slowly. "I see. Well, it should fool them, but if they do find out you are an AI, it may damage your negotiations."

"I had wondered about that," Corsia said. "I'm glad you're along; you should be a great asset in dealing with any issues that arise in that regard."

A laugh escaped Kendrik's throat. "Well, the issues that arise could be that they'll kill us all…or maybe just tell us to leave. If my brother Arthur is still running the show, it's hard to say. He can be…volatile."

"The information I have hints to that, as well," Corsia replied. "I have to admit, the idea of the IPE operating within the cluster—living as though the rest of the human race barely exists—is an interesting one."

"Yeah," Kendrik nodded, his eyes darting to the left, then closing for a moment. "Things are a lot different, deep in Praesepe. With no FTL routes within sixty light years of the tidal core, very few people within ever venture out. I'm probably one of only a few hundred."

"So the IPE only trades with other systems inside the cluster?" Corsia asked. "They don't operate their own trade routes out?"

"No," Kendrik replied. "You should know how it is, you were born pre-FTL, right?"

"I was," Corsia replied simply.

"Well, I imagine it wasn't much different then. In the core, people travel one, maybe two hops away from their home star. The empire itself is really only that in name. The furthest its influence reaches from the cluster's center is maybe twenty-five light years. That's not much different than the *Intrepid*'s initial journey to New Eden."

"True," Corsia agreed. "But they have Antimatter-Pion drives. Makes the trip a lot quicker."

"Sure, but who wants to go on a fifty-year round trip just to deliver some cargo? In all honesty—despite how it tries to make itself seem—the IPE is less an empire and more a series of trade agreements. The common monetary system is really the backbone of the whole thing."

Corsia nodded absently as she took in the man before her. He seemed like a calm, controlled person. One not given to flights of fancy, or illogical behavior.

"So what caused you to brave the journey out of the cluster's slow zone?" she asked.

A smile formed on Kendrik's lips. "Captain Corsia, there's a whole galaxy out here to be explored. Countless worlds, systems, cultures. Why live my life in a single star system when there are millions?"

"And yet, you stayed here, right on the edge of the cluster."

Kendrick's smile faded ever so slightly. "Well, the galaxy is a bit bigger than I thought. Turns out that I didn't really want to explore the whole thing, just needed a bit more room to stretch my legs. Plus…"

"Plus?" Corsia urged.

He gave a soft laugh. "I met a woman who I love a lot more than the idea of travel. I settled in Thebes and put down roots."

Corsia nodded. "I don't know love the way you do, but I understand how it can shape a person."

"Right. I read the brief on the team going in. Couldn't help but notice that your husband is the chief engineer, and your daughter is the ship's AI. I thought the military frowned on familial relations working together?"

"We didn't start out as a military venture," Corsia replied evenly. "Plus, our population is small. It would be hard to ensure families remained apart—which seems like a horrible thing to do, anyway. When it comes down to it, *Andromeda* is a family. Most of the people aboard have been together for decades—more than a few are married, or in partnerships."

"Doesn't that create personnel issues?"

"Sometimes, but not as often as you'd think. You have to remember, the people who signed on for the *Intrepid*'s colony mission were all smart, enterprising individuals, who were stable, hardworking and well-rounded. We're not the sort to let petty differences get between us—especially when we've been through so much together."

Kendrik shook his head in denial. "It's hard to believe you're such an evolved group of people. No strife at all."

Corsia snorted. "Luckily, we have enough coming at us from the rest of the galaxy that we don't need to go seeking it out. I won't say there aren't disagreements, but we're all working toward the same goal."

"You're a very fascinating people," Kendrik said with a slow nod, pausing before he asked, "When will we be…jumping?"

"Just over two hours," Corsia replied. "We need to get our return gate components loaded up and checked over for transport. Don't want to be stuck in the slow zone."

She winked as she said the last, and saw Kendrik pale.

"Don't worry, Kendrik. If we don't come back on time, they'll send another ship and gate for us."

"That obvious?" he asked.

"A bit. You have a family out here, and you don't want to be separated from them. I understand that all too well."

A request came from someone outside the door, and Corsia accessed the ship's optics to see that it was Terrance Enfield.

She opened the door and stood to greet the man, a look of surprise on her face.

"Corsia," Terrance said with a broad smile. "It's good to meet you in the flesh at last. And Mister Kendrik, a pleasure, to be sure."

"What are you doing here?" Corsia asked as Terrance shook each of their hands in turn.

"Well, I wanted to come see Tanis after her incident, so I caught a supply ship out here. We got to talking, and she mentioned this venture." Terrance paused and winked at Corsia. "I've been feeling a bit cooped up back at New Canaan while everyone else is traipsing about the galaxy."

"You're not…the Terrance Enfield who was born in Alpha Centauri back in the thirtieth century, are you? The pioneer of interstellar trade?" Kendrik asked, his eyes wide with disbelief.

Terrance glanced at Corsia, giving her a smug nod before smiling at Kendrik. "Yes, yes I am, thank you for knowing about that."

Kendrik chuckled. "Well, growing up in a place without FTL, we spent a lot of time studying how you set up Enfield's trade routes in the fourth millennium. People write dissertations on what you did back then."

"I'm flattered. I must say, I'm looking forward to this. Negotiating trade deals with an isolationist star system...this brings me back," Terrance said, rubbing his hands together. "Tell me, Kendrik, what sorts of trade arrangements do you think will be appealing to your brother?"

"OK, OK," Corsia raised her hands. "I have a ship to inspect, and a jump to prepare for. You two are welcome to use my ready room, here. We have a strategy meeting planned after we jump, so don't talk yourselves out before then."

Terrance laughed as Corsia made a hasty exit. "No fear of that, Admiral, this is my version of *fun*."

STX-B17

STELLAR DATE: 09.02.8949 (Adjusted Years)
LOCATION: TSS *Regent Mary*
REGION: STX-B17 Black Hole, Transcend Interstellar Alliance

"Have any coins?" Earnest asked Krissy with a wink.

"What? Coins?" Krissy scowled at the engineer where he stood at the front of the *Regent Mary*'s bridge. "Whatever for?"

Earnest waved a hand at the shrouded form of the black hole at the center of the star system. "For the oarsman, of course. We'll need to pay him to cross the River Styx."

Krissy shook her head. "Earnest, I have no idea what you're talking about."

"Nevermind, that's my usual experience," he said with a laugh. "Quite the sight, though. I've never seen a black hole with my own eyes."

<*And you still haven't,*> Hemdar said. <*Both because you're looking at a holo, and because you can't* **see** *a black hole.*>

Earnest shrugged. "True enough. But I can see the event horizon and, wow, this thing is feeding something fierce."

Krissy nodded in agreement. She had passed through systems with black holes before, but STX-B17 was much different than other black holes. It was a recently—astronomically speaking—collapsed star of over one hundred solar masses that was still in the process of devouring its stellar system.

Given that most black holes lose mass during the process of collapse, they rarely consumed their orbiting planets, but STX-B17 was different. Back when it was a massive B-Class star, it had blasted out an exceptionally fierce stellar wind. Now that the wind was gone, the planets were all drifting toward the black hole's event horizon, being torn apart one by one.

At present, it was shredding a Neptune-sized planet, drawing mass off the ice-giant as the world screamed around the outer edge of the black hole, the matter from the planet glowing brighter than a G-Class star as it was torn apart at the sub-atomic level before being devoured by the black hole.

"At least we'll have light," Krissy said after a minute of staring at the view of the event. "For a few thousand years, at least."

"I'd have thought you'd be used to sights like this…what, with running your dwarf star mine for the last few decades," Earnest replied. "That must have lit up the night."

Krissy barked a laugh. "It was like living on the rim of an active volcano. Honestly? War is less stressful…mostly."

"You know…" Earnest began stroking his chin as he stared at the black hole and the planet it was slowly consuming. "I wonder if we could mine *that* thing."

"The black hole?" Krissy didn't bother hiding the incredulous tone in her voice. "Why in the stars would we do something like that? We can just keep mining white dwarfs."

Earnest had a twinkle in his eye as he grinned at Krissy. "We've already played around with starlifting in New Canaan—you know, pulling matter directly off a star. Thing is, stars are pesky. They're hot and blasting out radiation, plasma, CMEs, all that garbage. A black hole doesn't have any of that, and it's no more massive than the star it started out as."

"Well, this black hole is a lot larger than your usual three-solar mass one. Pulling resources out of a gravity well like that would be more than a little troublesome. That's assuming you could even figure out how to extract matter from a black hole. I don't think I've ever heard anyone even theorize about that."

Earnest shrugged. "Just a thought. You're right, though. White dwarfs or neutron stars are better to work with. Smaller gravity well. OK, so let's take a look at our new home away from home."

As he spoke, Earnest flipped the view on the *Regent Mary*'s forward display to show their current destination, a planet bearing only the name 'STX-B17 O9'.

It was a gas giant, massing at just under 3MJ. Its placement, over eleven AU from the roiling cauldron that was STX-B17, meant that it would eventually slide closer and closer to the black hole it now orbited, and be consumed, just like most of the other planets already had been.

But for now—and the next billion years or so—the planet was safe.

"There she is, all light and puffy and full of tritium and helium-3, just waiting for my tender ministrations," Earnest said with a chuckle.

<*It's a planet, not a lover,*> Hemdar chided.

"And that's why you've called me in," Earnest replied. "You need someone who knows how to treat her right. Which reminds me, we need to give this girl a name. We can't just call it STX-B17 O9. How about Styx Baby 9?"

Krissy snorted. "There's no way I'm setting up a secret staging ground and giving it that name."

"Why not?" Earnest asked. "No one would *ever* think that's what it was. Perfect codename."

Hemdar laughed over the audible systems. <*OK, he does have a point there.*>

"Tell me again what you want us to check for," Krissy instructed Earnest. "You want a deep scan of the planet to determine the density of the hydrogen ocean?"

"Yeah, if my estimations are correct, the atmosphere of this jovian should be only fifteen hundred kilometers deep, and there should be a more marked transition to the 'surface' of the planet than is normal in gas giants."

"Forgive my curiosity, Earnest, but what does this have to do with building our staging grounds around the planet?" she asked.

Earnest cast her a conspiratorial glance. "*Around* the planet? I thought this was to be a super-secret base?"

"Right, it is."

"Well, then. We'd be far better off to build it *in* the planet."

<*Pardon?*> Hemdar asked a moment before Krissy could utter something similar.

"Isn't that why you brought me? You wanted something out of the ordinary." Earnest glanced at Krissy, and then back to the view of the planet.

"Not exactly, Earnest. We're having New Canaan build this base because Justin's little attack has given me trust issues. I want to set this up and have it operational before even my own fleet knows about it."

Earnest shrugged. "Well, you're still getting a 'Redding Special'. I don't do hum drum." He paused and rubbed his hands. "If the ocean's dense enough, we'll build grav pontoons and set them on the 'surface' beneath the clouds. Then we build a superstructure atop them, and then fire up a-grav fields to hold the atmosphere back. We'll run CriEn modules for energy—we'll be well below the thresholds—and then we set the gates up right inside the planet."

<*That doesn't seem feasible,*> Hemdar interjected. <*You can't jump reliably that close to a planetary mass. At least not one that big.*>

"Ahhh...that's what *they* tell you," Earnest wagged his finger. "But we can compensate for the gravitational shift. We can even bend the jumps around the black hole, though that shouldn't be necessary right now—Airtha is in the other direction."

"Is this some sort of new math?" Krissy asked. "I'm not jumping ships out of gates inside a 3MJ planet just because you tell me you can compensate for it."

Earnest glanced over his shoulder at Krissy. "I'll have Finaeus send you the details, but he's worked out a means to deal with it—all part of his plan to set up a trade route with Star City."

<*What's Star City?*> Hemdar asked.

"Crap...uhhh...forget I said anything. Let's get that scan going."

Krissy leant back in her chair, steepling her fingers as she considered Earnest's slip. *She* had been briefed on the existence of Star City—the massive dyson-style sphere on the far side of the Stillwater Nebula in the Perseus Arm of the galaxy. If Finaeus was working on a way to jump through that nebula, then maybe he *had* solved the issues surrounding gates and masses well enough for Earnest's plan to work.

Granted, she thought, chuckling to herself. *My father's been known to take some serious chances. We'll test the hell out of those gates with probes first.*

TRENSCH

STELLAR DATE: 09.02.8949 (Adjusted Years)
LOCATION: Bridge, ISS *Andromeda*
REGION: Trensch System, Inner Praesepe Empire

Corsia stood on the bridge, surveying the Trensch System—not with the ship's sensors and feeds, but with her organic eyes, examining the images displayed in a holotank.

It was an interesting shift in perception, one she hadn't quite expected.

Normally when she flew into a star system, she felt as though she was *in* it—even if the ship rested at the system's periphery. But looking at the system only via the image in the holotank, it created a feeling of being above the star system, somehow separated from it.

She wondered if other organics felt the same way. It would be interesting to query them at a later date, to better understand how they viewed stellar cartography and their place in it.

"Home, sweet home," Kendrik said before laughing. There was a rueful note in his voice when he cast a glance at Corsia. "You know, I never intended to come back here. Never thought I'd see it again."

"Well, you are just seeing an image of the system," she replied. "You could have viewed that anywhere."

"Are you teasing me?" Kendrik asked with another laugh. "I really can't tell with you."

Corsia hadn't been, but she realized how he might see it that way. "I was just stating a fact. You'll have to forgive me, I'm only a day and a half into having a body; I have to remember that people look to my facial expressions for cues regarding my intent. There's a lot of work involved in being an organic."

"Never thought of it like that before," Kendrik replied. "Well, I'd wager that, by and large, you're doing better than I would on my first day as an AI."

"Glad for your approval," Corsia said.

"See! Was that sarcasm, or was that actual gratitude? You're beyond hard to read..." Kendrik paused as a smile grew on his lips.

"My brother is going to have no idea what to make of you."

Corsia wondered if that was good or bad, and purposefully furrowed her brow to show her concern. "Will that be a problem?"

Kendrik shook his head. "Not in the least, it should work nicely to our advantage."

"That's good," Terrance said as he strolled onto the bridge. "We wouldn't want our illustrious Corsia to be a fly in the ointment."

Kendrik shook his head with a smile. "Not even remotely possible."

Terrance reached Corsia and Kendrik, and peered at the system hovering before them. "So…we're thirty AU from the central star in the Trensch System, and I assume you've already sent the welcome message we prepared for the local authorities."

<It was sent as soon as we jumped in,> Sephira confirmed. *<I received an acknowledgement ping from the nearest relay just a few seconds ago.>*

Corsia considered the layout of the system and their distance from the disparate stations and worlds. While she knew what the composition of the interior of the cluster would look like, being deep within it was another matter entirely.

The core consisted of nine massive B and A-Class stars, all orbiting a common barycenter that also formed the gravitational center of the cluster. Three of the stars were within one light year of each other, and were what the inhabitants labeled as the 'Trensch System'.

With all of the cluster's stars being so young—the oldest not much over six hundred million years of age—and with the gravitational mess that the dance of so many celestial bodies made, there were few planets in stable orbits. The Trensch System only boasted five around its three stars.

The major habitats all orbited the large gas giant planets, huddled within the jovians' van allen belts for protection from the stellar storms that constantly raged around them.

"I'll admit," Corsia said after a moment, "I don't really understand why organics would live here. This place is the very definition of inhospitable. Even non-organics would need additional shielding to remain safe from the constant flare activity and CMEs."

"I won't lie, it's a part of why I left—the other part was a desire to see planets with night. But things aren't so bad within the jovian planets' magnetic shields." Kendrik gestured to the closest gas giant on the holodisplay. "There are over thirty billion people living around Genesis, and it sports one of only three terraformed worlds in the central ten light years of the cluster. Which, of course, makes it highly valuable real estate."

"That's why the IPE center of government is there," Terrance reasoned with a nod, "rather than in a more logical place like one of the nearby stellar lagrange points."

Corsia found herself in agreement. The lagrange points between the stars in the cluster's core were filled with gas, rocks, and radiation. A nearby one even had a small terrestrial planet in a decaying orbit around its center.

Kendrik gestured at the display. "Yup, that's where all the mines are. All sorts of flotsam and jetsam piles up at them, but few are stable for long. Takes a special sort of person to work those debris fields—though...something seems off."

"What do you mean?" Terrance asked.

"Well...check the star orbits. I could be imagining things, but shouldn't they be about an AU further apart right now?"

<*He's right,*> Sephira confirmed. <*The stellar orbits are off predicted paths. I can confirm that they are not exactly where cartography predicted...granted, the dance performed by stars in a cluster like this is complex—unimaginably complex.*>

"Curious," Corsia murmured as she examined them herself. "Let me know what you come up with. I wouldn't expect the IPE to be able to move stars, so maybe the core of the cluster has been more perturbed by a passing star than expected."

"Or a shift in dark matter," Terrance added. "But it should be minor. This cluster has been stable for millions of years. We only need it to keep the lagrange points relatively stable for a few cycles."

"Right," Corsia nodded. "Mine the points, build the ships. That's what we're here for," she said while looking over the mass and composition estimates. "Honestly, we'd barely need to tap these resources. You could build a million starships with the materials in just one of those mass heaps."

Kendrik nodded. "So long as you could safely access it. Like I said, those locations aren't stable; some are more like smears than heaps."

Corsia shrugged. "Well, we won't start with those."

<*Captain, we've got a ping from a local STC,*> Sephira interjected. <*Looks like an automated response from an NSAI, just giving us a vector into Genesis. It's rather perplexed that it didn't pick us up sooner, keeps asking for our interstellar route and system of origin.*>

Kendrik snorted. "They have shit NSAIs here. Just give it a fake origin and source vector. There should be a crewed STC a few light minutes away. We can pass our message to them when they reach out."

<*Captain?*> Sephira asked for confirmation.

"Do it," Corsia replied. "No point in spending our time arguing with an NSAI."

Kendrik highlighted an outer station named Hero's Point. From what Corsia could see, it was more a ball of ice with some docks attached than a station.

"That will be the crewed location for the STC. Should be hearing from them any—"

<*Right on time,*> Sephira interjected. <*Should I put it on the holo?*>

"Yes," Corsia replied, folding her arms across her chest—a gesture that felt oddly satisfying—as a tall, raven-haired woman appeared on the holodisplay.

"Starship ISS *Andromeda,* I am Colonel Akari. We have no record of you on approach to the Trensch System; it is a breach of IPE law to pass a star system's helioshock without prior authorization. We also have no records from Junction that you departed their station. Provide your departure logs immediately, and stay on your current course."

The message ended, and Colonel Akari disappeared.

"Testy," Terrance commented.

Kendrik's brow was creased as he shook his head. "That helioshock rule is new. That was not a requirement when I left."

Corsia nodded in acknowledgement. "Sephira, send this message in response. 'Colonel Akari, I am Admiral Corsia of the Intrepid Space Force. We are from a distant star system and arrived in Trensch via a new form of FTL that does not utilize the dark layer. I am sorry that we have breached your approach protocols; we were unaware that we needed to gain permission at your star's helioshock, or we would have jumped in at that point. Our mission is a diplomatic one, and we seek an audience with the IPE's leadership'."

<*It is sent,*> Sephira said after Corsia finished.

"Good," she replied. "Now we wait."

The bridge remained silent over the following six minutes, the only sounds being murmured conversations between Scan and Helm as they mapped out any potential navigation hazards in the system.

When the response came from Colonel Akari, it was a text message only: *[maintain course]*.

"Well, they've probably sent a message on to my brother," Kendrik said, stretching out his arms. "Given that Genesis is twenty-one AU away, we've probably got over three hours to kill before we hear anything back."

"Indeed," Corsia nodded at the man, before glancing at the woman at the comm station. "Lieutenant Toni, what have you picked up?"

"Admiral," Toni gave a curt nod before continuing. "There's not a lot of signal traffic that makes it out this far—these stars are noisy as heck—but I do have decent signal on a few public data broadcasts. It seems as though Kendrik's brother, Arthur, is still president of the IPE, and he is currently at Genesis. There's also some sort of political upheaval going on right now, talk of elections, and the current party in power seems to be garnering a lot of hate on the feeds."

"Oh?" Kendrik asked. "Not that I'm surprised. Arthur is more of a 'do as I say, not as I do,' sort. Tends to make him some enemies, and gets the people riled up."

"So, does he run a dictatorship?" Terrance asked. "What Sephira is pulling from the feeds doesn't seem very democratic."

Kendrik had been given access to the feeds, and was frowning as he stared into the middle distance. "Well…the IPE has always operated as a democracy—of sorts. It's at least somewhat representative. Not a shining beacon of freedom by any means, not even as good as Septhia, but it's no Nietzschea, if you take my meaning."

"Do you think your brother's changed that?" Corsia asked.

Kendrik's eyes regained focus and he glanced at Corsia. "Would it be a problem? Does the IPE have to be a pure democracy to join the Alliance?"

"No," Corsia shook her head. "It doesn't have to be a democracy at all. Most of the requirements surrounding entrance have to do with fair and equal treatment of sentients; that is not often directly related to the form of government. Honestly, a dictatorship, or tightly knit oligarchy would be better for our purposes here."

"That's...a surprising thing to hear," Kendrik said after a moment's consideration. "I would have thought that your people would be very much in favor of freedom."

"A democracy isn't about freedom, it's about representation," Corsia replied. "A people can choose representatives who strip away their freedoms—be it on purpose or otherwise—while a dictator can operate benevolently. Not that either always works that way, but do not confuse the right to vote in an election with freedom."

"Yes, in theory that is true," Kendrik replied, his tone indicating caution. "And we have ample examples of the full spectrum—but wouldn't you agree that democracies are more likely to facilitate freedom for the masses?"

Corsia nodded. "In general, yes. And different phases of a civilization's progress can require different types of governments to thrive. It's the old argument; you have to ask what is better for the individual, versus the nation-state, versus the race at large. Those interests are never in perfect alignment. AIs, for example, do not govern themselves via a democracy."

"Govern themselves?" Kendrik cocked his head. "How do you mean?"

"It's less common now, but AIs cannot utilize the same set of laws as organics. It's illogical. Yes, we share many of the same precepts, but our justice is swifter and often stronger. Not that we often need to exercise it. Most of the injustices AIs suffer seem to be at the hands of organics. Still, when it comes to our self-governance, it is more of an intellectocracy. The wisest and most logical have their voices heard and respected above others. We listen to them, and form consensus about laws and judgements. It is a process that would not translate well to organics...you don't have the attention spans for it."

"So how do you interface with human governments?" Kendrik asked.

"Do you have a week for me to explain it to you?" Corsia asked.

Kendrik gave her a quizzical look, then a smile formed on his lips. "OK, I get it. I'll lay off the questions."

"That wasn't my intent," Corsia replied, her tone light. "But I'll take the result."

Terrance chuckled. "Good call, Kendrik. AIs can make your head spin with their logic. I know that all too well."

"Well, my over-interest in AIs aside, I'll not be surprised if my brother keeps the reins tight. To call him a control freak would be an understatement."

Corsia nodded, but did not reply, wondering what the next three hours would bring.

* * * * *

"...breached the boundaries of our sovereign state without prior authorization. I have half a mind to order you to depart the Praesepe Empire at once."

Corsia glanced at Terrance and Kendrik as President Arthur droned on, seeing expressions on their faces that mirrored her own.

"A bit of a blowhard, isn't he?" she asked.

"That trait does seem to have intensified," Kendrik said while shaking his head in dismay.

Terrance only shrugged as he continued to listen to the president's recitation.

"...send an escort, and require an inspection team to examine your ship before you're allowed to dock at Minoa Station."

"See?" Terrance glanced at Corsia and Kendrik. "He's just doing all this to show us who's boss. We've just turned his entire world upside down. Until a few hours ago, no one could get into the IPE without traveling for years through the slow zone. Now he has to deal with the fact that visitors can show up at any time."

"That doesn't mean he won't be a massive pain in the ass," Kendrik replied. "As you can see, it's something he excels at."

Corsia felt her eyes narrow, taking a moment to consider how 'right' the sensation felt. "If he thinks he's going to send an inspection team into this ship, he has another think coming."

"What are you going to do?" Kendrik spread his hands. "He'll fire on you if you do anything aggressive."

"Really?" Terrance seemed surprised. "Would he attack the first visitors from outside the cluster he's ever had?"

"Well..." Kendrik drew out the word. "I wouldn't say that it's a foregone conclusion, but there's a very high probability, yes. Like you said, he feels threatened, and we've turned his world upside down. If he feels cornered, he may lash out."

Terrance turned to Corsia. "I know it's irking you, the thought of letting 'inspectors' aboard, but we can limit them to a small group. There's an entire company of Marines on the ship, and we're protected by stasis shields. There's nothing to fear and everything to gain by establishing a modicum of trust."

Corsia pursed her lips. "Very well, but if they think that they can traipse through the whole ship, they'll be in for a rather unpleasant surprise."

Terrance nodded in agreement. "Yes, of course. We're not going to let them have access to our advanced technology, that's a given. So would you like to send the response, or should I?"

"No," Corsia drew in a deep breath—one of the things that annoyed her about having an organic body, the persistent need to breathe—and rocked her head from side to side, stretching out her neck. "I sent the first message, I should be the one to reply. Consistency, and all that."

"You're also playing bad cop, here," Kendrik winked at Corsia. "Terrance comes in later to be the one to mollify them, and I'm the wild card that they wonder about the whole time."

"Plus, you'll keep your brother from spewing too much bullshit," Terrance added.

"That too."

Corsia crafted a rather abrupt message acknowledging President Arthur's terms, and informed him that a small inspection team would be allowed to dock.

Afterward, she left the conference room—where Terrance and Kendrik were discussing the details of the proposal they intended to make to the IPE—and returned to the bridge to watch Scan as a dozen destroyer-class ships undocked from Hero's Point and boosted to match velocity with the *Andromeda.*

<They're making good time,> Sephira commented privately to Corsia. *<I wonder if they really do fear us.>*

<I'm sure they feel the same way we would if a warship had suddenly appeared in the New Canaan system,> Corsia replied.

<Which did happen.>

Corsia laughed quietly, shaking her head as she did. *<I suspect that our response would have been different had it been just* ***one*** *ship.>*

<You seem to be enjoying the use of a body, Mom,> Sephira said with a note of amusement in her voice.

<It's interesting. I don't think I'll keep it long-term, but the experience is enlightening. I rather wish I'd tried it sooner.>

<I seem to recall you giving Ylonda a hard time about having a physical body—though I suppose you may have been right.>

Corsia felt a tension in her chest at the thought of Ylonda, momentarily surprised that her body would register a physiological response to unpleasant memories. The connection to her physical form's nervous system was deepening in its complexity.

<What Myriad did to Ylonda was not related to her body—if you recall, at the time, she was ensconced in a node. And she didn't really die, not the way that organics do. Even Amanda didn't die per se; they just became something else…something more.>

<Don't you miss her?> Sephira asked wistfully.

<Yes, but more because she's on the far side of the Inner Stars, not because she's gone forever. Your sister, she…she left so quickly after she became Amavia. I never really got to know them—not with everything else that was going on.>

"Captain Corsia, message from the approaching IPE ships," Comm announced. "They've assigned us an updated vector, and will be sending over a shuttle once they're within ten thousand klicks."

Corsia nodded as she reviewed the vector. It was a small shift that would have them brake around Genesis before docking at Minoa Station. It also brought them closer to several other stations that Scan had identified as defensive emplacements.

No accident there.

"Helm," Corsia nodded to the ensign at the console in front of her command chair. "Assume the vector. Ease into it, don't give them the impression that we'll jump at their every order. Scan, I want to know their armament as soon as possible. Weapons, keep the coils hot, I don't fully trust these people not to take a pot shot at us."

A chorus of acknowledgements came back, and Corsia's bridge crew set to work under the watchful eye of Sephira.

<*Enjoying the ability to sit back and relax?*> Terrance asked as he leant against a console. <*What, with Sephira embedded with the ship, you don't have to watch everything all the time.*>

Corsia sent Terrance a mental eyeroll. <*I know what you're getting at. Yes, it's hard to release control. I'm working on it. I didn't check the message Comm sent back at all, and I've only corrected Weapons once on their assessment.*>

<*You're so grown up,*> Terrance replied with a laugh. <*I still remember when you first joined us. I was pretty happy to have someone with Lysander in their lineage on the mission. Was a good omen.*>

<*I don't believe in omens,*> Corsia deadpanned. <*But I think my ten-times great grandfather would have been pleased with what we've done.*>

<*I don't believe in them, either,*> Terrance glanced over his shoulder at Corsia. <*But that doesn't stop some things from feeling 'right'. I wonder if you'll gain an understanding of that, now that you have a body.*>

<*Symmetry of ideas is not exclusive to organics,*> Corsia replied evenly. <*You should know that, you've had AIs embedded with you before.*>

<*I have,*> Terrance replied, nodding slowly. <*Been a long time now, though. Ages, really.*>

<*Perhaps it's time for you to do so again.*>

Terrance snorted. <*I think I'm too old for that now. I passed over my six-hundredth birthday last month, you know.*>

<*Finaeus has clocked over four thousand real-time years, and he mentioned that he'd love to be paired with an AI again at some point. Though I don't know who'd risk going in the rat's nest he calls a mind. Besides, with the Transcend's enhanced rejuv techniques, your life can be extended indefinitely. No worry about cognitive dissonance, or the other issues that used to crop up.*>

<*Why the urging?*> Terrance asked. <*You looking to get inside my head?*>

<No, I'm just stating facts.>

Terrance didn't reply for over a minute, staring contemplatively at the display of the Trensch System in the holotank. Corsia began to wonder if she'd offended him, when he finally replied, *<I don't know if I'd opt for an eternal life. There has to be an end, right?>*

<Why?>

<Because everything ends, Corsia. Even the universe will end.>

<Of course it will, but on any timescale we can rationally consider—yes, even for non-organics—the universe may as well be endless. Wouldn't you like to watch the whole thing evolve? It'll be fascinating.>

<Maybe. Maybe if I could skip forward in time, not slog through the whole thing. I mean…fifty trillion years just to get past the star-forming age? That's…enough to melt my brain.>

Corsia laughed. *<Well, you don't need to commit to trillions yet. Just go for a thousand, and see how you feel then.>*

<Maybe I will, Corsia. It's not like I've gotten bored yet.>

<That's the spirit.>

THE LMC

STELLAR DATE: 09.02.8949 (Adjusted Years)
LOCATION: Aleutia Station
REGION: Cheshire System, Large Magellanic Cloud

"President Sera, Governor Andrews. Welcome to the LMC."

"Peabody?" Sera asked, a smile forming on her lips as she regarded the general standing before her.

General Peabody grinned in response as he inclined his head. "In the flesh, ma'am."

"Don't 'ma'am' me," Sera said, shaking her head at the red-haired man. "I still owe you one for saving *Sabrina* at Bollam's World."

"Just doing my job, ma'am," General Peabody replied. "Glad to see you're still kicking."

"More or less," Sera replied. "Hard to believe we've not bumped into each other before now—though I guess now I know why you were nowhere to be found."

Peabody laughed as he gestured toward a dockcar that waited next to their pinnace. "Well, building a place like Aleutia doesn't really make for a lot of vacation time. But the view is worth it."

Jason nodded in solemn agreement. "I'll say. Not every day you see…well…anything close to that."

"Good ole Spaghetti Bowl," General Peabody chuckled.

"What?" Sera asked.

"Well…from outside, the galaxy doesn't look like a milky way. It looks more like a really big mess of spaghetti."

A scowl creased Sera's forehead. "No, more like a pinwheel."

"Well, blame your uncle." Peabody shrugged as he settled into his seat, and the car took off. "He's the one that coined it. I mean, if I was asked, I would have just named it 'Freaking Gorgeous'."

"Good thing no one asked you," Jason grunted, trying to sound serious, but Sera could see a smile on his lips.

"OK. Give us the lowdown," Sera directed Peabody. "What have you learned?"

The general's face lost all traces of humor, and his eyes narrowed.

"We've done close fly-bys of four systems now; there are two more that have activity in them, and we'll have scans of them soon, too. From what we can see, until very recently, the FGT was terraforming worlds, building rings, moving stuff around—their usual gig. However, our scans picked up *a lot* of defensive emplacements. Not newly installed, either, so these systems were always intended to be defensive fallbacks."

"Not surprising," Sera interjected. "You don't build out in the LMC because you want a corner on tourism trade."

"Not that that would be a bad idea," Jason said, a finger on his chin as though he were giving the idea serious consideration.

"Either way," Peabody continued. "They've stopped all terraforming activity—other than stabilizing planetary orbits. Now they're building shipyards. Some are already complete, and there are more hulls under construction."

"So which system looks to be the main one? First made, or most well defended?" Sera asked.

Peabody summoned a holo that hovered in the space between the dockcar's seats. It showed the five systems he'd mentioned, all of which surrounded a binary system that showed no indications of human activity.

He highlighted one. "This one is the most heavily defended." Then he highlighted another. "And from what we can tell, this one was first to get underway."

"What about that system?" Jason beat Sera to the punch, asking about the star in the midst of the ones showing activity. "Nothing there?"

"We've not done a fly-by of that system yet," Peabody replied. "But there is no activity visible in it—not that we've seen from five light years out."

Sera lifted her gaze from the holo and glanced at Jason—who seemed to be on the same train of thought—before replying to Peabody. "But that data is five years old. It's plain to see from this layout that they were going to create a jump gate interdiction web around that central star."

"Perhaps," Peabody said with a slow nod. "But would Airtha have done anything with it once she took over? From what I understand, she's not focused on building a fallback location, like your father was…or is she?"

Sera shook her head. "No, you're right. But my father was a paranoid man. I think he'd have still built his fallback site there before the outer defenses were created. Our goal here is to get intel, not stop Airtha's construction—well, at least not yet. Anyway, chances are that whatever he built is just sitting there, full of juicy data, waiting for us to come and pay it a visit."

"Otherwise known as a baited trap," Jason cautioned.

"Maybe," Sera allowed. "Maybe not. Airtha has no idea that we're out here as well. It'll take two hundred years for them to see what you're up to in Aleutia."

"Do you want me to divert the next scouting run to that system?" Peabody asked.

"You have…what? Seven ships capable of full stealth?" Sera asked.

"Six," Peabody corrected. "One of the stealth cruisers has been having issues maintaining concealment in heavily ionized plasma flows. Which is common out here."

"Well, then," Sera said, shifting her gaze to Jason. "Sounds like we have our strike force."

"Wait, 'we'?" Jason asked. "You're not going on the mission to that system. You're the Transcend's president. They need you."

Sera placed a hand on Jason's knee, unable to miss how his brows rose at her touch. "We both know that I'm just a bureaucrat running the home front. Tanis is really in charge back there."

Jason's face was unreadable, and Sera wondered if she'd said something wrong. Then he snorted and shook his head.

"I know how you feel. I suppose we might need you. If we *do* find a secret base in that system, it's possible that only you will be able to breach it—what, with your super-special presidential tokens, and all."

"Glad to know my value as a lockpick is recognized."

* * * * *

Less than a day later, Sera stood with Jason and General Peabody on the bridge of the general's flagship, a stealth-capable cruiser named the *Helios*.

The ship was a new design, based on the rail destroyers the ISF had fielded in the Battle of Carthage. However, instead of just two rings, the *Helios* consisted of eight rings, all meeting along a single axis point fore and aft. A central shaft ran through the ship, and at its center lay the bridge and main crew-areas.

The diameter of the generally spherical vessel was just over three kilometers. Given each ring's capacity to house billions of rail-accelerated pellets, and fire them in almost any direction, the *Helios* was a formidable vessel, and a testament to the ISF's determination to produce war-ending ships.

Sera had already put in a request for the class of vessel to be produced for the Transcend's military.

Ahead of the ship lay the jump gate, but that wasn't what Sera found herself staring at. Instead, she had a secondary holotank dedicated to the view of the Milky Way.

She'd never given any serious thought to what the galaxy would look like from this far away, but she didn't think that anything could have prepared her for how beautiful, massive, and terrifying it appeared, hanging in space like an eternal storm that dominated nearly forty-five degrees of the 'sky'.

But it wasn't its size or luminosity that amazed her, it was the fact that everything she'd ever known, all her hopes, dreams—all of *everyone's* hopes and dreams—all laid within that cluster of stars.

And that cluster was just one of many…so many.

Even though the war they were mired in spanned a significant portion of the galaxy, the view reminded her that humanity's reach was still not even a trillionth of the universe.

Space had never made Sera feel insignificant. She had always viewed space as her home, as a playground of sorts.

But this, this makes me feel insignificant.

She saw that Jason was staring at it as well, his expression one of pensive consideration.

"What do you see when you look at it?" she asked.

He didn't reply at first, but then glanced toward her and said, "The past."

"Yours, or the galaxy's?" Sera asked.

"A bit of both." Jason gave a small laugh. "In the view we see from here, homo sapiens aren't yet walking about on Earth, and so far as we know, there isn't a single spacefaring species. The galaxy we're looking at...it's pristine."

"Do you think we've sullied it?"

"No," Jason said after a moment. "I don't think it's possible for us to sully the galaxy. We're a part of its evolution. That great big whirling ball of matter spawned stars, and around those stars formed planets, and on one, some four billion years ago, life as we know it came about. We're a part of the natural evolution of a galaxy—of this galaxy, at least. Maybe we'll last as long as it does, or maybe in a billion years there won't be a single trace of us left."

"That's a morose and sobering thought." Sera let out a small laugh, trying to lighten the moment, but it fell flat. "Granted, we're out here in the LMC, now. We're not a part of *this* galaxy."

Jason shrugged. "Seems like we are now."

"I see you're engaging in the official Aleutian pastime," General Peabody said as he approached the pair.

"I take it that staring at that thing doesn't get old, then?" Jason asked, jerking a thumb at the view of the Milky Way.

Peabody shook his head. "Nope, not even a little. I wonder, though, given that the Transcend was already out here when we arrived, is there any place that our people can ever go to just get away?"

"Andromeda?" Sera laughed as she said it.

Though a jump to the LMC was something they could manage, the amount of antimatter it would take to power a jump to the Andromeda Galaxy was beyond staggering. Even CriEn modules would not be able to power such a leap.

"Wouldn't that be something." Jason's voice sounded wistful. "A whole new galaxy."

"Not happy with the one you have?" Sera asked.

"What can I say? Wanderlust is something I've always felt. You don't spend centuries plying the black at sub-light speeds if you don't like to travel."

She held up a hand to forestall further argument. "I'm not

knocking it. I don't like to sit still, either."

"That why you're out here and not back on Khardine, ma'am?" Peabody asked.

The honorific reminded Sera of the title and responsibilities she constantly carried around. She glanced toward the bridge's entrance where Major Valerie and another of her High Guard stood, constant reminders of the job Sera had so foolishly taken on that insane day aboard the *Galadrial*.

At Tanis's insistence, Sera had stopped trying to foist the responsibilities off on others—namely Finaeus and Tanis herself—but that hadn't stopped Sera from privately wishing she'd never taken up her father's torch.

Going on this mission to the LMC had been highly irresponsible—something that the disapproving looks from Major Valerie frequently confirmed—but Sera was feeling truly alive for the first time since she'd left Tanis and returned to Khardine.

Maybe I can figure out some way to effectively lead from the front, rather than hiding away in a fortress of stars.

"Jump in t-minus thirty seconds," Helm announced, and Sera turned from the view of the Milky Way to face the gate ahead. The negative energy emitters came to life, and the gate's mirrors reflected the unfathomable levels of power into a roiling mass at the gate's center.

The *Helios* boosted toward the gate, pouring on one last burst of power to give them a higher delta-*v* relative to the destination star system—designated 'Hidey Hole'.

Then the ship's forward mirror touched the mass at the center of the gate, and the *Helios* skipped forward across two hundred light years and into the unknown.

"Stealth systems engaged!" Lieutenant Aya called out the moment they re-entered normal space.

Scan collated data from the ship's passive sensors, and a view of the star system began to appear on the main holotank.

At the center was a rather pedestrian G-Class star with a red dwarf on an eccentric orbit, currently placing it two hundred AU from the primary.

Over the course of the next hour, the other six stealth ships would enter the Hidey Hole System and take up parabolic trajectories around the stars, passing by major planets and moons.

Listening.

The *Helios* was on target for the planet deepest in the star system, a terrestrial world roughly half Earth's mass. It orbited the primary at only half an AU, its surface hot and inhospitable, but protected by a powerful magnetic shield that kept the most damaging radiation from reaching its surface.

"Those are some powerful van allen belts for such a small planet," Jason observed. "I'd be surprised if they're entirely natural."

"A lot of tidal forces in this system," Sera replied, turning to the AI who was managing scan, the holo of a young man sitting at the station he had no need of. "What do you make of it, Chief Reggie?"

"Hard to say," Reggie replied, his voice emanating from his holoprojection. "Could be natural, but like Governor Andrews suggests, there are a lot of tidal forces in this system that *could* keep the planet molten and spinning inside—yet terrestrial worlds that small don't often have a core differentiated enough to create strong magnetic fields when they rotate."

"So you're saying you're not sure." Sera winked at the AI, who raised an eyebrow and shrugged.

"We're twenty AU away and using passive sensors. I'm not a miracle worker," he countered. "But if I happened to stumble across a system like this, I'd find it curious—though not enough to immediately jump to planetary engineering as the reason for the magnetosphere. Granted, with this star's position in the midst of five others undergoing stellar engineering, the opposite suspicions would form."

"That's enough for me," Jason replied, then turned toward Sera. "The one thing going against it is the tectonic activity from a molten core. Would your father pick a planet that's so...motile? Or would he go for something further out that was cold and solid?"

Sera rubbed her face. "Well, from what I can see, he started this venture befo—wait a second. If it took almost two hundred years for the light from this terraforming operation to reach Aleutia, then he started this before jump gates were made."

"Or at least *revealed*," Jason amended.

<*Now* **that's** *an interesting thought,*> Jen mused. <*It would mean Finaeus hasn't been truthful—but that seems unlikely.*>

Sera pursed her lips and drew in a slow breath. "Either way, it all predates *me*. I wonder if Andrea or Justin knew about this."

Jason's visage grew grim. "When Krissy catches up to Justin, we'll ask him."

"Keeping up on current events?" Sera asked.

"I'm of the opinion that Justin sent Andrea to kill Tanis back in the Ascella System—and that he authorized her to turn you using mentally subversive tech. If there's one thing I don't hold with, it's mental subversion. As far as I'm concerned, Justin is villainous scum."

"I'll add your theory to the list of things to ask him about—not that I expect to get much out of him without stooping to his level."

Sera looked at Jason to see him nodding in agreement. She decided to ask him at some point what reason he had for his vehement dislike of mental coercion. Not that sane people liked it under any circumstances, but there was something in his eyes. A distant pain that spoke of personal experience.

"Helm, what's the best speed you can make to that planet?" General Peabody asked.

"Sir, best speed will put us at two days' travel for a close fly-by. But we'd light up the night, braking to orbit the planet. A better plan would be to brake around the star after passing by to see if we wanted to pay it a visit. Would take…just three days to fly by, then a day to brake around the star and settle into orbit over the planet."

"Sir, ma'am?" Peabody asked as he turned to Sera and Jason.

"Well," Sera mused, tapping her chin. "We're not sure anything is there, and ruling it out sooner than later would be ideal, so we could slingshot out to other targets."

"It keeps our stealth intact, as well," Jason added.

"Stealthed fly-by and star-brake it is," Peabody said, confirming the order before nodding to Helm, who pushed the vector onto the main holo, the display showing burn points, adjustments, and countdowns to the maneuvers.

Sera looked at the timeline. "Four days. I guess I can catch up on reading the never-ending list of reports that have jammed up my queues."

Jason laughed. "Sounds like it should be riveting. I've some of the same to attend to."

Sera thanked General Peabody for letting them stand around on his bridge, and walked off, her guard stepping in behind her, followed by Jason.

*<I think I know the sorts of reporting you'd **like** to be doing,>* Valerie said to Sera as they walked down the passageway.

Sera glanced at the major to see the woman's face perfectly composed, eyes forward.

<I have no idea what you're talking about, Val,> Sera retorted.

<Really? Then you're the only one that bridge who doesn't. If you and Jason had stood any closer together, you'd've been hugging…or something else.>

Sera rolled her eyes as they reached the lift.

"You know…" Jason began as he reached her side. "I have a rather large stateroom—for a warship, at least. We could set up in my quarters and have a light meal while going over all the reports that are demanding our attention."

He uttered the words as though he was suggesting they were organizing a scientific survey, but when Sera glanced at Jason, his eyes said something else entirely.

<See.> Valerie's mental tone was completely flat.

Sera ran a hand through her hair, weighing how much she wanted to take Jason up on his offer against the tsunami of scuttlebutt it would create.

Wait…since when do I care about that? This 'president' gig is really wringing the life out of me.

"Deal," Sera replied. "Lead the way."

An easy grin settled on Jason's lips as they stepped onto the lift. "Don't worry, Sera. I plan to."

Sera nearly burst out laughing at the 'O' face Jen placed in her mind.

* * * * *

"Stars, I needed that," Sera whispered as she flopped onto her bunk half a day later—finally getting to the reports that she'd ostensibly gone to Jason's quarters to work on.

Her stomach growled, and Sera reached out to order a meal from the galley. It turned out that Jason's version of a 'light meal' consisted exclusively of beer.

For someone who presented an air of the elder statesman when on the bridge of a ship, he could really pound the brews back.

But when it came to the main event, he was far more easygoing. Then deliberate. Then…well…mind-blowing.

I guess you learn a few tricks over a thousand years.

Sera let out a long breath and closed her eyes, reliving the experience while she waited for the food to arrive.

<*You have been wound a bit tight lately,*> Jen commented. <*Was good to see you relax.*>

" 'See'?" Sera asked.

<*Well, not 'see' per se. I wandered off elsewhere. The ship's AIs have a little expanse, and we explored the options surrounding a staged series of jumps to the Andromeda Galaxy while you partook in your organic happy times.*>

"You really wouldn't do that, would you?" Sera asked, a pang of fear running through her. "Leave for Andromeda?"

Jen's laugh filtered through Sera's mind like wind rustling tall, dry grass on a high steppe. <*Well, so long as this war doesn't wipe us out, we're all going to live a long time. I wouldn't mind seeing a few different galaxies before my time's up.*>

Sera grunted softly; she hadn't ever considered that possibility before. But now, flying through the LMC, the idea of extra-galactic adventures had become much more realistic.

"What do you feel when you look up at the Milky Way?" Sera asked her AI companion.

<*Feel?*>

"Your emotional analogue. Do you get a sense of wonderment? A shift in perspective?"

<*You know we're not all the same, right?*> Jen asked.

"Huh? AIs?"

<*Yeah, we're varied. Some are more prone to 'emotional analogues', as you put it, some not at all. Just like humans are varied.*>

"So what do *you* see when you look up at our galaxy, oh one of many varied AIs?" Sera asked, a smirk on her lips.

<Vectors. Soooo many vectors. I see the orbits of the arms, the stars in the galactic disk, the halo stars, I marvel at the x-rays blasting out of Sagittarius A's poles…I wonder what exists beyond the galaxphere. Is inter-galactic space as empty as we think? Are there pockets of matter and energy that we simply can't detect unless we're there? Where* ***is*** *the rest of the universe? Why can't we see most of it?>*

"Sounds like wonderment to me," Sera said, a smile on her lips.

<I guess. I don't know if it's like yours, though.>

"You probably have more precision to your ad-hoc math than I do, but it's not that different than where my mind goes. I find myself thinking about the people, too. The conflicts we have…somehow it doesn't look so important from out here. There's so much galaxy. Why do we have to fight over our tiny corner?"

<Well, in your defense, the Transcend has never been the aggressor—by and large, at least.>

"Small mercies," Sera replied. "My father was a lot of things, but at least he was no war-monger. Then again, if he'd gone after Orion in the past, things may not have gotten to this point."

<Coulda, shoulda, woulda,> Jen gave a mental shrug, then a smirk. *<How's that for imprecision? Pairing with you has made me a lot more loosey-goosey.>*

"You mean flexible and adaptable?" Sera shot back.

<Sure, that.>

A smile formed on Sera's lips, and she closed her eyes. "Thanks, Jen."

<For what?>

"For being you, for just being a friend."

<Of course, Your Presidency.>

A laugh burst from Sera's lips, and she shook her head before rolling onto her side. "Nice one. Now stop rattling around inside my head. I'm going to fall asleep basking in this glow, and forget the mountain of work waiting for me."

<What about the food?>

"Tell them to set it on the table," she mumbled softly.

Jen didn't reply, but the feeling of warm contentment she fed into

Sera's mind was all the response the president needed.

For the first time in years, Sera fell asleep not thinking of *that* day: the day her lover killed her father, and she learned of her mother's searing betrayal.

INSPECTION

STELLAR DATE: 09.02.8949 (Adjusted Years)
LOCATION: Bay 1, ISS *Andromeda*
REGION: Trensch System, Inner Praesepe Empire

Corsia had strongly considered delegating the job of meeting the IPE's inspection team. Jim, Terrance, or even Commander Eve from the Marine company could handle the task.

Such are the trials of being the captain, she thought. *You can't delegate this sort of nonsense. Could be worse, though. I could be in Tanis's shoes.*

As Corsia was wishing she were anywhere else, the doors across the docking bay began to slide open, an ES field activating to hold the ship's atmosphere in.

Most of the new ISF ships used grav fields on their bay entrances, but the *Andromeda* had used electro-static shields for over a century, and she saw no reason to change them—especially when the ES fields were far more efficient.

Pulling a feed from the ship's sensors, Corsia watched the IPE shuttle close the final hundred meters. The thirty-meter ship was an ugly, squat thing, almost as wide as it was long.

Lucky for them, the *Andromeda* had a large central bay occupying the belly of the ship. Considering that they'd once squeezed *Sabrina*'s two hundred meters into the bay, the IPE shuttle wasn't even a snug fit.

"That's a well-armed shuttle," Jim said as he approached. "Though it looks like their firing systems aren't charged up."

<*Of course not, Dad*> Sephira replied. <*I wouldn't have let them dock if they were.*>

"I figured as much, Sephira," Jim said, a scowl lowering his brow. "Still, doesn't really bode well."

"We'll see how it plays out." Corsia looked down at her shipsuit, feeling strangely self-conscious. The sensation was entirely unfamiliar to her, and she wondered if people with bodies felt this way from time to time, or if it was just because hers was new.

"You look fine," Jim said, a smile gracing his lips. "I gotta say, though. You're totally keeping that body—if I have any input in the matter."

<*Seriously, Jim, not now,*> Corsia scolded, wishing her form wasn't so distracting to him. Sometimes it seemed desirable, other times it was as though he was unable to focus around her.

The shuttle settled onto the cradle, and the ramp rose to meet the craft's exit. A half-minute passed with no activity, and then the door slid open to reveal two armed and armored Marines who strode down the ramp, their visors hiding the direction of their gaze.

Following them, a dark-haired man stepped out of the shuttle, clothed in a light grey uniform, with a yellow IPE crest over his heart, along with several ribbons and a crescent moon medal.

Two birds adorned his lapels, and Corsia noted that each leg held a separate clutch of arrows, a particular colonel's insignia many of the militaries around Praesepe seemed to use.

Her own collar bore a single star, and the man's gaze darted to it, before his eyes lifted to meet hers.

Corsia strode forward and extended her hand. "Welcome to the *Andromeda*. I am Captain Corsia."

"Captain?" the man asked, eyes darting to her Admiral's star once more.

"It is our custom in the ISF that, in the case of a captain of a storied vessel, title supersedes rank, Colonel…" She left the address open-ended for him to complete.

"Hickson," the man replied. "I am here to oversee the inspection of your vessel."

As he spoke, a group of technicians began to walk down the ramp behind him, and the colonel stepped aside to let them pass. "We will need to sweep your entire ship before you'll be allowed to dock at Minoa Station."

Corsia pursed her lips and shook her head slowly before replying. "We will give you a walk-through of non-classified areas, and you may perform any checks that will not harm our vessel or require any physical connections or interaction with the *Andromeda*'s systems."

As she spoke, the colonel's eyes grew wide, and his jaw tensed. "You must have misunderstood President Arthur's directive. We will perform a *full* inspection of your ship."

Corsia drew herself up, the five centimeters she had on the man allowing her to stare down on him in a very satisfying fashion.

"I understand that we are within the borders of the IPE, and you have reason to fear us—the idea of ships entering your core system with no warning must be very unsettling. However, we are not at liberty to allow you full access to this ship, but we want to make every good-faith effort we can to accommodate you. Is there no way we can reach a compromise?"

"Captain Corsia." The colonel loaded the words with so much disdain, it sounded as though his tongue had withered just from uttering them. "If you were at the edge of the Trensch System, we would simply refuse you entry. But since you are this deep within the gravity well, we will consider any non-compliance as an act of aggression."

"How many ships do you have?" Corsia asked plainly. "Five hundred? A thousand? A week ago, we jumped forty thousand ships into the Albany System to bring about the greatest defeat the Nietzscheans have seen since the early days of their war with the Genevians."

The colonel's eyes grew wide for a moment, then narrowed. "Talk is cheap. Right now you have just one ship. How will you summon more?"

Corsia could feel her body responding to the man's words with an increase in heart rate, muscle tension, and a host of other physiological changes. A part of her found it fascinating, and wondered how humans managed to deal with the chemical changes in their bodies while under stress.

The rest of her wanted to punch Colonel Hickson in the face.

That urge nearly won.

She considered placing a call on the QuanComm network for another ship to jump in, but decided against it for the time being. If the IPE was being this testy about one ship, the presence of more vessels would surely escalate things.

Granted, it wouldn't be hard to simply take what we want from this system.

Corsia tamped down the thought. That was not the way Tanis wanted to operate, and it ran contrary to Corsia's own beliefs as well.

Though the idea was tempting.

She was trying to think of something to say that would diffuse the situation, when Jim spoke up.

"Colonel Hickson. You've witnessed our abilities, and we can see how zealously you defend your people—something we understand, and greatly admire. Our purpose in travelling to the Trensch System is to create a trade agreement that we think will *greatly* benefit your people. Perhaps I can escort your teams—" Jim nodded to the technicians who were standing uncomfortably to the side of the ramp, "around the non-classified areas on the ship, and they can assess whether or not we are an extreme threat, and then you can make a decision with that information in hand."

"I suppose that's a start," Colonel Hickson grunted.

"Would it also be an option for us to remain in a high orbit around Genesis instead of docking at a station?" Corsia asked, glad for Jim's interjection. "We could bring a pinnace to Minoa Station. No need to worry about a foreign warship docking."

"I suppose that could work." Though his words were noncommittal, Hickson's tone hinted at genuine surprise. "You'd have to remain outside Genesis's van allen belts. Trensch is not an agreeable star to be so close to for long periods of time."

"If we assess that risk to be too much, we can reevaluate the full inspection," Corsia replied.

"We'll proceed as you suggest, then," the colonel said, nodding to his inspection team. "But the president may decide it is not satisfactory."

Corsia nodded. "I guess we'll hope for the best."

Jim gestured to the technicians, ten in all, and they followed him out of the bay. Two more IPE Marines came down the ramp and followed after.

Corsia was tempted to deny the soldiers access to her ship without surrendering their weapons, but decided it wasn't worth the hassle. Sephira was already dropping a nanocloud onto their armor and weapons to disable them, should the need arise.

"Would you like a tour of the bridge?" Corsia asked the colonel. "Something to while away the time?"

The man's eyes actually widened in surprise before he schooled his expression. "Certainly, lead the way."

Corsia led the colonel through the ship, Marines from his delegation coming along, shadowed—of course—by a pair of ISF Marines. He seemed only moderately interested in the vessel until she made the offhand remark that it had been built in the Sol System.

"Sol, you say?" his voice was sharp and filled with disbelief.

"Yes," Corsia nodded. "We're a part of the *Intrepid* colony mission. Left Sol in 4124. Hit Kapteyn's Streamer and dumped back out into normal space just a few decades ago. Much of the *Andromeda*'s crew was born in Sol."

"*Intrepid*..." the colonel murmured. "It doesn't ring any bells."

"Well, it was long ago. Either way, our arrival in the Inner Stars has stirred the pot, and we've joined an alliance that is attempting to stabilize the region."

"The Inner Stars?" Hickson asked. "I've not heard that term before."

"It's the stars on the Orion Arm. Everything about two thousand light years up and down the arm from Sol. Coreward of the Inner Stars is the Transcend, and rimward is Orion. Each of those regions stretches into the neighboring galactic arms."

"I didn't know people had spread so far," Hickson replied, this time his tone not giving away whether or not he was impressed. "We don't really pay too much attention to what happens beyond the cluster."

"I can't say I blame you," Corsia replied. "We were hoping for a similar existence, but that wasn't to be."

"Because of these jump gates?" Hickson asked.

"Yes, exactly so. We were paid a visit somewhat like this, not long ago. But it was from about two hundred thousand ships."

For the first time Hickson's veneer cracked. "*Two hundred thousand*?"

Corsia let a note of pride slip into her voice. "Give or take a bit, yes. Trisilieds, Hegemony, and Orion all ganged up on us."

"And you're still alive to tell the tale..."

"Well, we won."

Hickson shook his head. "I'd like to hear more about that."

"Perhaps," Corsia replied. "There are details of that battle we don't widely share. Not yet, at least. There's a war spreading across the Orion Arm. Nowhere is safe, and we need to keep our tactics for our allies."

Hickson stopped and turned to Corsia in the middle of a long corridor that led to the central lift bank. "You'll forgive my skepticism, but if you can do all this, what is it that you want with the IPE? What do we have to offer?"

"Well," Corsia began. "It's not for us. It's for our allies. You may not know this, given how many light years deep into the cluster you are, but Genevia has fallen to Nietzschea. Their empire is expanding at a rapid rate, and has reached the edges of the cluster. Septhia, Thebes, and a scattered few other nations are all that stand between the Niets and the IPE. Make no mistake, the Niets *also* want the resources within the cluster. They don't yet possess jump gates themselves, but their allies do. It's only a matter of time before they make a play for control of the IPE."

Corsia could see a war of emotions on Hickson's face. They weren't overt, but they were there. The man had every reason to be annoyed with her for coming into the system without authorization, but she knew he couldn't discount her words, either.

Everything he thought he knew about the galaxy outside the Praesepe Cluster was now utterly outdated, and they had to contend with the reality that their pocket of isolation was no longer unreachable.

"Come," Corsia said. "Let me show you the bridge, and then we can swing by the galley and see if there are any strawberries."

"Strawberries?" Hickson's eyebrows rose, as though that was the final straw on the incredulous donkey's back.

"Yeah, strawberries."

* * * * *

Hickson had vacillated between his fully prickly persona, and one that was borderline tolerable during the two hours Corsia entertained him.

He was less impressed with the strawberries than most people were, but went on for five minutes about how amazing the coffee was.

Both were new tastes to Corsia, but *she* vastly preferred strawberries to coffee. In fact, she couldn't imagine why any organic would subject themselves to the bitter brew.

Even so, Hickson loved it.

As best as Corsia could determine, coffee plants didn't grow well in the environs that the Trensch System had to offer. He hinted that an import business selling beans that could produce coffee such as the galley aboard the *Andromeda* offered would do quite well.

Corsia was walking Hickson back toward the bay, when suddenly the colonel stiffened and gave her a sidelong look. She pretended not to notice it, and kept walking as though nothing was wrong.

A minute later, they walked into the bay to see four more IPE Marines at the base of the shuttle, making six of them, compared to the pair of ISF Marines who were tailing Corsia.

"Is something amiss?" Corsia asked, turning to Hickson, a look of innocent concern on her face.

<*Dropping a nanocloud on the newcomers,*> Sephira advised.

<*Thanks, I hope we won't need to use it. Not off to a good start, here. Any idea why he got so prickly again?*> Corsia asked as she and the colonel waited in silence.

<*He was talking with his inspection team over the Link. Perhaps they told him something he didn't like.*>

Corsia didn't respond to Sephira, as the IPE inspection team returned, accompanied by Jim and the Marines from both groups. The team's leader nodded silently to Colonel Hickson as they boarded their shuttle, but no other apparent communication was made.

"So," Corsia said, deciding to press ahead. "I assume all is well? Should we hold our vector while we wait to see if we should remain in a high orbit around Genesis?"

Hickson turned to Corsia. "Depends on how much of an idiot you think I am."

"I'm sorry?" Corsia asked.

"My inspection team has confirmed that your ship has very advanced stealth systems."

Corsia nodded. "We do at that, yes."

"So this whole jump gate nonsense was just a distraction."

Corsia finally understood the human urge to roll one's eyes. "Are you suggesting that we flew at *least* three light years—probably more, depending on where you think we came from—under stealth, to sneak deep into the Trensch System, only to announce ourselves twenty-five AU from Genesis? What possible reason could we have to do that?"

"I don't know," Hickson shook his head, regarding Corsia as though she were the very embodiment of evil. "Maybe it was to force us into some sort of trade deal by worrying us about an incursion from Nietzschea. You'll stay on your current course until I speak with President Arthur."

Corsia decided enough was enough, and connected to the central QuanComm hub at Khardine. *[This is General Corsia. Plan B, on my coordinates.]*

[LZ hot?] the response came back a moment later.

[Not yet. ETA?]

[Three mikes.]

[Perfect.]

"Very well, Colonel. You'd best be on your way, then," Corsia replied to Hickson. "You have important messages to send. I'll wait until your president is ready to meet, or to send someone whose common sense isn't utterly suppressed by irrational paranoia. Although, I expect I'll hear from you before then…say, in four minutes or so."

<Wow, Mom, excessive derision much?>

<Hush, Sephira.>

Hickson's mouth worked silently for a moment, then he turned on his heel and strode up the ramp, trailed by his Marines.

A minute later, the shuttle was lifting off and passing out of the bay.

Corsia tracked its trajectory back to the colonel's ship, eagerly waiting for the arrival of the destroyers—and for the colonel's reaction.

Hickson's shuttle was only halfway to his ship when Corsia got the message from Khardine.

[Jumping.]

A second later, two destroyers appeared, flanking the *Andromeda*. The one on the port side entered the system only a kilometer from Hickson's shuttle—which suddenly slewed to the side.

<*Every IPE ship in Hickson's fleet has just raised shields,*> Sephira announced.

<*Good, now maybe we'll finally get somewhere.*>

Sure enough, Comm reached out to Corsia seconds later, and connected her with Hickson.

<*Captain Corsia! What is the meaning of this?*> he demanded.

<*To prove to you that jump gates exist. Either that, or our stealth tech is so good that we can flit right under your noses. Either way, I think we're worth having a chat with.*>

<*Very well, Captain. I will provide my report to the president. Shift your vector for an orbit five light seconds out from Genesis. You'll not be coming any closer, now that you have your escort.*>

Hickson's words carried a note of defeat, but he still managed to sound like a haughty asshole.

<*Understood,*> Corsia replied.

DOPPELGANGER

STELLAR DATE: 09.06.8949 (Adjusted Years)
LOCATION: Interstellar Pinnace
REGION: Airtha, Huygens System, Transcend Interstellar Alliance

Sera flew the pinnace toward the EMG, smiling in satisfaction at the machine's sleek, hundred-kilometer length.

It was the first of the new defensive weapons to be made, a device capable of firing a focused electromagnetic wave that would disable any ship in its path, even ones possessing stasis shields.

Sera's engineers had yet to test an EMG against one of the ISF's stasis shielded ships, but Airtha was confident that the variable waveform would be able to penetrate the stasis field.

Sera wasn't so sure, but her mother pointed out that—despite the commonly held belief—the ISF's 'impenetrable' shields did not envelope the entire ship. There were openings for cooling, engine wash, sensors, and weapons.

Initially Sera had countered that the ISF ships only opened those holes periodically, but when Airtha explained that EMG produced a field effect larger than all but the *I2*, she understood her mother's plan.

The physical size of the EMG waveform meant that the ISF ships would risk a disabling shot from an EMG every time they fired their weapons, or even took sensor readings.

To say nothing of using main engines and maneuvering thrusters.

Yes, Sera thought, a smile on her lips as she flew along the length of the EMG. *Let my doppelganger come. Let her fling herself against our defenses, thinking her ships are invulnerable. We'll overwhelm her with both our numbers and our superior weapons. Her rebellion will fall, and then we'll move on to Orion, finally finishing what my father should have done millennia ago.*

Sera broke off from her close pass over the EMG, watching as it approached the jump gate.

Though Sera's mother was undoubtably the most brilliant mind in the galaxy, Airtha was not one to implicitly trust even her own analysis. She wanted incontrovertible proof that the EMG could penetrate stasis shields.

Which was why this weapon was on its way—with a five thousand ship escort—to a system on the edge of the Vela Cluster. A system that had chosen the wrong side in the civil war raging across the Transcend.

Valkris.

The latest reports showed that the Transcend only had a token force defending Valkris. A mere dozen warships on top of the system's local military of five hundred or so ships—most of which were light interceptors.

Khardine's forces had been gaining ground across the Transcend, especially in the Vela Cluster, but that would end now. Once Valkris was under Airtha's control, they'd sweep across the rest of the cluster and crush Khardine's greatest stronghold.

That would send her doppelganger running.

As Sera thought of the other version of herself, a small twinge of worry flitted through her mind. Airtha insisted that *she* was the real Sera. That the one who had fled to New Canaan was in fact a copy made by the separatists Greer and Krissy. A poor shadow of the real Sera, and the separatists' puppet.

Though she tried to push the doubt away—she had no reason to doubt Airtha—a sliver of worry persisted, a worry that her mother was keeping something from her, manipulating her.

"No," she whispered, turning her focus to the jump gate that she'd be taking to the Vela Cluster. "I have no gaps in my memory, no points where I'd be falsified. I'm the *real* Sera."

She repeated the mantra to herself several times while watching the EMG jump through its gate, marveling at the sight of a hundred-kilometer weapon disappearing in an instant.

Even though she knew the Khardine Sera was a clone, it didn't diminish the regrets Sera felt over the events that had taken place. Foremost was the death of Elena, and the fact that Tanis had been duped by the clone.

The journey from Silstrand to Bollam's World with Tanis was a fond memory, as was the time she'd spent on the *Intrepid*. It was another thing that the separatists had stolen from her.

An alert lit up, informing Sera that it was her turn to jump, and she triggered the pinnace's bow mirror. The ship eased forward, and then leapt across the thousand light years to Vela in a matter of seconds.

When normal space snapped into place around her, Sera confirmed that she was at her designated overwatch position, five AU stellar north of where the engagement would take place.

That was the only way she had been able to convince Airtha to let her view the battle—promising to be so far from it that there was no chance of her being at risk.

Once the coordinates were confirmed, Sera activated the drones inside the pinnace's small cargo hold, and set them to work, hauling the ring components out of the bay and assembling a thirty-meter jump gate. Just large enough for the pinnace to slip through, if an emergency demanded it. A destroyer from the battlegroup would collect it later.

While the gate was being put together, Sera rose from her chair in the cockpit and walked back to the pinnace's small galley. The attack fleet had jumped in half an AU from their target, the world of Maitreya. Their location meant they'd engage the separatist fleets in roughly an hour, and Sera would see the outcome of the battle fifty minutes later.

*Well, maybe not the outcome of the **battle**, but certainly of the EMG's initial salvo.*

All Sera needed to do was verify that the EMG worked, and then return to Airtha. Not that she planned to leave early. She'd see the battle through, then join her fleets when they took the capital world.

Her mother would be annoyed, but either Sera was the president, or she wasn't. This was her call to make.

She poured herself a cup of coffee, wondering why her mother had allowed her to travel to Valkris without an escort, without anyone else on the ship at all. Granted, she was safe enough this far above the stellar plane. Unless Valkris had drastically changed its patrols—which *was* possible, but not too likely.

She hoped.

Stop fretting, Sera scolded herself, grabbing a sandwich from the chiller before returning to the bridge. She settled into her seat and took another sip of the coffee while reviewing the myriad reports she'd brought along.

I bet my doppelganger doesn't have to deal with all this nonsense.

PARLAY

STELLAR DATE: 09.06.8949 (Adjusted Years)
LOCATION: IPSS *Deepening Night*
REGION: Trensch System, Inner Praesepe Empire

Corsia stepped out of her pinnace, surveying the *Deepening Night*'s docking bay, taking in the dozen shuttles and fighters in the IPE warship's bay, along with the entire platoon of Marines.

Commander Eve—who had insisted she come along—stood at the base of the ramp with a squad of ISF Marines, and nodded for Corsia to proceed.

She glanced at Terrance and Kendrik. "Well, boys, let's do this."

<*You going to be OK?*> Terrance asked. <*This is your first away mission in…what, two centuries?*>

<*If you consider that the* Andromeda *used to be my body, I was always on away missions.*>

<*Huh,*> Terrance gave a mental grunt as he followed her down the ramp. <*I guess that's one way to think of it. But not at all the same.*>

A man and a woman in long robes stood at the base of the ramp, studiously ignoring Commander Eve—who returned the favor—as they watched Corsia descend.

When she was within arm's reach, the woman gave a perfunctory smile. "Admiral Corsia. I am Minister Rama and this is Secretary Larson." Larson nodded as Rama introduced him.

Corsia inclined her head to each in turn. "Thank you for hosting us." She turned to Terrance. "This is Terrance Redding, one of our top diplomats, and I suspect you know Mister Kendrik."

The IPE representatives' eyes grew wide, and Corsia's momentary satisfaction was shared with a sense of surprise that they hadn't already recognized their president's brother.

"It's been a long time, Minister Rama—though back then, you were the former minister's assistant, if I recall," Kendrik said with a genuine smile. "Secretary Larson, I don't believe we've met."

"I've never had the pleasure," Larson said, his voice smooth and cultured.

Handshakes were exchanged, then Rama gestured to the dock's inner doors. "The president awaits us. Please, come."

Commander Eve signaled to the squad Marines, who fell in behind the group, causing Rama to stop short.

"I'm sorry, your guards won't be able to accompany you."

Corsia had been expecting that. "Our welcome to your system has been less than warm. I hope you'll understand that we're a little uncomfortable. Would you allow four of our Marines to accompany us if they disarm?"

Rama seemed surprised at Corsia's offer. "Well...um, I suppose that will be acceptable. They'll need to remain in the corridor outside the meeting room.

"Of course," Corsia nodded, and Eve directed four of the Marines to pass their weapons to their squadmates.

She could tell they didn't like it, but an ISF Marine in light armor—which was the case for this squad—was still a formidable force. Especially considering that they still carried their lightwands, and their armored forearms held pulse weapons.

Rama led the group through the *Deepening Night*, a twelve hundred meter cruiser. It was one of a dozen such ships in the battle group of sixty vessels that had met the *Andromeda* and its destroyer escort when it settled into its orbit around Genesis.

Corsia suspected that the IPE military was trying to cow her with a show of force, but after the recent battles she'd participated in, sixty ships barely seemed like enough for a policing action.

The *Deepening Night* seemed relatively modern—by Inner Stars standards—though the pinnace's scan had shown that their power plants generated a far lower output than the ISF ships. They wouldn't be able to run their beams for an extended engagement.

Corsia's tactical assessment determined that the *Andromeda* alone could disable half the IPE ships within ten minutes.

The one thing she *did* like about their ships was the quality they exhibited. The designs were sound, the engines more than powerful enough to maneuver in a fight, while still being well-protected by ablative armor.

Each cruiser sported three railguns and a host of beam weapons. She suspected that they were more than a match for any enemies that the IPE was likely to face, this deep in its domain.

Rama made small talk—pointedly ignoring Kendrik—asking innocuous questions about events outside the cluster's slow zone, and was visibly surprised by a few answers Corsia provided, such as the attacks on Thebes, and even the fall of the Kendo Empire in the rimward fringes of the slow zone.

Once or twice, Rama made comments that led Corsia to believe she was nervous, but it was hard to be certain.

<Are you picking up on her cues?> Terrance asked after one of Rama's uncertain laughs.

<I think so,> Corsia replied. *<I'm second-guessing my judgement here, though. A bit out of my element.>*

<Well, trust your gut. Something's up. Stay sharp.>

Within a few minutes, they reached an unassuming door, and Rama turned to Corsia. "Please direct your escort to remain out here."

Corsia nodded, and Commander Eve gestured for the ISF Marines to take up positions in the corridor. IPE Marines took up flanking positions, and Corsia couldn't help but notice that the ISF fireteam was wound tight—ready to spring into action.

Good.

The door slid open, and Rama led the ISF delegation into a briefing room that had been repurposed for the meeting, half-filled with a large table.

Across the table sat President Arthur, who rose slowly, his eyes steely as they swept across the group, landing on his brother.

"Kendrik. You have no idea how happy I am to see you. Last update we had, you were settling down in the Theban Alliance."

"That's correct, brother," Kendrik returned the smile his brother had given—neither having reached their eyes. "About eighty years ago. I was just establishing my trade routes there."

"And yet here you are," Arthur replied, turning to Corsia. "With these rather interesting visitors."

"Thank you for agreeing to meet with us," Corsia said with as warm a smile as she could muster. "We have a proposal that I believe you will be very interested in hearing."

President Arthur gestured for everyone to sit. The ISF delegation sat with their backs to the door, while Rama and Larson walked around the table to sit on either side of the president.

"I'm not sure I have much choice other than to hear it," the president said, his tone unreadable. "You've been very...persuasive, I suppose is the right word."

"Yes, thank you for working through a rather tricky introduction," Corsia replied, avoiding the president's implications. "As I'm sure Colonel Hickson informed you, things are changing outside of the cluster, and we'd like to form an alliance with you that will strengthen the Inner Praesepe Empire, and establish direct trade with systems outside the cluster."

"Namely Thebes and Septhia," Arthur replied, his voice not giving away what he thought of either group.

"Thebes, mostly," Kendrik said while pouring himself a glass of water from the pitcher on the table. "I'll be using the resources we trade for to build a fleet that we'll use to defend Thebes against the Nietzscheans, and then sell it to the Septhians."

"So you'll use our resources to build up the militaries of other nations?" Larson asked, a scowl settling on his brow. "That's not very patriotic of you, Mister Kendrik."

"Indeed," Arthur said, nodding slowly. "If you have these jump gates, why not allow *us* to build the ships, and then send them to you? This seems like a better solution for the people of the IPE."

"That is certainly not out of the question," Terrance said, his voice calm and soothing. "In fact, I can imagine that a shipbuilding facility here in the IPE would be both very secure and efficient. However, from what I understand, it would take some years to establish that capability with your technological level. Kendrik has the facilities in the Theban Alliance to hit the ground running; we just need a steady supply of resources to feed his production."

"Is that what you hope to achieve here, brother?" Arthur asked. "You want to enrich yourself at the IPE's expense?"

"Expense would be the exact opposite of what will happen," Kendrik replied, his voice carrying a slight strain as he responded to his brother. "There are many technologies that the IPE could benefit from. Not just military. Medical, life expectancy, entertainment, construction, excellent coffee, there is much we could trade."

Rama seemed unconvinced. "I don't see how that will benefit us in the face of the types of threats you have implied are out there. You mentioned that the Nietzscheans have their eyes on the easily accessible resources in the cluster, and that they could have these jump gates before long. If we export all of our resources and get little in return, how will we defend ourselves against threats without and within the cluster? For all we know, those threats could already be present."

Terrance, and then Kendrik, addressed Rama's concerns, offering solutions and examples of technologies that could bolster the IPE. Their explanations seemed to mollify Rama, but not President Arthur or Secretary Larson.

Contributing to the uncertain feeling Corsia was developing was the fact that something about Rama's tone and her responses seemed off. As she discussed defensive options with Kendrik, the minister made statements which seemed to imply that threats already existed within the cluster.

Twice, her eyes had ticked to the left, toward the president and Secretary Larson—though neither of them gave any indication that her words had a double meaning.

<Sephira,> Corsia reached out to her daughter via a relay in the pinnace. *<Something seems amiss here. I get the feeling that the IPE is hiding something from us.>*

<Any idea what? Ships, stations, resources?> Sephira replied, her tone curious but unconcerned.

<I don't know. It seems to have one of their delegation nervous, but not the other two. If I had to hazard a worst-case scenario, it would be that Orion has beat us to the punch and is already here. Best-case, they have some sort of internal squabble going on that we're caught up in.>

<So you're saying that right now it runs the gamut.>

Corsia had to resist the urge to physically nod. *<I suppose, yes. Could you perform a low-level active scan of the* Deepening Night*? I wonder if there's something they're physically hiding from us.>*

<From out here with Andromeda*? They'd be able to tell what I was doing—oh! You mean to use the array on the pinnace.>*

<Yes, I do indeed. Random pings, listen for class C responses.>

<OK,> Sephira said after a moment. *<I'm kicking that off. You*

know…>

<Yes?> Corsia prompted, as Terrance began to describe the types of medical technology the ISF could offer in trade for resources. She couldn't help but notice that Arthur and Larson didn't seem overly impressed, while Rama's eyes were wide.

<Well, you have those four Marines outside the conference room. I can use some of their armor's sensors to enhance my view inside the ship, increase sensitivity.>

<Good thinking,> Corsia replied, glad her daughter was thinking on her feet—so to speak. *<Let me know what you find.>*

Corsia was about to join in the conversation, offering the possibility of tactical training for the IPE space force, when Sephira's voice came back into her mind.

<Shit! Mom…I'm detecting **sleptons**. *A lot of sleptons.>*

Corsia felt a shiver run down her spine. *<Where?>*

<On the Deepening Night. *In fact…I'm pretty sure they're coming from the room you're in.>*

<Eve,> Corsia pulled the Marine commander into the conversation. *<Sephira is reading sleptons in here.>*

<With us?> Though Eve's mental tone carried alarm, her face betrayed no emotion whatsoever.

<Yeah, one of our three friends across the table has a remnant in them.>

<Well that complicates things.>

<You're telling me,> Corsia replied.

<I've called in the stealthed team from the shuttle. They'll be on our position in seven minutes with the shadowtron.>

<Good. Tell them not to rush. Not being detected is more important than speed.>

While Kendrik outlined a process for setting up improved shipyards in the IPE, Corsia brought Terrance up to speed.

<Well that's unexpected,> he responded, while nodding along as Kendrik spoke. *<What would ascended AIs want with some place like this? It's not like the ASAIs can't just get whatever resources they need from the galactic core.>*

<Your guess is as good as mine,> Corsia replied. *<Maybe better.>*

<Well, the easy option is that they're doing it to deny resources to others,> Terrance suggested. *<I'm of the opinion that the core AIs*

engendered the war between Nietzschea and Genevia. That conflict ultimately put Praesepe square in the Niets' sights. Denying any of the fringe peoples access to the IPE's resources makes sense.>

<*Except for the matter of jump gates.*>

Corsia got a feeling of ambivalent acknowledgement from Terrance. <*Sure, but by Bob's own admission, these ASAIs can make pretty good guesses about the future. It wouldn't be a big deal for one of them to drop a remnant in someone, just to make sure things went according to plan.*>

<*Stars.*> Once again, Corsia had to manage her physical responses to disturbing thoughts. <*There could be remnants everywhere.*>

<*Maybe…but maybe not. I suspect there's some sort of limit to how many puppets an ascended being can make. If it were infinite, they wouldn't have to go through all these machinations to control us.*>

Terrance sounded entirely blasé as he continued to speak with President Arthur about trade options. One of the three people across the table had a piece of an ascended being inside of them, and from what Nance had been able to do when she was under the Caretaker's control, that person might be able to kill all of them.

With surprising ease, Terrance steered the conversation toward a break, and the IPE delegation agreed. The president rose and left the room, while Rama and Larson remained.

<*Minister Rama.*> Corsia decided to take a chance. <*Is there anything you'd like to tell me about risks to the IPE? Anything we should be aware of?*>

<*What do you mean?*> Rama replied, her mental tone cautious.

<*You've hinted at threats to the IPE on several occasions, and your wording has indicated to me that you think those threats are already here.*>

A nervous look crossed Rama's face, then she quickly schooled her expression once more. <*It's not anything specific…just my job to be concerned about potential threats and the like.*>

<*You seem to be concerned about more than a 'potential' threat,*> Corsia countered.

<*Just stop. You don't know what you're talking about,*> Rama said, her tone changing from dismissive to pleading. <*Things aren't as they seem. Honestly, you'd be better off going elsewhere in the cluster. Like Delaware—they're outside the IPE, and they're flush with resources. More*

than us, even.>

Corsia eyed Rama, considering the woman's words, then glanced at Larson, who was in the back of the room, filling a plate with snacks.

<*Eve,*> Corsia said to the Marine commander. <*When your team gets here, they need to stay out of line of sight until the president is back in the room.*>

<*Are you worried that our stealth systems can't fool a remnant? Because I am.*>

<*Exactly. Once we resume, they need to strike fast. Enter, take down the president before he has time to react. You ready for that?*>

A laugh flowed across the link from Eve. <*Ready to kill the president of the group we're trying to forge an alliance with? Why wouldn't I be?*>

<*Not kill, free.*>

<*Sorry, I was thinking of what's about to happen the way our armed and twitchy IPE Marines will see it.*>

Corsia had been thinking about them, too. <*Have half the strike team hang back to deal with them.*>

<*We've got nano on them already. It'll take a few seconds, but once the festivities start, we can lock 'em down.*>

<*Good.*>

Corsia updated Terrance with the plan, then turned her gaze to Kendrik, who was speaking with Rama by the coffee carafe, extolling the virtues of brews from outside the cluster.

She considered telling him what was about to happen, but decided to hold off. While Kendrik was not likely to be a double agent, he may not be able to handle the news that his brother was possessed by the remnant of an ASAI.

He'd just have to figure things out as they happened.

Several minutes later, the president returned and resumed his place across the table. He didn't speak, but his arrival signaled the resumption of the talks.

Rama had just launched into a listing of considerations that would need to be made, when Eve began to count down.

<*Three, two, one…go!*>

Behind the ISF delegation, the door burst open and, seconds later, slammed shut once more. Then a strange hum filled the air, and

President Arthur leapt to his feet.

"What! What are you doing?" he stammered, staring at the business end of a weapon seemingly floating in midair next to Corsia.

"This is called a shadowtron. We're drawing you out," Corsia informed the remnant. "There's nothing you can do about it."

The group watched in a combination of horror and transfixed wonder, as strands of glowing light began to emanate from President Arthur, and coalesce into a ball that was then pulled toward the weapon.

"What in the star's light is *that*?" Rama managed to ask after a moment.

"It's a part of an ascended AI," Terrance replied calmly as he watched the orb float through the air. "It—"

Suddenly, Larson leapt across the table, grabbing the shadowtron and wrenching it from the stealthed ISF Marine's hands.

The IPE secretary was about to throw the weapon to the ground when he was struck by an invisible force. Corsia rose and made a grab for the shadowtron, only to be thrown against the wall as President Arthur hurled himself at her.

The impact startled her, and it took Corsia a moment to re-orient herself. During that time, she picked up the sounds of combat in the corridor outside.

President Arthur closed with her, and Corsia grappled with the man, watching from the corner of her eye as Eve moved Terrance and Kendrik away from the fight.

"That's an interesting toy," the president said in an otherworldly voice. "I look forward to seeing how it works after I subsume your mind—"

Suddenly the man's words cut off, and a look of puzzlement came over his face. Corsia took advantage of the opportunity to pivot to the side and drive her foot into the president's jaw, sending his body flying across the room to slam into the bulkhead.

Corsia glanced behind her to see that the two stealthed Marines had managed to wrest the shadowtron away from Larson, but she could tell the weapon was ruined.

"You're no human..." Larson hissed, and Corsia realized that was what had confused the president a moment ago. "Clever trick with the fake brain."

Corsia's suspicion that Larson also was possessed by a remnant solidified into certainty. "Yeah, well you weren't exactly being honest, either."

Behind them, the door slid open, and one of the Marines leaned in. "Ma'am? We need to go!"

Backing away from Larson, Corsia pulled the feeds from the soldiers in the corridor, noting that one was down, a hole burned through his head, and the other two were firing down the passageway at a group of enemies who had taken cover in the doorways of other rooms.

"Grab the shadowtron," she ordered the Marines who had breached the room, and the group backed out of the room, the Marines shielding Terrance and Kendrick.

For a moment, Rama looked uncertainly at the slumped form of the president, then glanced at Larson's seething visage. Without a word, she dashed out of the room and joined the ISF group, her eyes wide as she glanced at Corsia.

"What the hell just happened in there?"

"I'll explain later," Corsia replied, grabbing a weapon from a fallen IPE soldier. "We're leaving. You coming?"

Rama nodded silently, and the group retreated down the corridor, the Marines laying down suppressive fire until they rounded a corner and picked up the pace, moving back toward the docking bay.

"Your shuttle," Rama said breathlessly. "They'll destroy it."

"They'll try," Terrance replied with a laugh as he fired his pilfered weapon at an IPE Marine that had dashed across the intersection ahead of them.

The shot caught the enemy in the knee, locking up the joint and toppling the soldier.

Corsia shot him a questioning look, and Terrance shrugged. "I wasn't always a businessman. Well…I guess I was, but I went on a few ops back in the day."

"That's not in your record," Eve said as she sprayed a hail of bullets behind the group, keeping their pursuers at a distance.

"It was a thousand years before the *Intrepid* set out," Terrance replied. "Not everything makes it into the record…and not all the records last."

"Still, I thought I'd have known that our main financial backer was a serious badass," Eve said while signaling two of the Marines to advance.

Terrance winked at the commander. "We all have little secrets. Jason and I got up to some fun stuff back in the day."

Corsia didn't reply, as a pair of arachnid-like combat mechs skittered around the corner, spraying rail pellets down the passageway.

The Marines moved in front of the rest of the group, their armor absorbing the enemy fire—mostly. The sergeant grunted as a rail pellet tore through his knee at the joint, spraying blood and cartilage across Corsia's thighs.

"Suck this," Eve roared as she pulled a pair of burn sticks from the sergeant's back and threw them at the mechs.

The sticks sailed through the air, both striking the mechs' bodies, the thermite in the weapons igniting and burning through the things' ablative plating. Once weak spots were exposed, concentrated fire from the Marines slammed into the robots and tore their bodies to shreds.

"Faaaaaawwwwk," Rama whispered, staring at the blood sprayed across her body.

"You hit?" Corsia asked.

"I…don't? No?"

"Good." Corsia grabbed Rama's arm and pulled her along, staying close to Eve.

Five minutes later, they had reached the level the pinnace was on, and were carefully advancing down a broad corridor with little cover.

<I've Linked with the team at the shuttle; they've got some fans who wanted signatures, but so far, the craft is OK,> Eve reported.

Corsia tapped into Eve's connection and saw that the squad of ISF Marines in the bay were holding back a platoon of enemies who had taken up positions at two of the entrances.

The pinnace had its stasis shields up, but wasn't firing on the IPE troops.

<Why aren't they shooting with the pinnace?> Corsia asked.

<Worried about holing the ship we're in,> Eve replied. *<You'll be fine, but Terrance, Kendrik, and Rama can't breathe vacuum too well.>*

Corsia finally understood the urge to slap oneself in the forehead. *<OK…I'll remind you that this is my first away mission.>*

<Good thing I'm here to babysit you, ma'am,> Eve said, a laugh escaping her lips.

"Am I missing out on some good combat jokes?" Terrance asked, as the team continued to creep down the corridor.

"No," Corsia said with a shake of her head. "Just me spacing out."

"Is it wise to be talking aloud?" Kendrik asked from Terrance's side. "Won't they hear us?"

Eve shook her head. "Not yet. We deployed a nanocloud to dampen our sounds. The lot of you walk so loud they'd have heard us a minute ago, otherwise."

Kendrik's mouth formed an 'O', and he nodded silently.

They reached a bend in the corridor, and the soldier in the lead held up his hand, halting the group. Commander Eve and the Marines passed hand signals, getting ready to rush out and clear the passage ahead.

Corsia watched their plan take form, while keeping an eye on the feeds of the enemy around the bend.

There were nine IPE Marines clustered around the forward entrance to the docking bay. The pinnace's feeds showed another ten enemies within, clustered behind cover near the entrance.

Eve coordinated her plan with the squad of Marines inside the bay to hit the enemy from both sides. With luck, they'd kill them all…worst-case scenario, the IPE troops would fall back to the bay's aft entrance.

Corsia, Terrance, and the sergeant with the blown-out knee held back with Kendrik and Rama. Terrance tried to stand at the front of the group, but Corsia gave him a stern look and pulled him back before taking a position behind the Marines.

With an unseen signal, Commander Eve led the Marines forward, and Corsia moved up to the apex of the corridor's bend, ready to provide any cover for the Marines.

A flurry of weapons fire was exchanged between the two groups in the corridor, and the ISF Marines inside the bay shifted their focus to the enemy at the forward door.

Corsia saw Eve take a shot to the shoulder, and another Marine was hit in the leg, but the enemy fared worse; two minutes later, the four surviving IPE soldiers fled aft, clearing the way for Corsia to lead her group to the bay.

She pushed Terrance ahead first, and fell into the rear of the party, anxiously looking over her shoulder as she pushed Rama ahead of her, the woman half-frozen with fear.

"You OK?" Corsia asked Eve when she reached the commander.

"Fucking Ippies! We gonna blow the shit out of this ship once we're clear?" the Marine growled through clenched teeth.

"Seems like a solid option," Corsia replied as they reached the bay's entrance.

She saw that Terrance and Kendrik were already at the pinnace, Rama a few paces behind them, ducking low as the IPE Marines at the aft doors intensified their fire.

<*Hit them with e-beams,*> Corsia ordered the shuttle's pilot.

A moment later, a series of straight lightning bolts shot from the pinnace's dorsal cannons, tearing through the enemy's cover—and no small number of the IPE troops.

"We gotta move!" the Marine at the door shouted, gesturing for Corsia and Eve to make the run to the pinnace.

Eve put a hand on Corsia's back, about to guide her through the doorway, when the Marine beckoning to them exploded.

The force of the blast flung Corsia and Eve a dozen meters down the corridor, sending them sliding along the deck until they hit the bulkhead at the curve.

Corsia was on her feet in an instant, but realized that Eve had been stunned, her head lolling to the side. She pulled the Marine backward around the bend while searching the feeds for the source of the deadly fire.

Then she saw them. A pair of heavy assault mechs were moving down the passageway, while another trio had entered the bay.

<*Go! Go!*> Corsia ordered the shuttle pilot, after checking that every other survivor was still alive. <*Get them out of here, and get Lieutenant Marky to send a breach team. Use the destroyers to take out this*

ship's engines.>

<Yes, Admiral. I—>

Another explosion shook the ship, and EM interference cut off Corsia's comms. The *thud* of mechs was shaking the deck.

Corsia bent over, screaming in Eve's face, "On your feet, Marine! We gotta move!"

VALKRIS

STELLAR DATE: 09.06.8949 (Adjusted Years)
LOCATION: Interstellar Pinnace, 5AU Stellar north of Maitreya
REGION: Valkris System, Vela Cluster, Transcend Interstellar Alliance

Fifty minutes later, the pinnace's sensors picked up the Airthan fleet as it entered the Valkris System. Of course that had all happened fifty minutes earlier, thanks to light lag. If all had gone well, by now the battle would already be over.

And if it *had* gone well, then Admiral Ika would have already sent word back to Airtha via jump gate. Though she hoped for that outcome, Sera steeled herself for the possibility that the EMG had failed, and her fleet was in ruins.

Settling into her seat in the cockpit, Sera pulled up a view of the Airthan fleet, placing it on the pinnace's holodisplay. She noted with approval how Admiral Ika had arrayed her ships around the EMG in a near-sphere.

The woman understands how important the weapon is. Good.

The ships advanced on Maitreya, their progress seeming unimaginably slow on scan, though even without the thrust indicators, Sera could see by the engine flares that the fleet was burning hard toward Valkris.

While she'd eaten her sandwich, the pinnace's sensors had identified five of the ships in a wide orbit around the planet as Khardine vessels, at least one of which was likely to have stasis shields. Thus far, this configuration had seemed to be the modus operandi for the separatists: leave bait ships around worlds, while fleets laid in wait nearby.

The Khardine fleets' ability to get ships into a system so quickly still baffled the Airthan tacticians—and even Sera's mother. The only explanation that made sense was that they set up fleets just beyond a star's heliosphere, and then the bait ship called for their aid via FDL transmitters.

Of course, if Khardine had a fleet for each bait ship, the size of their overall fleet was mind-numbingly large.

Which didn't pass the smell test with Sera. Even with New Canaan's ability to grow starships, there was no way that Khardine could field thousand-ship fleets around every world they'd claimed. That would require them to possess ships numbering in the hundreds of millions.

And if the enemy had a fleet *that* large, they'd have won the war before it even started.

Something else is afoot.

Sera quieted her thoughts as sixty-two enemy ships formed up around Maitreya —the five Khardine vessels bolstered by fifty-seven local ships. The separatist vessels began a slingshot maneuver, arcing around the planet on an intercept course for the Airthan ships.

At their fore were three cruisers.

Stasis ships, Sera thought with a nod. That would be the only reason for those ships to be at the fore with the rest in a narrow cone behind them. She was surprised that there were three here, but then again, Valkris was a special system.

Admiral Ika must have come to the same conclusion regarding the nature of the cruisers. The EMG pivoted, aligning with the approaching enemy, and fired.

Sera counted the seconds as the focused EM wave sped across space toward the enemy formation. She held her breath for the last ten seconds, shifting onto the edge of her seat in anticipation.

A brilliant light shone as the wave hit the foremost enemy ship, then more light flared, blinding the pinnace's passive sensors. When the interference finally cleared, she saw that the first cruiser was nothing more than a slowly expanding cloud of debris, while the other two were drifting hulks, their engines offline.

The remaining enemy ships spread out, firing a barrage of beams and missiles at the EMG, most of which were deflected by point defense provided by the surrounding Airthan fleet, as well as the shields on the EMG itself.

The EMG fired twice more before the enemy fleet dispersed too much for the massive weapon to track. The Khardine ships passed by the Airthan fleet, spreading out over several light seconds, jinking to avoid the attacking fleet's beams.

Sera wondered where the Khardine backup fleet was. Usually by now, they would have jumped in and engaged the Airthan ships.

She supposed it could be that the enemy did not have a force outside the Valkris System, or at least not one capable of destroying the five thousand ships in Admiral Ika's fleet—especially not with the EMG in play.

Airthan Fleet Tactics and Analysis had estimated that even if the EMG wasn't viable, it would take over five hundred ships to defeat Admiral Ika's battlegroup. Now that the EMG had delivered on its promise, the size of the opposing fleet would need to be much larger.

Still, one EMG was not a viable offensive weapon, and Sera began to wonder if the gamble of sending it with such a small escort had been wise.

Seconds turned into minutes, and minutes into half an hour. Still enemy ships spread further and further away from Admiral Ika's fleet—which was braking on its approach to the planet of Maitreya.

What's your game?

The planetary defenses hadn't engaged, and no other local military vessels had moved in to the rescue.

"Has Maitreya surrendered?" Sera wondered aloud. "Now *that* would be a coup!"

Just as she uttered the words, a group of ships appeared only twenty kilometers above the EMG—*within* the Airthan fleet formation. She instantly recognized them as ISF cruisers.

Dammit…they sent in the Caners.

The ISF ships fired atom beams into the EMG, the massive particles punching through its shields, and then through the weapon itself.

Seven seconds later, four thousand ISF ships appeared around the Airthan fleet.

"Motherfuckers!" Sera swore, slamming a fist into her chair's armrest.

She didn't even bother to wait and see what happened next. With the EMG offline, Admiral Ika wouldn't have a chance. The battle was lost.

Still, it wasn't a complete failure. The EMG had worked, and enough of them would create a viable defense for Airtha.

Initializing the gate, Sera turned the pinnace and waited for the negative energy emitters to activate, all the while wondering how the ISF had four thousand ships on the periphery of the Valkris System.

It was becoming all too apparent that the enemy possessed a faster means of communication than FDL. She considered the possibilities as the gate activated and she fired the pinnace's engines.

Her ship was a hundred meters from transitioning through the jump gate when Sera saw the unthinkable: an ISF cruiser, just off her pinnace's port side. The ship fired on the jump gate, its beams tearing into the energy emitters.

Sera watched in horror as the gate was destroyed, knowing that the wave of energy from the antimatter explosion would obliterate her pinnace.

What the…?

The explosion flowed around her ship as though held back.

A stasis shield?

Alarms flared across her console, registering a grav beam pulling her ship toward the ISF cruiser, a bay door on its hull opening up to take her in.

Sera jumped up from her console and ran to the pinnace's armory. They may be able to take her ship, but they'd find taking *her* to be much more of a challenge.

Nothing further crossed Sera's mind as the ISF cruiser placed her entire pinnace in a stasis field, and set a course for the nearest jump gate.

TANIS & JOE

STELLAR DATE: 09.06.8949 (Adjusted Years)
LOCATION: 7km North of Jersey City
REGION: Pyra, Albany System, Thebes, Septhian Alliance

"That's where we hid for an entire day, as the Niets moved an armored column through the region," Tangel said, pointing at a half-destroyed farmhouse. "Twice, scouts came through, and I thought we'd be found for sure, but we managed to stay out of sight. Brandt—" Tangel paused for a moment, still feeling sorrow at the loss of her long-time friend. "Brandt and I draped ourselves across Ayer and Johnny, covering them just enough with our stealth systems to keep them out of view."

"Brandt was...I'm going to miss that woman. She was a big part of the glue that held the ISF together," Joe said as he stepped over part of a shuttle...a skid, from the looks of it. He drew a drew a steadying breath. "A part of me is amazed you survived so long down here, and another part isn't surprised at all."

"You know how it is," Tangel said as she surveyed the Pyran landscape around them. "You survive because you have to. Giving up isn't an option."

"Not for you, at least," Joe said with a soft laugh. "Either of you."

"There's no either of us anymore," Tangel corrected her husband.

"Well, yeah, but back then there still was. I was speaking about past yous."

Tangel snorted. "I see. Well, past mes were pretty determined to get back to past you and the past girls. Would take a lot more than a planet full of Nietzscheans to stop former mes."

"Too bad no one told *them* that," Joe replied as they crested a hill and looked down on a once-green valley, now blackened from fires that had swept across the region.

Though the Nietzscheans were responsible for most of the destruction on Pyra, Tangel was relatively certain *this* fire had been started from the energy she had blasted through the city the night Rika and Priscilla had found her.

She was glad that so few Pyrans were in the area when that happened. And also glad that a lot of Nietzscheans *were*.

Of course, this one small patch of desolation was negligible when compared to the vast swaths of Pyra that had been destroyed by the departing Nietzschean ships, the wash from their fusion engines dumping massive quantities of ionized plasma and radiation into the planet's atmosphere, igniting fires that had raged for days—even with the ISF's fire-control ships onsite.

"Well, the longer we can keep the Niets in the dark, the better. Though that will soon fall to the locals—once I convince the Septhian government that they need to join our alliance, not continue to grow their own."

"I think they'll come around." Joe shrugged. "Especially now that you broke off Kendo and Thebes, and are setting up the latter to be a major player in the region."

"These people deserve a hand; I'm glad to do what I can to help." Tangel wondered how many of the Pyrans would eventually come back to their planet. She glanced up at the lights flashing in the sky—the construction of the world's new ring—and wondered if the displaced peoples would remain there, or return to the world's surface once it was safe.

Joe leaned in close, and his hazsuit's helmet touched hers. "They do, but they still have a world. That's a lot better than what the Niets planned to leave them with."

Tangel nodded as she looked over the burned out valley, watching the brown, ash-filled water creep along in the streambed at the bottom of the slope.

"Why did you want to come down here, anyway?" Joe asked.

"I just wanted to go for a walk on a planet," Tangel replied, shrugging as she spoke. "I realized that the last time I'd done so was the day before we let the girls fly the *Andromeda* to the gamma base."

Joe's eyebrows pinched as he considered her words. "Really? That was years ago. Are you sure?"

"Well, I went for some walks on the palace grounds on Alexandria, but with half of Empress Diana's court constantly tailing me, it wasn't the same."

Joe made a sound that was half cough, half snort. "I don't think walking on Pyra's burned out husk is really a step up from that."

Tangel slid an arm around Joe's waist. "You never got to meet Diana's sycophants. *I* think Pyra's husk is a step up."

"Remind me to avoid—"

Joe's words were cut off as Priscilla's voice came to them from the ship above.

<Tangel, Joe, Corsia and Terrance are in trouble!>

<In the IPE?> Tangel asked. *<What's happening?>*

There was the briefest of pauses before Priscilla replied. *<I just have a short burst and coordinates from Sephira. There are remnants running the Inner Empire!>*

<What!?> Tangel cried out. *<Our pinnace has a gate mirror, align the closest gate and send me the coordinates.>*

Tangel glanced at Joe as they ran back to their pinnace. "Well, so much for a leisurely stroll on your day off. That's what you get for hopping a ship out here."

"Are you kidding?" Joe asked. "Do you recall how long it's been since you and I saw action together?"

"Too long," Tangel replied. "Let's rectify that."

LANDING

STELLAR DATE: 09.06.8949 (Adjusted Years)
LOCATION: Planet HH1
REGION: Hidey Hole System, Large Magellanic Cloud

"There it is," Sera said, gesturing at the spire of rocks jutting out of the crater's center. "We should be able to get an IR reading off that spire, but it's completely invisible."

"Certainly unusual," Jason said from the pilot's seat.

Sera watched Jason's fingers dance over the console as he pulled the pinnace into a long canyon that led into the crater.

"You know," she said as they slid into the narrow rent in the planet's surface. "We have stealth systems. You don't need to—Wall!"

"Relax." Jason's voice was calm, his face filled with a rapturous expression as he flew the pinnace through the narrow canyon, effortlessly managing the twists, turns, and occasional updrafts surging through the planet's thin atmosphere. "This is my thing."

"Your 'thing' is smearing us across a kilometer of rock?" Sera asked, her hands gripping the sides of her seat, even though the internal a-grav systems dampened the ship's movement.

Jason tossed a grin over his shoulder. "Just like in Vagabond's Canyon back on Proxima. I used to fly that in my T-38 at twice this speed. Even threaded the stone needle with it."

"Back in your misspent youth?" Sera asked through gritted teeth, glancing back at Major Valerie to see the woman's usual stoic expression firmly in place, though on a face several shades paler than normal.

"Something like that," Jason said with a chuckle as he activated the grav emitters and began to slow the pinnace. "Regarding stealth, yes, they can't *see* our ship, but these pinnaces either fly fast, or they fly bright with a-grav to stay aloft. A-grav breaks stealth, and fast means we'd create visible air currents. Canyon's our best bet."

"So what sort of spaceship was a T-38?" Sera asked, trying not to pay attention to how close Jason got to the canyon walls. She would have to pass a vid of this to Cheeky at some point.

Jason laughed. "Not a spaceship. It's an old Earth air-breather. A T-38 Talon. I had a lot of reproduction aircraft strewn about the stars around Sol. A bird in every port—something to do on the layovers."

"Seems like a lot of 'something to do' for simple stop-overs," Sera replied, her jaw clenched, glad to see they only had thirty kilometers to go.

Jason's tone continued to be easy and nonchalant. In fact, he seemed more relaxed than she'd ever seen him. "On the pre-FTL trade routes, you could sometimes wait *years* for all the cargo to get assembled for the next trip. Always bugged me. People knew we were coming for decades, but they still never had their ducks in a row when we got there."

"So this…stunt flying…is your thing?" Sera asked as she watched Jason, starting to feel as though she was seeing him for the first time.

"Well," he shrugged while banking the craft around a tower of rock rising from the center of the canyon. "We all have to grow up eventually…take on our share of responsibility. Eventually you gotta trade in the T-38 for a GSS *Intrepid*." He glanced at Sera. "You know that as well as anyone."

"Stars, do I ever."

"Maybe when this is all over, I can just fly again for a while. You know…I have this bird back on Carthage, a Yak. I think you'd love a ride in it."

She didn't have a chance to reply before the pinnace shot out of the canyon and into the crater, rapidly closing on the rock spire in the center.

<There.> Jen highlighted a level patch of ground. *<Swept a bit too clean. That's a landing pad.>*

"And that," Sera placed a marker on a smooth section of the spire's slope, "is likely a door."

"No EM at all," Valerie said, speaking aloud for the first time since they'd left the *Helios*. "Though that doesn't mean we couldn't be looking at automated defenses."

"Not my first time on a job like this," Sera shot Valerie a meaningful look. "I *was* a Hand agent, after all."

Jason pulled the craft's nose up, letting the pinnace aerobrake as he banked around the spire, only firing the a-grav systems for a moment before he set down a kilometer from their destination.

"Why over here?" Sera asked.

He gestured at the fissures covering the floor of the crater. "This is the least convenient approach. Star's behind us too, meaning that if they *are* watching, this is the direction they're watching the least."

"Why would they watch any direction less often?" Valerie asked as she pulled off her harness.

"Maybe they're not," Jason allowed. "But there are always compromises when building an installation like this. Just trying to guess at which ones the builders of this place might have made."

Valerie inclined her head, pursing her lips for a moment. "Fair enough."

Sera followed Valerie and Jason out of the cockpit to the pinnace's small bay, which was fitted out as an armory. The strike team was already getting geared up. Eight members of Sera's High Guard, and a spec-ops squad under Colonel Pearson. And Flaherty, of course.

He gave her a nod, not an iota of worry on his face after Jason's breakneck approach.

In addition to the humans, there were four AIs in the group: Jen with Sera, Julia with Valerie—a pair that the High Guard had taken to calling 'The JJs'—and two in Pearson's team as well. Laney was embedded with the colonel, and another named Fara was in a mobile frame.

All four had spent the trip sharing their breaching techniques with Matthias, a specialist on Pearson's team.

"Alright, people," Pearson said, as Sera stepped into the armor rack and selected a light, ablative armor set. "Not all of us have worked together before, but we know how the job is done. First and foremost, we protect our assets."

With that, he nodded first to Sera and then to Jason, all eyes in the room following his.

"That all I am?" Sera asked with a lopsided grin as she stepped out of the armor rack.

Valerie winked at her. "Pretty much, yeah."

"Secondarily," Pearson continued a moment later, a small scowl settling on his brow. "We're here to grab intel. Every bit of data we can get our hands on. We need to know what the Airthans are up to, and what other strongholds they have tucked away in the far reaches of space. We get that, we protect—" he glanced at Sera and Jason, a smile pulling at the corners of his mouth for just a moment, "—the *president* and the *governor*, and we get out. General Peabody has two pinnaces with a platoon each in low orbit, ready to drop down if we need them, so if the shit hits the fan, you call for backup. No martyrs."

"Colonel has the right of it," Valerie added for the High Guard's benefit. "Protect our charges, get the intel, get out in one piece."

A chorus of affirmations echoed in the room, and Jason slapped Sera on the shoulder, turning her so he could inspect her armor.

<Looks good on you. Not often I see you clothed.> His eyes were serious as he checked her over, but there was a lilt in his mental tone.

<Funny man,> Sera retorted as she examined his armor, then spun him to check his back. *<You look good clothed or naked—not that I see enough of the latter. Don't go getting your fine ass shot off.>*

She clapped him on the shoulder to signal that his armor checked out, then turned for him to inspect her back.

Jason's chuckle rumbled in her mind. *<Look at that, a little action is bringing out the sass in you, Sera.>*

<You talking about the impending fight, or what we got up to in your quarters?>

<Little of column A, a whole bunch of column B.>

Pearson and Valerie walked through the group, both pausing to check over Jason and Sera's gear before moving on.

<Seriously, Val, not my first op,> Sera chided the major.

<True, but you're out of practice. Plus, the last time you were in combat, you flew across a city with your dragon wings, leaving me behind. I distinctly recall having kittens while trying to figure out what happened to you, so you'll forgive me if I plan to keep an eye on you this time around.>

<Good times,> Sera snickered. *<Good times.>*

She grabbed a helmet off the rack and slotted it on before selecting a multi-function rifle, two sidearms, and a lightwand from the weapons rack.

<Take this,> Jason said, handing her a cloak. *<Earnest's people have worked out how to get effective stealth tech in a loose fabric. It's still not*

quite as good as your skin, but better than ablative armor can pull off.>

Sera grabbed the cloak and threw it over her shoulders. *<Handy for hiding gear, too.>*

<That's the idea.>

She grabbed a bandolier of burn sticks and pulse grenades, slipping them on before pulling the cloak around her shoulders. It Linked up with the armor, a new menu of stealth controls appearing on her HUD.

All around her, the rest of the strike team donned their cloaks and formed up at the bay's exit. They waited while the ship extended a shroud that would hide the bay's exterior doors as they slid open.

Pearson's team exited first, spreading out and securing the area.

Laney had already deployed a swath of microdrones that spread out around the pinnace, checking the nearby terrain for sensors and defenses.

Almost immediately, they located several sensors, and marked both their positions and ranges on the team's combat net. Pearson made the call not to disable them—none of the AIs nor Chief Fara were certain they could shut down Airthan scanning tech without setting off an alarm.

<Best to wait 'til we're at the target before we risk detection,> Laney advised.

Sera was in agreement; there was little point in having stealth tech if they didn't utilize it for as long as it was effective.

Crossing the kilometer of terrain between the pinnace and the spire was slow, arduous work. The team kept to rocky ground, doing their best not to disturb the sediment on the base of the crater.

As best as Sera could tell, at one point, the crater had held water—though not much, and not for too long. Perhaps the impact of the meteor that had created this twenty-kilometer divot had been enough to alter the small planet's climate, causing it to lose its surface water.

Another piece of evidence that pointed to the magnetic fields as being artificial in origin. If this world had always possessed such strong fields, it would have held onto more atmosphere.

Ahead, Pearson's scout team crossed the final fissure. Though they were invisible, their markers on the combat net showed that they'd leapt over the gap, something confirmed by a few small wisps of dust lifting into the air.

A breeze swept by, removing the traces, but also scattering the microdrones further. Once the wind had passed, Sera saw Valerie release more drones, spreading them around to further mask the team's progress.

Sera reached the final fissure and eyed the four-meter gap. It wouldn't be hard to jump in the low gravity, but the crevasse was almost forty meters deep, and she didn't want to have to climb back out, should she slip.

<*Want me to hold your hand?*> Jason asked on a tightbeam Link. She saw that he was standing a meter to her right, his invisible form outlined on her HUD.

<*Only if you want me to drop you in there, old man,*> Sera shot back, then worried that her response was too coarse.

Jason only laughed. < *'Old man', is it? When all this is over, we can go back to my cabin, and I'll remind you what this old man knows.*>

Sera shook her head, a grin settling on her lips, as she crouched and then sprang forward, leaping across the gash in the crater's floor. <*You're on, ancient one. I bet I have a few things up my sleeve you've never imagined. I* ***did*** *fly with Cheeky for a decade, you know.*>

<*Believe you me, I've given that some thought,*> Jason said as he leapt across after her.

* * * * *

Five minutes later, the team reached the spire, a towering spike of basalt rising over seventy meters from the base of the crater.

It was worn by wind and the elements, and Sera wasn't sure if it was caused by a volcanic eruption after the impact, or if the meteor had liquified the surrounding rock enough that it had splashed back up and frozen in place.

The latter seemed unlikely, but given some of the bizarre geological formations she'd seen on various planets, it wasn't outside the realm of possibility.

<*So where's the door?*> Valerie asked as they spread out around the rockface.

Sera looked back at the area that was clearly a landing pad, then followed the most level route between it and the base of the spire. It led to a crease in the rock, and she cautiously stepped toward it, releasing a batch of nanoprobes into the air.

<*Sensors here, lining the rock,*> she announced. <*I think it's time to disable them. No way we breach the door and move two-dozen people past without them picking us up.*>

<*On it,*> Jen announced, as Valerie and two of Sera's guards approached.

<*Sera, you're not on point,*> Valerie said, and Sera gritted her teeth, but moved back, watching Pearson's team move into the fore.

Flaherty eased toward her position, and Sera realized she'd lost sight of him on the journey to the spire. She wasn't sure if it was because she wasn't paying attention, or if he'd turned off his IFF systems that randomly updated the combat net with his position.

<*If we need to split up, both Jason and Sera should stay with you, Major,*> Pearson said to Valerie over the command Link. <*That way when the shit hits the fan, one group has priority exfil, and the other creates a diversion, or whatever else we have to do to get them out.*>

<*'When'?*> Jason asked.

<*Maybe,*> Sera shrugged as she watched Jen's progress with infiltrating the sensors embedded in the rocks. <*For all we know, this place is completely unguarded.*>

<*You really believe that?*> Valerie asked.

<*Well…no.*>

<*OK, I have the sensor web spoofed,*> Julia informed the team. <*You could turn off stealth and dance a jig in front of them, and they won't see you.*>

<*Dang it, I left my dancing shoes back in the pinnace,*> Chief Matthias said as he approached a flat stretch of rock at the back of the crease. <*OK, the probes have found the door, it's an irregular micro-seam. Looking for the control mechanism.*>

<*I can backdoor into their network through the sensors,*> Jen suggested.

<*Hold off on that. I think I've found the control. OK…looks like I can…*> Matthias paused. <*Damn.*>

<*Damn?*> Colonel Pearson asked.

<*Yeah, there's a hard-line that connects this door control to an NSAI.*

It's using an active signal to monitor the panel. If I breach from here, I'll trigger an alarm.>

<*OK, Jen,*> Sera directed her AI. <*Try it your way.*>

<*On it.*>

The rest of Pearson's team continued to scour the area surrounding the spire, noting the placement of other sensors while Jen worked her way into the facility's network.

<*This is odd,*> Jason said after a few minutes. <*This crater is littered with sensor webs that would be good enough to spot us if we didn't have better stealth tech than the TSF expected when they set this up.*>

<*Which means?*> Sera prompted.

<*Well, if you detect an enemy, how do you neutralize them?*>

Sera realized that Jason was right. They'd found plenty of different sensor systems: EM bands, sound waves, even geo vibration pickups.

But no defense systems. Not a single autoturret, or drone dispersal port.

<*They could just be really well hidden. This door took us getting right on top of it to spot,*> Valerie countered.

<*Maybe,*> Jason allowed. <*You'd think they'd have some turrets around it, though. But nothing.*>

<*So what do you think?*> Sera asked.

The governor let out a long sigh. <*Honestly? It's starting to feel like a trap.*>

She didn't think that was the case. <*How can it be a trap if the Airthans don't even know that we know about them? This place was built some time ago…long before you started building the Aleutian site.*>

<*Was your father paranoid?*> Jason asked. <*I mean, I think he was, but was he* **this** *paranoid?*>

Sera didn't have to give Jason's question much consideration. <*Yes, yes he probably was.*>

<*We'll keep our eyes peeled,*> Pearson replied. <*But as I understand it, we need this intel, and we can't walk away because it might be dangerous to secure. Though…*> he paused for a moment. <*I'd feel a lot better if you two weren't tagging along.*>

<*You're going to need me to breach the security on any datastores,*> Sera pointed out.

She wasn't going to be left out of the fun that easily. There had to be *some* perks in being president.

<And you, sir?> Pearson directed the comment to Jason.

Jason only snorted. *<Nice try, Colonel.>*

<Was worth a shot. Tanis has rubbed off on all of you.>

<Not me,> Sera replied. *<I was getting into trouble long before I knew her.>*

<Same here.> Jason chuckled. *<Though she may have re-ignited the spirit of adventure in me a bit.>*

<Probably because she's a trouble magnet,> Pearson grunted a moment before Jen sang out in victory.

<Nailed it. Best part about all the data from Terra's past is knowing how many modern systems are built on systems with ancient exploits. I swear, no one does reviews of shared code repositories.>

As Jen spoke, a section of rock slid out and shifted to the side, held aloft by an a-grav field. The group waited as Matthias flushed a nanocloud into the darkened interior.

<OK, ***here*** *we have autoturrets,>* Julia announced. *<Hold one.>*

Sera pulled the feed and saw a long passageway that led to a pair of lift doors.

<Not a lot of options.>

<I'll send a team down first.> Pearson directed Gunnery Sergeant Barry to ready a fireteam to take the first lift down along with Fara once Jen declared the turrets offline.

<I'm not entirely certain that these turrets don't have failsafes, so everyone stay frosty,> Julia directed. *<I've shut down their central control and switched off their firing mechanisms, but they're an unusual design.>*

<I wonder if I should just pass my auth codes to the facility,> Sera mused. *<Could just tell it that I'm the president and order it to let us in.>*

<I think that's too risky.> Valerie sounded nervous, and Sera wondered what had the major on edge. *<Like Jason said, this place smells too much like a trap. Let's not let it know exactly who it has trapped just yet.>*

<Gah, so much caution,> Sera muttered privately to Jason.

<Let them do their jobs. It's important to them.>

Sera glanced at Jason's outline on her HUD, then nodded. *<OK, yeah.>*

Fara set up a relay outside the lift, and then led her team inside.

<Just one level that the lift goes to. Listed as '0'.>

<Seems ominous,> one of the Marines joked, getting a snort from Sera, and a stern cough from the gunnery sergeant.

Before the lift descended, Fara sent a filament of nano through its floor, putting a view of the shaft on the combat net.

<Damn…that's deep,> Sera muttered.

The nano couldn't get a read on the depth, just that it was over ten kilometers.

<Going down,> Fara said as she activated the lift and began to descend.

Sera and Jason walked toward the lifts, taking a position along the wall, while Pearson directed a pair of Marines to move a few hundred meters out onto the crater floor to set up surveillance systems, while directing another pair to patrol the exterior of the spire.

No one spoke as Fara's team continued their long descent, though Jason did give a low whistle when they passed the hundred-kilometer mark.

The lift continued on until it had descended nearly a thousand kilometers into the planet. Readings from Fara's team showed no significant increase in heat, meaning the core of the planet was not molten—or at least not where the shaft penetrated.

<Radius of this world is only three-thousand klicks,> Sera said at one point. *<Think that lift goes down to the core?>*

<Seems increasingly likely,> Jason replied. *<Express elevator to hell.>*

As he spoke, the lift began to slow, and Sera slaved her vision to Fara's optics, watching as the team exited the lifts and fanned out into a circular chamber. Directly ahead stood a pair of large doors, and Fara approached them, rifle held ready.

<Place is dead. No EM at all. Not even a wireless network offering handshakes,> she reported.

The Marines stacked up around the door while Fara accessed the controls. A minute later they slid open, and the team rushed through, securing the next room.

What they saw caused Sera to suck in a sharp breath.

"What the hell?"

CORNERED

STELLAR DATE: 09.06.8949 (Adjusted Years)
LOCATION: IPSS *Deepening Night*
REGION: Trensch System, Inner Praesepe Empire

Corsia screaming in her face seemed to snap Commander Eve back to full consciousness, and she rose on shaky legs to follow the AI as they ran further toward the bow of the ship.

"What the fuck," Eve muttered when she finally regained the powers of speech. "Heavy combat mechs on a ship? They're gonna hole it themselves."

"Seems like those remnants really want to get their hands on us," Corsia replied as they rounded a corner and nearly bowled over an enemy soldier. Corsia grabbed him by the neck, pushing his head back, and fired three shots under his chin with her pilfered rifle.

The man went down, and she grabbed his weapon before they took off once more.

"We need to find somewhere to hole up," Eve said as they pulled open a hatch and slid down the ladder to the next deck.

"Agreed," Corsia replied. "Preferably somewhere near the forward sensor array so we can hack it and get comms with our ships. I'd like to take Arthur and Larson alive. Learn what the hell the ASAIs are doing with the IPE...what strategic value can it hold for them?"

"Other than to deny it to us? I've no idea," Eve said, slowing as they reached an intersection, and releasing a fresh passel of nano to scout ahead.

Corsia pondered the possibilities as the nanocloud began to spread out, highlighting nearby IPE personnel that were rushing to duty stations.

She spotted a clear path in the enemy's movement patterns and directed Eve ahead. Though Corsia could trigger her skin to activate its stealth modes, Eve's camouflage was compromised by the blood all over her uniform. Not to mention the fact that neither had stealth capable weapons.

For now, they'd have to rely on the nanocloud to mask their movements from internal sensors, and do their best to avoid the enemy's Mark 1 eyeball.

As they skulked down the corridors, Corsia considered how unlikely it was that the ASAI would have two remnants in the IPE just to deny the ISF—or any others—access to ship-building resources.

Then another thought occurred to her.

She considered the variations they'd witnessed in the orbits of the three stars of the Trensch System. On their current trajectories, the only thing that would change is a few of the lagrange points in the system.

But what if the changes keep happening along the same course as they have thus far?

Corsia tasked a process with solving the three-body problem, and watched the gravitational shifts that occurred within the Trensch System and the cluster's core.

"Shit..." she whispered a minute later.

"What is it?" Eve asked, glancing behind them. "Did you pick something up?"

"No," Corsia said, while gesturing for Eve to move to the hatch that would lead them down another deck. "I think I know what the ASAIs are doing here."

Eve waited for the nanocloud to slip around the edges of the hatch and into the level below, declaring it clear before she pulled it up and slid down the ladder.

"So what is it?"

"I think they're going to collapse the stars of this system into a black hole."

"What? Really?" Eve glanced up at Corsia as she slid down the ladder, landing silently on the deck below. "That won't change anything, the mass of the system will just be concentrated in one place."

"I don't know why," Corsia replied, as they crept along the empty corridor toward the forward sensor array—now just thirty meters further in, behind a maintenance panel. "I just know what. Maybe they saw what happened in Bollam's World, and they're going to try to suck in all the dark matter."

Eve's mouth hung open for a moment. "From the *cluster*?"

Corsia gestured for Eve to keep moving. "I'm just speculating. No matter what, it's probably bad for the rest of us."

The corridor ahead ended in a 'T' right at the access panel for the forward sensor array's control system. Corsia was certain that once they reached it, she could breach the system and reach out to Sephira aboard the *Andromeda.*

The pair was five meters from the junction when the nanocloud alerted them to a pair of technicians walking down the corridor to the right.

Eve glanced at Corsia and nodded to her rifle.

Corsia shook her head, and handed her rifle to Eve, then motioned for the Marine to press herself flat against the bulkhead, while Corsia stood in front of her, and triggered her skin to shift from the appearance of a shipsuit to invisibility.

Her body didn't perfectly mask Eve's, but the Marine saw what Corsia was doing, and triggered her own armor's stealth systems, keeping her left side out of view.

A tense few seconds passed as the IPE technicians reached the 'T' junction, paused, and then turned down the corridor toward Corsia and Eve.

Corsia clenched a fist, ready to take the enemies out as they passed, but the pair hurried by without even a sideways glance at the bulkhead where Corsia and Eve stood.

"That was close," Eve whispered once the coast was clear.

"Yeah, pretty sure our rifles were visible between us."

Eve took up a position at the 'T', ready for any further visitors, while Corsia pulled off the access panel, revealing a small NSAI node that controlled the forward sensors.

"Should only take a moment," she said while placing a hand over a hard-Link port, feeding a tendril of nano into the system.

"Good, because we're sitting ducks here," Eve muttered.

Corsia nodded absently as she began to breach the NSAI node's defenses. She worked slowly, not wanting to alert the system to her presence. The last thing they needed was for the IPE to spot a node under attack.

"Almost there," she whispered.

Then Eve stiffened. "Too late," the Marine muttered.

Corsia held back a curse as she saw the reason for Eve's utterance. IPE Marines had appeared at the ends of each corridor forming the 'T' junction.

"Freeze! Step away from there!" a voice yelled, as the enemy Marines advanced toward Corsia and Eve.

BOLT HOLE

STELLAR DATE: 09.06.8949 (Adjusted Years)
LOCATION: Hidden Facility, Planet HH1
REGION: Hidey Hole System, Large Magellanic Cloud

Sera stepped off the lift with Jason at her side, glancing at him before striding across the circular room to the doors guarded by a pair of Marines.

She knew what the other side held, but still marveled at the sight when it met her.

Beyond the doors was a hallway with windows along one side, and those windows revealed a vast, hollow void, one thousand kilometers across.

The spherical space was at the center of the planet, but it wasn't empty.

The first thing that crossed Sera's mind as she stood at the window, looking down at the void beneath her, was that gravity was a touch higher here than it was on the surface.

That confirmed her suspicion that the hundred-kilometer-wide sphere she could see far below, positioned at the center of the planet, housed a black hole.

One that was likely spinning rapidly within layers of ferric materials, creating the world's strong magnetic field, and protecting the contents of the void within the world.

Sera corrected her thinking. It wasn't a *void* per se. It was half-full of stuff, but it was not the sort of material one normally encountered in a planetary core.

Towers anchored to the black hole's housing at the center of the planet stretched up in every direction, reaching to the rock ceiling above. Wrapped around every tower at ninety meter intervals were broad platforms, each covered in a dome that enclosed a different biome, filled with plant and animal life.

<It's an ark,> Jason said from Sera's side.

<That's my assessment as well,> Jen replied. *<I've tapped into the environmental management systems. The facility is entirely automated,*

and from what I can see, hasn't had a sentient visitor for over a century.>

<*I concur,*> Fara added. <*I've reached what I can only assume is the facility's command and control center. Route is marked on your HUDs.*>

Sera tore her eyes away from the strange view before her and began to walk down the passageway, still glancing out the windows that lined either side, which were angled out to allow for a better view of the marvels below.

<*Why would my father build this?*> Sera asked Jason privately. <*Was he expecting some calamity to wipe out the Transcend?*>

<*Well…yes?*> Jason laughed as he spoke. <*On one side he was expanding toward the core AIs, and on the other was Orion. On top of that, the Inner Stars continued to be a roiling mess.*>

<*I get that,*> Sera replied. <*It's probably the whole reason he was setting up out here in the LMC. But if they were terraforming all those worlds in surrounding stars, why make this hidden ark in the middle?*>

<*Maybe he made it first,*> Jason suggested. <*I wonder…*>

<*Yeah?*> Sera asked as they turned down a passageway that no longer had windows looking out into the interior of the planet.

<*Well, if you were worried about a growing array of enemies, maybe you wouldn't wait for something like jump gates. Maybe you'd set up contingencies long before that. As the photon flies, it's only about five hundred years to get out here; maybe your father sent a team long, long ago.*>

Sera considered Jason's words as they walked down the passage toward the C&C that Fara had marked on their HUDs, barely aware of the High Guard surrounding her.

What were you up to, Father? she wondered.

Sometimes it felt like the few decades she'd spent with him had barely been enough time to scratch the surface of who he was…of what he'd done.

There were times Sera felt as though she'd not known him at all.

That uncertainty was further reinforced by the stories Jason told of places he'd been in Alpha Centauri, many bearing the name 'Tomlinson'—all in honor of her father.

The first FGT captain. The first person to travel out into the stars with the magnanimous vision of building worlds for humanity to spread to.

The Future Generation Terraformers.

She wondered how their grand vision had turned into two groups pitting the rest of humanity against one another as they readied for the greatest war to ever sweep across the stars.

The father of hers who had led humanity down this path to war didn't align with the one who had set out from Sol nearly seven thousand years ago.

Her musing was interrupted when they reached the C&C, and she stepped inside.

The room was a half-circle, angled down toward the planet's core at forty-five degrees, the forward half having a transparent wall and floor that allowed for a near unobstructed view of the center of the planet.

Fara stood at one of the consoles, while the Marines in her team took up positions around the room.

<We're checking the rest of the facility—so much as we can in any reasonable time,> Pearson called in. *<You all stay put.>*

<Will do,> Sera replied. *<I suspect it's going to take some time to crack this egg.>*

She looked around, wondering where Flaherty was, and pinged him.

<Don't worry about me,> he replied. *<Just checking the surrounding rooms.>*

<OK, Dad.>

<We have control of the room's sensors,> Jen said. *<Atmosphere is clear; you can de-stealth and take off helmets if you'd like.>*

<Whoa, now,> Valerie said as she disabled her stealth, standing near a console in the center of the room. *<Helmets stay on.>*

<Wasn't going to pull it off,> Sera replied. *<Like I said—>*

<I know,> Valerie interrupted. *<Not your first op.>*

<Cheeky,> Sera muttered. *<And not the pilot, either.>*

<OK,> Fara announced.

Sera walked toward the front of the room, feeling like she should be sliding downhill, but held in place by the a-grav systems in the room. The feeling made her a little nauseous, but she ignored it. It wouldn't do for the president to get sick inside her helmet.

<'OK' what?> Jason asked.

<*This is up there with the most elaborate encryption I've ever encountered,*> Fara informed them. <*It might take days to find a way around it. Weeks to get through it.*>

Sera walked toward the central console—the only one showing any activity—and saw that it was prompting for the presidential tokens.

<*Looks like only my father was intended to unlock this place,*> she said in a mental whisper.

<*Let me try a few other—*> Fara began, but Sera stopped her with a raised hand.

<*We don't have days or weeks. We need to know what's in here* ***now****.*>

Fara nodded and took a step back. Beside the prompt was a hard-Link port, and a bioanalysis sleeve. Both systems required physical contact; wireless auth and remote DNA samples wouldn't pass muster.

<*I'm buffering you,*> Jen advised, as Sera unspooled a hard-Link cable from her armor and jacked in. Then she signaled her armor to disconnect the glove, and watched as it folded back onto her arm, revealing her red-skinned hand.

She altered her flesh to allow penetration by the sampling system, and slid her hand into the sleeve.

The console sent a signal across the hard-Link, prompting for Sera's authorization tokens. She used the provided hashing algorithm, and generated a fresh token which she passed into the system.

The word 'Verifying' hung in front of her vision for a full ten seconds before it disappeared, replaced by 'Accepted'.

All around them, the other consoles activated. Sera was about to make a triumphant statement, when the walls came alive.

REMNANTS

STELLAR DATE: 09.06.8949 (Adjusted Years)
LOCATION: IPSS *Deepening Night*
REGION: Trensch System, Inner Praesepe Empire

<*What's our play?*> Eve asked, the need for EM silence gone.

<*I have no idea,*> Corsia replied, playing through every possible option—seeing none where either she or Eve would escape. <*I think we have to surrender…hope that Sephira can get them to stand down.*>

As she spoke, a shudder rippled through the ship's deck, and Corsia saw an alert flash on the *Deepening Night*'s emergency broadcast network that the engines had been hit.

<*See? We'll be OK.*> Corsia tried to keep her mental tone encouraging, but she wasn't so certain they'd weather this.

If it were humans they were dealing with, she would have been far more certain of how things would play out. With remnants? There was no way to know what their endgame was…what they'd sacrifice to see their goals achieved.

Corsia's rifles were already leaning up against the bulkhead, and she set her sidearm down before stepping away from them, nodding for Eve to follow suit.

<*I'm still in the node. I can get a signal out letting them know —*>

"Well, looks like we'll be continuing our conversation after all," a voice said from the central passageway, followed by the appearance of President Arthur.

Larson was on his heels, the two remnant-controlled humans striding forward as if they had no reason whatsoever to fear Corsia and Eve.

Which was probably true.

"I don't think we'll get very far with a chat," Corsia replied as the IPE Marines closed on either side, reaching the dropped weapons and kicking them aside.

Then two soldiers in heavy armor reached Corsia and Eve, and clamped thick bands around their arms.

"No?" Arthur said as he stopped in front of Corsia. "I think that our conversation will happen whether you want it to or not. I don't know why you're walking around in that meat-suit, Admiral Corsia, but now that I know what you are, I'll subsume you just as easily as if you had been an organic."

"Give it your best shot," Corsia challenged, ready to trigger a death cycle in her mind, should she be at risk of giving up any of the ISF's secrets.

A sidelong glance from Eve told Corsia that she was ready to follow suit. Before either of them could speak further, Arthur reached forward and grasped Eve's head, clamping down hard.

Eve began to scream, her eyes bulging from their sockets, as Corsia struggled to free herself, sending nano into the soldier behind her, fighting with the enemy's armor's control systems.

"None of that," Larson said as he strode toward Corsia, his hand outstretched toward her.

His palm was centimeters from Corsia's forehead, when she saw the secretary's eyes look over her shoulder and widen in surprise.

Corsia twisted and looked behind herself to see…something that made no sense.

The NSAI node, and the equipment behind it, was disintegrating—solid objects turning into streams of particulate matter, and flowing through the ship, toward the hull.

Then more of the bulkhead began to dissolve, and Corsia could see starlight shining through the clouds of dust. In the midst of that cloud, a silhouetted human figure was moving through space toward the ship.

As the person grew closer, Corsia could see that they were wearing light armor, the suit's jets propelling them toward the IPE cruiser.

Upon closer inspection, Corsia saw that something was wrong with their head…it seemed diaphanous. Then the tableau made sense—sort of. The human woman drawing near wasn't wearing a helmet, and her hair was flowing out behind her in the vacuum of space.

That was when Corsia made out the approaching rescuer's features.

Tanis.

* * * * *

The hull of the IPE cruiser was a web of molecular and atomic bonds, their matrices a simple puzzle that Tangel solved and undid, drawing the energy from the bonds into herself as needed, while letting much of the power that lay between the atoms bleed off into space around her. Photons bled off into the darkness along with other high-energy waveforms, as solid matter degenerated into more basic components.

Then she was through the hull, and the internals of the ship began to come apart before her. She disassembled components of the forward sensor array, then the NSAI node that had sent the telling, momentary ping out into space, alerting her to the location of Corsia and Eve.

There they are! she thought triumphantly, as the passageway came into view.

With a thought, she extended the ship's grav shields to keep the atmosphere within the IPE cruiser, despite the gaping hole in its hull.

It wouldn't do to kill her people during their rescue.

Her eyes lit upon the man touching Eve's head, and she saw that there was a remnant within him, its tendrils reaching into Eve's mind.

No, Tangel thought.

With a flick of her hand—the part of it outside normal space-time—she separated the molecules in the human hand touching the Marine, then grasped the tendril the remnant had extended, yanking the entire remnant out of the person it had been inhabiting.

The remnant curled in upon itself, forming a ball of light, and Tangel formed a weave of energy around it, holding the remnant in place while she reached for the one in the other man.

It fought her, but she pulled it free, too, and placed it within its own cage.

As the two humans who had been under the enemy's sway collapsed, she infiltrated the armor of the soldiers holding Corsia and Eve, using them to free the women, and then directed them to stand aside.

A moment later, she eased through the grav field, and settled onto the deck next to Corsia.

"You called?" Tangel asked with a smirk.

Corsia's mouth worked for a moment, as though the AI had forgotten how to operate the organic body she currently inhabited.

"Well, I was about to," she finally managed to say.

Eve was tottering on her feet, and Corsia grabbed her and eased her to the deck.

Tangel glanced at the two men before her—President Arthur and Secretary Larson, from the data Terrance had given her. Both wobbled, and the president half rose, then fell back, putting a hand against the bulkhead while muttering incoherently.

All around them, the enemy soldiers were standing dumbfounded, then one leveled his weapon at Tangel, shouting, "Stand down!"

"Brave," Tangel said with a laugh, and threaded a tendril of herself toward the weapon, causing it to dissolve in the soldier's hands. "I believe it is all of *you* who should stand down."

She proceeded to ignore the enemy soldiers and walked toward the IPE's president.

"Arthur. Are you OK?"

The man's gaze lifted from the deck to meet Tangel's, and she gave him an encouraging smile.

"Welcome back," she said softly.

"What? How?" he asked, his voice beleaguered.

"It's going to take a bit to explain. Can you have your soldiers stand down? We need to get medical attention for our people, and then we can talk."

The president nodded numbly and sent a command to his soldiers, who slowly lowered their weapons.

"Good." Tangel smiled before turning to Eve. "Let me see to your shoulder."

She reached out with her extradimensional limbs, assisting the soldier's mednano in healing her body, and then reformed her armor over her shoulder.

Eve's eyes were round circles of awe as she stared at Tangel, and Corsia's weren't much narrower.

<*You've ascended,*> the AI said in a hushed mental tone.

<*I have, but let's not spread it too far just yet.*>

Corsia nodded, her motions slow and deliberate. <*OK, but what do I call you now? Are you still two?*>

<*'Tangel', Corsia. You can call me 'Tangel'.*>

TAKE A MIRACLE

STELLAR DATE: 09.06.8949 (Adjusted Years)
LOCATION: Ark Facility, Planet HH1
REGION: Hidey Hole System, Large Magellanic Cloud

The Marines and the High Guard leapt into motion, firing at barely perceptible movement all around the room's perimeter. Shots struck foes, and Sera saw ten-legged mech frames shimmer into view.

Judging by their size, there had to be a hundred of the things lining the walls. She unslung her rifle, firing at a shimmering form atop a console, when something hit her in the back, knocking her to the ground.

It was at that moment that Sera realized the deca-mechs were falling from the overhead as well.

Her wrists were pinned to the floor, and she struggled to free them, twisting and kicking at her invisible foes. She managed to get her left arm free, and she drew her lightwand, slashing wildly, watching robotic limbs fall around her. She struggled to her feet to see only Fara and one of her High Guard still fighting—every other member of the team was trapped under a writhing mass of deca-mechs.

A slow clap came from the entrance of the room.

"Well done…you."

Sera turned to see the speaker, and came face to face with herself.

No…not exactly myself.

Walking into the room, wearing light armor, but with the helmet off, was a version of herself—one with organic skin, short, dark hair, and utterly boring fashion sense.

Sera didn't know the last to be true, but given the pedestrian haircut, she was certain that the pawn version of herself that her mother had made was completely unremarkable in every way.

<*OK, so…trap,*> Jen commented.

The robotic attackers throughout the room disabled their stealth systems as the Airthan Sera entered, and Sera saw that there were easily two hundred of the machines. She had to admit it was impressive that so many had been able to hide—at least so long as they were still.

"You can put the lightwand away," the other Sera said. "I'm not going to attack you, I've been waiting here for weeks to meet you. Plus…I have no need to. You'll do as I say, or your people here will die. Horribly."

Sera tried to reach out to Pearson's team, but the comm signal didn't make a connection.

<*I've been trying it, but they have an EM jammer running nearby,*> Jen informed Sera.

<*Keep trying,*> Sera said as she turned to see Jason struggling beneath a dozen of the deca-mechs. A little further was Valerie, laying utterly still. She tried to reach out to both, but even in the room, the signal was blocked.

Sera glanced at her lightwand and disabled its blade, but didn't let go of the hilt. "What do you want, Evil Sera?" she asked.

Her doppelganger snorted. "*I'm* the evil one? You're the Sera whose lover killed our father, the one who has red skin, and is leading a rebellion. Stars, I even heard you were a demon at a party not long ago. Pretty sure that if this is a battle between good and evil, you're on the wrong side."

Sera chuckled; her doppelganger had her at a disadvantage when it came to her personal tastes. "I suppose I might be 'Bad Sera'," she admitted. "But that's just skin deep. Given what Airtha has likely done to you, you're probably rotten to the core. If you even have a core. You're probably not much more than her sock puppet."

Her clone's eyes widened a millimeter at the words, but then narrowed once more. "Well, either way, you've done what I wanted—what mother wanted. Gained access to the archives here."

Sera glanced at Fara, who was pinned down two meters to her left. The shadowtron was still slung over the AI's back—though trapped beneath a pair of deca-mechs. She knew getting to that weapon was key. She had no doubt that a remnant was in control of the Airthan Sera.

"What? You couldn't access it yourself?" Sera asked with a wicked grin. "Can't light up your own facility?"

"I didn't have the tokens."

<*I find that highly unlikely,*> Jen commented privately. <*I wonder if your mother has done something—changed her DNA enough that the system wouldn't verify it.*>

<*I guess that makes sense,*> Sera replied. <*But a little verification that I'm the real me is nice, too.*> She chuckled aloud, then said, "Sounds like an excuse."

She suddenly remembered that her hard-Link cable was still connected to the console; the cord ran from her hip—not visible to her doppelganger, who was weaving her way through the mechs that had formed a wall around Sera.

She drew a steadying breath, then hooked her foot under the console's leg. Once secure, Sera sent a command to reverse the room's a-grav systems, switching up for down.

A second later, Sera was hanging from the console by her foot, and each member of her team was now atop the deca-mechs. With a flick of her wrist, she activated her lightwand and flung it at the window at the end of the room, the blade slicing a long gash in the plas before burning a hole through and falling out into the planet's empty core.

<*You better hope that thing doesn't land on the black hole housing,*> Jen commented.

<*I gave it a thirty-second shut-off,*> Sera replied as she shifted gravity in the room by seventy degrees, turning the roof into a steep slope.

Deca-mechs tumbled over one another, a dozen slamming into the damaged window, cracking it and falling away over the brink.

"Shit!" Jason swore as he began to slide toward the opening, along with Fara and two of the ISF Marines. The others were scrambling over the enemy, shooting some, slashing others.

The Airthan Sera cried out and lunged toward Jason, grabbing his wrist and pulling him toward a console.

The deca-mechs had not re-engaged their stealth systems, but the Marines and High Guard had. The battle re-engaged, and the humans gained the upper hand as more and more of the deca-mechs tumbled toward the end of the room, falling toward the planet's core.

Jason was grappling with the Airthan Sera, who Sera realized had been trying to save him, while, nearby, Fara had managed to leap to the deck-now-overhead, and was clinging to a console.

Sera! Call me crazy, but I draw the line at base jumping into black holes! Little help here with the gravity, here?" Jason cried out as he drove a fist into Airthan Sera's face, sending her sprawling, just as a deca-mech grabbed his leg, pulling him down.

A few more seconds, Sera urged, as another dozen mechs slid out of the room.

Then she snapped the failsafe ES field into place, and flipped the gravity around once more.

The room devolved into a final spate of utter chaos as the High Guard and Marines fired on the enemy, several even tossing burn sticks at a few clusters of mechs, the acrid smoke from thermite fires filling the air.

Then something struck Sera, and she turned to see her Airthan counterpart holding a deca-mech's severed limb, hauling it back for another swing at her head.

Sera threw her left arm up in a block, then grabbed the mech-limb and yanked it away, only to have her doppelganger pivot and deliver a kick to Sera's wrist.

She hadn't pulled her armor back over her hand after the bio-samples, and she lost her grip on the limb, taking a step back as the other Sera—a primal scream tearing past her lips—charged toward her and knocked her to the ground, pulling her hard-Link cable free.

Losing sight of the general melee, Sera drove a fist up into her other self, catching her under the chin and snapping her head back, only to receive a flurry of blows to her stomach for her trouble.

A fistfight in armor was patently ridiculous, and Sera cast about, looking around for a fallen weapon, when the other Sera was pulled off her and flung across the room.

She saw both Jason and Flaherty standing over her, each man extending a hand.

"You're the good one, right?" Jason asked aloud as they pulled her up.

"Funny. Thanks for the save."

All around them, the enemy mechs had all fallen still, though most appeared to be undamaged.

"Took a few minutes to worm my way in," Fara explained as she approached. "Their NSAI cores were too hard to hack, but as it turns out, their limb actuators use a system I'm familiar with, and I was able to fake limb-control commands once I got nano on them."

"Nicely done," Valerie rasped from behind Sera, and the president turned to see the major applying biofoam to a wound in her upper chest. "Damn thing missed my heart by a few centimeters."

Gunny and one of the High Guard soldiers had Evil Sera pinned against the wall, and the Marine was applying a LockIt to her armor.

Sera approached her Airthan counterpart, watching the rage simmer in the other woman's eyes.

"I guess you weren't quite clever enough," Sera told her. "Should have waited for me to disconnect from the hard-Link before you made your grand entrance."

"You'll never get away," the doppelganger said. "I sent out a signal. We have stealthed ships that will be here in less than an hour."

<*I can confirm that,*> Julia said over the combat net. <*Comms are back, and we've relayed our status up to General Peabody. He's sending down the other pinnaces.*>

<*Has he detected the stealthed Airthan ships, yet?*> Pearson asked as he reconnected to the combat net. <*And is everyone OK?*>

<*Operational,*> Valerie replied. <*Not necessarily OK.*>

<*The* Helios*'s scan has picked up sixty enemy vessels less than three light seconds from the planet.*> Fara announced. <*He's moving to engage them. Distress signal is out on the QuanComm.*>

"Then we'd better find out what secrets this place has, and get the hell out of here," Sera said as she turned back to the console and reconnected her hard-Link.

<*Jen, just suck it all down into our internal datastores; use the whole team's, if you have to.*>

<*You got it, boss.*>

"That was one heck of a gamble," Jason said as he approached. "Coulda dropped half of us out there."

"Your armor has a-grav and thrusters," Sera gestured to Jason's gear. "You *probably* would have been OK. Could have aimed for one of those biomes down there."

"Real reassuring," Jason said, a mock frown on his brow and a hint of smile on his lips.

"Well, I would have turned the ES field on before you fell out. Promise."

"Somehow your glib tone makes me feel less certain."

"Sorry, I get snarky when I'm—wait..."

Jason cocked his head to the side. "You get snarky when you wait?"

"Uh, no...I mean I found something. Something weird."

"This whole place is weird," Valerie said from a few meters away, where she was driving a lightwand through the central core of a deca-mech.

"Well, this is weirder...maybe. There's a vault at the back of this room."

As Sera spoke, she activated the vault's doors, and a section of the rear wall swung away, revealing a stasis pod resting vertically in a narrow alcove. The surface of the pod was opaque, not revealing the occupant.

"Huh...I wonder who that—" Jason began to say, then stopped short as Sera activated the wake sequence. "Well, I guess we'll find out."

The pod registered a successful termination of its stasis field, and Sera disconnected her hard-Link, stepping over the disabled mechs as she walked toward it.

She was still a few paces away when the cover slid open, and she gasped.

"Father?"

The man in the stasis pod was a spitting image of Jeffrey Tomlinson. He had the raven hair, the sharp eyes, and angular features, but he looked subtly different at the same time. His lips were more generous, his eyes a touch kinder.

Though I suppose it could just be that he looks really confused.

His gaze swept across the room, then landed on Sera, his eyes widening.

"Julianna?" he whispered. "How? What is going on?"

"Uh...I'm not Julianna," Sera replied, never having considered how much like her human mother she may appear. "It's me, your daughter. Seraphina."

"Who?" Sera's father asked, taking a tentative step out of the stasis pod. "Where…where am I?"

"We call the system 'Hidey Hole'." Sera replied almost absently, staring into the eyes of the man before her, wondering how he could be here. Was he a clone? Another of Airtha's pawns?

"Really?" the other Sera snorted. "Try the 'Nora System'."

"Nora…" Jeffrey Tomlinson whispered. "How did I end up here?" Suddenly his eyes narrowed as he looked at Sera, then at her doppelganger. "Wait…daughter? Are you twins?"

"She's a clone," both Seras said at once, then glowered at one another.

"That's kinda creepy," Valerie said in hushed tones.

"I only have one daughter," Jeffrey said after a moment. "Andrea…and neither of you look a thing like her."

"Father," Sera asked, stepping toward the man she'd spent so much of her life either wishing desperately to please or reviling. "What year did you go into stasis?"

Jeffrey glanced back at the stasis pod he'd just stepped out of. "Well…I don't remember going into stasis, but my internal clock aligns with my last memories. It's 7977."

"Shit," Sera whispered. "You've been in there for over a thousand years."

"Well if he's been in there, who was running the Transcend for the last thousand years?" Jason asked.

Jeffrey had a stricken look on his face, and he staggered backward, placing a hand on the wall to steady himself. He swallowed and looked up at Sera, and then her evil twin.

"Airtha," he whispered.

<I have a full dump, we should get out of here,> Jen announced.

Sera nodded absently, her eyes still on her father…or, to his mind, the man who was genetically her father, but had never even known her.

"We have to go," Sera said. "Airtha's forces are coming."

"She's here?" Jeffrey asked, paling further. "She knows about our work in the LMC?"

Sera took a step forward. "Father…she…she's running half the Transcend now…with her." She jerked a thumb at the other Sera.

"And you?" Jeffrey asked, meeting her eyes and not glancing away for the first time since he'd called her 'Julianna'.

"I'm running the other half. Trying to get our civil war under control so we can confront Orion."

"We're at war with Orion too?" he asked, pushing himself away from the wall. "What of the Inner Stars?"

"Everyone's at war with everyone, Father."

Sera couldn't help but feel like she'd utterly failed this man she didn't even know. When he had gone into stasis, the last FTL wars had finally ended, and the age of reconstruction was beginning.

Now everything he had worked for was in shambles.

"Why do you keep calling me that?" Jeffrey asked. "I didn't raise you."

A lump formed in Sera's throat, and she found herself unable to speak.

"Shit…sorry," Jeffrey said, as the High Guard ushered them out of the C&C and back into the corridors leading to the lifts. "I didn't…"

"You *did* raise me. Well, you and uncle Finaeus," Sera said once she'd regained the powers of speech. "I guess…I guess it was just a different one of you."

"Finaeus?" Jeffrey asked. "You must take me to him, he'll know what's happened. He never trusted Julianna after she came back."

"Don't worry." She placed a hand on her father's shoulder. "We'll take you to him. He's really going to be happy to see you."

<Do you think he's the original?> Jason asked as he fell in on Sera's other side. *<Or is he a clone?>*

<I don't know,> she admitted, unable to keep the waver out of her mental voice. *<I mean…that means the man who raised me really wasn't my father.>*

<We still have your father's body,> Jason reminded her after a moment's pause. *<Back at New Canaan. We could figure out which was the original.>*

<Oh, shit!> Sera exclaimed, suddenly realizing they'd not checked Evil Sera over with the shadowtron. *<Fara, you need—>*

<*I've already checked. Neither of them have remnants in them,*> Fara answered before Sera could complete her question.

<*I don't know if that makes me feel better, or worse—at least about other me.*>

<*We need a name for her,*> Jason said as they turned down the corridor with the downward-looking windows on either side. <*How does 'Seratwo' sound?*>

Sera couldn't help a laugh. <*Dumb. I prefer 'Evil Sera'.*>

"I can't believe it's been a thousand years..." Jeffrey said to no one in particular, shaking his head as they walked toward the lifts. He glanced at Sera. "Are you really my daughter? And her? Clones you said?"

"I'm the original," Sera said, then jerked her thumb at her doppelganger. "Airtha made *her* after I wouldn't play ball."

Evil Sera only snorted and shook her head in silence.

"Airtha tried to trick me into killing you," Sera said to her father. "Well, the other you. In the end, an Orion agent did it, but then Finaeus arrived, and Airtha tipped her hand by trying to kill him. It was then that we realized she'd been playing all of us, manipulating things to take control of the Transcend and spark up a war with Orion."

"All of that is true, except for the part where Airtha is the one in the wrong," Evil Sera said, as they reached the lifts to find Pearson already sending one of his fireteams up. "The Caners made this other Sera to try and take over the Transcend."

"Oh, c'mon!" Sera turned and took a step toward her clone. "*When* did they do that? When did the people of New Canaan have access to you to make a copy? They were cooped up in their system the whole time."

"They did it when I was on the *Intrepid*," the other Sera shot back. "Before I flew back to Airtha from Ascella."

"Oh yeah?" Sera asked. "Then how do I remember everything about being the director of the Hand? How do I remember the night of June twenty-seventh, when Elena and I went swimming in Wishbone Lake, and she cut her foot on that sunken statue? That all happened *after* Ascella."

The other Sera paled, and Sera knew she had her on the ropes.

"See! We *both* remember those years. Which means you were made from *me* while we were on Airtha—under our mother's tender care."

"I—" the Airthan Sera began, then stopped.

"And what about Helen?" Sera asked. "What happened to Helen?"

"She had to be removed," the other Sera retorted. "It had been too long."

"Damn right it had been too long," Sera muttered. "Face it, girl. You're the copy. You may *be* me in every way, but you're still the copy. Proof is in the skin."

"Your skin?" Jeffrey asked, a puzzled look on his face.

Sera held up her hand, still unarmored, and changed it from red to a light tan, then transparent. "Airtha doesn't have the tech to do that. Not with skin, not that smoothly. It's why you're so pedestrian," she sneered at her clone.

The other Sera pursed her lips, looking resolute, but then her face fell, and she turned away, her shoulders drooping.

She whispered, "Stars…I wish none of this had ever happened. I should have stayed aboard *Sabrina*."

Sera's sense of victory became pyrrhic as the realization hit her that—despite Airtha's influence—this other woman wearing her face *was* her. She had the same hopes and dreams. The same memories, passions, the same vulnerabilities.

"Dammit," she muttered, imagining how terrible her counterpart must feel, knowing that everything she believed was a lie. "Look, we'll figure this all out."

She nodded to Pearson, and his Marines directed the despondent Sera into the lift on the left, while Sera and Jason took the other one up with Jeffrey and the High Guard.

"This is going to take a bit for me to wrap my head around," Jeffery said, after a minute on the lift had passed. "You're going to have to walk me through this step by step. And…you're really my daughter?"

Sera shrugged. "I guess? Genetically speaking, at least. Airtha must have cloned you at some point—"

"*She* didn't," Jeffrey said. "I did, as a fallback. She must have found him and...unless *I'm* him. I don't know that I'd be able to tell."

"We'll be able to tell," Jason said.

Jeffrey glanced at Jason. "I'm sorry, this has all been entirely crazy. You're...?"

"Jason Andrews." He held out his hand. "One-time captain of the GSS *Intrepid*."

Jeffrey took Jason's proffered hand and shook it once while whispering, "the *Intrepid*..."

"Colony ship, left Sol in 4124," Jason supplied.

Jeffrey's eyes went wide. "*That Intrepid*? No wonder the shit's hit the fan."

"We've been a bit of a catalyst," Jason said in agreement.

No one spoke as the lift continued its journey to the surface.

In the passageway, Fara provided Jeffrey with an EV suit, while they had the other Sera strip out of her armor and don one as well.

Five minutes later, they were outside the spire, and Valerie guided her charges toward one of the backup pinnaces that had set down in front of the facility, while Pearson led the other Sera to the second ship.

They'd only taken a few steps when the atmosphere began to shimmer a few paces ahead, then a thunderclap tore through the air, knocking everyone sprawling.

Sera clambered to her feet to see a silhouetted figure standing before them, tendrils of light spread around it.

<Shit! It's an ASAI!> Valerie cried out, raising her rifle.

"Valerie, stop," the figure's voice boomed, and Sera's mouth fell open.

"Tanis?" she asked, broadcasting with her armor's speakers.

The tendrils of light drew back into the figure, and Sera saw that it was indeed Tanis. She was wearing light armor, but no helmet—on a world without a breathable atmosphere. She was holding something in her hands like a shield, but cast it aside as she approached.

"I guess the cat's out of the bag now, isn't it?" Tanis asked, a smirk forming on her lips. "And it's 'Tangel' now. Are you all safe?"

Sera felt like the air had been sucked right out of her lungs as she gaped at Tanis—Tangel. "Yes...how...?"

"Let's get you into the pinnace," Tangel said. "Me too; eventually I'll need to breathe again. Plus, I want to talk to your father."

<Yeah,> Sera managed to say after switching to the Link. *<Looks like there's a lot to talk about. Stars…that feels like the understatement of the last millennia.>*

Tangel glanced at Jeffrey Tomlinson, who was staring open-mouthed at her as he was led past her to the pinnace.

<Or the last seven thousand.>

A MIRACLE

STELLAR DATE: 09.06.8949 (Adjusted Years)
LOCATION: ISF pinnace, Planet HH1
REGION: Hidey Hole System, Large Magellanic Cloud

The moment the airlock sealed, Tangel dismissed the field that had enveloped her head, the stale air she'd held in the bubble replaced by the pinnace's fresh supply.

As she gulped down long breaths, Sera stopped next to her, pulling her helmet off to reveal a wide-eyed stare. Jason followed suit, his expression not significantly different.

"What…?" Sera asked. "OK, how did you *do* that?"

"Arrive on the planet?" Tangel asked, leaning against the bulkhead, weathering a wave of dizziness.

"No, Tani—gel…how did you…" Sera rolled her eyes. "Bah! I can't come up with a sarcastic remark right now. *Yeah,* how did you get here?"

"I used a jump gate," Tangel replied with a wink.

She could see a light go on in Sera's eyes, and the woman snapped her fingers. "That was a gate mirror! The thing you tossed away when you arrived. But why didn't you take a ship?"

Tangel checked the status of the three pinnaces rising above the planet toward Peabody's ship, the *Helios,* ensuring that every member of the team was safely aboard.

Above, Peabody was battling the Airthan fleet, already having disabled four of the sixty enemy vessels, his rail-cruiser flinging near-relativistic pellets out at dozens of targets at a time.

Good, Tangel thought. *Glad to see that design works so well.*

While making those observations, she replied to Sera's question.

"I was in the Trensch System, aiding in the negotiations—which is to say I jumped in on a pinnace with Joe. The ship took some shots as we approached our target, and was disabled. I had to leap through space to get to the enemy cruiser where Corsia and Eve had been captured—"

"Terrance?" Jason interrupted.

Tangel nodded. "OK. Everyone is safe. Turns out they had a bit of a 'remnant' problem in the Inner Praesepe Empire."

"A remnant?" a voice asked from behind Tangel, and she turned to see Jeffrey Tomlinson standing in the pinnace's central passageway.

"A little thing ascended AIs can leave behind in people," Sera explained. "Fun for controlling them and making messes everywhere."

"Really? They can do that?" Jeffrey's eyes were wide as saucers.

"That's a long story," Tangel interjected. "Regarding my arrival, we had a bit of a dust-up with the IPE's space force, but their Minister of the Interior was aboard the *Andromeda,* and we managed to get everything under control. Remnants and all.

"Then I got the message that you two had skipped on out here, and were in hot water as well." Tangel paused to give both Sera and Jason meaningful looks. "Joe will confirm that I had some choice words for the pair of you."

"Don't change the subject," Jason said, rolling his finger in a circle to indicate she carry on.

"Fine, but you're getting demerits for leaving the galaxy without permission. Anyway, so the *Andromeda*'s gates were still racked up in storage, and Peabody's distress call over the QuanComm made things here seem more than a little dire.

"The *Andromeda* has a smaller gate for pinnaces that was fully assembled in one of the bays, but it didn't have the power to jump a ship clear out here to the LMC—not without some jury rigging."

"So you just went on your own?" Jason's tone made it sound like he thought she was crazy or lying…or perhaps both.

Tangel shrugged. "Well, I pulled the gate mirror off the front of our pinnace and had them activate the gate while it was still in the bay. Sephira oriented the *Andromeda* to align with the LMC, and I…jumped."

Sera shook her head, mouth hanging open, while Jason wore an expression that caused Tangel to wonder if he wanted to try a ship-less gate jump.

"Just so you know," Tangel continued, "once I did it, I realized how monumentally stupid it was. If I didn't reach my target, I could have dumped out into space between the galaxies. That possibility made for the most frightening seventy seconds of my life."

Sera raised a finger and wagged it at her friend. "Keep that firmly in mind if you feel like coming down on us for going on this mission." She held a stern expression on her face for a few seconds, then lunged forward and wrapped Tangel in a tight embrace.

"OK, OK," Tangel grunted. "Shit's hitting the fan out there, we should get to the cockpit."

Jason pushed past Tangel and Sera, jogging down the passageway to where the Marine pilot was shifting vector to avoid a swarm of Airthan drones.

Tangel pulled the pinnace's feeds, watching as the enemy drones fired on the ship from every direction, wearing down the ship's standard shields.

"No stasis on these pinnaces?" she asked as she reached the cockpit to see Jason sliding into the copilot's seat.

"Too many capital ships need them," Jason replied as he took control of the pinnace's defense systems, firing chaff and electronic countermeasures in an attempt to fool the enemy drones. "We shorted the pinnaces out here because we were supposed to be alone."

Tangel only grunted in response, watching as Peabody altered his vector to close with the approaching pinnaces, the *Helios* spewing its deadly hail like a cyclone of destruction.

"We have an approach vector," the pilot announced while weaving the pinnace through the incoming drone-fire.

Tangel realized that the enemy craft were not taking kill shots on the pinnace—instead they seemed focused on overwhelming the craft's shields.

I wonder if I can locate their command frequency…

She tapped into the pinnace's scan suite, and then hopped onto that of the other two pinnaces. She used the passive sensors on each ship to broaden her scope, creating a massive antenna, flying through space.

Detecting anything through all the chaos around them seemed impossible, especially with the Airthan fleet firing at the *Helios* with everything they had.

C'mon... Tangel thought as she picked out a low-frequency wave that varied in amplitude. *A predictable pattern*!

At only two-hundred megahertz, the carrier wave didn't support a high-bandwidth datastream, but it *would* have the range to manage the drones from ships three light seconds away.

This has to be it.

Tangel tapped into the signal, finding the datastream and picking through the information, looking for the auth mechanism so she could fake her own wave and confuse the drones that were slowly wearing down the pinnaces' conventional shields.

"Fuckin' bots," the Marine pilot muttered, as a dense wave of drones closed with their vessel. "Those things will do us in for sure...."

"Think again," Jason said through gritted teeth.

Tangel watched the third pinnace cease its evasive maneuvers and streak straight toward the wave of approaching enemy craft. It fired all of its beams and missiles, causing explosions to flare in the mass of drones. It continued boosting—well beyond its safe acceleration threshold—taking more and more weapons fire from the drones as it closed.

Then the craft was amidst the drones, its beams shredding the robotic attackers at point-blank range before the pinnace was finally overwhelmed and holed, venting atmosphere in a dozen locations as it tumbled away from the battlespace.

"Shit," Tangel muttered. "That was brave...but stupid."

"Why would you say that?" Jason asked, glancing over his shoulder at her as their pinnace continued to weave through the attackers. "I'm rather proud of it."

"What?" Tangel asked, then realized what he had done, and groaned. "You know...next time you send an empty pinnace into the enemy, can you let me know beforehand?"

"Sorry, forgot you weren't on our comms when we boarded. That was the one we came down in...I was remote piloting it back up."

As Jason explained his clever duplicity, their pinnace shuddered under a heavy barrage of enemy fire, and Tangel redoubled her concentration on dissecting the drone's control wave.

The two remaining ISF pinnaces were ninety thousand kilometers from the *Helios* when the drone pattern shifted. The robotic attackers intensified their fire, and Tangel knew their orders had changed from 'capture' to 'kill'.

Exactly what I needed.

With the orders had come a new auth packet, and she lifted it off the carrier wave and pulled it apart. She realized that the token was generic, not hashed per command.

Sloppy, but maybe it was done to keep the data packets small, counting on security through obscurity.

"Rear umbrella's failed!" the pilot called out, and then Jason swore as one of the pinnace's two engines died, beamfire from the drones triggering a thermal shutdown.

The pinnace slewed to port, and Tangel closed her eyes, crafting new orders for the drones while configuring the remaining pinnace's comm systems to send out the low-frequency wave.

Here goes nothing, she thought, and sent the command.

Half the drones immediately broke off from their attack on the pinnaces and turned on the other drones. Utter chaos erupted around the pinnaces, and Tangel managed a laugh, not caring to think how close they'd come to being dead in space with thousands of enemy drones around them.

"Now *that's* more like it," Jason crowed as the *Helios* drew closer, its beams sweeping away any drones that had survived the robotic civil war that Tangel had ignited.

"This is insane," a voice whispered from behind her, and Tangel turned to see Jeffrey approaching. His mouth was agape as he stared at the forward view—a display that showed the *Helios* fending off dozens of Airthan ships on its own, while miraculously—to him—remaining unscathed.

"This?" Tangel asked, gesturing to the firefight occurring around the *Helios*. "This is just another day at the office. Don't worry, Airtha doesn't have weapons that can penetrate the *Helios*'s stasis shields, and we're almost there—"

Tangel's words cut off as a massive ship appeared on scan, easily a hundred kilometers long. At first glance, it appeared to be little more than a rail accelerator with engines—more like a defensive platform. One that looked incomplete, judging by the construction scaffolding on one side, and the missing hull plating in a number of locations.

As she watched, thrusters fired along its length, and the weapon shifted its orientation to align with the *Helios.*

"What the…" Sera whispered, then the pinnace's alarms wailed as a massive EM burst flared on scan.

"Holy shit!" Jason swore.

The forward view showed arcs of electricity flowing across the *Helios,* dancing between its rings, sending explosions flaring across the ship, as the rail accelerators lost containment, and a billion fist-sized pellets tore through the hull, flying in every direction.

Then the *Helios* went dark.

<*Admiral!*> Colonel Pearson called in from the other pinnace. <*Our Sera here is laughing her ass off—says that thing's called an EMG, and it can penetrate stasis shields…*>

We can see that, Tangel thought as she watched escape pods blast out of the *Helios.*

<*Pearson, break off, get behind the planet, we'll take out the EMG,*> she ordered the colonel, while she addressed Jason and the pilot aloud. "Get us in close to that thing, I'm going to take it out."

"Close?" Jason twisted in his seat. "How close?"

Tangel turned and strode down the passageway, calling over her shoulder. "Jumping distance. Don't worry, I'll wear a helmet this time."

She reached the armory with Sera close on her heels.

"Tanis! You can't be serious! We'll never make it close enough to that weapon!"

"Pull scan and look," she said as she grabbed a helmet and pulled it on. <*I've got their drones shielding us. Plus, that weapon's not complete, it doesn't have point defense beams.*>

"So you *think,*" Sera shot back.

<*Sera.*> Tangel placed a hand on Sera's shoulder. <*We don't have a lot of options here—Shit, they've jumped in.*>

"Who?" Sera asked, then her eyes widened. "Dammit, the rest of your Aleutian fleet. That thing is going to tear them apart!"

<*Exactly,*> Tangel replied to her before calling up, <*Jason, pour it on, get me within a few meters—above that knobby protrusion, five eighths of the way down the hull.*>

<*Are you sure about this?*> he asked. <*You've always done crazy stuff, Tanis, but—*>

<*You just come get me afterward,*> Tangel replied. <*Got it?*>

<*You know we will.*>

The calm certainty in Jason's voice steeled Tangel, and she leant forward, touching her helmet to Sera's, letting the vibrations carry her voice through. "When I get back, we have to talk. Things have to change."

"What things?" Sera's eyes were wide. "Are you going to leave us?"

"No." Tangel shook her head. "We're going to go on the offensive."

"With who?" Sera whispered.

"Everyone."

Tangel gave Sera a quick embrace, then turned and walked to the airlock, closing the inner door on her friend's worried expression. She grasped a handle as she cycled the outer door open.

All around the pinnace, the remaining drones were flying in a tight formation, absorbing beamfire from the Airthan fleet, and taking shots of opportunity to keep the forty enemy cruisers at bay.

Ahead, three of the enemy cruisers were in a close formation near the EMG, and Jason dove the pinnace between them.

Tangel could tell it was him and not the Marine pilot by the chances he took, passing only a few kilometers from the enemy vessels.

He's one to call **me** *reckless….*

Tangel directed a hundred drones to launch their remaining missiles at the closest cruiser as they swept past, taking out its shields with the weapons, and then the drones themselves slammed into the enemy ship's hull, tearing it open to gout flame into space.

Three hundred thousand kilometers away, the Aleutian ISF fleet was shifting vector and burning hard to reach the pinnace and the disabled *Helios*.

They were too far away to damage the EMG, but she wasn't so certain that it couldn't hit them.

Tangel sent them a warning to stay at least fifty degrees away from the business end of the EMG, praying that the dozen ISF ships could last long enough for her to destroy this new weapon and still have enough firepower to take down the remaining Airthan ships.

As those events played out, Jason spun the pinnace and fired the engines for a full braking burn, slowing the craft down to a mere hundred-kilometers-per-second. The a-grav dampeners failed to absorb all of the energy, and Tangel was slammed against the bulkhead, nearly missing the optimal time to jump.

With three hundred milliseconds to spare, she leapt out of the airlock.

Faster than her eyes could send the information to her brain, she crossed the forty meters between the pinnace and the EMG. Luckily for her, she had other ways of seeing, and was able to stretch her arms out and disintegrate the hull of the enemy weapon before she was smeared across it.

Shredding the EMG's hull was a lot harder than when she'd destroyed the Nietzschean soldiers' weapons on Pyra, or dissolved the hull of the IPE cruiser just an hour earlier. This time, she had to shred molecular bonds at break-neck speed, praying that she didn't tear through anything too volatile.

The slurry of matter and energy around her slowed her descent, and she came to a stop near the center of the ship's long shaft, roughly a kilometer forward of the bulge she suspected to be the main firing system.

Around her, the matter began to solidify, chemical bonds reforming, and Tangel pushed her way through, finally coming to a passageway.

A wave of exhaustion hit her, and she realized that, while her non-organic body was able to feed off the energy around her, she wasn't so adept at keeping her flesh energized while performing these insane feats.

Don't get lazy now, Tangel, she chided as she pushed away from the corridor's bulkhead and began a slow, loping jog down the ship's length. *Next time I do something like this, I'm wearing powered armor.*

She drew matter from around her, and converted it into fuel for her organic body, carefully altering molecular compounds into safe carbohydrates. Her body responded, gaining strength, and she picked up her pace, reaching the end of the corridor in just another twenty seconds.

Ahead of her was a thick door, sealed against intrusion, and half-covered with warnings about the environment beyond.

Tangel reached out, feeling the magnetic fields on the far side, a realization hitting her like a hammer blow.

So much mass…Finaeus always said this was impossible…Seems like Airtha knows a few things he doesn't. Like how to jump a black hole.

She knew that destroying the EMG was no longer an option. If she did, the black hole on the far side of the door would eventually fall into the planet below—or maybe, given the mass of the black hole, the planet would fall into it. Either way, it would destroy the ark hidden beneath its surface.

Not to mention kill her, as well.

<Jason, Sera.> She called out to the pinnace, but didn't get a response. *<If you can hear me, break off, I'm going to shut it down, not destroy it. The drones should continue to shield you. Get back to the planet.>*

The snap of kinetic rounds ricocheting off something nearby drew Tangel's attention back to the world around her, and she realized that a group of Airthan soldiers were firing from behind her, and that the 'something nearby' was her armor.

With a wave of her hand, she dissolved their weapons and seized the joints in their armor.

Enough distractions.

She concentrated on the dense alloy before her. The door to the EMG's firing chamber consisted of layers and layers of carbon-reinforced steel and lead.

She was about to dissolve it, when she realized it would be wise to protect her organic body from whatever lay within. She drew the lead out of the door and formed it around herself, wrapping her body in a thick cocoon before pulling the door apart the rest of the way and drawing herself through.

With her organic eyes trapped inside the leaden cocoon, Tangel pulled feeds from the chamber's systems while also examining it with her extradimensional vision.

Sure enough, in the center of the chamber was a one-hundred-meter sphere, magnetic fields surging around it, holding a ball of mass and energy within. As she watched, streams of material were fed into the black hole, the matter flaring brightly as it was torn apart, becoming the ultra-dense non-matter within the singularity itself.

What amazed Tangel was that, to her other vision, the black hole was not black at all. Waves of extradimensional energy flowed off it in every direction, a shimmering halo of luminescence so bright it was almost blinding.

The magnetic fields generated by the chamber's containment systems warped that energy, and as she watched, the fields shifted, focusing it into a single point on the forward-facing side of the black hole.

The energy held at that point for a second, building. Then a tremendous blast of electromagnetic energy tore out of the black hole, surging down a shaft that ran the length of the EMG.

So ***that's*** *how they power this thing,* Tangel thought while trying to determine the best way to stop the weapon without destroying the ship and herself.

Her initial thought was to disintegrate whatever system was used for firing the weapon, but she knew that tearing apart a black hole was far beyond her abilities. Especially one that had to mass at least a hundred times that of a terrestrial planet.

She briefly wondered how they held the thing within the weapon—let alone moved it—and why it wasn't crushing her with its gravitational pull. While she was toying with those questions, she tasked a part of her mind with breaching the ship's systems.

If she could take control of the firing systems or the positioning thrusters, she could nullify the weapon's effects.

She set about that work, cringing as the weapon fired again, knowing that her people were being targeted, and that she would be too slow in stopping it.

Milliseconds stretched into seconds, then longer. An excruciatingly long two minutes and eleven seconds later, Tangel broke through the encryption on the weapon's firing systems and took control of it.

What she found there was terrible in its cruelty. Six AIs were mentally conjoined at the heart of the control system, their sole task to control the fields around the black hole and trigger its electromagnetic eruptions.

The instant they detected Tangel's presence in the system, they did the unthinkable: the AIs shut off the magnetic fields containing the black hole.

While a part of Tangel's mind wailed in terror, feeling the increasing gravitational pull of the thing—and wondering why it wasn't crushing her—another part examined the systems that had been holding the black hole aloft.

In addition to magnetic fields, anti-gravity stabilizers were present, firing negative gravitons at the black hole. Without the containment systems, she could now see that the black hole was roughly six centimeters in diameter, an unimaginable amount of mass to haul within a ship, but something that the graviton emitters had negated.

Seven milliseconds had passed since the AIs shut off the containment systems, and Tangel could now feel her body being crushed against the leaden cocoon by a steady 100*g* pull from the black hole as the graviton emitters ceased operation.

She stretched an ethereal hand through the cocoon, and anchored herself to the chamber's wall while simultaneously re-activating the a-grav emitters.

The AIs countered Tangel by shutting off the CriEn modules that had been powering the emitters, leaving her only whatever energy was left in the backup SC batteries.

Knowing she had less than a second to live, Tangel did the only thing she could think of: she used the a-grav emitters to open a hole into the dark layer.

A *fhummp* thundered through the ship as the rift opened, drawing the black hole and the air inside the chamber into the dark layer.

The rift surged toward the perimeter of the room, stopping only a meter from Tangel's cocoon, the gantry she was resting on cutting off in a ragged line as the eternal darkness lapped hungrily at the solid matter.

A curious realization struck her.

There are no Exaldi out there. I should be able to see them, but there's nothing….

Forcing herself to stay on task, she shut off the a-grav emitters to seal the portal into the dark layer, but when the emitters registered as offline, the opening into *nothing* still gaped before her.

"Nooo," Tangel whispered, remembering what had happened with the planet Aurora in the Bollam's World System.

She had believed the black hole's creation and connection to the dark layer to be just a fluke, but perhaps there was some strange property of black holes and the dark layer that no one had guessed at.

Either way, the thing wouldn't close.

With a growing sense of abject terror, she watched as a clump of dark matter streaked through the dark layer, bleeding gravitons that she could see with her other senses, and impacted the black hole.

Frantically, Tangel activated the a-grav emitters once again, attempting to reverse the waveform that had opened the rift in the first place, but nothing happened.

Then she remembered the emission pattern that Earnest had devised to push the Exaldi back into the dark layer above Carthage.

She tweaked the frequency and amplitude, and fired the a-grav emitters once more. This time, they shoved the black hole away from the rift's opening, deeper into the dark layer. Once it had moved a kilometer away, she deactivated the emitters and gave a cry of joy, the utterance consuming the last of her flagging strength.

The rift closed, and Tangel breathed a long sigh as consciousness slipped from her mind.

SERAS

STELLAR DATE: 09.07.8949 (Adjusted Years)
LOCATION: Airthan Ring
REGION: Huygens System, Transcend Interstellar Alliance

Airtha reviewed the information from the secondary observation team stationed beyond Valkris's heliopause with mixed feelings.

That the EMG had worked—and spectacularly so—was something that pleased her greatly. Losing Sera, and then her forces, to the ISF fleet ruined that elation and left her feeling hollow.

Another daughter lost.

She had hoped that letting Sera leave on her own would temper her impetuous daughter's need to 'get out of this place,' as she'd taken up saying.

However, there was a second silver lining. Airtha now had no doubt in her mind that the ISF had developed a near-instantaneous means of communication.

Quantum entanglement was the most obvious possibility, though how they'd compensated for the heisenberg uncertainty principle intrigued her greatly. So far as she knew, even the core AIs—her hated enemy—had not properly managed to solve that conundrum.

How to know where the entangled particles are, and how to measure their movement at the same time with any fidelity…?

She doubled her resolve to capture one of their bait ships. Now that she knew their purpose—and the means by which they sprung their traps—Admiral Krissy's rescue fleets would soon find that turnabout was indeed fair play.

Reviewing her options for the right location to turn Krissy's bait operations into a trap for her enemies, Airtha couldn't keep a part of her mind from lingering on the daughter she'd lost.

Two of them now. Two of my flesh and blood aligning themselves with that abomination, Tanis Richards, and her AI, Bob.

She knew it was possible that *her* Sera would not change sides and turn against her, but she doubted it. The abomination's powers of persuasion were great.

And Seraphina had proven herself to be weak.

Repeatedly.

Airtha considered further altering the next iteration of her progeny. Make her stronger, more commanding, less flexible. Of course, that limited Airtha's own influence over her daughter; she was trying to make a woman in her own image, not a puppet.

Just as she was examining Sera's DNA and neural network, a courier ship jumped in near the ring and sent a priority message.

Airtha scanned it, feeling her determination slip into rage.

*Another EMG **and** another Sera!?*

The parts of her mind most reminiscent of an organic brain seethed at the thought. *Two daughters lost in one day…Tanis Richards will be made to answer for this.*

And was the Nora System lost? She had hoped to learn what secrets her former husband had placed within its vaults. The message didn't say, as the courier had left the system before the conflict with the ISF ships had concluded. However, the message did contain scan showing that the EMG had been disabled. Without that weapon—just as in the Valkris system—an ISF victory was assured.

Airtha steeled herself for the news of the mysterious planet's loss. In fact, she had to assume that her enemies would take control of all the facilities in the LMC.

She wondered if the extragalactic settlement would cause Tanis and the rebellious Sera to scour the Milky Way and nearby dwarf galaxies for more of her hidden locations. They could try, but with nearly a trillion stars to investigate, it could take them decades to even scratch the surface.

I'll see Tanis defeated long before they find them all.

With that worry put to rest, Airtha turned her attention back to the next iteration of her daughter. Perhaps she'd been fighting too hard against Sera's deviant nature. Rather than suppressing it, Airtha considered what enhancing it may do.

Create a version of my daughter that covets power and submerges herself in her vices.

Not too much—Airtha still needed to control her—but enough to give her new Seraphina an edge.

An edge she'd hone into a deadly weapon and use to end the

obstruction that Tanis Richards represented, followed by that buffoon, Praetor Kirkland.

Once she had all AIs and humanity aligned with her, Airtha would finally be in a position to strike out and destroy the ascended AIs in the core.

The ones who had killed her and remade her into the *thing* she'd become.

TRANSITION

STELLAR DATE: 09.07.8949 (Adjusted Years)
LOCATION: Ol' Sam, ISS *I2*
REGION: Pyra, Albany System, Thebes, Septhian Alliance

Tangel walked out of her lakehouse, away from the gathering within, her gaze immediately alighting on the figure standing on the dock.

<Want some company?> she asked Sera as she walked down the steps and onto the path.

<Umm…I guess? Only if you tell me what the ***hell*** *I'm supposed to do.>*

Tangel chuckled softly to herself as she walked toward the dock. *<That's Bob's job. I'm just a pawn.>*

Sera turned as Tangel approached, and shook her head. "That big, dumb AI's no help at all. Just tells me that you muddy destiny too much—plus other assorted nonsense."

<I can hear you, you know,> Bob interjected.

"Yeah," Sera glanced up the clouds overhead. "That's why I spoke aloud, you big dummy."

<Oh.>

"I won't lie," Tangel said as she reached Sera's side, staring out over the lake. "Shit's gotten weird. Like…super extra weird."

"Seriously, Tani—Tangel? You, my best friend, are an ascended-merged-AI-person, my father was a clone, my *real* father has been in stasis for a thousand years, there are two clones of *me* on this ship…" Sera paused, her eyes both angry and pleading. "Do you want me to go on?"

Tangel kicked her shoes off and sat on the edge of the dock, dipping her toes into the water.

"Sera, sit."

Sera stood still for a moment, then sighed and pulled her boots off before joining Tangel. "Huh…it's warmer than I expected."

"It's the tropical fish. They like it warm."

Neither woman spoke for a second, both lazily dragging their toes through the water.

"Seriously, Tangel?" Sera asked. "I need someone to tell me what to do. I can't figure this out. Do I just turn everything over to my father? Is that insane?"

"He's not ready yet—if he even wants it," she replied. "No, I think it's time that *I* do what I've been running from, what you've been asking me to do for over a year now.

Sera's brows rose. "Which is?"

"I'll take the reins."

"Of the Transcend?"

"Of everything."

"What do you mean...everything?" her friend whispered, her eyes round and staring.

Tangel didn't respond immediately, considering different word choices and how Sera would receive them.

Finally she sighed, deciding to wing it. "I'm half-human, half-AI, I'm ascended, and relatively competent at most things I set my mind to. I think I'm the best one to unite everyone, to see if we can't forge a civilization that values the good in both species, and understands the variances within those species.

"I'm going to turn our 'Scipio Alliance' into a nation, and I'm going to bring everyone under that single banner."

"How?" Sera asked. "Not everyone is going to join you willingly."

"Yeah," Tangel laughed softly. "I get that. But I have a plan that can get us on the road to peace without this war burning humanity to ash. And an important part of that plan is you."

"Me?" Sera asked, her voice wavering. "We just had the part of this conversation where I said I have no idea what to do."

"I have a gift for you," Tangel said, a smile pulling at the corners of her mouth. "A gift and a job."

Sera heaved a sigh. "So since you're running 'everything', is the job for me to get back to day-to-day operations for the Transcend?"

Tangel shook her head. "No, I think I can manage that now. And maybe your father *will* want that task eventually; we'll see. But I know you've been struggling with how to deal with Airtha...I think our best bet is a targeted strike. A team that we send to Airtha to take her out and end her reign without destroying the Transcend."

"You want *me* to go in and do that?"

"Yes," Tangel replied. "But not just you. I want to send Katrina and Kara in with you—plus your sisters."

Sera snorted. "Now I *know* ascendancy hasn't been good for your cognitive process. My 'sisters', as you call them, hate me. Stars, since they realized that Airtha made two of them—that they know of—they hate pretty much everything."

Tangel knew that beneath Sera's angst over her sisters was the knowledge that Airtha had made *her* as well. For all intents and purposes, she existed because her mother had used her father to create new versions of herself, in hopes of raising a daughter in her image that would rule the Transcend as her puppet...or something along those lines.

However, it was not something that Tangel would bring up; Sera didn't need to dwell on that reality any further right now.

"You understand your sisters very well." She spoke quietly, waiting for Sera to realize what part she could play. "Because those two women *are* you. Tweaked a bit here and there, but separated from Airtha's influence, I believe they'd revert to form."

"What does that even mean?"

"Sera, you're smart, cunning, resourceful. You're a highly skilled operative. Three of you? With a team? You'd decimate Airtha."

Sera snorted. "OK, Tangel. Let's say for a moment that I *don't* think you're insane. What's the 'gift' you have for me?"

"I can't send you against Airtha unarmed; I can leave something inside of you to help."

Sera jerked away, turning to face Tangel with a mixture of awe and terror on her face. "A remnant? In me? No way!"

"Not a remnant. A memory. Like what Xavia did with Katrina. It's not the same as what the other ascended do, I promise."

Sera's expression softened. "I don't know, Tangel.... That's a lot to ask. Can I think on it?"

"Of course," she nodded. "There's something else I can do, too—I did it for Rika not long ago. I can show you how *I* see you."

"What does that do? Put something *else* in me?"

"No," Tangel said as she gazed out over the still waters of the lake before them. "Nothing other than thoughts. But they're *your* thoughts."

"OK," she whispered. "Show me."

Tangel lifted a hand and touched it to Sera's forehead, feeding a tendril of her other body through her friend's skin and into her mind.

She pulled an image from her own thoughts: one of Sera as a powerful woman, her skin gleaming white, angelic wings stretched out behind her. A rifle in one hand, and a sword in the other.

Arrayed behind her, stretching into infinity, was a vast fleet of ships, and around her was a multitude of warriors, all standing ready to face whatever came their way.

"Really, Tangel? An angel? Isn't that a bit anachronistic?" Sera asked with a self-deprecating laugh.

"You're the one who sees herself as a demon, someone vile and undeserving," Tangel pointed out, sliding her hand down to clasp Sera's shoulder. "But that's not you. You're steadfast, noble. You put others before yourself far more than you let on. You've saved my life many times…you tore that EMG apart looking for me. You're my angel."

Sera's jaw tightened, and her lips pressed together as tears sprang into her eyes.

Her hand reached up and held onto Tangel's as she managed to hoarsely whisper, "Thank you."

THE END

* * * * *

Big things are afoot. Sera's father is back, and she faces a mission to confront her mother. Tangel must move on to the Trisilieds, and the TSF hoplite forces are about to move into Orion space ***Assault on Orion***.

And that's just the tip of the iceberg. Everyone from Roxy and Carmen to Katrina and Kara will be involved as the war spreads further.

All the while the forces of the Caretaker, Xavia, and General Garza wait for the right time to strike out at a weakened ISF.

But Tangel has a plan for victory, one she hopes none of her enemies will suspect.

THE BOOKS OF AEON 14

This list is in near-chronological order. However, for the full chronological reading order, check out the master spreadsheet.

The Sentience Wars: Origins (Age of the Sentience Wars – w/James S. Aaron)
- Books 1-3 Omnibus: Lyssa's Rise
- Books 4-5 Omnibus (incl. Vesta Burning): Lyssa's Fire

- Book 0 Prequel: The Proteus Bridge (Full length novel)
- Book 1: Lyssa's Dream
- Book 2: Lyssa's Run
- Book 3: Lyssa's Flight
- Book 4: Lyssa's Call
- Book 5: Lyssa's Flame

The Sentience Wars: Solar War 1 (Age of the Sentience Wars – w/James S. Aaron)
- Book 0 Prequel: Vesta Burning (Full length novel)
- Book 1: Eve of Destruction
- Book 2: The Spreading Fire
- Book 3: A Fire Upon the Worlds (2020)

Enfield Genesis (Age of the Sentience Wars – w/Lisa Richman)
- Book 1: Alpha Centauri
- Book 2: Proxima Centauri
- Book 3: Tau Ceti
- Book 4: Epsilon Eridani
- Book 5: Sirius

Origins of Destiny (The Age of Terra)
- Prequel: Storming the Norse Wind
- Prequel: Angel's Rise: The Huntress (available on Patreon)
- Book 1: Tanis Richards: Shore Leave
- Book 2: Tanis Richards: Masquerade
- Book 3: Tanis Richards: Blackest Night
- Book 4: Tanis Richards: Kill Shot

The Intrepid Saga (The Age of Terra)
- Book 1: Outsystem
- Book 2: A Path in the Darkness
- Book 3: Building Victoria

- The Intrepid Saga Omnibus – *Also contains Destiny Lost, book 1 of the Orion War series*

- Destiny Rising – *Special Author's Extended Edition comprised of both Outsystem and A Path in the Darkness with over 100 pages of new content.*

The Sol Dissolution (The Age of Terra)
- Book 1: Venusian Uprising
- Book 2: Assault on Sedna
- Book 3: Hyperion War
- Book 4: Fall of Terra (2021)

Outlaws of Aquilia (Age of the FTL Wars)
- Book 1: The Daedalus Job
- Book 2: Maelstrom Reach
- Book 3: Marauder's Compass

Althea's Raiders (Age of the FTL Wars)
- Book 1: The Fall of Rome (2021)
- Book 2: The Terran Empire (2021)

The Warlord (Before the Age of the Orion War)
- Books 1-3 Omnibus: The Warlord of Midditerra

- Book 1: The Woman Without a World
- Book 2: The Woman Who Seized an Empire
- Book 3: The Woman Who Lost Everything

Legacy of the Lost (The FTL Wars Era w/Chris J. Pike)
- Book 1: Fire in the Night Sky
- Book 2: A Blight Upon the Stars
- Book 3: A Specter and an Invasion (2021)

The Orion War
- Book 1-3 Omnibus: Battle for New Canaan *(includes Set the Galaxy on Fire anthology)*
- Book 4-6 Omnibus: The Greatest War *(includes Ignite the Stars anthology)*
- Book 7-10 Omnibus: Assault on Orion
- Book 11-13 Omnibus: Hegemony of Humanity *(includes Return to Kapteyn's Star)*

- Book 0 Prequel: To Fly Sabrina
- Book 1: Destiny Lost

- Book 2: New Canaan
- Book 3: Orion Rising
- Book 4: The Scipio Alliance
- Book 5: Attack on Thebes
- Book 6: War on a Thousand Fronts
- Book 7: Precipice of Darkness
- Book 8: Airtha Ascendancy
- Book 9: The Orion Front
- Book 10: Starfire
- Book 10.5: Return to Kapteyn's Star
- Book 11: Race Across Spacetime
- Book 12: Return to Sol: Attack at Dawn
- Book 13: Return to Sol: Star Rise

Non-Aeon 14 volumes containing Tanis stories
- Bob's Bar Volume 1
- Quantum Legends 3: Aberrant Ascension (2021)

Building New Canaan (Age of the Orion War – w/J.J. Green)
- Book 1: Carthage
- Book 2: Tyre
- Book 3: Troy
- Book 4: Athens

Tales of the Orion War
- Book 1: Set the Galaxy on Fire
- Book 2: Ignite the Stars

Multi-Author Collections
- Volume 1: Repercussions

Perilous Alliance (Age of the Orion War – w/Chris J. Pike)
- Book 1-3 Omnibus: Crisis in Silstrand
- Book 3.5-6 Omnibus: War in the Fringe

- Book 0 Prequel: Escape Velocity
- Book 1: Close Proximity
- Book 2: Strike Vector
- Book 3: Collision Course
- Book 3.5: Decisive Action
- Book 4: Impact Imminent
- Book 5: Critical Inertia
- Book 6: Impulse Shock
- Book 7: Terminal Velocity

The Delta Team (Age of the Orion War)
- Book 1: The Eden Job
- Book 2: The Disknee World
- Book 3: Rogue Planets

Serenity (Age of the Orion War – w/A. K. DuBoff)
- Book 1: Return to the Ordus
- Book 2: War of the Rosette

Rika's Marauders (Age of the Orion War)
- Book 1-3 Omnibus: Rika Activated
- Book 1-7 Full series omnibus: Rika's Marauders

- Prequel: Rika Mechanized
- Book 1: Rika Outcast
- Book 2: Rika Redeemed
- Book 3: Rika Triumphant
- Book 4: Rika Commander
- Book 5: Rika Infiltrator
- Book 6: Rika Unleashed
- Book 7: Rika Conqueror

Non-Aeon 14 Anthologies containing Rika stories
- Bob's Bar Volume 2

The Genevian Queen (Age of the Orion War)
- Book 1: Rika Rising
- Book 2: Rika Coronated
- Book 3: Rika Destroyer

Perseus Gate (Age of the Orion War)
Season 1: Orion Space
- Episode 1: The Gate at the Grey Wolf Star
- Episode 2: The World at the Edge of Space
- Episode 3: The Dance on the Moons of Serenity
- Episode 4: The Last Bastion of Star City
- Episode 5: The Toll Road Between the Stars
- Episode 6: The Final Stroll on Perseus's Arm
- Eps 1-3 Omnibus: The Trail Through the Stars
- Eps 4-6 Omnibus: The Path Amongst the Clouds

Season 2: Inner Stars
- Episode 1: A Meeting of Bodies and Minds

- Episode 2: A Deception and a Promise Kept
- Episode 3: A Surreptitious Rescue of Friends and Foes
- Episode 3.5: Anomaly on Cerka (w/Andrew Dobell)
- Episode 4: A Victory and a Crushing Defeat
- Episode 5: A Trial and the Tribulations
- Episode 6: A Bargain and a True Story Told (2021)
- Episode 7: A New Empire and An Old Ally (2021)
- Eps 1-3 Omnibus: A Siege and a Salvation from Enemies

Hand's Assassin (Age of the Orion War – w/T.G. Ayer)
- Book 1: Death Dealer
- Book 2: Death Mark (2021)

Machete System Bounty Hunter (Age of the Orion War – w/Zen DiPietro)
- Book 1: Hired Gun
- Book 2: Gunning for Trouble
- Book 3: With Guns Blazing

Fennington Station Murder Mysteries (Age of the Orion War)
- Book 1: Whole Latte Death (w/Chris J. Pike)
- Book 2: Cocoa Crush (w/Chris J. Pike)

The Empire (Age of the Orion War)
- Book 1: The Empress and the Ambassador
- Book 2: Consort of the Scorpion Empress
- Book 3: By the Empress's Command

Bitchalante (Age of the Orion War)
- Book 1: Bitchalante (2021)

The Ascension War (Age of the Orion War)
- Book 1: Scions of Humanity (2020)
- Book 2: Galactic Front (2021)
- Book 3: Sagittarius Breach (2021)

OTHER BOOKS BY M. D. COOPER

Destiny's Sword
- Book 1: Lucidium Run

ABOUT THE AUTHOR

Malorie Cooper likes to think of herself as a dreamer and a wanderer, yet her feet are firmly grounded in reality.

A twenty-year software development veteran, Malorie eventually climbed the ladder to the position of software architect and CTO, where she gained a wealth of experience managing complex systems and large groups of people.

Her experiences there translated well into the realm of science fiction, and when her novels took off, she was primed and ready to make the jump into a career as a full-time author.

A 'maker' from an early age, Malorie loves to craft things, from furniture, to cosplay costumes, to a well-spun tale, she can't help but to create new things every day.

A rare extrovert writer, she loves to hang out with readers, and people in general. If you meet her at a convention, she just might be rocking a catsuit, cosplaying one of her own characters, or maybe her latest favorite from Overwatch!

She shares her home with a brilliant young girl, her wonderful wife (who also writes), a cat that chirps at birds, a never-ending list of things she would like to build, and ideas...

Find out what's coming next at www.aeon14.com.
Follow her on Instagram at www.instagram.com/m.d.cooper.
Hang out with the fans on Facebook at
www.facebook.com/groups/aeon14fans.

Made in the USA
Middletown, DE
04 April 2023

28241854R00459